THE MARK OF THINGS UNLEASHED

ALEX CLIFFORD

ALSO BY ALEX CLIFFORD

THE WITCHES OF WYLDEDEN CHRONICLES

The Mark of Things Unwanted

The Mark of One Unending

The Mark for Those Unbound

NOVELLAS

A Love of Books and Leather

A Tale of Scars and Rebels

A Dream of Thornes and Sunflowers

THE MARK OF THINGS UNLEASHED

THE WITCHES OF WYLDEDEN CHRONICLES

ALEX CLIFFORD

E-book: ISBN: 978-0-6454799-2-8

Paperback: ISBN: 978-0-6450201-9-9

Alex Clifford

www.alexclifford.com.au

spcafcs@gmail.com

Nir
Ahrenhale
QIRI
North Mountains
Northern Spine
sarn
ERVEDA
The Vein
Pirevia
VERTLYN
Womb
Heart Lake
Soul Lake
Orhn
ANFAR
eppa
Southern Spine
Wyldeden
Dividing River
BERNT
Hyrsch
Belden
OFORD

THE MARK OF THINGS UNLEASHED

DEARMEAD

THE ENTIRE WORLD HAD BEEN REDUCED TO THE MADDENING ITCH IN Dearmead's bones. It was the foundation of the universe, the lie that was time, and the only thing waiting for them at the end of it all. And like the birth of a star, the itch bloomed, consuming vein and muscle and flesh.

Fractured dreams of waterfalls were forgotten as consciousness returned, bringing with it a near perfect darkness and an unbearable cold. The stone floor against his bare back sapped the heat from his body, while the listless fire sprite trapped in its jar barely lit the small cavern.

Dearmead stared at the sprite's dull form and envied its inevitable death.

For the first time in hours, his lungs filled, and with oxygen came pain. Its return was a relief for only a moment—at least it was something besides *itching*—but the novelty wore off quickly. The pressure in his chest where the stake pierced through to the cave floor was an anchor in a sea of agony, his shaking hands grasping it tightly as he came back to the reality of his body.

He did not want to be here, but wanting was a useless endeavor. Oblivion would only return when the cycle of beasts had run their course again. Only when the shtryg had sucked every drop of blood from his veins, when the packs of lupanis had torn the meat from his limbs and the harpies picked out his spleen and liver, when the monstrous beetle-shelled nightmares had snapped his bones to slurp out the marrow, and once the cawkers and ratki had finished with the scraps . . .

Only then did consciousness let him go.

Only then could he go to the other cave, small and damp, turquoise light filtering through the heavy downpour of a waterfall. It was sunny there, and the quiet was gentler. Honey eyes watched him from under a furrowed brow. Warm hands cradled an old book, long fingers turning the soft parchment pages.

Home.

In the same breath that he yearned for it, he mourned.

His home was gone.

Burning.

"What's your name?"

The voice was rasping, choking around her still-healing throat, but the dark-haired woman was the only one of the imprisoned kinner who'd retained her sanity enough to acknowledge him.

Dearmead reeled his spinning thoughts back to the present, back to the world outside of his body, working his own aching throat until he managed to croak, "What?"

"Your name."

When he had first arrived at this cesspool of a base camp, the kinner woman's black hair had been long and matted, but somewhere over the hours, days, millennia since then, it had been lost. Which beast exactly had developed a taste for *hair*, he couldn't recall, but unlike the rest of her body, it had not grown back. It was only a matter of time before his own knotted braid was taken as well and he eyed her stubbly scalp with trepidation.

Mottled blue-green eyes scalded him, waiting for his answer. In a way, the severity of her face reminded him of his ma. Calla Bayfield had done everything in her power to ensure her children lacked softness, and—perhaps for the first time—he was grateful.

"Bayfield." The surname was another anchor, as painfully effective as the one in his gut. "Dearmead Bayfield."

"Good." Her dry lip split around the word. There had been no food, no water, and Dearmead's head throbbed from the lack. "Don't let your name slip away or you won't make it through this. You have to keep your mind strong. Conquer it and you'll survive anything."

The words were a variation of a well-practiced mantra. Dearmead thought she must have repeated it to herself for so long that she didn't know how to say anything else.

"What's your name?" he asked.

"Vy." Like violet. Like violence. "Vy Tacenda."

2

A cacophony of growls and hissing echoed from the tunnel. The fire sprite twitched and dimmed until Dearmead could barely see the way Vy pointed her chin toward another of the chained kinner.

"That one over there was my husband, Ru."

Was. Though the male breathed and blinked and drooled, he was not there.

"I'm sorry."

"Don't be," Vy snapped viciously. "His weakness is his own fault. Times like this show that I had too high expectations of him."

Dearmead didn't have the energy to react to her calloused assessment, but yes, Vy reminded him very much of Calla Bayfield.

The beasts' echoes grew distant, but that was not a relief. In their stead approached heavy footsteps, and Dearmead knew exactly what that meant.

He closed his eyes.

There had been a single break from the cycle of feasting that took place on the cavern floor. One of the harbingers had come, pulled the stake from his belly, and dragged him deeper into the network of caves inside this insidious mountain. He had been stripped and cleaned, made presentable, only for something else to take their turn with him. Something which, upon witnessing, had Dearmead's mind collapsing.

He wasn't sure if he simply couldn't understand what it was, or if the thing didn't have a shape. Two blood-red orbs gave the impression of eyes, but nothing else was consistent. Was it cloaked in shadow, like the shtryg, or leathery like the lupanis, or somehow both? Did it have legs or claws or wings? All three, or none? Sometimes darkness oozed from it like sap, while other times it glistened like obsidian glass.

Dearmead hadn't known what it was at first, only that the world blurred around it, and that it liked taking its time eating away at him. Only later did he hear the harbingers call it "master."

King of Beasts.

Chaos.

The footsteps stopped right beside his head and Dearmead waited for the agonizing tug of the stake that would yet again bring on the itching. Instead, a boot nudged his side. Dearmead hissed through his teeth.

"Time to stop lazing around down there," the one called Byron mocked. "And don't look so glum. I come with good news: you're going to see the sun again."

Vy had gone silent.

Gasping down a thin breath, Dearmead opened his eyes. The

harbinger standing over him hadn't sported large dragon wings when they'd first met and fought in the sky above the Womb, and the way he stood—appendages drooping and scraping along the floor—suggested he hadn't had them long enough to grow comfortable yet.

It didn't stop the violent smirk pulling at Byron's thin lips as he crouched, hand gripping the stake, stroking it slowly.

"We're all going for a little walk."

PART I

THE QUEEN IS DEAD, LONG LIVE THE QUEEN

CHAPTER ONE

CINN

RADLEY'S HEARTY SNORE ROUSED CINN FROM SLEEP. THE DUSTY wooden floor he lay on was better than any down-stuffed mattress because, on his left, his brother's smoke-and-stale-whiskey scent promised their reunion hadn't been a cruel dream. On his right, cheap apricot soap and sweat brought the ache back to his tear-swollen eyes; Edwina had barely stopped crying long enough to thank the Copelands for bringing him home, and the crack in her voice had broken the dam inside Cinn too. Even in sleep, the possessive arm she wrapped around his waist echoed the morning's grief-fueled promise:

I'll never let you out of my sight again.

William and Sarah had opted to return to the Turlough's inner-city home, allowing Cinn, Radley and Edwina some privacy. He didn't remember falling asleep. Tangled together on the floor, Edwina had been fussing and talking about breakfast, unable to let go of his arm, while Cinn had let his weight rest on Radley.

And then he was waking up. There was not an inch to move with his two siblings curled around him, their deep breathing a sign they were as heavily asleep as Cinn had been.

For a few precious minutes, nothing else existed. The moldy smell that no amount of elbow grease could rid the ramshackle apartment of was as comforting as cinnamon, the whistling breeze through the broken door a lullaby. The sun was once more sinking low outside, the heat that baked them while they slept giving way to dusk shadows. Cinn would gladly lay on the floor and doze the entire night away as well—except he really, really had to pee.

The crust welding his eyelashes together was unexpected; he didn't know the last time he slept deeply enough, and it blurred his vision as he peeled his lids apart. Radley's mouth was wide open with another hearty snore. With his face buried as they'd cried and hugged the morning away, Cinn hadn't gotten a good look at his siblings, but now, with the golden evening light coming through the sheer-laced windows, his chest squeezed painfully.

Radley looked different. It had been almost three years, but still, he didn't like that his brother's anger marred his face even in sleep. The carelessly shaved stubble, the frown lines between his brows and across his forehead—features that had once been hints were now pronounced. His dark blond hair was dry and brittle, as was his skin, and though Radley had always been bigger than Cinn, there was less strength in his broad frame than there had been three years ago. Not thin, the way their childhoods had left them—the way Cinn had only just begun to grow out of—but deeply tired. Demi-kin didn't get sick, but Radley's body was trying its very best to be.

Gently pulling his arm from under Radley's head, Cinn eased him to the floor and turned to his sister. She too had changed.

Edwina's bitterness had always been quieter, a simmering pot rather than a screaming kettle, but where their brother withered, Edwina had hardened. There was a lean strength beneath her conservative dress, the fabric of which was far nicer than anything Cinn had seen her wear before. Her dark brown hair was full and thick, skin bright with health. Slavery had calloused all the demi-kin's hands, but as Cinn carefully lifted her arm from his waist, he saw how they'd changed too. He knew the marks weapon training left; his sister had been fighting.

And her eyes were open. The blue of them were storm clouds, but on Edwina's face, it was a storm that thundered outside while he lay wrapped in blankets by a crackling fire.

"You're still here," she whispered.

Ignoring the pain in his bladder for a moment, Cinn forced a shaky smile. Her eyes dampened again as she touched his face.

"You grew up."

They both knew where that growing up had taken place and he did not want to talk about it. Not when he was home, with his family.

Their voices disturbed Puddles. The tabby cat had found the brightest, warmest spot beneath the window to curl up, stealing the reverence of the moment with a small, annoyed meow. It was for the best. Cinn couldn't put it off any longer. He pointed to himself, then to the small bathroom. Edwina's lips pursed at the way he couldn't voice his need but wriggled aside to give him space to climb up.

The simple room and its lack of plumbing was a harsh contrast to the comparative luxury of the Copelands' farmhouse, and somehow worse than the indignity suffered while traipsing through forests and mountainsides and deserts. After emptying his bladder into the refuse bucket and covering it with cloth to mellow the smell, he went to the kitchenette to wash his hands.

The space felt smaller than he remembered. It was home, but it wasn't. It was exactly how he remembered, but he no longer fit.

On the windowsill above the sink sat three twine dolls the size of his thumb, looped and twisted into the vague shape of a person. Children's toys for demi-kin. Running his finger over the musty old twine, the sensation prickled at a memory buried too deep to truly recall.

Quietly, Edwina joined him. She stared at the dolls a moment before letting her voice crack through the room.

"It feels like so many lifetimes ago."

Swallowing against the lump in his throat, Cinn nodded. The quiet settled between them again as Edwina watched him look around in disbelief, refamiliarizing himself with the little kitchen. The storm in her eyes grew tempestuous.

"I looked everywhere for you. I'm sorry. I'm sorry I couldn't . . ."

Tears fell as she trembled. His hands were just as unsteady as they cupped her face, his own twisted in a grimace. Just a few words of comfort were all he wanted, but something about being back in this city had stolen them from him again. All he could do was shake his head and hope she understood how little he blamed her.

A gasp, and Radley sat up on the floor, wild eyed and fists clenched.

"He's gone."

"He's here," Edwina called softly, removing Cinn's hands from her face. "It's okay, he's here."

Twisting on the floor, Radley's panic didn't ease until he'd blinked a few times, and Cinn wondered how long it would be before any of them believed their eyes weren't lying.

Radley opened his mouth but, before he could speak, there was a heavy rapping on the door. The sound barely registered before Cinn was tripping over his own feet, backing away. With the door's latch and handle broken, Radley had pushed their dining table in front of it after the Copelands left, but Cinn knew the shoddy barricade would do nothing to keep out the guards who had undoubtedly come for him.

Eyes too wide, breaths too quick, he reached for a knife at his hip that wasn't there.

"It's okay," Edwina said. "It's just your humans. They said they would come back, remember?"

That Puddles only swished her tail and closed her eyes again hinted at that truth, but still, Edwina stepped between Cinn and the door, one hand deep in the pocket of her skirt.

Radley was still rubbing sleep from his eyes, but he too came to the kitchen for a blunt knife. He took one pained look at Cinn, who'd backed all the way into the corner, before facing the door, grumbling, "Not on my fucking watch."

Sweat soaked Cinn's clothes and no matter how many breaths he took, he couldn't seem to get any air. He shouldn't have come back. He shouldn't have fallen asleep. He still didn't really understand how he'd gone from almost killing the princess in the rubble of a strange castle to waking up in Hyrsch, but staying had been a mistake.

The window nearby would get him out to the street. If he rolled into the landing, he might not break his legs. The fall might break *something*, but it didn't matter as long as he could still run.

No.

Like a leash on a rabid dog, the word brought his panic to a halt.

No running. The knock on the door might have decimated whatever control he'd gained over himself in Qiri, but he could hold on to the one promise he'd made himself. He would not leave Eddy and Rad behind. Not again. Besides, even if it was the guards, even if they took him—his breath caught at the thought, a high-pitched ringing deep in his ears—Cinn had already established that Eaon would come for him.

The name brought feeling back to his face just in time for dread to rush down his spine.

Where was Eaon?

Radley pushed the dining table away from the door and yanked it open, knife pointed at where William and Sarah stood holding plates of food.

"Oh, Mother have mercy," Sarah gasped.

William flinched but held his ground, looking from the knife pointed at his barrel of a chest to the man holding it. "Feel free to lower that, son."

Radley narrowed his eyes to the plates and spat, "What is that?"

"Dinner."

"Why?"

Slowly, William took a step forward. Knife still raised, Radley mirrored him.

"Rad, stop it. Let them in," Edwina scolded, leaving Cinn frozen in the corner as she stomped to the impasse at the door. Then, to the Copelands, she said, "Sorry about him."

"No need to apologize," William said, low and slow, like speaking to a skittish horse. The way he used to speak to Cinn when he'd first found him. "We understand."

"Neither of us could sleep much, given the daylight," Sarah added, forcing a smile. Her graying hair was tied back into a tight braid, her clothes fresh and fancier than what she normally wore. "So, we just started cooking. The witches really appreciated it, poor darlings, and we figured you three might not have much stocked here."

Placing the plates on the crooked table, Sarah met Cinn's wide stare for the first time. The strained smile fell away.

"You alright, sweetheart?"

Silence fell thick as Cinn found himself unable to conjure enough sense to even sign.

Edwina explained, "He got a fright at the knocking."

"Of course. It can't be easy being here. But I brought your favorites."

Sure enough, one of the plates was laden with large, flat biscuits. William added two more to the table, stacked with sandwiches and pastries, ensuring he was between his wife and Radley at all times. There was more salt in his salt-and-pepper beard than the last time Cinn had seen them, deep lines of exhaustion framing William's wary eyes.

Despite having backed off, Radley still brimmed with hostility. "How do we know you didn't poison them?"

"Rad!" Eddy barked.

"Don't snipe at me," he bit back. "They're humans, Red."

Loosing a shaky breath, Cinn stepped out of the corner. He went to Radley's side and wrapped his hand around the fist clenching the knife. His brother wouldn't relent at first, but Cinn was just as tall as he was now. With all the weight he had put on, they were about the same size, too. Cinn dug his fingernails into his brother's hand until he released the knife, then he went to the table and took a biscuit from Sarah's plate. She smiled and flattened the sweaty hair curling behind his ear; an affection he couldn't help but lean into.

"Thank you for the food," Edwina said, though the last word was cut off as Radley stormed to the kitchen and slammed a cabinet door.

He didn't come back out.

Cinn frowned, but Sarah squeezed his shoulder.

"It's alright," she whispered gently. "We've housed many demi-kin in our time, including plenty as angry as him."

One side of Cinn's mouth quirked, but instead of biting into the cinnamon biscuit, he returned her squeeze and followed Radley to the kitchen.

A red haze still stained the sky above the distant city walls, signaling the forest fire's continued burning. The golden light filtering inside lit up dust motes like flickering embers. Radley stared out the window, leaning against the counter with his hands braced on either side of a half-full bottle of amber liquid.

Cinn stepped to his brother's side and tried to catch his eye, but Radley turned away, pulling the bottle out of Cinn's reach. For a long time, neither spoke. Only the hushed small talk taking place where the Copelands and Edwina had settled on the sagging couch eased the quiet.

Radley let out a harsh breath. "I'm not out of line. I don't know them, and I don't trust them. I know they helped you or whatever, but they're human, and you . . . You're different. How do I know they didn't hurt you too? You can't even tell me, right? I heard you don't speak at all anymore."

Finally, Radley looked at him, and the bloodshot eyes weren't the product of the drink in his hand. Not tonight.

There was so much to say. Not just the words stuck in Cinn's throat, but the ones burning behind Radley's eyes too. Instead, Cinn took Radley's hand off the bottle and placed the biscuit in it instead. His brother stared at the middle ground somewhere just left of it, voice cracking when he spoke again.

"I didn't think I'd ever see you again."

Cinn pressed his lips together to keep the pain from spilling. He desperately wanted to tell Radley that he understood. That he'd thought the same. That he loved him, and he was sorry. He could speak, he knew he could, but the pressure of doing so right now was too much. His mouth, his throat, his voice—none of it would cooperate.

"I . . . I wanted to be the one to go in. The night the rebels got you out." Radley didn't seem to be having the same problem, still unfocused on the biscuit held between them. "We tried, Ry. We tried every day to find you, I swear it. But it was like you disappeared. Eddy searched every nook and cranny of the palace at least ten times, and I wrung every bit of information I could out of anyone who worked there, but it was like you never existed.

"And then we finally had information on where you were, and I didn't care where it came from, I was going to light the whole fucking palace on fire if that was what it took to get to you. But Siobhan and Wendy were better spies, so I led the distraction. Eddy made sure . . ." Even lost in his rant, desperate to get as many words out as quickly as possible, just in case fate ripped them apart again, Radley hesitated over the name he somehow knew not to speak. "Eddy made sure there was enough wine consumed that nobody would be down there that night.

"We were there. We thought you'd make contact when you could, tell us where you'd escaped to so we could come find you, but when you didn't . . . We thought maybe they got you again. Or maybe something else did."

Being torn open by a lupanis would have hurt less than listening to the desperation pouring out of his brother. And maybe he wasn't ready to stop being a coward, because he couldn't bring himself to tell Radley that, while they had spent years searching for him, he had forgotten them. Had wanted to forget them.

Radley's other hand—the one not holding a cinnamon biscuit with gentleness unprecedented—gripped Cinn's sleeve and pulled him close, whispering in his ear, "If we were right, if these humans did something to you and you're just afraid to—"

Vehemently, Cinn shook his head.

Warm and bitter breath exchanged between them as Radley stepped back to meet Cinn's eye. "Blink three times if you need me to get rid of them."

Again, Cinn shook his head.

When Radley made to protest once more, Cinn decided he had to prove it. Prove they were safe and prove that he really was home. Prove to his brother that, yes, he was different, but he was still Ryson too.

Snapping off a piece of the soft biscuit between them, Cinn shoved it into Radley's open mouth. Reeling back, his brother choked on it for a second, but as Cinn failed to suppress a mischievous smirk, Radley's hacking morphed to a single shocked laugh.

"Little shit." The words were muffled around the biscuit he spat out into cupped hands, soggy and half-chewed. "Come here."

The apartment was too small to play games but having spent the past six or seven months running around Nir, it was easy as breathing to duck under Radley's reaching arm, twisting out of his grubby hands. His face ached from the wicked grin plastered there as Radley lunged again, cussing beautifully. With the wall behind him, Cinn had little choice but to jump nimbly on top of the kitchen table, scattering loose papers and empty inkpots.

"No shoes on the counter!" Edwina barked from the couch, but the effect was lost to the laugh behind it.

Radley gave up trying to catch him and settled for flinging the biscuit at Cinn's head instead. It hit with force, but Cinn was too busy cackling to care about the crumbs in his ear as he climbed down. Putting his arm over his brother's shoulder, ducking when Radley ruffled his hair, Cinn led him back to the picnic the others had set up on the floor by the hearth.

The joviality dampened as they sat down. Radley shot a dark look at William, but there were no more remarks. Instead, Radley took another biscuit and ate.

CHAPTER TWO

CINN

HE KEPT HIS MOVEMENTS SLOW AND HIS VOCABULARY SIMPLE SO THE Copelands could keep up, reciting his story aloud for Edwina and Radley. Cinn was keenly aware of his siblings watching his hands, both picking at their food with less and less enthusiasm.

First, he told them about the Copeland farm. How Sparrow soldiers had come looking for him, so they'd fled to the witch territory of Wyldeden for sanctuary. How he had thought the only way to fix things was to fulfill a Morvish prophecy and go to Ahrenhale, so he'd left the Copelands behind and made his way to the Northern Mountains and through the wards.

He told them what the wards really were—not a bubble around Qiri, but a bubble around the rest of Nir, keeping the primordial deity of Chaos caged. He told them about the unrest in the city, about the Unifiers and the Separatists, and how there was no outside help coming. He told them about Moyra. About Gatty and Lula, Dida and Nena, but left out the selkies and his bargain. His fingers reached for the bare skin at the base of his throat as he remembered them, though; the amulet he'd gone back into the lake to retrieve, along with the rest of his things, were still in his pack at the bottom of the Womb. The loss of his trinkets grated more than he wanted to admit, but he thought William noticed anyway. The man who had become like a father to him had found the three dolls on the windowsill, taken them, just to place them in Cinn's hands with a sympathetic look. Cinn fiddled with the twine lumps now as he mulled over the rest of his story.

He did not tell them about what happened with Moyra in that shack by the lake. He did not tell them about the Kinner at Orhn. He skipped past all the discoveries he'd made that did not concern them. He picked up his story again with trying to find the Copelands and ending up in the ruins of Dusarn instead. He fumbled as he told them who he had found there. About the beasts and the monsters and all the blood he had spilled. He did not remember how he'd gotten from there to Hyrsch, which is when Sarah took over the story.

She told them about the perfect beauty of Wyldeden, the generosity of its people and the wonders of magic witnessed there. She told them what it was like to hear that the forest was burning. The evacuations, and the people who had refused to leave their home. The way the trees had grown faces and moved aside, but no matter how easy their path was made and how fast they moved, the fire was on their tails.

Which is when Eavha arrived. Eavha, and *her*.

Sarah averted her eyes and kept her explanation of the portal *she* had opened brief. How the clan jumped through a hole in Celeste's realm to come out closer to the Dividing River. The crossing had been an ordeal, as had their venture through the ordinary forest of Oford, but they made it.

She wasn't sure what happened between arriving in Hyrsch and the scene in the palace courtyard, but she managed to fill the gap in Cinn's memories: *she* had returned from her home city with an unconscious Cinn on her back before collapsing.

Sitting on the floor in front of the empty fire, Cinn felt very, very small in a world that was so very, very big.

Eaon and Moyra and Edwina and Radley and Sarah and William and Siobhan and Eavha and *her* . . . All his worlds were colliding, and he was drowning in the mess of it.

Find something to anchor yourself, Moyra had told him back in her cabin. *When you're feeling lost in your head, just find something to hold onto. Something real.*

It was the slave bread that came to mind. It was missing from their picnic, but he remembered making it for Moyra. Remembered the texture in his hands, the smell of yeast and butter and heat. Remembered deciding that it was okay for all these separate parts of himself to converge. He had greeted them, one by one; the slave, the prisoner, the refugee. The little boy lost and alone in knee-high snow somewhere in the Southern Spine.

The lanky cadet full of naive love and loyalty. The coward who left his friends behind when danger came knocking. A monster capable of committing genocide against his own people.

He was all these things at once, and that was okay.

{Are you okay?} he asked when Sarah finished.

"We're alright." Sarah yawned. "Tired, but alright."

"Word is most of the witches who left the forest made it to the city," Edwina added.

Most, but not all.

Cinn's hands shook. {Eaon?}

Tell me you've seen him. Tell me he is close and safe. And in the same breath, *Tell me he is nowhere near this city. Tell me she doesn't have him.*

William cleared his throat. "He's here in Hyrsch."

"Who is?" Edwina asked, looking between them.

Cinn barely heard William's explanation of who Eaon was over the ringing in his ears.

"Eaon is a Wyldeden witch Cinn met during the spring," William said, pausing to chew on the crust of a pork-and-cheese sandwich. He beat at his chest a little when it got stuck halfway down. "He's a good man. Stayed with us during the summer. He's the one who taught Cinn how to sign."

It didn't seem like enough to describe who Eaon was to him.

As if they could see the way Cinn's heart was beating through his skin, upper lip damp with sweat, they gave him a moment to wrangle all the little parts of his mind that went fleeing in a billion directions at the news. Eaon was here. Eaon was in Hyrsch. Was it relief or terror or some sickening combination that had him pushing away his dinner?

Radley picked at the dry skin of his knuckles until he couldn't hold back his question any longer. Clipped and tight, he asked, "So . . . Cinn. Is that what we're calling you now?"

Hearing his new name out of his brother's mouth was disorienting.

William looked to Cinn, rubbing his left shoulder. "I forgot that's not your real name."

"Why?" Edwina asked. "Why Cinn? What does it mean?"

"He couldn't tell us," Sarah answered for him. "When he first came to us, we didn't know what to call him. But he loved the smell of cinnamon, so we nicknamed him."

Burning red, Cinn grimaced at his siblings. It was so stupid. But Edwina and Radley didn't laugh, matching puckers deepening between their brows.

{It's not that I wanted a new name,} he began to explain, despite knowing they couldn't understand. {I don't think I even remembered it at that point.}

Sarah shuddered, hand fluttering to her throat. William stilled, swallowing anger with slow, measured breaths. They'd seen him at his worst—had dragged him kicking and screaming back to civility—but he had forgotten that he had not told them the same things he had told Eaon. They didn't know how bad things had been inside his head; that he had buried his own name deep in the fog. They didn't know that sometimes the sight of his own body was jarring, because he forgot that he wasn't seventeen anymore. How every time that happened, the last three years came crashing down all at once to leave him heaving.

"I don't think that's why they're upset, sweetheart," Sarah said, leaning across the plates of food to take his hand. Her own eyes were as glassy as Edwina's and Radley's were growing again.

{Why are they upset with me then?} Cinn asked.

"They're not upset *with you*."

"What is he saying?" Radley asked, gentler than he had spoken to the Copelands yet.

Sarah held his gaze, waiting for permission to translate. Confused, but trusting her, Cinn gave it with the smallest nod.

"He thought you were upset with him for going by a different name," Sarah explained, continuing even as Edwina shook her head. "He also wanted you to know that he didn't want a new name. It's just that he couldn't remember his at the time."

A small cracking sound slipped from Edwina's lips before she slapped a hand over her mouth, turning her face toward the window and the darkening city beyond. Radley placed a hand on her shoulder.

Eyes wide, Cinn looked between them all. {I'm sorry. I didn't mean to—}

"You don't apologize," William interrupted sternly.

"No," Radley agreed. "Not for a damned thing."

Edwina couldn't turn to meet his eye, but took a steadying breath as she asked, "Would . . . Would you prefer that? Would it be easier for you if we called you Cinn from now on?"

The question was so unexpected, Cinn could only stare. For at least five minutes, he couldn't get his brain to make words. He didn't know what to say. He didn't know what he wanted. He was Ryson, but he wasn't. He was Cinn, but he wasn't.

In the end, he simply shrugged.

"Doesn't matter," Radley said, unusually mellow.

"It does, Rad," Eddy began to argue, but he squeezed her shoulder.

"It doesn't, because no matter what, we're still the Triple R Threat. Right? Maybe we'll call him Ry-Cinn."

The snorting laugh that came out of him was inhuman. It was contagious too; soon they were all chuckling. With that settled, Cinn turned to the Copelands once more. No matter how sidetracked they got, he still had questions to ask.

{Do you know where Eaon is? I need to see him.}

The laughter died as suddenly as it came on.

"Sweetheart." Sarah's tone set off the swell of panic that was always waiting for a reason to rise. "Eaon isn't well. He's hurt. Eavha is treating him in the palace infirmary."

All the heat left his body. Sagging back against the lumpy, sodden couch, he closed his eyes against the maelstrom in his head.

"Breathe, kid," William said softly.

"It's alright," Edwina added. "It's okay. I . . . I should go over to the palace anyway. Check on things. I'll tell him you're asking about him. I . . . I'll find out as much as I can."

He had dreamed of this. Of Edwina in the palace. Of Edwina in the dungeon, in that cell. On that table. How it was all his fault that she was dying, dying, dying . . .

Before he could think, before he could get a grip on himself, his mouth opened.

"*No.*"

The word was a crack in the foundation of the city. It silenced the entire world.

Opening his eyes, everyone was staring, but he couldn't explain. He couldn't speak again or sign. The fear eating his body from the inside out —*Eaon, Eaon, Eaon, Eaon*—was only made worse by the thought of Edwina going anywhere near the palace. Of her being out of his sight for even a second. They'd only just found each other again. He couldn't bear to let her go.

Sarah petted his hand and kept her grip tight before turning to Edwina. "I think that would be a good idea, love."

No.

No, no, no.

No.

Breaths too quick, too shallow.

Skin too tight, too damp.

Vision blurring, Cinn wrenched his hand from Sarah's and lunged for his sister. He didn't really think about why. Didn't think about what he was going to do, just that he had to stop her.

Radley caught him mid-leap, hauling him aside, crushing him against his own body.

But then it wasn't Radley at all. It was that big hulking guard of *hers* that was always in the shadows, watching. Waiting. That day he'd been shot by a stray bolt, after the conversation in the parlor soured and Cinn realized where he was being led, he'd made a run for it, but that brutish guard had been lurking. He'd grabbed Cinn around the waist like a ragdoll and half thrown, half dragged him the rest of the way down into the dungeons.

He would not go without a fight.

"I got him, Red." The man grunted as Cinn's elbow connected with something hard and unflinching. "I got him. Just go."

"I'll be back. I promise, okay? I'll be right back. You'll be glad I went."

Throwing his weight sent the man to the floor, grip slackening enough for Cinn to wrench free. The man was quick though, snatching his wrist. Pure instinct had his fist flying. He had bettered a pack of lupanis and shtryg, had scared off those monstrous beetle things, had almost beaten *her*; it would take more than one man to stop him now.

All he needed was a weapon.

"Easy, kid. Easy."

A second, larger man bullied him into the corner. The broken door banged closed, and Cinn remembered why he was fighting. Edwina. Eddy. Red. His sister was going to the palace.

Where he wasn't, right now.

He was too late to stop her.

The apartment swam back into focus: William, a veritable wall between him and everyone else; Radley, nose bleeding and watching Cinn with an expression he didn't understand; Puddles, tail puffed up but inching across the floor toward him.

Sarah appeared at William's side and placed a gentle hand on Cinn's shoulder. He flinched beneath the touch, but it was so light, so careful, that he didn't pull away. His chest hurt, and he realized he hadn't taken a breath in a minute. When he sucked one in, it was wet and raspy and entirely unsatisfying.

"Head between your knees, sweetheart," Sarah encouraged, pressing down just enough to encourage him to the floor.

His knees gave out too quickly. William was there to catch him, to lower him down steadily. Radley remained close, taking up the world.

"I'll fucking kill her," Radley growled to nobody in particular.

An apology sat leaden and bitter on Cinn's useless tongue. Shutting his eyes, he buried his head in his knees.

CHAPTER THREE

AISLING

THE TATTOOS ON AISLING'S HANDS WERE RUINED. THERE WAS something poetic in the kinner being the one to rob her of the spellmarks' protection after all she had taken from him. Sunset glistened on scar tissue as she turned her palms over, but she truly couldn't bring herself to care about the damage. Instead, something akin to relief sat heavy on her shoulders; she didn't need these particular marks anymore. They had served their purpose.

Eavha's careful ministrations had repaired the nerve damage inside, but Aisling wouldn't let Eavha push herself to breaking point again. The Wyldeden healer could stomp her feet and scream she was "fine" until blue in the face all she pleased, but The Key Mark for Those Unbound etched on Aisling's flesh would remain twisted to uselessness.

The palm tattoos were the first gift Davina had given her—freedom from her brother's awful curses. She could be bound by him no longer, nor by anyone ever again. She had kept them secret with silk gloves but had walked the castle halls in Dusarn a little less afraid.

Now, Nevan was dead.

Her parents were dead.

Davina was dead. Beyond dead. The used moonstone was a lead weight in her pocket. One she would carry for the rest of her days.

At the top of the palace's western tower, Aisling lay on the chaise by her balcony and traced the lines on her palm with her nails. There wasn't time for moping, but Eavha had threatened to tie her to the bed if she didn't rest, didn't let herself heal, didn't let her magic recoup. Scraped raw, her body still felt incorporeal; a strong breeze could very well scatter her cells like dandelion seeds. There wasn't enough left to even scry for Kaelean, Wyldeden's missing high priestess.

Normally, such a threat would have earned a scoff. Would have tasted like a challenge, a dare. But ever since the fire in Anfar began to burn, Eavha had—in the most eloquent terms Aisling could think of—been on the verge of irrevocably losing her shit. Considering the shenanigans that beautiful creature got up to when she was in a good mood, Aisling wasn't tempted to find out what Eavha was capable of when pushed too far.

But being alone with her thoughts was not ideal. There was too much silence. Too much space for wanderers.

Slowly, the way one noticed footsteps on a staircase, awareness of the lost souls wandering the void grew. Wrathful curses echoed from deep in the void—one voice in particular was familiar, turning her heart stony, her skin tightening into the shield she desperately needed whenever faced with her mother's temper.

There was satisfaction, though, knowing Queen Tallula had not received the Lover's embrace into peaceful eternity. Why would she have? The Mother had turned her back on Chaos and his cruelty to form Balance with the High Spirit of Death, evermore known as the Lover. The Sparrow Coven had been formed in devotion to that Balance, to tackle the abomination that were the Kinner. When and why Queen Tallula had turned traitor, Aisling could only guess.

"*Fool.*"

The voice echoed from so deep in the void that Aisling barely heard it. Slamming down her mental shields, she cut herself off. There were no ghosts left that she wished to speak with, and she was not ready to deal with the ones she didn't. Perhaps later, if Aisling was very clever and very careful, she could trick the queen into telling her more about Chaos and what she was about to face, but not yet. She was too tired to build the mental space required for such interrogation. Could hardly walk among the people she needed to prepare for warfare, let alone tangle with her mother.

Heaving a great sigh, she looked longingly to the drinks cart by the window. It had been a while since she had turned to her vices, and if getting to her feet was any less effort, she would gladly drown herself in them.

Aisling was weighing the consequences of calling for Eavha's company when the hair on her arms began to rise. Though it made her head throb immediately, the dregs of her magic stirred when coaxed, and Aisling felt the air's disturbance when the door to her suite opened. She didn't hear the heavy wood creak, but she did hear the rustling of skirts and slippered footsteps trying to be silent. Not Clayton, then, who she had ordered to rest before he became utterly useless; his footsteps were heavier and lacked caution. Not Eavha, either, since she could hear them at all, but it was someone well practiced in moving around unnoticed. Since she had also ordered her handmaiden to bed and Larissa was not in the habit of disobeying, there was only one person it could feasibly be.

"You're not a servant anymore, Miss Red. You do not need to hover by the door, waiting for me to beckon you."

At the sharp inhale, Aisling turned. Her new second-in-command stood in the doorway, hands clasped tight on the handle to smother its noise.

An interesting little bird, Edwina. Always had been. Demure and proper in the way good servants were, but with just enough spine not to balk at the unsightly things Aisling sometimes needed help with. It was why she was chosen to be Aisling's primary handmaiden, why she had been allowed present during Aisling's meetings with Nora, planning the defense of the city. Quietly clever, secretly ruthless—Aisling could see it more so now than she had before; the nerve it took to betray another rebel in order to get closer to Aisling. Closer to her brother. It was present, now, in the cold stare Edwina leveled. If there was any remnant of cordiality the ex-handmaiden felt obligated to produce before royalty, she didn't offer it.

"If I were you, I would not be so hasty to invite people closer."

Aisling didn't lift a brow or quirk her lips, mirroring Edwina's blank stoicism. "Are you going to stab me again?"

"I never stabbed you once."

"Is today the day, then?"

The slightest twitch beneath her eye gave away Edwina's seething rage. "My brother cannot speak."

"He can," Aisling assured, ignoring the cold sweat beading down her spine. "He just won't."

The door closed with a heavy click as Edwina stepped fully into the room. It was instinct for Aisling to look down at a potential threat's hands; Edwina may not have taken a stab at Aisling yet, but she had held a knife to Clayton's throat and seemed awfully comfortable doing so.

There was no weapon clutched there, but Edwina's hands were balled into tight fists.

"That is an attitude you'd best guard a little closer to your chest," she spat. "He *cannot*. Just because I am working with you, does not mean I have forgotten or forgiven what you did."

Since that day in her throne room when she'd appointed Edwina, it was an image Aisling saw every time she fell asleep: the look on Edwina's face as she waited to die, spitting vitriol freely.

"*I scrubbed my brother's blood out of your clothes.*"

Aisling wished she could say Edwina's mask was so perfect that she couldn't tell how traumatizing those nights had been for the handmaiden, but the truth was that Aisling had been too blood-hazed and drunk to notice. In her dreams, though, she saw clearly the way Edwina would have stood in stunned terror as Aisling stripped and piled her soiled clothes in her arms. The tears she must have shed while laundering away the evidence of her brother's suffering. The nights Edwina had stayed in the suite in case Aisling woke with needs, silently plotting her murder.

"Would you like your pound of flesh, Edwina? Would that make it better?"

Her tone was mocking, but the offer was sincere. And surprising. She hadn't meant it until she said it, but Edwina wasn't the only one cracking. Aisling's mask had been slipping since the day she met Eavha, and in the gaps weeds of guilt and shame had taken root. Without her vineyard-grown poison to kill the wretched things, she was splitting open.

She didn't hate her own destruction as much as she thought she should.

"I want nothing from you." Edwina's cold fury was a thunderclap. "Especially anything that would debase me to your level."

At that, Aisling smiled. Doing so elicited flared nostrils and another threatening step forward, but Aisling couldn't help it.

"It is nice," she explained, "to find myself surrounded by so many people unwilling to do harm no matter how angry they are. Mean's I've been making better choices."

The storm raged on in those big, blue eyes for another long moment. When it passed, Aisling was doused in the humidity it left behind, her robe clinging to her skin.

"I heard you were the one who brought him back home."

The summer night did not harbor a breeze, but Aisling shivered anyway.

"Yes, well." She could no longer hold Edwina's gaze, her heart doing terrible, painful things at the reminder of that night. "I couldn't leave him in Dusarn for the beasts, could I. Handing over a weapon like that to the enemy is not good war strategy."

He will have healed perfectly after what she and Davina had done to him; that spell Aisling didn't know, yet fell from her possessed lips to shatter every bone in his body. She knew exactly how long it would have taken; the sounds it would have made as his body put itself back together. She had broken him before, so she didn't need to ask how he was. Not that she would dare. She had no right to know or care. Wasn't sure doing either was good for her sanity.

"Is that all he is to you? A weapon?"

Not since Eavha had made her speak his name.

"Do you know many people who drink themselves into a stupor to numb what they did to a weapon?"

"I don't know many people who would do what you have done."

"Lucky you." She needed tea, or water, or *something* to get the bitter taste of her own self-pity off her tongue.

"I won't thank you for bringing him back."

Edwina had reached the chaise, but she wasn't looking at Aisling anymore, brows furrowed instead at the distant red haze out the window. The dusk hour used to soften summer's sun, but the fire saw the days darkened, nights aglow—a reversal that wouldn't be righted until either the Mare-blessed witches' rain dances proved fruitful, or the forest was razed.

"I didn't expect you to." Aisling forced herself to sit up. To stand. She moved slowly but steadily to the drinks cart and poured herself a glass of water. "What I do expect is for you to fulfill the duties you agreed to when you became my Second. Are you going to be able to do that?"

The silence that followed was weighted.

"Promise me you will not touch him again," Edwina asked, the quiver in her voice sharp as glass. "Promise me you will not speak to him. That you won't even look at him. Just leave him alone."

Aisling had to wet her tongue before she could speak. "He's still here, then?"

"I swear to every god, Aisling—"

"I promise," she interrupted before Edwina could lay down her threat. There was no magic behind the words because, unlike the fae, promises were not inherently binding for a witch; marks and rituals had to be used to make them so. Regardless, this was not one she intended to break. "And if, for some reason, I have need to speak to him, I will not do so without asking you first."

Edwina sniffed, and Aisling gave her a moment to compose herself. She returned to the chaise, swallowing a relieved sigh to be seated again.

"I said that I didn't believe in the gods, but all it takes is a look outside and I can deny no longer that Chaos is coming," Edwina finally said, still facing the balcony. "We will be at war soon and you are not at your best. I can begin the preparations."

Aisling nodded. "I only need a day or so, then I'll be back."

"I will manage until then."

Edwina turned to leave, but another question demanded to be answered, for no other reason than curiosity.

"Does he know?" Aisling watched Edwina pause. "Does he know what position you hold in my court?"

The burning red of Edwina's ears was all the answer she was going to get, hurried footsteps and the slam of her suite door her only farewell.

CHAPTER FOUR

EAVHA

E<small>AON COUGHED AND</small> E<small>AVHA SLAMMED CLOSED THE THICK TOME SHE'D</small> been reading. The puff it caused blew out the nearest candle and it was all Eavha could do not to scream obscenities at it. Instead, she stood from the desk she'd been working at and stormed back to Eaon's bedside.

The palace infirmary was a stark contrast to the clinic in Wyldeden. The cabinets used to be well stocked before they'd been raided for the influx of injured witches outside, but the dark stone walls were suffocating compared to the tall, bright white ceilings she was used to. She missed the open, arching windows too. Whoever had designed the palace hadn't considered that fresh air and sunlight were important parts of the healing process.

As was patient cooperation.

The day had brought out the severity of Eaon's injuries. Dark purple bruises discolored the ridges of his skull: eye sockets, cheekbones, jaw and brow. It was worse on the parts of his body that had taken the brunt of the fall. The bones in his legs might be back in their right places, but every inch of skin was mottled, joints swollen with fluid. The lines of his ribs, his collarbones, his shoulder blades, were all a blackish blue and every breath grew more strained. There was soot in his lungs, and it was hard to tell if the shivers that wracked his body were an undercurrent of the Lover's blessing or a fever.

Either way, consciousness was proving difficult for Eaon to hold onto, yet he always found it whenever Eavha drew too close.

"Yvette has done all she can," Eavha said, fists curled at her sides. "You have to let me work."

"No." Breathless and rasping, Eaon had said the word so many times that Eavha wasn't sure he remembered any others.

"The gloves work," she reminded him. Briefly, in small doses. Too much contact and the leather began to break apart, but that was a risk she was willing to take.

Sanni, her patron spirit of healing, hovered closer than ever before. Every whim was permitted, so Eavha knew she could whittle her power down quickly, spear it through veins and marrow and nerves efficiently, and get out again before the necrotic magic poisoning her brother could touch her.

She could do it.

"No."

"It will take months to heal on your own." The petulant stomp of her foot had no effect at all, but the truth in her words hit home. "We don't have months."

Eaon's jaw clenched but he didn't say "no" again.

It didn't feel like progress.

Especially when she reached for the gloves and the room temperature dropped—the first sign that the hideous seed of power inside him was rearing its deadly head.

But she was out of ideas. It wasn't just frustration and exhaustion that had her eyes burning, but the hours upon hours of reading. More reading than she had ever done in her life. Every book that so much as alluded to healing had been brought to her, but not one of them was helpful; there were four vials of unicorn blood up in Aisling's prayer room and not a single recipe to tell her how to use it.

Glancing over to the other workstation, Eavha caught the phouka's gaze. She may have been in this infirmary for almost twenty-four hours, but so had the seven-foot-tall goat-man. Black as a starless night, eyes like slitted yellow moons, he'd been mostly useless, lurking in the shadows with his bag of bones like a ghost story personified. Eavha had tossed the bones Cinn found at the bottom of the Womb—used to stabilize Eaon's injuries —aside, but as soon as the phouka was no longer needed to control Eaon's surging, he had collected them from the courtyard, cleaning them reverently.

To say it was unnerving was an understatement. She had met the phouka briefly in passing when they'd been in Pirevia, but she'd been too distracted to really care what he was doing there or about the shimmering silver mark on the back of his neck. Now, spending so much time in close quarters with a powerful fae, an Old One, a creature who had been wandering the world since the dawn of creation . . . Unnerving didn't begin to cover it.

But as always, when the room began to chill, he left his bones on the desk and stepped forward. He looked from Eavha to Eaon, from the gloves to her abandoned book.

"I have an idea."

Eaon shuddered, eyes fluttering closed, and Eavha wondered again if it was a sign of infection or some visceral reaction to the phouka's voice.

She had already made one bargain without thought to consequence. Sanni's continued presence, her unhindered power a painful pulse through her veins, was proof. She had also spent far too long listening to Eaon lecture about the danger of fae to simply ask the phouka what his idea was. So she stared, waiting.

He didn't notice her caution.

"There was a game we used to play, back in the dawn days. We would tie a string of humans together by their hands and a nymph would send a spark of magic into one end to see how far the effects traveled. Admittedly, things often got out of hand. Humans are such flimsy things. But the idea is the same. If you're strong enough to get your magic to pass through, use me as a conduit to heal him. It removes the risk of contact."

Eavha blinked, unsure she understood fully what was being said and equally unsure that she wanted to. The story caught Eaon's attention, but he was either too tired or too sore to manage another "no."

The concept of conduits was not new—crystals had been used by artisans in Wyldeden for centuries—but there had never been a need in the healing field before. All her training had been based on direct, physical contact: the search, the diagnosis, the repair. Doing it remotely had never worked, and the idea of using another living being as a conduit . . .

She didn't know. She had never tried. Wasn't sure anybody ever had, since, until now, there had been no need. But just because something hadn't been done, just because she didn't know how, didn't mean she couldn't try. It hadn't stopped her before. So much of her learning had been instinctual; it was what made her so good at it.

"Will it hurt you?" Eavha asked.

"Quite likely."

Regardless, the phouka held out one large, claw-tipped hand and clamped the other around Eaon's wrist.

Do it, Sanni whispered. *I know this phouka. He can be trusted.*

With a nod, Eavha placed her slim hand in the phouka's and wrangled her magic into something she could use.

"It might take me a minute to figure this out," she warned.

A needle. Threading it through the phouka's flesh, through vein and sinew, her blessing told her of the phouka's health. Not a single weak joint or lingering bruise, his soul firmly locked in the heat of his chest. Coating it all was the shimmery tang of unicorn blood. The magic stemming from the mark on his neck was a familiar flavor, her needle blending seamlessly on its way through. There was no distress for either of them, but there was also no apparent way to leave the phouka's body any way other than which she'd come.

More, Sanni nudged.

Taking a steadying breath, Eavha withdrew her needle and drove back in with a scalpel. Cutting through to the other side, she could feel the point of contact between the phouka and Eaon.

"Don't be afraid, little one," the phouka teased, tension coiling in his body in preparation.

Eaon watched with heavy eyes, breath rattling.

More.

Sweat soaked her already soiled healer's uniform as her magic hit the phouka with all the subtlety of a hammer. The only sign that he noticed was the hitch of his breath.

The point of contact loomed like a wall, and when her hammer hit, it bounced off, ricocheting back through the phouka to burn in her own bones. The gasp she made was involuntary. Eaon narrowed his eyes.

"It's fine, it's not you," she panted, releasing the phouka's hand so she could shake out her own. "It's just a new technique. I'll get the hang of it."

Her assurances didn't land, but she left Eaon to his suspicion and closed her eyes, grabbing hold of the phouka with steel.

More.

Burrowing deep into her reserve, she went back like a battering ram.

A mistake.

The magic recoiled back to her with enough force to shake her organs, bile rising before she could stop it. Vomit now joined the gray soot and dark witch blood staining her skirt and chest binding.

The phouka dropped her hand and glared down at Eaon, who didn't have the energy to do more than twitch.

"Why isn't it working?" Eavha asked, wiping her mouth on the back of her hand and swallowing down the lingering taste.

31

The phouka kept his fierce glare leveled at Eaon and ground out, "We will keep trying."

Shivering, Eavha went to the bedside table and poured herself a fresh cup of ginseng tea. "Give me a minute."

It had been a while since she had failed at something. She didn't like it.

～

"Stop," a voice called in Nirnish from the door. "Eavha, stop."

Their most recent attempt to breach the barrier between the phouka's hand and Eaon's wrist had stolen Eavha's balance, the rebound of her magic leaving her crumpled on the floor. Still, Sanni was a warm blanket over her shoulders, urging her to try again. She was halfway back to her feet when Moyra Thorne rushed into the infirmary.

Grabbing her arm, Moyra helped her up and cupped her face. "Stop. Your nose is bleeding."

Wiping at the dribble, Eavha pulled away. The Qiri witch may have been of assistance triaging out on the streets, but she had no business touching her with such familiarity.

"I'm fine," she hissed. "As soon as I figure out how to do this, everything will be fine."

"You need to rest."

"I need to help my brother."

Moyra glanced to Eaon's shivering form. There was definitely an infection setting in. Time was not on their side.

"I'll brew—"

"I've already brewed everything I can," Eavha interrupted, turning to down the last dregs of tea. "It's not enough."

Moyra raised her hands. "Let me help, Eavha."

"And what help are you?" she spat back, head squeezing tightly with the promise of a migraine. "Are you going to spout some nonsense prophecy that will miraculously cure him of infection? No? Then go away somewhere you are—ah!"

Cutting herself off with a startled shriek, she stared at the shadow melting beneath the bed, reforming into the shape of a large cat—a cat that solidified as it leaped upon Eaon's bed and thumped its heavy tail on the mattress.

"Careful with that tongue, child."

Eavha stared, heart beating too loudly to be sure she really heard what she thought she had heard. "You spoke."

"I bite, too."

"Gatty, stop it," Moyra chided. Then to Eavha, raised hands placating. "Please."

"You have a talking cat."

"He is my familiar. Ignore him—he gets grouchy when tired. We're talking about you and the fact that you're pushing yourself too hard."

She had heard of neither familiars nor of talking cats, but judging by the sudden tension in the phouka's shoulders and the arm he placed between the cat and Eaon, she guessed it was a type of fae.

Pretending it wasn't there was in her best interests. Don't engage, don't provoke.

"I am not burning out." Eavha lifted her chin. "Sanni guides me."

Moyra dropped her hands and grimaced. "No offense to your spirits, but I'm not sure they understand your mortal limits. There is a tea I learned in Ahrenhale that helps with fever. It uses elderflower—"

"Tried it."

"—soaked in lemon juice and steeped in ice water."

Eavha blinked, her jaw clenching. When she didn't interrupt Moyra again, the Morvish witch sighed.

"I have ingredients in my pack. Let me try it while you rest for a while. Get your strength back, change your clothes. Eat something. He will be okay."

"No." As soon as the word left her lips, she winced at the hypocrisy. Looking down to where Eaon was desperately clinging to consciousness, she huffed through her nose and scowled. Spite and pettiness were enough to change her mind. "Fine."

Every muscle in her body quivered as she backed out of the room, her stomach plummeting as soon as she stepped over the threshold. Only the hope that some fresh clothes and dinner would be enough to figure out how to heal her stupid brother made her walk away.

Not wanting to bother Aisling or climb all the way up to her suite, Eavha hunted the halls on the infirmary's level until she found a small room. If she had to guess, it looked like a servant's bedroom, with only a small cot under the window and a chest of drawers. Also, there was a servant there, frozen and blinking owlishly as she made the bed.

"Can I help you, Miss? Are you hurt?"

At first Eavha thought she was misunderstanding the Nirnish—of everyone, she was the least hurt—but then she remembered the stains on her clothes and the filth on her skin.

"No. Is this your room?"

"No, Miss. If you need somewhere to rest—"

She didn't. Her eyelids clicked when she blinked and her limbs felt twice as heavy as they should, but she did not need to rest.

Since it wasn't that particular servant's room, Eavha went to the drawers and pulled them open. Clothes. Perfect.

"Miss!" The servant gasped as Eavha stripped out of her soiled skirt, unwinding her chest binding, and leaving both in a heap on the floor. A pair of suede trousers were snug around her hips, the legs too long, but if she rolled the hems, she could keep from tripping over. The short-sleeved blouse was also tight around her breasts, so she yanked at the collar until it split, giving her room to breathe.

"Miss!"

"What?" Eavha snapped. She glared at the human woman while untwisting the bundled knot of her hair, shaking the curls loose before retying it.

"Those . . . Those are stablemen's clothes."

Again, Eavha wasn't sure she understood—she didn't know what a stableman was—but she vaguely recalled that people were expected to pay for things in the city. She could not just have what she needed. Frowning, she didn't know what she had to trade.

"I will pay later," she promised instead, bundling up her healer's uniform and leaving with as much urgency as she'd arrived with.

Feet silent on the marble floor, Eavha jogged for the nearest washroom. Though she had not spent much time in the palace, she had explored enough of it to remember what the little symbols on the doors meant and quickly found somewhere to wash her face. The reflection in the small mirror was startling, not because of how sooty and bloody she was, but because Eavha hadn't realized she'd been crying until she saw the fresh trails down her dirty cheeks. Her light-brown eyes were red-rimmed and watery, and she wasn't entirely sure why.

Except, the longer she stared at herself, the heavier the bundle of fabric in her arms became, and she began to recognize the feeling weighing down her lungs. She'd felt it the morning she had woken up in her childhood bed to a silent house, Eaon and their father away on a trip, her mother lying dead on the floor. She'd felt it when she'd arrived home after a long day at the clinic and found Eaon sitting on the porch, head in his hands, Kailevi collapsed in front of the sink where their dirty breakfast dishes lay untouched.

There wasn't time for this.

Before, she had not understood how Eaon could shove his grief deep enough to go through the motions of a funeral, faking a smile for everyone who congratulated them. Now, she thought maybe she did. There were things that needed to be done and she did not have time to mourn everything they'd lost.

Stuffing her uniform under her arm, she used the small sink to splash her face and neck clean, ready for fresh spellmarks. Perhaps the problem with the conduit was that she had been relying entirely on Sanni's willingness and not enough on her own rituals. Incantations were designed to induce and control the blessing within, and maybe it wasn't right to assume that just because Sanni's realm was wide open to her that she didn't need spellmarks anymore.

Eavha stood taller with the new idea of how to approach Eaon's healing. As she jogged through the halls, winding her way back to the infirmary, she only slowed long enough to dump her Wyldeden uniform in a garbage chute.

CHAPTER FIVE

EAVHA

Whatever Moyra gave Eaon had settled his breathing and eased his pallor; by the time Eavha returned to the infirmary, a deep, honest sleep had claimed him. The difference between this unconsciousness and his previous bouts was the absence of the deadly chill that had hovered in the room all day.

Heaving a sigh, Eavha dragged her hands down her face.

"Feel free to apologize whenever you're ready," Gatty purred from where he'd curled up on the end of Eaon's bed, pointedly ignoring the way the phouka remained sentinel between them.

Heat burned Eavha's cheeks. She was saved the humiliation of actually having to apologize by a light rapping on the door. It cracked open almost immediately, and both relief and disappointment fell heavily when it wasn't Aisling who entered—relief, because it meant Aisling wasn't so unwell she'd had to return to the infirmary, but disappointment, too, because she missed her.

Only a few steps from the door herself, Eavha forced a smile for Edwina, who returned the expression tight-lipped and wary.

"Is everything alright?" Eavha asked.

The breath Edwina took before speaking hitched, catching her words before they escaped. Blinking once, she started again.

"Cinn is awake and asking about Eaon. I thought I would come check on him."

"Cinn's awake?" Moyra asked, standing from the chair by Eaon's bedside.

Edwina closed the door as she stepped inside, eyeing the two faerie creatures with appropriate caution. The cat grinned toothily, but the phouka vigilantly ignored them all.

"You must be Edwina," Moyra said, wiping her hands on her soot-stained skirt as she limped forward. "Cinn told me about you."

Eavha watched the two shake hands, distracted by the small holes that embers had left in Moyra's clothes, her bare feet wrapped in weeping bandages. She hadn't noticed the Morvish witch was hurt.

"He . . . He told you? He speaks to you?" Edwina's voice dropped to a rasp.

The smile faded from Moyra's face as she shook her head. "Not really. In his own way, I meant. Sorry, I didn't—"

"No," Edwina interrupted, waving the apology off. "I know. It's just that seeing him again, seeing him like he is, has been difficult. Is this Eaon?"

All eyes turned to the bed. Nothing else needed to be said. Edwina had come to see how he was doing, and words could only dilute what was obvious: he was not well.

"We're just catching our breath, then we're going to try some more healing," Moyra explained.

"Has anybody brought you any food?" Edwina asked, looking around the otherwise unoccupied room. "I could bring some sandwiches. Some tea."

At that last word, Moyra's eyes lit up. Retrieving food was one of the things Eavha was meant to have done, but hadn't, and her stomach growled at the reminder.

"That would be wonderful. Would you join us? I'm sure you have questions, and if I can, I would like to answer them."

Edwina had taken a step toward the door at the request but stopped to frown as she reached for the handle. "Why would I have questions for *you?*"

"She's Morvish," Eavha explained, biting her tongue to keep the rest of her words private. *And full of nonsense.*

"Oh." Edwina hesitated for a moment, brow puckered with a frown. "I shouldn't stay long. Cinn was quite upset. But it would be good to bring back better news about Eaon, I think."

"Linger, then," Gatty said as he jumped off the bed, padding in near silence across the stone floor to rub against Edwina's knees. "I found a deck of Sol cards while I was exploring—"

"Snooping," Moyra scolded.

Gatty ignored her. "I could fetch them. We could relax a little while we wait for the witch boy to wake."

"Sol cards?" Edwina asked, her sentiment mirrored in Eavha's frown.

The idea of relaxing chafed, but admittedly, there wasn't much else to do for the moment. Eaon was stable, she was hungry, and though she didn't *need* rest, it certainly couldn't hurt.

"I'll teach you," Moyra said with a soft smile.

Gatty sat and swished his tail, looking to the phouka. "What do you say, Old One? Shall we play?"

The two fae creatures stared at each other for a long minute, tension tighter than a hamstring about to snap. Finally, the phouka nodded.

"Let's."

Three hands into the game and Eavha still did not understand it. Moyra's familiar had been banned from playing after the first round since he'd failed to disclose that he could read minds. The phouka wanted to gut the cat sith for the indiscretion, but since—technically—nobody had asked if he could, it wasn't considered cheating, and thus a ban was an appropriate compromise. Apparently.

Eavha was so far out of her depth.

Keeping her cards close to her chest, she picked another off the pile in the middle. Moyra immediately smacked it out of her hand.

"Um, ow!"

"It's not your turn."

It was meant to be, she was sure, but she had stopped arguing the rules with Moyra an hour ago.

"This is a stupid game," she hissed in her native tongue, watching Moyra claim the card she had dropped.

The Morvish witch didn't understand the language but the phouka grinned.

"I am quite enjoying it," he answered, Terranian as natural for him as Nirnish.

For a moment, Eavha forgot to be wary, rolling her eyes at the old faerie. "Of course you are. You're winning. And I'm fairly sure you're cheating, too."

Gatty cackled maniacally from his spot on Moyra's lap—a sound that would have been disturbing coming from anyone, let alone a cat.

Sitting across from Eavha, Edwina looked between the faerie creatures nervously. She was faring better at the game than Eavha, but her comparative meekness suggested she was far more intimidated by their company, especially as the phouka's yellow eyes narrowed.

"I do not cheat. You just don't understand the rules."

"Then explain them again," Eavha demanded.

"Can we stick to Nirnish, please?" Moyra frowned at both of them, placing one of her cards down. Painted on it was a constellation Eavha didn't recognize.

A cough sounded from Eaon's bed.

All five of them froze, turning to watch Eaon's chest rise and fall. Not as deeply as Eavha would have liked, but at least he breathed.

Once he settled again, Eavha covered a yawn and reached for her tea. Moyra also sipped at a cup, though each time she did, her nose wrinkled in distaste.

"Where were we?"

"The phouka was going to remind me of the rules," Eavha said. Clearly something was getting lost in translation because she had no idea what she was doing wrong.

"Honestly, Eavha, they're not that hard," Moyra scolded. "We take turns clockwise, unless the player before you plays a new moon card, in which case you miss a turn. First to empty their hand wins."

"But I played a new moon card before and you didn't miss your turn!"

"Because I had the sun card." Moyra's sigh of exasperation grated Eavha's last nerve. "The sun cancels out the new moon's power."

Eavha scowled, muttering in Terranian. "Stupid game."

It was Edwina's turn next, her card depicting a comet. The phouka hummed thoughtfully, then grinned, placing down another seemingly random constellation of stars.

Moyra winced.

"Pick up another card, Eavha."

"What? Why!" Tossing all five cards in her hand, she crossed her arms and huffed. "You're making this up as you go. I'm not playing anymore."

"Onribleq." Rolling her eyes, Moyra dropped her cards too.

"I thought we were sticking to Nirnish." Eavha resisted the urge to poke out her tongue.

"I take it you both forfeit," the phouka said. He set his sights on

Edwina, who immediately put her cards down. Gleefully, the phouka took the small pile of berries they were using as currency.

Eaon coughed again, this time with vigor.

Jumping to her feet, only too glad to forget about the game entirely, Eavha rushed to the bed. The phouka was right behind her, winnings abandoned.

"Sit him up," Eavha said as she pulled on the pair of gloves left on the bedside since Yvette's retreat. The leather was discolored in spots where the elder healer had lingered in one place too long, the seams fraying.

Eyes still closed, Eaon's brow furrowed in pain as the phouka pulled his body upright. The dark bruises across his shattered ribs were a gut-churning sight, a black-and-blue backdrop for the pale scars peppering his chest and back.

"He's burning up," the phouka ground out.

Eavha placed her hands carefully against Eaon's back. Magic spooled out readily to assess the damage—the infection was in his lungs, his temperature reaching dangerous levels. Urging it on was the roiling cold wrapped around his bones; the seed the Lover had left in him was a volatile, sentient thing, and as soon as it sensed Eavha's presence, it lunged.

Eavha flinched back, breaking contact, grimacing at the sharp wheeze Eaon made at the sudden and tactless withdrawal of her magic.

"Damn it," she hissed, ripping off the gloves so she could better grasp the bowl of pre-ground herbs on the bedside tray, measuring a spoonful into a pitcher of distilled water.

Moyra's hands stilled hers, grip tight. "Try the conduit again."

"It won't work, and we don't have time." Though she also knew the herbs would not work either. Not for long.

Glancing over to the bed, the tattoo on Moyra's forehead shimmered briefly despite the lack of sunlight in the dark room.

"He's asleep now. It might."

"What difference does that make?" Eavha snapped, pulling her hands free to mix the herbs into the water. "I have Sanni's blessing and permission. I have her under my very skin, and I still can't do it."

She wanted to try spellmarks to focus, but faced with the severity of the infection, she didn't want to waste time trying if it would continue to be fruitless.

Except, when Moyra bit her lip like that, Eavha was stunned with the sudden memory of her father with that exact expression on his face—

usually when he knew something she didn't and was debating whether to share.

Secrets burned behind Moyra's eyes, and Eavha wavered.

"I will explain when he is awake, but please, just trust me. You'll have better luck while he is asleep."

"We must try," the phouka said. One arm still holding Eaon's limp body against his chest, he extended the other out to Eavha, palm wide. "I'm ready."

Eavha hesitated, only until she heard Sanni whispering again.

Yes. Do it.

Dipping her fingers into the herbs, Eavha drew smudgy marks on her face and the backs of her hands. There was a seed in her too. One named stubbornness. It was a seed that thrashed and roiled with the utter refusal to let Eaon die. As long as she was with him, she would not allow it. Not again.

Slapping her hand into the phouka's, she closed her eyes. Magic bloomed like a white-hot sun. Their previous attempts had discerned that finesse would not work, so she pushed the mass of her power into the phouka in a way her teachers had always warned not to.

The phouka flinched but his grip tightened.

"Oh." Pushing through vein and muscle, she found the barrier of flesh between the phouka and Eaon permeable, the resistance she'd been met with before entirely gone. "Oh, thank the Mother."

"It's working?" Moyra asked.

A grunt from the phouka is all either of them could manage as Eavha focused, refining the magic as it passed into Eaon, letting it trace the fractured lines of his ribs to leave healed bone in its wake. Pulling each bit of infected tissue from her brother's lungs, she imagined the healthy tissue left behind knitting together. Focusing became increasingly difficult when Eaon began to wake, hacking the diseased bits from his lungs.

Moyra blanched, stumbling back as the tattoo on her forehead shimmered again before going dull.

"What are you doing?" Eaon wheezed.

As soon as he spoke, the threads of her magic snapped, recoiling back through the phouka. Sweat soaked through her fresh clothes as Eavha pushed back, but she may as well be trying to push through a wall.

"Damn it, Eaon," Eavha gasped, letting go of the phouka to lean on her knees, trying to catch her breath. "We were getting somewhere! Just go back to sleep."

"Your nose is bleeding," he growled back as the phouka eased him down onto the pillow.

Eavha wiped her upper lip. Sure enough, a smear of dark blood stained her fingers again. She hadn't felt it—the crumbling her teachers talked about when a Terranian witch pushed too hard—yet her nose bled nonetheless.

"I'm fine," she told Eaon. "I promise. Just let me—"

She made to take the phouka's hand again, but Eaon wrenched away so hard he nearly toppled out of the bed. His skin paled, and when he turned back to growl again, his eyes had darkened, pupils too large.

The phouka pulled away from her too, crowding the bed. One of his large hands grabbed Eaon under the chin. The cat sith, once more perched on the end of the bed, thumped his tail and watched the interaction closely.

"You will stop. This boy is under my protection. You will leave him be."

The words made no sense and yet, the darkness eased, his skin regaining color. When the phouka let him go, Eaon pulled the blanket up to his shoulders, shaking the chunks of infected tissue onto the floor.

"What was that?" Eavha asked quietly.

"The seed has grown," the phouka answered, as if that explained everything.

"What seed?" Moyra interjected.

"If you're all going to talk about me and my seed, can you at least do it elsewhere?" Eaon grumbled. It was the most he'd had the energy to say in more than a day, and the sound of his sarcasm lifted a weight from Eavha's shoulders.

"No. No, I think it's important we talk. This seed . . . I think I've seen it. In the dreamscape, I saw your soul, Eaon." Moyra stepped closer, pausing only when Gatty gave her a stern look.

"Not now," the cat sith muttered. "It's not the right time."

"Seconded." Eaon sighed and stared up at the ceiling, taking slow breaths that were deeper than any Eavha had seen him take since he'd been in the infirmary. Then he raised a limp hand and shooed at them. "Let's never talk about it."

Eavha frowned. Considering the circumstances, Eaon's lethargy made perfect sense except that two seconds ago he'd been angry enough for the seed to rear its head. It could be nothing, but she'd seen these kinds of rapid mood swings before—Eaon was likely off his tonics. Which, again, considering the circumstances of the past few days was understandable, except she hadn't sensed any of his usual withdrawal symptoms during their brief healing sessions. He mustn't have been taking them for a while.

"Perhaps we should wait until everything stabilizes before discussing any stressful topics," she suggested.

Everybody stared as Eaon burst into hysterical laughter.

"What, like Wyldeden and the entire Anfar forest burning to the ground? Like the impending invasion of a deity? Or like the fact that Dearmead was . . . He was fucking . . ." Another bout of laughter shook his bruised body. "He was fucking kidnapped by a dragon! And our high priestess is missing! But by all means, freak out about the state of my pathetic soul and my stupid fucking leg!"

By the time he was done, he was back to rage. All five of them stared as Eaon blinked at the ceiling, fists curling at his sides.

Stepping into Moyra's space, Eavha spoke low enough that Eaon wouldn't hear. "You made him sleep before, didn't you? Can you do it again?"

She shook her head. "I did, but . . . No, I don't think I can right now."

There was that look again. Secrets.

Eavha took a steadying breath and prepared herself for the argument she was about to have. To Eaon, she said, "I'm going to brew something to help you sleep more."

"I don't need to sleep, I need to find Dearmead," he spat, then tried to sit up.

The phouka placed one finger on his collarbone and stared down dully as Eaon huffed and scowled. It was nice having an ally, so Eavha left them to each other and moved for the apothecary table to scavenge for herbs.

It was easy to forget Edwina, standing by the wall, watching. It was less easy to ignore the way Moyra took the chair by Eaon's bedside, staring at her familiar, face twitching with microexpressions. There was a silent conversation being had between the two of them and Eavha didn't like being left out. Especially when Gatty flattened his ears and thumped his tail. Moyra straightened her shoulders.

"I know you all have a lot on your minds right now, but there isn't going to be a good time to have this conversation for a long while. All our fate lines are very busy for the foreseeable future and there's something I need to discuss with you both."

"It really can't wait?" Eavha pushed, shaking a jar of ground lavender to assess its contents.

"No." It was her tone that gave Eavha pause, the hair on her arms rising. "No, I'm afraid it cannot."

CHAPTER SIX

EAON

THE PHOUKA'S FINGER ON HIS COLLARBONE MIGHT AS WELL HAVE BEEN A spear through his chest for all he could move beneath it. His lungs hurt as if they'd been scrubbed with lye, his ribs bruised and aching, but at least they didn't scream every time he drew a breath anymore. The breaks were healed, but he was far from whole. Both legs were deadweight, the pain unlike any he'd felt before, and it took every shred of self-respect not to beg for more poppy milk. Not only did he doubt Eavha would allow it, but he also didn't trust her not to try and touch him again while he was unconscious.

He didn't trust anyone else in the room either. The phouka had a gleam in his eye that suggested he rather enjoyed watching Eaon squirm. That there was a second fae in the room set his teeth to grinding; the cat sith on the end of his bed hadn't said anything yet, but he knew the loathsome creature could talk. He had met one before. Besides, Kailevi had told him enough horror stories about cat sith during their long months of traveling that, even through the haze of pain and herbs, even through the chill in his bones and the heat of his skin, through the claws of the seed raging in his chest and the claws of his brain raging against his bitten tongue, Eaon knew to guard his thoughts.

He didn't trust the young woman standing by the door, watching as if any of this was her business, and he certainly did not trust the witch sitting at his bedside. The constellation tattoo on her forehead marked her as Morvish, and her strange pink eyes were vaguely familiar.

"Do you remember when we spoke in the dreamscape? I said I would explain things later."

The rabid cold that dwelled inside Eaon's body bristled. It was sentient enough not to bother rising with the phouka's heavy finger holding him to the bed, but it didn't stop a shiver running down his aching spine.

That was why she was familiar. This was Moyra Thorne.

"I remember falling asleep in the middle of a conversation with my friend. I remember you telling me my sister was in danger, then waking up." Eaon scrambled for a scrap of concentration; she spoke of "the dreamscape" as if he should know what that was. "Is that what you mean?"

Moyra nodded, tucking hair that was already tucked behind her ears.

"Yes. The place I brought you is called the dreamscape. It is one of Morvia's realms. Sorry it was overwhelming, but it was the only way I could think to communicate with you from so far away."

"It was fine." He honestly hadn't given it a moment's thought, too concerned with the danger Eavha and Dearmead were in and everything that happened after.

Moyra grimaced. "It could have gone very badly. I'm not entirely sure yet that your lucidity in the dreamscape hasn't affected you. I took a risk."

In his periphery, Eavha stepped closer, eyes narrowed in what was undeniable hostility. "You took a risk."

Lover have mercy—why was his sister always worrying about the wrong things?

"It's fine," Eaon assured them both. "It worked out fine. I got there in time to help."

At that, the phouka snorted; they both knew the only reason Eaon did so was because of the Old One's interference. He still didn't understand what the phouka was doing or why he had helped, but that was a problem for when his brain wasn't a pendulum, swinging between a hurricane of urgency and being doused in thick syrup.

"I'm glad." Moyra nodded and averted her eyes. "But I think you need to understand why it was such a risk. And why everything turned out fine."

Eaon's sigh deflated his chest so completely that refilling it was almost too much effort. "I really don't think this matters right now—"

"It matters," Moyra insisted. "It's why I came."

No matter what he said, she was going to talk, and Eaon didn't have the energy to argue anymore. He found enough to move his head when Eavha took another step closer, warning her away with a pathetic glare.

But Eavha wasn't looking at him. "I thought you came because of Cinn."

One word. One name. That was all it took for the fog to clear, his heart thundering so loudly he was surprised the phouka didn't flinch from its ferocity.

"It's true that I would never have gotten here without him," Moyra went on, oblivious to the adrenaline now coursing through every fiber of Eaon's body.

Cinn was here. He remembered now. He remembered seeing his ruined body laying beside Aisling's and—

"Easy," the phouka growled.

The room had gone quiet.

It was strange, the way he barely noticed the seed anymore. As if every time they warred over control, they became a little more intertwined. Whatever effect he'd had on the room waned as quickly as it crested and Moyra cleared her throat, staring down at Eaon again.

"I came for you. For the both of you."

Silently cursing his useless legs for leaving him incapable of getting up and walking away, Eaon tried to wrangle his spinning thoughts. There was a bright haze fogging the room and he couldn't shake the feeling that something was happening. He didn't like it. He wanted it all to stop, for everyone to go away until he could make his head slow down again.

"Why?" Eavha asked.

Palms out, as if placating a wild animal, Moyra asked, "How much do you know about your father?"

The haze found a shape—colored lines weaving between everyone and everything—but Eaon didn't care. His attention was thoroughly fixed on the nervous bob of Moyra's throat.

"What does he have to do with anything?"

As intimate with grief as he was, he recognized its weight in the hitch of her breath.

"Everything."

He didn't like this. He didn't like it at all. Thoughts spun too quickly to grasp until they fell out of his head entirely, spilling all over the sheets. Leashed by colored strings and pulled taut by urgency, all he could do was stare at the impossible things in his lap.

"Da was from a different clan," Eavha said, because the silence had gone on too long. "He met our ma at a trading festival and followed her back to Wyldeden. He . . . He was low-blessed, and since he was from somewhere else anyway, the high priestess made him a traveler."

Moyra nodded, but it was a gesture of acknowledgment rather than agreement. "He never told you where he was from?"

The look of concentration on Eavha's face as she tried to think was annoying because *couldn't she see where this was going?* Time was a twisted thing as he stared at the trail of this conversation in his lap, a conversation that hadn't truly been had yet. It was a labyrinth of color and shape he could pick through, if only he could make sense of it.

"Um, I don't remember. I don't think he ever said."

"North." The word fell from Eaon's lips, cold and hostile. "He only ever said he came from the north."

Moyra tucked her hair. "True enough. Qiri is north, after all."

Eavha flinched, but everything inside Eaon had gone very still. Very quiet. One by one, he picked up his scattered thoughts and shoved them back inside his head, into the dark corners where he couldn't see them anymore.

"Sorry, what?" Eavha breathed.

"Kailevi . . ." Moyra spoke his name with an affection she had no business having. "He was my brother. When he was eighteen, he saw the fate lines guiding him south of the wards. He and my sister, Olyvia, cracked the wards in the mountain range to get through. She didn't survive the spell, and he . . . I guess he found what he was looking for."

Moyra's pretty eyes were glassy and radiating a warmth that was not for them. It was a love that echoed through their lineage, for a brother who was gone. Though the Nemuse siblings had inherited their mother's coloring, Moyra would see Kailevi in the set of their mouths and the roundness of their eyes. In Eaon, she would see their father's jawline, his nose and brow.

"You're our unt," Eavha wheezed, face graying. The Wyldeden word was a slip, but it was close enough to the Nirnish version that Moyra understood.

"I am." She smiled at Eavha briefly, but when she turned back to face Eaon she knew her pleasantry was not welcome. As if she could see the mess his mind had made on the sheets a few moments ago, could see exactly the conclusions he'd jumped to the moment she started speaking, she braced herself, broken heart on her sleeve. "Ask."

Everything was still. Everything was quiet.

"I think you should leave." He barely heard his own voice, but it must have been loud enough because Eavha was frowning at him now, still pale as a corpse as she scolded him.

"Eaon, we have family."

"We have to talk about what this means," Moyra pressed.

Eaon's teeth snapped shut with such force he felt it in his temples, but as always, everyone ignored him.

"What it means?" Eavha asked, crossing her arms to hide her shaking hands.

Knowing it was safer to speak to Eavha than Eaon right now, Moyra turned away from him to explain.

"Your father was not low-blessed. He was a rather powerful Morvish witch."

"That's . . ." Eavha shook her head, curls tumbling from the knot twisted on top. "He can't be. He didn't have a tattoo."

"Because he never graduated from the academy."

"But he never . . . He never did anything. He never said anything." His sister turned to him, eyes wide. "Did he say anything to you?"

Prying his jaw open with sheer force of will, Eaon ground out, "Leave."

Eavha's hair came completely undone as she shook her head again, but this time she wasn't ignoring him. More than anyone else still living, she knew what he looked like when he was about to snap. Lifting her chin, she put on a surprisingly steady voice and decided, "I think we both need time to process this."

"I agree." It was only then Eaon noticed how focused the cat sith was on him. Noticed the way the phouka's hand had moved, still touching but no longer restraining as he positioned himself between the other fae and Eaon.

Moyra didn't leave. She looked Eaon right in the eye and said, "Your father was Morvish, and so are you."

Still. Quiet.

Heat pooled in his stomach, his throat, his hands fisted in the sheets.

Eavha stumbled back and screeched, "*What?*"

"I saw it," Moyra continued, unflinching in the face of Eaon's stillness. "In the dreamscape. Your soul is bright with power, but Kai's own magic has it bound in a tight coil. It's a rudimentary binding spell, only used in emergencies by witches who aren't tattooed or don't know what they're doing. He must have cast it while you were young, because as you grew, your magic grew too, and now . . . The binding is bursting at the seams and your magic is spilling through the cracks. You need a suppressant until we can remove the binding safely."

White noise. Her mouth moved, but he barely heard a word. None of it touched him.

Distantly, he was aware of Eavha talking about his tonics: the ones he took for his moods, and the daily "all-rounder" he was supposed to take to keep him "balanced." He didn't listen as she rattled off the "family recipe," the incantations she'd been taught, the blessings done to the herbs. He ignored her stuttering as she recited words from the spells that she'd never understood, assuming her vocabulary would catch up when she was older. The way it had been Ma who'd taught her, but Da was always there, watching.

"Our parents run an apothecary in Ahrenhale," Moyra said. "They serve the untrained, to help with their magic. What you're describing . . . It's one of their tonics. You said he takes it every day?"

"Well, he's supposed to, but things have been difficult lately."

"How long have you been off them?" Moyra asked, and it took Eaon a moment to realize he was being included in the conversation again.

He took a steadying breath. Picking out the parts of the conversation he was interested in and shoving everything else away, he looked to Eavha instead.

"The brewer Kaelean recommended take over for you didn't brew them right. I've been in withdrawals since you left Wyldeden."

Eavha balked, and there was satisfaction to be found in seeing the lethal rage seething in his gut reflected on her face.

"I *showed* her how to do it!"

"I don't think Cleo likes me very much. Reigan said the herbs weren't blessed."

"That rogue bitch! I swear to both the Mother and the Lover that if the fire didn't kill her, I'm going to make her wish it had."

"We're getting off topic," Moyra interrupted, raising her hands in that placating gesture that made Eaon want to snap her fingers.

Glaring at him, the cat sith hissed. The phouka growled back.

Eaon ignored them both. "It doesn't matter, because you're wrong."

More than anything else that had happened during this whole ordeal, he hated the pitying look they both leveled at him.

"Eaon . . ."

"Da wouldn't do that to me," Eaon spat. He hadn't meant to say it, but the quiet was fracturing, the stillness trembling. "So whatever you think you know, you don't. The Lover put a seed in me. That's what you saw."

As if speaking to a child, Moyra's tone was soft and careful. "I did see that, but whatever the Lover has done to you looked very different. I saw long, black leeches made of void, sucking at your soul, and tethering you to another realm."

Eavha flinched. "What?"

"Right," Eaon deadpanned, all the heat that had risen smothered by a blistering cold. "If you insist on worrying about something, worry about that. Or even better, do something useful, like finding Dearmead."

Moyra opened her mouth, but the cat sith leaped off the bed onto her lap. "Moyra."

"This has to be dealt with," she argued.

A shiver blistered his spine and the phouka's hand came sliding back to grab his chin. Ignoring the command in that touch, Eaon warned Moyra, "I don't want to hear any more of your bullshit."

"Eaon, why would I lie?" she tried.

"Fuck off."

"It's not—"

"Leave, or I swear on the Mother I will kill you."

The oversized black cat on Moyra's lap flattened his ears and growled deep in the back of his throat. Moyra glared down at her companion, but her complaints were cut short by the cat sith's furious explanation.

"He means it, and I will not allow it."

"Go back to licking your behind," the phouka said, gentle tone somehow more violent than the cat sith's threat.

"Both of you stop it," Moyra scolded. Then, "Eaon, just do one thing for me and I promise I will let it go."

"Why would I do anything—"

"Just think," she spoke over him. "Kai bound your Morvish blessings when you were young, but as you grew so did your power, and the bindings couldn't contain it completely. The first time it cracked, you would have felt it. You didn't know the blessing was there, but magic is such an innate part of what a witch is, you would have tugged at it inadvertently. You needed something badly enough that the binding couldn't stop your magic from giving it to you. It would have felt like . . ."

Moyra struggled for a metaphor, but as she twirled her hands, encouraging her brain to come up with something, Eaon's life was flashing through his mind.

There were so many times he had *needed* magic. Times he so desperately wanted a way to make other witch's spells *break*. A spellmark drawn on his back, forcing truths until his lips bled, the magic so potent he vomited and vomited and vomited, talking throughout it all. A small house in Wyldeden with locked doors and warded windows and nobody to hear him calling for help. He'd gotten out. The smashed bottle and dark stains that could have been wine or blood. Broken roof hatching. Fractured hands and twisted ankles as he ran to the only place he had ever truly been safe. Dearmead hadn't been there and Eaon didn't want anyone else. He wanted to be left alone. He wanted to disappear. He didn't want anyone or anything to touch him—especially not magic.

And something inside him had snapped. It had hurt, but it was *relief*. Like taking a piss after holding it for hours. And later, Dearmead had told him the whispering leaves his family tried to send him that night wouldn't work.

Soon after, he had started hallucinating colors. The healers said it was part of his worsening frenzies. They said the stress of his life was driving him mad. They weren't wrong, but the colored lines he saw connecting things, people, ideas . . . They always led him to what he needed to find. They told him secrets that were always true.

The cat sith was grinning. "Spell-cleaving. And way-finding. I would bet everything I own that you have dream-weaving abilities too—a gift from each member of the coven your sire was part of when he spawned you. No wonder Kailevi's crude bindings couldn't hold you. There's a reason coventry is meant to be careful controlled."

Eaon scowled. "Well now I need to know what you own, because a fae's word is binding and you are wrong."

The vicious panic in his words made no sense because he didn't believe any of this bullshit. Refused to believe it.

"Eaon, I know this is a lot to take in—"

The sound of her voice lashed his blood, his skin a flaky dam. Sweat soaked the sheets, fists trembling where they pressed against his thighs, and he relished the pain it caused his still-healing bones.

"I swear to every fucking spirit, Moyra, stop talking."

This whole thing was stupid. This conversation was a waste of time. Dearmead was missing. Cinn was in the last place he should be. Chaos was coming. His legs were fucking useless. What the point was of spinning these conspiracy theories, he didn't know, nor did he care. He didn't have time for it. Didn't have time for the thickness in his throat, the cold blistering his veins. His exhale tasted like mold.

"Kai—"

"Get out!"

The dam broke and his insides spasmed with release. The tonics on the bedside curdled in their vials, the bedframe groaning as the wood rotted. The phouka hissed and clambered atop him, pinning him to the thin mattress, muscles rippling and convulsing with the effort of absorbing so much deadly magic.

Through gritted teeth, the phouka ground out, "Eavha, why don't you get some fresh air."

Eaon didn't see his sister leave, nor did he see Moyra, her cat, or the servant girl by the door slip from the room, but he felt their souls growing farther and farther away. Sharp claws hooked into his lungs, seething at the loss.

"You want to kill your sister? What a drastic change of heart." The phouka's grip tightened, the world narrowed to the wall of black flesh and fur above him. Yellow eyes bore into him, the wrath behind them mirroring the boiling cold inside.

This was not a blessing. This was not a gift.

But it was his. It was truth.

"Don't you dare surrender to it," the phouka growled, grip tightening until Eaon's hands numbed.

"What difference does it make to you?" Eaon spat, bucking futilely. "I thought you said it felt good. Thought it *tingled*."

Sharp, blackened teeth were bared an inch from his face, but the phouka did not have an answer.

With nothing to do and nowhere to go, the seed eventually settled, leaving the room silent sans the rasping breaths between them. Eaon knew better than to bother with self-pity, but Moyra's accusations continued to riot.

She was wrong. She had to be, because the alternative was impossible.

The alternative meant his da had sat there silently and watched the clan tell him he was useless, that he was barely a witch at all, that the only thing he was good for was serving others so they could concentrate on being productive members of society. That he was a leech. A waste of resources. That because he didn't have much magic, he was worth less than filth. That trading him for a chicken was to rob the clan who'd be burdened with him. The alternative meant his da had lied to him. Had let Eaon believe he was going mad when he sometimes saw things that couldn't be there. It meant Kailevi had bound him, poisoned him, so that his magic could not be detected.

And that . . .

Kailevi wouldn't do that to him.

So Moyra was a liar.

End of discussion.

CHAPTER SEVEN

MOYRA

MOYRA'S LIFE WAS RIDDLED WITH REGRETS. AS THE INFIRMARY DOOR snipped shut behind her, she thought this may be another on the tally. There wasn't time to do this gently, but the phouka's muffled growls behind her and Eavha's furious gait down the hall suggested it had gone about as poorly as it could have.

"Eavha, wait."

Eavha did not wait, and Moyra could not chase her. After the adrenaline had worn off, the burns on her feet from her melted boots had become something she could not ignore.

"I warned you it was not a good time." Gatty sighed. "News like that should be delivered when the recipients are not already on the verge of imploding. She is overwhelmed."

Moyra hummed, watching Eavha disappear around the corner. She hadn't realized what a wound her confession would cause. There wasn't time, but she feared if she tried to speak with them again while so raw, it would only push them farther away.

"Is it really that dire?" Gatty asked as Moyra began hobbling down the hall.

"The sooner he wraps his head around the truth, the sooner I can help him."

Way-finding was not her strongest skill, but the fate lines burned so brightly inside the wards that they weren't hard to follow. She didn't see a lot of good paths for her nephew. Even less if she didn't do something about the fraying state of his soul.

The infirmary was on the ground floor, tucked away at the end of a quiet hall. With healthcare spread throughout the city there weren't many people to encounter until farther along; exhausted servants rushed in and out of kitchens, courtiers lugging suitcases up and down stairwells, guards keeping order as best they could. Angry and confused arguments about having to vacate the palace rang through the foyer as Moyra stepped out, half leaning on the wall to take weight off her feet. Used to a life of comfort, many of those who regularly dwelled inside the palace abhorred having to make room for the masses of witches now milling about.

Gatty blended into the dark stone like a living shadow, padding forward only when Moyra was ready, leading her to a wide hallway. Lanterns lit the windowless way, illuminating paintings in gilded frames. The faces peering back as the two slipped along were unfamiliar, but details tugged at the magic sitting ready at Moyra's fingertips. Letting it surface, she tuned into the fate lines weaving a rainbow web between paintings, but the only one that really drew Moyra's attention was of a stoic witch with an undeniable resemblance to Princess Aisling.

The plaque beneath it announced the female as Queen Tallula Aurnia. The lines connecting her to the other paintings were inconsequential, but at her throat lay a ruby pendant with its own web. Moyra paused, frowning at the silvery line that started strong before splitting into seven threads. Six disappeared into the distance. One tied the gem directly to Moyra.

"Come back later when you're not staining the rug," Gatty said, stalking to a nearby door. He melted into the shadow cast by a lantern, and a moment later the door creaked open.

Knowing better than to argue with her familiar when her health was at stake, Moyra limped to the room Gatty had decided was theirs. It had been a full day since she'd arrived in Hyrsch but this was the first time she had stopped. She'd lost a little time in the courtyard outside while Eavha initially treated Eaon and Aisling, overwhelmed by how loud the stars had been shouting, how strong Morvia's blessing pulled at the pile of bones Eavha discarded. Old and inhuman, they had lured her like the tide to the moon, enraptured until the phouka returned to snatch them away.

Perhaps she had spent too many years at the lake; she didn't know how to focus around so many distractions anymore. It seemed like everywhere she looked, someone or something stood out as *important*.

So she had gone back to what had always grounded her—mixing herbs and bandaging wounds, she'd helped move the injured witches off the street. Every distraction was ignored until Gatty came to fetch her; Eavha needed help in the infirmary.

Now, it was time to take her own advice. She needed to rest. To bathe. To clean and rewrap her feet.

The window in the room Gatty had snagged gave them a view of a little garden and not much else, but Moyra didn't mind. She didn't need to see more of the chaos outside, nor did she need to see the orange haze in the night sky. The carpet was a plush white, soft beneath her feet, which were in fact leaving pink smears in her wake.

"I will fetch a servant to bring supplies," Gatty said, disappearing again.

Collapsing onto a couch, it wasn't long before a wide-eyed young boy came bustling in with a large bowl of water, towels, bandages and herbs. He placed it all down on the small table nestled between the two couches. The moment his hands were free, he dragged a delicate cart from the corner that Moyra hadn't spared a look at. Before she could ask, the boy hurried from the room, nearly tripping over the threshold in his haste.

"What did you say to him?" Moyra asked as she began peeling the fraying bandages from her feet.

Gatty curled up beside her and thumped his tail. "To be quick."

Clicking her tongue in disapproval, she opened the little doors on the cart's side. The noise that left her was somewhere between a gasp and a sigh.

"Tea."

"Can't have you in withdrawals at a time like this," Gatty drawled.

"Oh, look," Moyra said, raising an eyebrow. "A honey pot."

Smug, Gatty purred.

For a few minutes, they worked in silence, her familiar cleaning the honey pot while Moyra brewed a decent cup of tea and prepared the herbs for her feet. When it came time to clean the weeping wounds though, Gatty began chatting again.

"On another note, tell me I wasn't the only one who noticed."

Grateful for the distraction as she piled soiled bandages on the floor, Moyra grumbled, "You'll have to be more specific. There was a lot happening in that room."

"The Old One." Gatty's ears flattened. "Did you notice the phouka's behavior?"

"Can't say I know enough about phouka to say."

"One needn't know much about phouka; knowing the nature of fae is enough. When have you ever seen a creature of such might invest himself in the well-being of a witch? Not even a bargain could elicit such devotion."

Moyra frowned, replaying the past few hours over. As usual, Gatty was right, and when she looked over to meet his wary gaze, her breath shuddered.

"Is it . . ."

"Yes."

It wasn't often that something ruffled Gatty. Moyra watched his fur twitch, the muscles bunching and releasing underneath. "What's wrong?"

Gatty extended his claws and picked at the sofa's cushion, his words slow and pointed. "You know that the power of a witch correlates to the kind of familiar they attract. Phouka are rare, but this is also an Old One. He was one of the original fae who banded with the first rebellion against Chaos. He took Sanni's marking alongside the Kinner to make him immortal. He is one of the oldest living things in existence. And he is drawn to Eaon."

Slowly wringing out the cloth she was using to clean her feet, Moyra let the gravity of that settle.

"Then there is the matter of this *seed*," Gatty went on, rippling with tension. "A dangerous second power of unmeasurable strength. He is not strong enough to contain it, nor can he hold Morvia's blessing. The coil Kailevi bound him in is fracturing, and the seed grows stronger every day. It is inevitable; that boy is going to surge, and it will be devastating. I am wary of your proximity."

Nothing she said would comfort Gatty, so she focused on wrapping her feet in clean cotton. Her mind wouldn't stay present though, and she thought back to their brief meeting in the dreamscape again. To that whip of power that had lashed her, filling her head with sevens. A clue from Morvia, from his blessing to hers.

"I can help him," Moyra finally said, sitting back and taking her teacup from the tray. She blew at the steam before sipping, the warmth an immediate balm. "I just have to figure out how."

CHAPTER EIGHT

CINN

CINN SHUT HIMSELF IN THE BATHROOM ONLY FOR A SUDDEN claustrophobia to take over; the ferocity with which he threw the door back open nearly took it off its hinges. He settled instead for aimless pacing, sometimes to the window to see if Edwina was on her way up, sometimes to the door as if to chase her down, but mostly just wall to wall, needing to move. Needing to *breathe*.

He wanted to run. It was hard for any other thought to take space in his head. He wanted to leave, to put as much space between himself and this city as physically possible. And he wanted everyone to come with him —Radley, who'd situated himself by the front door, watching Cinn's restless pacing with crossed arms and fathomless rage; William, who was inspecting the damage to the bathroom door; Sarah, who was trying desperately to clean the rotting kitchen.

Somewhere, Siobhan and her unborn baby were resting.

Somewhere, Edwina was searching.

Eavha. Moyra. The Copelands had told him what they'd seen outside the palace before taking his healing body from the courtyard, and he cared enough about them both to plan their escapes too. They were in the palace. With Eaon.

Eaon, Eaon, Eaon.

Reaching the wall, Cinn made for the door again. Radley straightened. Before they could get into another fight, a gentle knock on the door stilled them both.

Cinn was going to vomit. Retreating, his hands twitched, silently screaming at the absence of his dagger.

"It's okay, honey," Sarah said, leaving her scrubbing, approaching with outstretched arms. William watched them, a clear warning that he would not tolerate any of the violence Cinn had shown earlier.

Sweat soaked his shirt once more as he forced himself to still. To not flinch away from Sarah's gentle embrace, her back to the door. To not react as Radley peeked through a gap in the framework.

"Who is it?" he snapped.

"Rad?" a familiar voice called back. "It's Siobhan."

It was just Siobhan.

Why wasn't it Edwina?

Opening the door, Radley stepped aside to make room, furtively checking the stairwell behind her to look for their sister. When it was clear Siobhan had come alone, he shut them inside, gaze roaming down to her swollen belly.

"Well, shit."

"Yeah." Siobhan smoothed the fabric of her dress. "Four months."

"Owen's?"

A hesitant nod and a shuddering breath left her words fragile. "I heard he and Nora went to Pirevia. That . . . That Nora died."

Radley grimaced.

"Wait, Owen went to Pirevia too?" William frowned, turning his attention from where Sarah still held Cinn in the corner. "Horseshit. He wouldn't go back there. Not willingly. Not when Sarah and I had to put that kid back together by the scraps of his skin."

Siobhan noticed the others in the room for the first time. "It wasn't willingly." Her eyes widened at the shivering ball of tension that was Cinn. Flicking her gaze away again, she said, "We'll discuss it later."

All four of them shared a look that said discussing why Owen and Nora ended up in Pirevia in front of him was a bad idea.

Confused as to how everybody seemed to know everybody, Cinn embraced the distraction from his panic and raised trembling hands to ask.

"Oh." Siobhan pointed around the room as she explained. "Rad and I were part of the same rebel sect. He roped Edwina into it, and I got Owen involved. He wasn't fully in yet, but he was the first step in figuring out how to bring Nora and Clayton into the fold."

"And we know Owen because he stayed with us for a while as a kid," William said. "He came to us from that revolting northern city, back when we spent more time smuggling people *into* Hyrsch rather than keeping them out."

Pressing her lips together, Siobhan frowned at Cinn. "I expected you to return here as much as we expected Owen to go back to Pirevia. I don't like it."

William snorted. "Nobody does."

"What brought you out, dear?" Sarah interrupted, releasing Cinn to rest a hand on Siobhan's shoulder.

Relieved at having conversation move away from him and his presence in Hyrsch, Cinn sagged against the wall.

Siobhan cleared her throat. "There's going to be a meeting. With so many strangers in the city right now, we didn't trust normal methods of communication, so I came to get . . . Where's Edwina?"

Any semblance of calm Cinn had found dissipated. He turned to the window again, searching the street below. Despite the dark hour—late or early, he wasn't sure—people still filled the roads. Most were demi-kin, but there were working-class humans too, the only noticeable differences between them being the slightly paler strip around their throats and the way the demi-kin stuck to the edges of the footpath, flattening themselves against walls so as not to get in anybody's way.

"She went to find information about Eaon," Sarah said carefully. "She'll be back soon."

"Oh."

He didn't want to know what kind of silent exchange was taking place behind him as he scoured the streets for Edwina, but he wasn't surprised that, when the quiet was broken again, it was by Siobhan.

"Cinn? While we're waiting, if you're up for it, I want to show you something in town."

Forehead against the glass, eyes squeezed shut, he shook his head. He couldn't leave, because if he did, he would run. He would bolt straight to the river that cut so close to part of the northern wall that Siobhan had once managed to push a laundry cart all the way to its edge without drawing suspicion.

For a second, he was drowning inside the laundry sack again, tumbling across the bottom of the Dividing River. He was burning under the first rays of sunlight to touch his skin in almost two years. He was vomiting dirty river water as he dragged his starving body through the Oford forest, no idea where he was going except *away*.

Wiping the mess from his chin, Cinn blinked at the floor. He didn't remember falling. Didn't remember making his way back to the corner.

The room swam as his breaths came too fast, too shallow. Putting his back to the wall, his hands made fists in his hair. He wished he could squeeze the memories right out of his brain.

Puddles meowed, pushing against his shins.

"It's alright. It's okay," Sarah soothed, gentle hands prying at his clenched fists. "Let go, sweetheart. You're alright."

The pain of his tearing scalp was real. Recalling Moyra's encouragement back at the cabin by the lake, he forced himself to suck down a deeper breath. Sarah smelled like cinnamon biscuits and soap, and that was real. The sound of her voice reminded him of long nights spent in front of the fireplace while she read him stories. Those were better memories.

Puddles meowed again, more insistent. Cinn let go of his hair and scooped the cat into his lap, trying not to squeeze too tight as he buried his face into her fur. Soft. The sound of her purring reverberated into his chest.

"I'm sorry. I didn't mean—" Siobhan started.

"No, that is not your fault," William assured her, endlessly tired.

Footsteps on the floorboards. Cinn opened his eyes at the smell of stale smoke and whiskey to find Radley crouched in front of him, holding a knife. Not one of the kitchen ones, but nothing as formal as the dagger William had given Cinn, either.

"See this?" Radley held the blade in a loose grip between them. "I stabbed her with it."

There was no confusion as to who he meant. Cinn didn't want to think about her, but if he had to, he didn't mind thinking about her bleeding.

"And I'll do it again," Radley continued. "I'll do worse than stab her with it if she dares come anywhere near you again."

Radley had stabbed her. The Copelands had told him how Siobhan stabbed her too, right after William had hit her with a branding iron and scarred her face. Edwina had refused to administer a poison's antidote and watched her choke on her own blood.

And Eaon . . .

"I'll make what happened in Pirevia look like a scolding compared to the lashing I will unleash upon her city."

Cinn would not be taken quietly again. He would not go missing, left to rot.

One by one, he pictured their faces—the people who would come for him. The people who loved him so much they risked violence against someone as powerful as *her*.

60

Closing his eyes, he replayed Dusarn. Every blow he had landed against her. How it felt to hold her life in his hands. Maybe he hadn't won that fight, but it had felt good to get so close. He had been *so close* to her, and yet here he was.

Free.

Safe.

Home.

His next breath came easier, and when he opened his eyes again, Radley's wore a savage smile.

"There you are. Now, let's go for a walk."

With Sarah holding one hand and William holding the other, Radley at his back and Siobhan leading from the front with Puddles, walking the streets of Hyrsch again was almost bearable. Cinn still scanned every face they passed, hoping for Edwina, dreading the guards, but he put one foot in front of the other without falling back into the cesspool of his mind.

They'd left a coded note for Edwina, telling her where to meet them, and Cinn had room to be curious by the time they reached a nondescript double-story crammed on a street of nearly identical houses. Siobhan led the way in without knocking, using a key she pulled from her pocket. She stopped just inside the door and pointed to a little hallway table, waiting for Cinn to get close enough to look.

"This is where we found the note telling us where you were," Siobhan said, watching his face carefully. "It was in our own code, but the writing didn't belong to anyone we knew. This was where the witch's amulet was left that would let us through the spellmarks hiding the cell's entrance. That red-haired witch, the important one I don't like very much? She was behind you getting captured again in Pirevia, but she was behind this, too. She's the reason we could finally get you out. This house? This is where we hatched the plot to free you."

It was easier to breathe when he wasn't drowning in guilt, and so he hadn't often lingered on thoughts of the rebels. In the weeks they'd spent together at the Copeland farm at the beginning of this cursed summer, Siobhan had only once alluded to the consequences the other laundress had suffered when caught. She hadn't gone into detail, but she didn't need to. Cinn knew too well what the princess was capable of. He had not slept for three days, stewing in it all, and Siobhan hadn't mentioned it again. But in this place, with Radley and Edwina's stories about that night fresh in his mind, it was impossible to ignore the enormity of what had been done for him.

As they led him deeper into the house, there was a framed cross-stitch of a seven-pointed star. Each of the four people with him kissed their fingers and pressed them to the glass as they passed.

"In here," Siobhan said, holding open the door to an ordinary, empty living room. "This is where Rad and Eddy told us stories about you. About a real kinner boy, living among us. Your people are legend. Proof to the demi-kin that they descended from something incredible, worth so much more than the life Sparrows forced them into. To Rad and Eddy, you were their family. To everyone else, you were hope."

Cinn blinked and saw a ruined city. A dark tunnel and a warded archway. He saw Moyra, kneeling before a lone candle, muttering.

His people had been turned into something monstrous.

His people were gone.

"Telling the stories kept you alive to Rad and Eddy, and they gave those of us with access to the palace an idea of who we were looking for," Siobhan went on. "My job was to spy on Nora, and every time they spoke of you, this is where I would relay the information to everyone."

"It took months." Radley's eyes had grown unfocused, staring at the unlit hearth. "But it was the first time someone else admitted you'd ever existed. When you didn't come home that first night . . . Even the commander of your cadet group, Porter, looked me dead in the eye and said he had no recollection of you. Siobhan's efforts brought proof that we weren't too late. That she hadn't shipped you away somewhere we could never reach. That you were still *here*, somewhere."

Cinn could barely feel his body, but he reached for Radley's hand and squeezed. He was here. He was real.

Behind them, the front door opened. Cinn's heart leaped into his throat as an elderly human stopped mid-yawn in the threshold. Physically, he bore no semblance to the man who'd been his master, but the age was about the same and the stranger's presence did nothing good to Cinn's blood pressure.

Radley's eyes narrowed, but his posture stayed relaxed. He might not like the human, but he knew him.

"Radley, is that . . ." The man's voice was brittle with awe.

Slowly, Radley nodded. "Ry. Goes by Cinn now."

As others began to filter in, the exclamations of shock and awe began to overlap until it was all just noise. William herded him to the far wall of the sitting room, standing with his body angled, ready to step forward should any of the curious rebels get too close. Sarah stayed by his other side, holding his hand while Radley and Siobhan fielded questions for what felt like hours.

If the mantle clock was to be trusted, it was only thirty minutes before a familiar face finally joined the small crowd. Cinn's knees nearly buckled as he locked eyes with Edwina. Pushing aside people who greeted her by name, she made a beeline right to where Cinn had dropped Sarah's hand. If not for the wall at his back, the force of her embrace would have sent him to the floor.

"I told you I would be alright," she said into the crook of his neck.

Cinn couldn't even nod, his grip bruising.

"How did it go?" Sarah asked.

The room was too busy talking to pay them any mind, but Cinn still wished there were less eyes on him when he felt Edwina stiffen. Peeling apart enough to see her expression, Cinn's stomach twisted.

"He's not okay."

Three words. All it took was three words and that killing calm he'd found in Dusarn washed over him again. He didn't care that he didn't have his knife, if *she* had laid a single finger on Eaon, he would shred her to pieces with teeth and nails.

"His sister was with him in the infirmary," she added quickly, holding Cinn's shoulders, as if that would keep him grounded. "Whatever happened out there left him in bad shape, but they were starting to make progress healing him. But then that Moyra witch showed up and told him something about his father and . . . He didn't take it well. The room got cold and the big fae thing was getting pissed off, so I had to leave. I'm sorry I don't have more information."

Cinn shook his head at her apology, the calm melting away now it was clear Eaon's trouble didn't have anything to do with *her*. It was replaced, however, by need. A base kind, like hunger or thirst. A need to find Eaon. To be with him. It couldn't wait.

Across the room, he caught Siobhan's eye and jerked his chin in silent request. She quickly excused herself from whatever conversation she'd been having and made her way over, brow creased.

"You alright?"

Cinn glanced at Edwina, who repeated what she had learned in the palace. Once she understood, Cinn raised his hands.

{Can you help me?}

"What do you need?"

{Eaon. I need . . . I need to go . . .}

His hands were shaking too hard, vision spotting at the mere idea of where he needed to go. But it was enough. They understood.

"We'll get you to him," Sarah promised.

"I'll talk you through every step," Siobhan agreed with a sharp nod.

William placed a strong hand on his shoulder, looking around the room at all the rebels starting to settle onto the furniture. "Someone should stay."

"I will," Edwina offered, cupping Cinn's face and smiling warmly. "There are things I need to ask the rest of the rebellion, and Radley won't cope with you out of sight. He won't let anybody hurt you, okay? I'll meet you back at the apartment later. Be safe. I love you."

I love you, too, he wanted to say. Instead, he pressed a kiss to her cheek and forced himself to let go.

Siobhan passed Puddles to Edwina, the cat having fallen asleep in her arms at some point during their walk through town. She growled indignantly at being disturbed.

This wasn't goodbye. Eddy had walked into the palace alone and come back unscathed. Everybody would be with him. He could do the same.

CHAPTER NINE

CINN

ANOTHER STEP, AND HE WAS OKAY.

Another step, and he was still free.

Another step, keeping his eyes on his feet as Siobhan said, "And this is the side gate where the guard almost stopped us. Do you remember that? How me and Wendy faced that obstacle and still got you past it?"

He remembered.

Another step, and they were at the gate. The hinges didn't creak, but he knew someone opened it by the swooping in his gut. In the trembling in his legs as they begged him to run.

Stuck, he took a deep breath. He had thought the city smelled of fresh air that night, but after spending so long in the wilderness, the air in Hyrsch was suffocating. The sweat of thousands at the height of summer, the baking horse shit on the streets, the underground sewers. Or maybe that was just him. After years locked in a cramped cell too small to lay down in, he had reeked of waste. He had choked on it until his mind finally blocked it out and he stopped being able to smell anything at all.

"We're with you," Sarah said softly, squeezing his hand.

Nodding, Cinn raised his head to look at the sky. The smoke left the early dawn hazy, but it couldn't hide the fact that he was still outside.

"We're going to see Eaon," William reminded him.

Cinn nodded again and took another step. Another, past the gate and the guard watching them.

"That door ahead will take us directly into the laundry room. We'll take the servant's hallways through the palace to the infirmary. Nobody will see us," Siobhan reassured, walking backward to keep her smile visible.

The servant's door opened.

Before it even finished registering, Cinn was surrounded by bodies, a shield between him and the palace. Strong hands landed on his shoulders, keeping him in place. His heart rolled over and threatened to come bursting out his throat, but a familiar face poked out from the ajar door.

"Oh, thank the Mother." Moyra practically fell out the door in her hurry to reach him, hobbling along on bandaged feet. Cinn stepped out of his protective circle to catch her as Moyra threw her arms around his shoulders. "You're alright."

Without words, all he could do was nod and pat her arms, her back, her face, checking that she also was in one piece.

"I'm okay," she said, letting him go. "I was just about to come find you, but Gatty said you were already on your way. He's off spying again. I . . . I wasn't sure you'd actually . . ."

She trailed off, noticing the others hovering nearby. One by one, she took them in, gaze unfocused. Whatever she saw in his motley family pleased her as she turned her smile back to Cinn.

"I'm so proud of you for getting this far. Come on. The path's clear."

He'd only made it this far because he had people with him—people he trusted to get him out again—but he was glad Moyra was here to finish this. One step inside was all it took to forget all their promises. To forget all the courage he'd mustered up to this point.

One step, and he was plunged into a storming sea of unfathomable pain.

Moyra's hands on either side of his face, her rose quartz eyes glazed as she stared directly into his, were his only anchor. She held on until the cold eased, until the pain wracking every inch of his body was only a memory once more, then she removed one hand from his face and reached for something.

A hand. Someone else's hand. She placed it against his face.

"Breathe," she told him, and Cinn breathed.

Cinnamon and sugar and smoke and whiskey.

"This is real," she told him.

It took a while for Cinn to find his way through the panic fogging his brain. To remember to nod. Moyra let him go and Cinn found more hands —gentle, warm, familiar—on his back, in his own. He was not alone.

A second step. A third.

They left the door open behind them. Not a single stranger stood in the laundry room, nor did anyone linger in the halls. The bareness of the floor, the walls, was nothing like the parlor where he'd first met *her*, but its cleanness was nothing like the prison she'd kept him in either. If his lungs weren't soaked in the terror of the familiar, they were soaked in the terror of strangeness, and every step deeper into the palace felt like a shackle around his throat.

But the memories did not descend. His body stayed in the present. Be it the ceaseless presence of the people with him, their smells and voices, or Moyra's influence over the dreamscape, Cinn didn't know. Only that he was grateful.

When they finally left the winding halls and Cinn faced the infirmary door, he was grateful a hundred times over. That day, he had been in the infirmary for a little while; it didn't frighten him now, because on the other side he could hear Eaon bickering.

Cinn's hand did not tremble as he pushed it open. The rest of the palace ceased to exist as he saw Eaon sitting up in bed, bandaged and bruised, but alive.

Mid-word, Eaon stilled, all color draining from his face.

"What are you doing here?"

At his side, the strange night-dark fae who'd plucked them from the Womb stood with a hand on Eaon's shoulder. Though Cinn had only seen the fae half-burned or in bird form, this man-goat was undoubtedly the same creature.

"He wanted to see you," Moyra explained as she slipped inside beside Cinn.

At the sight of the Morvish witch, Eaon's fists curled in the sheets, but as the rest came in—William and Sarah, Siobhan and Radley—his animosity eased.

Cinn left them in the doorway. He didn't understand the look on Eaon's face as he sat on the edge of the bed. Not until he said, "Are you alright? I told them to get you out of this place."

When Cinn nodded, it felt like the truth. He was alright.

Better, when Eaon reached out to touch his arm. Better still when he pulled his battered friend into a careful hug. There were so many questions brimming between them, but for a few minutes Cinn was content waiting for Eaon's pulse find a steady rhythm. Shattering on the bottom of the Womb had not hurt as much as finding Eaon down there, just as hurt and drowning in death. Healing was less of a relief than seeing Eaon whole again.

"We'll give you two some time," Sarah called softly from the door.

"We'll bring back some food," William added, taking his wife's hand.

Cinn let go of Eaon, skin too hot, heart flipping uncomfortably in his chest. He didn't like the idea of them wandering around the palace. He didn't like the idea of them being here at all. Not when *she* was here somewhere. Not when she knew what they meant to him.

Flinching at the sudden press against his leg, Cinn looked down and scowled at the cat sith who had not been there a second ago. Gatty grinned toothily; black fur and yellow eyes, the cat sith and the phouka were unnervingly alike.

"I might be inclined to keep an eye on them, for a price."

The ease with which he nodded was frightening, but he had watery memories of what Gatty had done to the selkies back in the lake by Moyra's cabin. If there was someone he could trust to keep his family safe, it was the cat sith. Especially if there was a jar of honey in it for him.

Reading the offering in his thoughts, Gatty purred and flicked his tail before padding across the infirmary. "This way, humans."

Sarah and William stared.

"Did that cat just speak or have I lost my bloomin' marbles?" William muttered.

"If you have, then so have I."

Moyra laughed quietly. "Mr. and Mrs. Copeland, I assume? My name is Moyra. Gatty is my familiar, and fae. When you reach the kitchen, fetch him a jar of honey and he will guard you with his life."

William immediately narrowed his eyes at the large black cat as it sauntered by, putting an arm in front of Sarah as if that would be enough to protect her should Gatty become hostile.

"I will not wait for you. Keep up," Gatty told them, unperturbed.

Sarah looked back to Cinn, who nodded encouragingly. Also by the door, Siobhan and Radley shared a few murmured words.

"I'm going to go back to the meeting with Edwina," Siobhan announced, giving Radley's shoulder a squeeze. "Rad will stay by the door to make sure nobody bothers you."

Hand wrapped around the hilt of his knife, the danger Radley posed to anyone stupid enough to come near the infirmary was as trustworthy as Gatty's guardianship. Cinn gave him a grateful smile and nodded. The four left, and his heart stuttered, but being this close to Eaon again made their absence bearable.

The phouka stayed, though he didn't feel the need to stand quite so close.

"It is a pleasure to see you again, son of Ru and Vy," the phouka said, giving Cinn a long appraisal.

Eaon raised an eyebrow. "You two know each other?"

"Retrieving you from the bottom of the Womb was a joint effort," the phouka explained.

Brow dropping, Eaon shook his head. "I don't . . . I'm not sure I remember what happened. How did you even get here? How did . . ."

Eaon's questions tapered off as he glanced to where Moyra had pulled up a chair at one of the healer's stations, busying herself with herbs and pretending not to listen.

So much had happened since they'd separated at the Northern Mountains, Cinn didn't know where to start. Didn't know how much he was ready to talk about yet. So he started with the moonstones, and how Moyra took him to an island he wouldn't name—not even to Eaon, not yet—to take care of something personal. How he was stuck there when the forest started to burn. The phouka didn't understand the sign language and turned away, bored, so it was up to Cinn to tell Eaon about arriving in the forest, about the phouka crawling half-burned for the Womb, begging Cinn to help. He told him about jumping into the Womb, about getting back out with the phouka's help, and about forgetting his pack down there.

Then he told Eaon about going in search for Kaelean and winding up in Dusarn. About the ruined city and the beasts in the tower and finding . . .

His hands wouldn't make a sign. They trembled, and Eaon covered them with his own until it stopped.

"I'll kill her."

Cinn steadied his breath, pulling his hands free. {I almost did.}

Then it was Eaon's turn to talk, and Cinn got the impression he was leaving parts out too. He told him about being lured to a faerie circle where he met the phouka, and how the fae hadn't left him alone since. About Moyra finding him in the dreamscape, about going to Pirevia to save Eavha. He told him about Dearmead being turned kinner too, the two of them going to investigate the fire together on the phouka's back. He told him about the dragon.

Eaon's voice cracked as he explained how he'd lost control of the magic they were now calling *the seed*, and how that lapse had killed part of the sky coven. How Dearmead had tried to fight the dragon rider and lost, and now nobody knew where he was. How the next thing Eaon knew, he was waking up in Hyrsch, laying across the courtyard from a broken Cinn.

"You shouldn't be here," he finished.

{Edwina said you weren't okay.}

"I . . ." Eaon stopped to swallow, once again flicking a look to where Moyra was working. "I might have overreacted to something."

{She's your aunt,} Cinn signed.

Eaon pressed his lips so tightly they bleached but nodded.

{And you're Morvish.}

"I'm not."

Cinn blinked and sat up straight. It wasn't often Eaon spoke with such vitriol, especially not to him. The denial was a surprise too. Eaon was too smart to not know Moyra spoke the truth.

Cinn left the matter alone for now. {Did she tell you about the wards?}

That dulled Eaon's defensive edge. "What about the wards?"

Moyra glanced over her shoulder at the direction their conversation was taking, but didn't interrupt as Cinn went on to explain how Nir was encircled in a giant faerie ring, and they were all trapped inside with a murderous deity.

Eaon took that better than he'd taken the news about his lineage, sinking deep into thought.

"That . . . explains a lot."

{It does?}

"I never once wondered what was beyond Nir, and it never occurred to me that a lack of curiosity was strange. Did you know, phouka? About the wards?"

"What about them?" the phouka asked.

"That they're around Nir, and not just around Qiri? That there's a world beyond?"

Slowly, the phouka looked from Eaon to Cinn, expression unreadable on his long face. "You did not know this?"

"Since I asked? Obviously." Eaon huffed.

"Wait, how do *you* know?" Moyra interrupted quietly. Cinn could read her nervousness in the way her hands folded and unfolded on the table.

"I was there when the circle was formed, and I do not easily forget."

Moyra blinked, paling slightly. "Oh. I see."

Eaon ignored their entire exchange. "It also explains why Chaos would do something like trap himself in a mortal body, if it's the only way out of the wards."

"Wait, *what*?" Moyra stood from her chair, paling even further. "He did what?"

Eaon refused to look at her, to acknowledge her at all, but Cinn met her wane expression. Without Gatty around to translate, he signaled for a piece of paper and a pen, which she brought to him quickly.

Someone needs to tell the council, he wrote. *Qiri needs to prepare in case he gets out.*

"I . . . I'll try to find someone in the dreamscape," Moyra said, taking his note back to the table and turning her back.

Cinn watched her a moment before looking to where the phouka had started pacing, his large body twitching and tensing, fists curling. The anxiety in the room was palpable, so Cinn tapped Eaon's hand to get his attention.

{Don't worry. I have a plan to get you out of here.}

Eaon tilted his head. "What do you mean?"

{We'll find Dearmead and Kaelean, get Eavha and my family, and then we use a moonstone to get out of here. There's a couple left, I think.}

Eaon's frown grew deeper, and when Cinn didn't have anything to add, said, "That . . . That's not a plan, Cinn. What about everyone else?"

{Who?}

Eaon didn't answer right away and Cinn wasn't sure he'd ever seen that particular look of disappointment directed at him before. He didn't like it.

"I have friends in the Southern Mountains. The Northern Mountains. In the planes and the river clans. What about them? Who is going to get them out?"

Shame was an ugly, bitter thing in his throat, because if Cinn was being honest, he had not given a single thought to the well-being of anybody else.

"I know your instinct is to run, and believe me, I don't want to be here any more than you do, but there are very few people who might be able to do something to stop this. If you need to get Sarah and William out of here, I completely understand. I'd even ask you to take Eavha with you. But I have to stay."

Closing his eyes, Cinn sat back. After a moment, he covered his face, too.

"Hey. Cinn, listen. You do not have to be a part of this. I understand. Cinn." The tug on his sleeve was a demand, and when he met Eaon's gaze, the seething rage in it was startling. "You were dragged into this against your will, and I will bury anyone who argues that you have to stay and be a part of this fight. You don't."

{I won't leave you.}

The declaration was dousing. Eaon looked away.

71

Grief was something Cinn had long ago become intimate with but could only recently name. He felt it now, for the death of his escape.

Where Eaon was, Cinn would stay. Even if it meant facing Chaos.

Even if it meant staying in this palace.

Even if it meant facing . . .

He made himself think it. If he was going to be here for a while, if he was going to be staying in this city, he had to swallow the sound of her name.

Aisling Aurnia.

He flinched at the weight of Eaon's hand on top of his, but Eaon only held it tighter. There was a darkness in his eyes that had nothing to do with the seed festering inside him and everything to do with an echoed promise.

CHAPTER TEN

EAVHA

PEOPLE WERE STARING AS EAVHA STORMED DOWN THE STREET BUT there wasn't space in her head to care about any of them. The shock was wearing off. She knew the signs. Her skin was clammy under the summer night sky, her blood a furious torrent, yet she shivered. It had been a while since something had made her feel so *delayed* and she didn't like it. Part of being a healer was to act quickly, confidently, but as soon as Moyra had opened her mouth, Eavha had been stunned still.

She had an unt. A living, breathing relative.

Tucking her arms tighter around her body, she narrowly avoided colliding with a human couple strolling past, both bewildered at her callous glare. Could they not see that she was in the middle of a crisis? Could they not have moved for *her*?

Huffing, she roughly pulled her hair back into a pile atop her head, wrapping a long curl around the mass of it to keep it bound.

Moyra Thorne was her unt. *Aunt*. Mother of all, how often had she teased her da for the slip in his accent? She had been so young, had thought he was mispronouncing words on purpose, to be funny, but . . . Terranian was not his first language. Possibly not even his second. What language did they even speak in Qiri? Eaon probably knew.

Eaon.

As quickly as she had started her rampage down the city streets, she stopped. Someone walked right into her back, knocking her aside, cussing her out as they hurried on their way. Eavha didn't care. Squeezing her eyes closed, she found the very small amount of self-control she had and shoved every ugly feeling threatening to make an appearance as deep as she could.

Eaon was Morvish. Whether he wanted to admit it or not, he was.

Nasty things swarmed in her belly at the thought. They did not deserve her time or energy.

Opening her eyes, she looked back to the palace. To the tower where Aisling would be. Going would be selfish. For so many reasons, hiding away with Aisling was so incredibly selfish that her feet started moving again. She needed to do something good. Something helpful. Something to distract her from the fact that she had an unt, that her father had been Morvish and powerful, that her brother was Morvish and powerful, and everything that meant. She needed to do something that didn't make her feel like the worst sort of person.

Eaon was angry, but Eavha . . .

No. She would not name the feeling. She would not give it that power. She would bury it, smother it, and do something good instead.

So she walked.

~

In the time Eavha had been squirreled away in the infirmary, Yvette had organized. The injured witches had been moved off the street into an old entertainment hall; nothing special, like the theater Aisling had taken her to, but large enough for a hundred hastily built cots.

For every herbalist and brewer tending to the many burn victims, there was a Hyrschan medic, both human and demi-kin alike, helping. The combination of burned flesh, bile and medicine was familiar and grossly comforting. Here, she knew what to do. Here, she was still Eavha Nemuse, renowned healer.

Checking her hands were steady, Eavha crossed the floor to Yvette's workstation. Eating had helped. The tea had helped. She didn't feel strong by any means, but she didn't need to be. The metaphorical book of realms was open to Sanni's page, and Eavha barely had to focus to find her, the connection between them running strong.

I'll give you anything.

A promise to a spirit felt more binding than a promise to the fae. A stupid promise she couldn't be bothered thinking too hard about. Certainly, she hadn't told anybody. Eaon would kill her. Possibly literally.

A favor.

Sanni had yet to collect. Had yet to abandon her either, despite their initial deal only including enough power to heal Eaon and Aisling. Though the exchange was dangerous, she couldn't regret it. The spirit of healing was a warm, comforting presence curled against her soul that had never once led her astray.

"You're back," Yvette grumbled, cold gaze sweeping over Eavha's borrowed clothes. "How is your brother?"

"Annoying," she snapped. It was the kindest word she had at the moment. "Distract me. Point me at something."

"Have you slept?"

"Yes," she lied. "I napped during the day."

"How are your reserves?" Yvette asked, scanning the crowded hall.

"Replenished." It was true enough. She wouldn't be bringing back the dead any time soon—Sanni's presence wasn't an indication of what she could physically endure, apparently—but it would feel good to heal someone who actually wanted to be healed. To use magic and see the results.

She had spoken too loudly. Whispers were starting.

She didn't care, she'd heal all of them. There wouldn't be so much as a bruise left by the time she was done. Eaon wanted to be stupid and annoying and make her feel incompetent? Fine. He could suffer and she would prove her mettle.

Eavha took a slow breath. Those were cruel thoughts. Unfair. She needed to stop it.

"Cot thirty-two, over by the window. Go finish what you started," Yvette said, tilting her chin in the direction she meant.

Unsure what Yvette was talking about, Eavha nodded and left for the cot. She soon remembered. A woman with a reed sticking out of her throat lay silently. At her side, a child clung to her clammy hand.

Eavha closed her eyes. She had promised to come back and had been so thoroughly distracted by Aisling and Eaon that she had forgotten. But she was here now. That had to count for something.

"Hi," Eavha said, crouching by her side. "I'm ready now. Sorry it took so long."

The woman flickered heavy, tired eyes, grimacing when Eavha placed a palm against her neck's reddened skin. Moving quickly, holding the reed pinched between two fingers, Eavha closed her eyes.

Throats. Esophagus. Veins. Tendons. Magic unfurled inside her, whittled to a thread and soft as moss. Eavha pictured what she wanted the female's throat to be and asked Sanni, *May I?*

The answer came as a sigh—relief and love. *Yes.*

At the same pace her magic began to repair the damaged flesh, Eavha carefully withdrew the reed. Once it was out, the woman gasped, grating and deep. Eavha splayed her hands down her chest, searching for smoke damage, for burns, and soothing them away with little more than a thought.

"Thank you," the woman croaked, one hand at her throat, the other pulling her child closer. "Thank you."

Eavha smiled as she stood. Satisfaction was a balm like no other.

The witchling's tiny voice was a fresh burn.

"Ma? I can't find Da."

"I know. It's alright. He's with the Lover now."

Frozen, Eavha couldn't breathe as she watched pain flicker across the young one's face. Couldn't look away as the female's eyes turned glassy despite the false smile.

"It's an honor he has been chosen."

The witchling gave a single sob before their ma hushed them, and Eavha couldn't take it. Lowering herself once more, she shook her head.

"What happened was not the Lover's bidding. What happened is a tragedy, and you are allowed to be sad about it. You are allowed to mourn."

A deep frown creased the witch's brow. "But, that's . . ."

"I know. I know it feels like blasphemy, but Lorelei twisted our teachings to serve her own ideas. Kaelean has told us it is alright, and she is the true high priestess of our clan. She loves us, and I trust her over Lorelei a hundred times over. Do you trust me?"

The female nodded but the frown remained. Behind her, Eavha's name was being called. She didn't have time to preach; there were others who needed her help.

Still, as she petted the witch's hand and rose to her feet once more, taking a long look at the hall filled with injured people trying to quiet their grief, she knew it was going to be a problem.

～

Healing her people felt good, even if her head was pounding. Having Sanni's hand on her shoulder didn't mean the spirit of healing was allowing her unrestricted access to power—as soon as the headaches began, Eavha felt the magic furl up like a night rose protecting itself from the scorching daylight.

Just one more, she pleaded silently, looking around at the dozens she had yet to reach.

Rest.

The command was impossible to disobey.

"I'll be back," she said to the next witch in the row, climbing shakily to her feet to find some tea.

Yvette's expression was hard as she watched Eavha approach. "You do more than you need to."

"Is that supposed to be a bad thing?" Eavha lifted a brow, taking a mug of tea to sip at. The ginseng had become such a staple of her diet that she barely tasted it anymore.

Yvette opened her mouth to retort, but at the loud groan of the entryway doors, she snapped it shut again. Somehow, her gaze found deeper pools of cold. Or, more likely, it had been so long since the elder healer had leveled such derision at Eavha that she had forgotten just how cutting Yvette could be.

Eavha glanced over her shoulder and stilled.

Lorelei stood in the hall, observing the witches recovering in their beds. She did not speak to them, nor was she carrying anything to offer; she simply watched the wounded with detached curiosity as she approached the workstation.

The only sign of her surprise at Eavha's presence was a long, slow blink.

"Weren't you supposed to go to Pirevia?" Lorelei asked tightly.

Eavha swallowed against the stubborn lump in her throat and begged her knees not to shake. "I delegated."

For a long minute, Lorelei's inscrutable gaze held the gravity of the earth. The weight of it was crushing. Without Kaelean as a buffer and with Lorelei's magic unbound, there wasn't much stopping the ex-high priestess from lashing out. She certainly hadn't cared about their audience the first time, when Eavha had been arrested for necromancy.

It was Yvette's toneless voice that broke the tension, holding out a stack of clean towels.

"If you've come to help, you can hand these out."

Lorelei released Eavha from the prison of her stare and turned on Yvette, nostrils flaring. "No, I did not come to labor. I came because there will be another Imsa soon regarding what is to be done, and I need to speak with each of the elders before I go. You ignored my summons."

Yvette remained unmoved. "I've been busy."

Another Imsa. She hadn't heard anything about it, but she had also been singularly focused. If Aisling was calling for Imsa, Eavha would be there. Kaelean's absence may have left a vacuum in the clan's leadership, but the idea of Lorelei representing Wyldeden was not only absurd but offensive.

Just as Yvette saved Eavha from that horrible stare, Eavha took a deep breath to return the favor. "I am already on good terms with Aisling. Perhaps I should go to Imsa instead."

The slow blink Lorelei filled the silence with reduced Eavha to a bug-like panic, faced with death-by-boot. With an assuredness fit of a high priestess, Lorelei declared, "I am in charge."

Eavha's mouth turned dry. Yvette looked between them, eye twitching.

Technically, Lorelei wasn't wrong. Kaelean left her as emissary, but only because Eavha was meant to go to Pirevia. Since she didn't . . . Eavha really wasn't sure who was in charge. As heir, was it her? Or did Kaelean's order supersede that, even if the stipulations were moot?

Did it matter? If Lorelei claimed to be in charge, did Eavha have the authority to say otherwise? Not without the elders to back her up. And why would they? Half of them hated her.

If there was one thing Eavha was sure of, it was that the technicalities of law came second to Kaelean. What would the true high priestess do? What would she say? What would she want?

"If you say so," Eavha allowed, fully intending to go to every meeting regardless. With Aisling at her side, she could speak over Lorelei if need be. "When you speak with the elders though, I think you should organize a funeral."

It had been increasingly obvious as she'd treated the witches in the hall that what was hurting the most was their grief. Not everyone had acclimated to Kaelean's ideas that mourning was acceptable. Eavha herself still felt the need to hide it, because she didn't know how to let it out. She could cry and scream and rage, but what was there to do with all of that? Where did it go? Where could she put it and not have it ruin her?

Wyldeden needed a funeral.

"Do you, now?" Lorelei's facade was cracking. "Are you an elder? Did I ask for your input?"

Yvette cleared her throat. "There is a lot of anxiety—"

A scoff. "A few months with Kaelean and everybody has forgotten what a gift it is to be chosen by the Lover."

Eavha bristled despite herself. "They weren't chosen, Lorelei. It was not their time. This was violence, and the people are mourning—"

"Blaspheming, you mean."

"Do you honestly feel nothing?"

"I am pleased."

Eavha wanted to smack her. Only the fact that she felt two feet tall stopped her. "You fought for us in the forest—"

"There was no reason for us to just stand there and die, but I will not mourn those who didn't make it. Wanting to live and accepting death are not mutually exclusive."

She was never going to get through to her. Eavha changed tact. "Regardless of theology, we have always held a funeral for the passed. The people need one now."

"And I need breakfast. Fetch it for me."

Eavha blinked. "I . . . The castle is hosting breakfast in the banquet hall for all the refugees."

"You think it is appropriate for *me* to eat amongst the rest?" Lorelei smirked. "Kaelean unbound me. With my power restored, I am no longer subservient, and you'd best remember that before you speak so freely to me again. Now, whether you fetch my breakfast or get a slave to do it, I do not care. Just get it done."

Eavha blinked again. The audacity left her borderline speechless, but when words did come, they did so unbidden.

"You have learned nothing."

Lorelei turned slowly, her gaze dark. "Your impertinence is annoying me."

Eavha's body ached with remembered bruises. "I . . . I am heir. You . . ."

Stepping closer, Lorelei let the significant blessing in her veins swell until Eavha's stomach turned.

"I am what? A laborer? Tell me, what exactly gives you the impression I am of the same pathetic, useless breed as your brother?"

Like a candle blown out, all the fear itching Eavha's skin dissipated. Her mouth tasted of metal.

"Eaon is a hundred times the witch you have ever been."

"Get out."

"You are not in charge."

Lorelei's next step put her within striking distance. "Say that again."

As quick as the steel had straightened her spine, it left. She remembered too clearly the beating Lorelei had ordered, had gleefully watched from the edge of her prison cell. Fear whittled her down to nothing and it was all Eavha could do to keep her knees from quivering.

It didn't matter. Lorelei knew. The part of her that thrived on asserting dominance ran rampant in the smirk pulling her upper lip.

"Where did that Nemuse arrogance go? I do miss seeing your family strutting around like peacocks. You may be Kaelean's heir, but you were never mine, and I am in charge here. Defy me, and I'll turn your innards into shrubbery and watch you choke."

Sheer cowardice had Eavha crumbling. It didn't matter who saw; she fled the hall, heart thrumming like a hummingbird.

CHAPTER ELEVEN

AISLING

THE SUN'S BREAKING OF THE HORIZON MARKED A DAY SINCE EAVHA HAD healed her, but it was Edwina's knocking that marked the end of her rest.

"The evacuation notice has been sent," Edwina said while Aisling pulled her hair into a tight braid, accentuating her harsh angles. "Not everybody is happy about it, but the guards are making sure order is kept."

"What did you decide to tell them?" Aisling asked.

"A foreign clan from Bernt has harnessed an army of beasts and is invading. That leaving is just a precaution. Temporary."

It was the truth without the horror.

Nodding her approval, Aisling finished dressing. Choosing an outfit while the world was on fire was the vainest thing she had ever done, but one of her earliest lessons was the power of fashion. At the very back of her closet sat the dress she had worn her first day in Hyrsch—the day she had sat on her throne for the very first time and declared slavery abolished.

High necked with a sharp collar, long sleeved with a tight fit, the black fabric shone metallic and gave the illusion of armor. The loose, blood-red skirts were a warning, concealing weapons strapped to her thighs, accessed easily through slits hidden in the many folds. Wearing it again brought with it a violent nostalgia. She would resort to that level of bloodshed again if required.

"I must tell you," Edwina said while Aisling toed on her shoes. "When I returned to the palace an hour ago, there were people gathering at the

81

gates. The guards were already on their way to disband any protests but that wasn't why they had come. They wanted to volunteer. They had been out all night gathering names of people who wanted to fight."

Aisling's reflection could have been a painting for how still she had gone, first at the idea that she would have to beat down a civil resistance and then at the surprising turn it had taken. It was like that night she'd spent in Dusarn, distracting her mother while Eavha stole the unicorn blood, when a guard had cornered her; she had expected the worst, steeled her spine for a fight, only for Foley to whisper support.

Closing her eyes, she prayed to anyone listening that he had made it out of the city before the harbingers arrived.

"How many?" she asked.

"I heard a thousand. More were still signing their names." Edwina's voice softened as she explained. "They love what you have made this city and they want to protect it."

Aisling took a moment to steady her hands before picking up the insulated vial of bird's blood to paint her lips. With every breath in her body, she would try to be worthy of her people's devotion. There wouldn't be time to get them all battle-ready and she refused to feed bodies to the beasts as fodder for the sake of numbers, but there was work to be done outside the city walls, and when the fighting started the soldiers would need shield bearers.

Another knock on the door announced Clayton's return, and with him, a messenger. The young boy didn't need to speak; the pallor of his face told her all she needed to know.

"They have arrived," she guessed.

"Yes, Your Highness." The boy bowed deeply. "They wait in the throne room, as requested."

"Thank you."

The messenger left but Clayton lingered, the heavy bags under his eyes eased since she'd ordered him to rest. Knowing full well what they were about to walk into, her guard lifted his chin, ready.

Many of the final preparations were well within Edwina's means as second-in-command, but hosting this meeting was not a task Aisling would subject her to.

The lords of Oford had arrived, and it was time for them to kneel.

~

Middlemen of the hierarchy, there was a lord to rule over every town the Sparrow Coven had claimed as their territory. They were meant to keep order, keep civilians safe, but also to report back to the reigning royal in the nearest city.

As soon as Aisling had regained her wits after Dusarn, she had sent the summons. Messengers on horseback had ridden all the previous night, and the lords had ridden back with equal urgency. Not all could make it on such short notice, but the nearest towns were those she had immediate need of anyway.

A council room would have been more comfortable, but Aisling needed the authority of the throne room. All five waiting men turned as Clayton pushed open the doors, watching her stalk down the long red rug. They stayed silent as she climbed the dais, Edwina to her right, Clayton to her left. The morning light through the stained-glass windows behind her illuminated the pinched expressions on their faces as she sat on her gaudy throne.

Hands folded in her lap, back straight as a board, she stared each of them down until they bowed. She did not care about etiquette at a time like this, but they did, and she would play their game if she had to.

Rather than bother with greetings, she got right to the point.

"As you know, the Anfar forest is currently burning. The river clans and the Northern Mountain Clan are working to control the blaze, but it will likely rage for some time. The disaster is not a natural one, rather one of dragon fire, and an act of war committed by the harbingers of Chaos."

The mocking scoffs were expected and immediate. Aisling didn't give them time to add words to their disbelief.

"I have neither the desire nor the time to convince you of the fourth high spirit's existence. It only matters that you do what I say."

Lord Dustin of Belden took a step forward, the whiskers of his large orange mustache obscuring his mouth as he spoke.

"I beg to differ."

"You're welcome to, but it will go unheeded. Save your knees the trouble." Aisling had long perfected the art of deadly softness. Of the hard quiet. She did not need to raise her voice beyond a bare whisper to have Lord Dustin stepping back. "War is coming, here, to this city. I am ready for it. As a precaution, I have mandated an evacuation of all non-essential persons."

They had to have seen the beginnings of it upon arrival—human and demi-kin families alike packing clothes and photographs, favorite teddies and stashes of coins.

83

Unable to contain himself, Lord Dustin balked. "Where do you expect them all to go?"

This time it was Lord Hawthorne who interrupted her, not bothering to step out of the pack. A little less than six years ago, upon Aisling's quarter-century birthday, the wiry man had been demoted from Lord of Hyrsch to Lord of Porton. He too wore a mask of faux serenity as he held her gaze.

"Isn't it obvious? She expects us to take them in."

Immediate outrage broke out, but Aisling only waited, unblinking. When their protests petered out, four of the five shifting their weight nervously under her steely gaze, she continued.

"I have taken Pirevia from Prince Nevan and am sending most of the civilians there until Hyrsch is secured, but there is a small percentage of people who cannot go there."

"Wait, you *took* it?"

"How? When?"

"Where is Prince Nevan?"

Aisling raised her voice only a little, the word ringing with warning. "Dead."

The room went quiet. Someone's breath hitched.

"You said some people cannot go to Pirevia. So I am right; you expect us to take them in," Lord Hawthorne repeated.

"Yes. My second-in-command has procured a list of demi-kin who escaped Pirevia to move here. They do not wish to return." Prompted, Edwina stepped forward with five scrolls in her hands, ready to hand out. "Eighty, to each town. You are to make accommodations for them, and, I cannot make this clear enough, they are to be treated as free people. Not slaves."

Lord Hawthorne curled his lip. "You may have authority to make those decisions within your city walls, Princess, but the towns of Oford are not your jurisdiction."

There wasn't much to smile about given the state of the world, and Aisling didn't let her face actually move, but it must have shown in her eyes regardless because Lord Hawthorne blanched.

"Actually, they are."

In the silence that followed, the creak of the throne room doors could not be missed. Aisling only dared look after everyone else had, and when she saw Eavha peeking through the gap, red faced and teary, her stomach sunk.

"I am so sorry."

"No. Come in." Aisling nodded but kept her face sharp and empty. She waited until Eavha had closed the door, putting her back to the wall, before attempting to speak.

Lord Hawthorne interrupted. "Who is this and what business does she have here?"

"Eavha Nemuse, Heir Apparent of the Anfar Forest Clan," Edwina announced.

"And her business here"—Aisling let her tone drop to chilling depths—"is none of your concern."

"Everything concerns me," Hawthorne spat. "Where is your council? Why haven't they—"

"Dead."

More shuffling. A few of the lords eyed the door.

Hawthorne continued, spluttering, "King Phineas and Queen Tallulah would not have given you free reign over all of Oford—"

"They didn't. They are dead."

"The . . . The high council . . ."

"Dead." Aisling relished the bleaching effect the word had on her predecessor's face. She wasn't entirely sure about the high council, but given the state of Dusarn when she'd arrived, it was a safe assumption. "They are all dead. There is only one authority left, and that is me. So if I say the demi-kin—all the demi-kin in all of Nir—are *free*, then they are free."

As she said it, as she watched the lords' shock and fear take hold, the true weight of the crown settled in. It took all her strength not to sink beneath it.

She was the only royal left. She was the only member of the Sparrow Coven in a position to hold power. Their empire was in ruins, but what remained of its control was hers, and she would hold it. Until Chaos was gone, she would hold it.

"Impossible." Lord Dustin gaped.

Another cried, "Lies!"

"Did you kill them?"

"What witnesses can attest to this?"

Their outrage was predictable and boring. Her attention shifted to where Eavha crept silently along the wall, cheeks tear-stained, chest and shoulders shuddering with an emotion Aisling hated. Whatever had caused such distress would be dealt with fittingly.

Clayton lunged, and Aisling snapped her gaze forward. Lord

Hawthorne had taken a step toward the dais, quickly backpedaling as Clayton drew his weapon.

It was not surprising that it was Lord Hawthorne rising to challenge her. He had enforced Sparrow law in Hyrsch for decades until the city was gifted to Aisling. Proper inheritance laws meant Hawthorne should have been demoted to her second-in-command, her right hand as she adjusted to government, but Aisling had argued with her father tirelessly to have him removed from the city entirely. She was unwilling to work with someone so opposed to demi-kin freedom.

King Phineas had humored her, as he always did, with equal measures of amusement and disdain. *Coddled*, the queen would accuse. With Davina's death so fresh, her seemingly blasphemous decisions were excused as a temporary defiance borne of grief. It wasn't a story that would hold forever, but she hadn't needed it to. She only needed six years.

"My apologies, Your Highness," Lord Hawthorne ground out, hands raised and head lowered.

Clayton didn't lower his sword. "Try *Majesty*."

The neck to throat coverings of her dress hid the gooseflesh that pimpled at those words, and though Aisling didn't dare look away from the scene at the bottom of the dais, it was a comfort to feel Eavha's warmth reach her left side.

"Not yet," Lord Hawthorne spat. "This information needs to be corroborated, and there will have to be a coronation."

Aisling blinked. "Given the state of things, there is hardly time for—"

"There *will* be a coronation, Princess Aisling." The utter disrespect had the order for Clayton to cut him open leaden on her tongue. "If we throw away our laws simply because they are inconvenient, how are we any different from this Chaos you fear so much? The coronation ensures Balance is kept, and so there will be one."

The urge to flay them all open until they *did what they were fucking told* boiled beneath her skin, but reappointing lords would take longer than simply seeing the process through. Still, she spent a moment imagining it, letting the five men below her remember how easily she had spilled blood when first claiming the city. How easily she could do it again.

Hosting a coronation in this climate was a joke. Nobody outside the throne room gave a damn about official recognition, and yet Aisling had known it would come to this. Formalities didn't matter, but she would do it. Queen was a title she would only have to wear for a little while.

"For the sake of Balance, then," she acquiesced.

Clayton didn't move as each of the lords bowed their heads. As if sensing that Aisling was one wrong word away from killing the lot of them, Edwina stepped forward, scrolls still cloistered to her chest.

"Rooms have been prepared for each of you. We will summon you again for the ceremony once arrangements have been made."

Hawthorne wrinkled his nose as if the act of being spoken to by a demi-kin was somehow distasteful. He didn't speak to Edwina, aiming his warning at Aisling instead.

"Tonight."

Clayton bullied them from the room then, but even once the door was closed and it was only the four of them left, Aisling couldn't relax her shoulders. She stared through the heavy wooden doors as if she could still see her prey.

"You prepared their rooms?" she ground out.

Edwina sniffed. "Small ones. We are quite crowded, after all."

Finally, as Eavha's hand rested atop of her own clenched fist, Aisling let out a long, deep sigh and turned her attention upward.

"You've been crying. I don't like seeing you upset."

With her other hand, Eavha wiped at her cheeks. "I don't like seeing you like this, either."

Another measured breath, and she managed to release some of the tension in her jaw. "I don't want to be."

"I know."

"What happened?"

"Can we talk about it upstairs?"

Aisling nodded and took Eavha's hand properly, petting it gently. Turning to Edwina, she asked, "After I left for Dusarn, what happened to my father's body?"

Glancing away from the pair's linked hands, Edwina blinked twice before grimacing.

That was answer enough.

"I need it."

"That might be a problem."

"Edwina, *I need it*."

Swallowing, she nodded. "I'll take care of it."

Aisling stood and rolled her shoulders. Releasing her hand, Eavha slipped her fingers beneath the collar of Aisling's dress, letting a tendril of warm, healing magic find its way to the taught muscle of her neck.

"Thank you," she whispered, then to Clayton, "Stay with Edwina. I don't trust the lords."

"I don't need a babysitter," Edwina groused. "I can take care of myself."

"I'm well aware." Aisling gave a pointed look to the concealed weapon in Edwina's skirt. "And yet, Clayton will go with you."

"What about you, Your Majesty?" Clayton asked. "Another guard can stay with Miss Red—"

"You will stay with her," Aisling repeated, done with the conversation.

Neither argued again, and though both Clayton and Edwina followed her to the stairwell winding up to her suite, they let Eavha and Aisling go alone.

CHAPTER TWELVE

AISLING

Sequestered in her suite, door locked, the city's pandemonium far below, Aisling couldn't rip off the dress clinging to her sticky skin fast enough. Shrugging back into her robe was the best she'd felt all day. While she changed, Eavha took herself to the balcony where the daylight exposed fully the toll of too many long days and nights. Shadows darkened the otherwise flawless brown skin under Eavha's eyes, her lips chapped.

Aisling tied her robe closed and took Eavha's hand, moving a stray curl aside. Knowing she was more comfortable using her native Terranian language, Aisling told her, "You are going to come with me. I am going to run you a bath. You are going to tell me what upset you. We will find a solution, and then you will take a nap."

Mischief lit Eavha's light-brown eyes as she smiled. "Is that an order from the queen?"

Aisling only lifted a brow. "Will making it so encourage obedience?"

Grinning wider, Eavha shrugged, but when Aisling tugged her hand, she followed to the bathroom willingly. She watched curiously as Aisling turned the handles, releasing hot water into the large tub. It was quite the feat of engineering to get hot water so high up the tower, and not a demand Aisling herself had made. The royal chamber had seen many Aurnias before she arrived.

There wouldn't be any after she was gone.

"There's a bath salt in here somewhere that you'd enjoy," Aisling said, frowning at the row of polished wood cabinets concealing an array of additives she had no clue about. "I don't want to disturb Larissa—she's saying farewell to her family—but for the love of the Mother, I wish I'd paid more attention when she used to run my baths."

"The true burden of princess-hood," Eavha teased, though it lacked her usual energy.

Ignoring the jab, Aisling hunted through the cabinets until she found the salt she wanted, adding it to the steaming water.

"I'll be on the balcony when you're done," she promised.

Shoulders dropping, Eavha's lip quivered. "Won't you stay?"

It took a moment to be sure Aisling's voice stayed steady. "You want me to?"

Her own face might have been heating at the suggestion, but one look at Eavha's glassy eyes and the sudden drop of her full mouth told Aisling the request was simply one for company.

"I know I was the one who told you to stay up here and rest, but I . . . I don't know who else I can talk to. About everything. If Kaelean was here, she would know what to do . . ."

Eavha pressed the heels of her palms into her eyes in an attempt to smother the hitch of her breath.

"As soon as Celeste allows it, I will portal back to Dusarn to find her."

"She has ways of letting me know she's okay. I don't understand why she hasn't sent a whispering leaf."

Gently taking Eavha's hands away, Aisling wiped at the first tear spilling over. "Bath. Talk. We can solve it all together."

Nodding, Eavha began to undress. Aisling left to fetch a large cushion; the tile on the bathroom floor was cool despite the summer and the velvet made a pleasant buffer between it and Aisling's bare legs as she sat on the floor beside the tub. Watching Eavha approach the water with all her golden-brown skin on display, her mess of curls tangled and heavy around her face, turned the bathroom into a temple. Even grimy with the remnants of soot and blood, she was a creature of such organic beauty that staring was involuntary.

Eavha poked at the hot water pouring from the tap. "Still fascinating."

In the short time Aisling had been permitted in Wyldeden, during the night they had spent at Eavha's family estate, she had noticed the lack of bath. The tepid stream that snaked by the house connected the central lake to a source beyond the settlement's limits and was the sole source of water. There had been pipes in the kitchenette and the sinks in the bathroom, but the water was unheated. At first Aisling had been endeared by its rural charm, but as she'd exposed herself in the privacy of the forest the following morning to wash before returning to Hyrsch, something intrinsic had settled. Something deeply buried had washed through her body, alive again in a way it had only ever been while flying over the gray deserts of home. A rightness. A homecoming. A sense of grounding that she reveled in over and over every time she touched Eavha.

Like King Phineas once told her, in the safety of the sky, where he was, momentarily, simply her father: "The Sparrow Coven may insist you abandon your element once you take the Passing rite, but you will always feel better in nature. Celeste blessed you, so the sky is where you belong, but you can find solace with the soil and water too. The seven elemental spirits are connected. Together, they are the world, and so are we."

It had been confusing to her later, in the classrooms, when her teachers had detailed the same man's ravings about the savagery of elemental witches. Temple visits had been marred by the priests echoing of Phineas's mockery of the seven, and his promises that blessings from a high spirit was proof of their entitlement to all of Nir's land.

Had the conflicting views been a deliberate attempt to confuse her, to weaken her to Sparrow indoctrination? Had he done it to keep her from the throne, or because he, like Aisling, wore an array of masks?

It didn't matter anymore. He was dead, and she had hated him right up to his final breaths. Those brief moments in the sky, riding the winged horses he bred together, were but a dream.

Eavha sighed as she slipped into the water, resting her head on the lip of the tub. Aisling's fingers walked the bare skin of Eavha's shoulder, warm and soft.

"I am sorry about your home."

The rise and fall of Eavha's chest stuttered. "I'm sorry I interrupted your meeting today."

"I'm not." Aisling propped her chin on the edge of the bath and watched the rippling water climb the side of the porcelain. "You gave me something to focus on beside killing everybody in that room."

Eavha didn't comment on that. "Who were they?"

"The lords of Oford. Some of them at least. They watch over the smaller towns and villages in the area and report back to me if anything becomes relevant to the Sparrow Coven. It was how I learned about the demi-kin smuggling chain. Walking the line between appearing to condemn it and ensuring the rebels involved were not disturbed on their way into the city was . . . challenging. The lords are challenging. They are Sparrows; they are loyal to the coven and its cause, not to me."

For a moment, the only sound was the water splashing into the tub, and when it was full and Aisling turned off the tap, there was only a rhythmic drip remaining.

Finally, Eavha took a steadying breath. "We haven't really had a chance to talk since you came back. I didn't know about your mother. I'm sorry."

"I am not. I always hated her, and all of this is her fault. She brought Chaos back."

There was only the paradoxical swirl of rage and boredom in her belly as she thought of her mother. That, and the distant echoes of her wrathful screaming deep in the void.

"You will be a much better queen," Eavha promised.

Aisling hummed. The word still fit like a six-fingered glove. "Not that there is much of a coven left, and not that it matters, except I need what's left to listen to me. But they won't. Not until a coronation is held."

"Why do I get the impression a coronation is more than just a crowning ceremony?"

Aisling sighed. "Because it almost always is. Don't be surprised if there is another assassination attempt."

Sloshing the water, Eavha sat up. "What?"

Grimacing, Aisling found comfort in Eavha's fretful face. "Nevan may be dead, but there are plenty of people left who hate me. I will be alright."

Reaching out of the water, Eavha took her hand. "Yes, you will be. I won't let you die."

As always, the thought of Eavha anywhere near that level of danger left Aisling hollow.

"You don't have to be there. In fact, it's probably safer if you're not."

"I wouldn't miss it if you portaled me all the way to Dusarn and left me there." It wasn't an exaggeration—Eavha would find a way. "Though, if I disappear at any point, it's because Lorelei is also likely to be there."

The fear Aisling sensed whenever Eavha spoke of Aadya was also present whenever the retired high priestess was mentioned. It was sometimes easy to forget that, for all her bravado and senseless courage, Eavha was deeply afraid of many things—heights, wide open spaces, death.

"Tell me about her. What happened today?"

Shrinking in on herself, Eavha's grip on Aisling's hand tightened. "You have so much on your plate already, I shouldn't have asked you to listen to me."

"I'm not asking you to give me your plate, too. I'm asking you to tell me what's on it, so that I may give you some advice on how to tackle it. You're young, Eavha. I may not have been doing this as long as Kaelean, but I have been playing the politics game for some time now. Let me help."

Eavha's teeth bit into her soft bottom lip and Aisling resisted the urge to pull it free. "It's complicated."

"It always is."

"The Imsa you organized . . ."

Eavha glanced at her questioningly, so Aisling explained, "It's a part of the plan Nora and I made a long time ago. Edwina has initiated many things for me, since I was ordered to rest."

Not remotely apologetic, Eavha nodded. "Well, Lorelei heard about it and tried to speak with the elders. She didn't like that I was still here in Hyrsch, didn't like that I told her I would be at Imsa regardless of who she thought was in charge of the clan right now, and she especially didn't like when I suggested we take the time to host a funeral."

"She threatened you," Aisling guessed.

Eavha's breath hitched as she nodded.

"You do not have to put up with that. You are her superior."

Eyes shut tightly, Eavha repeated, "It's complicated. Kaelean left her in charge."

"Because she thought you were going to Pirevia."

"Still . . ."

"Still, you are her superior."

Aisling's own politics only mattered to ensure she was obeyed. Eavha's had deeper repercussions; the Anfar Forest Clan had lost their home and whoever rose up to lead in the vacuum would make or break them.

"She doesn't see it that way, and while I know it is technically true, she . . ." Eavha opened her eyes again to stare at the intricately molded ceiling, the crystal chandelier sparkling in the sunlight that poured through the window. "I idolized her while growing up. I wanted to be her. She is centuries old, and I have not even reached maturity yet. She is skilled beyond anything I could hope to achieve and . . . And she is cruel. I never saw it until it was directed at me. Her whole attitude is blasphemous to the peace we aim to achieve. When I brought Eaon back, she had her guards punish me, and I will never forget the smile on her face when they first drew blood. The glee in her eyes as she branded my hands and banished me from the clan."

The raised lines on Eavha's palms seemed to burn against Aisling's own, and though she didn't want to disentangle their interlocked fingers, she wanted to see them up close.

She knew the official, public story. Aside from the unprecedented and untrained feat of necromancy, nothing about it had struck as particularly extraordinary, but hearing the crack in Eavha's voice as she spoke of being "punished"—of bleeding and burning—the tale sat differently. The oily violence that thrived in her heart, the one she had tried to bury in the face of such bright goodness, seeped through. Once again, she wished she could breathe deadly curses with Nevan's ease, because she had the most delectable ideas for Lorelei.

"Would you like me to kill her?"

"Aisling!"

"It would not burden me at all to do so."

"*Aisling.*"

Running her tongue across her teeth, Aisling took the obvious "no" in Eavha's tone with a grain of salt. They could discuss it later. Running her thumb over the scars, she considered instead how the spellmark's power would have faded with the shift in power in Wyldeden, and now lay dormant with the rift between realms closed entirely. The place Eavha had been barred from no longer existed, but the shiny pink lines still told a story of that pain.

"Can you heal these?"

Eavha squirmed. "Possibly. Healing myself is a lot harder than having someone else do it. But even if I could . . . I don't want to."

"Why not?"

"Because I can't heal Eaon's." Her voice grew thicker, blinking rapidly as she stared at a fixed point on the ceiling. "He only bears them because he chose to protect me. I had only ever left the Boab for burials, and that was with a large crowd, with guardians to protect us. I would have died alone. He knew that. The clan would have forgiven him for my crime, but he chose me. He chose to share my shame, and I won't leave him alone in it for vanity's sake."

Considering Nevan, Aisling had never had high opinions of siblings, but whatever had gone wrong between the two of them seemed to have gone right between Eavha and her own brother. Eaon's power and his affection for Cinn made her nervous, but he made the very short list of people Aisling respected.

Eavha's hand reached up to cup Aisling's jaw and her attention returned to the honey-brown eyes now staring at her cheek.

"I think I could heal yours, now."

"No. They are my own penance. Back to the point, though," she said, not wishing to discuss her feelings about the whole kinner situation again. "That Lorelei was so keen to get rid of you only proves that you are within your rights to claim power over her. She does not represent what your clan stands for, and while she may have more experience, she does not have more magic than you. Kaelean appointed you heir apparent. While she is missing, you are in charge. If Lorelei has some sort of power here, you need to take it back. Prove to everyone, including yourself, that Kaelean chose you for a reason. Put her in her place."

"I can't."

The words were so meek, so *wrong*, coming from Eavha that Aisling saw red.

Rats. She would make Lorelei watch while rats ate her, piece by piece, starting with her hands. She would keep her conscious as she fed them her eyes. Rip all the teeth out of her vile mouth, keep it pried open while rats ate her tongue.

Violence wouldn't comfort Eavha. Aisling's anger would not reassure her.

Measuring breaths in counts of four, she kept her voice level as she said, "You have forgotten who you are."

"No, I—"

"You have forgotten that you have never been confronted with an unbeatable challenge and walked away anything but victorious. You faced Death and said *no*. You faced banishment and said *no*. You jumped into an arena of murderous rioters in nothing but your gauzy skirt and walked away intact. You are extraordinary, and capable, and you have *forgotten*."

A pretty pink blushed Eavha's cheeks. "I had you and Dearmead and Eaon to thank for that last one."

"And you will have me at your back when you challenge Lorelei, too."

Eavha's chin dimpled as she closed her eyes again, and though she didn't verbalize her uncertainty, Aisling countered it anyway.

"You can, and you will. At the coronation."

"Tonight is your night."

"Historically, Sparrow coronations have always been a time for shifts of power across the board. It would be tradition for you to speak up."

The shudder than ran through Eavha's body was visceral enough to disturb the water. Aisling leaned up over the tub and took her face in both hands, waiting until Eavha opened her eyes again.

"If she even thinks to hurt you, I will kill her on sight. Do you trust me to keep you safe?"

Nobody had ever looked at Aisling with such unadulterated honesty shining on their face. "Unquestioningly."

She had asked, had been sure of the answer, and yet hearing it left Aisling sick to her stomach. She didn't deserve that trust. She didn't deserve to be kneeling before a creature like Eavha and have her look at her like that.

Throat almost too thick to speak, she said, "Then take your crown."

CHAPTER THIRTEEN

EAON

GOSSIP SPREAD QUICKLY AND LOUDLY ABOUT THE EVENING'S coronation. It was quieter about the confrontation between Lorelei and Eavha, but whispers and speculation still reached Eaon through the servants who came to refresh his bedsheets.

He knew his sister. Better than anyone. He needed to be at that coronation.

Standing at the foot of the bed with his large arms crossed tightly, the phouka watched Cinn help Eaon swing his legs over the side. "It is too soon."

Ignoring him entirely, Eaon took a slow breath through the worsening pain, hands trembling around his bruised thigh.

"We need something to make a splint," Eaon told Cinn. All the hours he'd spent quizzing Eavha for her exams were worth it as he planned his own rehabilitation. "Try that cabinet. And get those long things in the corner—the crutches."

Cinn nodded, and while he collected things, Eaon tested the strength in his legs. Both had broken, but the one where the femur had protruded through was impossibly heavy. Muscle twitched and spasmed, a limb possessed as he tried to lift it.

"Do I need to break your ankles as well to keep you in this bed?" the phouka growled, puffing his chest.

"Death will not keep me in this bed," Eaon snapped back. Despite the sweat dripping down his back already, he forced a smile when Cinn came back and began to strap a splint around his thigh.

The scrape of a chair reminded him that Moyra still lingered, cloistered away at the desk. Her book closed heavily as she rose, making her way over to inspect Cinn's work.

"May I?"

"No," Eaon bit out, finding a spot on the floor to stare at while he swallowed down the necrotic rush of his blessing. It had always taken advantage of the way strong emotions chipped at his focus, and as much as he hated her for the garbage she'd tried to sell him, he did not want to kill her.

He almost lost control when she reached for the worn leather gloves, but she did not try to touch him, just guided Cinn's hands to better wrap the splint.

"I'll get you some pain relief," she said once satisfied.

"You're going to allow this?" the phouka asked, glaring at her as she passed.

"Thornes are known for their stubbornness. The best you can do is get out of our way," Moyra said, fetching one of the many vials she had brewed over the hours. "Or, if so inclined, help ensure we don't get ourselves killed."

Eaon changed his mind. He did want to kill her.

"I am not a Thorne."

Moyra grimaced apologetically but she didn't retract the sentiment. It was only Cinn's hand wrapped around his wrist that stopped him from smacking the pain relief tonic from her hands. He refused to take it from her though, and refused to meet Cinn's chastising look as the kinner took it from Moyra to pass to him.

Had he always been this petty and bitter and violent? He wasn't sure, and right now he didn't care. Drinking down the pain relief, only mildly disappointed it wasn't poppy milk, he stretched as much as he could while waiting for it to kick in.

Without another word, Moyra returned to the work desk and opened her book again. The phouka glared between them, nostrils flaring when Eaon reached for the crutches. Considering only yesterday the bone was protruding, his quivering legs did surprisingly well to hold him up.

He should thank Eavha, even if she was unbelievably stupid for having risked so much to heal him.

For five seconds he stood before needing to sit again. Allowing only a minute to rest, he stood again. Again and again, over and over. Cinn could barely keep his steadying grip on Eaon's sweaty arm as the witch shook violently with effort.

When he was sure he could stand without Cinn's support, leaning heavily on the uncomfortable crutches, he shifted his more injured leg forward. The awkward shuffle-hop he managed brought him an inch from the bed. It also brought him such bone-deep pain that his vision spotted.

"You know, if you're that desperate to attend, you could ask me to carry you," the phouka teased.

"Go rogue," Eaon spat back.

Sipping the water Cinn handed him, Eaon set his sights on the other bed a mere four feet away and stood again.

Inch by inch, he shuffled. The cold stone against his bare feet was a nice contrast to the hot throbbing in his thigh, the fresh sheets against his sticky skin equally pleasant as he finally collapsed onto the other cot.

"Ridiculous." The phouka huffed, flinging his hands up in defeat.

Eaon managed to raise a middle finger as the phouka returned to polishing his bag of bones.

~

Without windows, the only indication of time passing was how often servants stopped by. Every time the door opened, Eaon caught sight of Cinn's brother standing guard, and when lunch arrived, he told Cinn to fetch him.

Radley Lightman looked the way Eaon expected demi-kin to look— brimming with equal parts anger and exhaustion, the strip of paler skin around his throat the source. Shadowing Cinn, hand resting on the knife at his hip, it was a relief to see others taking Cinn's continued freedom in this city seriously.

While Cinn took the tea tray from the servant over to Moyra and began pouring a couple of cups, Radley dragged a spare chair from across the room to where the lunch tray balanced on Eaon's bedside.

"It's nice to meet you," Eaon offered once Radley sat down.

Judging by the disapproving glare aimed his way, the sentiment was not reciprocated. Without a word, Radley snatched up a sandwich and tore into it.

Cinn rolled his eyes at his brother's antics, setting one of the teacups by Eaon.

"Thanks." Eaon picked through the tray beside him and found a soft-cheese and cranberry-jam sandwich. "Here, you'll like this one."

Taking a curious sniff, Cinn bit the corner, audibly moaning when he did in fact like it. Eaon smiled and found a second sandwich in the pile, setting it aside, closer to Radley.

"There's another one there, in case you're a sweet tooth like Cinn."

Finishing his mouthful, Radley sat back in his seat, wiping the crumbs from his chin with his sleeve. "You're awfully friendly for a stranger."

Making no attempt to be subtle, Cinn kicked Radley's boot. Eaon frowned questioningly but was ignored in favor of the series of pointed glares Cinn and his brother shared. A language all their own, those twitching brows and pursed lips.

"Why wouldn't I be?" he asked. "You're Cinn's brother, and Cinn is my friend."

"Why?"

"Why what?"

"Why are you friends with him? What do you want from him?"

It was more than a question—it was a flat-out accusation. The flare of annoyance in Eaon's chest didn't have room to grow dangerous, though the phouka stopped cleaning his bones long enough to glance over.

The bite in Radley's tone was understandable. Eaon reminded himself that he too grew a sharp tongue when the people he cared about were in strange, untrustworthy company.

"I don't want anything from him. We found each other at very difficult times in our lives and we helped each other through it. I care about him."

Eaon's passive tone did nothing to subdue Radley's.

"People say they care about demi-kin, but they don't. We're just fun ways to pass the time to your kind."

Cinn scowled and slapped Radley's knee, signing furiously. Rather than translate, Eaon considered the man sitting before him. It wasn't unusual for people to dislike him; beyond his status in the clan, he'd been told often how whiny and moody and sour he could be. Eaon didn't need to be liked.

But this hostility wasn't about him.

In the very first conversation he'd had with Cinn—as one sided as it had been—Eaon had tried to communicate with the outlawed demi-kin language to no avail. It was a secret shared only among rebels, of which Cinn had never been one.

Radley was.

"What is this really about?" Eaon asked, the language awkward on his unpracticed tongue. He remembered enough, apparently, because Radley's eyes widened impossibly.

"Get our language out of your mouth."

"It was trusted to me long before you knew it."

At nineteen, Eaon hadn't been traveling long. The first time he saw Hyrsch was his first time in any human city and the first time he'd met demi-kin. It was a few months before Aisling took it over from Lord Hawthorne, who'd been acting as the Sparrow Coven's representative in the southeast. It wasn't where Kailevi intended for them to go, but the small sea clan at Oford's coastal port town was as wary of foreign witches in their territory as the Anfar Forest Clan was protective of Wyldeden. They had gone to discuss a trade arrangement, and Hyrsch was middle ground.

The rare herbs Eaon had picked in Anfar had depreciated in value since Kailevi's last visit, so the inn they'd stayed at was cheap. There were still slaves working there, though, and Eaon had *hated* that. Hated the metal collars locked around their necks, hated their lowered eyes and bowed heads, and most of all, he hated that they cleaned up after him. As if he wasn't one of them.

He still remembered the wide-eyed terror of the young demi-kin he'd tried to talk to. Eaon's fascination with language had thoroughly taken root and his Nirnish was almost fluent by that point. He'd been growing bored waiting for Kailevi to finish scoping out the agreed-on meeting place, so he'd asked if the demi-kin had a language of their own he could learn. The slave reacted like Eaon had pulled out a weapon, their days-long silence abandoned for nonsensical denials and desperate pleas for mercy.

That was how Eaon learned about the rebellion working quietly in the shadows to overthrow the Sparrow Coven. Where he learned that life could be cruel and unfair no matter where you were from.

He didn't have much to offer the slave who eventually calmed down and explained, except to teach them the few medicinal remedies he knew from traveling. He gave them his coins, too, and would deal with the consequences of that later. In exchange, they taught him their language so that, wherever he went, the rebels there would know he was a friend.

"You don't know me," Eaon continued. "So this cannot be about me. What is the real problem here?"

Cinn was staring at both of them, mouth agape, but Radley was too busy seething at Eaon to notice.

"That's exactly it, though. I don't know you. All I know is that my brother is fond of you when he has never been close with anyone. All I know is how people treat my kind; once the novelty of the forbidden has worn off, we're worthless. I will not let him be hurt like that. So what exactly are your intentions?"

Whether the barrier was linguistic or cultural was irrelevant; Eaon had no idea what was going on. Or, he sort of did. He knew very well how laborers were treated in his own clan, and he had the feeling Radley was insinuating the same thing. To have that accusation leveled at him, though, was entirely foreign.

Cinn tugged on his sleeve and signed, {What are you two talking about? Is he being an asshole? Should I hit him?}

Shaking his head, Eaon took a sip of tea before speaking in Nirnish. "We're just getting on the same page. Give us a minute."

It didn't seem to reassure Cinn much, narrowing his eyes at his brother.

Radley ignored him.

"My intentions." Eaon rolled the word around in his mouth, its connotations, revolted by the taste in any language. "Your brother has only ever wanted to be my friend. I want nothing else from him. In fact, as his friend, I would gladly ruin myself to keep him safe and happy. There is very little I wouldn't do. I have no *intentions*."

If Radley believed him, his face revealed nothing.

"If you hurt him, I will kill you."

"If I hurt him, I will give you the blade."

Satisfied, Radley picked up his sandwich and ripped off a bite. Eaon turned away and caught the phouka watching, head tilted curiously. Before he decided whether or not he wanted to know how much the phouka understood of what just transpired, Cinn smacked Radley's knee again.

"Ow! What was that for!"

{You were being an ass. I just know it.}

Eaon snorted, almost choking on his tea. It took almost a whole minute of chasing his composure before he could translate.

"Little shit." Radley poked Cinn hard in the ribs.

"If we get any spare time, I'll teach you to sign," Eaon offered. "Curse words first, obviously, since they're Cinn's favorite."

There was a glimmer of amusement in the way Radley looked at him, nodding once. Eaon would take it as a white flag.

When they were all done and a servant came to remove their dishes, Eaon pulled his crutches closer.

"I'm ready to walk some more. I need to get out of this room."

Slowly, Cinn placed down his glass of water. Despite how carefully he moved, the shaking of his hands had the liquid sloshing over the lip.

{I can't come with you tonight.}

"I know." He had never expected Cinn to. Wouldn't want him to. The thought of Cinn and Aisling in a room together made Eaon nauseous.

{I don't think I can walk . . . around . . . out there.}

Eaon's fingers were dry as chalk as he lay his hand on Cinn's once more. It both warmed and sickened him that Cinn had come to this place for him, and every second he lingered was a second more than Eaon would have ever asked him to endure. If he'd had enough, Eaon was not going to ask him to stay.

"I know."

From where she had been pretending not to watch, Moyra stood from the desk and closed the book she'd been reading. "Why don't Radley and I take you home for a while. Edwina will likely have news by now. I can escort you back again tomorrow."

Swallowing thickly, Cinn looked from Eaon to the phouka and back again, lifting a brow in silent question.

Eaon sighed. {I'll be fine. He's an asshole, but he's safe enough. Go spend some time with your family.}

For a moment, Cinn deliberated. Eaon ran his fingers through the tangled hair at the back of Cinn's head and gave him a gentle push.

"Go."

{I'll come back.}

Another push, and Cinn finally stood. Radley and Moyra rose on either side of him, the latter already muttering distractions. It was an odd dance of relief and misery to watch the door close behind them.

"You should rest longer," the phouka said.

Rather than bother with an answer, Eaon gripped the edge of the bed and pushed himself to his feet.

CHAPTER FOURTEEN

EAON

EAON STOOD IN THE THRESHOLD TO THE GROUND FLOOR'S GRAND FOYER and watched dozens of servants scurry in and out of halls, up and down the stairs, helping the residents of the palace prepare to leave. Not one of them paid him any mind.

Nobody beat the young girl who tripped in her hurry, dropping a tray of dirty plates. Nobody scolded her when she cursed loudly and viciously at the stain on the rug. Nobody stopped her when she declared to no one in particular that she'd had enough and was going home.

Eaon leaned against the wall, sweaty and sucking down shallow breaths, watching her stomp across the crowded foyer and straight out the main doors into the afternoon. He watched, and smiled.

Aisling Aurnia might be scum, but she had done at least one thing right.

The palace was an architectural enigma—beautiful, in a claustrophobic sort of way. While Nevan's castle in Pirevia was open to summer sunlight and salty sea breezes, its towers a blinding white broken only with dashes of royal blue and gaudy gold, Aisling's palace was older, darker, with its gray stone and heavy drapes, veined in rich reds and deep purples. It should have felt oppressive and violent and full of secrets, but it wasn't. Or not any *more* violent than Pirevia, anyway. Eaon knew the kinds of things that happened in the dungeon below. He'd sat through long nights beside the aftermath of those clandestine horrors.

He could have studied the architecture for days—the blown-glass chandeliers, the elaborate molding, the gilded railing—but the impatient huff of the creature behind him warned him not to.

Not that the phouka, with his thick arms crossed over a furred chest, yellow goat eyes slitted in annoyance, approved of this venture. No, his impatience was more about wanting Eaon to hurry up and fall on his face so they could return to the infirmary.

Ignoring him, Eaon shuffled into the foyer. The shadow cast by the phouka's long, curling horns stretched out before him, scattering courtiers and servants alike. The path to the grand staircase leading up to the second floor was clear, and when he reached the base, he stuck both crutches under one arm, clutched the railing and grit his teeth. Slowly, agonizingly slowly, he lifted one leg onto the bottom stair. Sweat beaded his brow as he shifted his weight and dragged his more damaged leg up behind him.

The phouka snorted.

"Shut up or fuck off," Eaon snapped, though it lacked bite. He was too tired for it.

"I am not required to do either of those things."

"You are not required to be here at all," Eaon reminded him.

The following silence was not a surprise—every time Eaon tried to bring up the phouka's completely unwanted presence he was met with silence. Since learning about Chaos, Eaon understood that the phouka could not walk away; as an Old One, he had faced this beast before. He was one of the fae with enough of a conscience—despite the phouka's insistence that he did not have one—to fight for human freedom back in the First War. One of the fae blessed with The Healing Mark of One Unending, just as their human counterparts, the Kinner, had been. So Eaon understood why the phouka was still here, in Hyrsch.

He did not understand why he was here, hovering over Eaon.

Except, Eaon supposed, he did have the Lover's seed growing inside him, and the phouka seemed adamant it should not be allowed to bloom. Aside from Cinn, who could only handle being in the palace for small bursts, and . . . Dearmead, who was not here . . .

Eaon swallowed, losing his train of thought. He forced his body to climb another step.

Another.

Another, and his knee buckled. Catching himself by the railing, Eaon swallowed the pain radiating from his ankles, his knees, his thigh. It was nothing compared to how it felt when the bones had been fractured pieces inside him, yet he couldn't seem to get back upright.

The phouka huffed, but stayed at the bottom of the stairwell, leaning against the railing.

Eaon glared back at him. "No, I insist, don't help."

"I will not aid in this stupidity."

"So you're just here to watch. Typical fucking fae, getting off on pain and suffering."

The phouka did not answer.

Eaon probably wasn't too far off the mark; he had met the thing in a faerie ring after all. Perhaps he *should* be nervous to be alone with the phouka since just the other day, he'd wanted to kill him. But then they'd been flying to rescue Eavha, and Pirevia happened, then Anfar . . .

"Haven't you got anything better to do?" Eaon snapped, returning his attention to the stairs. Focusing on this pain, on the impossible task of climbing the stairs, was easier than thinking about things out of his control.

He could not go back and do better. He could not save the forest. He could not save Dearmead.

"Many, many things."

Too tired to come up with another retort, Eaon forced himself to take another step.

Over the hour it took him to reach the crest of the stairwell, he only had to pause twice, dizzy and nauseous and unwilling to vomit on the rug for someone else to clean up. But finally, mouth dry and head throbbing, he made it to the landing.

The phouka sighed directly behind him. "Where are you even going?"

Eaon ignored him, out of petulance, yes, but also because he didn't know where he was going. The pounding in his head was almost worse than the burning, pulsing agony in his legs as he leaned against the wall to catch his breath. Everything was too bright, too loud. In the space of a blink, there were suddenly too many lines of pure color fogging his vision. Threads as tactile as a rainbow's reflection weaving between everyone and everything, until none of it made sense.

The brightest lines would lead him to Cinn. To Eavha. To Dearmead, who Eaon knew, somehow, was *far away, far away*. As soon as he was able, he would follow it. He would find Dearmead, since nobody else seemed to care enough to try.

Hallucination. That's what his ma told him it was. What his da agreed was a side effect of his wild moods. To accept any other explanation now was to admit they were liars, and that . . . He couldn't . . .

The phouka had not been surprised by Moyra's—not "confession," because it wasn't *true*. Moyra's accusation.

"You knew," Eaon managed between scraping breaths. He didn't want to think about it anymore. He shouldn't have said anything. Needed to change the subject. Needed to clear his head. "You knew about the Lover's seed."

The phouka watched him struggle with himself for a long moment. Eaon refused to meet that stare in case the phouka could somehow read the thoughts right out of his head, like the cat sith could.

"I suspected," the phouka admitted. "Now I am sure."

"You talk to it like it's sentient. Like it's separate from me."

"Is it not?"

Eaon closed his eyes, needing the spinning to stop. Needing his brain to slow down.

He had not realized for too long that magic wasn't supposed to be something that could throw a temper tantrum. He'd never had it before. Not really. To learn that this thing he'd come back from the void with was not an average Lover's blessing but something trying to take possession of his body . . .

"Do you know what's going to happen to me?"

The silence felt different, and when Eaon opened his eyes, he flinched at the undiluted rage festering on the phouka's face. It didn't smooth out the moment Eaon was looking at it either, and he had enough sense to stay quiet. To stay still.

He had things to do. He could not afford to get murdered by a faerie. Death would probably not be permanent, but the fire in his shaking legs was proof that an inability to die did not make him invulnerable.

"I have never hated a creature as much as I detest you," the phouka snarled.

What was he supposed to say to that? Sorry? Good to know?

He said nothing.

Nostrils flaring, the phouka snatched the crutches and grabbed his arm, and Eaon couldn't help but flinch. Any second, the cold of the void would consume him, and some poor servant would have to clean the blood out of the carpet.

The phouka half-dragged, half-carried Eaon along the hallway.

"No, I don't know what might happen to you." Words sharp and low, they hesitated outside each closed door for less than a second before moving on. "I only know such a thing is possible because the Lover has tried it before. During the First War, there was a human man Sanni was particularly fond of. He died, and though she did not know it was possible, she attempted to resurrect him. She managed it to some degree, but he was not the same. He said he could hear the dead whispering, and the weight of magic on his mortal soul was too much. It drove him mad, and he killed himself, but he returned again of his own accord, spluttering about an unimaginable void. He said Death spoke to him—wanted to end the war through him.

"Sanni kept him close after that. Kept him safe. He was the first human she turned Kinner, and I do not know what happened to him after that. But I remember how he smelled. Your scent is strongly reminiscent, and when I witnessed your return after the mountain clan tried to burn you, I knew. Given the timing, after Aisling told us about Chaos, it was not difficult to deduce what the Lover is up to. After all, has the world not made art of the horrors we commit in the name of love?"

That was a lot to process, and Eaon's brain had stopped being able to do that. It was static and numb, like the time he smoked too much papaver with Tomaii in the northern mountains and they'd lain dumb for hours, incapable of more than blinking and breathing. But this wasn't that. This was uglier, his chest too tight with thoughts he didn't want to have.

"You . . ." Eaon clawed his way out of the haze. "You speak of Sanni like you knew her. Personally. As if she is something you could know."

The phouka stopped outside the next set of closed doors and looked down at him.

"I did know her. I knew them all. I walked beside them on the great trek east. Before they were your spirits, they were Fair Folk. Mother was so grateful for their sacrifices during the First War that she asked her Lover to give them something special in the after-realm, and so new realms were carved out for each of them, space from the void turned into something new. They were made gods over their dominions and left to an eternity of watching their descendants from beyond."

Somewhere inside his paradoxically sluggish and rapidly firing brain, the words rang true. Which, of course they were—fae didn't lie—but he had also heard something of the sort before. Maybe a book he'd thought fiction but was in fact not. He couldn't remember.

"This room," the phouka said, shaking the handle until it opened, leaving Eaon in his spinning mind. "It smells like your sister, and your . . . lost boy."

Eaon frowned.

"How did you know this was where I wanted to go?" He hadn't even known this was where he wanted to go.

Inside, the phouka dumped him into the nearest chair and smirked. "You are sometimes predictable."

Looking around, he could not see Dearmead in this place—this room, with its fancy furniture and large paintings and expensive rugs. And yet he had been here. This was the suite he and Eavha had boarded in when they had come for Aisling's Imsa.

Awkwardly, still seated in the plush chair, he picked up his crutches from the floor where the phouka had tossed them. Every fiber of his being protested, but now that he was in this room there was something he desperately needed to find.

Slowly, silently, as if afraid to disturb the ghost of people who were not here, he crept to the nearest door and pushed it open.

Eavha's things were thrown haphazardly all over the place, the bed unmade and clothes hanging off every free surface. Candles and flowers, both fresh and dried, lay scattered in a rudimentary altar on the floor by the window. The luxury suited her. Leaving it, he went to the next door.

Dearmead's things were tidy. Organized. Spare leathers were folded on the dresser along with a few sets of civilian clothes—Wyldeden cloth, worn and familiar. Eaon brushed his fingers against it and could almost feel the warmth of Dearmead lingering.

And there, by the bed. A notebook so full and used the pages had thickened.

Dearmead had told him he could read it, but now it felt like a violation; Dearmead was gone and Eaon could not help him. Not yet.

Maybe it was masochism. Maybe he wanted to punish himself by ripping this wound open at the worst possible time, when his head was already unraveling, raw and aching.

The phouka lingered in the doorway as Eaon shuffled to the bed and sat down. He took the notebook in his hands and held it to his lips, breathing in the smell of parchment and ink.

What did Dearmead dream of? Eaon needed to know he'd had hope. That he'd imagined a world where they were safe and happy. It wouldn't be real, but he needed it anyway.

Cracking the cover, he took in the familiar, messy scrawl and nearly gagged on the grief that flayed him open, made worse by the very first line on the page—the first word, scratched out and rewritten a dozen times before he'd finally settled on it.

"Fear made a coward of me only once, because regret is a far sicker feeling."

Minutes slipped into hours as Eaon read Dearmead's uneven scrawl.

It was Dearmead's regret for not having followed Eaon into Anfar the day of his excommunication. It was a story of another life. One with a happier ending. A wish. A dream first confessed in a servant's room in Pirevia:

In the end, I stay. I stay with you.

Reading that hope on the page wrung a pain unlike anything Eaon had ever truly let himself feel before. Because this was a dream that could never be. It was a life that only existed in a world where Eaon had never died, and Dearmead had never had to turn himself kinner just to be close. One where Eaon wasn't destined to play host to the Lover, and Dearmead wasn't captive to a dragon and its rider, suffering unimaginably. Neither of them would ever be the males Dearmead had so painstakingly written about, no matter how much Eaon wished, too. Even if they found Dearmead and won this battle and Eaon somehow survived the Lover, they would never be happy. It wasn't in the cards for them.

"You should eat."

The phouka had remained a quiet, passive observer while Eaon devoured Dearmead's dreams. His presence had been intermittently noticed, and when Eaon was aware of him, it was more of a guardian's vigil than the sort of prying nosiness one might expect of the fae. To say it was a comfort would be overstating things, but it was not unwelcomed company, either.

He'd certainly had worse when a fatigue hit.

"I'm too tired." To eat. To make it back down the stairs. To get up off the floor.

The phouka scoffed derisively, but Eaon knew what the weight in his bones meant. The thickness in his thoughts, the sluggishness of the hollow muscle beating in his chest. Grief was such a dangerous thing to allow, because he didn't have *time*.

His body did not care. Eaon put the book on the floor and closed his eyes.

He was done.

"Get up."

"Just go away," Eaon said, fingers braced on the floor that was about to become his bed for the next few hours, days, weeks.

"I will drag you."

"Okay."

His head weighed a thousand tons as he lowered himself down. His hips and legs protested, a sharp, lancing ache wrapped around his bones, pulsating in every muscle and tendon and nerve. A vial of poppy milk wasn't even enough to motivate him, though with his eyes closed and his body heavy, he could remember the opiates taking him far away from pain.

The phouka's footsteps were both heavy and silent as he loomed over Eaon, who couldn't find the energy to care if the phouka really did drag him all the way down the stairwell by his broken leg. The idea of lifting his arm to swat him away was laughable. In no time at all, he'd lost the energy to do much more than breathe.

"I will make a bargain with you, witchling."

The phouka hadn't phrased it as a question. There *will* be a bargain. In flashes, Eaon remembered the way the phouka's commands could drill inside his head, impossible to deny. He had said things and done things he did not mean to say or do, because the phouka had told him to.

He may not have the energy to breathe too deeply, but that didn't stop his pulse fluttering with nerves.

"I will help you." The words were dragged through the faerie's teeth, like he hated saying them.

"I don't want your help," Eaon managed.

"What you want is irrelevant."

Eaon snorted. Wasn't that the truth.

"You are a disaster in the making," the phouka went on. "Untrained Morvish magic wrapped in shoddy bindings, while Death's seed grows inside you with the potential to bring the living world to ruin. You are unstable and unprepared and in desperate need of guidance."

If the insults were meant to touch him, they didn't. He was too far away.

The phouka crouched, his shadow darkening what little light seeped through his closed eyelids.

"You will accept my help."

The words didn't have that sucker-punch quality that a true command had. Not yet. Eaon figured he could only refuse for so long before the phouka would force this on him. But . . .

"Why?" Eaon asked.

"That you do not know proves how stupid you are."

"I don't believe mind-reading is one of the Morvish abilities, bound or unbound."

The phouka's sharp, yellowed grin didn't need to be seen. "You admit you're Morvish."

Eaon snapped his mouth shut and opened his eyes. Such a wicked grin on an elongated goat's face was a stark reminder of exactly what he was dealing with. The phouka had been amenable for longer than could be expected, but Eaon would be unwise to forget his lessons on the fae.

Mother made them to care for her non-living creations. There were fae whose sole purpose was to share their life force with the trees, to perform rituals in the rivers to keep them flowing, to care for the fungi and the flowers and the soil. However, Mother also made them for Chaos. They were capricious, clever, tricky things, and she made mortals to entertain them.

The rituals were beautiful things to witness. If not for his da's guidance early on, Eaon would have easily been lured with fruits and songs, trapped in faerie rings and favors and promises. Not all of the fae could make commands without knowing their victims' names, and in another life, the phouka would not have hesitated to feed upon and use his flesh however it entertained him to do so. The grin on the phouka's face proved how fundamentally he enjoyed teasing Eaon, twisting the proverbial knife in this wound Moyra had inflicted.

So why? Why was this ancient beast offering to help instead of harm?

"Why do you even need my permission?" Eaon rolled his head from side to side in a pathetic mockery of a headshake. "You could be a nuisance without a bargain; not that you've told me what you expect from me in return."

There was a flash of *something* in those yellow eyes that rose the hair on the back of Eaon's neck, but the phouka's next words were back to sounding like he did not want to say them at all.

"Because fate is a cruel, wicked thing."

Eaon stared, waiting.

"They say Morvia does not make mistakes. That the potential of a witch is evenly matched to the power of the fae she chooses for them. That the bond is perfect in every way. But I was born at the dawn of creation, and you are the single stupidest thing on the face of the world."

When Eaon continued to stare blankly, the phouka almost vibrated with rage.

"*The familiar bond,*" he spat.

Somewhere, deep in the only part of Eaon's brain that was still functioning, he recognized the concept. A story his da had told him once to distract them both from the frigid chill of a winter's night spent in the mountains.

There was enough room for shame in Eaon's chest that his very first thought was how disappointed he was that he did not know enough about familiar bonds to extort this. But he didn't think it was an irrational response. The fae were dangerous. This phouka was likely one of the most dangerous, and he had some kind of fate-bond to Eaon? It was not ideal. He did not like the idea of someone so much stronger being in a position to control him. It gnawed at a part of him that screamed *trapped*.

"I don't want it," Eaon said.

The phouka spat back, "That makes two of us."

"Then I'll do you a favor. Whatever bargain you want from me, the answer is no. Leave me alone."

Eaon shut his eyes again. He didn't care about the coronation anymore. He just wanted to sleep.

If the phouka left, he didn't hear it.

CHAPTER FIFTEEN

CINN

"I THOUGHT IT WOULD BE DIFFERENT," MOYRA SAID, ARM LINKED WITH Cinn's as they finally reached the Turlough home.

The cat sith had appeared when Moyra called. Apparently, Sarah and William had returned to the large inner-city house with extra food taken from the palace kitchens, and as much as Cinn wanted to go back to his own shoddy apartment, if he couldn't be with Eaon, then he wanted to spend time with the Copelands.

He looked up from the smudges his shoes left on the footpath, the roads coated in a fine layer of ash, to find Moyra staring at the sky rather than the house. Frowning, he followed her gaze. The noon sun sat heavy and orange in the hazy sky, as far from normal as he had ever seen it.

{It is different,} he signed.

Nobody understood him, but after a moment, Gatty heaved a long-suffering sigh. Reading the thought out of his mind, the cat sith spoke it aloud for him.

"The boy says it is."

Moyra's other hand dangled low as they climbed the porch, letting her fingers brush through the soft fur of her familiar's tail.

"I mean, sure, there's a lot of smoke in the atmosphere, but it's the same sky. The same sun. I don't know why, but I thought the world would be different here inside the wards."

Behind them, Radley scoffed, kicking the step to shake loose dust and ash that had stuck to the bottom of his boots. "Typical."

Cinn glared back at his brother. First Eaon, now Moyra? Was Radley going to be an ass to all Cinn's friends?

"Excuse you?" Moyra asked, lifting a brow.

"I said, typical elitist, thinking those of us born in cages live in an entirely different world from you. Easier to ignore us that way."

Pulling his arm from Moyra's, Cinn clipped his brother over the head. Radley scowled and smacked him back.

"Onribleq," Moyra sighed, ignoring them both to push open the door.

Gatty flicked his tail in annoyance, giving Cinn a pointed look. "Just when I thought there was nobody as insufferable as you."

Torn between defending Radley and defending Moyra, Cinn settled for silently promising Gatty another jar of honey in exchange for not attacking his brother. In a way, Radley was right; not all cages were prison cells and metal collars, though the demi-kin had seen plenty of both. Nir was a land so large that Cinn could spend years exploring it and never run out of new views, but with the wards locking them in with Chaos, it qualified. But spending fifty years isolated to a lakeside shack with only hostile fae creatures for company was a cage of its own, too. It wasn't elitism that had Moyra thinking the sky should look different inside the wards—Cinn knew too well how foreign fresh air could feel. That it didn't meet those expectations spoke legions.

The Unifiers in Ahrenhale were right. It was one Nir.

"There is only so much honey in this city, boy," Gatty growled, flattening his ears. "Your brother would do well to watch his mouth before I take his tongue for my collection."

Not one to be perturbed by the threat of violence, Radley opened the offending orifice to spit back. Desperately, Cinn made a cutting motion across his throat, but was saved from having to intervene by the call of their names from down the street.

"Rad! Ry! Hold on a moment!"

Standing on the porch with the front door wide open and Moyra lingering in the threshold, the four waited for Edwina to catch up. She jogged with her skirt hitched in her fists, but the hems hadn't escaped the ash entirely. They would all be covered in it for a long time to come.

Behind her, a large male in a heavy cloak with the hood pulled so far over his face there wasn't an inch of skin visible, followed. His long strides came to a halt when he was still a long way from the front gates.

"Let's go inside, Moyra," Gatty said, swishing his tail. "Privacy is needed, and there is honey to be had."

Judging by Edwina's stiff shoulders and pursed lips, Gatty wasn't wrong.

The small amount of peace Cinn had found after spending time with Eaon lodged in his chest like a cork, keeping his panic from bubbling too quickly. Still, it stirred: Had something happened at the palace? Was it Eaon? He never should have left.

"I'm going to go introduce myself more thoroughly to your farmers," Moyra said, fingers brushing Cinn's wrist. "I have a lot of work to do, but I want to give them each a reading while I'm here. Remember to breathe, and remember to anchor if the dreamscape descends. I'll come find you if you need me."

If she meant it to be comforting, it wasn't. He watched her wander into the house proper, wishing she wouldn't leave.

"What's wrong?" Radley demanded, voice low as he moved back down onto the street. He only gave the large man a fleeting glance before clenching his jaw, tenser than Cinn had seen his brother since arriving home.

Following him down to the footpath, Cinn tried to see who the cloaked man was, but Edwina stepped between them.

"You wait here," she snapped over her shoulder, grabbing Cinn's arm and leading the way to the nearest alley where they had more privacy.

For the first time in many years, the thunderstorm in Edwina's eyes mellowed. She couldn't quite meet Cinn's concerned curiosity as she let him go, smoothing her fingers down his arm where she'd grabbed him. An apology, as if anything she did could ever hurt him.

Bracing herself, she faced their brother instead. "I need the body."

Radley grimaced.

{What body?} Cinn asked before remembering there was no point. They didn't understand. Settling for universal gestures instead, he held his hands out in question.

Radley cleared his throat, averting his eyes. "The Sparrow king's. Red, you know I—"

"I know. But we need it."

It took Cinn a minute, but when the conversation finally churned its way into sense, he stepped back. All he could do was stare, eyes so wide they were at risk of falling out of their sockets.

Scratching the back of his neck, Radley shook his head. "If I get it, and she sees . . . She'll kill me."

They didn't have to say the name for Cinn to know who they were talking about. His fist was clenched in Radley's sleeve before he knew he'd moved, heart pounding so loudly that all he could hear was its visceral demand to *run, run, run.*

Edwina's nervous glance at Cinn was laden with apology, but her words were still for Radley. "That won't happen."

"Red."

"It won't. There are far more important things to be concerned about right now, and she knows that crossing me is not in her best interests. She might be pissed, but she can't do anything."

Cinn had no context, but he knew that Edwina was wrong. His bones ached with memories of the many, many things she could do.

"Breathe," Radley reminded him, hand wrapped around Cinn's wrist, which was shaking where he still gripped his shirt.

"It's okay," Edwina promised, fingers pressed to her lips. "Things are . . . Shit, I have to explain this properly. Cinn, listen. You know how I was her handmaiden, right? I was present, or hovering, for most of her conversations with Nora, including the ones preparing for war. And you know how I told you that, when you didn't make contact with us after escaping, Rad and I thought she had captured you again. How we confronted her, exposing ourselves as rebels?"

Cinn nodded.

"Well, when we were caught, when she brought us out for sentencing and I gave her a mouthful, instead of executing us she . . . She offered me the role of her Second. With Nora dead, she needed someone to follow through on all the plans they made should anything happen to her, and she knew I was the only one who could."

Cinn stared.

"I took the job not because I want to work with her—gods know I hate her—but . . . This is real. And at least if I am in charge, I can make sure the demi-kin aren't left behind. I'm doing this to protect them. To protect all of us."

Cinn could taste his heartbeat.

"I need the body. Not for the rebels, but . . . but for this. As Second. There's political things going on, and . . . I just need it."

The fabric of Radley's shirt tore beneath Cinn's nails. The dark look on his brother's face held all the rage Cinn couldn't feel.

"Don't look at me. I'm only part of this to make sure Red doesn't get killed."

"I swear, Ry." Edwina's voice cracked on his name. "The moment we don't need her, I will kill her myself."

She moved closer, arms open, but Cinn released Radley's shirt and stepped back. He didn't want to be touched right now. The nauseating swirl of soundless thoughts spun and spun until he was too dizzy to even try to pick it all apart. He couldn't think. Couldn't do anything but try to breathe. To anchor. To hold it in.

Arms crossed tightly, he couldn't quite look at his sister, picking a spot on the wall behind her head to stare at instead.

"You have to know I would never side with her."

Cinn nodded. He did know. It didn't help.

"Go do what you have to do," Radley said to her. "I'll get the body."

She didn't move right away, blowing out a heavy sigh. Her eyes watered as she offered a quiet apology, unable to turn her back until she stepped out of the alley.

Cinn just stared at the wall.

"Hey."

Shaking his head, he squeezed his chest a little tighter, ribs creaking.

"*Hey.*"

Cinn's shoulder blades hit the brick wall. He hadn't even realized he'd been moving. Crowding his space, a shield against the world, Radley tilted his head until he was all Cinn could see.

"I'm going to give you a choice. One, you can go back to the Turlough house and try to relax with your humans and your witch, and we can talk about this whole second-in-command thing later. Or two, you can come with me, and I will show you why you shouldn't be mad at Edwina. Not going to lie, I'm hoping you pick number two, solely because I'm about to go dig up a dead body and I could use the extra pair of hands."

It shouldn't have been a decision that needed considering. Obviously, sitting with a cup of tea and letting Moyra push back the dreamscape, watching her read cards for the Copelands before he joined Sarah in the kitchen to bake a fresh batch of cookies, was the only choice worth making.

"I'll take you out drinking after," Radley promised in an attempt to sweeten the pot.

Cinn closed his eyes and smacked his head against the alley wall.

In their youth, Cinn had been too afraid of discovery to make friends, and Radley had been too abrasive. Not much had changed. The demi-kin who met them outside the oil factory wore a silver seven-pointed star the size of a thumbnail pinned to his collar, his nod one of solidarity rather than comradery.

"Where is she?" Radley asked.

"Little Miss Ackford has her hands full for the next hour at least."

It had never sat right that one of the only jobs Radley could land was under their old master's daughter. The same one who'd been happy sneaking kisses in the shadows, letting Radley take the punishment when caught, right up until the moment the demi-kin were freed. Without a collar, she wasn't interested. Whether her employment of him at the oil factory was a kindness or a cruelty, nobody had figured out.

"Good," Radley nodded, checking over his shoulder that Cinn still followed before shouldering through the side door.

At least he didn't spend too much time in the factory itself. Radley was a lamp lighter, carrying oil through the city to replenish the streetlamps, lighting them at dusk. Cinn wanted to ask why they were there, but he supposed he would find out soon enough.

The hall was stone, both walls and floor, giving the sounds of the factory a solid surface to echo from. Chatter was low beneath the dripping of oil, the sloshing of it as it was poured into barrels. The lack of windows or other exits had Cinn's skin tightening, but he trusted Radley, so he followed his brother down a basement stairwell. At the bottom, the stone floors gave way to soil, the walls boarded. Hundreds of empty barrels lay waiting, stamped with the Ackford Oil seal.

"Watch the door," Radley grunted to the other demi-kin rebel, who gave another nod before leaving.

They waited until the door above closed. At the latch's click, a full-body flinch rocked through Cinn's bones, his lungs bruising from the force of his swallowed scream. It was dark, and he was underground, and . . .

He could breathe. Pressing his fingertips to the wall on his left, he stretched his right arm out as far as he could. He couldn't touch the other wall. He had space.

"You alright?" Radley asked, watching with a frown.

Cinn nodded, forcing his shoulders to straighten, unsure when they'd begun to curl in. Despite the assurance, his brother gave him a moment to steady his hands.

"Slaves built this factory," Radley started, opening a large chest. "Didn't quite get to laying the floor down here before the collars came off, and the cheapskates didn't feel like paying that kind of labor."

Cinn rolled his eyes. He'd heard all about Radley's gripes with the factory during the many, many nights he'd come home drunk. It had stopped being an interesting story before he'd finished telling it the first time.

"If only they knew the shit we hid in the dirt down here."

From the chest, Radley pulled out two shovels. He left one leaning against the wall for Cinn to grab when he was ready, taking the other along the rows of barrels to poke at different parts of the ground.

"Rebel-turned-traitor somewhere around here," he said. "And here, some asshole who still had a few collared kids in his basement. Ah, this is the spot."

Slamming the tip of the shovel into the soil, Radley stomped on the step, sinking the blade halfway in. Cinn waited for the reasons he shouldn't be mad with Edwina, though he still wasn't sure that's what he was, but the only sound Radley made was the heavy pants of exertion as he began to dig.

Pushing off the wall, Cinn grabbed the other shovel.

The basement was sticky with humidity, and within five minutes, Radley's shirt was dark with sweat while Cinn's hair stuck to his forehead. Despite how freshly the grave had been dug, the ground was hard, every impact shooting through his wrists.

At least it wasn't deep.

The moment Radley's shovel hit meat instead of soil, the basement exploded with the distinct smell of decaying flesh. Cinn wrinkled his nose and shallowed his breaths. It was a reek he had grown uncomfortably accustomed to with how frequently he found Eaon post-surge. When the necrotic magic was potent enough to leave little more than mist and bone in his wake, the tang was ignorable, but this fresh rot pervaded deep into his skull. Still, his flinch was nothing compared to the way Radley stumbled back, gagging.

Waiting until his brother composed himself, Cinn rolled his eyes again.

"Give me that face again and you can finish this yourself."

Cinn threw one hand out, waving around at the mounds of soil. *This was your idea.*

Mouth and nose buried in the crook of his elbow, Radley scraped at the two-foot hole they'd made until Cinn could see what lay beneath. He had never seen the king of Sparrows in person. Hadn't even seen any good paintings. But even if he had, he didn't think he'd recognize the gray, sallow face looking up at him form the ground.

"Red might not be one to get her hands dirty, but she watched. For a nag, she was viciously smug when we put this prick in the ground. The marks were her idea. Considering how much he hated us, leaving our mark on him was the most offensive things she could think to do. A carving for every one of us we said goodbye to over the years."

Cinn's fingers found the mark at the back of his neck, pinching hard.

He was used to the curving silver lines feeling like a curse, their freckle-brown mirror on his sibling's flesh ensuring it was generational. He'd grown up hearing his kind's name used as a slur. Seeing it all turned back into a weapon was unsettling in a way he didn't entirely hate.

He thought of the callouses on his sister's hands and the storm in her eyes, and he thought of her standing beside the witch haunting his every sleeping moment. It left his heart skipping a beat, the sweat on his palms having nothing to do with the heat. Perhaps, deep down, betrayal had nicked him, but it wasn't fair. She was fighting a fight he couldn't. She was there because of him, and if the witch hurt her, that was because of him, too.

And she was just as angry as he was. As Radley.

At least in that, nothing had changed.

It took another half an hour to remove enough dirt that Cinn could get a grip on the corpse's ankles, helping Radley heave it out of the ground. Every joint in his knees and shoulders popped and burned as they lifted him out, the deadweight loose and heavier than expected. Radley dropped it as soon as it was free of the hole, stumbling back to gag again.

The demi-kin keeping watch poked his head in to hurry them up, so Cinn rolled his neck and helped Radley wrangle the naked, mutilated body into an empty barrel. When Radley finally lost his war with his stomach, Cinn left him to it, tipping the barrel on its side and rolling it to the staircase.

Never again was he getting roped into something like this. He should have stuck with tea and cookies.

Their vague, one hour window to get this done was well and truly over by the time they got the barrel up the stairs. Radley was so exhausted his legs were shaking, barely able to hold himself up. They shoved open the door into the hall. Radley took a single step out and stilled, hand whipping back to grip Cinn's shirt. A restraint and a shield, keeping him hidden.

"Oh, so you do still work here?" a feminine voice crooned. "Did you enjoy your unapproved leave the last few days? Almost a week?"

"Fuck off, Ruby."

"That's Miss Ackford to you."

"Sorry. Fuck off, Miss Ackford."

A huff of laughter and the clack of heels against the stone floor; Cinn gripped Radley's wrist in a plead to let him go. This was one person he wasn't afraid to face, and he'd be damned if he was going to let Radley apologize to her, even insincerely.

But his brother knew him too well. His grip only tightened.

"You know, I could consider not firing you. All sweaty and dirty like that . . . Put the collar back on for one night, and you can keep your job."

"Counteroffer: go fuck yourself. And I quit."

"You can't afford to quit."

"How out of the loop are you?"

Another step. Cinn couldn't see much from where Radley was holding him behind the doorway, but he saw a pale hand reach for his brother's face. He saw Radley flinch back and smack the hand away.

"Do not touch me."

"Did you just hit me? I will have you arrested."

Snorting, Radley's face broke into a foul grin. The pulse in his wrist rabbited under Cinn's fingers. "You really have your head so far up your own ass, you truly have no idea what's going on in the palace, do you? Go on, Ruby. Have me arrested. See how well it sticks."

The deep breath she took was the sort that preceded a scream. Cinn's body flushed with cold, every ache and twitch of tired muscles ebbing to numbness.

In his mind, he could see Radley in the cramped cell deep in the palace bowels. He remembered, viscerally, the day when they were still children, and Radley had nearly been taken. Demi-kin organs were in high demand on the black market and too many in their area had gone missing.

It would not happen.

Over his dead body.

Shoving Radley, Cinn squirmed out of his grip and through the doorway, ramming his shoulder straight into their old master's daughter's now-grown body. The breath she took to call for help wheezed out as her back hit the wall and Cinn slammed his forearm into her throat.

"Shit." Radley's hand fell on his shoulder, tugging slightly. "Ry."

Right then, he decided he didn't care what name they called him. He was both Ryson and Cinn and every iteration of himself between. With Ruby pinned, eyes wide and terrified, gaping in recognition, he felt more like the feral child who'd murdered a grown man in the back alley behind their master's house rather than let them take his brother, but he had enough sense to restrain himself this time.

Shooting a look over his shoulder, Cinn looked between Radley and the barrel. He couldn't bring himself to make sound, but he mouthed the word *go*.

It took a moment, but Radley left him to begin rolling the barrel toward the exit. Satisfied the path was clear, Cinn turned back to hold his captive's gaze. Her throat bobbed tensely against his forearm, but he held her unflinchingly until Radley was out the door.

The second he released her, she ran. Cinn spat on the floor in her wake.

If there were to be consequences, it was better they were for him.

"Are you done?" Radley called from the door.

Wiping his hands on his pants, Cinn nodded and followed Radley outside. He barely spoke as they rolled the barrel through backstreets, the encounter having sapped some of his fire. There would be drinking, later, but not for Cinn. Not the fun kind, either. It was the one part of his old life he had no nostalgia for; as he and Eddy had done ever since Ruby had lost interest in their brother, Cinn would be spending the night cleaning up the fallout.

CHAPTER SIXTEEN
AISLING

ANOTHER BLACK DRESS PLUCKED FROM THE DUSTY CORNER OF HER wardrobe—one she'd nearly burned years ago. Gold threaded the skirts in a pattern of in-flight sparrows, and as Larissa helped pull taut the laces of the corset bodice, Aisling's deadened gaze stared back at her in the mirror, haunted.

The cut of the bodice was low enough to display the arrangement of tattoos on her chest and throat. The first time she had worn the dress she'd paired it with a tight velvet undershirt that covered her from wrist to chin, hiding the raw marks Davina had etched. There had been only two left to tattoo, her Morvish lover so exhausted from the outpouring of magic that she fainted during the ceremony.

This dress was what Aisling wore during her Passing rite, when she had reached her quarter-century and taken the plunge into the void. The Lover had blessed her with visions of ghosts, as if the High Spirit of Death knew it would be only hours until she'd need to be able to speak with one.

She'd been wearing this dress when she'd become a true Sparrow. She'd been wearing this dress when Davina died.

She wore it now, with her hair pulled back tight and her eyes shadowed, to remind the lords of Oford who she was. Of what she was capable of. It didn't matter if they bowed and called her queen, it only mattered that they listen and obey, and she didn't know how else to do it.

In the mirror, Aisling watched Eavha step up behind her. Larissa managed a small smile for the heir, bowing deeply before leaving the room.

The warmth in Eavha's gaze met Aisling's cold stare, chin resting on her shoulder.

Everything had already been said.

Reaching back, Aisling rested her palm against Eavha's cheek. She couldn't afford that undeserved warmth to bleed into her right now, but she also couldn't help but cherish it.

A knock on the door signaled Clayton's arrival.

It was time.

In the hours since Hawthorne had called for the coronation, word had spread, but only a select crowd had been permitted inside to bear witness. The setting sun was too low to bathe the room in the colors of the stained-glass window, the chandeliers and sconces kept dim. Darkness was encouraged during Sparrow ceremonies. The void was not something to fear when one was devoted to the Lover—a realm to pass through on the way to the final embrace, to eternal rest.

A deep-red carpet led from the grand entry doors to the marble dais and was kept clear of spectators by rows of guards. In the space between the crowd and the steps to her throne, a shrouded body lay on a stone altar, filling the cavernous room with the reek of rot. The courtiers gathered—both human and demi-kin alike—held handkerchiefs full of herbs and scented oils to their faces. Some spectators were likely rebels, and the number of guards lining the walls did nothing to ease Aisling's vigilance. Wyldeden guardians and elders were present as well, their gazes landing on her for a moment before finding their heir, only a step behind.

It was not the time for public displays of affection, but when Eavha shuddered, Aisling let the back of her hand brush her knuckles.

"Clayton," she muttered, but her most loyal guard heard. He placed two hands on Eavha's shoulders and bodily moved her to where the elder guardian waited.

"Hey!" Eavha hissed, shrugging against the guardian's vice grip as he dragged her deeper into the crowd. Her protest was drowned out by the heralds, who began blowing their horns on either side of the dais the moment Aisling's heels touched the carpet.

It wasn't that she didn't want Eavha at her side, it was simply too dangerous to allow her to be so. Despite the dozens of guards, the crowd's proximity meant an assassin—be it hired by rebel or lord—would have their best shot during the approach.

The thick, swishing layers of her skirts as she walked made her hands' disappearance into the folds seem natural, hiding the white-knuckled grip she had on a pair of long daggers. The pendant at her throat was one she had enchanted a long time ago to deploy an air shield with little more than a thought; a precaution for if the time came where she was too weak to use her Celeste-blessing.

Clayton scanned the crowd as he followed her, stiff shouldered and hawkeyed, but Aisling missed her invisible guardian too. Never again would Davina's ghost wander the crowd, a private alarm to any brewing trouble.

It was not a relief when she reached the altar unmolested. It simply meant the attack was yet to come.

As she turned back to face the crowd, the heralds finished their announcement and Hyrsch's citizens bowed. In the front row, the lords of Oford also lowered their heads, some further than others.

Only the Wyldeden witches remained standing. They were a free people, and they were not there for her.

By the time everyone rose and silence dampened the room, Edwina had stepped from behind the dais, coming to stand at Aisling's right. The Second's uniform sent a heavy pang through Aisling's chest; Edwina's new garbs were identical to those Nora once wore, and while Edwina was perfectly adept for the role's duties, Aisling missed the unconditional friendship Nora had offered.

Behind Edwina, Radley stopped, weapon held loosely at his side.

Letting the silence stretch until movement in the crowd proved their discomfort ensured Aisling had the room's undivided attention when she finally lifted her chin.

"In this time of great upheaval, the Sparrow Coven has not been exempt. King Phineas, Queen Tallula, and Prince Nevan have all been met by the Lover."

For some, the extent of the loss was news. Small whimpers echoed briefly, dying quickly as Aisling stared coldly out at the masses.

"Before new leadership can be crowned, let a representative of the Oford lords come forward to bear witness with me the legitimacy of my claim."

Her eyes fell on Lord Hawthorne the same instant he stepped forward, but his own gaze was locked on the hidden form prone on the altar. This close, the decay of her father's body was so potent that, had she not been conditioned against it, the smell would have watered her eyes.

Hawthorne's mask didn't break as he approached, but the twitch of his nose and heavy blinking gave away his discomfort.

All upper-level Sparrow members learned to view a corpse's final living moments, and it made no difference to Aisling that it was her father as she pulled the shroud down to reveal his face.

Or what was left of it.

While Hawthorne stumbled slightly, fighting to maintain his composure, Aisling shot a scathing look back to where Radley stood with a smug little smirk. Edwina grimaced, but there was no apology on her face either.

"What has been done to him?" Hawthorne managed, steadying himself.

"By the looks of it, I would say rebels happened," Aisling said, stoic.

Sightless, lidless eyes stared up from a soil-stained face. The fecal matter filling his mouth was crawling with maggots, but it was the bloodless marks carved into each cheek, into his forehead, and likely into every inch of skin still on his body, that gave the defilers away.

Two S's, mirrored and overlapping. The Mark of One Unending. The mark of the demi-kin. The mark of the Kinner.

"How could you allow this to happen?" Hawthorne accused.

Aisling waited for any hint of nausea, of regret or outrage, but she felt nothing. The brief flash of annoyance she'd shot back at Radley had nothing to do with what had been done to Phineas and everything to do with the fact that she now had to deal with the consequences.

Meeting Hawthorne's furious stare, she said, "As you are about to see, I had other concerns."

Narrowing his eyes, Hawthorne let his voice carry for all to hear. "Where has the Aisling who strung rebels up on her gate disappeared to? Where is the princess with her iron fist? The king of this land, of our coven—your own father—lays mutilated and defiled before you, and you do not call for retribution? Has your association with the Wyldeden heir softened you so much?"

Seeds of doubt. He was already playing the game.

A game that, if she lost, brought all her plans crumbling down.

To call for Radley's head now would look like pandering, but to do nothing was to allow those seeds to take root.

"Tell me, Hawthorne, do you play chess?"

"Excuse me? What relevance—"

"I already know who is responsible for this," she said, flicking her fingers over her father's corpse. "Retribution at this time would be like taking out the pawn who stole my rook, endangering the rest of my pieces for the sake of petty revenge. I will win the game, not by reacting thoughtlessly to every slight, but by biding my time. It's called thinking. Something you might try, sometime."

Hawthorne's nostrils flared, and Aisling leaned closer, voice barely a breath.

"I don't think you play, Lord. I don't think you should have sat at this table with me."

"Let us not bicker publicly at a time like this," he spat, placing a reverent hand to the king's face.

Aisling straightened, resting hers against the other side. She already suspected what she was about to witness as they delved into their Lover blessings. As tired and depleted as she was, the incantation needed to be vocalized, but at least her voice was not louder than Hawthorne's. Eyes unfocused, the Hyrschan throne room blurred, shifting into the larger one near the top of Dusarn's castle. The late evening sun was temporarily blinding, her other senses muddied by the enveloping memory.

"What have you done, Tallula?"

King Phineas was not a meek man, but his voice wavered on his wife's name. In the eyes of the coven and the world at large, the two were equals, but in the privacy of their intimacy, he had always deferred to her. Aisling held no love for either of her parents, but while her mother had been suffocating and disdainful, her father had given her a longer leash.

"What have I told you about questioning me?" the queen panted between labored breaths. "And now, of all times."

Aisling's eyes cleared slowly, Lord Hawthorne beside her, blinking rapidly against the sun's glare. Vision returned to them both in time to witness King Phineas flinging a leather-bound book at where Queen Tallula lay swollen and pained on the dais, her belly growing by the second —so large her dress had split open, skin mottled and bruising with the force of the thing inside her, pushing to get out.

"You ordered our troops to *stand down* when there were dragons approaching the city, and now it is in ruins! Our people burn! Half the guard has disappeared, and the rest are being torn to shreds by the swarms of cawkers, ratki and lupanis now prowling our city. Our castle is crumbling, and you allowed it! Tell me why!"

"I am in labor, Phineas!"

"With what beast? Because nothing of mine would do that to you. Nothing of mine would have you drinking gallons upon gallons of human blood these past months."

Blood coated Tallula's teeth as she bared them. "I will not be shamed for the master's appetite."

Phineas balked.

"Master? What master? We rule most of Nir—" His breath caught, his entire being going still. Slowly, he gave her deformed body another appraisal. "Aisling was right, wasn't she? It's Chaos. He's real, and you . . . Tallula, what have you done?"

He took a step to find his balance and Tallula drew her blade, pointing it futilely. "You will call him master, or you will refrain from speaking of my child."

Aisling saw the decision in her father's eyes. He may have bowed to her on many things, but he was loyal to Balance above all. Before he even moved, Aisling knew he would reach for the silver-and-iron sword at his waist. He had barely drawn it before Tallula was screaming. Half rage, half pain, she forced herself to sit up enough to fling her own small blade.

It struck true.

Phineas stumbled, blood spilling too quickly from the wound in his gut, but he lunged for her anyway. The pointed tip of the sword slid harmlessly off her undulating flesh, near translucent with how thin it was stretched.

A spattering of blood burst from the queen's mouth, coating them both as she cackled. Her eyes were wild as she grabbed the hilt in Phineas's belly.

"My master will return this world to its former glory, and those devoted will rule with unimaginable power." She twisted the knife, sticking it as deep as her trembling arms could manage. "The vermin that we have kept at heel these centuries will become nothing but our playthings once more, and our son Nevan will rule them all. He may be stupid, but he will bow to Chaos."

She twisted the knife again. "I am glad you got to see the first fruits of my sacrifice feeding on the buffet I readied in this sand-blasted city, but before you meet your precious Lover, I want you to know this, too. This is not the end for me. Chaos will defeat Death, and when he takes over the void, I will return. I will return in time to see the harbingers fulfill their promise: that our blaspheming daughter will suffer greatly before he tears her apart."

Ripping the knife through his gut, Tallula pulled it out and shoved Phineas away. Slipping on his own blood, the wide splay of his fingers was barely enough to keep his intestines inside.

"You wretched thing," he gasped.

Tallula gave one more hearty laugh before a spasm of pain wracked through her so severely her body arched off the floor. Magic crackled through the room, crashing like thunder as a portal opened.

Tallula wheezed, pointing her bloodied knife in his direction. "Don't you dare!"

Phineas had no strength left. He said nothing as he fell through the portal.

He died on Aisling's throne room floor a moment later.

Aisling opened her eyes.

Lord Hawthorne stared at her father's desecrated corpse, white as a sheet, but she held no pity for him. There was no satisfaction in proving she'd been right when the game was afoot, and every second they spent arguing was a second less she had to prepare.

"Perhaps it is time to open your mind to the possibility that I know what I'm talking about," Aisling hissed. Louder, she announced, "King Phineas died by Queen Tallula's hand, who is herself a traitor to the Sparrow Coven. Even if she had not died birthing the spawn in her womb, she would be unfit to rule based on her shifting allegiance. Lord Hawthorne sees this truth."

"I do." Lord Hawthorne swallowed thickly, turning from the corpse to meet the heavy gazes of his fellow lords.

"King Phineas is dead," Aisling repeated. "Queen Tallula is dead. Prince Nevan is dead. And so I, Princess Aisling Aurnia, lay claim to the throne by right of being the only living blood entitled to it."

Not a single murmur from the crowd. Not a single argument.

Except, of course, from Lord Hawthorne. "I rebuke your claim."

Movement. To the left.

A thought, and her pendant exploded. A dart hit her air shield and clattered uselessly to the floor.

Shocked sounds echoed in the otherwise silent room, but Aisling feigned indifference as guards speared into the crowd, wrestling the would-be assassin down. People moved aside, frightened chatter rising as the young man cursed and thrashed against the restraints shackled to his wrists.

Remaining aloof took such effort that it sparked a headache, exacerbated by the lone figure shoving their way through the crowd toward her. More guards made to stop her, but Eavha Nemuse was recognizable enough that none mistook her as another assassin. The raging man being dragged through the shadowed doorway to her dungeon held almost everybody's attention, the noise drowning out Eavha's fury at being prevented beyond the front row.

"I need to make sure she isn't hurt," Eavha snapped at the guards holding her back.

One of them looked to Aisling for approval, but Aisling shook her head.

Not yet.

Lord Hawthorne had stilled the moment the dart clattered on the marble, but once the throne room died down again, he asked, "Will you accuse me? The timing would lend itself."

Repressing a smirk, she tilted her head. "I would hope any attempt you make on my life would be far more creative."

Clayton had his weapon drawn. He could not be expected to stop a poisoned dart midair, but he was ready to cut into Hawthorne if need be.

"Any attempt I make will be within the confines of the law," Lord Hawthorne countered. "As I said, I rebuke your claim to the throne."

Expected. She had seen and done this dance often enough that the rebuttal bored her. The script was predictable, its conclusion inevitable.

"On what grounds?" she asked, letting her mouth purse with an amusement that was sure to chafe. "Have you the king's secret love child to present?"

Lord Hawthorne's eye twitched but was otherwise unperturbed. "No. On grounds of you being unfit."

With the lazy roll of her wrist, she said, "Elaborate."

"You have been in power here in Hyrsch for little less than six years and you made a mess of it. You have brought war to our walls." His voice climbed in volume with every word until he could no longer mask the loathing he held. "I ruled here for decades before you arrived, and I followed Sparrow laws and ethics to the letter. There was never so much discord."

It was true. Lord Hawthorne had curried favor with King Phineas in Dusarn by being both a merciless bull and his most brown-nosed advisor. He had been trusted as emissary in the southeast, but he had never been permitted to touch the throne.

"You think you should be king instead."

Lord Hawthorne's eyes glittered. "I do."

Behind him, Lord Dustin of Belden raised his hand, but his eyes remained fixed on the quaking hairs of his own obscene mustache. "Seconded."

In the eyes of the law, a single vote of support was all that was needed for a challenge to be official, and as ridiculous as this whole farce was, it was the law that mattered to their witnesses.

"Experience over inheritance is a valid argument," Aisling allowed. "Shall we hold a democratic vote to see who the people think is a fairer ruler? Who they think is best prepared for the coming conflict? I've been preparing for six years. Tell me, what is your plan for Chaos?"

At the mention of a vote, Hawthorne paled, and by the time she was done speaking, he was downright sallow. The demi-kin were free to vote, and even the rebels couldn't hate her so much as to take Hawthorne back.

"I would prefer to settle this the old way."

Of course he would.

The law stated that the challenger chose the method of settlement. If she did not abide by it in this instance, the rest of the lords would have grounds to overthrow her. Of course, she could just slaughter them all the way she had gotten rid of her council, but with so many witnesses she could easily lose control over the situation. Besides, she couldn't personally oversee the towns as well as the city, and appointing new lords would take longer than simply playing along.

So Aisling dipped her chin.

Hawthorne smirked and turned to his posse.

Taking a moment to prepare, Aisling nodded to the guards restraining Eavha. Scowling at all of them, Eavha stomped bare foot up to the altar, not softening at all as she whispered in Nirnish, "What's happening?"

"Eavha, I know this is difficult, but I need you to leave. Just for a moment."

If things went wrong, the Wyldeden heir would try to intervene, putting herself in the line of fire. If things went right . . . She didn't want Eavha to see what would happen.

"I know what that look on your face means. I'm not leaving you."

"If I want the crown, I have to do this, and I cannot concentrate with you here."

"You sure about that? You seemed to concentrate just fine when we were in the arena. And what if you get hurt? Your magic is drained, and—"

"I have enough."

"You do not."

There wasn't time to argue, but just as Eavha claimed to know that the expression on Aisling's face meant trouble, Aisling knew the look on Eavha's meant she would not be persuaded.

Rubbing her thumbs into her temples, Aisling released a slow breath.

"Fine. If you insist on staying nearby, at least stand by Clayton."

Eavha didn't budge, but at his name, Clayton came forward.

"Lady Eavha."

"Remember what happened the last time you tried to stop me?" Eavha warned him, narrowing her eyes. "I'm not leaving."

"Neither am I," Clayton said, low and quiet, so the conversation didn't carry into the throne room. "But we undermine her authority in front of everyone who matters if we do not give her room to fight. Come with me. Be ready."

Nostrils flaring, Eavha looked between the two of them. Her suspicion was justified since they'd already enforced separation once tonight, but when her shoulders dropped, Aisling knew she had won this round.

Eavha stepped back with Clayton, joining Edwina and Radley closer to the dais a few feet back.

For once, Aisling didn't have gloves to remove. The marks on her palms and backs of her hands were ruined from the knife Cinn tried to kill her with, and if it weren't for Eavha's painstaking work knitting her skin back together, she had almost lost a great deal more across her back and shoulders. Those, she had allowed to be healed because she still needed them, but the Mark for Those Unbound was no longer required.

Bare arms turned outward, exposing the pattern of curved black lines from her wrists to her elbows, curling up around her biceps onto her collarbones, she reveled in the nervous bob of Hawthorn's throat.

Not nervous enough to withdraw, though. He knew her Sparrow blessing was comparatively harmless—that she would rely on the Celeste-blessing she was meant to have forsaken at her Passing. There had been no rumors of Aisling showing any exceptional power beyond that which her name gave her and some skill with a battle-axe.

She had not practiced with the gifts Davina gave her; never shown or demonstrated them publicly. But she knew what they did. She knew how to use a few, and she knew exactly how Hawthorn would attack. Unlike her, the lord had made a spectacle of himself.

"In the Second War, the Sparrow Coven took their power by force. Against all odds, they asserted Balance over an abomination against the Lover," Hawthorne recited. "And it is by force that power will be taken again today."

He had barely finished speaking before he raised his hands and clicked his fingers, a whispered *"vacu"* the only clue before the room was doused in complete and utter darkness.

Light had never existed in this place, and never would.

Except this was not the real void, and Aisling had been expecting it.

Pulling her blades, ignoring the confused murmurs from the crowd just as blind as she was, she focused on the marks down her sternum and let the air become her eyes. Every disturbance, every movement, every sound was heightened. The magic burned against her bones, but she could bear it.

Hawthorne had a weapon too. A blade of ice, forged right there in the dark and flung with all the certainty of the only person in the room who could see.

She could shield, but sweat was already beading down her spine as she pushed the marks on her chest to stay active. Swatting it away with the flat of her own blade was easier; it shattered on the floor like glass.

Mimicking the attack with a throw of her own would only lose her a blade, so she drew deeper from her Celeste-blessing, the marks on the backs of her wrists sinking into her flesh with the blistering cold.

There were so many ways air and death were intertwined, and this spellmark was one she knew how to use.

Giver and taker of breath, let me borrow command.

Celeste acquiesced, and Aisling snatched the air right out of Hawthorne's lungs. It only took a moment for his control over the void to slip, flickering candlelight bringing the room back into focus. Twirling her blades, she slid them cleanly back into her skirts and stepped around the altar.

"You know, I pulled this trick on Nevan, too," she taunted as Hawthorne clawed at his throat, collapsing to his knees. "In his own arena, in his own city. At least he knew how to counter me long enough to suck down a few breaths, but look at you, squirming on the floor like the leech you are."

His face matched her stained-glass windows, red and purple and lined with blackened veins. He was fighting it. Hard.

"You wanted to do this the old way. You wanted to die like a Sparrow. Well, look at you. As hideous as the rest of them."

"Aisling."

It was the softest of calls, right by her side. Aisling couldn't remember anyone ever speaking to her with such gentleness. Such forgiveness.

"Don't, Lady Eavha," Clayton warned a moment before a warm hand touched her shoulder.

Aisling shrugged the touch off. She could not stop now. Hawthorne wanted to do this by the law, so be it.

She held his breath until he stopped twitching, and then she waited another moment before letting the magic go. The mass of her skirt hid the small step she took to balance herself, the black of the fabric hiding the sweat dampening the bodice.

Then she looked to the rest of the lords.

"Who else is feeling old fashioned?"

Not one of them stepped forward, but Lord Dustin of Belden did dare to speak.

"We'll not blindly follow your orders, crown or not."

"Then I shall debrief you on the plan I have been working on for six years and see if there's anything you feel like adding in at the last minute."

The bunch of them exchanged glances, but she could see their resignation. Hawthorne had been the only one of them with a leg to stand on, and she had not even bloodied her knives on him. Her ribs ached when she breathed, but nobody else needed to know that.

One by one, they knelt again. Aisling moved to the dais, climbing it with a hand from Clayton, ignoring Eavha, silent beside her. The side door opened and a handmaiden passed a large velvet box to the herald, who passed it to Edwina. It opened with a soft click, and inside, a crown.

Aisling had worn many crowns, delicate and light, suitable for a princess. This one looked heavy. *Was* heavy, if she remembered her mother's complaints correctly. Tallula left it in Hyrsch to be forgotten the last time she visited, claiming she didn't want it anymore.

Made sense it was the one Aisling would wear.

Back straight, chin up, she curtseyed low enough for Edwina to place the crown on her head. She went through the motions of speaking her queenly oaths, the adrenaline slowly leaving her body. Her hands trembled, clammy as Eavha took one.

"May I present, officially, Queen Aisling Aurnia of the Sparrow Coven," the herald called.

With everyone's heads bowed low, Aisling dared to glance at Eavha. There was too much sadness there, and Aisling hated the way Eavha raised their hands to her mouth, kissed the back of her hand before bowing, too.

"Rise." Aisling's first command. She pulled Eavha upright, released her hand, and took a step back. "I believe our night is not yet done."

CHAPTER SEVENTEEN

EAVHA

Unsteady.

It wasn't a feeling Eavha had often, and she didn't like it.

She was far too small to be standing on the dais like this, front and center, despite Aisling's assurances that she was enough.

It was Lorelei. Nothing had shaken her this badly since she'd found herself tossed into Anfar without her magic—or, she supposed, magic the way she understood it. She was not the powerful healer she had grown up believing herself to be, but a powerful charmer who had built a Blessing Charm so strong she could bring back the dead.

How was that enough to lead her clan? When Lorelei could pull roots and branches from the ground to build bridges, when Kaelean could move earth to widen a river, could split open realms and carve out parts for herself, could shapeshift . . . How could charm work compare?

It didn't matter. Kaelean chose her.

Eavha's confidence may have taken a blow, but she knew she was a better choice than Lorelei. As she looked around the room for familiar faces, she caught each of the elder's eyes. Bodhi, their elder teacher, nodded quickly. Herbe, their guardian, stood straighter. Milnova, the elder keeper, lowered her shawl and closed her eyes, lips moving in a quiet prayer.

Yvette was among them. It might have been a trick of the poor lighting, but Eavha could have sworn the elder healer was smiling.

Near the very back of the room, a tall, dark figure stood, brimming with fury. When Eavha's gaze landed on her, she didn't look away.

"Lorelei."

Her voice was too high, too soft, in this place where Aisling had just murdered someone for her crown.

Murmuring swelled as the ex-high priestess moved away from the wall, separating the crowd with the sheer might of her presence. If this went the same way Aisling's coronation had gone . . . Eavha couldn't kill. Watching Aisling sink into the depths of her worst self left her stomach in her feet. Somehow, despite her best intentions, she had fallen in love. Loved Aisling, even when she was taunting a dying man. It was a cruelty Eavha didn't think she could ever emulate, even to do what needed to be done, and though she wished the violence wasn't necessary, it somehow only made her love Aisling more.

It took a different kind of strength to ruin oneself for a cause, and Eavha didn't have it.

Lorelei made her way to the deep-red rug running the length of the throne room and stopped only when the guards there raised a hand. The distance paired with the height of the dais gave Eavha a considerable advantage, yet she still felt the urge to cower at Lorelei's feet and beg for mercy.

"I give you fair warning, child," Lorelei said in Nirnish. "Do not embarrass yourself."

She had not been afraid, jumping into a killing arena to stand at Aisling's side in Pirevia. She only knew she had to protect her. Keep her safe, the way she had to protect all of Wyldeden now.

Her voice still tremored. "Stand down."

"On what grounds?"

"Kaelean left you as Wyldeden's emissary because she thought I was leaving for Pirevia. It is clear I have not, and so you can stand down."

If there were official words, she didn't know them. There had only ever been two changes in Wyldeden's leadership: when Lorelei took it from Kaelean, and when Kaelean took it back. Eavha had been so distracted by Kaelean's decision to bind Lorelei rather than excommunicate her that she had forgotten whatever else happened that day.

If there were official words, Lorelei didn't care for them either.

"She chose me because you have been heir for a handful of months, most of which you have not spent home with our people but here, seducing our enemy. She chose me, because you are a child. You are years away from maturity still, whereas I have ruled this clan for centuries."

Experience over inheritance. It was the same argument Hawthorn had made with Aisling. There was comfort in that, somewhere.

The newly appointed elder laborer nodded and Eavha grounded her feet. If for no other reason, she had to do this for them.

"You have ruled them poorly."

The throne room was so silent the wind outside was an audible rush. Every word that spilled from her loosened tongue smoothed Eavha's doubt, because every one of them was true.

"Kaelean told me her vision for Wyldeden. A vision of peace and community she said you used to share. Maybe seven hundred years is too long for any one person to be in charge, because you have perverted what Wyldeden was supposed to be. I don't know when you lost sight of what and who these people are, but you made Wyldeden about power, and you made my brother a slave."

It could not be allowed to happen again.

Silence reigned as Lorelei glared up at her. The chandelier groaned above them and Eavha prayed it wasn't made of wood. Not with Lorelei's fists curling at her sides, eyes alight with the same hateful rage she'd leveled at Eavha the day she'd brought Eaon back from the void.

Voice glacial, Lorelei said, "You will beg my pardon for such blasphemy."

"No."

The word was a whip. Lorelei flinched.

"No?"

"You do not pardon me. I do not acknowledge you as my superior."

For a moment, Lorelei only stared in stunned stupor. It passed quickly, and her face fell into a mask of dull boredom as she turned her back, hands splaying in supplication to the crowd of Wyldeden witches behind her. "Well, let us settle this the way all high priestesses of the past have been usurped. The council shall vote."

Why Lorelei would even suggest it was a mystery. She had to know how much they hated her.

For another fleeting moment, as muttering once more began to resound through the room, Eavha considered letting the vote play out. But what would that prove? That she had to be handed things? The council had already voted to appoint her heir apparent. They had voted to allow her to represent them at Aisling's Imsa. Some of them hated her, but she knew they wanted her regardless, and what they needed now was for her to prove their trust was not misplaced. That they didn't have to keep coddling her. That Eavha could fight for them.

"No."

Eavha could barely breathe through the lump in her throat, but the tremble in her hands didn't echo in her voice. The word returned the room the silence, and Lorelei turned back to face her, brow raised in amusement.

"No?"

"You are not high priestess, so there is no usurpation. There is only me, the heir apparent, telling you to get back in your place. You were warned when Kaelean left that if you did anything in her absence she disapproved of, you would be bound again. I am not afraid to enact her will."

The amusement dropped away immediately and nobody missed the single, threatening step Lorelei took toward the dais. Aisling's warmth was at her back in an instant, the sound of Clayton's sword being drawn again unmistakable.

None of it concerned Lorelei.

"You don't know how."

"As I said at the river, that has never stopped me before."

Reckless. Arrogant. That was what they called her because that was what she was. She performed necromancy before she knew the word for it. She made a new kinner in a feat that had only been done prior by the spirit of healing herself. Pushed, Eavha would bind Lorelei again.

War waged behind the flat mask on Lorelei's face, and Eavha waited. Waited, for her to assess how serious Eavha was and whether fighting back would garner her any favor. To weigh what could be gained against what could be lost.

When Lorelei moved her arm, Eavha couldn't help her flinch. But it was not an attack. With an exaggerated flourish, Lorelei bowed.

"So be it."

A mix of small gasps and shouts of victory came from the audience as Lorelei turned and stormed from the throne room. Eavha didn't realize she'd been holding her breath until Aisling took her arm to stabilize her.

"Breathe," Aisling muttered, putting her body between the room and Eavha, back exposed and vulnerable to attack. "Deep breaths, Eavha."

"I did it," she wheezed.

Aisling's smile was small. Hidden.

"You did. Don't go anywhere without a guard. I don't trust her."

Eavha nodded, grounding herself further by wriggling her toes against the cold marble floor. She was barely able to pull her gaze away from the newly appointed Sparrow queen as Aisling stepped away, letting the room see her once again.

The Anfar Forest Clan stared up at Eavha with a reverence usually reserved for the temples. All her life she had basked in the respect that came with being a renowned Nemuse healer, their awe of her blessing that ran so much deeper than any before her. But this was something else.

Home destroyed, high priestess presumed dead, their spirits seemingly having abandoned them to their fate—these were the faces of people with nowhere left to turn but to a young witch, still four years from maturity, who had never, not once, shown them doubt.

But she felt it.

Doubt swooped in her gut but didn't find a single mirror in the faces peering back at her. It was not reflected in a single Anfar witch, nor the Hyrschan civilians, and certainly not in Aisling, who tilted her chin and raised her brow in a silent command to take the moment.

Eavha swallowed the lump in her throat. Maybe she wasn't a born healer, but that was who she was in her heart, and it was who the clan needed her to be for them. Healing wasn't just about sewing wounds and treating burns.

"Until Kaelean returns, I will guide you," she addressed the room, the Terranian words not from any script or ceremony. "If you'll have me, I will keep us safe. To the very best of my ability, I will care for you. Like family, like blood, each and every one of you lies under my protection."

And they all knew the lengths she would go to for family. They'd all stood by to watch her branded and excommunicated for it; a suffering she would endure for any of them, despite it.

From the middle of the room, a dark brown fist rose. Eavha recognized the male as one of Dearmead's many older brothers, Trumard.

"I will have you," he called.

It was the beginning of a chorus. They would all have her.

An elder stepped from the crowd, muttering into her cupped palms. Eavha stood tall as the guards let them through, watching Milnova climb the dais to rest her hands against Eavha's temples. The tickle of petals caressed her brow, a floral perfume of peonies and baby's breath washing out the lingering rot from King Phineas's corpse.

Stepping back, the keeper smiled.

"Our heir apparent has risen."

CHAPTER EIGHTEEN

AISLING

"DID YOU SEE HER *FACE*?" EAVHA CACKLED AS SHE THREW HERSELF OVER the chaise by the balcony, catching her flower crown as it slid to the side.

Closing the door to her suite, Aisling wasn't fooled. Eavha may be laughing but she also hadn't stopped shaking since the moment she saw Lorelei. Leaning against the solid wood, she watched Eavha run her hands through her tangled hair, settle, then jump up again to skip in a little circle before crashing to the chaise once more.

"I can't believe I did that. Vindication is glorious." She turned her head, looking for Aisling. Finding her still at the door, that perfect smile faltered. "What's wrong?"

Aisling wasn't sure what her face was doing. That she had released control of her features was proof of her comfort, but she didn't like that it had taken the joy from Eavha's.

Softly, Aisling promised, "Nothing's wrong."

"Do you want to talk about what happened with Hawthorn?"

"Not remotely."

"I think we should. I know it's a defense mechanism, because you couldn't do the things you sometimes have to do without it, but talking about the fact that you killed someone today will help shed this . . . coldness. It's not who you are."

The things she sometimes had to do. Like imprisoning and torturing a young boy for two years. That, she felt things about. Killing Hawthorn? There was only numbness. Indifference. Perhaps Eavha was right, and it would hit her later, but she had killed a lot of people in her life and very rarely felt anything about it at all.

Assessing the impact of her words, Eavha tilted her head. The pucker between her brows—the one Eavha always got when something was troubling her—was a contender for first place on Aisling's list of nemeses.

Needing to rid her of it, Aisling said, "You are the most stunning creature I have ever met, and every moment I spend in your presence makes me crave life like I have never done before."

The small sound of Eavha's breath catching was all it took to pull Aisling away from the door; those wide brown eyes were a honey trap she would gladly fall into. When Aisling reached the chaise, she cupped Eavha's soft face in her palms, drinking her in. Something so beautiful had no business among the ugliness that was to come, yet Aisling knew there was no making Eavha leave. This girl, who stole horses and faced her fear of flying to chase Aisling across the world. This girl, who leaped into a battle arena with nothing to defend herself, so she could stand between Aisling and death. This girl, who ran fearlessly into a burning forest. Who refused to leave people behind.

"I have not enjoyed the company of many people in my life, and mourned the loss of even fewer." Aisling needed Eavha to know, and it did not frighten her to expose this weakness. Not to Eavha. "Davina stayed because she did not want me to be alone. She left to save me, but she did it too because she knew I was coming back to you."

Rising to kneel on the chaise, Eavha continued to stare at Aisling like she had never been admired before. Like nobody had ever declared themselves so utterly weak for her before.

Because they hadn't, Aisling realized, as she continued to hold Eavha's warming face and Eavha did nothing more than take tiny, shuddering breaths. She was so young. Perhaps too young. Maybe if Eavha had reached her quarter-century, if she had finished growing into the ethereal powerhouse she was clearly going to be, the nine years between them would not matter so much. But right then, with those honey-toned eyes devouring Aisling whole, it did.

Eavha's hands came to rest on either side of Aisling's face, fingers trailing lines of fire down her porcelain neck. Closing her eyes, Aisling pressed a kiss to the top of Eavha's head.

"Pretty wildflower," she mumbled into her hair, smelling of gardens and earth and heat.

Eavha hummed with contentment before letting her hands drop away, sitting back down and smoothing her hands across the chaise.

"Speaking of flowers, I need to make a new Blessing Charm." Eavha's hand hovered at her bare throat, and despite Aisling's best intentions, her eyes followed the movement. She barely heard Eavha continue speaking. "None will ever be as strong as the first one I made, because I don't have years and years to build it, but still, anything that can help is worth the time."

"What will you use for a base?" Aisling asked distractedly, sitting on the arm of the chaise. The hair-bound feather that hung from a long chain around her own neck was tucked neatly between her breasts, hidden and protected by her dress. It was frayed and tattered from her encounter with Chaos in Dusarn, but still, she had not discarded it.

"I liked the peony." Eavha sighed wistfully, eyes lowering to Aisling's chest. "It felt right."

If she didn't touch her, Aisling was going to explode. Reaching over, she tucked a loose curl behind Eavha's ear.

"The pink complimented your warmth nicely."

Aisling wasn't sure what was more beautiful, the smile or the blush tinting Eavha's cheeks. It was rare to elicit such a reaction from her. Eavha's confidence outshone almost everything else about her, but here she was, bashful under Aisling's palm. Her next words were out before she could think twice about them.

"I do not have the words to describe you."

Eavha blinked, blushing further before blurting out, "Jasmine."

At Aisling's raised eyebrow, Eavha ran her hands across her trouser legs, then through her curls, messing them all over again.

"That's what I would choose, if I had to pick a flower for you," she explained.

"Jasmine?" Aisling suppressed a smirk. "I'd have thought Lily of the Valley."

Eavha's fluster left her as she rolled her eyes. "They're similar in many ways—both very pretty—but I refuse to whittle you down to something known best as poison. So, no. You are jasmine."

Turning away, Aisling shook her head. "You're too kind."

The balcony usually provided a stunning view of the city, but it was spoiled still by the haze of smoke drifting across the river. Left unchecked, the forest would burn for days. Weeks, even. Ignatius-blessed witches were doing what they could, as were the Mare- and Celeste-blessed, and their collective effort seemed to be containing the spread, but still, none had the power to stop the blaze entirely.

Fleetingly, Aisling wondered if that was their fate, too. All of them, trying to eradicate Chaos from their land. Would they ruin themselves the way the spirits had during the First War, able to do nothing more than simply contain him again? Could they even do that much?

"Hey," Eavha called softly.

Aisling turned back. Eavha had a knowing look on her face.

"We will survive this," she promised. "And when it is over, we will spend a hundred years together."

Aisling pressed her lips together, smothering a smile. "A thousand."

"Greedy." Eavha's smile returned to full bloom. At least for a moment. Her eyes roamed over Aisling's face, her tattooed hands. Tenderly, she took one in her own, and Aisling watched Eavha rub her thumb over each of Aisling's broken nails. "Can I ask you something?"

"Of course."

"About the Sparrows," Eavha warned.

Aisling nodded, so Eavha took a steadying breath and fixed her eyes on their hands.

"You said a thousand years like that would be acceptable. And, I think . . . I think I wouldn't mind having that long to know you. To see you grow into the person I know you could be. But in Wyldeden, Lorelei taught us that a long life is a sign of being unworthy. A punishment. Kaelean even says the Lover is punishing her for stealing from Mother by letting her live so long."

"The curse in Kaelean's long life is that she has outlived everyone she has ever cared about." Aisling did not mention her concern that the high priestess of Wyldeden, of Anfar, may have finally had that curse lifted. She had not come to Aisling in the void, nor did any of the ghosts lingering nearby whisper of Kaelean having passed into the Lover's embrace, but that did not provide much relief. Not when all she had to do was send a whispering leaf, and rescue would find her.

"So, your priests and priestesses disagree?" Eavha asked.

"They disagree on everything." Aisling let herself smile, trying to ease some of the tension growing in Eavha's shoulders. "But if you want to know what I believe, then, yes, I disagree. I think it is the corruption of power that has placed the idea of 'worth' on a life. Life is life. It exists, and it is right, and I will protect it. Think of it like . . . Like a peach. You leave it on the tree until it is ripe, but if one peach takes longer to ripen than others, it is not less worthy. It just isn't ready."

Eavha frowned. "You protect life, but worship death?"

Aisling nodded. "Life and death, Mother and Lover . . . They are the two sides of the same coin. They are Balance."

Eavha took a long time to take that in, then nodded.

"I never used to question it." Letting go of Aisling's hand, Eavha began to wring at her blouse. "Never used to question the idea that mourning was blasphemous. Until Kaelean. She told me it was okay to feel those ugly things. That if we didn't miss the people who passed, it would be an insult to Mother; that her gift was not special, that we are happy to see it gone. The clan is slow to change, but . . . I want to teach them that there's a balance to everything when it comes to life and death. It's beautiful and hideous at the same time, and . . . It's okay that I wish very much to live a thousand years with you. It's okay to want to stay in this realm as long as I can, and to enjoy my time as much as possible. Death may be our purpose, but I will always defend life."

Unable to stay away, Aisling slid down onto the cushion beside Eavha and let her hand rest on Eavha's leg.

"If there was ever any doubt you are a true priestess, those pious words have erased it." Aisling chuckled. "Our philosophies are not that different. My coven was born out of hatred for those who refused Balance by not dying—a hatred that has poisoned generations. A hatred that I refuse to let define me. Or at least I try."

She did not cringe from Eavha's comfort this time when she leaned into her space, hands on Aisling's face so that she had no choice but to meet her sincerity.

"You are just as capable of hatred as I am, and just as capable of love."

Aisling's breath stuck in her throat. She could not deny it; not to herself, and not to Eavha.

"I would build you an empire. On every single street, there would be a temple in your honor."

Eavha's next breath parted her lips, and the one after that closed what little space was left between them.

CHAPTER NINETEEN

CINN

SOMETHING HAD HAPPENED. A STREET VIEW WASN'T POSSIBLE FROM HIS spot on the Turlough's sofa, but the cacophony building outside was evidence enough. Riots or celebrations, he couldn't tell. Maybe both. His nails dug so deep into the cushion he could feel raw stuffing, which was quite the feat since he'd chewed them halfway to the beds.

Two things kept him from running. Firstly, William had settled against the doorway to the hall, half an eye on where Sarah and Siobhan were making a mess in the kitchen and half an eye on him. Should Cinn cave to his flighty tendencies, William wouldn't let him get far. Second came reason. Outside was where things were turning dangerous—what sense did running out there make when he was warm and safe inside?

Edwina and Radley were out there. Eaon, somewhere in the palace. If there was trouble, Cinn ought to be with them.

He couldn't make himself move.

Kneeling by the window where moonlight spilled through open blinds, Moyra remained unaffected by the commotion. While her tarot cards were left abandoned on the small tea table, the rest of the Morvish paraphernalia brought from Moyra's cabin—small crystals, candles, bowls of herbs and paper etched with charcoal marks—were spread in an arrangement before her. The constellation on her forehead glittered dully, lips moving silently under Gatty's careful supervision.

She had been kneeling there since Cinn's return. Being in the palace was like wearing a cloak of thorns—the longer he stayed, the more it hurt

—so he'd agreed to wait at the Turlough house with the Copelands until his siblings finished whatever it was they had to do with the dead king's body. He'd been reluctant to let them go, but Edwina, with her looming, hooded guard hovering several feet behind her, swore up and down that it would be safe.

Plus, Radley had promised to retrieve him before finding some hole to drink away his feelings. A promise Cinn prayed he kept. The streets had never been safe for the demi-kin, especially at night and especially while intoxicated. Doubly so when Radley had been forced into the company of Ruby fucking Ackford. It gave him only a little peace to know that, should Radley forget his promise and venture out on his own—as he was wont to do—Eddy would know. But would she follow? She hadn't been much of a drinker before . . . *before*. But things had changed. Would she also wash away the evening with ale? Or would she leave their brother to fend for himself while she pandered to the princess?

That wasn't fair. Cinn wasn't being fair.

Nervously, he glanced to the door for the hundredth time that night. It remained stubbornly closed.

"I can't hear you," Moyra muttered, swaying. "Where are you?"

It was the first thing she'd said aloud all evening, and Cinn latched onto the distraction. The candles at her knees flickered. Gatty's ears flattened.

"Can you hear me? Are you a Unifier?"

Outside, someone set off firecrackers. In one of the other rooms, a young witchling squawked in terror. Cinn's own heart skipped several beats. Still, Moyra swayed, sweat dampening the back of her blouse.

"I can't hear you. I can't . . ."

"Enough," Gatty growled. "Don't push yourself."

Another minute of incoherent muttering went by before, with a frustrated huff, Moyra slapped a hand down on the nearest parchment and shoved it away. Once more aware of her surroundings, she blinked rapidly around the room, heaving a great sigh.

"Morvia's realms are so strange here inside the wards."

"You are tired," Gatty excused. "Rest and try again tomorrow night."

Moyra shook her head. "No, it's more than that. The fate lines are easier for me to see, the stars louder than they've ever been, but . . . While I can sense other Morvish witches dwelling in the dreamscape, I can't find them. I can hear them calling out, but the words are garbled. The interference feels . . . intentional."

Gatty hummed. "Morvia doesn't make a habit of meddling."

"No." The look the two shared was laden with silent communication, broken only when a door slammed open in the hall.

Cinn had barely blinked before finding himself in William's arms, held back from the witches running inside the house. Their quick, hissing language was unintelligible to him, but the energy behind it didn't seem hostile or afraid.

"It's not them," William muttered. "Breathe, kid."

His heart was trembling too violently for such a thing.

"Perhaps," Gatty purred, appearing at Cinn's feet to rub against his shins, "a walk would suit you better than idleness."

The cat sith had lost his mind. It was the only thing that made sense. Staring down, bewildered, Cinn's stomach turned at the mocking, sharp-toothed grin creeping across the faeries face.

"It's just a little crowd. A bit of noise. Nothing to be frightened of."

Cinn stiffened, nostrils flaring. Before he could think up something to say, William put himself between them and guided Cinn down the hall to the kitchen. Probably for the best. Nothing but foul curses came to mind, and he doubted the cat sith would take kindly to such insult.

Covered in flour and crushed tomato, Siobhan had paused her cooking to talk quietly with another rebel who'd slipped in the back door. Sarah held Puddles to her chest as the farm cat fluffed and hissed at all the noise.

Nothing had ever been so relatable.

Needing something to ground himself with, he took Puddles and cradled her against his own chest, burying his face in her fur. Focused on *soft* and *warm*, he managed to listen as the rebels discussed Aisling's ascension to queendom. As they detailed Eavha's rise to authority. There was no danger in the news, and yet his heart would not settle. The claws digging into his chest were a pain that he nuzzled the cat in gratitude for.

"That faerie cat thing is right," William said when he returned to Cinn's side. "Let's go for a walk. It's not going to stay any quieter in here than it is outside, and it sounds like whatever was happening at the palace is well and truly over. Do you know where your brother normally goes out to drink? We'll look for him."

Lifting his head, Cinn blinked. Twice. Put Puddles down.

{You'll come with me?}

"I sure as shit am not about to let you wander around on your own. Not under normal circumstances, and certainly not in this city. Come on."

William's hand in his hair—the familiar, affectionate way he ruffled the black locks—was as effective as a comforting blanket. Cinn spared a shaky smile for Siobhan, for Sarah, before following William out into the night.

~

The first tavern Cinn led them to was closed. The second had an equal number of patrons and rats crawling around on the floor, but no Radley. Streets crowded with gossipers and revelers, protesters and brawlers, meant Cinn kept close to the walls, grateful for William's broad frame buffering him from the mayhem. Grateful, too, for his guiding arm, his warm hand that never strayed from Cinn's shoulder as William pulled him away from wildly swinging doors and shadowed alleys.

The third tavern was busier, but after ten minutes of searching, it was decided they should keep moving. It would be a few blocks before they reached the next drinking hole Cinn remembered collecting his brother from before, so he tugged on William's sleeve to get his attention.

{I'm sorry.}

"What in the bloody world for?"

Lifting a brow, Cinn gave him a pointed look. Sorry was a state of being he'd been in ever since bringing trouble to the Copelands' door; surely he didn't need to start listing reasons.

He didn't. Scratching his beard, William hummed. It took him so long to say anything else that Cinn thought maybe he wasn't going to.

"We'll discuss your stupid guilt later, but what's brought it on all of a sudden?"

The answer was dread. As the spike of anxiety he'd been riding all evening softened, it made room for a heavy dread to thicken in his throat. More than anything, he wanted to go home. Wanted to go back to before he knew about Chaos and the wards and the shitshow about to go down in this city. Wanted to go back to before, when everything was easier, the four of them living peaceful lives on the farm. It was safe there. Quiet. He would have liked to have Moyra there, though. Radley and Edwina, too— he couldn't truly regret anything since it brought him to them. But, if that was how he felt, he could only imagine how much worse it was for William and Sarah. Forced out of their home, running in terror from forest fires . . . All of it was his fault.

{I want to go home,} he finally signed as they passed into the northern quarter of the city. {You should go home.}

"We will. Soon," William promised. "Moyra said as much."

He hadn't realized how thin his breaths had been until he managed a proper one. Relief was so, so sweet. Communicating his next questions was a little trickier as he hadn't learned signs yet for all the new terms he'd learned in Qiri. {When she did her cards? What did she say?}

149

William sighed, moving Cinn in front of him as they passed another alley, this one darker and quieter than the ones to the west.

"You know, only a year ago, witches were a rare sighting for us, and even then it was only the wild ones living in the forest, or ones like Lord Useless in Belden who didn't really do much. If not for their Sparrow uniforms, you'd never know they were witches. Now, I've got them coming out of my ears, reading my palm and cards and aura." A muttered complaint, and yet there was an undeniable fondness. "She said she saw us on a journey homeward soon, and to be careful who we let in our house. Said something about being careful with our hearts. She saw an ending of sorts, probably to do with our way of life, considering everything. Honestly, nothing I wasn't already expecting when we realized we were involved in all of this."

At Cinn's fearful expression, William ruffled his hair again.

"Stress less, kid. When I used to smuggle demi-kin out of Dusarn, someone claiming to be a prophet told me I was going to see a great death in the near future. Actually, that might have been a witch too, now that I'm thinking about it. But anyway, Sarah and I lost a crop on the farm that year. You can't take predictions like that too seriously. But, we'll be careful. I promise. Please, do the same. The greatest pain either of us can think of would be to lose you."

Everyone said the Morvish talked nonsense, but Cinn had too much respect for Moyra to not take her seriously. A new possibility was dawning, an ache starting deep in his heart, quickly spreading through his entire chest. If the Copelands were due to return to their farm soon, then maybe Cinn should steer clear. Maybe it would be better if he never went home again.

{Maybe you should get away from me. I'm dangerous to be around.}

William scoffed. "No more so than any other demi-kin we've helped."

{The warning of who you let into your home could be about me.}

Abruptly, William brought them both to a halt. Hands on each of Cinn's shoulders, any trace of humor was gone as William stared down at him.

"You will always be welcome. And if you ever doubt it, if you ever stray, I want you to remember the pebbles we left out for you, back before summer. It's proof that we wanted you to come back. We will always want you to come home. And, when you do, I want you to know that your brother and sister are welcome too. There's room for all three of you. And for Eaon."

Cinn missed his pebble.

The combination of grief and relief in his belly was nauseating. Hanging his head, he let it fall against William's chest. The farmer's breaths were steady. Full. Cinn measured his own against them.

It was all he'd ever wanted. A home and a family.

He was too weak to refuse it.

{Radley isn't easy.}

"Did you miss the part where we've been helping demi-kin for decades? Do you think any of them have been easy? You remember Owen, the one whose house we're refuging in? The one who spared us the first time Hyrschan guards came knocking, looking for you?"

Of course he did.

"He was a child when Damien Turlough brought him to us. After six weeks, he was still so distrusting that he tried to kill me in my sleep. Twice. He refused to eat anything we prepared for him, and his first winter, he killed and ate our dog. And yet, we got him well. We got him into a safe home here in Hyrsch. It wasn't perfect, but it was better than where he came from. So, I'm not worried about your brother. Radley can call us whatever he wants, can glare at me and point as many knives at me as he needs to. We'll still want to help him."

They would help him. Cinn closed his eyes, not even sure what he would say if he could. More than his own safety, he wanted a better life for his family. He wanted Radley to sleep through the night without drinking himself numb. He wanted to see him thriving. Happy.

William could help him. Sarah could help him.

Words failed, but Cinn wrapped his arms around William's middle and hugged him as hard as he could.

"It's going to be okay, kid," William promised, voice cracking slightly. "Come on. Let's keep looking."

~

Eventually, they found Radley.

The front door to the tavern was locked as the hour reached midnight, but the bang of the rear exit emptying into the neighboring alley brought William and Cinn's attention to the man being tossed out. Before the poor lamplight could show them his face, the string of foul curses spewing in a familiar torrent had the stress of the night releasing Cinn's worn-out heart.

"Hey!" Radley cheered as he spotted them, half leaning, half falling down the alley wall. "There he is!"

This wasn't the kind of jovial drunkenness that Cinn sometimes wished he could join in with. No, there was an edge behind Radley's glassy eyes, in the vicious way he pointed the empty bottle in his hands at them. There was rage in the way he sucked his teeth and wrinkled his nose, glaring at the hand Cinn extended as he reached for the bottle.

"Oh, don't look at me like that," he spat, pulling away. "I promised, I promised, I know. But what even is a fucking promise, Ry? The only thing a promise really promises is that it'll be broken. Maybe I didn't want you around me right now, did you think of that? Maybe I just wanted to feel sorry for myself in privacy. Is that alright with you?"

Dropping his arm, Cinn watched Radley try to drink more. Watched him realize the bottle was empty. Watched him hurl it at the wall, glass shattering in a cascade of glittering brown.

He didn't know what to do. This, too, was partly his fault. For being so stupid as to join the cadets. For getting caught. For abandoning his family. He knew, deep down, that returning would only bring burden to Eddy and Rad. It was what he'd always been; the two of them, children themselves, raising a child.

William's hand on his shoulder was both the weight that nearly buckled his knees and the only anchor in the world capable of holding him up. With William, he didn't have to feel guilty for not knowing what to do. The burden of his existence was in capable hands. Sarah's kindness, her mothering, was that of a wishful dream, while William's guardianship was the kind of offered safety Cinn had craved his entire life. Not even his birth parents had given that to him, and his heart swelled double its size as he watched William step forward, hands raised, shoulders bowed, trying to appear less threatening.

"The streets aren't safe tonight and your brother is worried about you," he said to Radley, low and slow, calm and soothing. "Come home with us."

William was careful to make it a request rather than a demand. Still, Radley cackled, rough and broken.

"Only a human would think the streets are ever safe. What fucking difference does it make? Just fuck off."

"You're angry—"

"I said fuck off, you dumb fuck!" Reaching down had Radley falling to the cobblestones, scrambling and huffing back to his feet, but he brought with him a shard of glass, holding it out as if to defend himself. "And stay the fuck away from my brother. I don't know what you've done to him . . ."

Cinn shook his head, throat too thick to persuade his brother otherwise. He made to put himself between them, but William put out an arm, holding Cinn back. The only reason he didn't duck under it, didn't insist, was because Radley was far too drunk to be a true danger to anyone but himself.

Unperturbed, William pressed on. "We can talk about this in the morning, once you've sobered up."

"We ain't going to talk about shit."

It was less of a lunge and more of a stumble, but Radley moved to swipe his shoddy weapon at them. William caught his wrist, holding it high, keeping him upright. The farmer could have easily stopped the second swing too, the one Radley made with nothing but a closed fist, but instead, he let it hit.

The blow was wild and weak, but as Radley realized he wouldn't be stopped, he swung again, harder and more furious. William was an immovable wall—grimacing, but immovable. Holding Radley up by his wrist, he let Cinn's brother treat him like a punching bag until the hits became nothing but exhausted smacks.

Without warning, Radley stilled, heaved, and puked amber liquid over Williams boots.

And Cinn knew the look on Radley's face then. The posture. The dawning realization that he had attacked a human male twice his size, a human who still stood, slightly bruised but mostly unharmed, had puked on his shoes, and was now at his mercy.

Master Ackford had beaten them all for speaking in his presence. For raising their eyes. Radley had begged their master to whip him in Cinn's place, desperate to protect the secret of Cinn's silvery mark. The strip of paler flesh around the demi-kin's throat had not disappeared in the past three—no, five . . . six—years, and the knot in Radley's throat bobbed as he waited for consequences.

Plucking the shard of glass from Rad's bleeding fingers, William tossed it aside. He didn't release Radley's wrist, but did lower his arm, taking hold of his elbow to keep the man on his stumbling feet.

"Dinner will be cold back at the house, but, I don't know about you boys, I don't much care. I'm starved."

The speed with which Radley glanced between Cinn and William was dizzying, the change in topic discombobulating as he stayed braced for punishment. "What?"

{It's okay,} Cinn signed before remembering his brother couldn't interpret him. So instead, he took his brother's other arm and pulled it over his shoulder.

∽

Bewilderment was still rife on Radley's face as they finally returned to the Turlough's house. What little conversation William had carried died a few blocks back as his breathing became labored, but that didn't mean they were silent as the trio stumbled in through the front door. Moyra was asleep on the sofa, remaining that way even as the door banged closed behind them, so they took Radley to the kitchen instead.

It wasn't a surprise to anyone who knew her that Sarah was still awake, sitting diligently at the island counter with a mug of steaming tea between her tapping fingers. As soon as she caught sight of them though, she was on her feet.

"Good gracious, I'll go find that witch again," she muttered, rushing from the room.

Red-faced and sweaty, William did most of the work getting Radley perched on the stool now vacated while Cinn focused on keeping his brother upright. Sarah returned with a witch in tow—one Cinn didn't know. He watched the Wyldeden refugee place two fingers against William's pulse, frown, snatch a pot off the window that once had herbs growing but now was just soil, and begin an incantation. A small sprout grew immediately, and the witch wasted no time stripping it clean and grinding the leaves.

"Is that blood?" Sarah gasped, pulling at William's sleeve.

Leaning heavily on the counter, waiting for the witch to steep the leaves in a cup of hot water, William ground out a quiet, "Not mine."

Shooting a not-so-subtle look to the shallow cuts the broken glass had left on Radley's hand, no further explanation was needed. Cinn wasn't worried about the wounds. They'd be healed by the next evening. Instead, he stood fascinated by the conversation William and Sarah were having entirely with their eyebrows.

"We should go," Radley slurred in a whisper that reeked of whiskey. "Before they remember us. Put us in the basement."

Scowling, Cinn smacked his brother up the back of the head.

"Let me fetch some bandages," Sarah finally said aloud, leaving her husband to the Wyldeden witch's care to pull out a first-aid kit from beneath the counter.

"Fuck off," Radley snarled as she rounded the island, barely getting the words out before Cinn smacked him again.

"It's alright, sweetheart," Sarah assured Cinn with a small, tired smile. Then to Radley, "I suppose you'll heal just fine on your own, but it can't hurt to at least wrap them up so you don't keep bleeding everywhere. I'll leave this right here."

Sliding the kit closer, Cinn pulled out a roll of bandages and wrestled one of Radley's hands into position.

As if the previous two reprimands meant nothing, Radley spat, "I don't need anything from you."

If Cinn was a little rougher than necessary as he tied off the wrapping, nobody noticed.

"Perhaps so," Sarah continued, indifferent to the hostility directed at her. "But I will insist on getting you both some dinner regardless. It's homemade pasta. Siobhan and I made enough for the whole house and the neighbors too, so there's plenty left."

Sputtering, Radley didn't say whatever nasty thing sat on his tongue, meeting Cinn's warning glare instead.

"You can't seriously trust this. *You*," he hissed. "Is it poisoned? Is it . . . Does the food brainwash you or something?"

Cinn rolled his eyes and shook his head, and when Sarah returned with large bowls of saucy pasta for them both, he thanked her and ate greedily. Ate, and nudged Radley's side until he, too, picked up his fork.

One day, he wouldn't hesitate. One day, Radley would thank Sarah too. As William drank the gross-looking water the witch had made, Cinn smiled. One day, they'd all be at home, and everything would be alright.

CHAPTER TWENTY

EAVHA

Sunrise brought with it a new era. One of Eavha and Aisling.

Of love and grief.

Today, they would hold a funeral.

Whispering leaves had been sent out via the elder messenger before Eavha had fallen asleep and by the time the sun brightened Aisling's suite, a leaf was waiting for her in return. The preparations she asked for were under way in one of the fields within the palace grounds.

"Davina promised I would not be alone when I faced Chaos, but she's gone now."

Eavha turned on the silk pillow beside where Aisling lay, watching the dawn warm her perfect, scarred face. Apparently, she wasn't the only one thinking about death this morning. Aisling's tone was indiscernible, but she knew Davina had been her saving grace and her passing had to be painful.

"She might be gone, but that doesn't mean she was wrong. I will be with you."

Aisling sat upright with far too much vigor for so early in the morning. Hair loose and tangled, sleeping clothes too thick in this summer heat, an unguarded Aisling was a sight to behold despite her incensed expression.

"Absolutely not."

"You can't stop me."

"I most certainly can."

"Name one time you've managed."

Aisling could not.

Sitting up with far less grace, Eavha smothered a yawn and rested her head on Aisling's shoulder. Amusement pulled at her lips when Aisling blew frizzy curls out of her face.

"It would be rather poetic, wouldn't it? You and me, death and life. Two sides of the coin, our balance, facing Chaos together. Sounds like fate. And we all know Morvia has more of a hand in all this than she will admit."

Aisling was silent for a moment, then she muttered, low and bitter, "Last night I said I had no words for you, but I thought of one. *Incorrigible.*"

Eavha sat up and flipped her hair over her shoulder. "Thank you."

"Will you be okay today?"

"Will you?"

"I have a lot to do to get ready for our second Imsa. The seaside clan by the port city and the west-side Dividing River clan have agreed to come, and . . . I need them to listen. I need people to believe me this time."

They would. They had to. A seed of worry planted itself between her brows though as she remembered yesterday. Remembered the lengths Aisling had gone to in order to get her way. It was difficult to reconcile the necessity of being believed with those actions, but Eavha knew Aisling well enough to know that display was not *her*. It was what she thought she needed to be in the moment, but it wasn't who she was. And so Eavha could forgive her.

"Do you want to talk about what happened with Hawthorne yet?"

Immediately, Aisling's face closed off. "There is nothing to talk about."

"You killed someone."

"You know full well he wasn't the first and he will not be the last. I know . . . I know you can't condone that part of me, but—"

"I love you," Eavha interrupted. "You don't have to explain yourself."

Aisling closed her eyes and Eavha let her bask in the confession for a moment. Let her love, the morning light, their warmth, soften all the hard edges Aisling bore.

"I will try very hard not to kill anyone else. Until the battle."

Eavha stroked her face. "Can I help you at all?"

Aisling took Eavha's hand to kiss, opening her dark gray eyes, looking over Eavha with unprecedented adoration. "You do just by existing. Can I help you today? I can be with you at the funeral tonight, if you want me there."

"I would really appreciate it if you were."

Aisling nodded. Kissed her hand again. "Let's go help our people then."

~

It wasn't a surprise to find Herbe, the elder guardian, conversing with Clayton outside Aisling's suite when the two of them finally emerged. Herbe smiled widely and stayed by her side as they made their way outside; Eavha wanted to return to the impromptu hospital, to finish what she could, and when they arrived she was glad to see the number of patients had declined significantly since yesterday. She was met with smiles and waves, and she stopped to crouch by each of them, Sanni's quiet presence stronger where she was needed.

Yvette was waiting at her workstation, packing away supplies.

"I checked on your brother during the night," she said in lieu of a greeting. "He has apparently started his own physical therapy but was almost catatonic with one of his moods. The phouka and I got some of your brew into him."

Eavha's good mood soured. "Thank you. I'll go see him soon."

"He was more lucid by the time I left. In pain, but speaking."

Eavha stood for a moment, folding clean bandages that were no longer needed. She hadn't been to see Eaon since Moyra's confession, which wasn't fair. Yes, there had been a lot going on the past few days, but the two of them needed to talk about it.

"I wanted to thank you," Eavha said softly. "For supporting me yesterday."

Yvette's face was as cold and uninviting as always. "We all did. Had it gone to a vote, you would have won."

"You already voted. I didn't see the point."

And there it was—a twitch at the corner of her mouth. A hint of that smile she'd seen in the shadows.

Eavha grinned at the sight of it. "You don't have to pretend you hate me. I'm very lovable."

Yvette snorted, refusing to dignify that with a response. Instead, she slung her bag over her shoulder and waved to the last of the witches leaving the hall.

"The families of the few who died here in the city want to do their burials privately, but the ceremony will be healing for all of us. I will see you at sundown, Eavha."

The brief reprieve from all the heavy things in her chest was over.

Distraction only worked for so long. For every life saved in this building, every witch who'd escaped Wyldeden's burning, there were too many who had not. Too many who had refused to leave their home, enveloped forever into Terra's realm, the pocket collapsed into nothing but energy. Too many had been left behind, burned to ash on the forest floor. Witches and dryads and animals alike.

They lost their lives. They lost their safety. They lost their entire way of existing. Anfar was a terrifying place, but in so many ways it had been beautiful, too.

~

At sundown, Eavha met her people in a field that was not the Lover's meadow. Nor was the ceremony being held in their temple, where all Wyldeden funerals had taken place for hundreds of years. The clan had gathered in a strange place, dressed in foreign, donated clothes, standing on a field used to train soldiers—not a single face that turned to greet her seemed comfortable. It was a stark contrast to every ceremony Eavha had ever attended, where death was celebrated as an honor. There were no smiling faces. There were no congratulations. There were no tears or outbursts of the grief written so clearly on each of them, either. Yet, as Eavha passed through the crowd, palms out, fingers brushing against their reaching ones, her people sagged to their knees.

In the center of the field stood a boab. Branches had been carefully grown from the ground, bound and arranged to mimic the convex curves of the trunk. It was nowhere near as high as the Great Boab had been, but still stood thrice as high as a man was tall. Magic tingled against Eavha's skin as she followed the sprawling canopy, every twist and bend an exact replica of the way their sanctuary had done, its shadows on the ground familiar. The dark purple sky was still tinged with red, the stars obscured, and yet the closer Eavha drew to the emulation of home the brighter it became.

Candles nestled in the roots built along the ground, a blanket of flowers softening the way underfoot as Eavha approached the makeshift dais at the base of the boab. Aisling, Clayton, Milnova and Herbe waited for her upon it, but she was distracted by a young witch placing a bouquet of dandelions into the crook of a root. She paused to watch the witchling mutter a Wyldeden prayer into their fingers, pressing them to their heart before rising.

"Oh," the witchling gasped, realizing Eavha's presence. "Sorry."

"Don't be."

Eavha managed a small smile and plucked a flower from her crown. Moving to the witchling's side, she placed her peony beside the dandelions, muttered her own prayer into her fingertips and pressed them to her heart.

"For safety, and for kindness."

It was what Wyldeden was meant to be. It was what Kaelean had made it for. It was the vision Eavha had for the clan's future.

When she looked back, the witchling was on their knees. The entire gathering had knelt as she passed, and Eavha's heart stuttered.

She could do this. She would be deserving.

In her hesitation, Herbe had climbed down from the dais. The elder guardian stood at her side, hand at her elbow, until she was ready to take the final steps toward the towering trunk. He helped her climb the dais, and Eavha knew this was the part in the usual ceremony where the priestess would raise her hands and begin the passing prayers.

Eavha knew them—could recite them from memory—but they did not feel appropriate. The hundreds of people staring up at her from their knees were not thankful for their friends' and families' embrace by the Lover. They could not take comfort in knowing there was an *after* where their souls would rest for eternity. Not while the sky was still blotted with smoke, the clouds wrathful embers.

Safety and kindness—everything her people knew had been taken from them.

Pacifists and peace makers—everything they stood for had been challenged and would continue to be challenged in the face of the coming battle. Eavha herself could barely stomach it, and the majority of people waiting for her to speak had seen considerably less violence.

Closing her eyes, Eavha sank to her knees. After a moment, she heard four other sets settle against the platform.

"Grief," she began, voice catching as her eyes opened, "has been forbidden to us for a long time. It is only these last few months that Kaelean has been able to show us that it is the most natural thing in the world. Yes, it hurts. Don't be afraid of it. It means what we lost was worth something."

The reminder, the permission, was all that was needed for some witches to break apart. Every audible sob was a knife to the chest.

As they took a moment to feel, Eavha noticed a shadow growing at the outskirts of the gathering. It grew until it seeped into the crowd itself, slowly taking shape into the familiar form of a phouka. Tall and large, the way he carried Eaon reminded her of the way a parent cradled a child.

Eavha could only stare as the phouka found an isolated spot to set Eaon down, kneeling beside him to keep him upright. Her brother's eyes were open but there was a sickeningly familiar vacancy to them.

He had hated Wyldeden. It had never been a haven to him. Yet he managed a nod before leaning heavily against the phouka. The phouka, who also knelt. Not for her—she was not so deluded. A creature like the phouka knelt for no mortal being, but the fae would mourn the forest.

As if his presence was a signal, the field came to life. Tiny creatures made of mushroom and dandelions, blades of grass and twigs, poked their heads out from the boab's trunk. A breeze blew across the grass, scattering flower petals, and in its wake stood beings of mist and cloud, faces drawn in pain.

Eavha could barely breathe as they threw themselves to the ground, wailing softly on the roots of the boab. Anfar had few fae within its wards —only the dryads, too integral to the trees to be forced out—and Wyldeden had been home to none. Not everyone had travelers in their families to tell them stories of what the fae were like, not everybody read the folktales written about them, and so rather than be struck with the fear crawling in Eavha's belly, her people stared in wonder.

Trembling, Eavha looked back to her brother. The phouka gave her a nod to continue, so she took a steadying breath. It was easier to speak to Eaon instead of facing the rest, and despite the exhaustion lining his face, he held her gaze.

"We have lost so much." She didn't hide the crack in her voice. "But we are not alone in this loss. You and I are in this together, and between us, there is space enough to carry the memories. Terra gave us Wyldeden so we could become the best versions of ourselves, so we could become who we needed to be, and even though it is gone now, what it gave us is not. No matter where we go, no matter the distance between us, we carry it with us. We carry that love in the safest of places."

She lay a hand against her own heart, where she had never forgotten the love of her ma. Her da. Her brother.

Eaon closed his eyes and bowed his head.

"With every breath we take, every heartbeat, we keep the spirit of Wyldeden alive. And with every step, every meal, every dance, we honor those who are now at rest. So rise, and let us dance together."

The drummers took their cue, beginning a slow, rhythmic cadence reminiscent of a steady heartbeat. Eavha stood, but she remained still as her clan climbed to their feet. Stamping in time to the drums, they moved, circling the boab in rings as witches joined hands. The dance was slow, the whispers growing louder as people cried out the names of the dead. Among them, the sprites spun and wailed, their pain too deep for them to cause any mischief.

The phouka stood but did not join in. Scooping Eaon off the ground, he turned and stalked away.

Before Herbe could stop her, Eavha jumped from the dais and chased after them.

"Wait. Eaon, wait," she huffed, barely audible over the drums.

The phouka heard her. Eyes narrowed, he let her catch up.

"You're out of bed," she noted, mentally berating herself for such an obvious statement.

She waited for Eaon's sarcastic reply and was met with only weary silence. His body was limp against the phouka, chest heaving with effort as he pulled in a deeper breath.

"Just wanted to see you. To tell you, they'd have been proud of you."

Eavha stilled, heart squeezing painfully. Instinct had her clamming up, swallowing it down, but she had just told the entire Anfar Forest Clan to let themselves feel their pain. She had to do the same.

"Thank you," she croaked, reaching up to straighten her crown. "They'd have been proud of you too."

Eaon's eye twitched as he turned away, a ripple of cold wafting from him. Considering they hadn't spoken since Moyra's revelation, and considering she very rarely understood what was going on in Eaon's head, perhaps she shouldn't have risked such a declaration. But it was true. The way Eaon had taken care of her during what was undoubtedly their hardest times, the way he cared about everybody, the way he tried so hard to manage the magic that had been thrust upon him . . . They would have been so proud. She was proud.

The phouka shifted, putting his shoulder between the two of them. "I'm taking him back to the infirmary."

"Alright. Send for me if you need me."

Neither confirming nor denying the request, the phouka left. A gentle hand on her shoulder stopped Eavha from watching after them. Covering the hand with her own, Eavha turned. The small smile on Aisling's face was softer, warmer, than anything Eavha knew the Sparrow queen to be capable of.

"Are you ready to dance with them?" Aisling asked, looking back.

"In a moment." Eavha took Aisling's hand from her shoulder and pressed her lips against her knuckles. "There's one more thing I need to do. Then, will you dance with me?"

Aisling's eyes widened—only a fraction, but she expressed so little that Eavha caught it. "Would that be appropriate?"

"I say it is, so it is."

She didn't wait for Aisling's answer, but led her back to where Milnova waited with a heavy bag of supplies. She held it open while Eavha withdrew a small cluster of clear quartz, tall red candles and an array of smaller black ones. Aisling's gaze was a comforting weight as she placed the crystal on the dais and arranged the candles until they formed an arrow toward the boab. From the bottom of the bag, Milnova handed her a jar of burnt herbs to mark her chest and face, which she did so with practiced efficiency. The rest she sprinkled around the makeshift altar, the sage and tobacco potent.

Lighting candles felt wrong considering the mournful revelry happening nearby, but not all fire was destructive.

"What is it for?" Aisling asked, keeping clear as Eavha went to her knees once more, head low and palms raised.

The lump was back in Eavha's throat. "For Kaelean."

The high priestess was not gone. Eavha would not accept that. Not yet.

It was a simple enough spell—one her ma had taught her when Da and Eaon were late returning from a traveling trip.

"It's a beacon. To guide her home."

CHAPTER TWENTY-ONE

KAELEAN

SEVEN HUNDRED YEARS AGO, KAELEAN CAESAREA WAS USURPED AS HIGH priestess of Wyldeden for stealing magic from the Mother. Cast out, branded, drained of almost all magic and labeled a "rogue," Kaelean found herself alone for the first time in nearly three centuries.

It was under the winter canopy of Anfar's sentient gray forest that she met the first true threat she'd faced since the Third War: a hungry lupanis.

Scales frostbitten, the lizard-like frill around its lupine face was scarred and shredded, but it's shoulders still rippled with muscle as it stalked her.

It should not have been there. The wards she had laid around the forest after her ascension to power should have kept the beasts out, the decades of hunting parties removing any stragglers. One must have survived the purge, but at the time, it hadn't mattered why the lupanis was there, only that it was. Barefoot in the snow with nothing but a heavy rock as a weapon, Kaelean had faced down one of the deadliest creatures in Nir —and she had *won*.

Taking down a dragon was not like that at all.

In all her years, Kaelean had never seen one in the flesh. Like Kinner, they had been reduced to myth or legend—a fiction, or something from an age long gone. She had not stopped to think about what she was doing when the beast stuck its enormous face through the broken window of Dusarn's throne room. She just pounced.

If anybody had been watching, they'd have seen her wolfish grin as she'd done it, too.

Now, Kaelean couldn't draw breath. The ache in her lungs was proof she was alive—at least for a few moments longer, anyway—but the weight of the tower the dragon crashed into while fighting for its remaining eye lay atop them. Memories of the crash were foggy; the buckling walls and ear-shattering roars, the world twisting and twirling in a dizzying spin of sunset and sandstone as Kaelean clung to the dragon's hide with tooth and claw. When they finally hit the ground, every scrap of air was knocked from her body, but she had used the second between impact and the crush of falling rock to roll under the dragon's monstrous leg. Pure instinct made her shift; the lupanis was a good weapon, but in a pinch Kaelean wanted her magic.

The tower had fallen, the dragon screaming into the purple dusk, and the world went dark.

It was still dark, but the awake kind now.

Cold scales surrounded her, scratching against bare skin. Tons of muscle and stone crushed in so tight there wasn't room to expand her lungs. She would only have a minute or two of consciousness unless she could get smaller.

Willing her body to turn to clay again, she thought of the dormouse whose tiny beating heart she'd swallowed whole so many new moons ago. The world was muddier through its tiny, beady black eyes, but in the dark it hardly mattered. Once smaller, she gulped down desperate lungsful of stale, hot air before scurrying through the rubble, looking for a way out.

It took longer than she wanted.

In her witch form, she could have manipulated the earth to move aside. Her blessing ran deep enough that she didn't need to incant the spell to do so, her training so thorough she could *will* her intentions to being, but she didn't trust there to be enough air to remain conscious long enough.

The first wash of fresh air came after hours of squeezing between rock and scale. Panic wasn't something she did often, and something she didn't realize she was doing until it receded. Pushing out from what would no longer be her tomb, Kaelean immediately began to shift, rising up once she had her feet back.

Beasts growled in the near distance, the low glow of a burning city washing the night in red. Every bone and muscle in her body ached so deeply she was sure she'd never been in so much pain before. None of it could stop the feral grin contorting her face.

Her name was Kaelean Caesarea, and she had defeated a dragon.

Not just any dragon, either—the one that burned her home.

She could not save the forest. She could not save the haven she had built with so much magic and blood that she *felt* every inch of Wyldeden in her body. Her blood sung with its rivers, her bones built of its boabs. She had never been good at asking permission from spirits, but Terra never held it against her; unlike Mother, the spiteful hag, the nature spirit had lent her personal shadow guardians to protect the tear in her realm. Terra had taken in the Anfar Forest Clan with an embrace that rivaled the warmth of the Lover's.

Kaelean wondered if Terra felt as empty as she did now. If the loss of the clan was as painful as the hollowness of Kaelean's bones, the stickiness of her blood. She had ripped herself apart to make Wyldeden, and now that part of her was *gone*.

Because of Chaos.

Because of his harbingers.

Because of the dragon she had just killed.

Almost.

The rubble shifted beneath her feet. An entire tower of the Sparrow Coven's castle had collapsed, but it was not enough to have buried the dragon in its entirety. Its dark yellow scales glittered under the full moon as it stirred.

There was nothing alive in Nir that could compare to its size, and for a brief moment, Kaelean was awestruck. She couldn't help it. Having enjoyed the boundless strength of the lupanis, she understood the power in the thick muscle contracting the dragon's serpentine neck. Having reveled in the ease her fangs and claws could shred bone and stone, the flash of teeth as the dragon huffed had her heart skipping. A dragon in Nir was what a lupanis would have been to Wyldeden—unmatched, unparalleled destruction.

Kaelean curled her upper lip and glanced around at her surroundings. Though her eyes remained black in her witch form, she had her normal vision. Whatever beasts lurked within the castle ruins weren't near enough to be a threat yet, but she would have to go in search of Princess Aisling soon.

Careful where she put her feet, *willing* the rock to support her as she clambered down, Kaelean made her way to where the dragon's head lay limp. Blood soaked the sandstone rubble—not enough to kill the beast for a while, but enough to weaken it. Every breath from its wet nostrils reeked of burnt flesh and sulfur, the accompanying steam adding humidity to the hot summer night. Kaelean basked in the sweat slicking her naked skin as she assessed the damage to its eyes.

The left was gouged completely out by something with claws that weren't hers. Judging by the circular pattern of the punctures and the inward dragging wounds, something with talons so large they put the lupanis's to shame. The right side was her handy work. Slashed to ribbons, there was still eye-goop seeping from the socket, the thinner parallel lines of her attack dragging down its snout from where she'd slipped during their freefall.

The dragon had to know she was there but did little more than huff, resigned to whatever fate lay in store. Crouching before it, Kaelean tilted her head.

Such a magnificent beast.

"Is it true? Are your kind intelligent?"

It wasn't uncommon. Shtryg could hold conversations, could taunt and prey on things with a cruelty only possible through intelligence. Harpies—human in appearance bar their winged arms, taloned feet and beaked faces—were clever enough to be bargained with, though that was often attributed to their part-human origins. Shtryg, too, were argued to have descended from the union of humans and a monster so fearsome nobody dared speak of them. Mother may have made four separate species—animals, for practice; monstrous beasts, for Chaos's amusement; fae, for the land; humans, to feed and entertain them all—but that was over three millennia ago. The Fair Folk were the product of fae and human mingling, and many breeds of beasts were borne of similar causes. Witches were a product of dilution—Fair Folk so many generations removed that they had no inherent magic. They had to be blessed.

There was nothing humanoid about a dragon, yet at Kaelean's question, it managed a slow, heavy movement that could only be interpreted as a nod.

The familiar crawl of an idea crept up the back of Kaelean's neck.

The dangerous kind.

"I'll be back."

She needed a moment to stew on it. Needed to check on the princess.

The tower holding the throne room still stood, though precariously. Despite the low growls permeating the night, the tower remained silent, its windows dark.

Kaelean shifted. The fox was nimbler than even she, and would be less of a target should a beast wander by. Like liquid, she slipped along the cracked courtyard and into the tower, slinking up the stairs.

The shadows could not conceal anything from her night-sharp eyes—the throne room was empty. Empty of anything living, anyway.

Death had visited.

Lupanis and shtryg corpses littered the floor, and on the dais, the mangled body of Queen Tallula. The fox's sense of smell wasn't as strong as the lupanis's, but just as she kept the dormouse's eyes in every form, the beast's nose came with her too. The lingering scent of burnt flesh raised her hackles, but it was nothing compared to the curdled milk of white beast blood. The darker, throatier scent of mulberry witch blood splattered the floor alongside something sweeter. Bright and rich, she crept closer and buried her nose in the red stain.

Cinn.

Cold washed beneath her fur, stomach clenching as she darted around the room, double-checking every dark corner, under the thrones and corpses, looking for the young kinner.

All she found of him was his silver knife, warped from heat but still sharp.

Confident in her solitude, she shifted back, measuring the finger-shaped imprints in the hilt against her own.

"What in all the realms did I miss?" she whispered to herself.

Cinn was not in the throne room, but he had been.

Aisling was also unaccounted for. If she had him again, if she had hurt him . . .

Wrath burned so hotly inside her chest she should be blowing steam through her nostrils, too.

Nobody was around. She was on her own again, and Cinn might be in trouble. The pain of her heart twisting was exactly why she had sworn to never form these kinds of bonds again, and yet here she was, gladly sinking into the depths of feral rage at the thought of the kinner she'd claimed. The twisting sharpened, turning into an incessant *pull* as she thought of each of the young witches she had also claimed—Eavha, Eaon, and Dearmead. A pull that had her turning southeast, aching for her clan, ripped from the only home they had ever known.

Her decision was made.

The danger didn't matter. Not if it got her back to them.

Stalking to Queen Tallula's body, she stripped it of fabric and fashioned herself a wrap, including a band to tie Cinn's knife to her thigh. The queen's abdomen was torn open from sternum to groin, most of her organs chewed upon. Her blood was strange. Kaelean sniffed deeply and caught both witch and beast scents, clumps of white sticking to ruined tissue.

Something to think on later.

All that was left on the dead queen's corpse was a necklace. Kaelean had never been one to care for the trinkets and decorations the Jem-blessed produced, but as she ripped the jewelry from Tallula's throat and held it up to the moonlight, something about it struck wrong. The single fist-sized ruby was hollow, unrefined, and little more than a lump of raw stone cradled in a golden clasp. Not exactly the adornment a Sparrow monarch typically favored.

Tucking the treasure into the strap with Cinn's knife, she grabbed the queen's now bare corpse under her stiff, graying arms and hauled her off the dais. Bodies were heavy, but she managed to half-carry, half-drag the corpse back down the stairs and across the mosaiced courtyard to where the dragon still lay limp.

With a final heave, she tossed the queen right in front of the dragon's maw and wiped her dirtied hands on the shredded dress draped over her dust-streaked body.

She didn't know how loyal dragons were, but its rider had left it behind. She could use that. She could win it over the way she won over every other injured, scared thing she had found lost in the wild—with food.

"Listen here, you giant-assed lizard. You don't get to die and leave me stranded. So open your mouth and eat."

She would have to find a way to move the rubble. She would have to be careful not to get caught by the numerous beasts lurking nearby until she managed it.

Because the dragon was her ride back to her family.

PART II

LINES DRAWN AND HELD

CHAPTER TWENTY-TWO

AISLING

As the council room filled, Aisling couldn't help but think this was what her first Imsa should have been like. Not that she wished the kind of fear permeating the whispers around her, but it was appropriate. They took this seriously.

The day was sweltering despite the early hour. Pitchers of ice water and sweet tea waited on the long, feather-shaped table alongside bowls of nuts and fruit. At the head, Aisling was in a good position to assess the room. For six years, she had been preparing—stockpiling—but those joining her hadn't had the same time. She would have to be gentle with them.

Edwina sat to her right, Eavha to her left. The former may have only recently learned why she was preparing for war, but she had always known it was coming, and, aside from Aisling herself, was the only person truly ready. The latter had been the first outsider to believe her. Eavha sat at the table this time not as a representative, but as leader of the only clan of witches who'd ever remained entirely outside of Sparrow government. The rest were left to their own devices for the most part, but they knew who owned the land they settled on. They knew that if a Sparrow came knocking, they were to submit. Not Anfar, though. Kaelean and the Third War ensured that.

The rest of the clans may bow for Aisling, but they had no respect for Sparrows. They did for Anfar, though. To have Eavha sit beside her was a victory worth the first Imsa's humiliation.

Clayton, as always, stood behind her with his hand on the hilt of his sword. Next to him, Radley scanned for threats to his sister.

Eavha's guard was not with them.

From what she understood, Dearmead had been taken by the enemy. Aisling sent a silent prayer to any spirit listening that they protect him. That, somehow, he could make his way back. In the short time she had known the male, he had earned her hard-won respect, as well as some of her even harder won trust.

Other Wyldeden witches lined the walls though—Herbe, the elder guardian, Milnova, the elder keeper, and Yvette, the elder healer, along with a handful of others she didn't know by name. A number of Aisling's commanders also stood to attention, as did some trusted servants. They were all waiting for orders.

Orders that would only come after Aisling had finished speaking with the rest of the witches sitting along the table. Down one side, a representative of the seaside South Shore Clan sat with their attendants, while on the other, a representative of the Western Dividing River Clan bit into a ripe peach. After last time, it was not surprising that Sar Vin of the Southern Mountain Clan had ignored her summons.

Moyra Thorne was the last to enter, taking a seat at the far end of the table. She had brought her own teapot, placing it down with great care, while the large black cat sith that followed her everywhere perched on her lap.

The doors closed and the charged silence that tended to follow Aisling every time she faced a crowd descended. It chilled the air despite the summer heat, the hair on her arms standing tall.

The crown on her head had never felt heavier. Her knees shook under its weight as she stood, but she schooled her face into the calm they all needed. Eavha's bare foot pressed against her heeled boot—not even the leather could keep her warmth from seeping through.

People needed their customs and traditions in a time like this, so she began the way it always began. Pulling an empty goblet closer, she took the spellmarked bone knife from its sheath and pierced the flesh of her palm. Holding the wound over the cup, she let a few drops fall.

"I, Aisling Aurnia of the Sparrow Coven, hereby offer my life forfeit should I break any of the three promises of Imsa." This time, the scars on her hands meant it would be binding. "To those who offer their blood to this goblet, I shall cause no harm. To those who speak the truth to me, I shall offer only truth in return. And to those who bring their grievances to me, I shall strive to make peace. In the names of Mother and Death, for the sake of the Creator and the Lover and their Balance, I pledge myself before your witness."

Nobody moved. Nobody spoke. The leader of the river clan spat out the pip of her peach and narrowed her eyes at the goblet as if it offended her. Both Mare-blessed water clans had refused to meet with her last time, and the then-king had not seen fit to enforce attendance. Their reasons had not since changed—there wasn't an oath in any language that would make them trust the Sparrow Coven.

Eavha stood, taking the goblet and the knife. Slicing the side of her arm, she added her blood to the cup.

"I, Eavha Nemuse of the Anfar Forest Clan, hereby offer my life forfeit . . ."

After that, things went easier:

"I, Edwina Red of the Hyrschan demi-kin, hereby offer my life forfeit . . ."

"I, Dominic Azgeda of the South Shore Clan, hereby offer my life forfeit . . ."

"I, Fior Damsa of the Western Dividing River Clan, hereby offer my life forfeit . . ."

Then Radley.

Yvette, Milnova, and Herbe.

Clayton.

Moyra Thorne.

The cat sith was not offered the goblet, but Gatty promised to be on his best behavior all the same.

Rather than have Milnova and the other keepers do it, Aisling took the heavy cup to the doorway and windows, dipping her fingers into the blood to flick splatters of it on the floor and sills. The magic was mild in its side effects but strong in its hold; inside this council room, Imsa was law.

When she returned to her chair, she took a cloth to clean her fingers.

"Let us begin."

First, Aisling explained to the river and shore clans what she had already explained to Eavha, and what Moyra already knew.

The story began with their creator—Mother once made a star, and her sister Morvia loved it so much that she made billions of them. Then Chaos wanted something too, so Mother thought very hard about what would make Chaos happy. And so she made life.

It was a story, but it was real. Chaos was real, and he was here. He was coming to Hyrsch.

Her audience was a captive one, especially when she told them in great detail of Chaos's birth into his mortal form and the shifting shape of it. What it was like to feel the fibers of existence, of reality, bending when he gave one of his harbingers wings. It was not an enemy any of them could fathom, nor was it something to be fought in ways any of them knew how to fight.

"If he cannot be fought, then what are we doing here?" Fior of the river clan asked, rubbing her thumb against the soft flesh of a second peach. She'd been holding it for some time, playing with it absently as she listened. "We should be evacuating."

"Evacuations are already underway," Aisling explained. "Some of the demi-kin in the city are moving east to the villages while the rest will be going with the humans to Pirevia as soon as we organize transportation. If you bring your people, we can send them as well."

Dominic of the South Shore Clan nodded his agreement, but Fior was not convinced.

"And how long until Chaos decimates the east? Before he goes to Pirevia?"

"That is why only civilians are evacuating, and only as a precaution." Aisling straightened in her seat. Gooseflesh rose across her skin as she finally admitted her secret aloud. "I have a plan to face him and his army."

"You have a plan?" Fior sneered, far too reminiscent of Sar Vin's condescension. "What authority do you have to be making plans?"

"Aside from being the Sparrow queen?" Aisling narrowed her eyes, gripping the arm of her chair. Eavha's hand was cashmere on steel as it settled on top. "I was given sage advice from a Morvish seer."

The room took a collective breath, except Fior, who scoffed. "What—"

"Who?" Moyra interrupted, her quiet voice so much louder than Fior's bark.

A hundred days and nights flashed through Aisling's mind. Memories of golden hair against brown skin, of too green eyes that saw too much, pulling Aisling apart at the seams until there was nothing she could hide. A bright, laughing compass forced into her hand, inked into her skin, giving Aisling's life direction. A purpose.

"Her name was Davina Downing." Aisling's voice didn't crack on the name, but it was a close thing. "Did you know her?"

"No. But . . ." Moyra looked toward the stained-glass window behind Aisling, gaze distant, as if she could see all the way across the razed land to

Ahrenhale itself. "Downing is Pearl's last name. She sent her own blood beyond the wards?"

The question must be rhetorical because Aisling couldn't possibly know what she was talking about. The rest of the room was fascinatedly silent as Aisling asked, "Who is Pearl?"

"The High Seer of Ahrenhale."

So little was known about Qiri. About Ahrenhale and the Morvish. So little was *remembered*. The stories Davina told her were memories blurred by what Aisling had chalked up to alcoholism, but now understood as the effect of the fae magic surrounding Nir. Had she been told before about the political system in Qiri? Had she once known what the position *High Seer* meant? Who Davina came from?

If she had, she didn't anymore.

"This Davina . . . Her magic was strong, then?" Dominic asked, breaking his silence, likely trying to decide how much of this he believed. Wondering how much stock to put into visions from a witch he'd never met. How much trust to place in a magic known for being cloudy.

"I don't know," Moyra admitted. "But she would have been trained well. As well as any Morvish witch can be."

Aisling didn't mention that one of Davina's visions had already been misinterpreted, moving the timeline for the attack up by six months, but considering how nonsensical all the Morvish who'd come to Dusarn before and after her were, perhaps Davina had done the best that could be done. It wasn't a lie to keep it to herself because nobody had asked, and the spellwork in the room would have forced the words out if secrets were the same as lies.

"What were these visions?" Dominic asked.

And that was something Aisling could not forget. The day Davina had *seen*. The terror, the grief, the desolation as she'd collapsed to the floor and heaved. Then the determination. The resolution. Her promises, ending in the tattoos. Ending in her death.

"Her first predicted the when of Chaos's arrival," Aisling explained, looking toward the window, grateful for the tight grip Eavha had on Aisling's trembling hand beneath the table. "She saw the ash, and saw that we would have two weeks after it fell."

Wyldeden's elder guardian, Herbe, gaped like she had slapped him. "You knew the forest would burn?"

Aisling frowned. "No. Of course not. The ash could have been from anything."

Before another pointless argument could break out, Fior asked, "What else?"

"She predicted Chaos would come here to Hyrsch and she saw the damage we can inflict on the beast army when he does. She saw what I needed to do to prepare." Every waking moment, every choice she made, from freeing the demi-kin to imprisoning the kinner, was to see those visions come to fruition. She regretted much, but it was too late to do things differently. She could only hope it would work out in the end.

She wanted to stop there, but this time, Imsa made her speak. This was not a secret she could keep.

"Davina saw me facing Chaos, alone, on the bridge above the Womb."

A moment of silence. She could see the questions on all their faces; the same ones she had been trawling over herself. If Hyrsch was where their final stand against Chaos took place, how did Aisling end up at the Womb? There was no way to know until it happened, but Aisling had to assume an opportunity to lead the King of Beasts away from the city would arise, and that it would be in her best interests to take it. What happened on that bridge would undoubtedly be the end of her, but she knew that if Chaos was going to kill her, she would be taking him to the void with her.

"So," Eavha said, and Aisling didn't miss the tremor in her voice, even as she tried to get conversation back on track. "What is your plan?"

Deep breaths. Slow breaths. There could be no doubt for this part.

"The attack will be messy," Aisling admitted. "Disorganized and chaotic. The five years I have spent in this city, I have had every Argon-blessed witch and silversmith working to make a stockpile of weapons and armor. Davina saw that they will come from the west, through the frozen wastes and the mountain pass. Meeting them in an open field would be a grave mistake; beasts don't do well in closed quarters, so we funnel the masses to the western gate where we have the advantage."

"Funnel them how?" Fior wasn't arguing anymore. Whether she was fully convinced or not, Aisling couldn't tell, but at least they were invested.

"The wards that were used to block beasts from Anfar. We lay them down along the river and by the shore, narrowing at a small enough degree that the harbingers don't realize until they're in the kill box—given the size of the troops I have, about five-hundred meters on either side of the western gate."

Dominic raised his brows. "You know Kaelean Caesarea's wards?"

Aisling turned to Eavha, who looked to her elders. Their conversation was hushed Terranian, and though unsure, the elders believed a male named Bodhi may know them.

"Wyldeden can assist with that," Eavha announced.

Another gamble paid off.

"Speaking of Kaelean." This time it was Yvette, speaking up for the first time. The elder healer had a hardness, a coolness, that Aisling found oddly comforting; it was an attitude she was familiar with. Right then though, there was a challenge in her tone that set Aisling's spine. "You left with our high priestess and returned with a kinner boy. We need Kaelean back, Your Majesty, so I need you to remember more than 'she went out the window.'"

"A valid point," Fior chimed in. "With your ability to move through Celeste's realm, why have you not gone back to look for her? It would take you no time at all."

"Of course it occurred to me to go back," Aisling said carefully. "And if we had received any word of her survival, I would in a heartbeat. But as it is, it is too risky."

"Too—"

Aisling cut the objection short. "If I were Byron, the harbinger Chaos gave wings to, I would have left a trap. If Kaelean is there, if she is alive, the only conceivable reason why she has not called for aid is because Byron is using her to lure us. All Kaelean needs is a leaf, and she can call us to her. It has been days, and we have heard nothing."

Eavha closed her eyes—the only outward sign of the pain Aisling's words caused. Her next would be more comforting.

"Likewise, if she is in hiding and we try to contact her, we could give away her position. If I'm right about this, he won't be able to hold her long. In fact, if he has her, I almost pity him."

The Wyldeden elders exchanged looks that suggested they agreed.

"We will hear from her soon, and I will retrieve her the second we do. Until then, returning to Dusarn is an enormous risk. We know for a fact that Chaos and his army are coming here, and we will need every weapon in our arsenal if we are going to end him."

There was no waver in her voice as she said it, because she would not accept any other outcome. The time she had to prepare may have been cut down, but the allies at this table could compensate if she could just get them to cooperate.

"If Kaelean needs our help, she will call for it," Eavha finally said. "If we risk everything to rescue her when she does not need it, she would hate it. If we risk everything when she is already dead, she would hate that more. Aisling is right."

Beneath the table, Aisling squeezed Eavha's hand.

"You said they had a dragon." Dominic brought the conversation back to preparations. "The wards didn't stop it from unleashing death on Anfar. It won't be enough to protect our lands, or your city."

The dragon had been a surprise, but Aisling was not required to admit that. All she could do was tell them the truth.

"I don't know what happened to the dragon in Dusarn, and I don't know if they have more, but I have commissioned large, long-range crossbows that are ready to be mounted on the city wall." There were other winged beasts she had been expecting, and ever since she'd been able to resume preparations, she had asked the Argon-blessed and the silversmiths to make adjustments.

"If what you said about its size is true, it won't be enough," Fior argued.

Aisling found a new level of stiff as she straightened further. "I have also trained in aerial combat."

Fior balked. "You are one witch."

"And I will be enough."

It was as good a time as any to finally remove the suffocating shawl and expose her tattoos. The black inked spellmarks etched into her skin were a burden she knew she needed to train with more—her failures in Pirevia and Dusarn proof—but they would be enough to defend this city.

In a rush, Dominic scrambled to his feet, muttering in Marian and warding himself in a complicated hand gesture. His guard was instantly at his side.

"Imsa is still in effect. You have no reason to be afraid," Aisling said, voice low and calm. "These marks are for Chaos, not for you. When the moment comes, I will lead Chaos away from the castle and face him where he cannot harm the rest of you."

Eavha was turning green, mouth pursed, and Aisling knew she would get an earful about this part of the plan later.

"I don't know if this is when we defeat Chaos," she went on. "Davina saw me face him on the bridge over the Womb and that is quite some way from here, even by wing. He was also much larger in the vision than how he manifested in Dusarn. But if the opportunity presents itself, I will take it."

"Futures are ever changing," Moyra said, looking at her niece rather than Aisling. "Just because Davina saw it as the likeliest path, does not mean it is the only path."

And at that, a thousand arguments broke out. Aisling shut her eyes and steeled herself against the stray words that found their way across the room. There were valid arguments: *"If none of this is certain, how can we really prepare for anything?"* While others grated at her already thin nerves: *"The second she said the Morvish were involved, I stopped trusting this."*

For a solid ten minutes, she let them debate, only drawing a decent breath when it seemed like things were turning in her favor. The risks were too high for them not to believe her.

It took another moment for them to settle, but when they did, Fior was ropable. "Chaos may be coming, but this plan is nothing. It's madness."

This was Davina's plan. This was Davina's legacy. Aisling's last nerve snapped as she stood from the table and slammed her palms down on the black wood.

"Feel free to come up with a better one in the five minutes you've known about the threat."

Slowly, like she was approaching a rabid animal, Eavha stood and placed a soft hand on Aisling's arm. Her words were gentle, but her gaze was as uncompromising as ever.

"The plan is good but you brought us all together for a reason. If the others have ideas to strengthen weak spots, it would be a waste not to listen. For instance, there is an archaic spellmark called The Barring Mark of Things Unwanted. We should cast it on the city walls as an extra layer of protection."

Murmurs went around the table. It seemed the spellmark Eavha spoke of was not well known, but Herbe was nodding again. "It would give the restless Wyldeden witches something to do."

"There are marks we use to attract certain beasts," Dominic added. "We lay traps to lure them in when one starts causing problems in town. We could lay them in the places you want the beasts to go. Control the flow."

"If I may suggest." Gatty jumped up on the table, swishing his tail. Aisling narrowed her eyes at the cat sith; she disliked having fae in the palace more than almost anything, but as long as Moyra was in the fold, this one seemed to be on a leash. "There are additional forces you have not tried to rally, and wards more powerful than those of witches. I can speak to the local fae."

"Absolutely not—" Fior began, and it was that outrage that had Aisling going against her better instincts.

"Fine," she snapped. "But there will be promises involved to keep them in line."

Gatty grinned.

The doors opened.

Every head in the council room turned, then blanched at the sight of the enormous creature hulking in the entry. All except Gatty, whose grin widened almost to the point of splitting his face in half.

The phouka walked in, then stepped aside to reveal Eaon limping behind him, a pair of crutches wedged beneath his arms.

"Heard a meeting was being held," he said. "If we're talking about how we're going to stop Chaos, don't you think I should have been invited?"

CHAPTER TWENTY-THREE

AISLING

DESPITE THE PAIN HE HAD TO BE IN, DESPITE THE SICKLY PALLOR TO HIS face and deep purple bags under his eyes, Eaon's glare was heavy as he met Aisling's across the room.

"You would make a formidable enemy," she had once said to him. Meeting the frigid hatred in his stare was proof it was truer than ever.

"Shouldn't you be in the infirmary?" Eavha asked, crossing her arms. "I planned to come back down there to try healing your leg again. I would have told you about it."

"I don't need to hear about it secondhand," Eaon snapped back, leaning on his crutches. "I need to throw my hat in the ring. There's no need to waste life. Save your armies. Put me in Chaos's path and I will end it."

Behind him, the phouka's eyes flashed. His clawed hand yanked Eaon's hair until the witch was forced to look up at him.

"That is not what you said you would say. And I will not allow it."

Eaon bared his teeth. "Why don't you go back to the mountains and mind your business?"

As they bickered, Aisling's head spun. Sometimes she harbored deep regret for how much she used to drink, because surely brain damage was the only reason she hadn't seen the new piece on her chessboard. The stories of what Eaon had done while escaping Pirevia the first time had circulated widely. Aisling had seen the damage to Nevan's face herself, the necrotic wave of magic finding him all the way up in his tower. She had seen, too, the damage he could do in the arena.

Eavha had lost all color. While she looked two seconds from passing out, her voice was level and determined as she argued, "If it was that simple, Davina would've seen it."

Aisling's control over her face was the only reason she didn't raise her brows at the blatant bullshit. Eaon hadn't bled for this Imsa, so he wasn't contracted to tell the truth and receive only truth in return. The rest of them had just discussed how subjective Morvish visions could be, but here was Eavha, acting like they were law.

Before Aisling had to decide how she was going to play this—back up Eavha, like she would normally do, or call her out for bending the truth, which would lead to the outcome she wanted—Moyra stood.

"Morvish visions are subjective, and what Aisling described is hardly a full picture."

Eavha bristled, and Aisling recognized the furious expression on her face. This wasn't going to end well.

But Eavha wasn't the only one fighting this idea; the phouka released Eaon's hair and snapped around to Moyra. Gatty's hackles raised in response, but Moyra offered her hands, back-tracking quickly.

"Regardless, it is still a bad idea. Until we understand what the Lover is doing, we should refrain from feeding the seed further. If the phouka is correct and the Lover truly is trying to possess your body, Eaon, unleashing Death in mortal form could be devastating."

"For the sake of argument, we don't know that it would be," Aisling said before Eaon could argue, ignoring the look of betrayal Eavha leveled at her. "The Lover has always been a benevolent spirit; as Mother's creations, we have value. I can try to convene with the Lover and find out what their intentions are."

"Irrelevant," Eaon said with a cutting gesture, sinking into an empty chair Moyra pushed out. He made a point of not looking at her. "Even if the Lover taking mortal form is dangerous, all you have to do is wait for me to kill Chaos, then someone kills me. Problem solved."

The flippancy with which he suggested his own murder had half the people at the table flinching. Aisling wasn't sure most of them even knew who he was, but they were listening. Putting the pieces together. Planning.

"That is not a solution," Moyra said lowly.

Eaon sucked a tooth. "Didn't ask you."

"Just stop it!" Eavha buried her face in her hands, unable to hold back tears any longer. "I didn't save you just for you to throw your life away like that."

"No." Eaon leaned forward onto the table, merciless as he stared his sister down. "You saved me because you didn't want to be alone. You have people now. So let me go."

Eavha dropped her hands, pained. "I saved you because you're my brother and I love you."

Eaon snorted and rolled his eyes.

Aisling felt the ricochet in her own body as something snapped inside Eavha, and she regretted allowing things to escalate. Eavha stood and slammed her hands on the table, baring her teeth, eyes rimmed in red. Neither sibling seemed to care that they had an audience. A war council, of all things.

"If this is some kind of self-destructive bullshit—"

"Oh, I'm sorry, is nobody else allowed to be useful around here? Are you the only special one in this room?"

"This has nothing to do with me—"

"Everything always has everything to do with you—"

"Just stop it, Eaon!"

"Oh, you *hate* that I actually have something to contribute—"

"What I hate is your self-esteem bullshit!"

Eaon threw his head back and cackled, and it was so bizarre that Aisling sat back in her seat and stared with the same unabashed fascination one might have looking at a crime scene. Both Moyra and Eavha's shoulders dropped at the sound of Eaon's dark laughter, matching frowns on their faces as it ended as quickly as it started. Eaon's fists clenched on the surface of the table and any trace of humor was swallowed by a black rage.

"I had to find out from the servant who changes my sheets that you confronted Lorelei, and that the elders crowned you. I had to hear about the funeral from a whispering leaf, like everybody else. You didn't want me to know. You didn't want me there. Because I might be your brother, but that has always been embarrassing to you."

"That is not true," Eavha snapped, but the fire had left her.

"You've been avoiding me since Moyra said what she said. You hate even the idea that I might—"

"No, Eaon. Just stop."

"It's fine, Eavha, because it's not true. I'm the same pathetic lump of uselessness—"

"Stop." The plead was a whisper now.

It did nothing to cow Eaon's bitterness as he stood, struggling with his crutches as he spat, "Just go back to being amazing. I'll be in the infirmary."

The phouka stood in his way, staring down with an unreadable expression. Eaon glared back, unintimidated but unable to move around him.

Steadying herself with a long, slow breath, Eavha moved around the table to approach her brother, stopping a mere arm's length away. She tried to be quiet, but the entire room was paying far too much attention to miss her question.

"Are you taking the tonics I brewed you?"

"What do you think?" Eaon spat back.

"Right now, I can't tell, because this kind of rubbish is what you spew when you're heading into one of your episodes."

"Right. Eaon's having emotions, so he must be losing his shit. Is that it?"

Moyra had also gotten out of her seat, ignoring Gatty's hissing. It wasn't until the phouka's hand wrapped around Eaon's bicep that Aisling noticed how cold the room was growing.

"He's not in his right mind," Moyra said to Eavha.

Eaon tried to turn on her but stumbled over his injured leg. "That's right. Blame the magic my father lied to me about. Or blame my fucked-up brain because of what he did to me. Or blame the Lover's influence that only lives in me because of what Eavha did to me. Maybe, just maybe, my fucking rage at my family is fucking justified." He turned his glare back at Eavha then, but she didn't flinch beneath it. "Maybe when I say I don't believe for one fucking second that you give a shit about me, it's a valid fucking point!"

The phouka hissed, grabbing hold of Eaon with both hands and wrenching him away from everyone else. The crutches clattered to the floor as the fae creature pinned Eaon to the wall, his body a shield.

And just like that, the fae was the only thing standing between Eaon's bad mood and an entire room of rotting corpses.

His power was incredible. And utterly useless.

Harnessed, he would be unstoppable, but as Eaon panted heavily against the wall and the phouka growled lowly in his ear, it was obvious that this was not something Eaon could control. He was as likely to kill everybody in the city as he was to take out Chaos's army, and that wasn't a risk Aisling would take. If he could not be managed, she would have to find a way to remove him from the picture.

"If you cannot control yourself, you will have to leave," Aisling said coolly. "If you cannot be a part of this Imsa, a part of a united front—"

"Do not threaten him," Eavha interrupted.

"I wasn't going to," Aisling lied. "But he either needs to work with us in finding a reasonable solution, a sensible plan of action, or he becomes part of the problem. What side of this do you want to be on, Eaon?"

The room waited for the chill to leave the air. By the time the phouka helped Eaon back to his seat, his face was wane and hollow. The phouka kept his claws tight on both Eaon's shoulders, gaze unmoving from the top of his head.

"I am trying to be reasonable," Eaon ground out. "I am trying to be sensible. I am trying to avoid as many deaths as possible. Unlike some people, I was raised to center life. To protect it. To be a pacifist. War will only bring death, so it makes sense that is your go-to solution. You would sacrifice thousands to stop Chaos, but I am telling you to sacrifice just one. Just me. Everybody else gets out."

Eavha had not returned to her seat. She stood in the space between Eaon and Moyra and leaned heavily on the table, shaking her head. "No."

"Why not?" There was no energy left in the words. "Why them and not me? I am not worth more than them. Especially not because you love me. How conceited do you have to be to think your emotions are more important than everything else? Grow up."

This conversation was too personal. They should not be having it in front of everyone. Aisling tried to meet Edwina's eye, but her handmaiden was watching raptly. Aisling wanted to stand and tell them all to get out, to give Eavha privacy, but this had already unraveled too far. If people left at this point, they would leave believing Aisling could not control her own meetings. She had to bring this back somehow.

Eavha's switch to Terranian was enough to cut out most of the room, but not everybody.

"How miserable do you have to be to not consider your emotions at all?"

"It's not misery, it's practicality," Eaon said, following her language choice. "And you know damn well where I learned it."

Eavha crouched to his level, jaw set. "Look me in the eye and tell me that, if it were me trying to sacrifice myself, you would stand aside and let me."

"If it would save everybody else? You bet I would. I'm not that selfish." Eaon's face twisted as he said it, like the words tasted foul. Nobody listening believed him.

"I am not selfish for wanting you to have a chance at a real life," Eavha argued.

"Why me more than them?" Eaon repeated, but it sounded less like an accusation and more like a real question. "Why is my life more important that theirs?"

"Why isn't your life just as important as theirs? Why won't you fight for yourself like you fight for them?"

Aisling thought that would be the end of it, but found herself shaking her head when Eaon only met his sister's gaze, unmoved.

"One tree to save the forest. Not the forest for a tree."

Eaon was unstable, but he spoke Aisling's own thoughts aloud. It was the same reason she was not afraid to go to the Womb when the time was right. Why she was not afraid to leave everything behind. Why she was not afraid of the grief eating her chest at the thought of leaving Eavha.

Regardless, she had to get this meeting back on track. The others were starting to mutter among themselves now that they couldn't follow along.

Aisling cleared her throat and spoke clearly. "You don't even know if you could pull it off."

Having Eaon face her in such an antagonistic mood was unsettling.

"Underestimate me. See how that turns out for you."

Before Aisling could find another way to bring the conversation back, Eavha stood. Shoulders straight, she looked down at Eaon and said, "No."

Eaon held Aisling's stare but tilted his chin in his sister's direction. "You stay out of it."

"No."

His eye twitched. "I am still the Head of House—"

"*No*. And if you want to play that card again, I'll renounce my last name."

Eaon opened his mouth, but Moyra raised her voice over them both.

"I'll consult Morvia. Let's table the idea for now."

Aisling held in her sigh of relief. She would find the best tea in this city to gift the Morvish witch later. The cat sith, who had not calmed, perched on Moyra's lap once again and flattened his ears.

"If you're done trying to kill yourself," he hissed at Eaon, "Maybe you could put that big brain I've heard you have toward a different plan. We can discuss maximizing our advantages later, but we should take a moment to talk about theirs. With the shtryg among them, the army will be strongest in darkness. We can expect a nighttime attack."

"Wait."

Aisling turned to Edwina, who had thus far not said a single word.

There was a tiny furrow between her brow as she counted quietly, then looked from her hands to Moyra, to Aisling.

"Do you think they know we have Morvish help? They are coming for Aadya, so they have access to Morvish knowledge, but do they know we do too?"

"Unifiers have been sneaking south of the wards for years, meaning to fight back against Chaos," Moyra said slowly. "I haven't noticed any around, but we have to assume the harbingers would assume we have aid. If any of the beasts around Dusarn saw you use a moonstone the other night, they'll be certain."

Aisling couldn't rule it out.

"It's not just Morvish magic that benefits from the moon," Dominic added. "Mare's blessing also fluxes depending on the lunar cycle. There are many protective spells that are stronger under moonlight."

"Then," Edwina continued, "they know that the moon would give us an advantage. Davina said we would have two weeks from the day the ash fell; that's the new moon."

Silence gnawed at the room, but something settled in Aisling. It was the knowing, the certainty, of a deadline. Of course they would come on the new moon. She should have figured that out earlier.

"Then we take it from them," Fior said, finding her voice for the first time since Eaon entered the room. Aisling was grateful to have that single-mindedness keeping things on track. "I know you planned to meet them at the city, but if we move this westward, we can meet them earlier."

"The pass through the Southern Spine is a natural funnel. It would be better than using Kaelean's wards along the river," Wyldeden's elder guardian, Herbe, added.

"I . . ." Moyra panted, and everyone noticed at the same time that her collar was damp with sweat. Her eyes were glazed, the tattoo on her forehead shimmering. "I can see that we would fare better at the pass than here at the city."

"I know," Aisling said coldly. "Unfortunately, Sar Vin was not cooperative during my last Imsa and has not deigned to respond to my latest attempt to communicate. We do not have the resources or the time to take the pass from him by force."

"A guerrilla force, then?" Edwina suggested. "To get into the pass unnoticed. We might not be able to stop the army entirely with so few, but we only need to slow them down. Delay them, just by a day."

"At the very least, thinning out the herd gives us better odds when Chaos reaches the city," Moyra conceded.

"I can make Sar Vin listen."

Everyone turned to look at Eaon. Whatever had overtaken him while arguing with Eavha seemed to have dissipated, his focus on the fingernails he was picking apart.

"I don't think threatening to kill his entire clan is conducive—" Fior began to mock, but Eaon didn't even raise his head as he spoke over her.

"I have a contact in the southern mountains who owes me a debt. Let me go to the pass and they will listen."

Now, that was interesting. Aisling's next question was genuine, and she was careful not to let any scrap of derision lace the words as she spoke.

"If Sar Vin will not listen to the reigning Sparrow queen, why would he listen to a Wyldeden traveler?"

"Because travelers are better at inter-clan relations than Sparrows. It's literally our job."

Eavha looked like she was about to say something, a deep frown between her brows as she assessed her brother, but Dominic had something to say.

"We can't put everyone in the pass. We can't make it our only front. That's bad battle strategy, especially if so much of what Aisling has prepared is too hefty to cart all the way to the mountains in the very little time we have to prepare. I think using the pass to delay the army is wise, but I think we need to prepare for them to get through. We need to split our forces, and I don't think, even if we bring everybody up from the port town, that our numbers will be enough."

Aisling was aware that their numbers were not enough, and the bitter words were falling out before she could stop them.

"Well, I did want to have an additional army of kinner, but that plan went askew."

She knew she shouldn't have said it the second the words were past her lips.

The fragile peace in the room splintered with the sudden, severe drop in temperature. The phouka once again pulled Eaon from his chair but didn't stop at simply pinning him to the wall; thrown over his shoulder, Eaon was hauled from the room.

Eavha looked from the door banging closed in the phouka's wake, to Aisling, disappointment rife. Aisling was too distracted by the guilt such an expression carved to notice Edwina trying to slap her.

Her hand stuck mid-swing. Behind her, Radley's grip on his weapon was shaking and frozen. They could not hurt her with the laws of Imsa in effect, but by all the gods, they wanted to.

"Yes, we all know what you wanted, but I'm afraid that is not an option," Moyra said calmly, though there was plenty of wrath behind her eyes too.

"Kinner?" Fior scoffed. "You may have brought me around to the idea of Chaos being real, and I can wrap my head around dragons, but you can't expect me to believe in Kinner, too."

Aisling leveled an exhausted look at the river clan representative. "Was there truly nobody more intelligent than you to speak for your clan today?"

"They're real," Eavha said before Fior could retort her indignance. "I know at least two, personally."

She had *made* one, personally, but nobody had asked so it wasn't a secret that had to be shared. The other was somewhere in the city, probably planning her murder. His siblings certainly were.

"As Moyra said, they are not an option," Aisling bit out. "Also uncooperative."

Radley looked like he was about to burst a vein from how hard he was fighting the Imsa magic.

"Bring up the kinner again, and I'll eat you," Gatty warned. The threat was a surprise. Not often did fae defend someone they weren't promised to.

"I think this is as productive as we're going to get today," Moyra said, and Aisling didn't miss the way her fingers had laced into Gatty's fur.

Aisling nodded. "This is where we stand then: Eaon will contact Sar Vin and ensure we can send a sizable force to the pass. Dominic and Fior, bring as many as you can, and we will integrate your fighters into the army before deploying west. You may also lay traps in the kill box—I will send you a map of the area to cover. The Wyldeden witches will raise wards north and south to funnel those who escape the pass into something we can manage, and they will also ward the city walls. Gatty may recruit fae, but as I said, each one of them is to make me a promise before I will allow them near my forces."

It seemed like so little had been decided in what had been one of the longest meetings of her life, but each of the remaining representatives nodded before disbanding.

Edwina and Radley were quick to storm from the room, and Aisling swallowed the urge to call them back. To apologize.

They wouldn't want to hear it.

Not even Eavha stayed.

CHAPTER TWENTY-FOUR

EAVHA

GOSSIP WAS BARBED AS IMSA'S ATTENDEES LEFT THE COUNCIL ROOM, THE other witches' stares a brand on her back. Fighting with Eaon was always unpleasant, but doing so in public, at a time like this, with her crown still fresh, was a particular shame she didn't have time for. They didn't understand what behavior like this from Eaon meant. They didn't grow up with him, composed and studious, his quiet but unshakable foundation the only thing she'd had to stand on when everything seemed to be falling apart. She could count on one hand the times she'd witnessed one of his meltdowns, though he undoubtedly had more of them in private.

He wouldn't do this. He wouldn't be like this. They didn't see the way he was unraveling.

"Eaon," Eavha called, chasing the phouka down a hallway, still with a thrashing Eaon tossed over his shoulder.

The dark fae slowed, glancing back with silent command. Be it an intrinsic fear that slowed her own feet or some actual power from the fae, Eavha couldn't be sure and didn't particularly want to know. She stopped a few feet from where the phouka put Eaon down, pinning him to the wall with one muscled forearm.

"*Calm down.*"

This time there was definitely magic lacing the words. Eavha felt it crawling against her skin, her stomach curdling. The command's impact on her brother was instantaneous—shoulders falling from his ears, fists releasing. Ire still flickered like candlelight behind the gold of his eyes, but his breaths came deeper, slower.

Stepping back, the phouka let his arm drop but kept his gaze trained, even as he spoke to Eavha. "Say your piece, little one."

Without knowing how long this false calm would last, Eavha chose her words quickly. "We are all going to have to figure out a way to work together. Cinn will follow you to the end of the world, and if you insist on involving yourself then he is eventually going to come into contact with Aisling. I need to know that, when that happens, you'll stop him from trying to kill her again. I need to know that you can see the bigger picture here, Eaon."

"I don't know how you can stand her."

"You don't know her."

"Apparently I barely know you." Eaon whirled around, calm decimated, the phouka's grip on his bicep the only thing keeping him from either losing balance or throttling her. "I know your selfishness runs bone fucking deep, but Lover be damned Eavha, do you have any idea what she did to him?"

The details of what occurred between Aisling and Cinn in the dungeon below the palace had not been shared with her, but Eavha had seen the aftermath. Silent and crippled with anxiety, she had seen the way Cinn was terrified of his own continued existence.

Nobody else seemed to care that Aisling had also hurt herself in the process. It tore Eavha's chest apart—lungs collapsing, heart shuddering— to even think words in defense of such cruelty, and she couldn't blame Cinn for retaliating with such hateful violence; but they didn't know Aisling the way she did.

And in the end, it didn't matter.

It didn't matter that nobody understood Aisling's pain. It didn't matter that every second Cinn spent in the city was a liability to everybody's well-being. Couldn't they see? Surely Eaon could.

"If the world ends," she said softly, "does any of it even matter?"

Gooseflesh prickled her bare arms as the temperature plummeted.

"You're disgusting. You deserve each other."

Failing to pull his arm out of the phouka's grip, Eaon turned and shoved at the giant fae creature instead, urging him to move.

"Where are you going?" Eavha called. "You promised to help with the letters."

"If I go back in that room right now, I will kill you and her and everyone else in this fucking palace."

It wasn't a threat, but a promise.

For a split second, Eavha nearly fled the hall, racing all the way to the very top of Aisling's tower where four vials of unicorn blood waited to be used. There would be significantly less sources of stress in Eavha's life if she used one to turn Aisling into a kinner. Her Blessing Charm might be tattered, but she had Sanni now. She could do it.

Would do it.

The hall blurred, but the tears welling quick and heavy were armed with anger. It seeped into her fists, curling tight, and into her words as she spat, "And you have the nerve to call *me* selfish."

Eaon gave up arguing with the immovable wall that was the phouka's chest and spun back to point a finger in Eavha's face.

"You *are*."

"And you're—" Cutting herself short, she pressed her lips together and seethed at the floor. She knew how deep the weapons in her arsenal would cut—words like *useless*, and *deadweight*—and though once upon a time she wouldn't have held back, she was a better person now. She wanted to be better.

But Eaon knew what she'd been about to say. She couldn't see his face as she aimed all her bitterness at the dark stone beneath her feet, but she felt the weight of his stare. Felt the tension between them wrought so tight that one wrong step could irrevocably snap any and all familial affection. Fighting like this wasn't new, but they weren't the same people they'd been growing up. She didn't know if she could count on Eaon's forgiveness anymore should she overstep. Didn't know if she had the time or energy to forgive him if he did either.

"Say it."

Shaking with effort, she forced a different word through her clenched teeth.

"Petty."

"Nice save."

"Cut the shit, Eaon." It was almost a plead. "Your temper tantrums are embarrassing, and nobody has time. You don't get a free pass just because you're mad at Da."

"And you don't get one for being heir. You can wear whatever crown you want, have any title you please, but you're still just a stupid, bratty, selfish child who needs to grow the fuck up."

"You are a hypocrite."

"And you are the bane of my existence."

"I hate you."

"I don't care."

"I have been busting my ass trying to keep you—"

"I don't remember once asking you to! I don't remember once asking you for anything!"

It was a spear through her chest to watch the Lover's seed take over. Skin ashing, eyes darkening, her brother was *gone*. His head tilted dangerously and Eavha's stomach turned at the prickle of deathly cold magic in the air.

Stepping back, her knee buckled.

The phouka wrapped an arm around Eaon's throat and hauled him back, his other arm pinning him tightly against his chest, but that empty gaze was locked on Eavha. Hungry.

The fae's sharp, twisting horns were both a barrier and a threat as he lowered his face to Eaon's ear, muttering softly. Seeing her brother trapped in the hold of the phouka, of an Old One, had her pulse fluttering sickeningly, and Eavha had to actively remind herself that it was safe. That the creature had and would continue to allow her to cause it pain to aid Eaon's recovery.

Whatever was said had Eaon's nostrils flaring, his body giving a single jerk in an attempt to pull away, but it also had him breathing for the first time since losing control. Color warmed his face one more, and between one blink and the next, his eyes returned to their familiar shade. Pain also returned, his legs shaking, buckling, until the phouka's grip was the only thing keeping him upright.

Eavha and Eaon took matching, shuddering breaths, but while she couldn't pull her gaze away, drinking up the promise that was his sun kissed tan, Eaon averted his eyes.

"Sorry."

Wiping her face with the heel of her palm, Eavha nodded. "It's alright."

"It's not." Hands curling and uncurling, eyes squeezing shut, he took a measured breath that still hitched in his chest. "I can hate her without taking it out on you. I can."

It was frightening to witness the sudden drop. As quick as his temper flared, he plummeted into the kind of emptiness she had too often seen in their youth. The frenzies and fatigues hadn't been this severe in a long time and though she was right—nobody had time for either end of the pendulum—it wasn't exactly something her brother could control. He was trying. She could see the male she'd known her whole life clambering to shove his wild moods down with nothing but too weak tonics and strength of will.

"We are returning to the infirmary. Now." The phouka allowed no argument, loosening his grip on Eaon enough to pick him up. "I hope you've both gotten it out of your system, because I will not allow this again."

Eavha blinked at such a parental warning, swallowing down a sarcastic retort that would undoubtedly get her killed. Instead, as they retreated farther down the hall, she called, "I'll meet you down there when I can. We'll try the conduit healing again."

"Whatever," Eaon called back.

"And I'll tell Aisling you'll meet her at sundown to help with the letters?"

Eaon's voice was barely audible, his apathy a final slap.

"Tell her whatever you want."

In the council room, Aisling stood at the window looking over the palace grounds with her forehead pressed to the glass. Only Clayton remained, but as Eavha stepped silently into the room, he moved to guard them from the hall. As lost in thought as she was, Aisling didn't notice Eavha's approach until she touched her elbow.

Flinching back, she hissed, "Eavha. Don't do that."

"Sorry. Are you alright?"

Turning to lean against the glass, Aisling shut her eyes. Strands of her slate gray hair had slipped loose of their pins, dark with sweat against her nape. "Things could have gone worse. They could have gone better. I shouldn't have brought up the Kinner."

"No," Eavha agreed, though things had been going pear shaped well before then. "I spoke to Eaon, though. I told him to come back at sundown to write the letter with you."

Tension turned Aisling's shoulders to granite as she stared at the opposite wall, the rise and fall of her chest slow and controlled. "I know he is your brother and, if we can find a way to work together, an invaluable ally, but Lover take me Eavha, I don't know how many more conversations I can tolerate having with him."

Chin down, Eavha swallowed the laughter that had absolutely no business rearing. "Someone tried to assassinate you the other day, but my brother giving you a hard time is the straw to break your back?"

Aisling finally turned to her, sporting a withering glare. "A hard time?"

Eavha shrugged, the tight purse of her suppressed smile drooping. "Yeah, actually, I take that back. In the hall, he threatened to kill you. Which leads me to the reason I came back to speak to you."

"I'd hoped you'd know you don't need a reason to keep me company. But go ahead."

Stepping closer, Eavha reached for the sleeve of Aisling's dress, rubbing the fabric between her fingers. Warm. Soft. "I want to use one of the vials of unicorn blood. I want you to wear The Healing Mark of One Unending."

The full-body shudder than ran through Aisling only drew Eavha closer, touch falling from Aisling's sleeve to her hand, fingers lacing.

"I have no right to wear that mark."

Tone flat but grip white-knuckled—Eavha recognized what fear looked like on the new Sparrow queen. They didn't have time for it.

"You had no right to do a lot of things, but you did them anyway. You will do this too. For me."

Aisling managed a smile, gentle and sad. "Is that an order from the heir apparent of Wyldeden?"

She could reply with the punchline—*Will making it so encourage obedience?*—but it wasn't a joke to Eavha. "I can't lose you too."

Cupping her face, so carefully it was hard to remember that she had killed a man a couple of days ago, Aisling ran her thumbs along the tired shadows beneath Eavha's eyes. "Alright. For you. But in the morning. I have things that need to be put in motion immediately, and you need rest."

"We should do it now, before you see Eaon again. I don't . . . It's not that I don't trust him, but he has no control. He is falling apart."

"People have always wanted me dead, and yet here I stand. Half a day won't change that, but if you burn yourself out trying to save me I will never forgive you. I can handle Eaon."

"I am not going to burn out," Eavha promised. Should she tell Aisling about her bargain with Sanni? Though that would only expose the fact that the bargain did not include protection against her own overuse of magic. But she had been pushing herself to do things she shouldn't be able to do without a decent Blessing Charm for days, yet she remained unaffected.

"Correct," Aisling agreed. "Because you are going to wait until morning."

The argument sitting on Eavha's lips disappeared as Aisling pressed her own against them. It was a chaste thing, but Eavha's face bloomed pink regardless.

"Alright. Morning."

Aisling smirked. "Finally. I have found the secret of getting you to behave."

Scrunching her nose, Eavha chose not to respond except to lean in for another kiss.

CHAPTER TWENTY-FIVE

CINN

HE HADN'T BEEN ABLE TO GO TO THE FUNERAL, NOR COULD HE GO TO Imsa. Not if . . . Not if *Aisling* was going to be there. The towering palace walls remembered his broken screams, and with Siobhan busy, with Moyra busy, with Edwina working and Radley once more at her side, Cinn was afraid if he went to back alone, its dark granite walls would echo the sound for him.

At least sitting outside in the Turlough's garden with Sarah and William, he could forget where he was. The picnic rug was anchored with teapots and jugs of lemonade, plates of biscuits and sandwiches; with nothing else to do, the Copelands had taken to feeding every witch they saw. Fresh fruit grew out of season on the kumquat and apple trees, a full selection of strawberries and tomatoes, cucumbers and pumpkin sprouting lushly. The sweet fragrance forced out the drifting smoke, and Cinn took deep, settling breaths as he watched Puddles pounce through the daisies and dandelions, chasing fat bumblebees.

A small smile begged to be set free on Cinn's face. The sight of the fluffy, white-topped weed reminded him of Dida, back at the shack in Qiri. Something so frail had no business being as fierce as that dandelion sprite, but at least Dida had Nena to keep an eye out. And the two of them would look after Lula.

Sighing, Cinn wished he had his pack. His treasure box, where the shell the sweet mushroom sprite had given him was hopefully intact. Maybe when this was over, he could go back. Take Eaon and live quietly for a while, away from people and trouble.

A Wyldeden witch sat cross-legged by a stone birdbath, running a gentle finger along a finch's dusty feathers, helping it clean itself, while two witchlings barely old enough to stay on their feet rolled across the lawn, racing each other to the backdoor.

It didn't seem real, this peace. It shouldn't exist in a city so stained with his pain, in a time where the sky was still hazed in orange.

"Oh, look at that," Sarah said, awed.

A flickering shadow fell over the yard and Cinn followed Sarah's pointed finger straight up to where a cloud of leaves spun through the air, carried on the breeze. With impossible intent, individual ones separated from the flurry, one twirling down to land on the lap of the witch by the birdbath. She brought it delicately to her ear, standing with a grace utterly inhuman.

All across the city, leaves were falling. Whispering. Within minutes, the streets were filled with witches moving with purpose, the air static with urgency.

"What's going on?" William tried to ask as the one who'd been with them hurried for the backdoor.

She slowed enough to shake her head, not understanding. Pointing at them, then to her eyes, she looked to the two children still giggling on the lawn.

"We'll watch them," Sarah said, nodding and smiling.

Assuming the Nirnish words were agreement, the witch left.

"It can't be too serious, or someone would have come to tell us, too," William assured them.

A small, throat-clearing cough startled Cinn, and he spun to witness Gatty's emergence from beneath an apple tree. Tilting his head, the cat sith watched Puddles catch a bee and let it go, just to start chasing it again.

"This must be the famous Puddles. What a stupid creature."

William heaved a sigh. "Nope. Never going to get used to that. *Talking cats.*"

Sauntering over, swishing his tail, the cat sith grinned at the Copelands, wide and toothy. "Hello humans. I see tea is served. Is there perhaps any honey about?"

"Yes, of course," Sarah said, hands shaking slightly as she made to pass the pot.

Cinn snatched it, glaring at Gatty. *What's going on?*

"Nothing that concerns you," Gatty assured, eyes focused on the jar in his hands.

The farm cat noticed the faerie for the first time, coming to a complete still. Ears flat, she slunk low to the ground and let out a low, threatening hiss.

Gatty spared Puddles a glance and chuckled. "Oh, I admire the audacity. Should I demonstrate who the superior feline in this yard is, or can you control your animal?"

Leave her alone, Cinn warned. *She just doesn't like you. Understandably. Now, are you going to tell me what's going on with all these leaves?*

"I don't see why I should," Gatty sniped, thumping his tail. "It's nothing to do with you."

Glaring, twisting on the picnic blanket to put himself between the cat sith and the Copelands, Cinn grabbed a spoon, opened the honey jar, and slowly pulled out a large scoop.

He had Gatty's undivided attention.

Mottled green-blue held buttercup yellow in unwavering eye contact as Cinn lifted the spoonful of honey to his own mouth and ate.

Gatty hissed.

"Cinn!" William chastised. "Don't piss off the faerie *on purpose!*"

"Lover have mercy," Sarah muttered, hands over her eyes.

Cinn's teeth would never recover from the sticky sweetness gluing his lips together, but he refused to look away as he dug out another spoonful.

"I will kill you," Gatty growled, thumping his tail. "I will find a way."

Cinn smirked and pried his mouth open, spoon dripping amber goop down his fingers.

"The leaves are orders from Eavha and the Wyldeden elders. Some to start training with the Hyrschan soldiers, some to report to the city walls to cast spellmarks in preparation for battle. The young ones will be evacuated with the magic-poor witches once Aisling has arranged transport to Pirevia. Now, you horrid thing, give me that honey."

Smug, Cinn put the jar down in front of the cat sith and grabbed a napkin to clean his hands. He'd be sucking honey off his teeth for hours, but it had been worth it.

Dipping his paw in the jar, Gatty settled on the picnic rug and began licking himself. Still unsettled, Puddles crept across the lawn to crawl into Sarah's lap, her low growl constant.

"Are . . . I mean, should we be getting ready to go to Pirevia?" Sarah asked her husband, stroking the cat soothingly. "I don't know that I want to go there."

"No." William shook his head.

Shoulders tensing, Cinn turned to face his family properly. {You can't stay here.}

"Listen," William said, hands out. "I've been thinking about this. I'm no soldier, and the last time we had to deal with a beast was that shtryg that broke into our house and nearly killed Sarah. So, no, we shouldn't stay here. But I don't think we should be going to Pirevia either. There are a lot of demi-kin we helped smuggle into this city that I can guarantee would rather die than go back, and they're going to need somewhere to go."

"Mm," Gatty hummed, licking his chops. "Aisling thought of that already. They're being distributed to the eastern townships instead. The lords have been instructed to treat them well."

Cinn shuddered at the sound of her name, blinking rapidly until he could focus on the look William and Sarah were exchanging.

"Lord Dustin is useless. He won't enforce that," Sarah said.

"No, he won't," William agreed. Another moment of silent communication between the two farmers. Then he turned to Cinn. "We're going to go home. To Belden. Keep as many demi-kin at the farm as we can fit, and talk sense to our neighbors until they do the same. It's the best we can do."

Belden was a few days' walk from Hyrsch, less by carriage and even less on horseback. It was too close. If things went wrong and the city was lost . . . It was well warded. Eaon had made sure. The Sparrows who'd come hunting for him back at the start of this cursed summer had not been able to get through.

Fists pressed into his thighs to hide their shaking, Cinn nodded.

"You can have your old room back." Sarah smiled. "Free up the cottage—"

She cut herself off when she noted the way Cinn's shoulders dropped.

"You . . . You're not staying, are you?" she asked in disbelief, eyes widening. Hand frozen on Puddles, her other gripped William's sleeve. "You're coming home with us, aren't you?"

Forcing his fingers to relax, Cinn signed the only explanation he had.

{Eaon's staying.}

He had never seen a heart break into quite so many pieces. The impulse to rip out his own to replace it was so strong that only William's hand in his left, Sarah's in his right, prevented him.

"I don't want this for you," William said. "Maybe if we speak to Eaon, he will come home with us too."

Cinn shook his head. Took back his hands.

{He won't go. And I won't leave him. But I will live, and I will come back to you when this is done.}

Eaon was a better person than Cinn was, and if the best he could offer was this—support, protection, loyalty—then it was simply returning in kind the gifts Eaon had given him.

"As revoltingly touching as all of this has been," Gatty droned, knocking over the empty honey jar. "I did actually intrude for a reason."

For a couple of humans who had such a pervasive fear of fae that they salted a line of earth around their farm, the Copelands managed a look of such profound annoyance that Cinn almost laughed.

"There is something you should see, kinner. Will you follow me?"

There was nothing he wanted to do less.

The cat sith grinned. Seeing it, Puddles hissed and swatted a paw in his direction, though she didn't leave the safety of Sarah's lap to do so. Amusement flashed across Gatty's face before his ears flattened too, eyes growing larger, pupils dilating until they swallowed the yellow. His mouth opened too wide, jaw unhinged and dropping low until Cinn thought his entire head could fit inside the cat sith's maw. Exposing long, needle sharp fangs, Gatty hissed.

This was the creature who'd followed Cinn into the lake by Moyra's cabin and tore a selkie to shreds. Who frightened the rest of the wild fae in that marsh so much that they left Moyra alone—with a few exceptions, of course.

No longer satisfied with the safety of Sarah's lap, Puddles fled to the house. William extended a protective arm in front of Sarah, his other reaching for Cinn, but the kinner shook his head and scowled.

{It's going to take days for Puddles to trust me again.}

Gatty's grin returned to its usual size, his eyes a bored buttercup once more. "Yes, well, that is not my problem. I asked you a question."

{Why would I go anywhere with you?}

"Because your chosen siblings will be there, and I have an inkling they'd like to see you after the fiasco that was Imsa."

His heart stuttered, and Gatty heard it, swishing his tail once in smug victory.

"I should stay to keep an eye on the little ones, but William will go with you—" Sarah began, but Cinn shook his head again. Whatever bullshit the cat sith was about to pull, he didn't want the Copelands anywhere near it.

{I'll be back before dark,} he promised, leaning over to kiss them both on the cheek.

CHAPTER TWENTY-SIX

CINN

IT WAS EASIER TO BE ANGRY THAN IT WAS TO BE AFRAID AS CINN stepped through the city's western gate and took in the open plain. The land between Hyrsch and the Southern Spine undulated with hills, marshes and small villages nestled in the shallow valleys, none of which Cinn could see from the crest bearing the weight of the iron barred gate.

There was no freedom in leaving the city's confines.

Uniformed soldiers stood alongside cadets, practicing drills. Their style was organized and precise, taught by Sparrow leaders in preparation for battles against other Sparrows or demi-kin rebellions. The youngest cadets were distracted by the Wyldeden guardians gathered nearby, testing the weight of their new silver-tipped spears. The guardians' movements were foreign, unpredictable and efficient, each one brimming with strength and power. It would have been more frightening had Cinn not known that most guardians had never left the Boab, and even fewer had experience fighting anything besides each other.

Civilian volunteers observed from the outskirts, some of them picking up weapons for the very first time, laughing at their own awkwardness. Scattered among them were rebels. Cinn only knew because he spotted Siobhan loitering at the edge of the crowd. Plus, Gatty had said Rad and Eddy would be here.

Time was a malleable thing. With every footstep, Cinn was both present and not. He was here, now, twenty years old and preparing for a fight he wanted no part in, but he was also seventeen, racing across the training ground as fast as his legs could carry him to avoid being any later than he already was.

Commander Porter paced in front of a group of cadets, barking criticisms: *"The beasts on their way will not spare you because you're inexperienced. Keep your guard up on the left, Raven."*

Yes, it was easier to be angry.

Cinn remembered Porter the way he remembered everything else from *before*—murky, like an abandoned anchor at the bottom of the sea, left so long that algae disguised its sharp edges. For a time, remembering the commander's frantic attempts to save Ryson's life as he lay bleeding on the field with a bolt in his throat had been comforting. Someone knew where he was meant to have gone. Someone would come looking.

Nobody had.

Stalking down the hill with his fists clenched tight, Cinn gave his head a small, sharp shake. That wasn't true. Edwina had come looking, and Radley *"wrung every bit of information I could out of anyone who worked there."* His brother knew who Ryson's commanding officer was, which only left one conclusion to draw: Porter had lied. For whatever reason, Porter had looked Radley in the eye and denied knowing anything. Convinced all his peers to do the same.

As he hit the flat valley, someone pointed at him.

Commander Porter turned. Stilled.

Why would you bring me here? Cinn thought at Gatty, stride quickening.

"Thought you could use the exercise," Gatty teased.

Resisting the urge to kick the cat sith all the way across the Dividing River, Cinn came to a halt two feet in front of his old commander.

Time had put lines around his eyes, his mouth, and though Cinn hadn't grown much in that small hole in the floor, the last ten months of freedom saw him standing eye to eye with the paling human man. Cinn had more freckles than he used to, and there was a vacancy in his eyes that his younger self had burned too brightly to host, yet Porter recognized him anyway. He looked at Cinn with all the haunted acceptance one might show an early death.

"Have you come to kill me?"

Violent, scathing words sat heavy on Cinn's tongue, but his throat was far too tight to allow them. He could not speak in this place. Right then, he wasn't sure he'd ever find the strength to speak again. It didn't matter that no harm could come if he accidently confessed the secrets he had so painstakingly protected—the Kinner were gone; she could not have them, could not torment them any further, could not unleash them on an unprepared world. To speak now bore no consequences, and yet, he couldn't do it.

Nails carving holes into his palms, his fists shook at his sides.

In his periphery, the cadets had stilled, muttering among themselves. A handful of soldiers were inching closer.

Cinn hated them all. It made perfect sense that the people who'd left him to rot in the bowels of the dungeon were now learning to work side by side with Wyldeden guardians, many of who had undoubtedly been cruel to Eaon at some point. With beautiful clarity, he imagined them all on the battlefield, disemboweled by lupani or bleeding from open shtryg wounds. Impaled on the end of a beetle-monster's long pincer and choking on their own bile.

For a moment, he reveled in the idea of them losing. Of the palace falling. The city in ruins.

"Actually," Gatty purred from his spot at Cinn's feet, "I brought him here to train with you. The kinner boy has invaluable experience with actual beasts that he wishes to share—for the sake of the family he still has living in this city. Especially the ones who will stay to defend it."

Cinn scowled at the cat sith. *I'm going to skin you and turn you into a hat.*

Eaon wouldn't walk away from this fight and Moyra wouldn't leave Eaon. Which meant Cinn was staying. And since Eddy and Rad had sworn to never leave him again, he supposed they would also be here when everything went to shit.

Gatty knew all that, and he was using it to fashion a noose around Cinn's neck.

"You . . ." Commander Porter took a moment to adjust to the talking cat at their feet before lifting his head to meet Cinn's glare. "You want to train?"

"Need help, Commander?" a soldier asked, close enough that, if he drew the sword his hand was so tightly wrapped around, Cinn was within striking range.

A body appeared between the soldier and Cinn.

"Back off," Radley growled. At his side, Siobhan arrived, dagger ready.

Cinn's heart beat madly as he grabbed hold of the back of Radley's shirt. He didn't want his very killable brother standing between him and a weapon.

If Radley felt Cinn tugging, he ignored it.

Between one breath and the next, Cinn's sudden frantic energy sharpened, the rest of the field falling away. Air filled his lungs deeper and cleaner than ever before, the magic that kept him alive a thundering promise.

It was newly familiar, this killing calm.

Knocking Radley's hand off the sword at his hip, Cinn pulled it right off his belt, drawing the blade and throwing the scabbard into the dry grass. He was no better trained than the cadets now stumbling back, and on a normal day, he would stand zero chance against the soldiers drawing their own weapons. A ring formed around the four of them—Cinn, Radley, Siobhan and Porter—half ready to help their commander and half anticipating either slaughter or a mildly interesting fight.

Radley turned to him, eyes wide. "Ry."

Ryson wasn't there. Ryson was deep underground, cold and undying.

Cinn was curled away in front of some mental fireplace, soaking up the smell of baking biscuits.

In Qiri, he may have begun consolidating all the different parts of himself, but the glue he used couldn't hold up under this kind of threat. No, the boy holding Radley's sword was something else. He was the feral thing his mother had raised. He was the product of a people who had suffered for centuries.

He was unfathomable rage.

He was kinner, and he turned to point his sword at Commander Porter.

"Son, think about what you're doing," Porter pleaded, drawing his own weapon. "I don't want to have to hurt you."

"Lay a fucking finger on him and I'll fucking kill you," Radley spat, trying to move between them.

Gatty pushed against Radley's leg, calm and self-assured. "He needs this."

"No, he doesn't," Siobhan argued.

Ignoring her, the cat sith looked over his shoulder, words heavy with demand. "Spar with him, Commander Porter. Witness for yourself what he has to offer."

Memories of his torn and burning flesh as he'd fought the beasts in Dusarn were dull, but he knew he'd survived that encounter through sheer force of will. There had been no skill then, and there would be little to demonstrate now as the kinner lunged forward.

Porter blocked easily, stepping back to give himself room, grating his blade against the kinner's as he pulled it free—

And then everything went red.

His movements were fast and hard, his swings wild, and at some point a searing hot pain slashed across the back of his thigh. It didn't stop him. The vague shape of his commander lost ground under the ferocity of the kinner's assault.

Another slice across his chest. It meant nothing.

A blow snapped the bone in his wrist and he lost the sword for a moment, but the itch in his arm was immediate, as was the way the kinner threw himself weaponless at the soldier. Someone was screaming as a blade pushed through his gut, but he ignored it, wrapping hands around the commander's throat.

Hands on his shoulders, on his legs, pulling desperately. He held on as long as he could, but soon found himself rolling in the grass, itching, itching, itching, scrambling for the hilt of the sword laying bloody in the grass.

Faces above him. He slashed, grinding his teeth against the weight of the steel, trying to get to his feet as soldiers surrounded him. Their mouths were moving, but he could only hear his pulse. Breath sawed, unneeded. Someone moved, and Cinn tightened his two-handed grip, swinging wide.

He had killed soldiers in Pirevia, when Kaelean had first betrayed him. Unbidden, the images came back crystal clear. The dry grass underfoot sprouted tall heather, his opponents' black-and-red uniforms shifting to gold-and-blue.

Steel pierced through his back, cutting right through his lung.

The force of the blow sent him to his hands and knees, but once steady, he threw his weight back, spearing himself deeper until the hilt was against his ribs and the soldier holding it was stumbling back.

Dark spots danced in his red vision. If he couldn't get the blade out of his chest, he'd just have to use it. Weightless, he rushed the nearest soldier, who flinched back, raising their own weapon only just in time to keep from being impaled. Their block sent the protruding sword carving sideways through his chest, and the pain was too much. He fell. There was a body underneath him.

Noise. Shouting he had no chance of understanding. Someone grabbed the hilt in his back and yanked the blade out, eliciting an itch so terrible he blacked out for a second.

Only a second.

Then he was rolling, moving. People were pulling away the soldier he'd hurt, but others were after him, trying to pin him down. Boots found knees, fists into throats, teeth tearing through ears until he got his hand on someone's dagger and ripped it right out of their hand. Only afterward did he realize it had been held to his jugular.

The dull demands for him to *stop* rang hollow.

Blood on his teeth, he spat into a looming face, bucking against the weight pinning him. So many hands pushing down, so many voices using up all the air.

It was rage that tore a scream from his throat as he thrashed on the ground, sticking anything he could reach with the point of his newfound dagger.

He would not go back.

He would *not* go back.

When Eaon found out they had him, they were all dead.

The name was a bubble of clarity in the violent torrent of his mind. A bubble that made space for one of the voices nearby to ring clearly.

"Get off him! Get the fuck off him!"

Not Eaon.

Radley.

His brother had found him. His brother was here.

His brother . . . was here.

No.

His fingernails caught on something, and he pulled. Blood warmed his palm, then the knuckles of his other hand as he plunged the knife into a body. Catching an ankle with the toe of his boot, he yanked them off balance, then kicked out at another, bone crunching on contact.

Then air. There was air, and there was nobody touching him, and Cinn rolled to his knees. The only person within striking range had their back to him, arms spread wide. Shielding.

But the soldiers had backed off on their own, assessing each other, themselves, for wounds, not quite putting their weapons away.

Gatty snaked between their legs, coming to sit beside Radley, who was sinking to his own knees. Risking a look back at Cinn, Radley's face was a mirror. Rage and fear and murder.

"Get him out of here." Voice rasping, Commander Porter limped forward. "I don't want him anywhere near my cadets."

"Have you ever seen a lupanis in the flesh, Commander?" Gatty purred, moon-bright eyes narrow. "Nine hundred pounds of muscle and teeth. Quick as a horse. Claws that cut through stone like butter. You think it will slow its rampage to parry your blade? It will not. If you knock it down, it will get back up. If you spear through it, you'd best hope it's a lethal blow, or you will only enrage it."

"What is your point?" Porter growled.

"The kinner has killed lupanis. He has killed shtryg. And while what you will face here on this field in a little over a week is not as impossible to kill as him, they will be just as vicious. Just as difficult. You are not ready, and there is much the boy could learn too. Teach each other."

Porter shook his head. "If he cannot follow a command to stop, then he cannot train with us. He endangered—"

Gatty snorted. "What part of this war do you think will not endanger your troops? Ignorance will not save them."

"We will not have any troops left at this rate."

"Nobody died."

"Six of my men are so wounded they've been taken to the infirmary!"

"And if Cinn was a lupanis, they would be dead."

It wasn't necessary to be a lupanis; if they hadn't stopped when they had, Cinn wouldn't need claws and teeth to kill them. But, through the ebbing haze, Cinn knew Gatty had a point. It took everything he had to fight those beasts. The soldiers may take a few down, but they'd eventually buckle. The cadets wouldn't stand a chance. The Wyldeden guardians were brutal, but most had never had to be truly violent before. And the civilians . . .

Sucking blood off his teeth, Cinn took slow, measured breaths. So much of his body was itching, but with every sip of oxygen he dragged in, the pain in his chest eased. He had gotten lost. The dreamscape had taken over his waking mind again and he had taken this too far. Gatty was right, but so was Porter.

Hand shaking, he tugged on Radley's shirt. Signed something he knew his brother wouldn't understand.

"Hey, cat," Radley hissed. "What's he saying?"

Gatty turned his moon-bright eyes on Cinn and waited. Read the thoughts right out of his head and nodded.

"If there was someone who could reach him if he loses his mind like that again, would you be more willing to cooperate?"

Looking past Gatty, past Radley, Porter met Cinn's gaze. Even through the pain and fear, there was regret weighing him down.

"You're telling me someone can control that?"

"*That* is my brother, you lying piece of shit," Radley spat. "The one you said you'd never heard of? Bet you won't be forgetting him now."

Cinn tugged on Radley's shirt again. He was ready to leave. Yes, he wanted to help, to learn, but not today. He wanted to speak to Moyra beforehand. Wanted to make sure that when he did, he wouldn't hurt anyone. Because the couple of weeks spent in Qiri, living in a shack by the lake with Moyra, far away from everyone and everything, had been a promise that, one day, he could heal—but that day wasn't this one. Wasn't one Cinn would see until he was far, far away from this city.

"Nobody controls a kinner," Gatty said, cold. "But take some time. Consider what just happened. I will know when you're ready to accept my offer."

Manipulative, horrid creature.

His offer involved volunteering Cinn and Moyra without having asked either of them, as if they were both pawns in whatever game the cat sith was playing. Worse was that Cinn already knew he would come back to the training fields if Moyra agreed. It was what Eaon would do.

Carefully, Radley helped Cinn to his feet. The gaping holes in his shirt exposed the bleeding flesh slowly knitting itself back together, and Radley couldn't pull his gaze away. One arm around his waist to keep him upright, he pressed his free hand to the weeping wound across Cinn's bare stomach.

"Don't ever do that again," Radley hissed quietly, both voice and hands shaking as they turned back toward the city.

Not knowing how else to comfort his brother, Cinn put his forehead against his shoulder and let him take his weight.

They made it through the western gate before the only other person Cinn could stand to be around right now came running down the main road toward them. Clutching her left wrist, Edwina was red faced and sweaty, running in a dress far too nice.

"What's wrong? What happened? Is that *blood?*"

"I thought you were at the palace," Radley grunted as Edwina slammed into them, patting them both down with frantic hands.

"I was between there and a meeting with the rebels. *What happened?*"

Cinn frowned, looking between them, taking Edwina's hand to assure her that he was alright. How could she know that anything was wrong at all?

Then he saw it. Dangling from her left wrist, the old charm bracelet she and Radley had been gifted when they were children, before Cinn had come into the picture. The ones made by a witch. The one that had alerted Edwina, back when they'd all been owned by Master Ackford, that something was terribly wrong with Radley. The one that had led them to the alley out back, where strange men were trying to take their brother, like so many other demi-kin who had been taken, organs cut out and traded on the black market.

211

Pulling at Radley's sleeve, Cinn touched the matching bracelet there, thread worn thin. Down in that cell, he had both wished for a matching one so that someone might find him, and been so thoroughly grateful that his family had no inkling of just how much he suffered. To this day, he had not settled on a side.

Pulling them close, an arm around each of them, he took a long, deep breath. Took a second. Opened his mouth. Closed it, wetting his tongue. Swallowed, and opened his mouth again.

Quiet. So quiet.

"I'm okay."

The immediate swell of panic and nausea that threatened to buckle his knees was only mitigated by the awful sob that cracked through Edwina. Was it wrong that his pain was eased by the presence of hers? Or was it just comforting to know it wasn't his alone to bear? Radley's grip tightened around the both of them, keeping them standing, though as his head came down to rest on Cinn's, the hitch in his warm breath exposed his hurting too.

They stood like that until Gatty caught up with them, winding between Cinn's feet. Glaring down at the cat sith, Cinn let go of his family and directed a loud thought toward the awful creature.

A heads-up would have been nice.

"You would not have come if I told you what I wanted you to do."

Radley quietly filled Edwina in on what had transpired out on the flat, but since Cinn was looking down at their feet, he didn't miss the way his brother tried and failed to step on Gatty's tail.

Don't you have better things to do than bully me into training?

"Yes, but this needed to be done. Consider it revenge for your stunt with the honey earlier."

Cinn huffed, straightening as they rejoined the throngs of people carting supplies through the city streets. Everyone seemed to have something to do, but that didn't keep them from staring openly at his bloodied clothes.

I hate you.

Gatty peered up, falsely innocent, and smirked. "Your mortal lies do not wound me, boy. I'll find you later."

With that, the cat sith melted into the nearest shadow.

"You have the worst friends," Radley grumbled.

Cinn wrinkled his nose, leaning on his brother all the way back home.

CHAPTER TWENTY-SEVEN

EAVHA

EAVHA NEVER DID MAKE IT DOWN TO THE INFIRMARY, THE HOURS LOST to the demands of the elders, and she doubted the broken promise was going to do much to bolster the fragile state of her and Eaon's relationship. Though, there was some comfort to be had knowing that the phouka didn't deem it a significant enough insult to fetch her. Not much, but some.

She wondered what kind of mood Eaon was going to be in.

A petty one, she thought, as the last of the day's rays dipped beneath the horizon.

The brass chandelier dangling high from the ceiling was already lit, and the glow of the burning forest through the council room's tinted windows bathed them both in a bloody red. They were both too tired for conversation as Eavha and Aisling picked at the dinner Larissa had brought them. The porcelain crockery could have been laden with quail eggs or mashed worms and Eavha wouldn't notice.

"I'll go fetch him," she sighed, pushing her plate away.

"Forget it." Aisling mimicked the motion. "I can write to Sar Vin without him."

Pulling the top piece off a pile of parchment, Aisling readied her quill and loosed a strained sigh. Watching her deliberate over words, careful not to smudge the ink as her hand moved across the page, Eavha folded her arms on the cool marble table and rested her head in their cushion, watching the looping scroll in a trance.

She was so tired. Each blink was heavier than the last.

A knock on the door pulled her from sleep, despite her eyes never having closed. Aisling lifted her chin as Clayton poked his head inside.

"Eaon Nemuse and the Old One are here."

Exhaustion melted away at the spike of adrenaline that ripped through her. Eavha gripped the edge of the table as Clayton stepped inside, allowing her brother through, the phouka inches behind him.

Leaning heavily on his crutches, trying to keep his gait even, Eaon limped all the way to the head of the table and took the seat at Aisling's left. The phouka settled against the wall, arms folded across his broad chest, assessing the arm's length of space between Eaon and Aisling.

Nothing had ever made Eavha as nervous as seeing the two side by side.

"Almost no point taking a seat," Aisling sniped. "I'm nearly done."

With gloved fingers, Eaon snatched the parchment from under her quill.

Eavha bit her lip at the way Aisling stilled, eyes trained on the spot where ink now stained the table. If Eaon noticed her silent rage, he didn't let on, simply scanning the letter quickly and snorting.

"The only thing less effective than a threat is offering to honor your father's deal if he reconsiders your request. Send this, and Sar Vin will deny you until his dying breath."

For a beat, Aisling continued to stare at the table. It took two full minutes before she could meet Eaon's taunting gaze. "That would have been good advice to have had a half hour ago when I started writing the letter. This war won't wait for you to get out of bed."

Eavha pressed her foot down on Aisling's boot. Hard. She didn't want to be caught in the middle. She didn't want to choose sides.

"Give me that." Eaon snatched the quill from her fingers.

At the closeness, Eavha flinched. Gloved or not, that Eaon would even risk contact spoke legions to how little he valued Aisling's life. Waiting until morning to cast The Healing Mark of One Unending was a mistake; she should have insisted on doing it before the two most important people in her life faced each other again.

Tossing the parchment aside, Eaon pulled forward a fresh page and began to write.

Aisling tucked her hands under the table, gripping Eavha's own tight enough to bruise. Face forcefully blank, tone clipped and dry, she ground out, "I can't wait to see what you think is more persuasive than the words of the Sparrow queen."

"See, that's your problem," Eaon said, his own handwriting far less swooping than Aisling's, yet just as elegant. "You think Sar Vin cares that you're queen? He never wanted the rights to the Southern Spine—it makes no difference who owns the land because nobody else knows how to tame it. Nobody else knows how to survive there. He just wanted to take something, because that's what he does. The taking, regardless of what it is, gives him power over you, and that is all Sar Vin has ever cared about. And appealing to some mutual need to protect against Chaos is pointless. He won't believe Chaos is real until the King of Beasts runs him through, and maybe not even then."

Signing his name, Eaon passed the letter back to Aisling. She waited until his hands were back on his side of the table before taking it.

"'Mustavrick. We are sending troops. Please don't kill them. Toad-face knows why, he's just being an ass. Eaon.'" Aisling slapped the parchment back down on the table. "What is this?"

"Give the messenger an hour's head start and tell them to hand that directly to Mustavrick Sar-son. Then send your troops."

"You must be joking."

"Not at all."

The stare down went on so long that Eavha couldn't help her squirming. "Aisling. Eaon knows what he's doing."

Neither said anything, but Aisling narrowed her eyes.

"He traveled to the mountain pass with our da many times," she continued, voice cracking with grief only a little. "He knows them. He knows how to speak to them."

If it was anyone but Eavha asking, Aisling would have bitten her head off. The tension around her eyes was familiar and the words that finally came from her mouth were strained.

"Who, exactly, is Mustavrick Sar-son?"

"A friend."

Aisling sneered. "You would risk the entire war effort on the power of friendship?"

Mimicking her expression, Eaon leaned forward. "I know it's a foreign concept to you, but since you're too busy to torture cooperation out of anyone right now, you might want to branch out."

"Mother above, Eaon," Eavha hissed. "For once, can you just . . . not?"

"I don't know. For once, can you not make moon eyes at people I really wish you wouldn't?"

Eavha's face burned. "You know what? I take it back. You're terrible at talking to people and are an absolute idiot and I regret ever sticking up for you."

"Makes no difference to me. Pretending you give a shit doesn't suit you anyway."

"Oh, go rogue."

Aisling's eyes followed the bickering, a single eyebrow rising higher with every exchange. "How have you two not killed each other?"

"Indoctrinated pacifism," Eaon snapped.

"Extreme willpower," Eavha hissed back.

"Seems healthy."

Whipping his focus from Eavha to Aisling, Eaon bit back. "You have no room to comment. Your brother tried to have you assassinated how many times since you came to Hyrsch?"

Aisling pursed her lips. "Fifteen."

Waving his hand around his head, Eaon scoffed. "I am literally a saint."

"You are literally uninvited from this meeting," Eavha said, pointing at the door.

"Fine by me. I didn't want to be here anyway."

Forgetting how weak his still-healing legs were, Eaon pushed up from the table only to buckle. The phouka was at his side in a heartbeat, getting him propped up on his crutches and keeping a clawed hand clamped on the back of his neck.

"Send the letter, Aisling," Eaon ground out. "And when the pass is open and waiting for you in a few days' time, you can thank me by turning the battlefield into your gravesite. It'll be a more dignified death than the one I'll give you."

From his post by the door, Clayton drew his sword. The moment metal scrapped against scabbard, the phouka's goat-slitted eyes became weapons, pinning the demi-kin guard in place.

"Threats to the queen will not be tolerated," Clayton managed, surprisingly steady.

Eavha could barely breathe as the phouka's face split into a horrible grin, black teeth and fangs glittering under the candlelight. Her heart wasn't going to last through this war if every day was going to be filled with this much homicidal promise. Turning back to Aisling, the phouka tilted his head.

"*Aisling Aurnia, you will not move until I return.*"

"No!" Eavha cried as Aisling's entire body stiffened, eyes stuck half closed in a blink. Climbing out of her seat, Eavha cupped Aisling's face, only slightly relieved that the command hadn't stopped her chest from rising and falling.

Blade fully drawn, Clayton aimed it at the phouka's throat.

"Release her. Now."

"Clayton," Eavha warned, shaking her head. "Don't make it worse. She's alright."

Ignoring the demi-kin entirely, the phouka placed a hand on each of Eaon's shoulders and marched him carefully toward the door. Walking as if the blade meant nothing—and truly, with the shimmering silver mark carved into the back of his neck, it didn't—the phouka only smiled at Clayton again as they passed. Sheer willpower kept Clayton's hand steady, but he did not attack as the fae closed the distance between them.

Eyes wide, pliant under the phouka's grip, Eaon looked back. The concern lining his mouth was the most Eaon-like her brother had looked for a long time, even if that concern wasn't for the only person in actual danger.

The next few hours were some of the slowest of Eavha's life. She sat at Aisling's side, dripping water into her eyes every couple of minutes to keep them from drying out. Doing so without tilting Aisling's head back was difficult—her lap was damp from failed attempts—but trying to move her resulted in a sharp whine forced between closed lips.

It was almost midnight before Aisling blinked. The phouka stood in the doorway, a cruel smirk on his mouth as Aisling sagged forward, resting her head on the table. Eavha made to rub her shoulders, but pulled back when Aisling shrugged her off. Instead, she watched the queen rub the scars on her palms, likely reconsidering Eavha's offer to remove them.

Grinning at Clayton again, the phouka sat at the opposite end of the table and folded his long, muscular legs.

Aisling straightened slowly. Eyes red from strain, she held the phouka's stare.

"What do you want?"

"At Imsa, you agreed with Eaon about taking advantage of the seed. I will not allow it. Try to use him, and I will kill you."

"Yes, I considered it," she admitted. "Briefly. His lack of control quickly changed my mind."

Whatever thought process it took for the phouka to be convinced of her sincerity took far longer than Eavha was comfortable with, but finally, he nodded.

"In the First War," he said, taking the subject in an unexpected direction, "Terra raised the spine and left only one passage through it for the approaching army. She stood there alone, and when the masses reached her, she tore the earth open. She opened the Womb and swallowed them whole. Her power, as was the power of all the Fair Folk who now reign as spirits, is unrivaled, but the idea is still a good one to mimic."

Was that . . . praise? Eavha rubbed her neck, aching at the whiplash. She hated not knowing the mood in the room. Was there going to be a fight? Did she need to be ready to heal? Or was the phouka more civilized than he pretended to be?

Aisling blinked and said nothing.

The phouka crossed his arms. "You remind me of her."

"I'll take that as a compliment," Aisling said.

The phouka nodded. "I fought with the seven Fair Folk during the First War. I fought with the Kinner."

Had another command been made? Eavha couldn't move. Couldn't breathe. Cinn may be second generation, but that wouldn't matter if the phouka was offended by what Aisling had done.

Aisling swallowed deeply, unable to hide her nerves at the enemy she'd likely made of this phouka, too. Clayton's presence was not remotely reassuring.

Lowering his voice, the phouka continued, "I dislike much of what happened today. I dislike what you said about the Kinner. I am, of a sort, one of them."

Eavha trembled with regret. She should have marked her. Should have *insisted*. Aisling was going to die.

"You wanted an army of kinner." The phouka stood. "I cannot offer that. But there are a few of the Old Ones who may be willing to fight again."

For a moment, Eavha didn't understand. When it finally registered that the phouka was not about to kill them, that he was in fact offering *aid* . . .

Eavha's vision was so spotted with panic that she barely saw Aisling nod.

"There will be a cost."

"Yes."

"Name it."

The phouka took a breath, eyes alight. "A vial of the unicorn blood I know you possess, and the dead moonstone in your pocket."

How did he know about those? It didn't matter.

The crease between Aisling's brows grew deeper as she closed her eyes. Her chest rose in a slow, practiced movement; not a breath but a bracing as she reached into the pocket of her dress and placed the small, sheer white moonstone on the table. The one Davina had sacrificed her soul to reactivate, giving Aisling a way back to Eavha.

"Deal."

The four of them traipsed all the way up the stairwell of Aisling's tower. The door to her prayer room was tightly sealed, and without the marks on her palms, Aisling had to draw and cast an unlocking spell like a common witch. Despite the Blessing Charm's tattered state, she used the sharp tip of the feather still hanging around her neck to prick her finger, streaking bloodied lines on the hardwood door.

Today, they needed two vials—one for the phouka and one for Aisling's mark—which meant there would be two left. Ideally, Eavha would like to mark Eaon, too. The Lover seemed inclined to keep shoving him back out of the void, but that couldn't go on forever, and each time, his return took a larger toll. The logistics of casting the mark on him would be a pain, but with the phouka willing to play conduit, she would figure it out.

Once inside, Aisling went to her cabinet while Eavha watched the phouka take in the enormous map pinned to the wall. Looking at it was different now they knew the wards were not a bubble around Qiri, but a dome over the rest of Nir. What lay beyond? What did the lands outside the wards say about them? Did they know what was happening?

The phouka pressed a clawed fingertip against the Womb, loosing a heavy sigh. "Terra."

Eavha kept a healthy distance as she watched the phouka trail his finger up to the Bleeding Mountain in Vertlyn. "Ignatius."

West, to the deserts of Dusarn. "Celeste."

Down, all the way to the frozen wastes and the pass between mountains in the Southern Spine. "Jem and Argon."

East, to the strait. "Mare."

Finally, he came to a stop over the island of Orhn. His eyes closed.

"Where is it?" Aisling hissed behind them.

Turning away, Eavha went to where Aisling was pulling open other cabinets, abandoning them quickly to rifle through the contents on overhead shelves.

"I swear, I put them down next to the belladonna. But . . . Maybe I . . ."

Suddenly cold, Eavha went to the first cabinet Aisling had opened and dug through the boxes and jars. But Aisling was right. The vials weren't there.

For twenty minutes, the two of them tore the prayer room apart looking for the unicorn blood, and with every nook and cranny that remained unfruitful, Eavha's pulse beat a little faster.

"They're gone," she wheezed, stumbling back to lean against the table. "They're *gone*."

Fists clenched, Aisling turned a dangerous look on the phouka.

"How did you know I had them?"

Fury had the phouka growing half a dozen inches, his deep inhale expanding his chest until he took up the entire room.

"I did not steal them, if that's what you're accusing. Hence why I bargained for one. How do I know that you haven't hidden them and are lying to me?"

"Because I need one too," Eavha hiccupped, her skin too tight, eyes welling so quickly she couldn't see. "I need them."

Heels clacking on the floor, Aislings steps were hurried as she pulled Eavha close, hand rubbing circles into her back. "Breathe. It'll be alright."

"I will find the thief who did this," Clayton promised from the door. "I will fetch one of the Wyldeden scouts to help scent the room. Or . . . Can you . . ."

The demi-kin guard seemed to realize what a bad idea it was to ask a favor of the fae a moment before doing so, but the phouka began hunting around, sniffing at things anyway. He wanted that vial more than he cared about further bargaining.

"Leave me," he said. "And go ask the Morvish one if she can *see* anything."

"Is that something she can do?" Eavha asked.

"I don't know," Aisling answered. "Only one way to find out."

CHAPTER TWENTY-EIGHT

MOYRA

IN A PLACE WHERE EVERYONE WAS PREPARING FOR BATTLE, MOYRA WAS as useless as a bellybutton. She did not have the seer powers of the Morvish witch who had been Aisling's companion, so could not aid the war efforts in that same way, but she had accumulated a list of things to do anyway:

Find Kaelean Caesarea.

Find Dearmead Bayfield.

Help Cinn and the Hyrschan soldiers.

And most pressingly, figure out what was going on with Eaon.

Between what she had seen of his soul and the information given to her about the Lover's seed, she knew her nephew was in trouble. Saving the city might be outside her abilities, but helping one witch was manageable, especially when half his problem was one she was intimately familiar with: an out-of-control Morvish blessing and a failing, rudimentary binding. As soon as Eaon stopped being stubborn and admitted the truth, she could help him. Until then, she could prepare.

The other half of his problem was something only the phouka seemed to have any ideas about, and the fae creature was hesitant to share more than he already had about his experiences with the Lover during the First War.

In a place where everything was foreign—even the tea—Moyra went back to her roots.

In the early morning moonlight, she set a few candles around the low table and sat on the floor with her supplies. From memory, she sketched out a portrait of Eaon. His features were so like Kailevi's that it was difficult not to draw her brother instead, but there were elements that were also uniquely Eaon. The serious awareness of his eyes. The studious, almost judgmental tilt of his chin. The curl to his now chin-length hair that he shared with his sister—a gift from their mother, along with the brown of their skin. She thought she had seen a hint of Kai's wanderlust when Eaon spoke of the places he had visited in Nir, a hint of something curious and adventurous. She imagined them clearly, her brother and her nephew, exploring their world, uncovering its secrets together, learning of its peoples. She remembered how often she'd found Kai standing on the crest of a hill or the shoreline of a lake, staring into the wild or up into the sky, searching for something *more*. Something new.

With the drawing satisfactorily detailed, Moyra smeared the damp tea leaves from the bottom of her teacup across her constellation tattoo before pouring a fresh cup. The portrait of Eaon flickered warm and dark in the candlelight as Moyra moved it aside, readying a fresh parchment.

"Seven." The word was a whisper in the silent room. "Seven seven seven. Seven."

She uttered the phrase over and over, waiting for the stars to show her what it meant. Gatty stalked from the shadows and settled at her feet—a grounding presence as her mind drifted back to her encounter with Eaon in the dreamscape. His soul, wrapped in Kailevi's fraying coil of binding magic, and a second foreign power, black limpets suckling, stretching far into the dreamscape. Perhaps all the way to another realm.

Charcoal in hand, she let her hand move in whatever manner it pleased, unsurprised to find herself writing the number seven, over and over.

Seven moonstones.

The seven-pointed star of the rebel movement against the Sparrow Coven.

Seven elemental spirits.

Seven was considered one of the two most powerful numbers in Morvia's web of fate, alongside the number three.

She couldn't see a connection yet.

"Close my eyes to clear them," she muttered as she let her lids slip shut. "Let there be nonsense so there may be sense."

Her mother had taught her a silly song when she was beginning her years at the academy. Noise to cancel noise, filling up her head so that it could find stillness. One thing could not exist without an opposite. Life and Death, Balance and Chaos. Time and dreams, stars and darkness. For there to be thought, there had to be no thought. It was basic Morvish rules—and for there to be rules, there had to be anti-rules.

Seven was Death's number.

It came to her with sudden clarity. Of all Mother's pious devotees during the First War, Death had chosen seven to reincarnate into something else. Death chose seven gods, seven spirits. Balance theology argued there were seven planes within the void, and seven layers of rest in the after-realm.

Seven. Seven seven seven. Seven.

It was almost a certainty that the Lover was trying to possess Eaon's body. Every time he died, the seed inside him became hungrier, louder, more vicious. During the swells of it, his skin turned ashen, his eyes going dark in the way the endless depths of space were dark. Spellwork had been done to bring Chaos to this realm, and it made sense that there would be spellwork involved in bringing Death to mortal form too.

Even with her eyes closed, her hand still scratching sevens into the paper, she felt the starlight through the open window tingling against her forehead. All Morvish witches could dabble in all ten avenues of Morvish magic, but one or two usually came more naturally. Star-reading wasn't something Moyra was exceptionally good at, but lately they seemed to scream so loudly that she didn't need to be.

Seven.

How many limpets had there been? Four? Yes, four. But when she'd looked again the other day, there had been five. Of that she was certain.

How many times had Eaon died?

Once, to the curse. Secondly, to a spear. Thirdly, to arrows. Fourth, to fire. Fifth, to a fall.

The Lover returned him, over and over.

Seven.

He would get seven deaths, the last one to be final. She knew this with the absolute certainty that only came from messy, spinning thought. Seven was Death's number, and seven deaths would unlock Eaon's body for them.

But it was more than that.

Seven seven seven.

The stars had screamed the number at her over and over, not in sound or image, but in the abstract knowing of what seven meant. The three sevens together were significant.

Three and seven, seven and three. The two most powerful numbers in Morvia's realm.

Her hand moved over the paper, three sevens so close together they overlapped, becoming one number.

One number.

Seven seven seven.

Seven hundred and seventy-seven.

How many lives had Eaon snuffed out with his Lover's blessing, their souls passing through his own to feed the seed? Was there a way to count? Every surge seemed to take more and more. Those initial surges in the forest, the prison in Pirevia, then again in the arena. The beasts in the pit.

So many. Too many.

How many?

Not seven hundred and seventy-seven. Not yet. Not if the seed was still hungry.

Moyra opened her eyes and found her wandering hand had filled the paper with so many sevens it was just a blanket of black pigment staining the table around it, her fingers even more so.

What the second lone seven in the pattern meant, she didn't know, but what she knew about the first two segments was a start. They could not let Eaon take more souls, and they could not let him die again. Twice more, and who-knew-how-many souls, was all the buffer left between Eaon's ownership of his body and the Lover's possession of it.

It wasn't just about morality anymore. She had to warn him that every soul he took, every risk he took with his own life, brought them one step closer to a confrontation nobody would survive. What happened when Chaos met Death? What happened when those two primordial deities stood before each other in a place where mortals had no way to protect themselves from the fallout? Surely not even the wards of Nir could contain it.

Sitting back against the sofa, Moyra picked up her teacup with trembling hands.

She had come to save Kailevi's children, but even with her coven's power at her fingertips, she didn't know if she could. Even if she bound Eaon's magic properly, it would only contain his Morvish blessing. It would take a Lover-blessed witch with immeasurable talent to bind the seed, and most of the Sparrow Coven had either died or gone missing in Dusarn. Aisling didn't have enough. Not even with her tattoos.

"I have a bad feeling about all of this," Moyra whispered to Gatty, who thumped his tail against the rug at her feet.

"As do I, my friend. As do I."

CHAPTER TWENTY-NINE

EAVHA

PEERING AROUND THE DOORWAY TO MOYRA'S ROOM, EAVHA HELD AN arm out to keep Aisling from interrupting. Sitting cross-legged on the floor, hands stained in charcoal, Moyra muttered the number seven under her breath over and over, eyes closed to the way the candles in the room burned higher, light flickering madly. The cat sith in her lap was still, watching Moyra's face reverently.

"What is she doing?" Aisling whispered.

Frowning, Eavha leaned farther into the room. On the table, beside where Moyra was destroying a piece of parchment with sevens, her brother's likeness stared up at her. She swallowed down the lump in her throat as she retreated once more.

"I think she's trying to figure out what's going on with Eaon."

A moment passed before Aisling took a steadying breath. "Don't take this the wrong way, but—the unicorn blood is missing, Kaelean and Dearmead are missing, and we're going to need every advantage we can get when Chaos arrives. As long as he's unmanageable, Eaon isn't useful to us —is this really the priority right now?"

Earlier, Eavha had wanted to throttle her brother. To his face, she had said she hated him. Yet, when she found the words to explain the rabbiting in her chest, they came quiet and hard.

"My brother has never been anybody's priority and look where that has gotten him. Where it's gotten all of us. He may not seem *useful* to you right now, but he still has worth, Aisling. He is my family, so yes, for me, he is a priority. If Dearmead were here . . ." Eavha's breath hitched. "If Dea were here, Eaon would be his priority, too. Clearly he is for Moyra, and he deserves that. He deserves to be saved. Let her finish."

When Aisling's reply didn't come right away, Eavha turned away from the tearoom. The weight of whatever she was thinking dragged Aisling's gaze to the floor.

"What?" she pushed.

"Eavha, I love how fiercely you love. Even those of us who don't deserve it. I don't wish it on you, but . . . not everybody can be saved. Eaon knows as well as I do that sacrifices will have to be made to ensure that other people get a chance to survive this."

Davina had seen Aisling at the Womb, and neither thought she would survive it. Eaon offered himself so easily at Imsa that it made Eavha sick. *One tree to save the forest, not the forest for the tree*. Utter bullshit.

"Eaon and I have sacrificed enough," Eavha said, adamant. "I will not lose either of you."

With enormous effort, Aisling lifted her gaze, pity creasing her brow. "Fate will take what it needs. It may not be a choice you get to make."

"Wrong. I do choose." She set her chin stubbornly.

"Eavha."

"You said it yourself. I said no to Death, and I will say it to fate too, if I must."

"Eavha?"

The call came from within the tearoom. Ears burning, Eavha poked her head around the doorway again to see the candles burning normally, both Moyra and her familiar looking expectantly in her direction.

"Hello."

"Is everything okay?"

They hadn't spoken since Eavha had fled the infirmary. They hadn't discussed the fact that they were family. That there was Morvish blood in the line, even if the blessing had touched her only as much as Sanni had bothered with Eaon.

"Not really. This isn't a social visit."

Nirnish was still awkward and clunky on her tongue, but with little choice but to practice if she wanted to communicate with half the people at Imsa, she wrangled her aching brain to concentrate.

Moyra climbed to her feet, dusting her blackened hands on her skirt. The constellation on her forehead throbbed once, twice, then dimmed. Morvish magic was so strange. It didn't nauseate her the way elemental magic could. Actually, neither did Kaelean's Mother-blessing when she shapeshifted, or Aisling's Lover-blessing when she spoke to ghosts or peered into the deaths of corpses. What Eaon did was different, was likely intentional on behalf of the seed.

If what the phouka said was true and the seven elemental spirits used to be Fair Folk, then elemental magic was fae in origin and the nausea likely stemmed from its effect on the human blood watering down witch genetics. It was an interesting idea from a priestess's perspective, and a philosophical discussion she could throw at Eaon the next time he needed distracting.

Assuming he was still speaking to her.

From the hall, Aisling joined them inside the tearoom and closed the door.

"Something has been stolen from me. Can you find it?"

At Moyra's feet, the cat sith flattened his ears.

"Do I look like a circus animal to you?" Moyra's nostrils flared, upper lip curling. "Maybe in your Sparrow city you could get away with *demanding* things from Morvish witches, but I am *busy*."

Eavha sighed. It would be nice if, just once, Aisling could have a conversation with someone and it didn't devolve into hostilities.

"I didn't mean to offend you," Aisling tried, but Moyra threw her stained hands in the air.

"Your existence offends me. Leave me to speak with my niece."

Aisling was done. Just, so done. Eyes closed and a short nod, she didn't even say goodbye to Eavha before letting herself back out of the room.

"That was rude," Eavha said, hands on her hips.

"I do not care."

"I thought you came here to help."

"Help *you*. Help *Eaon*. If that involves helping in this war, then so be it, but I did not come to do anything for that wretched cow."

"Because of Cinn?" Eavha guessed.

Moyra nodded as Gatty moved to an armchair, leaping onto the cushions in a fluid movement incongruous with his size. The cat sith didn't greet Eavha, turning his attention to grooming his paws instead.

"Well, fine," she allowed. "Can you answer me, then? Can you find something that's been stolen?"

Plopping onto the couch, Moyra tucked her straw-colored hair behind her ears. Tiny holes decorated the lobes but there was no jewelry to be seen.

"It is not what I am good at. As it stands, scrying for your missing high priestess and this Dearmead fellow is also beyond what I am trained in. But I can try. What was stolen?"

"Four vials of unicorn blood."

The Morvish witch stilled. Even Gatty froze, mid-lick.

"Why do you have unicorn blood?" Moyra's voice was barely a whisper.

Pride swelled. Eavha couldn't help it. "I've been making Kinner."

One. She made one kinner. She needed to make more.

Pressing her fingertips to her forehead, Moyra took a moment to gather herself. "I will look, but I cannot promise anything. And not tonight. I am tired."

"Thank you. And . . . understandable. Whatever you were doing seemed intense."

Moyra nodded. "I was trying to deduce the parameters of Eaon's curse."

"What did you learn?"

Turning her gaze to the ceiling, Moyra's lips turned white and thin with how hard she pressed them together. "I should discuss it with him first."

That was fair. And also, not what Eavha wanted.

"It's my fault." The words were out before she realized they were even ones she wanted to say. The thought had been sitting in her head for a while now, but there hadn't been any point in addressing it. Didn't mean it wasn't true. "All of this is all my fault."

Moyra looked to her again and frowned curiously. "How?"

Eavha blinked. She had expected Moyra to immediately coddle her, the way most people did. It was so rare that she made a mistake or did something wrong that she wasn't accustomed to being criticized.

Moyra's question was not a criticism, though. Eavha swallowed her nerves.

"I can't regret what I did, but . . . Maybe Eaon would have been better off if I'd just let him go last year. The first time he died I had been too afraid to be alone, but if I had let him go, his soul could be resting in the after-realm instead of being corrupted by the Lover. Sometimes I think he would prefer that."

Eaon resented her for a lot of things, but she was sure he also sometimes resented her for being the reason he was still alive. Still suffering. It didn't seem to matter that he had met Cinn, that he and Dearmead seemed to have worked things out—even if that reprieve had been brief. Every time she spoke to Eaon, she was left with the distinct impression that he would rather be dead.

Yes, initially, she had brought him back for her own sake, but now . . .

She wanted her brother to get a chance to have a life. A good life. He deserved that, and considering everything he had sacrificed for her sake, she would do anything to pay him back.

Moyra watched Eavha's face as if she could hear every thought in her head. The cat sith blinked slow and lazy, and she remembered that he actually *could*.

Huffing, Eavha tried to settle her thoughts.

"Would you like to see what would have happened if you had?" Moyra finally asked. "Would you like me to show you the lines of fate that would have unraveled had you made a different choice?"

"What? I thought you said you couldn't see the future."

"I can't." Moyra held up her hands. "But your father's magic leaned heavily toward way-finding—a skill that let him see the connections between people, between places and objects, and with enough practice, allowed him to follow those connections to all their possible conclusions. It's closely tied to *seeing*, the way all Morvish magic stems from the same spirit, but it's not the same."

Eavha swallowed. Hearing someone talk about her da having magic seemed like a fable. She tried to imagine it, to rearrange memories in her mind with this new information, but she couldn't see it.

She could see it in Eaon, though. She remembered too vividly the way he would behave in one of his frenzies. She remembered the mess he had made of their unk's office when it had just been the two of them left, papers and strings pinned to the wall as he tried to solve the mystery of their family's demise. It hadn't seemed like magic, and there had been no nausea, but hadn't she just deduced that there usually wasn't when the magic came from one of the high spirits?

"Way-finding." The words tasted foreign on her tongue. She didn't really understand. "What does my father's magic have to do with you?"

"It's complicated," Moyra said with a grimace. "But he and I and our sister bound ourselves together when we were young and stupid, and his affinity for way-finding means my own is better than it should be. Not at his level, but better all the same. I can show you what would have likely happened if you'd let Eaon die last year."

Did she want to know? Would it make her feel better or worse?

It didn't matter. Curiosity won.

Reading the answer in her face, Moyra stood, patting the cushion she vacated. Eavha took a seat and watched as Moyra rearranged her makeshift altar on the table, smearing damp tealeaves across her palms.

"I'm going to induce a dream that I can manipulate," Moyra warned.

"And then I'm going to unspool old fate lines that are no longer relevant. There is very little danger."

"But not none?" Eavha asked, tilting her head back to meet Moyra's gaze as she took position behind her, fingers fluttering on either side of Eavha's temples.

"Morvia's realms are . . . a lot. Many go mad. I will take care of your mind, but there is never no danger when dealing with Morvish magic."

Eavha swallowed. "I think Eaon is going mad."

Moyra said nothing. She already knew.

"Do you trust me?" she asked.

"I don't know you. But I trust your self-preservation instincts enough to keep me safe."

The threat was not of her own ire. Moyra knew that too.

"I do like living," Moyra agreed, then took a steadying breath and pressed her palms flat to either side of Eavha's face.

Eaon was dead.

The Wyldeden infirmary was bright with daylight, but the sun's warmth couldn't touch Eavha as she sat on her brother's abdomen, both hands on his chest, staring at his lifeless face. The Blessing Charm hanging from her neck was intact. To the side, Dearmead crouched with his back to the wall, face buried in his hands. The entire clinic was silent as they stared at her, at Apaete, her best friend, whose face hid all the grief Eavha's own couldn't mask.

Eaon was dead, and he was not coming back.

She buried him alone. Dearmead helped her dig, helped her lower Eaon's body into Anfar's cold, unforgiving ground, but she scooped the earth back over him alone.

Later, in the Lover's meadow, Aadya crowned her Head of House. A cruel joke.

A week later, Eavha couldn't breathe.

Life went on, though it no longer mattered much to her. Eavha was a ghost, a cloud, floating above the world, watching things happen that no longer affected her.

Aadya left Wyldeden in the middle of the night. Lorelei remained high priestess. Dearmead pretended he was alright, but he was just going through the motions of being alive now. There was nothing left that he cared about.

Winter went by in Anfar. Wyldeden remained in spring. Always spring.

A tiny new crack in the Boab's wards caused mayhem for a while, but nobody noticed the brownish-red fox sniffing around. Whatever it hunted for, it did not find, and it left as unnoticed as it had arrived.

Eavha floated away from Wyldeden, following the fox as it returned to a skinny, cowering boy hiding in the bushes with nothing but a thin bedsheet looped into a rucksack. As the fox's body turned to clay and reshaped into the form of a tall witch, their names swam to mind with slow murkiness:

Kaelean.

Cinn.

The two of them did not speak to each other as they scurried northeast through the forest. For weeks, they picked their way through Anfar, only stopping when Cinn threw a silent temper tantrum about something, gesturing back the way they came. The spats quickly ended when Kaelean snatched his rucksack and skipped away into the brush, staying just out of reach and leading him farther and farther north.

They emerged into Vertlyn. Eavha watched with a detached sort of sadness as Kaelean set her trap, cruel and cold as the Sparrow guards dragged Cinn to their prison wagon and hauled him back down to the swamp, to the glistening white city perched on the top of the seaside cliff.

She cried a little as she watched them throw Cinn in a cell. The kinner boy lost what little hold he had on his sanity. He was wild and violent when a Morvish witch named Yomra came to speak to him, and Eavha watched dreadful realization dawn on the old witch's face as she took in the state of him. Whatever she meant to tell him stayed with her. There was no point.

When Kaelean returned to break him out of the cell, he attacked. Kaelean knocked him out and dragged him from Pirevia, furious and spitting, killing anything that got in her way.

It was almost a day later when Cinn woke up. Kaelean had taken him back to the fields above the swamp and it was there that they brawled. Kaelean used her magic over the soil to try and mellow the kinner, burying him in an attempt to regain control, but Cinn held tight and dragged her beneath the surface too, both of them disappearing into the earth.

Neither reappeared for several hours.

Even then, it was only the kinner.

He ran north and disappeared into the trees, and Eavha didn't see where he went after that.

The clouds took her away, then. They took her all the way across the world to Oford, to another city nestled against the Dividing River. A palace with red and purple stained-glass windows.

In the throne room, Aadya knelt before Princess Aisling Aurnia of the Sparrow Coven.

Two weeks later, Aisling Aurnia was dead.

Eavha sobbed as the clouds took her away again. They took her over the spine, across a gray desert with bent over trees, to another throne room. Queen Tallula lay on the dais, her belly split open as a creature slithered from within.

For months, Eavha watched it grow. Watched the army of beasts organize, marching to the Womb, making the crossing—slow, so agonizingly slow with only the one bridge to get them across.

They ate everything in their path. Razed towns and trampled forests, leaving only bloodstains and chewed bones behind.

In the Northern Mountains, Chaos found Cinn.

And then he found the crack in the wards around Nir.

The sun had risen outside by the time Eavha realized she was awake, once more alive and real, sitting on a sofa in Aisling's tearoom. She blinked, and Moyra let out a heavy sigh.

"Thank the Mother. There you are."

"Was . . ." Eavha's voice cracked, frail and wispy. "Was I not here?"

"You had some trouble coming back, but you're alright," Moyra said, a muscle in her jaw ticking.

"Was that real?"

It couldn't have been, and yet her mind couldn't differentiate.

"It might have been, if things were different. But it was just a dream."

Slowly, Eavha nodded. The world still felt fragile, reality a fickle thing. Moyra handed her a cup of tea, and the heat of the ceramic in her hand, the sweetness of it on her tongue, was grounding.

"All of that, because Eaon died?" Eavha whispered into her cup.

Her brother, who had been called useless every day of his life, might be the single most important piece on the board right now. A shiver ran beneath her skin, tea sloshing over her fingertips. She sipped deeply.

"He died. You died." It was the cat sith that broke the silence, Moyra sinking into the carpet and rubbing her own temples, leaving traces of tea leaves in her wake. "Aisling died. Kaelean died. Cinn was dead in the way kinners die. All of you have a hand in this. No matter which way Moyra follows the fate lines, one thing is the same: if one of you falls, the rest go like dominoes, and then Chaos escapes. Even the one I haven't met yet, the kinner you made; he has the same silvery glow the rest of you do."

Eavha finished her tea and sank deeper into the sofa, pulling her feet onto the cushion to squish her toes against the soft velvet. "Dearmead. He was the only one who survived."

"Everybody dies, eventually," Gatty continued when Moyra didn't speak. The cat sith slunk from his armchair and padded over to his witch, rubbing himself against her knees. "It's the when that counts."

Eavha narrowed her eyes. "You think Eaon should do it. You think he should let the Lover have him during this battle."

Shaking her head, Moyra straightened her shoulders. "No. I don't see that ending well, but he won't listen to me. He won't even see me. I need to tell him . . . what to avoid. How to avoid this."

It was the fear in her tone that twisted Eavha's stomach. Whatever Moyra knew about Eaon's curse worried her greatly, and her worry was enough to spur Eavha's own.

"I'll talk to him," Eavha decided. "Again."

Moyra grimaced. "I don't know if you'll get through to him either. He doesn't seem to want much to do with either of us at the moment."

Well, she wasn't wrong.

"Don't take it personally. Eaon's relationship with family has been tumultuous since he was twelve."

Moyra sat with that for a moment, reaching for a cloth on the table to clean her hands. Exhaustion made her movements slow and Eavha wondered just how taxing the adventure they'd taken together had really been.

Finally, Moyra asked, "And yours?"

Eavha closed her eyes. "I was luckier."

Because that was the only difference between Eavha and Eaon—she had inherited their mother's leaning toward Sanni while Eaon had inherited their father's leaning toward Morvia. It very easily could have been the other way around. It could have been Eaon thriving, training as the heir apparent, while she was bound and miserable and suffering. He could have been the one hailed their family's hero while she had her face stomped into the floor.

"In Qiri, we don't believe in luck. You are who you are for a reason, as is Eaon."

"No reason is good enough to excuse what my brother has been through."

Not for one second had she ever thought Eaon deserved the treatment he received, but only because her ma and da made sure she knew. For the most part, she had been happy to ignore him. She didn't know how to make up for that.

"Well, I didn't say it was a good reason," Moyra grumbled, almost snappishly. "For as many bright paths we can take, there are at least as many dark ones. Some unfortunate souls have fewer bright paths than others, but I'm yet to meet anyone who had only darkness ahead. With guidance and favorable circumstances, there is a bright future for everyone."

"Favorable circumstances?"

"I did meet someone, once, whose only bright futures depended on a huge shift in government policy that hadn't changed in two thousand years and had no inclination to do so any time soon, so . . . While we can make good choices, sometimes our bright futures lay in the hands of change we cannot always bring about ourselves."

"Like how the laborers in Wyldeden needed Kaelean to come back before they were respected. How the demi-kin needed Aisling to be free."

"Exactly."

"And Aisling only did what she did because of the Sparrow Coven and Davina and a whole list of things."

"Cause and effect. The lines of fate connect everything."

"And that's what Eaon can see? These connections?"

"Yes. Likely he could do much more if I can get him safely unbound and trained."

Eavha's headache grew as she tried to wrap her mind around it, but . . . she wanted that, for Eaon. A chance to live a good life, and a chance to figure out who he really is. A chance to grow into his true blessing. A chance to be happy.

"And what do the fate lines say are in store for us now instead?"

"It's easier for me to see what could have been than what could be, because what could be is always changing. But, I know there is hope."

"Vague Morvish nonsense."

Moyra grinned. "I know our chances of surviving this are greater because of what you did. I know the chances of Chaos being contained once more are greater. And I know that there are as many bright futures for Eaon as there are dark ones. You saved his life that day. You saved all their lives."

"Except maybe Dearmead."

Moyra sighed. "Yes. Except maybe Dearmead."

CHAPTER THIRTY

DEARMEAD

THE CHAIN AROUND HIS NECK WAS TOO TIGHT FOR SOUND, YET HIS tongue was numb from incessant whispering. For days, he had repeated the Terranian words, magic burning through his starved body until his bones threatened to crumble.

Bones he had seen exposed after his flesh was chewed away. Bones he had felt being ripped from their joints and sockets. Bones the mutant witches sucked the marrow from before discarding to the packs of lupanis waiting their turn. Bones that had regrown over and over, not really belonging to him anymore.

The spell was simple; since the day Dearmead learned to walk, he had been manipulating the earth beneath his feet. Wyldeden had been a sanctuary where even Eaon hadn't felt the bite of sticks and stones as long as he stayed within the confines of the Great Boab, but Dearmead had learned how to firm the ground when he needed power behind his kicks, how to soften it when a blow knocked him down. With his arms bound behind his back, bare skin exposed to summer's burn, the small comfort he found in smoothing the path before his tired, bruising feet kept him moving.

The gray sands of Kerveda had given way to Bernt's forest a day prior, along with his view of the western tower by the Womb. Which was fine. There was enough pain in every breath—he didn't need the reminder of what had happened in the sky above that bottomless crevice. He didn't spend time examining Bernt's flora, either. After noticing the enormous toadstools standing amid the trees, the spores growing out of tree trunks in a spiraling staircase to the canopy, veins of them latticing over boulders and cliffsides, hunger panged so painfully in his gut that he didn't dare look again. Perhaps it was as otherworldly and beautiful as the stories said, and perhaps if he paid attention, he would notice the fae that dominated the territory watching the army passing by, but he couldn't afford distraction.

When he found the strength to glance over to the other kinner, each leashed to the back of the same wagon, and saw the bloody footprints left in their wake, the smear of it where one had collapsed, dragged mercilessly for miles and miles, Dearmead forced his magic to ease their way as well. A thick coating of moss had grown around the fallen kinner, who stared insipidly through the sparse canopy at the cloudless sky beyond.

He wasn't stupid enough to try an escape. Even if he managed it without anyone noticing, their wagon was situated in the middle of an army barely kept in order by Chaos's harbingers. He wouldn't make it two steps before something descended on him.

At least during the day, the shtryg weren't prowling. The memory of their venom, of their shadow-cloaks' vacuous weight, buckled his knee and left him stumbling. With the sun at its peak, the night masses hid in the hundreds of wagons being hauled by too large six-legged salamanders through the valleys of Bernt, winding along the bare swathes of plains between thickets of trees. Creatures he had only seen depicted in books, only knew of due to Eaon's stories, stalked between them: cawkers weaving under carriages, knee-high and carnivorous, dusty feathers tinged red with old blood, and ratki, swarms of them, tails whipping at the kinners' heels as the oversized rodents scuttled by.

Then there were the larger beasts like the lupanis, frills flat and claws out as they stalked along, hissing and growling at anything that wandered too close. Gryphin perched atop the wagons, thick fur and golden feathers glistening under the sun, keeping an eye on the masses with their eagle vision. Harpies soared overhead, swooping with the currents, screeching their warnings at any wild animals in their path. The sheer number of beasts had flattened the bushland as they bulled through, their winged brethren blotting out the sun more effectively than storm clouds.

That the harbingers managed to get so many different species to cooperate, to organize, was an impressive feat, though that may have had more to do with the monsters lurking toward the back. In none of Eaon's stories or any of the books he'd looked through had Dearmead seen anything like them: seven-feet tall and encased in shiny black elytra, their pincered limbs clicked as they skulked about, chittering and hissing in what was unmistakably a language. Between the layers of their exoskeletons, puss-white mucus lubricated bulging muscles, more of it seeping from the hole in its bulbous head, only identifiable as a mouth due to its ring of teeth. Guardians, of a sort, they congregated around the largest wagon.

The one housing the King of Beasts.

A shadow passed overhead, followed by a roar that rattled the trees. As one, the army came to a halt.

Dearmead's knees finally buckled, the muscles in his legs twitching with exhaustion as he squinted up into the sky. Larger than houses, three dragons descended, circling the army. A dozen smaller ones followed them down. With his arms bound behind his back it was hard to keep his balance, though that could also have been the tremors wracking his body. He knew what the call to halt meant.

The harbingers were hungry.

Creatures scattered as the dragons landed, shaking the earth, and from their backs the three remaining mutant witches dismounted.

"Watching you try to keep up with us on that runt is the best thing I've seen in weeks," one of them cackled, watching Byron slide off the smallest of the adult dragons.

The name was spoken freely enough that Dearmead had pieced together that Byron was their commander, and that he was the one who had burned Wyldeden. The one whose dragon Dearmead had tried and failed to take down. The one who had killed Eaon.

Anger swelled, and Dearmead latched onto it desperately. Anger was energy. Anger was focus. It was the familiar heat in his belly that had gotten him through his guardian training when all he'd wanted was to hide away in his waterfall. It was what got him through every fight with his ma, every battle of wills against his da. If fear threatened to be his undoing, it was anger that would hold him together.

The other mutant witch didn't laugh, looking between their commander and the orange-haired hybrid, whose feet were a pair of cawker talons, her ears long and pointed like a ratki. Byron settled on the ground and shook out the large wings sprouting from his shoulders; either he didn't know how to use them yet or doing so would be slower than riding a dragon. Dearmead didn't care either way, except that Byron looked livid.

The mutant commander had not made a secret of his outrage that his own dragon had not returned from Dusarn. Even missing the eye the phouka had snatched, it was a better beast than the one he was stuck with.

Eavesdropping on their gossiping, Dearmead got a small thrill knowing it was probably dead; Byron didn't know that the lupanis Aisling appeared to have "trained" was actually the high priestess of Wyldeden, but Dearmead did. He had shared the secret victory with Vy, the only other verbal kinner, whose smirk was so severe it bared her teeth.

If Kaelean had taken on Byron's dragon, she would have ruined it.

"I still think it would have been better to send Wert or Pryll on one of the small ones, then you could have used their mount to ride east," the dark-skinned one said, standing no taller than five feet.

"If Kari comes back and sees me on a dragon bigger than her, she'll get territorial," Byron argued, then pointed one clawed finger at the orange-haired one. "And not another word out of you."

Hands raised, the bold-mouthed harbinger held back a grin.

Aside from the fresh air and not being staked to a stone floor, the main benefit of the eastward march was that the army could hunt for food that wasn't him. The small witch hybrid let out a piercing whistle. If the wildlife and fae of Bernt knew what was good for them, they'd have fled the moment they caught the army's scent. If there were any villages nearby, they wouldn't be standing for long.

As a large portion of the army scattered, the harbingers approached.

"Stay strong," Vy hissed. "Conquer your mind. We will survive this."

Dearmead was so sick of hearing those words and all their variations that he almost wished his ears wouldn't grow back.

The other kinner were silent. Even when the harbingers hauled the fallen one to her feet and unlocked the chain around her neck, as they queried the moss cradling her body only briefly before ripping it free, as they pulled a long metal skewer from the back of a wagon and readied a roasting pit, the kinner were silent.

Dearmead grit his teeth and flexed his wrists.

The other kinner, Vy's husband, was pinned down and pulled apart, limbs taken to each of the larger dragons first, the smaller ones knowing they had to wait.

Byron stood in front of Dearmead, grabbing hold of his leash.

"I would say you should be honored to feed our master, but this is just a return to how things should have always been. All life belongs to him."

Dearmead's mouth was too dry to spit. To say anything at all.

But his silence wasn't like the other's. His wasn't surrender; it was defiance.

Or so he told himself.

More than anything, he wished he could find his way back to the waterfall. Back to stolen apples and secret books. To golden eyes and bony hands. But being outdoors awoke the part of him that was trained to pay attention, to be alert to threats, which right now, were everywhere. As Byron yanked him to his feet and led him through the clearing, Dearmead took note of how many beasts had stayed behind, hoping for kinner scraps.

How many had tasted his flesh? How many of the lupani watching him salivated at the memory of him pinned to that cavern floor? How many of the harpies cleaning their feathers had licked his blood from their claws? Pieces of him torn free, inside them, passing through, now nothing but waste left behind on their path of destruction. So much of him that, if they scooped it all into a pile, they could have made his body a hundred times over.

A small battalion of Dearmeads.

Giving himself a mental shake, he focused on the ground beneath his feet, counting steps on his way to the large, polished wagon. Byron tied the end of Dearmead's leash to the wheel of the carriage before climbing to the large side door. It was pointless, but Dearmead twisted his neck, his wrists, praying to any spirit who had not abandoned him to find some slack. If it had been rope instead of chain, he might have stood a chance. The harbingers were used to dealing with regular kinner, not witches, but he supposed even a regular kinner properly motivated could have torn through rope. Vy certainly seemed motivated enough.

There was strength to be found, thinking of the kinner woman. She had been in this company for a very long time, and as batshit feral as she was, she had not surrendered. Even when her own husband seemed to have broken, she remained ready. If his own anger could not hold up against this beast again, then hers would get him through it.

The creak of the door's hinges preceded the sudden swell of power. It was a visceral static felt in the soul, the sheer magnitude of it rolling from the carriage making Dearmead dizzy. For a moment, the grass beneath his knees glittered like glass, slicing into his skin like a thousand tiny knives. Then the blades turned sticky, glowing an unnatural green. The field swam in and out of focus, but it had nothing to do with how hard it was to fill his lungs. The world reflected around him like a warped mirror, snapping back into place as the King of Beasts emerged.

It was bigger than Dearmead thought it had been earlier. It seemed to have chosen to keep enough of a form for eight multijointed legs to jut out from the otherwise shapeless mass. The hard casing was reminiscent of the beetle-beasts' exoskeletons, but where their joints left exposed flesh, the gaps in this beast's armor only leaked shadows. Aside from the legs, the two red orbs that felt like eyes remained, immediately latching onto Dearmead. Mouths appeared from within the shifting mass of black, a dozen of them ringed with small, sharp teeth like the shtrygs'.

Byron said nothing, hiding behind the open door as Chaos descended.

~

"Please excuse the state of this one, Master." Byron's gravelly voice coaxed Dearmead out of the fog of non-existence. There were parts of his body still missing, itching maddeningly as he came back to the world. "Next time I will be prepared for your increased appetite."

Even between consciousness and oblivion, Dearmead knew the sound of Vy's rabid screaming. Not the sounds she made when in pain, her body being torn to pieces, but the sounds she made to make sure they all knew she was not like the rest. That they had not broken her where it mattered.

"Hungry."

The word was a feeling that echoed in the world without language. It was a knowledge so innate, so base, that it could not be mistaken as anything else.

"Eat, Master."

Dearmead peeled his eyes open, surprised to find they worked. He could see his hand nearby, three of his fingers still growing back, cell by cell.

The chains lay nearby. He had been eaten right out of them, and now he was growing beyond them. Blinking—twice—he forgot about the itching.

He was not chained.

Flitting his gaze to Vy, he watched her dig her heels in the dirt, screaming madly as the red-haired harbinger tried to drag her before Chaos. The King of Beasts raised himself on those eight legs to meet her face to face, his mouths twisting in undeniable glee.

Nobody was looking at him.

One by one, he tensed his muscles, testing his limbs to see what worked. He was not whole, not by a long shot, but he thought he might have enough of himself to run.

There wasn't time to think it through. He had to get up, quickly. His body might be in tatters but his soul was intact, and that was where magic came from. Gently, he asked it to tell him more about the ground he lay on, about the root systems nearby, and found them pliable.

The wagon was near the rear of the amassed forces, and aside from the two harbingers wrangling Vy, no other beasts seemed willing to come too close to their master. Certainly nothing was close enough to catch him right away, but he could not outrun a lupanis. The forest nearby was rife with them, hunting fae.

There wasn't time to think about it. There wouldn't be another chance. Chaos was getting ready to feed on Vy, and the harbingers would remember him soon.

He shifted his weight. Tensed his legs. The ground moved beneath him, supporting him, giving way where he needed it to. Roots writhed beneath the surface, winding their way over the boots of the nearest harbinger.

He breathed. And then he rolled to his feet.

Everything hurt. He didn't care.

It was the shock that saved him. The two seconds it took for the harbingers, for Chaos, to realize what was happening.

Vy didn't hesitate. She had been waiting for a chance for years, and now that it was here, she was *ready*. Whipping her head, the harbinger holding her chain let go. Shock. With her hands still bound behind her back, she sprinted for the forest.

Dearmead was half a step behind her.

CHAPTER THIRTY-ONE

DEARMEAD

THE SCREECH THAT SPLIT THE AIR WARPED THE TREES, BUT DEARMEAD'S breathless prayers kept the ground beneath his feet stable, their way free of roots and stones. As they passed the tree line, the branches behind him lowered and knotted into a wall.

"Don't stop!" Vy screamed back, uninhibited by the weight of the chain dragging behind her. "Don't look!"

Even without the warning, Dearmead wouldn't have chanced a look back as the sound of wood splitting cracked through the forest. A heavy crashing beat down on the earth, and Dearmead knew it was too heavy for it to be either of the harbingers. Chaos himself was chasing them, the world rippling as he passed through it.

Dearmead didn't stop. He didn't look back. He overtook Vy and fled on pure instinct into deeper brush. In his peripheral, paperbark trees fell, plumes of dust billowing in their wake, and his mind automatically calculated how far behind the King of Beasts had to be. How fast he was moving. The trees were slowing Chaos down, but not by enough. If Dearmead tried to get up into the branches where he knew he could move quicker, he would lose too much precious time.

"North!" Vy screamed behind him.

The only thing he trusted as much as his own training was Vy's survival instincts. He split north and forced his legs to move faster. Forced his lungs to pull in more air. They ran for so long that time stopped meaning anything. Breath sawed through him, but it didn't matter. His body's itching returned as he wore himself out, magic fracturing his bones as it continued to throw obstacles up behind them, but he didn't care. He ran, because to stop bore a fate worse than death.

The trees were thinning. He noticed it a moment before he noticed the cliff ahead. He barely had time to consider slowing before Vy was screaming at him to *go, go, go, go.*

Dearmead broke through the tree line and flung himself off the cliff. The rattle of chain was right behind him as Vy followed.

Below, the sky awaited.

Wind pulled his matted braid back so harshly his neck ached, and it took the entire ten seconds they fell for Dearmead to realize they weren't falling into the sky, but into a lake so perfectly still it became a mirror. So enormous in every direction he could not see the other shore.

Air whipped past too fast to pull in a breath as Dearmead speared into the silver surface of the Soul Lake.

The boom of the water boxed his ears, even with his arms raised to break the fall. The cold would have shocked him into uselessness if he wasn't so terrifyingly aware of the resounding crash of a second body hitting the water, the promise of a third on its way.

The water was clearer than glass. Not a spec of sediment muddied the view of bleached coral carpeting the floor a mile down, tendrils of seaweed frozen into stiff spears. So clear, in fact, that he saw with perfect clarity that they had run from one monster only to meet a dozen more.

Even Vy, whose heavy chains weighted her enough to catch up to him, balked at the pack of selkies that came slinking out of the bottom of the lake, which was riddled with holes like an enormous sea sponge. The fae creatures' bulbous eyes glittered, their large mouths split in toothy grins until a shadow cast over the lake. Each and every one of them slowed. Retreated.

No time. There was no time and no good options.

Lungs aching from holding his breath, Dearmead kicked as hard and fast as he could, aiming for the caverns at the bottom of the lake. The selkies watched for a moment, then turned and fled as the third boom hit and the water rippled under the weight of a mountain. Chaos's shadow stretched impossibly wide, tendrils of ink staining the perfect clarity of the water. Coordinating his body was getting harder as it begged him for breath, and only pure fight or flight kept Dearmead moving.

A lone selkie peeked out from the caverns, the rest of its herd long gone. It shrieked, clear as a bell, calling three more seal-skinned creatures out of hiding. And then they were flipping their tails, speeding upward with an agility Dearmead could only admire for a moment. His arms were almost too heavy to move, his mouth opening of its own accord to suck in air that wasn't there. Water burned his throat, his lungs, where it gave no respite, and yet his body continued to move. Poorly, but it did. His head was cloudy, but he held onto consciousness far longer than expected.

Long enough to see two of the selkies shoot straight by him and Vy, aiming for the looming darkness. The other two sunk their sharp teeth into the kinner's limbs. If Dearmead hadn't already filled his lungs with water, the cry of frustration that escaped him would have done the job.

At least, as the selkies dragged him to the bottom of the Soul Lake, there was comfort in knowing that if he was destined to be their meal for all of eternity instead, his brain would be too drowned to feel as much pain.

~

Fresh air hit him like a kick to the chest. Or perhaps that was the pelt-less selkie beating him, forcing more water out of his body than should be possible. Having shed her seal skin, her long limbs were powerful enough to crack his sternum, but it was almost a negligible pain at this point and one that brought with it untold relief.

Sucking down gasping breaths, Dearmead rolled onto his side and pressed his face into frigid stone. The selkie sat back on her haunches, watching with a tilted head.

Somewhere nearby, Vy was hacking out lungsful of water too. There was barely enough light to see her by. Distantly, he was aware the cave was made of ice, or glass, or perhaps some kind of crystal. Swatches of soft light glowed from within, casting everything in a peaceful, golden hue. He was also aware of how narrow the cave was, stretching into distant nothingness. Rolling over, the tunnel ended nearby in a pool of water that no doubt led back to the lake.

"You helped us," Dearmead managed between gasping breaths.

The selkie blinked large black eyes, slowly leaning over to sniff at him.

"Whispers." Her Terranian was high and rasping and utterly surprising. He hadn't expected her to understand him. "All waters are connected, and we hear our sisters' whispers."

Grimacing as he sat up, Dearmead turned toward the sound of Vy breaking the bones in her hands, squeezing them out of the chains. If she understood what was being said, she didn't show it.

He wasn't cut out for this. All he knew about the fae was the lore Eaon used to read to him. The stories he used to tell about his travels.

"You expect payment," he said, forcing himself to meet the creature's watchful gaze.

She hissed and spat in what could only be interpreted as offense. "Debts are paid!"

Dearmead shook his head in confusion. He had never met a selkie before. "I don't understand."

"You are the kind of the kinner, and we are the kind of the selkies. We are promised."

Once again, Dearmead looked to Vy. She was paying half attention to him now, the rest of it on the other selkie who fiddled with the links of the chain around her neck.

"They say the selkies are promised to the kinner. I think."

Vy frowned. "Fae do nothing for free."

"She said the debt was paid."

Vy shook her head. "I have no idea. Don't argue. Don't thank them, either."

Dearmead nodded, glad to have someone more knowledgeable than himself to talk things through with.

He looked once again to the pool of water. It was as still and clear as the lake had been. Nothing was coming. The other selkies that swum past them . . . They had gone to slow down Chaos, distract him, so their sisters could pull the kinner into the tunnels. They were dead. He felt the need to apologize.

"Did we really just escape?" Dearmead asked Vy. His heart still pounded as if he expected Chaos to rise from the water any moment. Being free didn't seem possible.

Vy didn't match his awe. As the chain fell away from her throat, she gathered it into loops and slung it over her shoulder, calloused and indifferent.

"Don't get cocky. We have no allies. No friends. We will end up right back as someone's meal if we don't keep moving."

"Where?" Dearmead asked. Certainly they were not going back into the lake.

Vy waved a hand in the other direction. "Where do you think?"

Standing on shaky legs, Dearmead nodded to the selkies. They hissed something at each other, then pulled their skins back on and jumped into the pool without another word.

"Do you have any idea where this tunnel leads?" Dearmead asked.

Vy sighed. "We don't have to be chattier just because we're away from the harbingers."

The tunnels were the kind of cold that reminded him of the cave where he had first been taken, and if it weren't for the glowing walls, it would be too easy to forget where he was. He couldn't decide which was more uncomfortable: the scalding heat of the summer, or the frigid cold of the underground. He longed for the perfect weather in Wyldeden.

He remembered that Wyldeden was gone.

"Let's move," Vy snapped. "The lake water is too salty to drink and we will not function well for long if we can't get some fresh water. Keep up or I will leave you behind."

"We left your husband."

"He would not have run. Move, Dearmead."

Tucking his hands under his bare arms, he wished he had even a scrap of clothing to hold in body heat. The light in the walls did not give off warmth, and Dearmead distracted himself wondering what emitted it.

He could almost imagine the exact tone of Eaon's voice—excited, whimsy—if he was here, explaining whatever biochemical reaction was taking place in the natural caves. But he was glad Eaon was not here. Also wished he was not still burning in the forest, but glad he was not where Dearmead was all the same.

CHAPTER THIRTY-TWO

KAELEAN

IT WAS QUITE POSSIBLE THAT, AFTER ALMOST A THOUSAND YEARS, Kaelean was losing her damned mind.

"Don't you use that tone with me," she hissed, throwing a fist-sized rock at the blind dragon's head.

Exhausted and miserable, the dragon huffed a cloud of hot smoke in Kaelean's face. It reeked of sulfur and rotting meat, but if it thought a display of petulance was going to make her back off then it was stupider than it looked.

Not that "stupid" was the adjective that first came to mind when up close and personal with a dragon. Its head alone was the size of a small hut, covered in dark yellow scale that was harsh and sharp as flint. Small spines framed its features, each as long as she was tall, reminding her of a deadly sort of whisker, the mass of them resembling a mane. There wasn't an inch of its being that wasn't dangerous, especially with its thick blackened teeth bared, tendrils of smoke unfurling in a display of frustration.

Kaelean scowled. "I'm hungry too, but you don't see me carrying on like a big, scaly baby. It's one more rock and we've freed one of your wings. You want to fly again, don't you?"

Without Terra's blessing, clearing the enormous hunks of debris would have been an impossible task. Even with, it wasn't easy. Kaelean was tired. She was hungry and dehydrated and hadn't had a chance to really recover properly from the expenditure she'd used at the Dividing River. It was enough, though. One chunk of sandstone at a time, Kaelean got the rubble to move, tilting the ground to ease the way.

With herculean effort, the dragon lifted its head and nipped pathetically in Kaelean's direction. If she didn't find food soon, she might become it.

"Eat me, and tomorrow you'll just be starving again. Unless you can get out from under these rocks on your own?"

A deep rumbling whine rattled loose a handful of stones, scattering down the mountain-worth piled on its back. One rolled across her bare foot and Kaelean hissed, picking it up and tossing it back at the dragon's dusty snout.

It did have a point though. Kaelean took a stumbling step back from the rubble and tightened the knot of her makeshift dress.

"Don't think this has anything to do with you. I'm only going because I, too, am hungry."

Laying its enormous head down again, the dragon bared its teeth in what Kaelean was certain was a smirk. Holding her tongue didn't come naturally, but she could do it knowing she would get her revenge.

There wasn't much food to find: a dead cat being ravaged by a one-legged crow. Wilted plants, mostly poisonous, suffocating under the debris. Nothing that would sate her, let alone a hundred-and-sixty-foot-long dragon. Nothing that would convince the beast not to eat her instead —all the intelligence in the world couldn't compete with a needy stomach.

Wandering beyond the courtyard to an entryway she hadn't yet explored, her right leg was stiff and heavy, a lead weight hanging off her hip. She hadn't noticed it at first, but as the days wore on, something deep in her thigh had begun to twinge. It was fine. Being injured was nothing new, and she had persisted through harsher climates in worse conditions.

For seven hundred years she had been unbound from the clan—a rogue. She had fallen in love, just to watch the Lover embrace them. She had made friends and called them family, called them *coven*, and watched them pass too, one by one. She had known so many people but had also spent so much time alone, lost in the only way a Terranian witch can be. She had wasted decades to drink and substances, trying to numb her losses. She had become a recluse, desperate not to feel again, hardening her heart so when it inevitably happened again, it would not hurt so much.

But it had. Gods, had it hurt.

Kaelean remembered what Aisling had told her during the princess's visit to Wyldeden—that Yomra lingered. She could not see her old friend's ghost, yet she knew she was not alone as she hauled herself over a crumbling step to the stable one above.

"Is this what you had planned, you crazy old bat? 'No Kaelean, don't save me from Nevan's curse, just go and fetch three annoying children and bring them here so I can tell them prophecies and then *die*.' How did that work out, hmm? Was this how it was all meant to go?"

The castle had mostly fallen apart, and the room she found herself in was no different. Some kind of kitchen, or at least a prep room. The ceiling had collapsed, crushing the workbenches and crates of spoiled produce, but from between the splintered panels she pulled free a half rotten beetroot. Enough to get her by for a minute, but she was fairly sure dragons didn't eat vegetables.

Rooting through drawers and the few cabinets still intact, she found some potatoes that were only a little green and tucked them into her makeshift dress. A jar of salt, another of pepper. The one filled with little green leaves caught her attention—too small to use as a whispering leaf, a quick sniff informed her it was oregano.

"Not my favorite mint," she commented to nobody, but an herb was an herb and she might need it.

Somewhere nearby, a scratching perked her ears. Sniffing deeply, she picked up on something musty and feathery, the tang of blood and mold. Alive. Meaty.

Perhaps a cawker still roamed, though the dead silence that had fallen over the city suggested the beasts had finished picking the streets clean and moved on. Stuffing the jar of oregano into her wrap, she drew Cinn's misshapen knife and crouched as low as her leg would allow.

Silently, Kaelean crept across the kitchen to the other doorway, half collapsed. Ducking under it, careful with her feet, blinking widely against the fading daylight, she took another deep sniff and peeked around the corner.

A hall, narrow and jammed with rubble. Tongue between her teeth, tasting sweat and fear in the air, Kaelean slinked a little farther until, barely audible, she heard a soft muttering.

"Where is it, where is it? This is stupid, Pryll, why would it be in the pantry? But it wasn't in the prayer room, so . . . Mother have mercy, it has to be here somewhere. It has to be."

Kaelean wasn't the only one in Dusarn losing her mind.

If the herbs in her dress were ground instead of whole, she could have used them, but as it was, she dragged her fingers through the sandstone dust coating everything and dragged the sediment across her face in practiced patterns. Low to the ground, she slipped farther down the hall. Whoever had snuck into the castle smelled like a beast but talked like a woman, and if Kaelean focused, she could taste magic fluttering weakly.

Witch. Hybrid.

How very interesting.

And then, fresh blood. Kaelean's nostrils flared as she looked down at herself.

"You have got to be kidding me." Words barely a breath, she stared at the blood dripping down her thigh. "Now?"

Her fourth century had been filled with poor decisions. Some were benign and temporary, like chopping all her hair off, while others were a never-ending nightmare, such as undertaking the fertility ritual. If she'd stopped to think about it for a minute, she could have figured that Mother would never bless her with a child. Not only was she to live an obscenely long life, losing everyone she loved over and over, but now she was cursed to bleed irregularly thrice a year as a cyclical reminder that she had scorned the deity of creation.

And of course, she had to be burdened with the consequences of that decision *right now*.

The spirits truly hated her.

In the nearby storeroom, the muttering stopped.

Carefully, quietly, Kaelean lowered herself even farther, practically snaking along the floor. Not as smoothly as she'd have liked, but still, when this Pryll witch came to investigate the blood she undoubtedly scented, it would be instinct to look at eye level first. For a fleeting second, Kaelean would have the element of surprise.

Movement. A boot, then a sliver of a face, nose pinched and hardened like a beak. Feathers lay smooth against her throat, as if they would be any kind of defense against claw or blade.

Grip tight on Cinn's knife, Kaelean sprung forward and sliced the back of the hybrid's knee.

Squawking a scream as her leg buckled, Pryll fell. Eye to eye, the witch-beast's golden gaze widened, fear soaking her scent.

"What are you looking for, little bird?" Kaelean cooed.

A booted foot swung for her head. Kaelean ducked and grabbed Pryll's ankle, but the hybrid was a tiny thing, slippery and panicked. She pulled her leg free, scrambled up, and fled. The girl was surprisingly nimble, hobbling on one foot and both hands. If she weren't the enemy, pity may have kept Kaelean from giving chase.

Yet she did. All the way back to the kitchen, out the door and down the stairs. Pryll turned to escape deeper into the city, but that would not do. Shucking off her dress and all the hidden things within it, Kaelean's body turned to clay, and she reveled in the strength of her lupanis. Running was effortless, as was the leap she took right over the hybrid, body twisting in a liquid movement to land facing her once again.

Pryll screamed, the shrill cry of a harpy, and spun back the other way.

Better.

Herding her toward the dragon took little skill. If all the harbingers were like this, the war would be a breeze. But even as she thought it, Kaelean knew that not everybody dangerous was a fighter. Her steps faltered slightly as she imagined it was Eavha fleeing through Dusarn's courtyard instead, injured and terrified, but there was nothing to be done.

Rather than balk at the dragon half crushed beneath rubble, the sight of it invigorated Pryll like nothing else; hysterical laughter tore from her as she scrambled for the giant beast.

"Kari!" the witch cried. "Kari, thank the king! Help me!"

Kaelean skid to a stop. Silently, she returned to her usual form, crouched and waiting to see how this went. Maybe it was foolish to take this risk, but Kaelean had spent as much time around beasts and fae as she had witches, and she thought she understood them fairly well. Perhaps dragons were different. Perhaps their loyalty couldn't be so easily stolen. Kaelean didn't think she was wrong, though.

Named and recognized, the beast shifted, sniffing in Pryll's direction, the small flap of scaled skin over its ears twitching.

"Byron will be so—Lover be damned, Kari. Your eyes. What has been done to you?" Then, remembering she'd been followed, Pryll turned with a wicked gleam and pointed. "She's there! Quick! Burn her. Burn her now!"

The blood staining her thighs made it easy for Kari to locate her among the rubble, but Kaelean held her ground. Loyalty and intelligence were attributes coveted in a companion such as this, but right now, they were in conflict. She could see it in the way the dragon hesitated, deliberating. Saw it steal the glee from Pryll's face.

"Kari?"

Pryll couldn't get Kari free. Pryll might not even try. How useful could a blind dragon be in battle? But Kaelean was helping. Kaelean had brought food.

And hunger was the true master of all.

Kari whipped her snakish neck and swallowed the harbinger whole.

Unable to wipe the smug smile from her face, Kaelean left the dragon to digest its food while she recovered her things. When she returned, Kari huffed, nudging gently against Kaelean's leg. A question. Concern for the blood slowly making its way past her knees.

Pressing a hand to Kari's warm neck, Kaelean let her lips brush against her scales.

"You beautiful, beautiful creature."

It had bothered her for a while, this curse of Mother's. It had bothered her until very recently when she realized she'd collected a brood of brats anyway. Her coven. Her family. Her children. Sometimes she feared the mere act of loving them would get them killed, but then all she had to do was look at Eavha and remember that the young witch had looked Death in the face and told them *no*. That her unparalleled stubbornness had been —and would continue to be—enough to keep Eaon and his incredible mind safe. All she had to do was remember the mark on the back of Cinn's neck, the one that would ensure Kaelean would never be without company, regardless of how reluctant and bitter it was.

She couldn't wait to see them again, to make sure they were safe. But she would. If she held out a little longer, she could bring them a gift to ensure they would never be in danger again.

CHAPTER THIRTY-THREE

AISLING

ONE OF THE THINGS AISLING HAD NOT QUITE WORKED OUT WAS WHERE to open the portal to Pirevia. It hadn't been a priority on her very long list of things to prepare, and she had expected to have a few more months to figure it out. Now, the problem was more urgent, and it was difficult to explain to a servant or guard what to look for. So, dressed in a light cloak, hood raised, she took four of her most trusted guards on foot to explore the northern quarter.

Eavha had wanted to come, but she wanted to take the opportunity to try healing via conduit again, moving her brother out of the infirmary and into her old suite where there was natural light and fresh air. It was always a subpar day when they were separated, but at least she had Clayton to keep her company.

Of her guards, he walked closest, eyes always scanning, but Aisling could tell his mind was elsewhere. There was a particular curl of his upper lip that had begun to show itself every time he spoke of Edwina post revelation of her rebel status. Her two closest people, aside from Nora, had never expressly been close, but they'd been friendly enough considering the proximity in which they worked together. Now, Clayton couldn't say her name without a snarl of disgust.

"Spit it out, Captain Grint."

"Sorry, Your Majesty?"

"What has Edwina done to scorn you now?"

When she had asked Edwina to fetch her father's body for the coronation ceremony, she had made Clayton escort her, both because it was unwise to have her second-in-command walking around unguarded, but also because Aisling needed to trust the people around her not to kill each other. She'd been hoping they would sort out their issues so she could stop thinking about them.

After another minute of deliberation, Clayton decided to say, "It's not my place to question your decisions, Your Majesty, but do you really think Edwina has what it takes to hold Pirevia for our people?"

Aisling smiled. It was a fond thing she normally wouldn't let touch her face, but she was tired. She didn't need to and couldn't afford to waste energy maintaining her usual composure when it was just her and Clayton.

"Yes, I am sure."

"She drinks in seedy taverns with her brother."

"I am aware."

"She has no history of leadership and has shown that she cannot be trusted."

"I know." All those things had been said about Aisling once, too, back when she was new to Hyrsch. "Consider, Clayton, that Edwina was my handmaiden for two years. I was torturing her brother in the dungeon the entire time and she knew it, and she kept herself in check so completely I never once doubted her. She hunted the palace for him every day, for two years, and I never noticed. She was a rebel under my nose, and I had no idea. She pulled a knife on you and you didn't see it coming. She knows what she needs to do, and she has the skill to act like she can do it. She will do wonderfully. And she will have you to protect her."

Clayton balked. "She'll have who to do what now?"

"You." Aisling petted his sword hand. "I want you to accompany Edwina to Pirevia. Keep her safe. Help her corral the city."

"Absolutely not," he hissed. A beat, and he remembered who he was speaking to, turning paler than the moon. "Deepest apologies, Your Majesty—"

"Accepted," Aisling allowed.

"I just think I would be of better service here, with you."

"You have trained me very well these past six years, Captain, and I will have many people at my side for what's to come. There are very few, however, that I would entrust not only my Second, but the well-being of Hyrsch's citizens. Pirevia is an ugly place full of ugly people, and she will need you. I can't lose another Second, Clayton. I need you there, so I don't have to worry about her."

It took him a moment to smooth his facade, but eventually Clayton nodded.

"I understand."

They walked in silence through the inner suburbs, the morning sun moving steadily across the sky. A few places presented as potentially good spots for casting a portal, but the proximity of storefronts was a concern. When she ripped open Celeste's realm, it would swallow up anything in its path and dump it on the other side. In the middle of Anfar, moving the Wyldeden clan to another part of the forest, the debris didn't matter. Accidently ripping out the glass windows and parts of stone walls, dumping them directly into the path Edwina would step into, however, was not ideal.

So she continued on, making her way through markets and into the outer rings. Each quarter had a main courtyard for larger gatherings, but she wouldn't know if the northern courtyard was as wide as some of the main streets were long until she got there.

"Your Majesty."

The ring of guards tightened around her, but Aisling recognized the voice. Lifting an eyebrow at the sweaty, red-faced Morvish witch chasing after them, she waited to feel something—a thrill, a pit of dread—at having Moyra call her "Majesty." But there was nothing. There was no power in being queen of a dying coven, in having her very own Morvish liaison, when the only thing stopping her from dissolving the entire Sparrow empire was the need for people to listen to her a little while longer.

"What's wrong?" Aisling asked as Moyra came to a stop, leaning on her knees to catch her breath.

"No, no," she panted. "Nothing's wrong. Mother of all, I am not built for running. Are you about to open the evacuation portal?"

Dipping her chin to her guards, they made space for the Morvish witch to enter their protective band. Aisling folded her hands and waited for Moyra to compose herself before answering.

"Not yet. Simply scouting for the best place to do so when Edwina is ready. Why?"

"After I spoke to Eavha the other night about your missing vials—which I have not been able to locate yet, by the way—we had a chat about a few things, and she asked quite passionately if I could look into your fate lines."

Controlled breaths. If it was truly terrible, she would have heard about it already from Eavha.

"Oh?"

Moyra grimaced. "I would like to make it pointedly clear that the only reason I care is because Eavha does."

"Duly noted."

"There were some splits along the path that were concerning. It's difficult to tell because it's not my area of expertise but the evacuation portals seemed to spark a litany of issues. I spent the morning thinking about it, and I decided that I am willing to temporarily put aside my distaste for you to solve the matter."

Considering the last conversation Aisling tried to have with the Morvish witch, Eavha must have had quite the conniption.

"You must love your niece very much. An impressive feat considering you only just met her."

"She is family," Moyra offered, as if that meant anything.

Rather than comment on the notion, Aisling said, "Walk with me."

Again, she waited for Moyra to tuck her frizzing hair behind her ears, the flush of her face cooling, before resuming her northward stroll.

"What is the danger of these portals?" Moyra asked once she'd sufficiently righted herself.

"Ripping holes in Celeste's realm is not easy," Aisling explained. "I can move one or two people long distances without problem, and I can apparently move large masses short distances without the magic becoming too cumbersome. Moving lots of people across Nir all at once is not something either of us feel confident about, but there aren't enough ships for the entire city."

Moyra nodded, as if all this made perfect sense to her. "I have heard the term 'burn out' being thrown around, and also 'crumbling.' There is much I don't understand about elemental magic."

"It's the same premise as Morvish 'unraveling.' When you use too much magic, or use it too long, or do something you don't have the ability to do, the magic kills you. For the Morvish, your mind unravels, your soul gets lost, and the body dies without those things. Burn out is an Ignatius term, because the Igni often spontaneously combust when they reach their limit. Crumbling is a Terranian term, because their bones break apart. The Lover-blessed rot. Celestians dissipate, and so on. 'Burn out' became a common phrase because the Igni tend to do it more than other elemental types. It's the nature of their blessing."

"I see," Moyra hummed. "You seem to know a lot about the Morvish."

"I know some," Aisling admitted. "I feel like I have forgotten more than I remember, which makes some sense now that I know about the wards being faerie magic. But I had a Morvish lover for a while. She taught me many things."

"Davina," Moyra remembered. "I'm out of the loop in Qiri politics, but I'm surprised Pearl would send her own relative as emissary, given how few of our people ever came back from Dusarn."

Aisling didn't want to talk about Davina. Didn't want the distraction. Her skin crawled with the weight of her tattoos, magic brimming just beneath the surface.

"How have you fared, contacting your people?" Aisling asked.

"Poorly. The dreamscape is behaving oddly. I didn't have any trouble finding Eaon when looking from the outside in, but now that I am here, it's as if it's full of fog. It may have something to do with the wards, but I also suspect there is some kind of interference. Gatty and I agree it is unlikely Morvia herself has anything to do with it, so, another Morvish witch, perhaps. Maybe a Separatist, maybe a traitor, muddying things intentionally. I'm trying to navigate it, and trying to find where the interference is coming from, but . . . I have a long list of things to do. My tattoo is the only thing giving me any kind of control, and it's exhausting to rely on it."

Aisling nodded. "I dislike how many Morvish witches became unaccounted for during their visits to Dusarn. If I can help at all, please send word. Perhaps a list of those I recall abandoning their duties?"

"It would give me somewhere to start."

Making a mental note to add that to her list of things to do, Aisling nodded again. "And don't overstretch yourself. I don't have any other Morvish allies to rely on."

When Moyra didn't argue the point of being allies, she continued.

"There is another Morvish witch besides Davina who lingered after death. She haunts Kaelean, the Wyldeden high priestess. Apparently they knew each other for centuries, and she will not take the Lover's embrace until she sees the fruits of her sacrifice. Her name is Yomra. Have you heard of her?"

Moyra looked up at the sky and took a steadying breath. "No. Only in that she was the one who sent Cinn to find me. I don't know how . . . The crack in the wards has only existed for fifty years. She must have been an earlier emissary if she knew Kaelean so long ago. There is no other way inside the wards except by moonstone, and those are heavily regulated."

"What about Aadya?" Aisling asked, fingers twitching. "As I understand it, she has been going from clan to clan, killing witches she believes may interfere with Chaos's plans, for more than a hundred years. I investigated our records when Eavha brought her here, looking for her name in Sparrow's history of emissaries, but she was never one."

Moyra wrinkled her nose. "Phara, your western neighbors, lost a handful of moonstones. Stolen, more likely. It was blamed on Unifiers trying to get inside Nir, but it could easily have been Chaos sympathizers. There aren't many of them, but they exist."

"You've mentioned Unifiers twice now."

"People outside the wards who want to bring the ring down. To assist with the war. Their opposition, the Separatists, want to leave Nir to self-implode and hope the wards will keep Chaos from spreading. They are currently winning the debate, but Unifiers have been slipping inside using the crack in the wards for decades. I've been trying to contact them in the dreamscape too, but . . ."

Aisling nodded. There was so much to organize before Chaos arrived. "I appreciate all your efforts. We all do."

"Well, that's why I wanted to catch you," Moyra said, standing a little straighter as they reached the largest northern courtyard.

A fountain stood two-stories tall, dribbling water serenely from marble spouts. There was a lot of empty space in the northern courtyard, which was ideal for a portal the size Aisling needed. It was also one of the least densely populated areas, since the seaport lay to the south and Oford's villages lay spattered to the east and west. Northward, there was only forest, the Dividing River, and Anfar, and nobody wanted to live that close to the fae and beasts lurking there. The northern part of the city was, thus, mostly demi-kin. Crowds of them stopped to stare as she approached the fountain, all of them packing and preparing for the evacuations.

Moyra perched on the lip of the stone base and crossed her ankles. "I might have an idea. A better way to move people, so you don't risk . . . dissolving—burning out, whatever—so close to war."

Tilting her head, Aisling was immediately curious. Moyra reached into her pocket. The sun glistened brilliantly off the glowing surface of the moonstone in her hand.

Aisling froze.

"This is—"

"I know what it is," Aisling interrupted, closing her eyes, trying to focus through the swell of grief clawing at her chest.

It was Moyra's turn to give Aisling a moment to compose herself. When she spoke again, she did so gently. "I've been considering the best use for them, and I thought if there was a way to somehow project the moonstone's power outward, stabilize it for a longer period of time, we could use it instead. Maybe some blend of the portal spell you use and the moon's magic. I'm willing to work on it together if you are."

Deep breaths. Slow breaths.

"I don't know how to do something like that, and the stones are too precious to waste."

"They are. Wasting one would be terrible, but I have a good feeling about this. You are able to cast a portal wordlessly, I've heard, but for lesser-blessed witches there is a ritual, correct? If there's a way to incorporate the moonstone into the ritual, and we cast it at night, it could work. I think it's worth trying."

Aisling wasn't sure. She already knew she could open a portal; what she had done for the Anfar Forest Clan was proof that one as large as she needed was possible. But to work up a brand-new spell, something that had never been done before, when the lives of everyone in her city was counting on her . . .

It was the kind of thing Eavha would do.

Weighing the risks between attempting the unknown or chancing a burn out, Aisling knew which one Eavha would prefer. Besides, if Aisling pushed herself too far again, Eavha would only push herself to heal her again, and that was unacceptable.

"Alright. We'll try it."

Moyra nodded. "This is a good spot. Lots of open sky."

"How many moonstones do you have?"

"Two," she lied. Her lip caught between her teeth, gaze finding a ripple in the fountains pool to stare at.

Three, most likely. Aisling didn't blame her for wanting to keep one for herself.

"Well, if this works, I think we should have a rendezvous for during the battle. I intended to announce at the next Imsa that, should things go awry, we all meet there so I can portal us out. But a . . . a moongate would be better."

Moyra raised her eyebrows. "Moongate. Is that what we're calling it?"

"Seemed appropriate."

"Sure. So if the ritual works, then for the rendezvous, we have everything set up and ready to be activated by whoever can make it there. Ready, but inactive. That way, if we don't need it, we haven't wasted a moonstone."

"Yes. There should be a way to have it so that I don't need to be there to complete the ritual. Anyone with magic will do. That way, if I don't make it, there's still an escape route."

Carefully putting the moonstone away in her pocket, Moyra watched Aisling for a moment, their guards forgotten. "Did Davina ever tell you about fate lines?"

"No." At least not as far as she could remember. "She was a seer, so she only explained how her visions worked. What are they?"

"Complicated. Fate is a convoluted thing; there is no single one for anyone. Always changing, so many possibilities. Some people have a running theme, though. Some people have far fewer potential happy endings than others."

Aisling nodded. "You don't need to dance around it. I already know mine must all be terrible. I have been ready to die for this cause for a very long time."

"Then why do you ache so much at the thought?"

Schooling her face into a mask of indifference didn't fool Moyra. Whatever she had seen in Aisling's lapse of self-control was too true to be forgotten. Still, she didn't let herself emote again as she thought of peonies and baby's breath, warm brown skin and pretty, hopeful eyes. Eavha was the only living thing in Aisling's marble world. She was air in an otherwise sterile place.

"I didn't expect to want to survive."

"Ah," was all Moyra said.

From the fountain head's shadow, the cat sith slinked into the morning sun, rolled onto his back to expose his belly and purred as Moyra reached down to scratch it. All Aisling's training couldn't keep her from flinching at his sudden appearance.

Her guards fidgeted, looking to her for instruction, but Aisling shook her head. Instead, she asked, "Cat sith. How goes your recruitment?"

"Fruitful. Also, you're about to have guests."

Sure enough, the guards turned to the main street that led from the courtyard to the northern gate. Security had doubled at the city walls, and two of the soldiers who were meant to be stationed at the watchtowers were instead escorting a trio of wild-looking witches. Two were children, but the adult male had his hands bound behind his back, arms straining against the grip of the soldier. The second of Aisling's men carried a burlap sack. A dark stain bloomed on its underside, a familiar weight swinging back and forth.

"Moyra, get back," Aisling muttered, one hand reaching for the dagger strapped to her hip.

The Morvish witch did as she was told, moving to a guard's side, the cat sith sitting by her feet. Clayton stepped up to meet the soldiers, drawing his weapon.

"What do we have here?"

"Rogues."

Shoving the male down, bent so far over that the soldier could splay the male's palm open for all to see, Aisling's stomach rolled at the pale brand stark on his pink flesh.

"Fuck you," the male spat. "Leave my kids out of this."

The children in question were young, not yet in their teenaged years, both wan and shaking, vacant expressions of shock on their sooty faces.

The soldier pulled the male back up while the other handed the burlap sack to Clayton. "He was carrying this. Strolled right up the gate."

One look inside the bag was enough. Clayton didn't flinch, but Aisling had shown him plenty worse things than what she knew was in that bag. He brought it to her. Held it open.

A decapitated head.

Female, dark hair. The neck wound was ragged and messy—torn rather than cut. The scent of blood was stronger than any initial rot; the kill was recent.

Looking to the rogue witch, Aisling's flat tone was a warning. "Tell your children to look away."

"They've already seen it," the male said, face twisting. "I—"

"You do not have permission to speak to Her Majesty!" The soldier holding his arms gave him a firm shake.

"She is no Majesty of mine," the rogue hissed back.

Fist curling, raised threateningly, it was only Aisling's presence that kept the soldier from openly beating the male right there in the courtyard.

"I want to hear what he has to say," Aisling said as she reached inside the sack and pulled out the female's head. Her eyes were closed, mouth slack. Just like the children and the male, her face was stained with soot from the fire burning freely across the river.

"Amnesty for my children, and I will bring every wild and unbound witch in the Oford forest here. We know something is happening. We've seen your gathering forces. We can help."

"Why would they listen to you? Rogues have no leadership." Aisling fingered the torn flesh of the female's neck. Teeth or claws, both thick and sharp.

"Strength has always come with numbers," the male said. "Even those of us against clanship know when we need to band together. That . . . That was my wife. Rumor has it you can see deaths. Look. It's all the proof you'll need."

She had intended to, but she didn't like being told what to do. So she held his gaze and pretended to consider it until he finally lowered his eyes.

"Clayton."

"Yes, Your Majesty."

It wasn't a question; he knew what she needed. This place wasn't secure, and when she looked into this female's final moments, she would not be aware of her surroundings. Clayton followed her to the fountain's edge, guarding her while she sat. Holding the dead witch's head up, Aisling took a steadying breath and dived in.

The family was moving east, steering clear of the river, now wider than it used to be. To their right, the towering walls of Hyrsch loomed, not close enough to be spotted by patrols, but not so far that the small family couldn't see the crossbows being mounted on the turrets.

"Stay close," the female said, pulling her youngest child closer.

"It's hot," the witchling complained. "My nose is itchy."

"What's happening to the forest?" the eldest asked, holding her father's hand.

"I don't know," he said. "We just have to get away from it."

Ahead, the ground sloped suddenly upward. Too wide to go around, almost too steep to climb, the female lifted her witchling onto her shoulders.

The moment her bare foot hit the hill, she knew something was wrong.

Aisling's heart flipped over as the hill moved, unfurled, a blanket of leaves and moss falling aside to reveal scale and leathery wings. The dragon lifted its enormous, sleepy head and blinked at the family of witches. A saddle was strapped to the base of its neck, empty.

Slowly, the female put her child back down.

"Run."

"Mama . . ."

"I said run!"

The eldest witchling grabbed her sibling's arm and ran for the bushes. Watching them, the dragon blinked lazily, huffing steam from its nostrils. It wasn't like the last one Aisling had seen; its coloring was different, more brown than yellow, its eyes smaller and farther apart. It still had both of them.

"What do you want to do?" the male asked, crouching slowly, palms flat to the ground. "I don't think we can take it."

"I'll distract it. You get the kids and go."

"What?" he hissed, looking back. "No."

"The river is close and I'm higher blessed than you. If I can lure it to the water . . . It might be our best chance."

The dragon's eyes widened, as if it understood the threat. Heat billowed like a cloud as it opened its mouth.

It was over quickly. That any of the family escaped was a miracle.

It was odd that the beast left the head for them. Purposeful.

Aisling put the remains back into the sack and wiped her hands on her cloak. Closing her eyes, she gave herself a moment. Just one, to find her foundation. Then she stood, lifting her chin to the soldier still holding the male tightly.

"Let him go."

The uniformed men exchanged glances, but at Clayton's pointed look, they obeyed. Unlocking the cuffs binding his wrists, the soldier stepped back, hand on his weapon.

"Two blocks south you will find Wyldeden refugees. Leave your children with them and go."

Nodding, the male pulled the two children close and led them deeper into the city. With relative privacy, Aisling turned to Moyra.

"I'll send someone to fetch you later to work on the moongates. There's something pressing I have to deal with."

"What's wrong?" Moyra asked, face gray, eyes stuck on the burlap bag.

Too exposed—there were too many eyes on them, too many shadowy alcoves and alleyways for someone to hide.

"We've been breached. There's a spy in the city."

CHAPTER THIRTY-FOUR

AISLING

SLAMMING THE DOOR OF HER PRAYER ROOM, AISLING'S SKIN PRICKLED with violation, and as her gaze landed on the cabinet where the unicorn blood was meant to be, she shuddered. Nobody besides herself, Eavha and Dearmead had known about the stolen vials from Dusarn's apothecary; why had it not occurred to her before now that if the harbingers had Dearmead, if they questioned him, he might have told them about the unicorn blood. Might have told them everything.

Snarling, Aisling ripped open every cabinet. This time she wasn't searching for the missing vials, but for hex bags. For witchmarks or spellmarks that would allow eavesdropping. For anything that wasn't supposed to be there, anything that might have been tampered with. She had spent too long suffering Nevan to not know what a cursed object felt like.

But her search came up with nothing. Nothing at all.

She had to trust herself. Trust that she had looked properly.

Moving on, she grabbed a stick of chalk and her collection of black candles, shoving her workbench out of the center of the room to clear space. Again, she had spent too long with her mother not to protect herself. Because it couldn't wait any longer. Aisling needed answers and had very few sources from which to get them.

She didn't need the sigil to look into the void, but after what happened in Dusarn, she could no longer trust the veil to be enough to protect her. Davina had been welcomed, but she would not let Tallula touch her.

Sitting in the center of the chalk circle, Aisling scattered her candles at equidistant points and lit them. Crossing her legs, hand on her knees, Aisling closed her eyes and opened her senses to the void.

"Mother," she muttered, shivering against the room's unnatural chill. "Can you hear me?"

It disgusted her, that Tallula Aurnia shared a title with their creator. Using Mother's name to describe those who also brought life to the world was meant as homage to the High Spirit of Creation, becoming such an integral part of their language that even those who did not believe in the gods used the term. Death, too, had their name used to describe the moment of passing from Mother's realm to the void. "The Lover" had only become the popular way of referring to the spirit who protected their final resting place after Balance was formed.

Tallula's screams of rage rattled the room. Aisling deadened her face as she opened her eyes, her mother's apparition translucent and fraying. The dead queen was little more than a smudged charcoal drawing, already succumbing to the emptiness of the void.

"I was promised! Get me out of here! I was promised eternity!"

"Oh, Mother, I think you'll find the void is rather eternal."

Tallula spun, searching blindly, unable to peer back. The sigil kept the veil between them impermeable, but Aisling still stiffened as her mother's fracturing face looked past her.

"Is that you, Aisling? Perhaps being here is a blessing after all, if we are in the void together."

The words were laced with faux affection that Aisling knew was truly a threat. Anything soft that came from her mother was a trap, and Aisling had not fallen for one in a long, long time.

"Alas, I am still in Mother's realm. Welcome to my séance."

The smudgy shadow withered and swelled, but before Tallula could break into whatever wrathful fit she was about to have, Aisling played her opening move.

"I need help, Mother." The words were vile on her tongue. "Help me, and I can help you."

As expected, Tallula cackled. All her royal decorum was gone, stripped away with her decaying soul. For the void to take hold so quickly, her soul must have been rotting already, which, considering what she had brought to life, was no surprise. With everything else peeled away, the venomous viper that had always lived beneath Tallula's skin roamed free. It was her truest self.

"You murdered your brother. Why would I trust you?"

"And you killed my father, but I'm willing to overlook that."

"Don't pretend you didn't despise him. Your father was a soft-spined fence-sitter, and I made sure to poison any bond he tried to form with you. Who do you think put a stop to your illicit flights over the city? Who do you think convinced him to ruin your Imsa? Me."

"Yet, in the end, he chose me. I may hate him, and he might have betrayed me at every conceivable opportunity, but when it mattered, he chose me. And you chose Nevan. You trained him, and looked the other way when he was tormenting me, and yet, again, when it mattered, it wasn't enough. I stuck him like the pig he was and left his corpse to the demi-kin. Father's, too. And yours? Yours was fed upon by beasts and left to rot in that crumbling throne room."

The prayer room shook with Tallula's rabid screams, pure rage and insanity made into sound. It twisted too quickly to hysterical laughter as her form solidified, pacing the edges of the sigil.

"You think you won? I gave Chaos a way into Mother's realm. She will surrender it to him or he will destroy it, and those of us who gave him back his throne will rule with a power you could never imagine."

There were so many things Aisling wanted to say. That all that promised power was a lie, because Tallula would never see it. That Chaos would never get beyond the wards, because Aisling had been planning her counterattack for years. She had questions, too. Why, with her dying breath, would she name Nevan king if a few days prior she had called him an "idiot child"? Aisling had assumed the fetus growing in her mother's belly was a replacement for them both. That Nevan must have finally done something to piss their mother off. That, perhaps, he had found out about the Sparrow monarch's affiliation with Chaos and had rebuked it. But then she had named him king—too late, Aisling had already killed him— so, why?

Retorts and questions brimmed, but they would die unspoken. Because Aisling had a game to play now, and there was more at stake than her curiosity.

"I know," she said curtly. Unsure just how blind her mother was, she forced herself to shrink, chagrined. "I know. That's why I called. Things are escalating and I don't think I can face this after all. Perhaps I would be better off . . . But I can't just . . . Mother, please. Explain it to me. Not just the promises, but . . . who can I speak to about shifting my allegiance? Who are the harbingers? Byron died in Dusarn retrieving the . . . retrieving Chaos, but there have to be more. Who else is there?"

Tallula stilled. "Byron is dead?"

"Yes," Aisling lied. "Chaos emerged from your womb ravenous. The dragon he rode was intelligent enough to accept orders to take Chaos back to their base, but Byron . . . Byron fed himself to Chaos. Such devotion . . . I've never seen anything like it. It made me think. Made me . . . reconsider."

For a moment, there was only silence. Sweat dripped down Aisling's spine as she let her lie sit between them.

"How did you escape? How are you still alive?"

Aisling didn't tell her how the harbinger had sneered and turned his back, deeming her unthreatening and unworthy of the effort it would take to kill her. She didn't tell her how, when the beasts terrorizing the city came for her, she had been so drained that death seemed inevitable. That it had been a kinner, the very one Aisling had brutalized, who saved her life. Saved it so he could take it himself, but saved her all the same.

"As always, you underestimate me," Aisling jabbed. Being too pathetic would only rouse suspicion. "You've always looked down on the blessing the Lover gave me, too, but now it might be the only thing capable of bringing you back from the void. Help me, Mother, and I can bring you through the veil. I can teach you to possess a body. We've never been close, but we could change that. We could rule together."

A child, wanting her mother. Tallula would no doubt be repulsed by such a desperate plea. Such a weak, pathetic daughter. This false desire was for the same bond that had almost formed between Aisling and her father, up in the clouds, riding winged horses together. That need for connection, for love, searched for a new direction now that Phineas was dead, and Tallula would want no part of it.

Aisling knew that.

A weak, pathetic daughter would be easy to manipulate, though. To ruin, once Tallula had a body again. The dead queen could take advantage of this, and with the void tearing her to pieces, with Byron supposedly dead, there were no other options.

Aisling had bared her throat. Now she just needed Tallula to take the bait. Let her find the poison coating the vulnerable flesh she was about to sink her teeth into.

"I only met two others, aside from Byron," Tallula offered. "Spies, opening up tunnels beneath Dusarn for their beasts to come when the time was right. They kept an eye on me, making sure I had everything I needed. The rest I don't know, but Pryll and Wert were reasonable creatures. If you can find a way to speak to them, they will bring you before our master, and he will cast judgment on you. If he finds you sincere, they will bring you into the fold."

Pryll and Wert.

Aisling smiled. "Thank you, Mother."

"Now, how do I—"

Slamming down her mental shields, Aisling shut out the void. She stood and stretched, shaking off the crawling down her spine. She was done with her prayer room, but she was not done with her questioning. Pinching out the candles, Aisling stalked across the hall to her suite to change.

~

Clayton walked with her down into the dungeon. In the dark, bare cells on either side of the long hall, Aadya's guards lay battered and bleeding. Still silent. Fixing the herb-stuffed mask over her mouth and nose, Aisling tilted her chin to them.

"Public executions for the lot of them. See if we can't draw the harbinger out."

Clayton nodded. He would see it done.

The spellmarks on her palms were ruined, so Aisling used burnt herbs and blood to cast The Key Mark for Those Unbound on the secret door in the furthest cell, returning the vials to Clayton for safe keeping once done. Shoving open the fake-stone door, she stalked down another flight of stairs to the hidden room where the reek of Aadya's ruination overpowered the rosemary in Aisling's mask.

Clayton shut the door behind them as Aisling stormed to the little hole in the floor she used as a cell, ripped back the bolt on the hatch, and flung it open.

Aadya's haggard breathing didn't hitch at the flood of fresh air that assaulted her. Her eyes stayed closed, lids twitching. The wound Aisling had left when she'd cut the constellation off her forehead and shoved the flesh down her throat was inflamed and leaking puss.

"Fuck," Aisling cursed, stepping back. Grabbing a bucket, she filled it with water from the tap in the wall and dumped it over Aadya's listless form.

Nothing.

"*Fuck.*"

Aisling threw the bucket at the wall with enough force to crack it. Dragging her gloved hands down her face, she paced for a minute, trying to think of literally any other solution than the first one that popped into her head.

But there wasn't time.

"Clayton," she sighed. "I need Eavha."

⁓

Clayton gave Eavha his arm as she navigated the stairs. Thick boots—*feet traps*—encased her usually bare feet, guardian leathers covering her clothes, a mask just like Aisling's clipped over her ears. With her voluminous curls tied back, Eavha's wide eyes were all Aisling could see as the two of them reached the landing where Aisling waited, leaning against the door, arms crossed tight against her chest.

"I need to ask you a favor."

"Alright."

"It is unpleasant."

Eavha looked around at the cold stone walls, the stained wooden door, and fixed the mask over her face. "I figured."

"After, it is okay if you hate me."

"Alright."

No argument. No assurances that Eavha wasn't capable of hating Aisling. She hadn't realized she'd expected the rebuttal until it didn't come.

Steeling herself, Aisling nodded and opened the door.

While Clayton had been preparing Eavha, Aisling had been preparing Aadya. Splayed naked on the table, scaled wrists and ankles bound, the mutant witch was still unconscious. Ready on the workstation waited two bowls, one of rousing salts and the other chloroform. If Aisling had no choice but to bring Eavha down to this filthy place, she would not allow there to be any risk. Aadya would not wake until Aisling wanted her to.

For two long minutes, Eavha stood frozen in the threshold, staring.

Aisling couldn't begin to imagine what was going through her mind. Holding herself apart, she waited patiently.

Eventually, Eavha stepped inside. She wouldn't meet Aisling's gaze as it followed her progress across the room to the table, and though Eavha had never given Aisling a reason to believe she was as soft on the inside as she was on the outside, the clinical way she inspected Aadya's wounds, detached and professional, was surprising.

There was still fear, though. Eavha's fingers trembled as she prodded the infected flesh on Aadya's face.

"I'm sorry," Aisling croaked.

"She murdered my entire family."

Whether it was a reminder to herself, a way to stomach this, or some kind of offering, forgiveness, an excuse, for Aisling, she didn't know. Neither option was pleasant.

Yet, that was part of the reason Aisling had inflicted that particular injury. No matter how she wished otherwise, there was too much Aurnia blood in her veins. Nevan had taught her too well.

"She is the reason they burned the forest. Why they are coming here," Aisling added.

"I doubt giving her back would stop them."

It had never occurred to Aisling to do such a thing. She had been so ready for this fight that avoiding it had never crossed her mind. Such was the sureness of Davina's visions.

Davina had been wrong before.

"Would it be worth trying?" Aisling asked.

"You're the strategist. You tell me."

Forcing herself to ignore Eavha's flat tone, Aisling thought on it. She didn't know enough about her enemy to predict them with any kind of accuracy; would Byron bargain with her? Or was he so confident that he wouldn't bother? Would he burn the city out of spite, regardless? There was no way to know.

The only thing that was certain was that keeping Aadya ensured the army's approach, but given what Tallula had said—if Mother didn't surrender this world, then Chaos would destroy it—it was a safe bet that any amnesty would be temporary.

"No," Aisling decided.

Magic curled in the air, twisting Aisling's gut as Eavha lay her hand over Aadya's infected wound.

"My da didn't have a constellation tattoo. Moyra said it was because he never graduated. He left before he finished schooling. To find my ma."

Eavha's soft voice was a nightmare in this place. She didn't belong here.

"I just spoke with Moyra. She said the wards made things difficult, and that she was relying heavily on whatever added control the constellation provided. Aadya said that without hers, she could not use her blessing properly. Perhaps that is why your da never displayed any of his Morvish power."

"Except Moyra also said he saw the fate lines like Eaon does. So perhaps it is more like a Blessing Charm. Focusing and strengthening otherwise aimless or latent abilities."

"Maybe," Aisling agreed, watching Eavha reach for a cloth to clean away the infected tissue she pulled from beneath Aadya's skin.

"The color of the constellation reminds me of the kinner mark. Of unicorn blood."

"It probably is."

"Perhaps a tattoo for Eaon would help him."

Aisling raised her eyebrows. "Maybe that's what the phouka wanted a vial for."

"Maybe," Eavha agreed distractedly. "Or maybe he wanted it to turn him kinner, too. Keep him from dying anymore. It's not good for him."

Aisling nodded. In all her years living in Dusarn, no Sparrow had ever taken the Passing rite more than once. No doubt for a good reason. Every time she saw Eaon Nemuse wandering the palace, stretching his poorly healed legs, he looked more tired. Sickly.

"If you haven't heard, there is a spy in Hyrsch."

Judging by the way Eavha's head whipped around, she hadn't.

"I believe they took the remaining vials. When I find them, I will recover the unicorn blood, and you may use as much as you want to turn whoever you like. I owe one to the phouka, as you know, but the rest are yours."

"I still want to turn you."

Aisling breathed. For the first time since Eavha descended the stairs into this cesspool, she found air.

"And I want to turn my brother."

"Of course. You should turn yourself, too."

If Aisling was going to survive this war, if she was going to allow Eavha to push her magic . . . If she was going to live forever, she wanted to do so with Eavha.

"I don't think I can." Eavha grimaced. "Self-healing is difficult, and . . ."

For a moment, Eavha was somewhere else. Listening to something else. Then she shook her head.

"No. It can't be done."

"I think you should still try."

"It would be a waste."

"You can't know that." Aisling would scour the world to find another Sanni-blessed healer if she had to. Would find a way to convene with the spirit of healing herself. "Nothing is impossible—"

"Sanni said it can't be done," Eavha snapped. "So drop it."

Aisling flinched back. "Sanni? You . . . you convened with Sanni, just now? So easily?"

Jaw tense, returning her attention to her work, Eavha gave a short, curt nod.

She had never been a good liar.

"What aren't you telling me?"

"Nothing."

"Eavha."

"I'm done," she said, stepping back, ignoring Aisling's stare as she moved to the tap to wash her hands.

"Eavha Nemuse, I swear—"

On the table, Aadya groaned.

Eavha flinched so hard she slipped, crushing her shoulder against the stone wall in an attempt to move away. Unaware of any decision to move, Aisling found herself across the room, grabbing a chloroform-soaked rag from the bowl to cover the mutant witch's face.

Eavha was sweating, the hair on her arms standing upright. "I . . . I . . ."

"She cannot hurt you."

"I can't be here. I can't . . . I . . ."

Leaving Aadya, Aisling took Eavha's arm and gently moved her away from the wall. Clayton would keep an eye on her prisoner until she could return, but she had to get Eavha out.

"Come on."

Up the stairs, through the dungeon, up more stairs, out into the hall, Aisling led Eavha far away from the witch who had taken so much from her. There were too many people about, staring curiously, and while Aisling knew Eavha was well practiced at containing her emotions, she was not perfect, so Aisling shoved open a door into the servant's halls and slammed it shut behind them.

"You're alright."

Pale and shivering, Eavha leaned heavily against Aisling as she caught her breath. Holding her gently, Aisling shucked off her gloves and stroked back her hair.

"Don't tell anyone," Eavha whispered into the crook of Aisling's neck. If not for the leather, the warmth of her breath would have stolen all of Aisling's remaining self-control.

"What?"

"Don't tell anyone how much of a baby I am. It would ruin my image."

Burying a smile in Eavha's hair, Aisling kissed her gently.

"Your secret is safe with me."

CHAPTER THIRTY-FIVE

CINN

FOR THE FIRST TIME SINCE WAKING UP IN HYRSCH, CINN WAS ALONE.

He didn't like it.

Well, he wasn't *really* alone; there were other people in the Turlough home, but nobody that was *his*. Everyone was busy getting ready to evacuate. William and Sarah offered to let him tag along while they spoke to Lord Dustin about the allocation of demi-kin in Belden, and it might have helped to have him at their side staring daggers at the incompetent Sparrow lord, but he couldn't do it. He couldn't be around one of them and not have some kind of breakdown—murderous or catatonic was a fence he balanced on far too precariously and he wouldn't risk the Copelands' safety if he fell on the wrong side of it.

Sarah had offered to stay with him while William went, but Cinn also didn't like the idea of them being separated. He was already losing track of where everybody was, and it seemed safer for them to be together. He had promised he would be okay—would stay at the house and help the kitchenhands make more food for everybody—but being surrounded by only strangers nagged at his anxiety.

He'd only just found everybody again. Separation was a splinter in his eye, and the longer it stayed there, the less he could bear it.

Edwina was doing something she either couldn't or wouldn't explain to Cinn, somewhere in the palace. It wasn't dangerous, she'd promised, but Radley opted to guard her anyway.

Moyra was also busy in the palace, Gatty undoubtedly with her. The cat sith hadn't bothered to check on Cinn since the fiasco in the fields outside the city, but he had gone back once, sitting on the crest of the hill where he could see witches dotting the empty plains that would soon be their battlefield, laying cursed traps. He watched the soldiers and cadets, the guardians and the rebels, learning to work together; observing and unwilling to go closer until he had spoken to Moyra.

A task he had not done yet, because she was in the palace, and he was a coward.

Eaon was also in the palace.

He could not beat down his cowardice for Moyra.

He would do it for Eaon, though.

Hours had passed since Cinn had tried to summon Siobhan, hoping she would lead him back through the servant's halls to the infirmary, but there had been no word. Busy, like everyone else. Everyone but him.

Maybe once he made it to Eaon, if his friend was up for it, he could take Cinn to Moyra. Last time, he couldn't bear the thought, dizzy and sick remembering what it had been like to walk the palace halls in reverent awe, moments before having his life torn from him. But . . . it might be okay to venture farther into that place if he had Eaon by his side.

He just had to find Eaon.

~

Find Eaon.

Just find Eaon.

It was the repetition of his self-dictated command that got him to the palace in one piece. The echoes of Siobhan talking him through every step—*this is the gate they took me through on the way to the river, and this is the door the laundry cart had barely squeezed through, and this is the laundry room the cart had come from, the smell of mildew my ticket to freedom*—got him inside.

Was it darker than last time, or was Cinn's vision spotting? Was he breathing? Probably not. He focused on his body, here, now, in the present. His lungs, expanding and contracting. The never-before-known strength in his limbs. The knife he had taken from the Turlough's kitchen, swinging from his trousers' belt loops.

He could do this.

He could make it to the infirmary.

Was it left at this hall? Or right?

He couldn't remember, but left felt like a good idea.

A good idea for a total of ten seconds, as he found himself in a hall he didn't recognize, and standing in it . . .

Standing there . . .

Mistake.

This had been a mistake.

Except . . .

Was that Eavha?

Was that Eavha with her?

Aisling was holding Eavha's head against her shoulder . . . An odd way to smother someone, but he wasn't about to try and make sense of the things she did.

He couldn't find the calm he'd found outside with the soldiers. The calm he'd felt in Dusarn, when he'd had his chance to kill Aisling and failed. There was only undiluted panic at the sight of her hands on Eavha. Of Eavha's hands holding her wrists, trying to get away, trying to breathe . . .

Cinn's footsteps were not quiet, drawing attention too soon. Aisling's eyes widened as she pushed Eavha behind her, raising a single hand toward Cinn. Scars marred her palm and his mouth filled with desire to see her bleed again.

Eavha shouted something, but he couldn't hear it. Whatever it was gave Aisling pause, though, withholding the magic she undoubtedly planned to hurt him with. Talking, talking, both of them talking, but Cinn didn't slow. And Aisling might not have blasted him with one of her spells, but she wasn't going to just let him stab her either. She blocked, shoving his arm aside, but Cinn swung his other fist before she could counter. Would have caught the side of her head, too, if Eavha wasn't pulling at Aisling, trying to get past her.

There wasn't time for this. Deep down, he knew there wasn't time to have this fight, here in the hallway. He had to get Eavha away. Get her safe. Grabbing her wrist, he pulled her out of the volatile space between him and Aisling, who didn't fight as he smashed his boot into the side of her knee. He barely waited to watch her crumple, tightening his grip on a thrashing Eavha to haul her down the hallway.

"Cinn! Slow down! Just stop!"

Not until they were safe. Not until they got to Eaon. Aisling couldn't touch them as long as Eaon was around.

Lost in the hallways, Cinn barreled through the nearest door and into an enormous kitchen. A skeleton crew were preparing meals, barely stopping to look as Cinn darted between benches, jumping over a mop bucket sitting unattended and in the way, glad Eavha was nimble enough to follow.

Out of the kitchen, he fled mindlessly down wider, carpeted hallways. No longer resisting, Eavha overtook him.

"Eaon's this way. Come on," she said in surprisingly clear Nirnish.

He didn't have time to wonder when she had learned. She, too, knew that their safety lay with Eaon and that was all that mattered.

A familiar hall came into view, and at the end of it waited the infirmary door, but Eavha ran right by it.

Cinn began to dig in his heels, but Eavha tugged more urgently.

"This way. He's up here," she promised, dragging him through a gut-churningly familiar foyer to a grand staircase.

Leather boots kept Eavha's swift footsteps from being silent as they clambered up the stairs, but she was still quieter than Cinn. Distantly, fleetingly, he wondered why she was wearing them—why she was dressed in Wyldeden guardian leathers at all—but it was overshadowed by questions as to how she had ended up in that hallway to begin with, and utterly drowned out by the need to get out of this place.

Another hall, dark and stuffy with the day's heat, and Cinn couldn't breathe, couldn't think, couldn't focus on where he was going . . .

A door.

Cinn didn't slow as he and Eavha burst through it. Barely registered the phouka, sitting in a velvet armchair and polishing an old, earthy brown skull, the furniture dwarfed by his imposing frame. At the sudden, frantic company, the phouka put the bone into a sack full at his feet and stood, following them through the reception room and into a bedroom the size of Cinn's entire apartment. The door banged loudly against the wall as Cinn barreled through, and in the bed, bundled under a pile of blankets, Eaon very quickly stopped sleeping.

"What—"

Cinn released Eavha, pushing her into the phouka's arms and turning his back to the room, holding his knife out. If Aisling herself hadn't followed them, she'd have sent guards.

Eavha's low Terranian words were impossible for Cinn to understand, but that was fine. Whatever language was easier to convey the danger they were in was fine.

But then, "Cinn." Eaon's gentle voice made no sense. "Cinn, look at me. It's alright."

Taking careful steps deeper into the room, he risked a glance over his shoulder.

The phouka had put Eavha in a chair where she had two fingers pressed to her lips, unmistakable pity directed at Cinn. Sitting on the edge of the bed, Eaon tested his weight, holding onto the bedframe for balance. Face gaunt, eyelids heavy, the skin underneath had grown dark.

"Come here," Eaon asked, free hand fluttering, too tired to reach out.

What was wrong? Had something happened in the days Cinn had been unable to come back? If he had known, he would have visited sooner. As it was, he shouldn't have dragged the shitstorm on his tail to Eaon's door.

Swallowing thickly, attention darting back and forth between the reception room and Eaon, Cinn made his way over. The phouka assessed for a moment before exiting the room, leaving the door open so they could see him peering out into the hall.

"It's alright," Eaon repeated, resting his hand on Cinn's cheek. Compared to the heat flushing Cinn's face, Eaon's skin was freezing.

{She was trying to kill Eavha,} Cinn explained clumsily, still holding the kitchen knife. {Did she not tell you?}

Sliding a pointed look to his sister, Eaon sighed.

"She wasn't trying to kill her."

Frowning, shaking his head, Cinn looked to where Eavha had turned away, eyes closed. A noise snapped his head back to where the phouka filled the suite's doorway, voice pitched low, blocking someone from entering.

Heart beating against his ribs so hard he was sure it was bruising, Cinn shook Eaon's hand off, needing him to understand.

{She was, Eaon. I saw it. She's followed us. She's out there.}

"Cinn, they were hugging."

Cinn thought, perhaps, he had stopped understanding Nirnish. Because that didn't make sense.

Unless . . .

Sucking in a breath, he stepped closer to Eaon. {Curse? Hex? Is that why your people are working with her? What do we do? How can I help?}

The side-eye Eaon gave Eavha was ten times more hostile than the one before. "A curse or a hex would be preferable, but unfortunately my sister just has horrific taste in women."

Cinn stared, waiting for understanding to hit. Waiting for the punchline. Because it sounded like Eaon was suggesting that Eavha had been voluntarily hugging Aisling, and that maybe hugging was the least offensive thing the two had been doing, and that . . .

Eaon's grimace deepened, and it hit Cinn like a volley of arrows.

There was no trick.

In the chair, Eavha was speaking, soft and apologetic and utterly indiscernible. If Cinn looked at her, he was going to scream.

"I'm sorry."

The words came from behind him, and the sound of them froze the breath in his lungs. Unable to move, Cinn could only see Eaon's eyes widening, nostrils flaring. His grip on Cinn tightened to something painful.

"Leave," Eaon hissed, looking over Cinn's shoulder. "Right now."

Eavha's being in the room was the only reason Cinn reached for Eaon's wrist, giving the roiling magic a safe place to go. He didn't know how he could ever look at Eavha again, but no matter what she had done, he wouldn't let Eaon hurt his sister. Even at his best, the Lover's seed was not something Eaon could control without gloves and cuffs and a wand, and right now he had none of those things. The magic hurt, eating away at his flesh, rotting his body from the inside out, but the distraction was a balm, and complaining would only force Eaon to pull that pain into himself. Cinn would not allow that. He could take it. He could endure the incessant itch that healed his body as quickly as it was being ripped apart.

"I know I am not welcome, but listen. If he is going to stay then we need to come to some sort of truce, because I cannot possibly fight Chaos and tiptoe around Cinn at the same time."

His name in her mouth split him apart.

He didn't let go of Eaon's wrist, but he wanted to. The phouka knew it, too. Appearing behind them, both clawed hands fell on Eaon's shoulders. He could command Aisling to leave—to do all sorts of terrible things, if he wanted to—so why wasn't he? Why had he let her in at all?

"*Leave*," Eaon warned.

"Please—"

"Do not look at him!" Eaon snapped, trying and failing to shrug the phouka off. "Do not speak to him!"

Cinn couldn't turn around. Couldn't look. Black spots danced in his vision and, in his head, he took a step back. A wall of cotton fell between him and the world, him and his skin. Conversation continued, but it meant nothing to him.

"I do not blame you for wanting to hurt me, Cinn, but this cannot continue. I can't let you kill me, but . . . If it brings some kind of peace, I can offer you your pound of flesh."

"Aisling!" Eavha hissed, but the Sparrow queen ignored her.

"I will put myself on that table and you can find your peace. All I ask is that you don't kill me. There's too much at stake."

"Aisling!" Eavha turned to stare wide-eyed at Cinn. "Please, don't."

On the bedside table, a tray of breakfast sat virtually untouched. The teacup was chipped. It reminded him of Nena the lake sprite. Her mischievous giggle echoing in the pipes.

Tearing his gaze back to Cinn's, Eaon asked, {Can I speak for you?}

Cinn blinked. He couldn't even sign, not with her in the room.

Eaon knew the answer anyway.

"He won't do it."

"Why?"

"Because you want him to."

Cinn couldn't bring himself to close his eyes, but his knees shook with the relief of being known. Of being understood. He wanted her screaming. Bleeding. Dead. But on his terms. Not because she allowed it.

"And to be honest, I'm glad he won't. You think offering yourself to him, letting him hurt you, somehow makes you even? That a settled score will absolve you? Maybe in your fucked-up head it does. Maybe to you, it would feel like forgiveness. But you will never have that peace."

Eaon's anger was a shield, and Cinn was so deeply withdrawn inside the dark corners of his mind that it felt like enough. If he had any of his own emotions, he wasn't aware of them. Floating somewhere just above his own head, he couldn't stop staring at the only thing Eaon had eaten off his breakfast tray. The broken shell of a boiled egg lay neatly piled inside the porcelain eggcup. It was just a chicken egg, unlike the delicate blue bird shell he kept in his trinket box. His nose tickled. He missed his feather. His paper fox. His shiny rock.

"I'm not stupid," Aisling ground out. "I just want to walk onto the battlefield and not have to worry about a knife in my back."

There was a knife in his hand.

He felt drunk as he stumbled back a step, the room falling completely silent as he did. Eaon reached out to steady him, but Cinn let go of his wrist and took the two steps needed to reach the bedside table.

There was a knife in his hand and a broken eggshell on the table, and he could feel something—something he was too blank to name—cracking his sternum.

In tiny fractions of moments, he had known peace.

He would make sure Eaon was right. She would never know it.

As if he was nothing but a spectator in his own body, he watched his hand put the knife on the bedside table and tipped the eggshell into his palm. When he turned around, he couldn't see the faces staring at him.

Nobody stopped him as he took clumsy, lurching steps across the room. Nobody spoke as he stopped an arm's length away from Aisling. His insides were colder than the chill seeping from Eaon, proof that he was dead in all the ways that mattered.

She had taken everything from him. His family, his voice, his name.

The worn leather diary on the credenza was something safe to look at, and he was grateful that all his other senses seemed to have shut off. He could not smell the blood on her leather bodysuit or hear the false calm of her measured breaths. If she was staring at him, if she was sweating, he couldn't see it. And if, as he held out his hand, emptying the eggshells into her waiting palm, their fingers brushed, he didn't feel it.

Somehow, he walked away. Somehow, he made it back to Eaon, the itching mild as he put his head down on his best friend's shoulder and retreated even farther away.

"I don't understand," she said softly.

"Don't look at me." Eaon's voice hummed against Cinn's cheek. "I don't know what it means, either. But you gave him a chance and he didn't take it. I hope trying to figure out why keeps you up at night."

A minute passed in silence. Or maybe it was longer. He didn't know. Time only started again once he knew she was leaving.

"I have to finish dealing with something. Send for me if he changes his mind."

"Hold your breath," Eaon answered.

The door snipped closed.

CHAPTER THIRTY-SIX

EAON

THERE WAS A SIGNIFICANT DIFFERENCE BETWEEN THE RELAXED, HEAVY weight of Cinn resting on Eaon's shoulder when he was tired and snuggling, and what he was doing now. This was not a search for comfort, it was surrender. It was defeat. This was too much fear and too much pain and the acceptance that he could not escape either.

Eaon held Cinn's head against his shoulder and glared at Aisling's retreating form, her brows still pinched as she stared at the eggshell Cinn had place in her hand.

In Eaon's sleep, seeing Cinn and Aisling in a room together always ended in bloodshed; a dream would mean it was Aisling's, while a nightmare meant it was Cinn's. Sometimes, he was a helpless bystander while the two of them tore each other apart. Other times, it was his own hands that were bloody.

Quietly, Eaon was grateful for the phouka's painful grip on his shoulders. The seed was rioting at another lost opportunity and Eaon loathed having to contain it. As always, though, what he wanted didn't matter. He couldn't kill Aisling right now; the war effort couldn't afford the loss. But, if the phouka hadn't absorbed the seething magic into himself, Eaon wouldn't be able to hold Cinn. The skin contact was probably still uncomfortable, but clearly not enough so for Cinn to pull away.

"She's gone," Eaon whispered, lips pressed against his ear. "She's gone, she can't hurt you."

"I'm so sorry," Eavha repeated for the hundredth time.

Ignoring her, Eaon took a few careful steps, encouraging Cinn to follow. It was awkward with the phouka shadowing him, but eventually Eaon got Cinn sitting safely on the bed. Cupping his face, he looked for any sign that Cinn hadn't entirely disappeared, but his limbs were deadweight, eyes hollow.

"I'm so sorry."

"Shut up."

"I . . . I'll get him something. For the anxiety. A . . . I think there were some—"

"He doesn't need a tonic, Eavha. He needs to not see people he trusts sucking face with people who tortured him."

In his ear, the phouka's hot breath warned, "You need to calm down. Now."

A ridiculous suggestion.

Yet, Eaon blew out a long breath through his nose. Ridiculous as the idea of calm seemed, it was also a necessity. He couldn't help anyone if he was bleeding poison into the room.

The sweat on Cinn's forehead was cold. Behind him, Eavha was crying.

"Could you fetch us some water and a towel?" Eaon ground out, swallowing as much of his temper as he could. It wasn't helping anyone.

After kicking off her boots, Eavha ran from the room.

"Hey," Eaon tried again, awkwardly lowering himself to his knees in front of Cinn, rubbing circles into the backs of his hands. Every muscle in his legs screamed at the position, but pain was secondary to the need to meet Cinn's empty stare. "Did I ever tell you about the time I traveled to Bernt and lost everything I was carrying to a cat sith? Not Gatty. This one was smaller and had these glowing blue eyes, fluorescent like the flowers in the northern mountains. Can you picture it? Da left me at camp to mind the heavy packs while he found us something to eat, and the cat sith offered protection from the other fae lurking in the area if I could solve their riddle in under a minute. Do you want to hear it?"

Cinn blinked. It was something.

"What is it that, given one, you either have two or none?"

Another blink.

Eavha returned, moving slower, carrying a bowl of water and a small towel. Already soaking it, she sat on the bed beside Cinn and brought the compress to his forehead.

Eaon saw the shift a moment before it happened.

Vacant Cinn was gone. Smacking Eavha's hand away, his other hand raised in a fist, already swinging.

He had barely moved before Eaon had a hold of his wrist. Heat, so foreign in his veins, flashed blindingly. He did not speak, but he did not need to—Cinn's entire arm fell limp, eyes blinking madly, neck reddening in shame. Cinn hadn't meant to react like that, Eaon knew, but it didn't matter.

"I am on your side, but that is a line you do not cross. Understood?"

Cinn nodded shallowly, lifting a finger to his mouth to sign an apology, but unable to follow through.

"I am so sorry," Eavha said again, this time in Nirnish.

The language change didn't matter. Cinn refused to acknowledge her.

Shooting his sister a pointed look, Eavha nodded and moved away. After a moment and a long staring contest, the phouka also backed off. For now, his magic was back under control.

Gently, Eaon put Cinn's hand back in his lap. Alertness didn't mean things were alright; echoes of a wild kinner boy who didn't know his name and bolted like a rabbit at the snap of a twig stared back at him, flushed and twitching.

"You can't be here," Eaon said to Cinn, who closed his eyes and shook his head. "Let me talk to Eavha for a minute, then I'll come home with you, alright?"

Eavha's latest attempt to heal him might have been a waste of time, but at least moping in Dearmead's bed instead had gotten him out of the infirmary. It couldn't continue, though. He had no energy, but sleeping wasn't a luxury he could afford anymore—it was time to get back to reality.

This time when Cinn slumped against him, it was with relief.

Eaon looked over his shoulder.

"Sit with him in the reception room?"

The phouka narrowed his eyes. "Are you asking for a favor?"

"No. It was a suggestion."

"I don't think you're calm enough to be left alone."

"Your nannying doesn't help."

Puffing out his chest in a display that no longer intimidated Eaon, the phouka glared. Assessed. Despite the vile things Eaon had said last time he spoke privately with his sister, he didn't think he was truly capable of hurting Eavha. He'd rather self-destruct.

The phouka knew that.

Huffing, the wretched fae watched with cruel amusement as Eaon struggled back to his feet. Cinn offered his arms as support and Eaon had little choice but to lean on them heavily.

"I'll only be a minute," he promised.

Cinn suppressed a shudder, eyes rimmed in red, but followed the phouka from the room.

The bed dipped as Eaon sat down. Chewing her nails, Eavha stared at her knuckles.

If Eaon thought about it, he couldn't remember the last time he had an easy moment with his sister. Every conversation they'd had in Hyrsch had been an argument, and before that, Pirevia had been sparse on pleasantries. Prior to that blood-soaked arena, Eaon hadn't seen or spoken to his sister in months, him on the farm with Cinn and her training as a priestess in Wyldeden. The celebration she had organized for his quarter-century birthday was probably the last time, and realizing it felt heavy.

"He hates me now." A declaration of fact.

Eaon sighed. Denying it was pointless. "Can you blame him?"

"No." Silently, Eavha began to pace the room. "Do *you* hate me?"

Well. Ripped from sleep, the pendulum of his emotions had swung fiercely between sheer panic, searching two of the most important people in his life for blood or bruises, and undiluted rage when Eavha explained what happened.

"Sometimes I really wish I could. But, no, Eavha. Even when I'm screaming at you in public and threatening to kill you, I don't hate you."

That earned a smirk, but she still wouldn't look at him. Exhaustion lined her face in a way he hadn't seen since their excommunication.

"Are you okay?" he asked.

"I'm fine."

"Eavha."

"What?"

The way she paced, the balding spot behind her ear where she'd been ripping out hair for her Blessing Charm, her fingernails chewed down to the beds—Eavha wore her stress on her sleeve for everyone to see. No doubt she was talking to Aisling about it, and it wasn't like Eaon was in a position to offer any sort of advice, but she was still his little sister. He still had a responsibility.

"Can we talk for a minute?"

Stilling, Eavha's eyes widened. "Are *you* okay? Did I hurt you when I tried to heal you? Do you need something for the pain?"

"I'm fine." Again, lying was pointless, but he did it anyway. "I just mean that, in the spring, I left you in Wyldeden, and then the next time I see you is Pirevia, and everything spiraled out of control from there. You're heir, and you're leading our clan, and pushing yourself further than you should be, and . . . I know I've been an asshole, a proper rogue even, and I'm sorry, but I still love you and I wanted to check that you were okay."

For a moment, Eavha just stared. Then she dropped her shoulders and sunk onto the mattress beside him, burying her head in her hands.

"I want to go home."

Eaon nodded solemnly. His own complicated feelings toward Wyldeden aside, he knew what it was like to long for a place of safety and belonging. For him, it had never been the Nemuse manor, but that didn't mean there weren't places in Wyldeden that had been a haven.

"I wish I could take you."

"This . . ." Eavha's voice cracked, and she tilted her face toward the ceiling to keep the tears from falling. "Being heir . . . It was everything I ever dreamed of—but not like this."

"You're doing a good job."

"Am I?"

"Yeah," Eaon promised. "You know, it wasn't that long ago that we were building that shelter in the willow tree in Anfar, and you were having a tantrum every two minutes because you hated the real world. Not even six months ago, you nearly wet yourself at the sight of an open field because the world was just *too big*. Now look at you."

Eavha huffed with what could have been laughter if she hadn't lost the fight with her tears.

"I am scared all the time. That hasn't changed."

Carefully, Eaon assessed the space between them, tucking his bare hands beneath his aching thighs.

"Me too." The admission sat between them for a moment, as much of a blow as it was a balm. "But it'll be okay. You know I'm not going to let anything happen to you."

Eavha bit her lip, worrying her fingers. "That scares me too."

"What does?"

"The lengths you'll go to," she explained, voice almost too soft to hear. Her eyes grew redder as she forced herself to say more. "I don't want you to die, and not just because I'd miss you. Not just because you're my brother. My whole life I have been so focused on myself and my goals that it feels like I'm only just now getting to know you. Truly. Properly. I see you. I see everything you've sacrificed for me, everything you never got to be because of me, and you deserve a chance to know you too. You deserve a chance to grow. To live."

Eaon looked away.

For years, "self-centered" was the kindest thing he could say about Eavha. Bitter and jealous, he had bled so she could stay sheltered and naive, and in return, she had, at every conceivable opportunity, rubbed her privilege in his face.

But his baby sister had grown.

She would be twenty-one soon—still years away from a witch's full maturity, but already he could see the kind of person Eavha was becoming. Not just arrogant, but compassionate. Honest. Inspiring.

"I meant it," Eaon said. "Ma and Da would have been proud of you. And I am too."

Eavha's lips parted around a shaky breath. "Thank you. I wish I could do more to help you. I . . . I wish I could hug you."

A shudder ran down Eaon's spine and the incessant chill beneath his skin stirred. For a fleeting moment, the absolute bliss his sister's soul would bring as the seed devoured it was tempting. She was so bright, the colors shimmering in and out of focus so vibrant—silver and gold twining in threaded patterns Eaon couldn't understand. One particularly pearlescent one tied her to him, and it almost tasted like permission. Their fates were tied. He could kill her now and it would be what was always meant to be.

Her death will be quick, the seed promised.

But there were five other threads just as shiny and strong, each stretching too far for him to see where they would lead. Logic promised the link between them couldn't possibly revolve around the seed's desire, so he took a thin, sharp breath and pushed the craving away.

Shoulders curling against the sharp dig of claws in his lungs, Eaon bore the brunt of the seed's disappointment in silence. Beside him, goosebumps prickled the bare skin of Eavha's arms—the only proof that his lapse in control was not entirely private.

She had to feel it, yet she sat beside him, tense and determined.

"Didn't I tell you to run from me when this happens?"

"I'm heir of the Anfar Forest Clan. You can't tell me what to do."

Eaon's mouth quirked in a grimace as the blistering cold carved apart his insides, but if he stayed very still, the expression could almost be confused for a smothered smile. "I'm still your Head of House, so actually, I can."

Eavha snorted. "Well, you're entitled to try, I suppose. See how it pans out for you."

"I already know. I can count the number of times you've listened to me on my thumbs." Every word was more and more strained as he caged the lethal magic seething inside. "But, seriously, Eavha. I need you to leave. I can't hold this in much longer."

Sighing, Eavha stood. "I'm needed at the war tents anyway. There's not much left in terms of supplies, but the med tent still needs to be organized. Come find me when you're ready to try the conduit again."

"Sure." He wouldn't. It wasn't worth the strain.

"I'll get Cinn for you."

"The phouka," Eaon forced between his teeth. "I don't want to hurt Cinn."

"But you'll hurt the phouka?"

"He likes it."

Eavha blinked but chose not to ask further questions. Which was for the best. She left, but Eaon didn't loosen his grip on himself until the phouka's sharp claws dug in his collarbones.

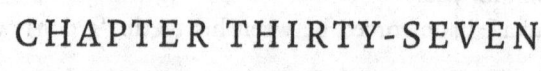

CHAPTER THIRTY-SEVEN

CINN

The evacuation was more evident as the trio wound through Hyrsch's streets. Shopfronts were shuttered closed, wares packed away. Grocers were turning people away, completely sold out of produce. Panic may have set in if it weren't for the guards redirecting people to the food halls and the throngs of Wyldeden witches pulling fresh fruits and vegetables right out of the ground, handing them out to whoever was in need. The streets were packed, and only the overbearing presence of the phouka kept the walk from the palace from becoming dangerous. For Cinn, because the world was still hazy and distant, his feet moving entirely out of muscle memory. For everyone else, because only the thin fabric of Eaon's clothes stopped a casual brush being a death sentence. But the looming fae walked behind them, a hand on each of their shoulders, ensuring a bubble of space around them.

Eventually, Cinn stopped in the alley where his family's little second-floor apartment waited at the top of a set of rickety stairs.

"This is where you used to live?"

The past tense scraped at an already festering wound. If it weren't for Aisling, he would still live here. If it weren't for her, he never would have known what it was like to come home and feel lost in it. It was a shithole, but it had been their shithole, and she had taken that from him.

"I wonder," a silky voice purred from the shadows, followed by the solidifying form of a black-furred cat sith. "Is it that this no longer feels like home, or that you've discovered the true meaning of the word. This is,

288

after all, nothing more than rotting wood and crumbling stone that you attached meaning to. And really, Cinn, surely there are better places to be fond of."

Through the veil of cotton between Cinn and the world, through the haze of his thoughts, something about Gatty's grating existence hooked him, dragging him back to reality. Rolling his eyes, Cinn sighed deep enough to drop his shoulders from his ears. Realistically, he couldn't be too annoyed, though. One fae friend was good. Two was better.

Gatty grinned. "I knew you liked me."

"You're a long way from your witch, cat sith," the phouka noted, moving closer until hot breath fluttered Cinn's hair.

"I am. Moyra is working on something that does not require my assistance. Meanwhile, our brethren have begun to amass. One of yours has arrived."

Raising his brows, Eaon looked between the two of them.

"Another Old One? Here?"

"Yes," Gatty confirmed, keeping his moon-bright eyes locked on the phouka. "She is asking for you, and I have it on good authority that there is no immediate danger to these two menaces. Allow me to escort you beyond the city wall, ancient one. We have things to discuss."

Cinn's shoulders tightened again as, slowly, the phouka loosened his grip and stepped away. Before he could begin spiraling again, Eaon laced his fingers through Cinn's.

"Go on," Eaon said to the phouka, waving his free hand. "Shoo."

Nostrils flaring, claws biting into the creature's palms as he clenched his fists, the phouka turned a look of undiluted hatred at him. "You are the bane of my existence."

Letting Cinn take his crutch, Eaon leaned on the staircase's wonky railing and hoisted his bad leg onto the first step. "Think of something original to call me while you're gone."

The phouka pointed a finger. "I will."

Cinn chewed his lip and watched the faeries turn away, disappearing into the crowd. It took Eaon tugging on his hand to pull his gaze away, the strained huff of exertion as Eaon struggled up the second step to get Cinn moving.

{He's going to kill you,} he signed after tapping Eaon's wrist for attention.

Amusement and anger warred as Eaon turned away, glaring at each creaking step they climbed. "Don't tell anyone but . . ."

Cinn was good at keeping secrets.

"He thinks he is my familiar. It's a Morvish thing, and I only know the very basic lore behind it, but . . . clearly he's gone senile in his old age because I am not Morvish."

Petulant. That's what came to mind as Cinn watched Eaon grind his teeth and glare. Again, he tugged Eaon's hand to make him pause.

{I think you know that's not true.}

Eaon couldn't meet his eye. "Don't you start. Please."

{I was there. In Qiri, in Ahrenhale. I saw Moyra helping witches experiencing things just like you do.}

"It doesn't mean anything."

{You're too clever for this, Eaon.}

"You want to know what I know?" he asked, though his voice cracked. "I know that the only proof of this Morvish theory is a stranger's story, and that believing it means I have to ignore truths that I have *known* for *years*. My da would not lie to me about something like that. He wouldn't."

Eaon said it, but his hand was growing colder, his voice pitching uncomfortably. Cinn squeezed tightly, putting his forehead on Eaon's shoulder. Tingles ran across his skin, but as the minutes ticked by and Eaon got control over his hitching breaths, it never became unbearable.

{Okay,} Cinn signed. The truth sat between them, known and unacknowledged.

"Come on. I'm tired."

Nodding, Cinn straightened and helped Eaon navigate the rest of the stairs until they finally reached the platform where the door had been rehung. A push had it swinging open silently—in the years Cinn had lived there, it had never done that.

Inside, the apartment smelled of lemon and vinegar. William had the old dusty curtains soaking in a bucket of water while he sealed up the gaps in the window frame. Sarah knelt on the hearth, scraping out the fireplace. She wiped her sooty hands on her dress as she smiled up at them, bright as the sunlight pouring in.

"Hello boys. Eaon, it's good to see you up and about. How are you feeling?"

Cinn felt about as well as Eaon looked, but while he couldn't do more than blink at the farmers, Eaon forced a strained smile.

"Been better. Been worse. Thought it would be a good idea for both of us to get out for a bit."

Already, parts of the day were distant and hard to remember. Eaon's hand on his shoulder got his feet moving again, to the couch, where he collapsed and closed his eyes. The apartment may have been cleaned, but the couch still smelled like stale whiskey and lamp oil.

"Very good idea," William agreed, then indicated around the apartment. "In the morning we're going with Lord Dustin and the demi-kin back to Belden, and we didn't think you'd feel comfortable in the Turlough home by yourself, Cinn, so we're just getting this place a bit more livable before we go."

"I was about to put together something for dinner, though," Sarah said, getting to her feet. "You boys hungry?"

The thought of eating made Cinn want to puke. One look at Eaon's face said he felt the same. Yet, easing into a dining chair, leaning his crutch against the wall, Eaon twisted his face into another smile-adjacent expression.

"That would be great, thank you, Sarah. I can help—"

"Just rest, sweetheart. There's not much to do anyway. It's too hot for soup, so, vegetable salad it is, and that's not a two-person job."

Despite the way Eaon's eyelids clicked with exhaustion, he opened his mouth to argue. William interrupted.

"You any good at stitching?"

Cinn frowned, but Eaon paused.

"What?"

"Stitching? These curtains are pretty raggedy, and I've got ham fingers."

As if unsure, Eaon looked at his own fingers, long and bony. "I can . . . Yeah, I can sew."

Bewildered, Cinn stared at William as he wrung out the curtains and brought them over to Eaon. It wasn't as if mending the lace was an urgent task, nor was it one that warranted asking Eaon to work when he was so unwell. If William felt that strongly about it, Cinn could figure out how to sew. But as he watched Eaon settle, shoulders dropping half an inch as he focused enough to thread the needle, Cinn's stupid brain caught up.

With everything a mess, Eaon needed to feel useful.

And William knew that. Had always known how to help people the way they needed to be helped. As William left Eaon to his task, he ruffled Cinn's hair on his way back. The smile Cinn found was small but genuine.

Not only did William reseal the window frame, he fixed the mechanism that allowed it to open and close properly. The night outside was cooling, and though they didn't need it, they lit a small fire in the hearth. The Copelands sat on the couch with their bowls of salad while Cinn nestled as close to the fireplace as he could stand. Keeping his distance from all of them, Eaon sat cross-legged on the floor too, cradling an untouched dinner in his lap.

"It's a good thing, what you're doing," Eaon said when the Copelands explained their reasons for leaving. "If my spellmarks are still holding, it's probably the safest place you could be."

"We would love it if you both would join us," Sarah tried.

"I can't." Eaon didn't hesitate. "But Cinn should—"

The glare Cinn leveled at him had Eaon ducking his head. Silence fell, broken only by the gentle crack of a log splitting and the endless chatter of people outside, conversations wafting through the open window.

"Well," William sighed, picking through his salad like he might find gold in there, "stay safe. And come find us when it's over."

Cinn nodded, unable to stomach another bite. He didn't feel safe. He'd forgotten over the past hour or so, but his brain was growing heavy again.

Gray eyes. Gray hair.

Blood in his mouth, in his nose, in his eyes . . .

Eaon shuffled closer, squeezing his knee.

Deep breaths. Cinn needed to take deep breaths.

Each one helped refocus the small apartment until Cinn could follow the movements of Eaon's hands. {You can go. I'll be okay.}

Cinn shook his head. Filled his lungs.

His hands shook. {I'm not running.}

Eaon leaned closer, his hands in the small space between them, both watching as he signed, {It's okay to run sometimes.}

It would have hurt having Eaon push him away like this, except there was a hollowness behind his eyes that promised this was less about keeping Cinn safe and more about sparing him from the end Eaon saw for himself.

{Then you do it.}

They weren't going to get anywhere, having this argument again, and they both knew it. So they didn't waste their last night with the Copelands rehashing it. Cinn changed the subject.

{You never did tell me the answer to that riddle.}

Eaon sat back and sighed. Turning to the Copelands, he said, "A fae asked me once: what is it that, given one, you either have two or none?"

All of them chewed on it for a while, but one by one they shook their heads. Cinn didn't even try to think up an answer. He didn't have the brain power.

"Yeah. I ended up guessing 'a name,' because I was on a time limit and it kind of fit the first part, but not really the second. And the fae have a thing for names."

"But that wasn't right?" Sarah assumed.

"No. The cat sith who asked disappeared after that and I was paranoid the whole night that by agreeing to attempt the riddle I had somehow given the fae permission to attack us."

"Did you ever figure it out?" William asked.

"Yeah, like, two minutes later." Eaon shook his head, annoyed with himself. "It's 'a choice.' When given one, you either have two or you have none."

William sat back and scratched his beard. "Huh. I don't know about that. Even if you don't like one of the options, it's still technically a choice."

"Well, how do you define choice?"

Blinking slowly, Cinn looked to Sarah, who gave him a sleepy blink in return. The riddle's answer wielded another well of anxious spiraling if Cinn thought about it too hard, so instead, he picked the shredded carrot from his bowl and let the numbness settle back in.

"It's the action. Choosing."

"And it is a synonym for option. So, consider, I've got a knife to Sarah's throat and Cinn has one to Aisling's. I tell you to choose who lives, or nobody does."

The carrots were surprisingly sweet. Definitely witch grown. Very crunchy.

"Still, it is technically, a choice."

"Is it? Or is it manipulation? A real choice is something balanced. Maybe you don't like the options, maybe both are awful, or maybe one leads to an outcome you'd prefer, but at the time of presenting them, both are equal. What I just said was me manipulating you to do what I want, because I know there is no way you're letting me kill your wife when Cinn's standing there two seconds away from vengeance. There's nothing to choose. There's just a script I wrote for you follow."

William looked ready to argue some more, but held his tongue when both Cinn and Sarah yawned deeply.

"It's a thinker," he said instead. "Come on. Let's go back to the Turlough house tonight. Bring a mattress from there back with you tomorrow. Especially when your brother and sister come back to stay too, there won't be room for four of you on this couch."

"There isn't room for three of you," Sarah grumbled, getting to her feet.

{The couch is Radley's,} Cinn explained as he fetched Eaon's crutch. {He's drunk a lot and usually needs to run for the bathroom quickly upon waking, and that's easier to do from the couch. I like the floor. Edwina and I curl up in front of the fire together.}

Nobody had anything to say to that. Sarah smiled and stroked his cheek, leading the way out into the night. William waited for Cinn and Eaon to navigate their way down, then took Sarah's hand.

"I don't know if I should sleep in a place where so many people are going to be," Eaon said quietly as they stepped out into the main street once more.

Cinn's heart beat painfully at the idea of parting ways again, but he couldn't stand the thought of going back to the palace with Eaon. {Stay with me. I won't let go of you.}

If the evening had brought with it any semblance of calm, it disappeared as Eaon stumbled closer to Cinn, narrowly avoiding brushing shoulders with a man. The phouka had not returned. The Old One who had arrived must be keeping him busy, but if there was a real problem, Gatty would have returned.

"Promise?" Eaon asked.

Squeezing Eaon's hand tightly, Cinn nodded. He'd stitch their skin together if he had to.

~

For once, it wasn't the terror of his nightmares that woke him. A different sort of dread settled in his bones as Cinn's eyes snapped open, the dark absolute. Night had truly fallen; the entire manor was fast asleep, the city quiet outside. Straining, he couldn't hear anything aside from William's snoring. The Copelands had taken the bed upon both Cinn and Eaon's insistence, the two of them opting to curl up tightly on the sofa that divided the room. Warm beneath his head, Eaon's breathing was soft and easy, undisturbed by whatever had roused Cinn. Puddles, too, purred loudly from the foot of the bed.

A floorboard creaked.

Cinn pushed upright.

"Ugh," Eaon groaned, eyes crusted closed.

Either everyone else was sleeping very deeply, or the sound was a figment of Cinn's imagination. Scanning the room, the minutes ticking by peacefully, he thought it might be the latter. When his eyes caught on a dark shadow by the drapes, he told himself to breathe. There was nothing there. It was a coat hanging on a hat stand or something similar.

"Cinn," Eaon grumbled.

He was in a memory—that night in the Copelands' home when a shtryg had gotten inside and nearly killed Sarah. The night they had discovered he was a true kinner. He'd been afraid, then. Afraid of what they would do with him. It made a twisted sort of sense that he was afraid again now, with the day he'd had.

He needed to go back to sleep.

Yet he couldn't look away.

The skin on the back of his neck crawled with cold.

Close your eyes, Cinn commanded himself, following Eaon's tug back down.

Curled into his side, laying half on top of him so they would both fit, Cinn clutched Eaon's hand like the only solid thing in a world turned hazy.

He closed his eyes.

The panic was immediate.

He opened them again.

The shadow was closer. He swore it was.

No it isn't.

Gritting his teeth, heart beating painfully fast, he closed his eyes again. He was safe. Eaon was safe. Sarah and William and Puddles were safe. There was nothing in the room with them.

Another creak, and then heavy footsteps marching quickly.

Before Cinn's eyes were even open again, he was rolling. Off the couch, lunging for the fire poker. The shadow rushed for him, heavy body thudding to its knees as it scrambled after him. On all fours, still a foot away from the hearth, Cinn kicked back, bare foot colliding with solid flesh. There was no vacuous gravity sucking him in—the shadow grunted and grappled for his ankle, yanking him flat to his stomach.

"Cinn!"

Eaon was up, the room temperature dropping. Across the room, a candle was lit. Hissing, Eaon shrunk back to the wall, arms wrapped tight around his chest. His face paled as he looked from where Cinn bucked and clawed at the body trying to pin him down to the Copelands, throwing back the covers.

He couldn't help without risking them. His bad leg was buckling.

Cinn screamed his rage into the floor and shoved back against the heavy body on top of him, wrapping a leg around theirs, an arm twisted behind their neck, rolling and pushing until he could scramble free. Grabbing the leg of the small coffee table, Cinn dragged it closer, hefted it over his head and slammed the wood down on top of what he now saw was just a man. A man with clawed fingers and a scaled throat, but a man all the same.

"What the—".

Cinn couldn't spare a glance at William's shock; if there was a second attacker in the room, he'd have to trust that the Copelands could handle it. As Cinn sprung for the fire poker again, the man began muttering under his breath.

The iron pole became blazing hot.

Cinn didn't care. He swung for the man's—the *witch's*—the *harbinger's*—head, missing only because they were quick enough to roll aside.

"I forgot what you kinner are like when there's still some fight in you," he snarled, mouth full of too many teeth. "When I heard you were here, I just had to come find you. It's been too long since I tasted fresh meat."

Burning flesh itched Cinn's nose, almost worse than the itch in his hands where the skin was trying to heal as quickly as it was being blistered away, but he missed again as the hybrid witch flipped onto his feet and lunged backward, onto the bed.

"Hand yourself over, and I'll let the humans live."

Sarah screamed, grabbing the candleholder and raising it above her head, ready to swing. There was no second attacker, but something was wrong with William anyway—red in the face and grimacing with pain, he tried to move toward his wife but stumbled into the wall instead.

Sensing the farmer's weakness, the harbinger changed his target.

"No," Cinn croaked.

He dropped his weapon. Raised his hands.

Eaon was across the room before the poker hit the floor.

Silent feet, quick as a fleeing deer, his sleeves had been rolled up to his elbows. Skidding into the space between William and the beast-witch, Eaon flung himself at the harbinger. No weapon, only bare hands. One touch was all it would take.

Upon impact, the beast-witch's claws found a home in Eaon's throat.

Blood splattered up the wall.

Cinn stood there stupidly as bodies hit the floor, Eaon's windpipe ripped out. The harbinger's chest was caving in on itself, rotting so slowly that the hybrid had time to look down and whimper.

The world had narrowed to the tangle of flesh and scale on the floor, the puddle of blood seeping into the rug. He needed to do something. Death wasn't permanent for Eaon, right? Eavha . . . Eavha could fix this, right?

From under the bed, the cat poked her nose out. Cinn took a shaky step forward.

"Honey? Honey, are you okay?"

It was her tone that was most alarming. His heart, already bruising his ribs in its desperate attempt to beat its way out, picked up a new sickening pace.

Sarah had very rarely shown true fear, but her terrified voice broke on a sob. Cinn turned to look at where William had collapsed into the corner, red and sweaty and gasping, clutching at his chest with his right hand while his left lay limp. There was no strength in his barrel of a body as he sagged to the side.

In his life of violence and bloodshed, in this time of war and beasts, Cinn had forgotten that, for some, mortality was also a threat. That age and shock could kill as suddenly as a crossbow bolt.

The strangled sound Cinn made was lost to the door slamming open, a wall of curious and frightened faces peering in.

"Mother above, someone fetch a guard."

Sarah wailed, screaming frantically for someone to help as William's hand went limp. The thud of his knuckles hitting the floor took Cinn to his knees.

CHAPTER THIRTY-EIGHT

AISLING

AISLING STOOD OUTSIDE THE TURLOUGH HOUSE WITH HER POSSE OF guards, watching a dark shadow against an already starless sky descend. The phouka flapped his enormous black wings to slow, then with a loud *pop*, changed back into the goat-man form she had grown used to, falling the remaining six feet to the ground to land in a crouch. Whipping his horned head around, he snarled at the civilians loitering on the lawn, among who waited Moyra; her cat sith flicked his tail anxiously at her feet. The two faeries locked eyes and every hair on the cat sith's body puffed out.

"You said there was no danger."

"I said there was no *immediate* danger. We were gone longer than expected."

The phouka managed to grow a foot taller, shoulders broadening as he sucked down a furious breath. Then, much like Eavha had five minutes ago, he turned his back and sprinted inside.

All the lamps in the Turlough house were burning, candlelight flickering across the front lawns in a failing effort to bring comfort to the small crowd outside. The echo of someone's frantic sobbing inside found a higher pitch.

Aisling waited.

The first two people to cross the threshold stumbled—a pregnant Siobhan, half carrying Sarah. They barely made it to the grass before their knees buckled. Sarah wept onto Siobhan's chest, heavy and listless, her sobs no longer panicked and desperate but full-body and exhausted.

It could have been relief, except Aisling was intimately familiar with what defeat looked like.

Touching the scar on her cheek, Aisling's stomach bottomed out.

William could not be saved, then.

Next to emerge was the phouka, dragging a corpse behind it. People screamed, flinching back as he heaved the body over his shoulder to slam it against the ground, bellowing wordless hatred as he sunk in shredding claws and tore off its arm. Most of the occupants of the house turned away as the phouka raged, throwing chunks of viscera into the bushes, but Aisling watched, dispassionate. Candlelight flickered off thick, beastly teeth and scaled flesh much like Aadya's.

A harbinger. Too dead to interrogate about the whereabouts of the stolen unicorn blood, but if the phouka left the head intact she could at least check if, in his death, he had revealed anything of importance about the approaching army. Soldiers had been searching the woods outside the city walls for signs of the spy's dragon, but it was either well-hidden or had moved on after its encounter with the rogue family.

Corpse sufficiently brutalized, the phouka went back inside. Clayton stepped out from among her guard and picked through the remains. With so many eyes on her, Aisling didn't dare relax so much as an inch as he returned with the head, skull caving in on the left side but otherwise intact.

It wasn't the male she had faced in Dusarn—Byron, who had flinched at the mention of Aadya. Still, she took the bloodied head from Clayton, muttering under her breath until the yard fell away.

"*I forgot what your kind were like with some fight left in you. It's been so long since I've had fresh meat.*"

"He knows something about kinner," she said aloud, frowning. The hybrid knew what Cinn was. Had hunted him, to eat. Was surprised by how energetically he had defended himself, as if he expected differently. Was used to kinner who'd lost the will to do so. "He knows where more kinner are."

What if, the whole time she had been looking for them, Chaos's harbingers already had the kinner? The Sparrow Coven's ancestors had somehow beaten the undying soldiers-turned-sovereigns during the Second War, but there had been no written record of what had been done to them. If knowledge was kept at all, nobody was talking—Mother knew Aisling had asked—but . . .

What if her mother knew? What if her mother had handed the kinner over when she turned traitor? How many did Chaos have? All of them?

She had played her hand with Tallula already. Unless she really did find a way to bring the dead queen back from the void, she didn't think her mother would be forthcoming with any more truths.

And then, a worse thought.

Cinn was just a small boy when he'd arrived in Hyrsch, no older that seven, discovered all alone by a hunting party looking for escaped slaves in the southern mountains. The party didn't know what they had found at the time, assuming he was demi-kin, but had still scoured the surrounding mountains looking for his parents to no avail. In that cell beneath her dungeon, she had questioned what happened to them. It was before he stopped speaking at all, and he had told her over and over how monsters had attacked their campsite. His parents had told him to run, and so he had, and that was all he knew.

Aisling closed her eyes against the echoes of a scream only she could hear—*"I swear, I swear, that's all I know! That's all I know."*

What if it *had* been all he knew? What if, the whole time she had been torturing him, he had been telling the truth.

Nauseous, Aisling opened her eyes and handed the head back to Clayton.

"Mind this for me, please."

A small frown creased his brow at her manners, but he took the head and tucked it under his arm regardless.

Speaking of kinner.

Edwina and Radley emerged from the house, the former clutching a cat to her chest while the latter carried a shell-shocked Cinn. As always, if Edwina had any feelings at all she was hiding them well as she led the way to Siobhan and Sarah. As they joined them on the ground, Sarah managed to lift her head enough to see Cinn and reach out a hand. He stared at it for a second before hooking his pinkie finger over hers.

Waiting a couple minutes to make sure they planned to stay there, Aisling nodded to her guards, who formed a veritable wall between her and Cinn as she approached the house. As long as the kinner had been inside, she refused to intrude, but now that he was out she needed to see if there was anything she could do to help Eavha.

There was blood on the ceiling. Ropes of it painted the walls.

Raising a hand for her guard to wait in the hall, Aisling stepped carefully into the room. Eavha was on her knees, chest seizing with barely controlled hyperventilation, hands over the gaping wound that was Eaon's missing throat. Skin to skin, and yet, she was not hurt. The phouka loomed over them, pacing the tightest circle ever paced, fingers flexing with restraint. He was ready to intervene the moment Eaon's magic returned.

Nobody bothered acknowledging her presence. Aisling stepped closer, trying to gage how focused Eavha was and deciding it was safe to ask, "Can I do anything?"

"Do not distract her!" the phouka snapped.

Eavha turned slightly, pale as a wraith, lip quivering. "Has anyone ever come back from the dead six times and been okay?"

There was no answer for that. The Sparrow Coven only allowed the Passing rite to be taken once. Necromancers were bound by law to never bring back a Returned a second time, let alone six.

"If I can help him at all, I will," Aisling said instead.

Bowing her head, sweat darkening the spine of her shirt, Eavha returned to her work. New veins and muscle grew from thin air, and Aisling watched in morbid fascination for a solid minute before noticing the bed sheet covering a large prone form by the corner.

"The farmer?"

"Heart attack," Eavha croaked. "He was gone by the time I got here and . . . I tried . . . I went into the void for his soul, but . . . I couldn't find him."

"May he find peace in the Lover's embrace," Aisling said softly, hand to her chest.

The phouka had stopped pacing, glaring at Aisling. "Be silent, or get out."

It wasn't a true faerie command, but the threat to make it so was evident. Was that how he convinced Cinn to leave Eaon's side? She didn't doubt it.

Aisling pressed her lips together and sat on the edge of the bed.

It took another hour before Eaon's chest rose, a rattling breath scraping down his new throat. Eavha hissed, flinching back, hands tucked under her armpits as she scrambled away from the emanating cold.

The phouka was there in an instant. Hands on Eaon's shoulders to absorb the wafts of necrosis, the phouka's body was a shield, whispering in a language Aisling didn't understand into the scrap of space between them.

Back to the wall, Eavha buried her face in her hands. The shaking of her shoulders was the only tell of her otherwise silent crying.

Slowly, Aisling slipped onto the floor beside her, pulled her hands away and pressed Eavha's face against her shoulder instead.

"He's going to be okay."

"I can't keep doing this. I can't. I can't do it."

"He's okay."

"I didn't know that this was what it would be like," Eavha went on as if she hadn't heard her. "I didn't know what it meant to be a healer. Always too late to prevent the wound, nothing to do but stitch it up, leave a scar as proof you tried your best."

The new skin of Eaon's throat was a paler shade than the rest of him— a lighter brown, unkissed by the sun. But it was Aisling's cheek that Eavha touched, pink and puckered from the branding iron.

"I'm so tired of being too late."

"I know," Aisling said, pressing her lips softly to Eavha's forehead.

It was all she had to offer as the night gave way to the gray light of dawn. The red haze that had brushed the city for the past week was mellowed by dark clouds moving across the sky. Lightning flickered, bright and electric, followed immediately by rolling thunder.

A summer storm.

~

The rooftops were laden with Wyldeden witches drenched by the heavy rainfall, watching the burning horizon turn to steam. Prayers of thanks to Mare, the water spirit, and Celeste, the sky spirit, echoed in a song that was equal parts joy and grief.

Aisling sent up her own silent prayer, then closed down the part of her that cared what the spirits thought of her.

Stalking back to the palace, the robe she had thrown over silk pajamas when Edwina came barging into her suite had muddied at the hem. Fingers shivering from cold, she tried and failed to wrangle the heavy length of her unbound hair into a twist, leaving it loose and plastered to her waist instead. Aisling didn't bother changing or cleaning herself up as she marched down the stairs to her dungeon, taking the severed head from Clayton as she went.

As she'd asked, the guardians who had occupied the cells were gone. Nose crinkling against the deep-seated smell of refuse and rot, she made her way all the way down to the darkest level of this place she called home and threw open the door to Aadya's cell.

Naked, chained and thrashing on the table where Aisling had left her, Aadya stilled, eyes widening with terror. Then she noticed the head dangling from Aisling's fist and loosed a sound purely animal.

"Friend of yours?"

Aisling was cold. To her bones, in her heart, she was marble and ice and steel. Standing at Aadya's side, she took the head in two hands and placed the wet edge of his neck on Aadya's stomach.

The hybrid witch screamed and thrashed a moment longer, finding the energy to level a hateful glare as she spat, "You will *burn!*"

Unblinking, Aisling held her stare. Carefully, she slipped a nail behind the spy's milky eye and eased it out of the socket.

"I must apologize, Aadya. I've been a terrible host these past months. Neglectful, even. You must be so hungry."

All the hate leeched from her face as Aadya saw what Aisling was doing, her body stilling. "Don't."

"It's what your kind does, isn't it? With the kinner?"

Slicing through the optic nerve with her fingernails, Aisling dangled the soggy eyeball above Aadya's face. Torn between terror and shock, Aadya's pale blue gaze flicked between the threat of her meal and Aisling's stony face.

"I don't know what you mean," she whispered, doing her best to speak without opening her mouth too wide.

Aisling was guessing, but she also doubted she was wrong. Releasing her grip on the head, she let it roll and thud to the floor, gripping Aadya's chin tightly instead. With force enough to crack the bone of her jaw, she pried Aadya's mouth open. The witch wailed and thrashed, shaking her head in a moot effort to shake Aisling loose.

Some string of panicked sounds came out, and Aisling held the eye a mere inch away from Aadya's chapped lips.

"What was that? Want to tell me something?"

Hatred seeped back into her face, but Aadya managed the smallest of nods. Releasing her jaw, Aisling tilted her head, the ratty tendrils of her wet hair falling in a curtain.

Aadya swallowed. Twice.

"We have kinner."

"How many?"

"Three."

Three was not an army. Three was more than she had.

If what the dead hybrid had said was to be understood, though, the three they had were merely food and unfit for fighting. It was hope.

"What else do you have? Dragons, apparently. How many?"

"How should I know? I've been here, or in Wyldeden, for decades!"

Grabbing the matted crown of Aadya's scalp, Aisling ripped her head back as far as it would go, curling her upper lip at the broken cry of pain it elicited.

"Your best guess, then."

There were at least two that Aisling knew of, but that was already too many. Over the years, she had commissioned large crossbows and trained hundreds of archers in preparation for whatever air force Chaos arrived with, but aside from that, there was just her. Her, riding Volya, with a battle-axe.

"There were five the last time I was there," Aadya admitted.

"And how many harbingers?"

Throat working, Aadya gaped for a moment before pressing her lips together firmly. Aisling raised her eyebrows. Gave her a moment to reconsider.

When Aadya closed her eyes, Aisling knew she'd have to work for the rest of her answers. Releasing Aadya's hair, she dug her elbow into her sternum, pried her mouth open and shoved the eyeball so far down Aadya's throat she had no choice but to swallow it. The mutant witch whined, arching off the table, but had accepted this fate before she chose defiance. Feeding her pieces of her friend wouldn't be enough to make her speak more, but one of Aisling's earliest lessons was that following through on a threat was important.

The second eye went down harder than the first and Aadya choked.

Giving the harbinger a moment to catch her breath, Aisling went to her toolbox and found a pair of pliers. Aadya's stomach made a shaky work bench, but she wanted the hybrid to feel it as Aisling pried open the corpse's jaw and began pulling teeth.

"Your friend was chattier," Aisling lied, calm and unaffected.

"He told you nothing," Aadya spat, doing her very best to buck off the pile of teeth accumulating in her belly button.

"His name was Wert." Aisling didn't pause as she removed the dead hybrids molars. "Another of your friends' names is Pryll. They were responsible for getting a portion of your forces into Dusarn."

Breath left Aadya in a rush, goosebumps spreading across her bare skin.

Tossing the head aside, Aisling selected an incisor from the pile and brought it and the pliers to the top of the table.

"So very chatty," she said, holding the tooth up. "I wonder, if you had his teeth, would it make you chatty too?"

It was a struggle to wrestle the pliers into position and keep hold of the tooth, but, calling in Clayton to help hold Aadya down, Aisling managed it. The ends of her hair pooled in the bloody drool collecting on the table as she yanked out one of Aadya's teeth and shoved Wert's in its place. A second tooth, and Aadya was begging her to stop.

"B-Byron," she stuttered, flicking her tongue against the foreign bones in her mouth. "Pryll, Wert, Urian, Denyse and Roal. That's all of us. That's all of us, I swear."

Aisling hummed. "So it does work. Any other spies or traitors I should know about? Like the ones Pryll and Wert made of my parents?"

"No."

Giving her a moment to rethink her answer, Aisling hovered, waiting, then went for a third tooth.

"No! No! There's nobody else! There's nobody!"

"I do not believe you," Aisling hissed.

Three, four, five teeth. Aisling moved on to the molars.

Gagging on spit and blood, Aadya fought for a breath and practically screamed into the room, "The pass! The southern mountain pass!"

Now they were getting somewhere.

"I already know they're coming through the pass." Aisling smirked and shoved another tooth into the empty spot she'd made, running the metal of the pliers down Aadya's tongue to keep her from trying to poke it out again.

Whimpering, Aadya managed to shake her head.

"There's a witch there. I . . . I convinced him to let us through."

Only practice kept Aisling's flash of hot rage from showing. "Sar Vin?"

Aadya shook her head. "No, no, too stubborn. One of the hunters. They'll attack and take the Sar's place before the army arrives and make the clan stand down. They're the only one. I swear. I swear."

Aisling held herself stiller than even the phouka's command could make her as her stomach twisted—"*I swear, I swear that's all I know.*"

Any moment now, the troops Aisling and Eavha had sent for the pass were due to arrive. No change in the Southern Mountain Clan's power was going to make Hyrsch and Wyldeden stand down, but they didn't need the added challenge of dealing with a coup.

Following through on a threat was important, but so was rewarding desired behaviors. Putting down the pliers, Aisling nuzzled against Aadya's ear, letting her lips catch on the shell, teeth pulling at the lobe.

"Good girl."

CHAPTER THIRTY-NINE

YVETTE

ELDER YVETTE WAS BORN TIRED, AND EVERY WAKING MOMENT SHE HAD spent in the company of Eavha Nemuse had worn down her already frayed nerves. From the very first day the young witch had walked into the clinic, she had been insufferable, and it felt like some kind of cosmic joke that she and Yvette were the last two remaining healers with any real power. Very different kinds, of course—Yvette was only nominally Sanni-blessed, enough to have good instincts and brew exceptional tonics—but regardless, circumstance had seen them thrust into comradery.

The urchin had grown on her.

It hadn't been a difficult decision for Yvette to offer to accompany the troops headed for the mountain pass in Eavha's steed. One of them had to go, and even if the Nemuse witch hadn't been heir, Yvette would have insisted she stay in the city. Her unrivaled Sanni-blessing would be a boon in times to come, yes, but more importantly, someone so young and with such clean hands shouldn't be exposed to the bloodshed that would occur in the coming days. It was the same reasoning that had brought Elder Herbe to lead the Wyldeden guardians. Human and demi-kin commanders had also been handpicked by the Hyrschan captain to march beside them; holding this pass, delaying the beasts by a day, was too important a job to not have the best in attendance.

Still, there was a collective shudder as the battalion crested the last hill before the steep incline toward the pass's entrance. The Southern Spine was a wall of harsh gray mountains tipped in ice, even in the tail of summer—between this stretch and its dustier northern mirror, Nir was split down the middle with only two ways to cross safely: the towers holding a bridge over the Womb, and this pass—a relatively narrow path that snaked between mountains. On either side, the mountains rose in a sheer vertical, and the harsh wind blowing through carried the crisp air of the frozen wastes on its western end.

They were lucky Chaos was not coming through during winter. The Southern Mountains could become so cold that, even at ground level, frostbite and hypothermia were severe issues. Wyldeden travelers almost never ventured this way during snowing months because, cloistered in their bubble of paradise, they had no chance of acclimatizing to such harsh weather. Yet, sometimes it was necessary, and in those times, it was the Nemuses who were sent.

Expendable, supposedly. Yvette had treated Kailevi once for a lost toe on his return and wondered how anyone who had spent any time with the male considered him a weakness to the bloodline. Without a scrap of magic to aid him, Kailevi repeatedly walked boldly into Death's valley and returned, for the most part, intact.

Struggling their way up the last incline before the pass's eastern mouth, every witch noticed the carvings etched into thin birch tree trunks and large boulders. Spellmarks that looked like eyes watched their approach, the tingle of magic alerting the Southern Mountain Clan to the battalion's arrival. For a few miles, there was no sign of life bar those scratches in the stone, and every step had the soldiers' grips tightening on the hilts of their swords, guard tightening around the wagons they'd dragged with them.

"They're watching," one of the guardians hanging close to Herbe said. One of the Bayfield brood.

"They are," Herbe agreed. "Here's hoping Nemuse knew what he was doing."

Yvette grimaced. "May the Lover have mercy."

As if the infamous name summoned him, a lone witch stepped out of a crevice in the mountain side, hands raised.

"Peace, brethren." The Terranian words were slurred beneath a deep, throaty accent. Someone repeated the words in murmured Nirnish, and the human commander of the Hyrschan troops called his men to hold.

"Are you the Sar-son?" Herbe asked.

"I am."

The male couldn't be any older than a quarter-century, yet he stood with unwavering spine before the thousand soldiers filling the pass. There was a hardness in his eyes, in the set of his jaw, that unnerved her even more than the scar twisting his upper lip or the bones pierced through his ears and nose. Animal, for sure. Some kind of bird. Large, like a vulture.

"And Sar Vin? Is he expecting us?"

"Expecting? Yes. Pleased? No. Who speaks for you?"

Mustavrick's gaze flitted through the masses, searching for a familiar face. He wouldn't find who he was looking for.

Herbe stepped forward and Yvette followed. The two commanders, one human and one demi-kin, also identified themselves.

The senior Bayfield guardian who Herbe had allowed at his side turned back and snapped his fingers. "The rest of us will take stock. Let's go."

The wagons were stilled, lids opened. Yvette didn't watch them count the arrows again, checking the shafts hadn't split in the haul. Instead, the four of them followed Mustavrick deeper into the pass.

It wasn't long before the whispering started, but it took an extra minute to realize there were two distinct types. Eyes peered out from cracks in the mountainside, narrow tunnels where witches hid, pale and harshly angled. They blended so well into the stone that nobody would have noticed their presence if it weren't for the tiny hand gestures drawing attention, a language of their own to compliment hushed conversations. They were communicating to those nearby, but also to those across the pass.

The second kind of whispers were different. Less verbal, and yet somehow louder. A sound Yvette felt in her bones and understood in the pulse of her blood.

"What is that?" Herbe asked in uncertain Nirnish, earning confused looks from the commanders. Clearly neither could hear what the witches heard.

The Sar-son frowned. "I don't understand the human tongue."

"Apologies. I was just asking about that . . . sound," he repeated in Terranian. Though there were different dialects of Terranian depending on clan, the Southern Mountain Clan's verbal language was close enough to Wyldeden's for communication to be a non-issue.

"The mountains," Mustavrick answered, intentionally sly.

"They talk?" Yvette pushed.

"And listen."

Somewhere, a horn blew.

Herbe's spear was off his back and in his hands in a second. The commanders also drew their weapons, though the demi-kin one moved slow, shoulders drooping.

"We're too late."

"No," Mustavrick assured them, but he too was frowning. "It's a call to gather the hunters. Which is odd."

Their pace quickened until a gaping hole in the mountainside came into view. A tunnel, much larger than the others they had passed. Moving quickly, the walls widened into a cavern painted with rich reds and browns, the floor smoothed by earthy mosaiced tiles. Yvette watched mountain witches trickle out of interconnected tunnels, rushing down spiraling staircases carved into the walls.

There was no throne like in Hyrsch, nor was there a stage like in Wyldeden. Identifiable by the sheer number of bones piercing his face and the fresh wolf's head perched like a vulgar crown on his own, Sar Vin shoved his way through the crowd to stand in the center. Briefly, he noted his son's presence with a scowl before promptly ignoring them all.

From the folds of his furred vest, he pulled out a leaf.

"This morning, a scout intercepted a message," he shouted, voice booming through the cave. "A warning from the Anfar Forest Clan that there is a spy among us. A spy, working for Chaos."

A chorus of chuckles. Yvette's stomach dropped.

"This, within hours of my son being convinced to allow Sparrow forces into our midst, to fight a supposed army of beasts."

Another chuckle. Beside them, Mustavrick paled.

"I don't know about you, but this reeks of infiltration to me. Of a petty little girl who can't take no for an answer and is now trying to take over our home!"

"*Fuck*," Mustavrick spat. Then, louder, stepping away from the wall, he shouted back, "Or maybe it's fucking true! And you're going to get us all killed with your unhinged paranoid bullshit!"

In Wyldeden, if someone had shouted at Kaelean like that . . . Well, it just wasn't done. Nobody would. Yet, here, nobody batted an eye at the way the Sar-son snarled up at his father in front of what had to be fifty hunters. And if the Sar felt public humiliation was out of bounds, he didn't show it.

"One day, boy, if you ever grow a fucking spine and take the Sar title from me, you can make these kinds of calls, but today you will be lucky if I don't throw you in the pit for a month."

Yvette had never seen much violence, and yet, the tension prickling the air was so visceral that, even sheltered, she knew what was brewing.

"Herbe," she whispered. "Hand me your knife."

Stone still, he gave her a bewildered look. Leveling a chilling one of her own, she stared until Herbe handed over the sharp bone knife at his hip.

Yvette quickly carved a spellmark into her palm, the sharp pulse of magic drawing the attention of everyone nearby.

Less than a year ago, her mentor had sacrificed herself on behalf of a young witch who couldn't defend herself, for the greater good of the clan. Yvette could do no less.

"I bear The Telling Mark of Truths Unveiled." She stepped forward, hand raised for all to see. "This news about a spy is the first I am hearing of it, but if the message is from our heir, then she can be believed. The only intentions she and Aisling have is to stop Chaos and his harbingers."

When Sar Vin had said it, the Southern Mountain Clan laughed. With the mark on her hand, Yvette's declaration was met with wary silence. They were listening. There was no need to descend into violence.

"What exactly did the message say?" Herbe asked.

Nostrils flaring, rage had Sar Vin's wide neck bulging like a toad. He said nothing, but another male, likely the scout who'd intercepted it, said, "It suggested that one of our hunters have been compromised. It's why I blew the hunters' horn."

Before the words were even finished coming out of his mouth, Sar Vin struck the male with a closed fist.

"Almost forgot to do that. Since I said to gather the *elders*, not the *hunters*."

Like the first beat of a drum signaling a dance, the blow was the spark that set Mustavrick alight. Drawing a blade of stone, the Sar-son made to lunge, but Herbe was quicker. One arm around the boy's waist, the other a vice around his blade-wielding wrist, he held Mustavrick back.

"The hunters—is this all of them?" Yvette asked, stepping into the space between Sar Vin and his son, a barrier of truth. "Tell them to mark themselves and declare themselves loyal to you. It's the simplest way to be sure."

In the end, there was no need for Sar Vin to do anything. One by one, ignoring Herbe and Mustavrick wrestling on the floor, hunters eagerly began marking themselves.

All but one, who started edging for the tunnels. The watchful eyes of his peers caught the movement immediately. They were on him like a pack of hyenas.

Sar Vin watched the chaos unfold with the same hard wall of fury and disgust Yvette had seen both Lorelei and Kaelean wield at times. More recently, she'd seen it in Aisling, too. In Eavha.

"I know our clans have not always seen eye to eye," Yvette said, hand still raised, rivulets of blood curling around her wrist down to her elbow.

Cutting her palm was stupid, but she could hardly claim to be thinking clearly in a situation like this.

Sar Vin sneered.

"Eye to eye? My people are fighters—here in the south, especially during the winter season, you kill or you die. Your people are pathetic, flower sniffing idiots."

"Maybe, but historically our numbers have been far larger than yours, so there is obviously some benefit to our way of life. I'm not here to debate that with you, though."

"Who even are you to debate with me at all? I see no high priestess. No queen. Not even that ridiculous child you all named heir. Why should I take any of you seriously?"

Lowering her hand, Yvette shook her head.

"Go ask your traitor who his master is. Then, when you're ready, we can talk."

Two hours. That was all it took before Sar Vin began moving people.

Mustavrick and the messenger sat against the wall, tending to each other's wounds with a skill that meant Yvette wasn't needed, leaving her free to follow Herbe and the other commanders outside. She couldn't entirely contain her smirk as Sar Vin began talking about Chaos and the beast army as if he had never doubted their existence, barking orders to his elders.

"Come on," Herbe said, passing her a pile of fur. "We're going to move to a section farther west. It's going to be a few hours' walk."

"How many is a few?" Yvette asked dubiously.

Herbe only grimaced.

"It's a long gorge, my friend. A very long gorge."

CHAPTER FORTY

DEARMEAD

IT WAS ONE THING TO BE STARVING AND DEHYDRATED AND IN PAIN when there was no end in sight, but lost in the network of caves deep in Bernt's underground, the need to find a way out, to find food and water, to *rest*, was maddening.

For the first few miles, Vy had led the way confidently, unperturbed by the dark and cold, but the moment they reached the first fork in their path, she hesitated.

As they reached their fiftieth, Dearmead sighed.

"Do it again," she snapped, pointing at the wall.

Only the years he spent growing up under Calla Bayfield made him bite his tongue—*No, I thought we'd stand here and pointlessly stare at each other. Of course I'll do it again.*

Pressing a palm against the cool wall of the cave, Dearmead closed his eyes and prayed.

The first time, he hadn't been able to feel anything. The walls were made entirely of crystal, which was more Jem's domain than Terra's. Many of the Anfar Forest Clan's dual-blessed witches were touched by Jem, but Dearmead was not one of them, so aside from *cold* and *less cold*, there had been nothing to learn. In the end, they had taken the *less cold* path.

The next time their tunnel split, there had been more rock to connect with; enough to tell him which way was north, which was east. The juncture after that offered more information again: *higher, lower*. Getting above ground would bring them to food, so higher was obvious, but choosing between north or east had fostered an argument.

Vy wanted to go north. Assuming the hunt for the two of them had been abandoned, Chaos and his army were delaying plans to break through the crack in Nir's wards to head southeast for Hyrsch instead, so that was precisely the direction Vy wanted to avoid.

It was the same reason Dearmead needed to go there.

He knew Aisling was expecting this. He knew she had a plan, and he knew, if they had survived the forest fire, that Eavha would be at her side.

He had promised Eaon he would protect her. Failure was not an option.

For a long minute, the two escapees considered splitting up, but since Dearmead was the only one who could vaguely guide them through this maze, Vy had little choice but to follow him unless she wanted to spend eternity wandering.

Now, as Dearmead splayed his fingers against cool, opal-threaded rock to ask the tunnel where to go, he was bombarded with information.

Without bothering to speak to Vy, he led the way up a steep incline, trailing his fingers against the rough-hewn wall just to feel something besides his stomach's complaints. Days had gone by since they'd escaped, and he had been held for many more before that; he could practically feel his body eating itself in compensation.

For Vy, it had been much, much longer.

Thinking of the kinner woman at his back, Dearmead frowned. He had not thought about it before, but . . . she should be thinner. After two years with Aisling, Cinn had come out of the dungeon a loosely connected string of bones wrapped in flesh, but the woman huffing breathlessly in Dearmead's footsteps now still had muscle definition. Not much, admittedly, but it was there. Enough to keep up with him during a mad sprint through the forest. Enough to carry the thick chain on her shoulder for days on end.

Bodies could last quite some time without food, but still, something didn't add up.

He had learned about it in biology classes and heard it proven in Eaon's traveling stories about that one awful time he and Kailevi had gone missing for months. It had been horrifying, when Eaon had finally managed to speak about it; so unlike his usual tales of adventure and culture. Dearmead had only ever been mildly curious about leaving the Boab, but those stories had planted a seed of fear that threatened to overgrow. The same fear that had smothered everything else the day Eaon had been excommunicated. The day Dearmead had abandoned him.

Penance. That's what this felt like. Fate had offered him a chance to fulfill his promise to Eaon—to take care of each other, to leave the Boab together—and he had turned his back on it. He'd been left scrambling ever since.

Behind him, Vy grunted and dropped her chain. Dearmead was almost too exhausted to look, but he did. For all her unyielding perseverance, the days of wandering in the dark were getting to her too. Vy had slipped, clinging to the wall to stay upright. Her hand shook as she reached for the length of iron coiled on the floor.

She didn't look like she'd been starved for Mother-knew how long. Then again, what use is a kinner to an army of beasts without meat on their bones?

He didn't want to think about it anymore.

"Leave it," Dearmead told her. "It's just slowing you down."

"We might need it."

"There's water ahead. We can come back after."

Her head snapped up at the mention of a drink. "Why didn't you say that?"

Dearmead shrugged, turning back to the steep climb and dragging his feet up another step. Loosing a sigh, Vy left the chain and followed.

~

A few hours later, they heard it.

Need had Dearmead's body surging with sudden energy as he scrambled the last few meters up the slope and crawled over the lip of the tunnel onto flat ground.

Water.

Delirium was the only explanation for why he lay down on the ground and laughed instead of rushing straight for the shallow pool in the center of the cavern, a stream of water dripping steadily from a crack in the ceiling to settle in a groove in the floor. Bioluminescent moss crept up the curved rock walls, its neon green overwhelming the soft amber of glowing crystals.

Dearmead laughed again as Vy dragged herself out of the tunnel and gave him a disgusted look. She didn't have the energy to follow it with a scathing remark, but he heard it in the roll of her eyes anyway. The stone beneath them was smooth and slippery, and rather than try to navigate it, Vy crawled her way to the pool of water.

Her deep, guttural moan of relief pulled Dearmead back to his senses.

His own feet were well practiced at managing difficult surfaces, and it wasn't long before he was kneeling beside her, the two of them drinking until their bellies were swollen.

Aching but satisfied, Dearmead left Vy to rub cool water over her skin and went to investigate the fungus growing on the walls instead. An array of mushrooms sprouted from thin cracks in the stone—sniffing deeply, inspecting their fronds, he passed over the hallucinogenic ones for a few that seemed safe enough. If he weren't kinner, he wouldn't eat them, but their mild poison wouldn't hurt for long, and he needed the calories.

Pulling a handful from the wall, he gave them to Vy, then went to find another patch for himself.

It was there, scouring the walls for mushrooms, that he thought he must have died. Mark of One Unending or no, Dearmead had to have died. He hadn't eaten anything yet, let alone a potentially hallucinogenic mushroom, but what he was seeing couldn't be real.

Eaon Nemuse's name was carved into the wall.

Dearmead blinked at it. Twice. Then he lifted his shaking fingers and traced each Terranian letter, just to be sure.

"How . . ." he whispered to himself before splaying his hand over the stone wall and asking again in prayer.

The cave couldn't tell stories, but it did tell him that if he followed the nearest of the many tunnels splitting off to the left, it would lead him to fresh air.

The Southern Spine. The Southern Mountain Clan, where Eaon had traveled numerous times.

People. Witches.

Help.

If he had anything in his stomach, he would have thrown up from the knee-weakening relief that rocked through him. Dearmead kept his palm on Eaon's name as he leaned against the wall, breathing haggardly into the stone, wrestling with the sudden waft of emotion shaking apart his skin.

He hadn't realized how numb he had been until he wasn't anymore.

"What?" Vy asked, tense.

Dearmead shook his head, reeling himself back together. They weren't out just yet.

"We're close to the surface," he choked out. "There's a clan nearby. They will help us."

Vy said nothing, and Dearmead didn't turn to see how she took the news. To see if hope seared her the way it did him.

Pulling himself together, he plucked mushrooms from the wall and ate, swallowing down the bile that rose almost immediately as the poison hit his stomach. It would do for now. Soon, they could eat something proper. Soon, they could rest.

~

The sun was in the same position in the sky that it had been when they first lost sight of it, and for a moment, the days spent below ground felt like a dream. It took a dozen blinks for Dearmead's eyes to adjust to the abundance of light, to the sun's reflection off the pale mountainside. A brutal gust of cold wind battered his shaky body, bare skin pimpled with gooseflesh, hair whipping out and around to strangle him. Gathering it, he wrapped it around itself and tied it out of the way, looking around to get his bearings.

Pointless, since he had never been here.

Standing at the bottom of a gorge, the hard-packed dirt warm against his bare feet, Dearmead could crane his head as far back as it went and never see the mountain peaks. Barren and dry, there wasn't a blade of grass or leafy bush to be seen. The passage wasn't wide; thirty steps and he could touch the other side, where more openings promised entry back into the maze of tunnels. Eaon's stories meant Dearmead knew exactly where he was—this was the pass. The only way to get through the Southern Spine between Oford and Bernt.

Chaos's army would have to travel through here. They couldn't be too far behind.

"Dearmead?"

His head whipped around, pulse rabbiting at the sound of a voice that wasn't Vy's. A male voice.

Standing at the entrance to another of the tunnels, dressed in full Wyldeden guardian leathers, spear in hand, the tip glinting with metal instead of stone, stood Trumard Bayfield.

That swell of emotion rushed him again, and this time it took him to his knees.

~

Someone put thick furs in his hands. Dearmead got dressed.

Someone put a bowl of steaming hot food in his lap. Dearmead ate.

Following his older brother back into a tunnel had been the hardest thing he'd ever done, closely followed by the hundred meter climb up a spiraling stairwell, but at the end of it, they emerged into what was unmistakably someone's home.

The south-facing wall was entirely gone, leaving the open-plan room exposed to the weather. No railings were installed to keep wavering-footed witches safe, nor was there any barrier to stop the roaring wind from grabbing hold of loose clothes and ripping them outside. All the furniture was carved of heavy stone and lacking any kind of cushion. Dearmead didn't care. He collapsed onto a bench that meant to be a sofa, pulled the hood of his fur-lined coat tight around his face, and closed his eyes.

"Did you just . . . fall asleep?" Trumard asked.

A grunt and a single raised finger were the only answer Dearmead had energy for. Briefly, his brother tried to hold a conversation with Vy, but Trumard didn't speak Nirnish and Vy didn't speak Terranian, and after a moment they fell into silence.

Dearmead drifted.

Maybe he slept a little.

Hurried footsteps on the stairwell pulled him back. It was a challenge to pull apart his heavy eyelids, to look at the doorway without moving his head, but Dearmead managed it as familiar faces piled through.

Elder Herbe.

Elder Yvette.

Behind them, more guardians. Hyrschan archers. Most ignored the newcomers, bracing themselves against the wind's tug as they approached the room's ledge, anchoring barrels of arrows and spears. Herbe spared him a shocked and worried glance before barking orders for the soldiers to rearrange.

Yvette crouched by his side, the elder healer draped in furs and mountain-colored camouflage. "You're alive."

Sighing, Dearmead nodded.

"Where have you been? Your friends have been worried sick."

Trumard hovered close enough to listen.

"We were captured by Chaos's harbingers," he managed. "Escaped near the Soul Lake. What are you all doing here?

"You . . ." Trumard paled.

Grimacing, Yvette took Dearmead's wrist to measure his pulse.

"We need to delay Chaos's army long enough that they don't reach the city on the new moon. Half of Wyldeden's guardians are here, along with a significant number of Hyrschan soldiers."

Waiting for Yvette to release his wrist, Dearmead forced himself to sit up. A deep frown pulled his brow as he looked around at the dozen people in the room. Beyond them, on the opposite mountain face, more open caverns filled with soldiers.

"It's not enough," he croaked.

"We know."

Shaking his head, Dearmead looked up at his brother, chest tightening. "This is suicide. You can't . . . This isn't . . ."

"The Southern Mountain Clan is preparing troop leaders to run escape routes through the mountains for when we inevitably get overrun. We're not here to die, Dearmead. We keep Chaos here for the night, then we run."

They didn't understand what they were facing.

From the doorway, a lone mountain witch strode in, tall and broad. His dark curls were tied back, white warpaint striped down his cheeks. Piercing through his stretched earlobes were two long, thick claws. Another smaller one curved through his septum, a necklace of them tight around his throat. It was the scar that gave him away, though; warping his upper lip, the blemish was another memorable feature from Eaon's traveling stories.

Mustavrick Sar-son.

Hard, dark eyes found Dearmead. The mountaineer's booted footsteps were heavy on the stone floor as he approached.

"Are you one of them? The wild witches from the tunnels?"

"They're not wild," Yvette explained. "Dearmead is one of ours."

"I see. And the other one?"

Vy was perched at the room's ledge, unperturbed by the daunting fall. The mark on the back of her neck was hidden by the thick furs given to her, but here, it didn't feel necessary to keep who they were a secret. Begging himself to stay steady, Dearmead got to his feet.

"She is kinner. Vy and I both are."

Trumard sucked down a breath, but Dearmead ignored him.

The news was water off a duck's back to Mustavrick.

"We could use you on the ground, then," he said. "Help to stop beasts from getting into the tunnels."

Dearmead was so tired. He was *so* tired. "Of course. You're the Sar-son, right? Vy and I have just escaped the army. You need to know what you're up against."

318

Narrowing his already smallish eyes, Mustavrick frowned. "You know me?"

"No, but we have a mutual friend. Eaon Nemuse."

The mountaineer's face softened. Dearmead *ached*.

"Ah."

"Have your scouts seen what's coming?" Dearmead pushed on, trying not to think about it. How was he this exhausted and still capable of jealousy? Such things shouldn't be allowed to fester when there were more important things to be concerned about.

"They have. The front lines reached the frozen wastes last night and have not stopped moving."

"So you know . . . You know the numbers. You know the breeds."

Whatever memory had softened Mustavrick's face vanished. "I do. This clan knows how to fight off beasts, and we know how to take advantage of the mountain. The numbers are . . . high, but the escape tunnels have been cleared. Don't fret, greenie."

The smirk was absent, but Dearmead heard it anyway. The scar warping the male's smart mouth made sense now; Dearmead was about to give him another one.

Don't fret.

Don't fret.

If Vy understood a single word being said, she would kill the witch herself, but since she didn't, and Dearmead didn't have the words to explain how fucking condescending that was—*don't fret*—

Only his brother's grip on his wrist stopped him from swinging.

"Walk it off."

"Don't touch me," Dearmead spat, yanking his wrist free. But he listened. Shouldering past Mustavrick, Dearmead ignored his brother's calls and stalked to the stairwell.

Walls. He was so sick of walls, caging him in. But it was a hundred feet to the ground and Dearmead's thighs were quaking with exhaustion. Looking up, the curling stairwell was riddled with beams of light. More doorways.

His skin was too tight. Anywhere else would do.

CHAPTER FORTY-ONE

DEARMEAD

His neck was hot. Itching. Scratching the skin there proved there was no blood, yet Dearmead could smell it. Taste it at the back of his throat. Shtryg venom pumped through his veins until every cell in his body was burning and—

Fresh air.

Shoving his hood off, Dearmead stalked through the bustling room. More of the same at this level as the one below: archers, guardians, stacks of weapons. They ignored him as he elbowed his way to the ledge and sat down, bare feet dangling freely.

To his right, the frozen wastes met Bernt's forests. He couldn't look.

To his left, he could see dark rainclouds emptying relief into the smoldering remains of Anfar's forest. A sickly mix of smoke and steam billowed into the late evening sky,

Eaon had fallen into that. The impact alone would have killed him, and if the Lover sent him back, the fire would have made quick work of him again. It couldn't go on forever, this back and forth between the living and after-realms, but Dearmead didn't know if he wished Eaon had survived or met a peaceful end at last. Nobody else had seen him go down. Nobody would know where to find him. It had been days, and even if they somehow did, the only people capable of walking through that inferno to pull him out were Dearmead or Cinn, and as far as he knew, the kinner was in Qiri.

Vy wouldn't do it. The phouka was also marked, one of the Old Ones, but Dearmead had seen the large faerie shapeshifter melted to nothing. How could he come back from that? How long would it take? And even if he did somehow heal down there in the flames, the fae weren't known for doing favors for free.

All the anger lingering in the wake of *"don't fret"* ebbed, but he didn't let the childish yearning that reared in its place to gain momentum either, shoving it deep into the dark corners of his heart.

"You look like a steaming pile of horse shit."

Dearmead raised his weary gaze to meet Trumard's. He didn't have the energy for a retort. He *felt* like a steaming pile of horse shit.

"You want to tell me how you ended up a kinner?"

It was the tone that raised his hackles. His brother sounded so much like their da that Dearmead couldn't help but shut down further, fists tucked under thighs to keep them hidden.

"Not really."

Sighing, Trumard sat beside him. "The world got scary very quickly."

Narrowing his eyes, shoulders stiffening, Dearmead snapped.

"I'm not going to run."

Trumard raised a single brow. "I know you're not."

The words lacked the threat that would have laced them coming from their ma. Calla Bayfield would have been an asset in the coming battle, and though the two of them had never been close, Dearmead missed her unflinching ferocity right now. In a way, he supposed that was why he had been so quick to fall into comradery with Vy. The ancient kinner reminded him in many ways of the calloused female his ma had been before Aadya's curse had taken her.

"I was trying to tell you that I'm scared too," Trumard said, unable to look at Dearmead as he said it. Calla had fought during the rogue attack on Wyldeden all those years ago and had always told her children they weren't strong enough, not fast enough, not brutal enough. Maybe she'd been right. "None of our training prepared us for this."

Dearmead agreed, but said nothing. All that sudden defensiveness drained out of him quicker than it built up.

"But we're still far more prepared than the rest," Trumard continued as if Dearmead's silence didn't bother him. "It will have to be enough."

His brother had been hardened by Calla before Dearmead was even born, but the uncertainty in his words, the confession of fear . . . Maybe Trumard was the perfect balance of what Calla wanted her children to be and an actual, feeling person.

"How is what we do okay?" he asked.

Trumard frowned. Not in disapproval, but confusion.

"Guardians are meant to be protectors of life," Dearmead explained. "Defenders of peace. Our people are pacifists, and yet we are trained in violence. We are about to kill."

He didn't mention that he had already killed. In Pirevia, when he'd tracked Eaon all the way to Nevan's prison and Kaelean had given him the key to get them out. In Wyldeden, in the Sanctuary, their holiest of places, he had killed the high guardians who'd caused Eaon's second death. Again, in Pirevia, when Eavha had rushed into that fighting pit barefoot, without armor or weapon, to stand at Aisling's side *like a fool*. He had killed and killed and killed, and praying for forgiveness had not done much to ease the stain of all that blood.

Trumard rubbed a hand over the thick stubble across his jaw. "Because it has to be done. To protect our way of life, someone has to do the ugly things. For our people to be able to live peacefully, gently, in a world that is neither of those things, someone has to keep them safe. We bear the violence so they don't have to."

And what if Dearmead wanted to live peacefully? What if Dearmead wanted to be gentle?

Too bad. Calla had chosen this role for him because guardianship was what Bayfields did.

"Besides," Trumard continued, "if what the new Sparrow queen says is true, then the Mother herself turned her back on the beasts a long time ago. She supported the First War; it is not too much of a stretch to assume she supports this Fourth."

Because that was what this was. The Fourth War.

"The new Sparrow queen?"

"Aisling Aurnia," Trumard said. "She was crowned recently. Apparently, the rest of the royal family are dead."

Suddenly there was room in his head for other things.

"You saw her? Was Eavha there?" The last he had seen of her, the two females had peeled away to deal with something farther south of the fire.

"Yes. She is well. She kicked Lorelei out and has officially taken power over the clan in Kaelean's absence."

"Kaelean . . ." He looked to the fire.

"She went to Dusarn with Aisling to confront the then-queen and did not return. Apparently, she took on a dragon in lupanis form and neither have been seen since."

A small gleam of satisfaction came at knowing the beast that had destroyed their home, their forest, that had taken him and left Eaon to burn, had met its match in a black-eyed rogue. It would've been nice to know Kaelean had survived the encounter, though.

"What about the rest? Did our family get out?"

"Many did. Some wouldn't leave, more perished to the smoke. A few died from inhalation after the fact."

"Frilla? Rumeard?" He wasn't close with many of his siblings or cousins —he didn't even know all their names—but Frilla and Rumeard had been kind in a home that didn't encourage such things. They had covered for him when he used to sneak out of training to meet Eaon.

"They made it."

"Good."

For a full minute, Trumard stared at him, but whatever question he expected was lost on Dearmead. His mind was replaying with crystal clarity what the Anfar forest looked like, burning. The heat of it, reaching them all the way up in the clouds. He was glad he hadn't been able to see the Great Boab succumb. The ache in his chest at the mere thought of his home turned to ash was enough.

Waterfalls crashed in his mind. The echo of a small, secret laugh. Mischief flashing behind amber eyes—so bright, so alive.

"You haven't asked about Eaon."

They had wasted so much time. All those years, neither of them realized their small pocket of paradise had an expiration date.

"You can ask, my brother. It hasn't been a secret for a long time now."

"Do you have news?" Dearmead managed, throat closing.

Dragon fire, so hot Dearmead's breath had burned inside his body. The plume of it spearing through the sky, swallowing the phouka whole, wings spread wide: a shield. A body, dropping. The ground so far below, burning, burning, burning—

"He'd be faring better if he would stop fussing—"

Dearmead was on his feet before he knew what he was doing. Every line in Trumard's face, the annoying curve of his mouth as he said Eaon's name, was suddenly the most important thing. "You've seen him?"

"Not personally, but even in times like this, people can't help gossiping."

"Trumard, be clear. Is Eaon in Hyrsch?"

Slowly, carefully, as if facing down a rabid animal, Trumard nodded. "Some nightmarish fae brought him. He fell to the bottom of the Womb, apparently, and he's being as uncooperative as he's always been, too busy worrying about you and everybody else instead of letting Eavha fix him properly or, Mother forbid, rest. What you see in him is beyond me."

Dearmead was going to vomit.

The feeling was made worse by the blaring of a horn.

～

Snatching silver-tipped spears from the nearest barrel, Dearmead and Trumard ran for the stairwell and spent the next ten minutes tripping over each other as they flew down. It wasn't a decision. No thought was involved, no spike of fear; the horn blew, and instinct kicked in.

It caught up to him by the time he reached the cave mouth, though. Cold sweat trickled down the nape of his neck, his shiver disguised in the roll of his shoulders.

Vy and Mustavrick were already waiting, the former with her own spear, the latter with two scythes. In Wyldeden, gardeners often carried wooden ones, the curved inner edge fused with sharpened diamond. This was not that. The handles were shorter, weighted, the blade a cruel, glistening silver. While the mountain native had his forehead pressed to the wall, lips murmuring against the stone, Vy stood snarling at her own shaking hands.

"What's going on?" Trumard asked, announcing their arrival.

Vy snapped her gaze to Dearmead, and the two of them shared a look that said, *I don't want to be here. I want to run. But we can't.*

Nodding his understanding, Dearmead took a deep, slow breath to steady his nerves.

"They've arrived at the first block," Mustavrick said, pushing away from the wall. "Depending how it holds, we have some time before they reach us."

The words were barely out of his mouth before the ground began to shake. Dearmead planted his feet, fingertips to the wall for balance, and stuck his head out of the cave. To the west, roughly two miles down, a cloud of pale dust billowed into the purpling sky.

"Well, fuck," Mustavrick hissed. "Alright, we don't have time, then."

"What's happening?" Vy asked Dearmead, twisting her grip on her spear.

"I'm not sure, hang on," he answered, then looked between the two males. "What is that?"

"Give me some space," his brother said, grabbing the back of Dearmead's thick furred vest. Trumard tugged him back into shadow before crouching in the entrance to scratch a familiar spellmark into the dirt.

Dearmead's stomach twisted, his head spinning,

Once, The Barring Mark of Things Unwanted had been something secret, something taboo—an archaic magic too easily misused. It had been taught to Dearmead with strict instruction to show *nobody*. He had shown it to Eavha, who had a conniption at the sight of it. Yet here was his law-abiding brother, scratching it into the dirt. Across the gorge, in the mouths of the other caves, Terranian witches bearing Marks of Concentration knelt and prayed to the ground, fingers making identical patterns.

"Each mile along the gorge marks a section," Mustavrick explained, one ear pressed to the rock as he spoke. "The Sar waits at the mile marker for section one and will let the clan fight as long as they can before calling the retreat. Then, he will bring down the mountainside to block up the pass, go to the next mile marker in section two while the fighters from section one retreat to section three. Repeat. Section two will retreat to section four, and by that point, section three is ready, etcetera. Should keep invaders busy for a while."

Dearmead relayed the tactic to Vy, who said nothing.

"What section are we in?" Dearmead asked.

"Thirteen."

"And how many are there?"

"Seventy."

Leaning against the wall, Dearmead did some mental calculations. At a walk, he could travel a flat mile in fifteen minutes, making the entire trek a seventeen-hour ordeal. At a full-blown run, he could do a mile in three minutes. Physically, he could not run like that for seventy miles without stopping, but if he could—and maybe as a kinner, it *was* possible; Bernt certainly proved his body was capable of unknown feats—the pass could be traveled in roughly three and half hours.

He had only seen the beast army at a steady march, but he knew from spending time with Kaelean how fast a lupanis could move. Knew she had run for two days straight without stopping when Eaon and Cinn had been in trouble. Uninterrupted and properly motivated, a lupanis could make it through the pass in an hour.

Breathing through the stutter in his heart, Dearmead reminded himself that the wagons the beasts were escorting would slow them down. So would having to get everything past each blockade when Sar Vin brought it down. Then there was the silver the army had brought with them, the archers ready high above.

Was it possible they could end this here? Would a large enough number of beasts even make it to Hyrsch to be a problem?

Dearmead remembered just how many creatures had fed on him. Remembered the way he had not been able to see the end of Chaos's force in any direction as they trampled Bernt. Any damage the clan could inflict tonight would be a blow, but it would not stop them.

The first mile was already compromised.

At least being in the thirteenth section meant Dearmead had time to calculate how long it was taking the army to move through each mile. Calculate if it would be enough.

"And what happens when we get to section seventy?" Dearmead asked, watching Mustavrick move away from the wall.

He could have sworn he saw a pair of stone lips depress back into the mountainside. Could have sworn one of the shadowed dimples in the cave wall looked like an ear.

"Tuck tail and bolt for the city." Mustavrick grimaced. "And stick to the Oford forest; the plains have been boobytrapped, apparently. There isn't a safe strip of land between the east entrance of the pass all the way to the city walls."

Again, Dearmead relayed all of this to Vy, who finally frowned.

"Why doesn't his father just bring down the entire pass now. Make Chaos take his army over the mountains. It would delay them weeks."

No matter how hard he tried, Dearmead couldn't get his eyebrows to come down from his hairline. "That . . . That is a lot of magic, Vy. I don't think even Kaelean could pull off a feat like that. Most witches can't rally enough to even pull down a landslide once, let alone seventy times."

"What, not even all of these witches working together at once?" Vy tossed a hand around the cave and snorted. "The blood really has been diluted."

Something about her tone rubbed him the wrong way. The nervous energy pulsing in his veins probably didn't help.

"If it's so easy, feel free to do it yourself. Oh wait, you can't. You're human."

The word *human* was barely finished before Vy was swinging her spear right at his head. Dearmead ducked, lifting his own to block a second downward blow.

"*Human*? I am two thousand years old!" she shrieked at him.

"Hey!" Trumard barked, chest puffed, ready to step in.

Dearmead held up a hand. Never, in all their training, had he needed someone else to defend him.

Straightening, Vy twisted her spear, over and over. "You would do well to remember, child, that I have already done this. I have fought this war before. I have done this *exact* strategy before. Back when I was *human*, we led Chaos all the way from the eastern borders of Dusarn to the very far edge of Orhn. And we ruined the land behind us, blockades of mountains and pits, deserts and floods. You will remember that, within days of being changed, the kinner *won*. Do not speak to me about what I cannot do."

It was a mistake to argue with her, but what was she going to do? Kill him?

"If you won, then why are we here?" Throwing his free hand toward the gorge, empty for a little while longer, he asked, "More importantly, how exactly did you manage this so-called "*win*"? Because, and tell me if I'm wrong, but I doubt simply killing his mortal form is going to cut it. Did he even have one, during the First War?"

The ground trembled, a handful of loose stones shaking loose from the walls. Section two.

Dearmead's internal clock told him it had been about fifteen minutes.

"No," Vy spat out. "He didn't. And no, it won't. If your best witches—if an entire clan worth of witches—can't bring down enough rubble to block the whole pass, then you don't have what it takes to end this."

Leaning back against the wall, Dearmead closed his eyes. Neither Trumard nor Mustavrick understood what the two kinner were talking about, yet by the time Dearmead rallied himself enough to speak again, to open his eyes, he saw they had their attention anyway.

"There is one witch," he said to Vy. "I don't know if . . . I don't know what she can do, but she is covered in spellmarks and witchmarks. She has a Morvish advisor and a plan . . . Maybe she can do it. Maybe." Heart in his stomach, he added, "And . . . There's another one. The Lover has taken a special interest in him. And his sister . . . she's the one who made me kinner—"

"You are not kinner."

Dearmead blinked.

"You must be from Kin to be kinner. You are marked, but you are not one of us."

Turning his head, Dearmead stared at her. That was the part she was going to comment on?

But Vy was deep in thought, brow furrowed. It took her a moment, but eventually her head bobbed in a slow nod.

"We will hold this pass as long as we can, and then you will take me to them. If they are as strong as you say they are, then I will tell them what I know. I will tell them how to defeat Chaos."

CHAPTER FORTY-TWO

DEARMEAD

SECTION TWELVE FELL.

From half a mile away, the small landslide Sar Vin brought down left Dearmead's teeth rattling. The survivors from all the odd numbered sections had bled into the halls, their warnings a cacophony of noise:

"Get shields up to the archers! The harpies pull you right out and then drop you!"

"The ice walls need to be thicker! The lupanis claws shred it like paper!"

"Where's the healer? Get this bleeding stopped, we need him back out there!"

"The sun's down! The shtryg will be out now! Get the torches ready!"

There was no word of the beetle-shelled monsters. No sign of the dragons or the harbingers. Nobody warned of the way the world shifted and rippled in Chaos's presence.

It wasn't a risk worth taking. If Byron had any brains at all, he wouldn't risk losing a dragon here. Wouldn't risk giving Aisling a clue to what was in store. Give her time to prepare.

There were not as many survivors as Mustavrick expected. Gritting his teeth, palms flat on the wall of ice he'd coaxed into place over the past hour, he poured more magic into the only physical barrier keeping beasts out of the tunnels. Judging by the shouts of the survivors, the whispers coming from the walls, the barricades weren't holding up as well as they needed to. Terranian spells had the internal cave network collapsing in on itself in their wake, trying to keep the leak from spreading too far east, but they were losing too many soldiers.

Claustrophobia had never been a problem for Dearmead before, but if he made it out of this, it would be.

Breathe.

Inhale for five. Exhale for four.

Shut it down.

Nothing else mattered but the spear in his hand. Holding this tunnel.

The ice wall was black as the night beyond, thick enough to muffle the mountains' rattling. But it was still ice; lighting the torches too early would signal the cave's location, so the dozen witches waiting did so in the dark.

Thousands upon thousands of feet stampeded through the pass.

Closer.

The cave wall rippled, stone mouths pressing through, echoing the cries from high above.

"Shtryg climbing up to the archers! Keep the ledge lit!"

"But the harpies—"

"They could see us at sundown, who gives a fuck if they can see us at night! Those shtryg so much as scratch you, you're done!"

"Rain silver! Rain silver now!"

Mustavrick flinched back as something hit his ice wall, the impact hard enough to crack it.

"Fuck. *Fuck.*"

"Get ready," Trumard said quietly at Dearmead's ear.

"Stay behind me," Dearmead muttered back.

On either side of Mustavrick, Vy and Dearmead held their spears crossed over their chests. They would take the brunt of it should the wall break.

Trumard didn't answer, but took Dearmead's re-braided hair and tucked it down the back of his vest, out of the way.

"Is that a harpy riding a gryphin?"

"They're going for the torches!"

"Spears out! Priority one is keeping the ledge lit!"

That was Herbe. Heart skipping at the sound of his elder, Dearmead braced against the thud of another body hitting the ice wall. A spine-curling screech resounded through the cave as claws sunk into the twelve-inch-thick ice, the guttural snarl of a lupanis far too close.

"Eyes and arteries," Trumard reminded him. "Aim true, hit fast."

"I know, Ma," Dearmead growled back.

Clicking his tongue, Trumard flicked Dearmead's ear but didn't offer any more advice.

"How are they getting past the marks? Send it down the line: the marks aren't working!"

"Harpy! Left, left, left!"

"Get another torch up! Now!"

Shaking with effort, Mustavrick stood in front of the crumbling patch of ice where the lupanis was digging, placed his hands flat and prayed out loud. Vy pointed the tip of her spear where the ice had grown thin, ready to stick silver into the beast's claws the second flesh showed through.

"Tunnel breached on the south side!"

"Close it up! Keep them out of the stairwells!"

Claw sliced through the ice. Vy roared, stabbing down. The lupanis howled, low and long. Not in pain—the wall shuddered under the weight of two more impacts.

"It's not going to hold!" Mustavrick warned, a single drop of blood racing from his nose along the line of his scar. Where his fingers pressed to the ice, his nails had blackened.

Eaon had taught Dearmead about hypothermia, about frostbite, after one of his treks to the south. He knew how serious it was.

"Save your strength," Dearmead told him, sinking into a wide stance. "Get back."

Taking three steps back, Mustavrick grunted as he pulled his scythes free. Then he shouted into the wall, "There's about to be a breach down here!"

"There's about to be a breach up here too!" Herbe shouted back.

"Someone get a fucking torch up!"

"Shtryg! There, up on the ceiling!"

"Shut down the stairwell! Do it now!"

"Yvette, stay away from the ledge! Let someone else get the torch!"

Dearmead didn't hear the rest. Another impact, and the ice wall shattered, replaced by an onslaught of scale and frill and teeth.

Lunge; spear through the eye.

Yank; tip pulled free, staff whipped into a second lupanis's face.

Slash; silver through scale.

Vy was painted in off-white beast blood, spraying from a sliced artery.

More scales, then feathers, too. Lupanis leaping high, cawkers at his knees, talons and teeth primed to tear flesh.

Dearmead aimed high. Behind him, Trumard aimed low.

Claw in his bicep. Didn't matter. The itch was a background to the growling, ripping, screeching of the swarming masses.

A step back. Ground lost.

Lunge, yank, slash.

Something hot sprayed across his face. Dearmead blinked his vision clear. Lunged.

Yank, twirl, slash.

Shadows clambered across the ceiling, hissing laughter.

Someone lit a torch. The shadows held back. Waiting.

Slash, whip, lunge.

Another step lost.

"Pull back! Get out! Section thirteen closing in two minutes!"

Spear stuck in the back of a lupanis skull. Dearmead yanked, yanked again. Back exposed. Claws catching on his ribcage. Red in his eyes.

Itching.

Yanking again, it pulled free and Dearmead whipped his spear around to smack a cawker into the wall. A wall that began to crumble, loose stone and dust filling the hall.

"Let's go!" Vy screamed from farther back.

A ratki was snout deep in Trumard's intestines.

Dearmead kicked it off, whipped his spear to block a lupanis. Screamed as he pushed up, pushed back, slamming it into the cave wall. Fist-sized rock crumbled from the wall, the ceiling, piling up at the entryway, but Dearmead couldn't move because the walls were growing mouths again, stone fingers curling out of the cracks to latch onto the lupanis he had pinned.

Stumbling back, gasping for breath, Dearmead watched the cave consume the beast.

"Dearmead, let's go!" Vy screamed for him again.

Dearmead ran.

~

Section fifteen was ready.

Dearmead should have been at the back of the tunnel, catching his breath, but he wasn't. Shouldering his way to the front, he waited beside the Mare-blessed witch holding the ice wall, spear tight in hand.

"Use the cave walls." His throat was raw. "Whatever magic you're all using to speak to each other . . . I saw it eat a lupanis."

Mustavrick had followed him, furs matted with blood, scythes loose at his sides.

"It's not . . . It's not a spell. The mountain just . . . does that. It . . . It ate a lupanis?"

331

Dearmead blinked, too numb to understand the expression on the other male's face.

Had Eaon told him about this? Yes, he had: *"The mountains whisper. Sometimes in Terranian or Marian or Jemian. Sometimes in the language of the fae. We had to sneak all the way down into the crystal caves together just so the entire clan didn't hear what we were doing."*

He hadn't said anything about the mountain absorbing things, though.

On his other side, Vy was grinning, stroking the cave wall.

"She's here. Terra is here."

The now familiar screech of claws digging through ice forced focus. Dearmead planted his feet. Someone lit a torch. No chances this time.

Section seventeen.

Mustavrick's scythes slid past Dearmead's feet. Whipping his staff, he cracked open the skull of a cawker. From there, he saw the Sar-son pinned to the ground by a shtryg, barely visible through its shadow cloak.

The vacuous weight of the creatures crawling in sent a fresh flood of adrenaline through Dearmead's veins. The torch bearers were too far back.

Thrusting his spear blindly, Dearmead found flesh. Hoped it belonged to the shtryg.

He didn't have time to wait and see.

Whip, slash—Slip. The floor was slick with melted ice and pools of blood. Dearmead rolled into his fall, snatching up one of Mustavrick's scythes. He didn't know how to use it.

The cave walls yawned, swallowing another lupanis whole. Dearmead ducked low; the air was growing too heavy, gravity crushing down. A lupanis bulldozed its way through the tunnel, heading straight for him. Something in his thigh snapped as he tried to push himself upright. Itching, itching, but he found his feet, the weight of the universe crippling.

Mustavrick threw himself onto the lupanis's back. From the knee down, one of his legs was missing, but his arms were thick, rippling with strength as he locked them around the lupanis's skull, every muscle in his body flexing taut.

Bone cracked, shattered, and the lupanis fell limp.

"Fall back! Fall back! Closing seventeen!"

Spearing up into the shadows above, a shriveled gray body dropped to the ground, splashing blood up the walls. Gravity lifted from his lungs enough for Dearmead to haul in a breath.

Tucking the scythe into the leather strap around his waist, he used his free hand to grab Mustavrick under the arm, dragging him deeper into the tunnel as the mouth began to collapse.

∾

Section nineteen.

Section twenty-one.

Section twenty-three.

Mustavrick couldn't stay upright. The torniquet around his leg was the only thing stopping him from bleeding out. Dearmead carried him up the staircase, looking for a healer. One finds them. Not Yvette. They crouch by him, but Mustavrick waves them away.

"Someone bring me a bow."

∾

Section twenty-five.

Pale and shaking, unable to lift his arms anymore, Mustavrick stayed behind.

Section thirty-one.

Section forty-nine.

Section sixty-seven.

There were no more tunnels.

There were no more archers.

There was Dearmead and there was Vy and there was Sar Vin.

The high priest couldn't get off his knees, hands pressed into the dirt, breaths wet.

"Go," he rasped as the tips of the mountains turned gold with morning light. Blood dripped from between his lips, spattering the ground. "Tell her . . . we gave her . . . the time. Make it count."

Somewhere not too far away, a lupanis howled.

Without a word, Vy turned her back and started running. There were still three miles until the end of the pass and nothing left to slow the beasts down. She still had a torch in her hand, burning low, but she had lost her spear somewhere around section sixty. Dearmead's need to stay close to the light had him stepping after her.

"Spirit of the earth, from thee I am descendent and to thee I give my all," Sar Vin wheezed into the ground, head bowed low.

Every muscle in Dearmead's body ached and itched as he turned his back.

"Terra, keeper of our foundation, bless me once more."

Tripping over his own feet, Dearmead ran.

Sar Vin's final words chased after him.

"Take my enemies."

～

The dust cloud from the final landslide was the largest yet, sticking to their sweat-and-blood-soaked bodies, but they made it the last three miles without seeing a single beast. It was only a matter of time, though. Once the wagons were through the mess, they would have a clear line to Hyrsch.

"We forgot to go back for my chain," Vy gasped, delirious and stumbling. She dropped the retired torch and dry heaved into the nearest scraggly bush.

They were through the pass.

The ground sloped down for a solid mile still, the brush growing thicker to the north. Straight ahead for as far as the eye could see were rolling hills, grass dry and brittle, spotted by small villages he hoped were abandoned. To the south, the hills gave way to marsh. It would frost in the winter. Not as thoroughly as the permafrost of the frozen wastes or the higher tops of the southern mountains, but cold enough to bite.

Dearmead had only ever known grasses that were lush and green. Only knew forests that were safe and bright. The cold of the past few days was nothing in the face of a southern winter; a fact he only knew because Eaon had told him. Eaon had been here. He had seen this, had felt it, had known the people who lived in the mountain—

Dearmead shut his eyes.

Inhale of five. Exhale of four.

Shut it down.

He could have feelings later. Right now, he had to get Vy to Hyrsch.

Taking a minute to check the state of his spear, he realized he had lost the silver tip at some point. The staff would do for the time being. At his waist, he drew the scythe. Handed it to Vy.

"Sharp," she noted.

Dearmead nodded.

"That way," he said, voice like gravel, dead and flat, pointing toward the thickening bushland that would evolve fully into the Oford forest. The plains were laid with traps, he remembered. Plus, they would need the Dividing River's water. Something to eat.

Vy swung the scythe and began jogging down the final slope of the mountain.

Dearmead followed.

PART III

WILD HEARTS IN RIB CAGES

CHAPTER FORTY-THREE

AISLING

Trading her filthy clothes for a fresh robe, Aisling shuffled to the balcony and collapsed into one of her wrought-iron chairs. The dawn hour was near, the moon barely a sliver, winking between the heavy rain clouds working to soften the horizon's red haze. Its light glittered on her glass chess set where the game she had started with Eavha sat untouched since their first Imsa.

The past month had been both the longest and fastest of her life. Every minute seemed to be crowding in, a weight on her weary bones.

Rest, Eavha had demanded. Was it coincidence that the healer chose this night, after Aisling had spent the day torturing Aadya, to spend the night running a crash course in triage? Did she know what Aisling had been doing? Did it matter? Aisling's aching for kind company and warm hands was another sign of how weak she was growing at a time when she could not afford to be.

Eavha was right, though. It was only two days until the new moon. No word had arrived from their eastern-bound troops since confirmation that Sar Vin had bent to their will, but if their plans for the mountain pass worked it would allow at least another day to prepare.

They needed it. They needed time as badly as Aisling needed to rest. Her body, her mind, her magic—she would need everything sharp and replenished when Chaos arrived. Yet, as the night promised to end, she could not find peace. Fingertip balancing on her glass queen, Aisling sighed; there wouldn't be time to finish teaching Eavha how to play. Their game, like everything else, would remain unfinished.

Davina never got to see how the rest of her visions would unfold. Her plans for the Kinner would never come to fruition. Aisling had a pit of dreadful knowing in her gut that her blossoming relationship with Eavha was another thing that would never find conclusion. There was too much uncertainty, too much danger, and the Wyldeden heir was such a delicate, breakable thing. Not in spirit—Mother knew Eavha could be sharp and abrasive, and anyone who spent a moment with her could see she was a creature of willpower. No, Eavha was breakable in a very mortal way. She was a healer, not a fighter, and their little self-defense lesson had not gone well enough to ease any anxiety.

If Aisling thought Eavha would listen, she'd insist upon sending her to Pirevia with the evacuees.

"Nice view."

Aisling did not flinch. At least not in any perceptible way. Inwardly, her body seized so thoroughly she wasn't sure her heart would ever restart. She had not heard the door. Had not heard *anything*. Yet, standing at the balcony's threshold was the second-to-last person she expected to see, only surpassed by the kinner himself.

Eaon Nemuse stared at the sky like one might stare at a corpse, and Aisling was struck once again by the enigma of him. He was the same sepia as Eavha, but where she was bright and warm, he seemed worn and aged. He was leaner than Dearmead or Clayton or Owen, yet infinitely more dangerous. Eavha was so decidedly *Wyldeden*, with its lush hills and ever-blooming flowers, its mantra of peace and pacifism and community. Eaon, however, reminded her of Anfar with its gray, misty trees and sharp thorny trails. He was like the hostile shadows that loomed just out of sight — the ones that had filled her mind with the need to get far, far away. Eavha had called those shadows "Terra's guardians," protecting the weak spot between Mother's realm and nature's paradise, and though Eaon had been trained as a laborer and a traveler, she saw that he was also a guardian of sorts. A guardian of his sister, of those he chose to love. Looming and hostile, he had come to warn her away.

"If you're here to fight, I'm not in the mood," she told him.

Dropping his gaze from the smoldering horizon, Eaon shook his head. "Neither am I."

Saying nothing, she waited while he limped farther onto the balcony. Aisling didn't move as he reached the little table, leaning on the back of the second chair.

"May I sit?" he asked quietly.

"Would be rude to deny you with a leg like that."

Dwarfing her with his long limbs and broad shoulders, he didn't seem to notice the way his presence left her shifting uncomfortably. There was not a shred of kindness in his cold eyes. Even when Eavha had detested her, there was warmth.

"What happened to your shadow?" she asked, noting the phouka's absence.

"He had other things he had to do."

Aisling raised a single eyebrow, gaze dropping to the splotch of paler skin where he had, just last night, been missing his throat.

"I doubt that's true, considering what happened the last time you were out of his sight."

Eaon's hand rested against his sternum, fingers tracing the edge of the healed wound.

"He did not want to. I didn't know fae could get anxious. He only managed to leave because he locked me in Dearmead's old room, commanded a guard to stay right outside the door, and told me to stay put."

Aisling pursed her lips. "Because you Nemuses are known for your obedience."

Did Eavha know her brother was wandering around unattended? Aisling couldn't imagine she would be happy about it. Even less so that the two of them were alone together.

"He *told* me to stay put," Eaon repeated, grinding the word between clenched teeth.

This time, Aisling understood the emphasis.

Unwilling to give away her discomfort, she refrained from rubbing at her dry eyes. "And yet, you're here."

That Eaon managed to defy the phouka's command was almost unsurprising considering who his sister was. Unrivaled stubbornness and an unwillingness to do what they were told must be a hereditary trait among the Nemuses.

What was confusing however was that, of all the people he could have gone to—his sister, his aunt, Cinn—he had sought out Aisling.

Because she was watching, she saw the way his throat bobbed, jaw tensing, fingers clawing into his skin like he wanted to rip it off.

"And yet I am here."

Forcing his hand down, he picked up a pawn that Aisling had taken during the game and placed aside, inspecting the craftsmanship. When it was clear he was not going to provide any further explanation, she began to move the pieces back to starting position.

"Do you play?"

Eaon considered before admitting, "I think I've played once before."

It took a second for the board to be reset, and Eaon listened attentively as Aisling ran through the pieces and their rules quickly and succinctly. The moment she indicated he could take the first move, Eaon slid his pawn forward two places.

Aisling mirrored the move. "So, what do you want?"

He didn't bother pretending he'd clambered all the way to the top of her tower for the pleasure of her company.

"You haven't heard from anyone at the pass for a while, have you."

It wasn't a question. He already knew the answer.

"Have you?"

"I think the phouka has. A nymph found us at the Turlough home and they had a quick conversation before he decided to drag me back to the palace. They didn't know I understand a little of their language. They were talking about a disturbance with the mountains. About beasts. I don't think it was good news."

Leaning back in her seat, Aisling pinched the bridge of her nose. At first light, she would have a scout or a spy find out more. Find out if there were survivors, unable to reach out for some reason.

"If I had been allowed to go, this wouldn't have happened." His anger was the defeated kind, grief swallowed. "I had friends there who didn't have to die. This could have been over."

"Maybe." Aisling allowed. "Maybe it would have been worse. You have no control. The Lover will not commune with me, so I have no way to ask the benevolence of their plans. If Moyra's had a chance to look into the consequences of you using your magic on the battlefield, she hasn't seen fit to say so. The risks are too high."

Pressing his lips together into a thin, tight line, Eaon stared at the chessboard for a solid minute before moving another pawn.

"You don't really think that," he finally said. "That's what everyone else thinks, but I saw your face. You agreed with me."

"I did, for a moment," she admitted, making room for her rook to come out. "I also know that if you wanted to do it, you would have. There are very few people who could stop you, and I'm not one of them."

"No, you're not," Eaon agreed.

"So what do you want from me, Eaon?"

"I want you to let me do what needs to be done."

Slowly, Aisling rested her elbows on the table, steepling her fingers. Completely absorbed in the game, Eaon didn't notice her piercing stare as he moved another pawn.

"What exactly is it you think has to be done?" she asked quietly.

His gaze lifted—the same brown as Eavha's. Where hers were life personified, his held an eternal melancholy as he said, "This seed. Regardless of what it does to me, it's a weapon we can't afford to waste. But they're not wrong—I lack control. I can't do it if our people are on the field. The majority are under your command; either evacuate them all, leave me here in Hyrsch alone, or if you can't trust me to get the job done, then I need you to hold everyone back while I try."

Aisling had made a large number of risky gambles over the past six years, but this was in a league of its own.

"It's your move," Eaon reminded her.

Moving her rook had much lower stakes than what Eaon was suggesting, but it was still surprising when Eaon made the bold decision to bring out his queen early. There was no hesitation. His gaze had a glazed quality, as if he wasn't really paying attention to his fingers, gently plucking her pawn from the board.

It put his bishop in direct line of her queen. She could take it, but putting such a valuable piece in enemy territory without backup was a mistake in the making. Shifting another pawn, she put it between the two instead.

"A sacrifice."

Eaon nodded. "You're prepared to face Chaos alone if it comes to it. I figured you would understand. And . . . Eavha might listen to you."

Aisling snorted. "If you think Eavha will let you martyr yourself because I asked her to, then you don't know her very well."

"Firstly, Eavha has been quite fine letting me make sacrifices for her for a very long time. She knows it's my job to do what has to be done, she's just being stubborn about it. But once it's over and she realizes I was right, she'll get over it. Secondly, I know her far better than you." His eyes darkened as he stole her knight. "She's twenty-one years old. She is years away from reaching maturity, and you are nine years her senior. You should not know her at all."

It wasn't the first time the age difference had crossed her mind; acknowledging it left her as conflicted as it always did.

"Of all the thing about me to get under your skin, you choose my age?"

She needed a moment to think. Distracted by the turn in conversation, Eaon had left his bishop, the one blocking her queen, open for the taking. She was reasonably certain it was a safe move. She took it.

"Stay away from Eavha."

"I don't think you have much to be concerned with considering I will be dead before this war is over."

Eaon moved his second bishop and took another pawn.

"Checkmate."

Aisling frowned, fingers frozen. "Where?"

"In seven."

"In *seven*?"

He waited patiently as she worked through every scenario, every possible move with the pieces she had left, but he was right. He had laid the perfect trap and she *hadn't seen it coming*.

"You said you'd only played once."

"Yes."

"Then, how?"

"I don't know," he admitted, crossing his arms. "It happens sometimes. I saw the path and I took it."

They both knew he wasn't just talking about the game. She watched a muscle in his jaw tic until he managed to turn to her. Somehow, the sorrow in his eyes had deepened.

"It has to be done. I know it."

She could not in good conscience ignore the warnings of a Morvish witch. Even a reluctant, untrained one.

Eavha was not going to like it.

Aisling reset the board.

CHAPTER FORTY-FOUR

EAON

THOUGH THE SUN HAD ALWAYS SHONE IN WYLDEDEN, EAON KNEW from the countless human books he'd read that rain during a funeral was cliché. If he'd had his way, he'd have left the forest to burn another day rather than watch Cinn, damp and shivering, say goodbye to Sarah and William. He stood in the same state of silent shock that he had been in since it happened, staring at the linen-wrapped body nestled carefully in the back of a small wagon. The horse Sarah would ride back to Belden waited patiently as she tucked Cinn's head against her shoulder and promised, for the umpteenth time, that it was not his fault. A heart attack was nobody's fault.

Yet, it was Eaon's. He knew it, even if nobody was saying it.

He had hesitated. Afraid of hurting them. Then, when he had finally moved, it had been too late. Too slow.

Hand stuck to the now paler flesh of his throat, Eaon swallowed down the need to shout at Cinn some more. His friend should be going home with Sarah, but repeating himself would only lead to more dead-eyed staring and Eaon couldn't endure it anymore.

"Come home," Sarah wept into Cinn's shoulder. "As soon as you can, come home."

Cinn touched her elbow in answer and led her to the saddle. Helped her up before holding out a hand for Siobhan, who waited by the reins. Boosting her up behind Sarah, the two exchanging silent demands.

Take care of her.

Make them bleed.

Eaon kept his distance, hiding under the porch of a closed-down store. A day of private mourning followed by a sleepless night left him cloistered in a heady fog, yet despite the beat of heavy rain on the cobblestone road, he heard three sets of footsteps approaching.

"Are you okay?" Moyra asked, coming to a stop beside him just as Sarah nudged the horse into movement.

Behind her, Edwina and Radley watched their brother with matching frowns of concern.

"Eavha's healing was perfect," he answered, hand still pressed to his throat. It wasn't entirely true. Eavha hadn't taken advantage of his trip to the void to finish healing his leg, and he hadn't had a chance to ask her why—wasn't sure he wanted to bring it to her attention. The pain of the awkwardly healing break took up fifty percent of his capacity to think, which meant he was fifty percent less capable of sinking into the depths of misery and self-pity. "What are you doing here?"

Moyra sighed. "I'm supposed to help Cinn train with the soldiers."

Sliding her a withering glare, he ground out, "I don't think now's the time."

A lot had been taken from Cinn, but he had never lost anyone this way before. Nobody he loved had ever died. Grief still felt taboo, but Eaon thought he knew something about how to deal with the weight that likely sat in Cinn's chest, and it didn't involve wielding dangerous weapons.

"Now is exactly the time." Sitting on the only dry patch of ground, eyeing the creeping puddle Eaon's bare feet were soaking in, Gatty was a small but deadly barrier between the two of them.

Eaon opened his mouth to argue, but Moyra got in first.

"I also wanted to let you know that I finally got a read on Dearmead."

There was no air in Eaon's body.

"He's alive," she said.

Obviously.

"And he's somewhere west of here. That's all I could get, though. I'm sorry. Scrying is not my specialty."

Looking away, hunting for Cinn, for something to anchor the screaming rage brewing inside him, Eaon managed to contain the maelstrom to a muttered, "Fucking useless."

If anybody heard it, they didn't say anything.

Sarah and Siobhan were gone, but Cinn still stood in the middle of the road, staring after them. Pulling up the hood of her cloak, Edwina went out to fetch him.

"Would you like an escort somewhere?" Moyra offered.

Again, before Eaon could lash out, he was interrupted by the dark, silky voice of the phouka. He stood in his horse form, waiting in the alley right beside the store, oblivious to Eaon's indiscretion a few hours ago. An indiscretion Eaon didn't want to think about too much. Refused to waste time pondering. Stuck in the armchair where the phouka had commanded him to *wait*, he had been broiling in hatred for magic. For every spell or spoken word that had stripped him of his autonomy.

No, Eaon didn't want to think about the *snap* he'd felt in his soul. The breaking that occurred, allowing him to struggle to his feet and bribe the guard to look away for a minute. Instead, he wondered whether it was a good thing that the dark faerie's presence had become so normalized that Eaon barely noticed him anymore. Wondered whether or not the relief he'd felt upon the phouka's return was something Eavha could brew a tonic for.

"That won't be necessary," the phouka assured Moyra. "We're going to the same place."

Eaon raised a brow. "We are?"

"The cat sith and I have our own troops to corral. Besides, that is also where your sister is, and I like having her nearby."

"Works for me." Moyra nodded to the phouka before setting those eerie rose-pink eyes back on Eaon. "I've been meaning to speak with you anyway."

That was his cue. "I have nothing to say to you."

Limping heavily, leaning on the wall, he took the two steps necessary to reach the phouka and refused to be embarrassed by how difficult it was to climb onto his back.

Hands settled on his hips, and Eaon froze. Looking back, he found and empty-eyed Cinn steadying him.

Eaon was by no means an expert on grief, but Mother of all, he hoped Cinn cried soon.

He wasn't in the mood to sit in the med tent that Eavha and the other healers had set up on both sides of the city's gate. They'd passed through it on the way out; the half outside set up for triage and quick fixes, to get soldiers back out as soon as possible, while the inside was for keeping the seriously injured stable and storing those who couldn't be helped. The human and demi-kin medics weren't bothered by their passing, but the Wyldeden brewers and low-blessed healers stared.

Eaon couldn't stand them. Couldn't stand being looked at like an invalid. Like he was even more useless now that he was dangerous.

It had to be close to noon, yet the sun hid behind the thick clouds still moving north toward Anfar, dousing the bushfire that had run rampant for almost two weeks. If the rain was cold, he didn't notice. He'd been cold for so long he didn't remember what it felt like to be alive anymore. To be conscious.

No, the shudder than ran down his spine had nothing to do with the cold; other Wyldeden witches walked the length of the city walls, carving a familiar spellmark into the stone, and the hum of magic was enough to make him nauseous. Being too close to the city wall was not an option, but he also didn't want to be anywhere near the faeries creeping through the muddied field, laying their traps and arguing with each other.

Least of all did he want to be near the soldiers sparring at the bottom of the hill, so he found an isolated spot halfway down, decided there wasn't going to be anywhere better for him to hide, and watched Cinn lose his fucking mind.

There was nothing healthy about the way Cinn tried his very best to kill the other soldiers with nothing but a blunt wooden sword, blind with grief and trauma. Radley and Moyra were doing their best but utterly failing to keep things civil.

Nobody ever listened to Eaon, but he couldn't seem to work up any outrage about it.

Truly, Eaon wasn't sure any of it was real.

He wasn't Morvish, he knew he wasn't, but, if he were—*he wasn't he wasn't he wasn't*—but if he were . . . It was as if he were watching a memory, where all the men and women down there were already ghosts, the field their graveyard.

Maybe he needed a nap.

He almost didn't notice when everybody stopped. Cinn stopped. Every face was turned south to where the road between Hyrsch and the southern port town curved through the valleys.

On it marched an army.

The phouka landed beside him, flicking water off his shiny black wings. "The sea-shore clan has returned," he explained. "And they brought reinforcements."

"Mm," Eaon hummed, resting his head on his knees.

Scoffing, the phouka *popped* back to his goat-man form and roughly hauled Eaon to his feet. Fighting his grip was pointless, so Eaon didn't bother as the phouka dragged him back up the hill to the med tent. As they reached the crest, allowing him a better view of who exactly marched toward them, Eaon became painfully awake. Among the sea-shore clan walked witches in a familiar dusty brown leather, and leading them were three faces he couldn't bear to see.

Injured leg or not, Eaon ran down the path.

"Killian?" The name was half awe, half terror in his mouth. "Reigan? Tomaii?"

The Northern Mountain Clan was here.

Overhead, the sky coven descended from the clouds on their delicate cunae mounts, whooping their glee, heads turned skyward as rain washed down.

Killian gave a two-fingered salute and shook his head. "Well, you look like shit."

"What are you *doing* here?" Eaon stopped his hobbling, and before he had time to regret not bringing his crutches, the phouka was there to take some of his weight.

The faerie creature gave the sea-shore clan pause, and even Killian and Reigan slowed, remembering the horror the phouka had inflicted on their people up north.

Tomaii grinned, rushing forward with arms extended eagerly.

"Heard there was going to be a party!"

Quick as a whip, Reigan grabbed the back of Tomaii's collar and yanked him back. "Do you learn?"

From the corner of his eye, Eaon noticed Eavha, Aisling and her guard catching up to him. The Sparrow queen could barely lower her gaze from where the cunae were circling, alight with a fire Eaon hadn't seen before. Her grin was wide and wicked, even as she forced herself to nod to Dominic, who returned it tiredly, commanding the rest of his clan to continue to the city.

"They arrived by ship just as we were preparing to leave," he said.

"Our high priest holds Pirevia—" Killian began to explain, but it was cut short as his older brother and the elder scout, Miika, dropped from his new wife's mount to land in a crouch before Aisling.

It was very dramatic. If he could find the energy to smile, Eaon would have at Killian's heavy eyeroll.

"Your Highness." Torn between bowing and keeping a straight spine, Miika dipped awkwardly, shooting Tomaii a murderous glare as his laughter pealed through the crowd.

349

"It's Majesty, now," Clayton warned.

Aisling waved her hand as if the correction were a particularly persistent blowfly. "Can I assume you speak for your clan, Elder . . . ?"

"Miika, and yes, I do. This is my wife and the alpha of her coven, Yasmin," he announced just as the ten remaining members of the sky coven landed.

Eaon felt ill.

He had killed some of them. Accidently, but he had. The gaps in his education meant he hadn't known it was possible for a witch to *push* magic away, else Eaon never would have flung an arc of deadly magic at the dragon rider. Not when three cunae riders and the mountaineers with them were close by.

Did they know it was his fault? None of them were looking at him, though he felt his friends' gazes like a brand.

Thank the Mother and her Lover it hadn't been Miika and Yasmin among them. Killian pretended he hated his brother, but gods knew that if Eaon had killed him, Killian would never forgive him.

"I was just explaining—" Killian started, but Miika held up a hand.

"My brother speaks out of turn." Miika lifted his chin, looking down to where Aisling stood, easily two feet shorter. "As emissary, our high priest has tasked me with presenting our offer to you."

"Oh?" Aisling tilted her head. "Pray tell."

"Our aid in your war, in holding your brother's city, and when this is over, you relinquish the Northern Mountains to us. We are to be free of you."

Aisling didn't even think about it. "Done."

Raising his eyebrows, Dominic opened his mouth.

"Done," Aisling said before he had a chance to ask. "When this is over, there will be no Sparrow Coven. All land is free."

The sheer number of loose jaws aimed at her was obscene. Eaon's wasn't one of them. He'd noticed it during the last Imsa—Aisling was prepared to do whatever it took to win this war, including forfeiting her own life. Land rights meant nothing to her anymore.

"Just . . . Just like that?" Dominic asked.

"Yes." Aisling was not interested in their shock. "Now, given the Northern Mountain Clan's arrival, another Imsa is due. There is news to be shared and plans to be made. I will officially announce the release of all Nirnish land then."

Eaon didn't miss the way Eavha's hand slipped into Aisling's. He didn't miss the harsh intake of breath and Killian's lethal glare at the link. But as the party began to climb back up the hill toward the city, it was Reigan who approached them.

"You must be Eavha," she said, extending a hand. "I've heard you're quite the healer."

"You have?" Eavha asked, looking over her shoulder to where the phouka was hauling Eaon up the slope. "Is this one of your friends? Oh, wait! Reigan, right?"

Reigan's usual scowl softened with surprise. "You know my name?"

"Eaon mentioned you. Is that Killian and Tomaii?"

Now Eaon was shocked. He didn't think Eavha was paying any attention to his dinner table stories back when he'd been traveling with their da, let alone capable of caring enough to remember them.

"It is."

"You're a brewer, right? Specializing in salamander milk? That is tricky work."

Eaon blinked. For a moment, he could see it: his sister and Tomaii's cousin bonding over their shared love of healing. Becoming friends.

"That is horrifying." Tomaii chuckled, powerful legs keeping pace with Eaon easily. "I vote we put a stop to it immediately."

"Are you kidding? Put them in a room with Chaos and this war is over," Eaon grumbled.

Another zealous bout of laughter lit up the valley, cut short only when someone pushed past Tomaii, nearly knocking him right into Eaon. The phouka had him half thrown over his shoulder before anyone could touch him.

"Well, excuse you," Tomaii sniped, but the male ignored him.

Eaon didn't blame him. Cradled in his arms was the familiar sight of a linen-wrapped corpse, this one stained and reeking of rot. Head down, clutching the body tight to his chest, the man bulldozed right past Reigan and Eavha, too. Right past Aisling, who stopped walking.

In an uncomfortably vulnerable voice, she called, "Owen?"

CHAPTER FORTY-FIVE

AISLING

OWEN TURLOUGH DIDN'T RESPOND TO HER CALL, BUT IT WAS HIM. AND in his arms, was Nora. Emotions had always been tricky things, either entirely absent or entirely too hot, and her range had always been rather stunted—the ones burning her now were relatively new, but she knew exactly what they were all the same.

Shame. Guilt.

"I didn't forget, I just . . ." Aisling didn't know what she meant to say. Her heart ached for her Second, for her friend, and yet she had not thought of Nora for weeks.

"I know," Eavha said softly, squeezing Aisling's hand. It was a different kind of warmth, like a blanket rather than a pot of scalding water. "Come on. We need to organize Imsa."

Aisling nodded, aware that while she had stopped still, Edwina was leading the party farther up the road. Yet Aisling's eyes lingered on Owen's retreating back. She didn't know what was appropriate. Should she offer a royal funeral? Should she invite him to the palace to talk? He had collapsed in her arms in the arena, had let her remove the collar with the key mark tattooed on her palm, but now that he'd had time to put himself back together? She wasn't sure he would want to see her.

"Aisling."

"I know. Just . . . Can you start setting up for me? I need a few minutes."

"Of course. But, Aisling, look at me for a second." Somber brown eyes waited patiently as Aisling wrestled her ugly feelings into something she hoped couldn't taint anyone else. When she managed it, Eavha placed her free had against Aisling's marred cheek. "She believed in you so fiercely. Hold onto that."

It would be easy to claim fault for what happened to Nora. A part of her clung to it as if penance was the path to salvation. But it wasn't. What happened was Nevan's fault. Was her parents' fault, for raising such a beast. Was the Sparrow Coven's, for punishing the demi-kin on the basis of their ancestors' existence. There was blame to lay everywhere, but doing so was a waste of time. It did nothing to help Nora now, and wouldn't do anything to protect anyone else from the same fate.

Closing her eyes, Aisling pressed a kiss to Eavha's palm and nodded.

~

Yesterday, the undertaker had removed a body from the Turlough home. Today, Owen took one back inside.

Clayton remained at her side as she followed Owen through the city, then knocked when she hesitated at the residence's front door. Relatively certain she wouldn't be welcomed, she didn't want to make the situation worse than it already was, yet she also knew she would be too distracted to concentrate on Imsa and Chaos if she didn't find some closure.

Shooting Clayton a pointed look, she smothered her annoyance the moment a servant opened the door.

"Y-Your H . . . Majesty."

"I just saw Owen come in. I need to speak with him."

"Yes, of course, he's . . . I think he just went into the backyard. Please come through."

Sheets had been laid over the furniture, and at first Aisling thought it must be some demi-kin mourning custom she didn't know about, but then she remembered her own servants doing something similar throughout the palace the last few days and realized it was for the evacuation. She supposed it was a promising sign that people were hopeful. They didn't want to clean up dust and whatnot when the war was over and they returned.

Following the servant through the house to the back door, Aisling stopped short of stepping outside. Owen was lowering the linen-wrapped corpse to the ground, so very carefully. The air was too willing to carry his words.

"You're safe now, my love. You're home."

Slightly jaundiced and highly worn, Owen's face was the kind of death the faithless feared. The strip of paler skin around his throat—the one almost all the demi-kin bore from their years wearing collars—had almost healed from the bruises he'd suffered in Pirevia. She felt like they should have healed already, given his genetic predisposition to quick healing.

"Owen," she called softly.

This time he paused. Slowly, tension pulled up his shoulders, tightening every muscle in his bulky body.

"What?"

He hated her. She could feel it.

That was alright. If he had to hate someone, it was best it be her. She could bear it.

"If you would like her memorialized here, I can make arrangements—"

"I want nothing from you."

That was fair. "I can send Edwina instead, if you prefer."

"I would prefer you to fuck off so I can bury my wife."

Behind her, Clayton vibrated with the need to pull his weapon, but even he could see this wasn't a man looking for a fight. This was a man in pain.

"Alright," she allowed. "Send word when you're ready and I can have you taken to Belden. You just missed Siobhan; she left for the Copeland farm this morning. She's doing well—"

"I don't give a shit."

Frowning, Aisling pursed her lips. Maybe it was just that her timing was terrible, but surely he still cared about his surrogate and the child they'd made together. As for going to Belden . . . He knew them, Aisling remembered. He had known the Copelands, had lived with them when he was a young boy, freshly smuggled from Pirevia's sewers. Now was not the time to tell him about William.

Prepared to walk away and try again in a few hours, Aisling took a step back, but apparently something had prickled enough to make Owen stand. Turning to look at her, shaking his head like he couldn't quite understand his surroundings, his shoulders fell.

"The world just keeps going for you, doesn't it?"

Her frown deepened. "What do you mean?"

Moving like his arm weighed a thousand pounds, he opened his palm in Nora's direction. "She's dead."

Careful not to let her own grief touch this moment, Aisling tightened her jaw and nodded. Owen choked on a sound that might have, once, in a different lifetime, been a laugh.

"Why am I bothering? You've never loved anything enough to understand that the world is *over* for me. It's over. I don't care about whatever war you've got going on and I don't care about Siobhan. I don't care."

Despite how stoic she held herself, Aisling felt her eyelid twitch. Vicious words sat on her tongue, because she *had* loved, she had loved Davina so much that it had changed her irrevocably. She *did* understand, but she couldn't just let the world move on without her, because then Davina's sacrifice meant nothing. That, too—*You can't be like this, Owen, or it meant nothing*—wrestled inside her for a moment, but she held her tongue. It wasn't fair to expect Owen to cope the same way she did. They were very different people. Growing up, Aisling had never, for a single day, trusted anybody. Lessons learned too young to remember, she had hardened her heart very early. She had refused to love anything because if she did, she knew with absolute certainty her horrible brother or her spiteful mother or her petty father would take it from her. She had been so angry, at first, to discover Davina had wormed her way through her armor, unable to soften Aisling's steel heart but laying claim to it anyway. She'd hated her for a while, because she knew she would lose her. And of course, she had. Davina's death had hurt, more than Aisling expected, but she knew how to be in pain. She knew how to stand still when all she wanted to do was throw herself in Davina's casket and bury them both six feet underground.

But Owen wasn't Aisling.

From what she understood, Owen was born in the literal sewers of Pirevia and didn't find a breath of fresh air until he was seven years old. He hadn't seen the sun, hadn't tasted food that wasn't the rotting meat of his neighbor. What he did have was a mother who somehow learned to love. Aisling and Nora had spoken of it once. It wasn't her business, and Nora didn't want to gossip about her husband, but she had needed help. She wanted to get Owen's mother out of Pirevia, and so had explained what she knew of the woman who had birthed and raised a child in such filth. A woman who woke up every morning and weighed up what was kinder: sharing what food she could claw their way, or putting the boy out of his misery. A woman who had held on to the hope that, somehow, she would get Owen out.

Aisling had inquired about the demi-kin at her earliest opportunity, grateful for the network of rebels and smugglers working to get people out of that city. It had been far too late.

But Owen *had* gotten out. He had seen the sun and breathed in the countryside. He had tasted chocolate, and fallen in love, and learned how to be happy. Had taken the life his mother gave him and, with the help of a strong, brave, fierce woman, built it into something enviable. He had believed in a future safe enough to want children.

And then that love, that safety, that hope, had been ripped away.

For him, the world had ended. And he was right, Aisling didn't know what that felt like, and wasn't sure she was compassionate enough to coddle him through it. Plus, she had something he didn't. Until a week and a half ago, she'd still had a part of Davina. The Morvish witch's second sacrifice to give Aisling a moonstone in Dusarn meant they would never be reunited in the after-realm, which had hurt all over again—hurt so much she woke sobbing nearly every night. But when she did, she had Eavha.

It wasn't her job to give Owen something to live for, but she took a slow breath and tried anyway.

"She's almost five months pregnant with your baby, Owen."

"I am aware," he ground out. "I am *aware* that she is pregnant, because that's the whole reason that Nora is dead."

Aisling tilted her head. "That's an interesting leap."

"Not really. It's the reason Nora didn't turn her in. It's the reason we ended up in Pirevia. It's why she is *dead*. I want nothing to do with it and nothing to do with her."

She'd tried. She'd tried to be kind.

"I understand that you're angry, but you need to find somewhere else to direct it," Aisling warned. "You don't want my help? That's fine. Bury Nora by yourself. You don't want to go to Belden to be with the woman you impregnated? Fine. Clean yourself up, get something to eat, take a nap, and then report to Commander Gogh."

Scoffing, Owen turned his back and stalked to the garden shed to fetch a shovel. "Go fuck yourself."

Anticipating Clayton's reaction, she reached back to still the hand on his sword.

For Nora. For Nora, she would make sure Owen stayed in one piece long enough to find a way out of this new dark hole he was living in.

"You've got until sunset to make your choice, Owen. You either report for duty, you go to Belden, or I'm putting you back in the dungeon until you reconsider the way you speak to the Sparrow queen."

Owen said nothing. He just began digging.

Turning her back, she made sure she had Clayton's full attention.

"Stay here. Watch him. If he doesn't make a move to the battlefield or to make travel arrangements, bring him to my room at sundown."

"What about you?"

"I'm going to Imsa. I'll be fine."

He didn't like it, but he also knew she'd had enough disobedience for one day. He nodded, and Aisling left Clayton to watch over Owen, silently digging a grave beneath the roses.

CHAPTER FORTY-SIX

AISLING

THE NEW MOON WAS TOMORROW NIGHT, AND EVERY MINUTE WASTED waiting for the council room to settle, for oaths to be spoken and blood to be spilled, was a minute Aisling didn't know they had.

Shutting away thoughts of Nora and Owen, Aisling took her seat at the head of the table and braced herself to share what her spies had discovered in the east. Or, more accurately, what her spies had learned from bargaining with the fae, who were far more capable of investigating the aftermath of Chaos's passage through the pass quickly and without risk.

Sensing her agitation, Eavha's hand found Aisling's beneath the table. Somehow there were both less people and more than last time. Edwina and Radley were accounted for, but Clayton was busy and there were significantly fewer Wyldeden witches lining the room. Only Eavha and Elder Milnova remained—and Eaon, though the way he was tucked between Moyra and Killian left Aisling wondering how clan-bound he truly was. The phouka, of course, hovered by Eaon's shoulder. Gatty had opted to stay with Cinn outside.

Loitering by the wall stood two Pirevian additions, boat weary and famished, judging by the way they attacked the small feast slapped together on the table. That Aisling didn't lunge across the table to throttle Rhosyn on sight spoke legions to her self-control. Nevan's whore really had the audacity to travel down to *her* city and sit at *her* council table when Aisling had been very clear that if she laid eyes on the jelly-spined bitch again there would be levels of agony inflicted that nobody alive had ever experienced before. Yet, there she sat, in a dirty dress, trying to be very small. When Moyra asked who she was, she had spoken so softly Aisling almost couldn't hear her explain that she represented all the Pirevian humans who had been glad to be rid of Nevan, who'd come on the dozen ships south to do what they could to help Aisling.

The second Pirevian also looked like they'd just spent two weeks on a crowded ship, a layer of grime settled into her scarred skin. Yellow-and-brown bruises were a ghastly framework for her wide, jaundiced eyes as she paced the length of the room—a starved predator on the prowl. It was Rhosyn who had to introduce the woman; as survivor and longest reigning champion of the arena, Cecelia had been chosen by the Pirevian demi-kin who'd also come on the ships to speak on their behalf.

Once Rhosyn shut her mouth, Aisling introduced Fior—emissary from the river clan—to Miika and Yasmin. Dominic had already had the chance to get to know their new allies, sitting patiently as the representative of the Northern Mountain Clan recounted their journey.

"A member of my clan—" Miika began.

"Me," Killian grumbled in Terranian.

"—received Eavha Nemuse's summons for aid. After discussing it with Yasmin and a few of those maintaining order in Pirevia—"

"Tomaii annoyed him into agreeing," Killian said to Eaon, who pressed his lips together in a desperate attempt to contain the laughter shining in his eyes.

"—we had any willing human, demi-kin, fae or witch board whatever ships were available—"

Killian snorted, cupping a hand over his mouth in an attempt to keep his mockery private. "Miika was so seasick he had to fly with Yasmin most of the way."

"Figures," Eaon grumbled back. "Did you like sailing? The sea?"

"Could you two hold off on gossiping until the adults are finished speaking?" Miika turned on them, red in the face. Killian rolled his eyes while Eaon had the wherewithal to blush, sinking lower in his seat.

Aisling was in agreement with Miika that their behavior was childish and inappropriate, but beside her, Eavha was beaming. It must have been a relief to see her brother doing something other than moping or raging, and that glee was the only thing that kept Aisling from scolding the males herself.

Eavha had made her so disgustingly soft.

"You made the journey rather quickly," Aisling said instead.

Holding Killian's stare for a moment longer, Miika turned back to face his audience. "Yes. The sky coven and the wind sprites did their best to give us speed. We were under the impression that time was of the essence."

"It is," Aisling agreed. "Our original timeline would see the army arrive tomorrow night, however we hope to have delayed them at least a day. It will give us the moon."

"For what reason? It won't be enough light to fight by," Killian asked, ignoring the murderous glare Miika shot at him.

"It takes away the advantage the new moon would give Chaos's beasts, but also gives the Mare-blessed and Moyra an edge. Fior and Dominic's people have laid traps in the hills between our walls and the faerie ring that will rely on the moon's sway," Aisling explained.

"But the moon will still not be enough light to counter a shtryg. Fighting at night is still a major disadvantage," the sky coven's alpha said. She looked to Miika, and the two of them had a silent exchange before the elder nodded.

"Killian, go find your bothersome friends. Tell them and the rest of the Igni to start making as many everlight amulets as possible."

The gift was a shot of adrenaline right to Aisling's heart.

"There are Wyldeden charmers congregated in the city's library making protection charms," Eavha said, smiling at Killian. "If you need supplies, they have everything available."

"Thanks," Killian said, returning her smile and nodding to Eaon before leaving the meeting, not bothering to hide the rude gesture aimed at his brother.

"What about aerial support?" Yasmin asked before anybody could get sidetracked by the animosity brewing between the northerners. Her accent was thick, and Aisling couldn't place it. The nomadic nature of sky covens made it difficult to pinpoint origin, but if she had to hazard a guess, she thought Yasmin may have spent more time near the southern borders of Dusarn than anywhere else. "My coven and I have made a hobby of taming beasts and know well how to manage them. We can integrate ourselves into your forces immediately."

Sucking down a deep breath, Aisling lifted her chin.

"I will meet you out on the plains first thing in the morning."

It took Yasmin a minute to understand that Aisling was, in fact, the entirety of Hyrsch's aerial force. When it landed, the alpha paled.

"You."

"Me."

"You are Sparrow."

"I am Celestian, also."

"Your coven . . . Not the Sparrows, but . . ." Yasmin waved a hand at the other witches who rode the cunae with her, but Aisling only shook her head.

"I've never had the privilege."

Letting her eyes close, Yasmin leaned into the back of her seat. "Then we will have much work to do. In the morning, you will join us for morning drills."

Something deeply buried thrilled at the invitation, and though there was so much to do, Aisling could hardly decline an opportunity—likely the only opportunity she would ever have—to fly with a real Celestian coven.

It had been a very long time since she'd felt the need to prove herself to someone in a way unrelated to her family's scorn. The desire to take her beautiful winged horse to meet the sky coven had nothing to do with asserting dominance. The coven would be more skilled in aerial combat than she was, and rather than be a source of shame, her blood bubbled with excitement. She wanted to be worthy of flying beside them. She wanted to learn.

"I would be honored."

Yasmin's small smile suggested Aisling's composure was not as stoic as she hoped.

"If we can shift our focus for a moment." Dominic placed his hands palms down on the table and looked to Aisling. "I brought all of the southern port town here, some to help and some to evacuate with your people. Have you a plan for that yet?"

"Yes," Aisling said, catching Moyra's eye.

The Morvish witch cleared her throat and removed a small velvet sack from her pocket. "Tonight, while we still have the waning moon, Aisling and I will open a moongate to Pirevia using a combination of portaling magic and a moonstone. If we keep people organized, it shouldn't take more than a few hours to move everybody."

"I'll send word to our high priest to expect an influx," Miika said.

"Edwina will be in charge of the organizing the evacuees," Aisling told him, then to her Second, she asked, "Can you be ready to leave tonight?"

"Of course. I'll have the city ready in batches by sundown."

Despite the confidence she exuded, Aisling didn't miss the tremor in Edwina's voice.

"Moongate?" the phouka asked, rolling the word in his mouth. "I have witnessed many feats of magic, but I am not familiar with this."

"Well." Moyra shifted in her seat, bringing her pouch back to her chest. "That's because I created them."

The phouka took a half step back, turning his slitted yellow eyes on her.

Nostrils flaring, Moyra tucked her frizzy curls behind her ear. "Don't look so surprised. Moon magic is one of the basic foundations taught in Morvish academies. I've been toying with it for decades."

"I don't doubt your skill, but I do know a few things about moonstones. Each has different properties, and the slight color and shape variations can have an enormous impact on the success of their use. If I may, I would like to see them. Perhaps I could identify which stone would give you the best chance."

Aisling narrowed her eyes at the same moment Moyra did. After the last time she had dealt with the phouka, Aisling didn't trust the polite request at all. Moyra, also, was too well versed in faerie mischief.

"Phouka," Eaon called for his attention. He had it immediately. "What are you doing?"

"Breathing. Blinking. Digesting. You'll have to be more specific."

"Why are you offering help?" Eaon snarked.

"Because I have a vested interest in doing so, obviously," the phouka sniped back. "Would you like a promise, witchling? I promise to inspect the moonstones and return exactly as many as are in there back to Moyra when I am done."

Nervous anticipation crackled in the room like static energy as Eaon and the phouka had a stare down that left Aisling shifting in her seat. Her eyes felt dry and itchy just watching them. There was no doubt in her mind that if it were anyone other than Eaon challenging the phouka, they'd be in a world of pain.

The knowing look on Moyra's face confirmed it.

Finally, Eaon said to Moyra, "Up to you. I don't think he means harm."

Hesitantly, Moyra slid the pouch of stones across the table. The phouka did exactly what he said he would do; picking up the pouch, he tipped the three moonstones into his hand, rolled them around, then slid them back inside. Passing them back to Moyra, he said, "The one with the blueish fleck will be more receptive to Celeste's will."

Knowing better than to thank him, Moyra nodded and put her treasure away.

"Hang on a minute." Miika reeled back in his seat, eyes wide. "Aren't you the same phouka that escaped our mountain?"

Half the room took a collective breath. Those who weren't familiar with the phouka glanced to those bracing themselves; it wasn't required to have felt the Old One's power to recognize that Miika's accusatory tone was a daring thing in the face of fae.

Tension tightened every muscle in Aisling's body. This was the first she was hearing of any history between the phouka and the Northern Mountain Clan, and the last thing this council needed was yet another personal vendetta slowing proceedings down.

In the ten seconds of silence that followed, Aisling learned all she needed to know.

Eaon's eyes widened, shoulders curling in slightly as he scratched one of the tiny burn scars on the back of his hand. In what was becoming a predictable reaction, the phouka wrapped his claws around the back of Eaon's neck. Glancing between them, Miika scowled, and the phouka seemed to grow six inches with the desire to rip the expression from his face. If it weren't for the oath taken by all, Aisling had the distinct impression there'd have been bloodshed.

But the real threat sat elsewhere, slowly rising to her bare feet.

"You tried to kill my brother," Eavha said, fists shaking.

Closing her eyes, Aisling bowed her head in defeat.

"It wasn't just me," Miika argued. "The elders all voted. He let loose a dangerous faerie responsible for kidnapping and murdering a number of our scouts! He endangered every witch in the warren!"

"And that warrants *death*?!" Eavha shrieked.

"It's their culture, Eavha," Eaon said, far meeker than he'd been at the last Imsa. "And it's not important right now."

"Not *important*?!"

Across the table, Fior dropped their head back to stare at the ceiling. "Not this again."

"No, Eavha, it's not important," Eaon insisted with a calm that was three-quarters exhaustion. "There are bigger things to worry about right now than some bullshit that happened, like, three weeks ago. Hasn't anybody told you yet what happened at the pass?"

Sucking down a sharp breath, Aisling straightened. Their truce was tentative, so very, very fragile, but Aisling would offer Eaon anything in thanks for getting them back to the point. Back to the topic Aisling had yet to figure out how to broach.

"Wait, how do *you* know what happened at the pass?" the phouka asked, leaning over Eaon's shoulder to catch his eye.

Rolling his eyes, Eaon scowled. "I have ears."

"You speak *fae*?"

"Are you going to tell them or am I?" Eaon snapped at his phouka before shooting a desperate look to Aisling.

"I, also, have been made aware of the situation to the east," Aisling admitted, tugging on Eavha's hand until she sat down again. Squeezing it tightly, she turned to tell Eavha directly. "The pass has been impeded with over a hundred moderate landslides. Chaos's army are struggling through the mess, but they are making quick work of it. We have, at most, an extra day." A rallying breath, not quite deep enough. "On our end, there are no signs of survivors."

It was a terrible thing to watch Eavha's face crumple. To see the immediate, enormous grief she felt for every witch she had sent to their demise fill her reddening eyes. Aisling may never have gone to war before, but she knew the costs. Had prepared herself for them. And maybe she was just too heartless to mirror the pain Eavha so obviously felt, but for that, Aisling was grateful. She sat stoic and immovable as Eavha fell against her, unashamed by the sob that broke free.

For several long minutes, nobody spoke. Nobody moved.

"We thank thee, Mother," Eaon said, head bowed low, the prayer well practiced yet cracking with fresh sincerity, "for the gift of our brethren and the time we were given to love them as you do. We thank thee, Lover, for the shelter of your warm embrace and the eternal rest you provide. For your Balance we live; for your Balance we die."

Elder Milnova spoke the words quietly along with him, but nobody else knew the prayer and Eavha was far too distraught to manage. It didn't stop the others from nodding their approval. Their respect.

They sat for a long minute of silence, remembering the soldiers and witches who'd gone to give the rest of the army the best chance of defeating Chaos. It wasn't meant to be a suicide mission, and if Eaon had been there, then maybe it wouldn't have been. Across the table, he was busy staring into the middle distance, lost to thought. Remembering his friends.

"Death is difficult in any circumstance. I am deeply sorry for your loss," Dominic said, easing them all out of their reverence.

Milnova nodded. "We will make time to pay respects appropriately."

Subdued, Fior asked, "How does this change things?"

"It doesn't," Aisling said. "We lost a thousand soldiers and however many others were living in the pass, but they died giving us the moon. They knew what they went there for. Though the plan had obviously included escape, anybody who stays to fight must come to terms with the possibility that they won't. I'd be more concerned if the sea-shore and northern mountain clans hadn't arrived this morning."

"Who else can we rally?" Yasmin asked.

"We have Hyrsch, Wyldeden, the Dividing River, the South Shore Clan, Pirevia, your coven, a hundred odd rogues, and a few hundred fae of varying types." So much of her time had been spent lately accepting promises from them that she had lost count. "There was supposed to be an unknown number of Sparrow defectors making their way here from Dusarn but with what happened there, I don't know if any of them got out. We have an Old One—"

"Two Old Ones. The swamp hag from Vertlyn arrived. She is a friend of mine and willing to fight."

Aisling nodded. Took a breath.

"And one kinner."

Beside her, Edwina and Radley were very, very still.

Miika immediately turned on Eaon. "I knew it."

"You didn't know shit."

"I knew he wasn't a normal demi-kin."

"Would you like a medal?"

"What are you even doing here?" Miika snapped. "Unless you've found a way to control whatever shitshow of a blessing you've got going on, I don't see how your presence here is useful."

As if she had been slapped, Eavha sat up, fire and brimstone.

"Do not speak to him like—"

"All of you just shut up!" Fior of the river clan stood, slapping her palms on the table.

"Excuse you," Eavha snapped.

"No, excuse *you*. The lot of you are wasting everybody's time—again." Fior straightened, taking her hands off the table to pour herself a drink. "And Miika has a point. Can you control it? We put a pin in this issue last time, but we really need to know if you're going to be a help or a hindrance on the field."

Across the table, Aisling met Eaon's eye. The shake of her head was infinitesimal, but he saw it. All other eyes had turned to Moyra, who had promised to consult her deity for advice on what to do about Eaon.

Grimacing, Moyra apologized to her nephew.

"Please keep in mind that I did try to discuss this with you privately first."

"Just spit it out."

"You can not be a part of this. I figured out two out of three parts of the Lover's curse on you, Eaon. I figured out what they need in order to possess you. Do you know how many souls you've consumed? Because seven hundred and seventy-seven is how many the Lover needs. That, and seven deaths. Then you will be ripe and the Lover can come to Mother's realm to fight Chaos. And before anyone says it, no, I still don't think it's a good idea to unleash Death themself into the world."

"Seconded," Fior grumbled.

"Did you even look to see if it would work, though?" Eaon argued, ignoring the visible way the phouka's grip on the back of his neck tightened. "Or did you just worry about the cost? Because a thousand of our people died the other night, the entire Southern Mountain Clan might be dead, because I wasn't there. What about that cost?"

"What of the cost if Death is allowed to walk amongst us?" Dominic countered. "We do not know what that would entail. From Aisling's story, the entire world bent to Chaos's mere presence, let alone his will. What do we risk allowing the Lover here, too?"

"A vote," Eavha called before Eaon could open his mouth to argue. "All in favor of keeping Eaon out of this, raise your hand."

The Pirevian woman named Cecelia was the first to shoot her hand up. "I don't really know what the fuck is going on, but I didn't fight my ass off in the arena just to let death bend me over here."

Murmurs of agreement, though nobody else felt the need to justify their vote. Relief was a palpable thing as Eavha sat back in her seat, heaving a sigh at the sight of every hand in the room being raised. Her faith in Aisling's agreement was so complete she didn't even look to her to check.

Nausea squirmed in Aisling's stomach. Could she really risk wasting Eaon's potential just to keep Eavha happy? How many more of their soldiers would die in his place? What about their families?

"Aisling?"

Edwina was looking at her, brow furrowed. This was a deviation from the plan—a plan so carefully put together over the past six years that changing it felt like blasphemy.

Slowly, all eyes turned to Aisling hands, resting flat on the table. The hint of smugness that had crept into Eavha's smile evaporated.

"I am not in the habit of making decisions based on fear," she said, choosing her words very carefully. "Especially not when there are avenues we have not explored."

The phouka wanted to kill her. She could taste murder in the air.

Absolute silence fell as hands slowly lowered. Everybody looked between Aisling's carefully composed calm and Eaon's grateful nodding.

"My brother Nevan had a proficiency for curses." Across the room, Rhosyn flinched. "And so I developed a proficiency for finding loopholes. Firstly, does anybody know anything about possession? I have limited experience, personally. I was possessed, once, in Dusarn. I reached through the veil into the void and touched the soul of someone who lingered there. They were able to possess my body for a short time.

"Now, Moyra said part of the spellwork involved seven deaths. Eaon, how many are you up to?"

Blinking, hand creeping up to his throat, he said, "Six."

The phouka cursed, loudly and colorfully, while Eavha had gone still in the seat beside Aisling.

"Not many people have my ability to interact with the void," Aisling continued, "but I imagine that actually dying is a sufficient way of breaching the veil, too. There are sigils to protect oneself. If we're making up spells to make moongates, perhaps we can make something incorporating those sigils to protect you against possession at all."

"We don't know enough about it," Moyra argued, shaking her head. "You and I are both experts in the magic we're using to make the moongates. None of us know anything about possession except that it's possible and involves crossing the veil."

From where she sat silently throughout the entirety of Imsa, the Wyldeden Keeper, Milnova, cleared her throat.

"That actually isn't true. I know a little bit."

Chaos himself could have flown by the window and nobody would have noticed, such was the focus of attention on Milnova.

"The lore surrounding the concept of possession is spotty at best because it is extremely uncommon. There aren't many entities powerful enough to do it, or in Aisling's case, the circumstances required aren't easily met. But, blasphemers have been avoiding death since the dawn of time, and like everything, the Lover has weaknesses. These sigils you speak of, if they're what I think they are, are derivative of faerie rings. They obscure the space between realms to make perception more difficult. With the Lover's seed already planted in Eaon, I don't think trying to hide him is going to work."

"What about a protection charm?" Miika asked. "Like the ones Eavha said her clan is already working on?"

Milnova nodded. "There are ways. Spellmarks and witchmarks, for one. They repel necrotic magic. Tattooing them on Eaon the way Aisling has hers would make it extremely uncomfortable for the High Spirit of Death to exist within. It would also stunt his power. However, you would need someone Lover-blessed to make the marks and I believe there isn't anyone immune to the effects of his skin able to do so."

No, there wasn't.

"In the Northern Mountains, there was a witch who made cuffs for him," Miika contributed. "They worked for a while. What about a full set of clothes like that?"

"Good for suppression of the blessing, not good for anti-possession," Aisling said. "The marks would have to be in his skin."

"Some kind of charm, then," Eavha suggested. Her first words since Aisling had voted against her. Goosebumps washed over Aisling's bare arms. "It is my specialty, apparently."

"Do you remember the story I told you?" The phouka managed to drag his yellow goat-slitted glare from Aisling's throat, softening slightly as he met Eavha's. "About the human the Lover once tried to possess, and how Sanni took a special interest in keeping them alive? She made a charm of some kind. Ask her what she used."

Looking at Eavha was like looking at the sun; Aisling knew she shouldn't, it would hurt, but she loved it too much to resist.

Throat bobbing, chin dimpled, Eavha shook her head. "I already did. We cannot get the ingredients needed to make it strong enough. I was hoping there was something else."

Milnova shook her head. "Nothing that's going to help someone already targeted."

Aisling bit her lip at the way Eavha's nostrils flared, a heavy curl falling out of her ponytail as she turned her head in Moyra's direction.

"What about you? Can't you do something? Bind it? Cleave it?"

Splaying her hands in supplication, Moyra looked genuinely sorry that she didn't have anything to offer. "It's like the tattoos. Only another Lover-blessed would have any hope, and, to be candid, Aisling doesn't have what it would take."

There was no offense to be found. Aisling waved Moyra's concern away. She had a second idea to share, anyway. Whether it could really it be that easy, though, she wasn't certain.

"Alright, so, a second loophole would be that, Eaon, on the battlefield, you take the seven hundred and seventy-seventh soul, and then one more. The seventy-eighth ruins it."

"Do you think you could take two souls in such close proximity that the Lover can't strike you down between them?" Yasmin asked.

Before Eaon could answer, Dominic was shaking his head. "That is a risk—trying to outrace a god."

"It's an option. It's a chance," Aisling argued. "The Lover can't take over, but you can still wield their power. Still bring the army to its knees."

"No, it's not." The phouka's guttural growl had everybody inching back. Releasing Eaon's neck, the phouka yanked Eaon's chair back from the table and spun it so he had no choice but to face him. If Eaon was afraid of the giant fae baring down on him, he didn't show it. "This is still a magic that does not belong to you. Even if it worked, it's a magic that will continue to devour your own soul until there is nothing left. You will be uninhabitable by the Lover, but you will never be yourself again either."

Eaon was already decided and everybody else was beginning to see it. "I've been living on borrowed time for ten months."

For the first time, it was Radley that spoke. "You shouldn't have to destroy yourself when we can win this anyway."

"But what if I do have to?" Eaon pushed. "What if, at the end of the day, that's what it costs? I'm okay with that."

"No."

Where Aisling's calm was designed to be a calm against which everybody else's fear could bounce against, Eavha's was one born of an anger so cold her features had frozen. She stood, hands clasped in front of her, chin raised. Even without her crown of peonies, everybody knew the heir of Wyldeden now spoke.

"No."

"Enough, Eavha." Eaon didn't care what role she had, he spoke to his sister as if nobody else was in the room. "My time has come and gone. You brought me back and gave me the ability to do something with my life. Let me do it."

"This is not what your life is for."

"Isn't it? Didn't this start with Yomra telling me to stop fighting it?"

Eavha's facade was cracking, the temper brewing beneath the surface peeking through. "That could have been about so many things!"

Eaon rolled his eyes and threw up his hands. "Moyra can't cleave it, but you won't let me use it, either. So what is the point? If fate has a hand in all of this, then what is the point of me?"

"No."

"You—"

"I am in charge until Kaelean returns and I said *no*. End of discussion!"

The two most stubborn witches in all of Nir stared each other down for an eternity. Stalemate. If it were just the two of them, this would have been an impossible impasse because neither would ever be persuaded. But they weren't alone. Eavha raised her chin, and the phouka nodded.

"I will not allow it."

Neither of them knew that the phouka's command wouldn't stop Eaon. Sharing a look, Aisling kept her mouth shut.

They had tried, but at the end of the day, not a single person in this room could stop Eaon. Not forever. Not even for long. The phouka may be able to physically restrain him, but his disinterest in the way the phouka roughly pulled him to his feet and marched him to the council room door promised such restraint wasn't a concern.

"So," Fior drawled as the door slammed closed behind them. "We're putting another pin in it?"

"No," Eavha said, stepping out from behind the table and pushing her chair in. "The matter is closed."

Without acknowledging Aisling's existence, Eavha walked from the room too.

"Is this meeting adjourned?" Miika asked.

"Not yet," Aisling sighed. "Let's discuss strategy and how we can best incorporate your forces."

And so they did. For hours. The sheer amount of ginseng tea consumed as everyone tried to stay alert was obscene, as was the number of bathroom breaks, but eventually they settled on a plan of attack.

The sun was sinking by the time they were done. From her pocket, Moyra removed the little sack of moonstones again and raised an eyebrow at Aisling.

"It's time."

CHAPTER FORTY-SEVEN

CINN

THE STREETS SURROUNDING THE EMPTY NORTHERN COURTYARD WERE overcrowded, which was fine by Cinn. Anonymity was a safety blanket considering that, a dozen feet away, standing at the fountain, Moyra and Aisling were building an altar of sorts. Candles and spellmarks drawn with chalk littered the bench of the fountain's edge, and among them glowed one of Moyra's coveted moonstones.

Since her offer of revenge and Cinn's refusal, Aisling had kept her distance. He no longer thought it was because she was afraid of another confrontation; after everything she had done, he couldn't imagine she was capable of *respect*, but he could see how the space she allowed him could be construed that way.

The night was disconcertingly quiet. Luggage at their feet and packs on their backs, Hyrsch's civilians waited with bated breath for the escape route promised. Plenty of South Shore, Dividing River, and Anfar Forest Clan witches also stood by; witchlings too young to fight were accompanied by the untrained low-blessed, exhaustion lining all their faces.

Tucked into the mouth of a nearby alley, Cinn watched over his brother's shoulder as moonlight caught on the luminescent stone in the center of the makeshift altar. On their knees, hands linked, Aisling and Moyra bowed their heads, muttering softly.

Something soft brushed against Cinn's ankle. Without thinking, he lashed out, kicking his boot into a small body that did not budge an inch.

Heart in his throat, he looked down to find Gatty, tail whipping in deep annoyance.

"Moyra says she doesn't see your sister having any serious problems in the north."

Radley cursed, looking down. "Fucking cat. I'm going to put a bell on you."

"Is that a promise?" Gatty grinned with too sharp teeth, and for a moment, the true monster that lurked behind those yellow eyes shone through.

Baring his teeth right back, Cinn inched in front of his brother, and when Radley opened his mouth to say something else, Cinn gripped his wrist and squeezed.

Deep down, he was moderately comfortable in the knowledge that Gatty wouldn't hurt his brother. But Cinn didn't trust his own judgment anymore. He couldn't trust his instincts, his senses, his mind. Doing so got people killed.

With a knowing look, Gatty's tail melted into shadow around Cinn's ankle, the rest of him not far behind.

"I hate that thing," Radley said, turning back to the fountain to where the faerie cat reappeared at Moyra's feet.

Cinn clung tighter to Radley's wrist. He didn't like this. Unbridled nausea had his body shaking apart. They'd only just found each other again —Rad, Red, and Ry—and he wasn't ready to say goodbye again. He didn't trust it to be temporary.

"We can go with her," Radley said, flexing his fingers. "It's not too late."

Cinn turned enough to take in the dark expression on his brother's face. Once again, he pushed a finger into Radley's chest before flinging it toward the fountain.

Radley's upper lip curled in a snarl. "We're not having this conversation again. You stay, I stay. The Sparrow-ass-licking traitor—Clayton, or whatever his stupid name is—is going with Red, and as much as I fucking hate him, he knows how to do his job. She will be fine. I don't trust you to be."

Huffing a hot breath through his nose, Cinn stabbed his finger into Radley's chest again. Cinn wasn't the one with a brown mark on the back of his neck. Cinn wasn't the one at risk of dying by staying. Cinn wasn't the one who wouldn't be okay.

"If you want me to go, then get your bag and let's go."

His teeth were going to break if he clenched them any harder. It was enough to make him regret ever loving anyone. If he had hardened himself the way his mother had wanted him to, he wouldn't be in this situation—having to choose between Sarah and Eaon. Between his siblings and Eaon. But he hadn't hardened himself. Didn't know how. He was soft and weak. A liability.

Radley was saved from Cinn's temper by Edwina's arrival. With a cloak pulled over her head, she managed to slip through the crowd unrecognized and join them in the shadowed mouth of the alley. She looked between her brothers questioningly, but Radley simply forced a brittle smile and pulled her in for a hug.

"Stay safe. Show those Pirevian assholes what the demi-kin are really made of."

"It's going to be much less exciting than you think it's going to be," Edwina grumbled, releasing him to pull in Cinn. Her embrace was a vice. "I understand why you have to stay, but I hate that you are."

Cinn only nodded. And with his face pressed into Edwina's hair, he swallowed down the lump in his throat and whispered, "We will find each other again."

Edwina squeezed him tighter, breath hitching as her hand cupped the back of his head.

"I love you."

Across the courtyard, a sharp crack of thunder had the entire city flinching back. Edwina let go of Cinn as blinding white light split the air, ripping open a portal the length of the fountain. For a moment, it wavered. Moyra and Aisling stood, keeping their hands raised, still muttering under their breath as they took synchronized steps backward. Each one had the portal growing longer, taller, until it rattled the storefront windows and signs.

Moyra lowered her hands first, nodding encouragement across the courtyard. Aisling hesitated, but eventually she dropped her hands too. The portal remained strong, rippling like moonlight on a lake, cool and inviting in the humid night.

"It worked," Edwina breathed. Fiddling with the braided twine bracelet around her wrist until it loosened, she rolled it off and took Cinn's hand. "Take this."

Blanching, trying and failing to snatch his hand back, he shook his head.

"I want you to. I'll feel better knowing that if either of you get into trouble, the other will know."

The twine was tight as Edwina rolled it over the meat of his thumb, but she got it on. Cinn shook his head again, but his sister had that look on her face that said this was not up for discussion.

"What about you?" Radley asked.

"I'm going to be fine." Pulling both of them in for another too tight hug, Edwina kissed their cheeks. "We're going to be okay."

Conversation filled the streets, excited and wary at the same time, but Cinn heard none of it. Aside from being pried off, he didn't think he was ever going to be able to let go. They stood in the shadow of the alley for too long, unwilling to part, until someone cleared their throat.

"Sorry," Moyra's soft voice interrupted. "Edwina, everyone's waiting on you."

The sudden tension in Radley's grip was a threat, thwarted by Edwina's gentle removal of his hand from her shoulder. Disentangling herself from Cinn had the steel of his grip crumbling until his knees shook like a new-born foal. He couldn't keep up. Could barely contain the panic swelling.

"Look after each other," Edwina said, eyes red and glassy. "And I'll see you soon."

Unsure who was holding who, Cinn and Radley watched their sister lift her chin and approach the moongate. Edwina looked into its light with a familiar determination—as if the idea of walking into a volatile Pirevia with a city's worth of refugees relying on her ability to enforce Aisling's ideals was no more intimidating than the bloodstains she'd helped Cinn scrub out of his shirt when they were children. It didn't matter that she had been born in the slave-breeding colonies, that she had been raised under the boot of a human master, that she had lived her adult life serving in the palace. Edwina had lurked in the shadows during every council meeting, every tactical planning session between Aisling and her old Second, and she had never been afraid of anything.

Edwina and the Sparrow queen exchanged a few quiet words before Aisling removed the diadem from her own head and placed it on Edwina's. Stepping back, she shook hands with her bull of a personal guard, who bowed deeply before moving to Edwina's side. With a small platoon of soldiers surrounding her, Edwina spared one last glance to the alley where her brothers watched, smiled, and stepped into the moonlight.

One by one, the rest of Hyrsch followed.

Edwina would be fine.

She would be fine.

Everything would be fine.

Cinn looked to Radley, giving him one last encouraging push to follow their sister, but his grip was unbreaking. Afterall, Cinn was the one who had disappeared and not returned once before. Cinn was the one with a history of getting into trouble he couldn't get himself out of. Cinn needed supervision more than Edwina did, and right then, he resented it. He hated every awful thing that had happened since being shot with that stray crossbow bolt because it meant that, right now, Rad was choosing him over Eddy.

The shaking beneath his skin wouldn't settle. He didn't feel the need to watch the rest of the departure. He wanted to go home.

~

The idea of eating while his stomach was in knots was ridiculous, but Cinn followed Radley through the emptying streets to a small tavern anyway. Moyra and Gatty tailed them, and though he didn't have the mental space to care much about the frown pulling at Moyra's features, he owed his friend more than silence.

Is she okay? Cinn thought loudly.

Gatty's ears twitched. "Ask her yourself."

Two sets of eyes found him, and Cinn's face burned hot.

"What is it?" Moyra asked, looking to Radley. "Do you understand his sign language?"

"Not yet," Radley grumbled as he pushed open the door to the tavern. "But he does."

With most of the city evacuating, the tavern was practically empty, yet sitting at the farthest table from the barkeep was Eaon and his Northern Mountain Clan friends. Despite Cinn's assurances, Eaon hadn't wanted to risk being around so many people, so had promised to wait nearby instead. The four witches were deep in conversation, Eaon's phouka sitting bored and restless, picking apart the remains of a cooked chicken. It wasn't obvious how tense Eaon was until he noticed Cinn's arrival; his shoulders dropped, his body sagging into his seat, eyes softening. At least, they did until he noticed Moyra following behind.

Judging by the suspicion on Tomaii, Reigan and Killian's faces, Eaon had filled them in on who Moyra was. It was difficult for Cinn to see hostilities aimed at his friend, but at the same time, he knew the situation was complicated. He knew, too, that aside from Dearmead, the three northern witches had been some of the first to show Eaon any kindness. Acceptance. Friendship. They were still some of the only people who knew about Eaon's curse and didn't treat him any differently.

For that reason, Cinn forced himself to be present. Lifting a hand in a meek wave, he met each of their eyes and slid into the booth beside Eaon.

"You alright?" Eaon asked quietly.

Cinn leaned against his shoulder and blinked. That was all the answer he could give. It was enough for Eaon, who slipped an arm around his shoulder, fingers threading through his hair to gently scratch his scalp. A full-body shiver ran from the top of Cinn's head to his toes, and in its wake, he was left boneless. If he were a cat he'd have purred.

Tomaii made a cooing noise and Eaon stopped his scratching to, presumably, cuss him out. Cinn ignored them both, as well as the venomous expression on his brother's face as Radley, Moyra and Gatty slid onto the opposite bench. More food was brought over, and though he wasn't hungry—was, in fact, nauseous with the sea of misery roiling in his belly—the level of training he was participating in meant eating was a cruel necessity. If he was going to be a part of this fight then he had to be at his best, so he ate what Radley pushed his way and tried to coax Eaon into having some too.

{Something's bothering Moyra,} Cinn signed once Eaon had finished chewing a piece of bread. {Gatty won't ask her. Or won't tell me.}

Asking Eaon to speak to Moyra was unkind, but her faraway gaze and deep frown was an itch that needed to be scratched. Sighing deeply, Eaon sunk lower into his seat and stared at the table as he grumbled the question out.

"Moyra. Cinn wants to know what's bothering you."

Gatty scoffed, but Moyra beamed as if Eaon had offered the moon itself, shifting eagerly forward and presenting the velvet sack she had brought from Qiri.

"When I was preparing the altar earlier, I realized one the stones had lost power." Tipping the sack, two moonstones tumbled into her waiting palm. One glowed brightly. The other did not. "They were all active earlier at Imsa. I've never seen moonstones behave like this before."

Questions from Reigan meant Eaon was spared having to converse further, safe in his role as translator between his aunt and his friends. Tomaii leaned forward, reaching for the stones, but Moyra flinched to stop him.

"They're too precious," Moyra explained. "I would hate for you to drop and break one."

"Break one?" Tomaii frowned, stumbling over his elementary Nirnish.

Smirking, the humor not reaching his eyes, Eaon said something in Terranian that earned a cry of outrage from Tomaii and cackling laughter from the other two. Cinn couldn't bear the sound of it. He turned instead to where Gatty was having a staring contest with the phouka, Cinn measuring his own ability to hold off a blink against theirs.

"Reigan wants to know if the wards could be affecting the stones," Eaon said once the laughter settled.

"Well." Moyra frowned. "Morvish magic does seem to be less reliable here. It could have affected the spell keeping the soul inside."

"There you go," Eaon grumbled. "Probably that, then."

Saving the two of them from further awkwardness, Cinn let himself lose the competition he'd invited himself to and loosed an enormous yawn. Done with his pittance of a dinner, he turned pleading eyes to his brother.

"We're going home," Radley announced.

"Yes, we could all use some rest. The new moon tomorrow will be trying for all of us," Moyra agreed, wiping her hands on a frayed cloth napkin. "Eaon, can we talk on the way back to the palace? I can find your friends somewhere to stay there, too."

"I'm staying with Cinn," Eaon said curtly.

Despite the weariness weighing Cinn down, he found the energy to anger when Moyra looked to the phouka for confirmation. Eaon's decisions were Eaon's decisions and Cinn was sick of people treating him like he wasn't capable of making them.

Regardless, the phouka nodded. Eaon waited for the verdict before speaking to his friends, the four of them breaking into a rather explosive argument. Maybe Cinn should ask Eaon to teach him Terranian. He was getting annoyed at not understanding what was going on half the time.

The bickering went on for a while and Radley quickly got bored. He stood up and stalked to the barkeep for an ale, glancing back every ten seconds to make sure Cinn was where he'd left him. Unnecessary, since Cinn had no intention of leaving Eaon's side.

The more the northerners argued the tighter Eaon's shoulders grew, but it wasn't until he turned to Cinn that the reason became apparent.

"They would rather stay with us, even though I told them your place is small and I . . . I am not exactly safe to be around. In fact, I think admitting that only made them more stubborn. But if you're not comfortable, or if Radley doesn't want them around, I can make them stay in the palace."

If Eaon had his way, he would isolate himself completely. As someone who had spent too much time alone, Cinn didn't want that for him. As long as they were together, the others would be safe.

The thought was a sucker punch to the gut.

The last time he promised not to let go of Eaon's hand so he could sleep peacefully, Cinn had failed. That wasn't where the danger had come from, but still . . . Cinn had let go, and Eaon had been too afraid of hurting the Copelands to move, and Cinn had been so useless at protecting anybody that Eaon's blood had painted the walls and William . . .

"I will be there to make sure it is safe," the phouka reassured them.

Trying to catch his breath, Cinn gave the phouka a once-over, trying to imagine the creature crammed into his tiny apartment with six other people. As if reading his mind, the phouka grinned and *popped*, shrinking into a knee-high goblin that was somehow even more menacing.

Still, Cinn called Radley back with the tilt of his chin. It was his home, too.

Radley returned from the bar and Eaon repeated his question, making it abundantly clear that there was no obligation to accommodate any of them.

"I'm not averse to a few extra sets of eyes around."

Cinn's eyebrows shot up, but when Radley didn't change his mind, Cinn shrugged. He too didn't mind filling the place with so many people that it would be hard for anyone to sneak up on him again.

The phouka perched on the windowsill, their silent sentinel. If his presence still bothered the three northerners, they did well to pretend otherwise. Radley rather graciously gave up his couch, opting instead to take first watch, and it wasn't until after his brother had set up outside the front door—a door that no longer hung crooked or creaked when opened —that Cinn realized it was the first time since arriving in Hyrsch that anyone had felt the need to guard his sleep.

Any amusement he might have felt as Killian, Tomaii and Reigan shoved and argued their way into some kind of comfortable pile on the small sofa died in his chest.

Maybe Radley shouldn't be out there alone. Maybe Cinn should be the one to keep watch. Except he couldn't stay with Eaon if he was outside, unless he came with him, which wasn't fair, because the exhaustion on Eaon's face made Cinn nauseous again.

Frozen with a fresh wave of panic, he barely noticed Killian losing the fight for a spot on the couch. Barely heard him and Eaon having a hushed conversation. But he noticed when Killian went outside to sit with Radley. Noticed Eaon settling on the floor by the hearth, tugging Cinn's hand until he went down too. Neither of them were doing well, but Eaon was by far the better actor; his face crinkled with a faux smile as Tomaii began snoring, truly and heartily, until Reigan smacked him so hard he choked.

Turning his back, staring into the empty fireplace, Cinn tucked his free arm under his head. Eaon curled up behind him, arm thrown over his waist, their fingers lacing.

Eventually, the room fell into a restful silence, the deep breathing of half its occupants a soft lullaby. Only in the privacy of their semi-aloneness did Eaon speak, lips against the back of Cinn's neck.

"Breathe. It's not your fault."

Cinn closed his eyes. His chest was a bottomless chasm.

"William wouldn't blame you for what happened. Nobody does. And . . . I know what he meant to you. I'm so sorry you lost him."

It was less than three months since the two of them had been living in the Copelands' most isolated cottage, neither sleeping well, trading stories and heartaches late into stifling nights. When Cinn had been nobody, when he'd had nothing and trusted even less, it had been William who'd coaxed him out of the forest and given him something to build a foundation on. Sarah had given him a name and William had given him a home and they had both kept him safe while he pulled a semblance of a self back together.

Throat far too tight to manage sound let alone syllables, Cinn pulled Eaon's arm tighter. On the back of his hand, letter by letter, he spelled out his new pain.

I'm going to lose everybody.

William was gone. Sarah had left. Edwina had left. It was only a matter of time before everyone he loved was gone. It was the curse of being kinner.

Cinn's breath shook, stomach tight.

One day, Moyra would take the mark off his neck. She had promised.

Rather than argue, Eaon simply pressed his lips to the silver mark there, holding him tight as Cinn finally began to cry.

CHAPTER FORTY-EIGHT

AISLING

AISLING WOKE AN HOUR BEFORE DAWN AND SHIVERED. THE NEW MOON was tonight, and though Sar Vin had bought them time, the knowledge that her own army was at their most vulnerable had riddled her dreams with a dread that followed her into waking.

Over the past two weeks, on the occasions that both she and Eavha slept at the same time, Aisling had grown used to waking to Eavha's light snoring, her eyelashes crusted closed with sleep. This morning, though, the bed beside her was cold.

Eavha hadn't come to bed last night. Hadn't come to the moongate or even spoken to her since Imsa. In any other life, for any other reason, Aisling would wrap Eaon in cotton wool and keep him in a padded room if it made Eavha happy. But this was not that life.

Sighing, Aisling rolled onto her back and opened her eyes. A flash of candlelight in her periphery drew a gasp as Aisling flew upright.

Sitting on the end of the bed, Eavha prayed softly to an ever-fresh peony in her hand, wrapping a hair around the stem. The tangle of brown curls was thick as her thumb—an impressive feat considering the first Blessing Charm Eavha had made had taken over a decade, whereas this one she'd built in a matter of days. The bleeding bald patches on her scalp were the consequence, and Aisling made a note to find more soothing cream for her.

"You decided to stick with the peony," Aisling said in lieu of standard pleasantries.

The moment she finished tying off the hair, Eavha pulled out another. "I did."

Tone clipped and eyes down, it couldn't have been more obvious that Eavha was still furious with Aisling if she wore a sign.

"It's okay that you're angry with me."

"Good, because I am."

"Is something wrong? Is that why you're speaking to me?"

"No," Eavha sniped. "It's just that someone pointed out to me once that ignoring people I'm pissed off with for weeks on end is hurtful. And also, I don't think we have time for me to be passive-aggressive about it for that long."

Aisling blinked. "Are you . . . Are you going to be just regular aggressive instead?"

Her voice was off. She heard it but couldn't stop herself from speaking. Eavha stilled, finally looking up from her charm.

"I'm not the aggressive type, Aisling. You know that."

"I do."

Flicking a stray curl out of her face, Eavha pursed her lips. "Right. So, no. It actually occurred to me that just because I am fabulous and you're soft for me, it wasn't fair to expect you to put my needs above your own. So I'm here to accept your apology for trying to get my brother killed while also offering my own for thwarting you. Though I am still glad I did. Then I thought we could have some breakfast before you meet with the sky coven."

Leaning forward, Aisling put her face in her hands and took a measured breath. Eavha thought she had won, and Aisling couldn't bring herself to correct her. Instead, she dropped her hands and reached for Eavha's closest, threading their fingers.

"I'm sorry."

"You're forgiven. Now, give me back my hand. I have a charm to work on."

Laying back against her pillows, Aisling watched Eavha pull another hair out. "Do you really need to hurt yourself so much? I thought Sanni was shadowing you."

"She is," Eavha admitted. "But there's no such thing as being too prepared."

It was something about the tone that gave away how uncomfortable the topic made her. Something about the way she blinked a little too quickly. Aisling's ribs contracted tighter.

"Can we talk about that yet?" she asked. "About why your patron spirit hovers?"

Pausing her ritual, Eavha lifted her pretty brown eyes. "Do you trust me?"

Surely that was rhetorical, but Aisling answered anyway.

"I have trusted very few people in my life, but of those I can, you are at the top of the list."

"Then trust that I know what I am doing. Trust me when I say that I am alright, that I am safe, and that of everyone in this palace I am the last person you need to be concerned about."

Aisling would not hesitate to put her life and soul in Eavha's hands, but what she was asking was too tall an order. There were not many people Aisling wasted time caring about, in whatever capacity she was capable of doing so, but of the people who made that list most could do a decent job of defending themselves.

"You're the only person in this palace I am concerned about."

Eavha pursed her lips. "That isn't true."

Swinging her legs over the edge of the mattress, Aisling got up. By the time she donned her robe and pulled the length of her slate gray hair over her shoulder, she had Eavha's full attention. Out on the flat, the sky coven was waiting, but Aisling took a moment to press her lips to Eavha's temple, fingers hovering over the clotting wounds on her scalp.

"Try and get some rest today." The shadows under Eavha's eyes weren't as bad as they had been a fortnight ago, but they lingered. "There won't be much time for it once night falls."

Soft and warm, Eavha's palm cupped Aisling's face. It was pathetic how quickly Aisling's shield melted under that velvet touch, gentle fingers sliding down her neck, trailing all the way down her arm until she held Aisling's hand and brought it to her full mouth for a kiss.

"I want to know what you're like when you rest. Not sleep, but rest," Eavha murmured into her skin. "I want to know you at peace."

All the anxious energy became heavy in Aisling's chest as she took Eavha's sunny face in her hands. She could promise nothing, but she could take another moment in the sanctity of her bedroom to taste peace on Eavha's lips.

～

As expected, Yasmin and the sky coven were perched on top of the city walls. Their cunae mounts had chosen the western turrets to nest, and with the bulk of the Northern Mountain Clan camping below, the sky coven had no reason to search out alternative lodgings. The morning air was heavy and humid, the rain having only overnight moved northward, but that didn't stop the dozen witches from pulling on full leather gear, gauzy veils over their faces as they went through dawn prayers. The language was foreign but the slow, smooth movements of their bodies brought about a surprising nostalgia.

On her quarter-century birthday when she undertook the Passing, Aisling had vowed to leave her Celestian heritage behind, but there had been a decade prior during which she'd been allowed to indulge her elemental origins. King Phineas, in one of his fleeting moments of fatherliness, had flown with her to a distant dune far from Dusarn's prying and taught her the prayer poses.

She didn't miss him—barely spared a thought for any of her blood relatives—but she grieved for the relationship she'd dared hope for in her very early youth. The one they may have had in any other life.

When the sky coven was done, Yasmin immediately sought Aisling by the stairwell. The alpha's dark eyes were piercing in a sharp way that didn't unsettle Aisling as much as it should have; there was honesty there, and if there was one thing Aisling appreciated, it was being free of having to play games.

"It occurred to me during the night," Yasmin said, accent thick, Nirnish uncertain. "If you didn't plan for aerial support, then you expected to hold the skies alone."

"Yes."

Yasmin's frown deepened. "The enemy has dragons."

"Yes."

Behind her, the coven began clicking their tongues in a rhythmic pattern, calling to their mounts. The cunae floated delicately from the turrets to the walkway where the witches began brushing their soft, velvety wings.

Yasmin barely spared her cunae a glance, head tilted as she gave Aisling a slower appraisal.

"I can't decide if you are brave or stupid."

"The word you are looking for is desperate."

The largest of the giant moths inched closer, clicking its mandibles and waving its long antennae in Aisling's direction. Palm forward, she reached toward the benevolent beast and gently stroked its furred body.

A northern breeze brought with it a heavy, musky smell that reminded her of the stables, both those she kept in Hyrsch for Volya and her non-winged mares, and those her father had kept, now abandoned in Dusarn. Closing her eyes, Aisling took deep, yearning lungsful. It was a smell that centered and grounded her when the pettiness and violence of the rest of her life threatened to consume her. Knee deep in shit, it reminded her that the sky awaited.

When she opened her eyes again, Yasmin was giving her a knowing look.

"Your mount?"

"Volya. A stableman is bringing her now."

"You don't look ready to fly."

Aisling nodded, rolling her silver-clad wrists to test their flexibility.

"I thought it best if we practiced in some of the armor I've had prepared. Silversmiths are bringing some for you to all try, though I admit, since I didn't expect to have any support, especially not cunae, I don't have anything to protect them."

"Armor." Yasmin wrinkled her nose. "We have not needed it yet, and the cunae will not like the weight."

In her mind, Aisling could too easily see those silky, patterned wings shredded to ribbons. Could too easily see the coven scattered and broken on the ground.

"Please reconsider. You and your people have no stakes in this fight—"

Cut off by the snarling show of teeth Yasmin offered, Aisling didn't dare move an inch. She had offended the alpha, somehow. She couldn't afford to lose allies now.

"There used to be more of us," Yasmin hissed. "They took Igni witches to Anfar when the blaze began and were struck down by a harbinger riding a dragon. For their lives alone, we would go to war. That doing so might benefit anyone else is a happy coincidence."

Once again, Aisling was struck by the effect love could have on a family. She remembered listening to Davina speak of it and scoffing at what sounded like weakness. She remembered the first time Eavha had spoken of it and feeling threatened by such an unbreakable bond. Judging by the prickling pain in her chest, both instances were born of what she now suspected was jealousy. Love, family, friendship—these were things not meant for her.

"I am sorry for your loss."

Yasmin dipped her chin before turning toward the lavender haze of the early morning's horizon.

"We will browse your armor. See if any of it is appropriate."

A weight lifted off Aisling's chest.

"Perfect. Down beside the med tent is where the smiths are working. I'll meet you down there with Volya."

Yasmin nodded, placing a foot into the stirrup of her mount's saddle and hoisting herself up in one smooth motion. "Then we see how a Sparrow flies."

Straightening her spine, she could barely contain a tiny smile. She watched the coven take to the skies, her heart lifting in a desperate need to follow. As she returned to the stairwell, she lost her composure entirely, unable to keep a giddy skip from her step.

~

Everything seemed so simple while three hundred feet in the air. The storm may have passed for the most part, but the cloud cover kept her metal armor from overheating as Aisling soared over the valley's flat below. A large number of the soldiers training stopped to salute her, and while she noticed Owen among their ranks, he didn't bother looking skyward. Barely bothered doing much of anything at all as he allowed his sparring partner to strike him over and over.

She'd have to deal with that later. For now, she urged Volya to catch up to the formation of cunae practicing drills. A flurry of motion, the cunae flapped their delicate wings, their speed surprising. Volya struggled to catch up to them until a northern current pushed through. The sky coven fought the shift in the air valiantly, but as nimble as they were, they couldn't compare to the power with which Volya plowed through.

Aisling envied the coven's veils, but the spellmarks on her skin provided enough of a shield to protect her vision against the buffering wind. Grinning at the witches who turned to gawk at the beast she rode, Aisling swooped to Yasmin's side.

At this speed, the roar of the wind was too vicious for talking, but Yasmin mirrored Aisling's glee before leading them all into a set of maneuvers. Lucky Volya was in tune with Aisling's every whim, and lucky Aisling was at her most alert while flying high, because nothing the coven did was familiar to her. She fell behind, the sheer mass of muscle that was her mare struggling with the agility of the cunae, but again, her disadvantage only lasted as long as the sky stayed settled.

Eventually, Yasmin made a hand signal that didn't need translating; a tug on Volya's reins had her tucking her wings, spearing toward the ground until it was safe to lower her hooves. Tufts of grass were ripped from the ground as their flight turned into a gallop, but Aisling quickly brought Volya to a stop beside the dainty moths.

"Hush, girl," Aisling panted, stroking Volya's neck as she caught the musky scent of so many strange beasts.

"You didn't say Volya was a winged horse," Yasmin accused, dismounting quickly. A look of pure wonder widened her eyes as the alpha approached, slow and careful. "I didn't know there were still any left."

Heavy, more awkward than she was used to considering her armor, Aisling got down from her saddle. Keeping one hand on Volya, she waved her other to encourage the coven closer.

"She's friendly," Aisling promised. "My father was infatuated with them. Purchased the very few he could find and kept them secret from the rest of the Sparrows. Bred them when he could. I—"

Her sentence trailed off as Yasmin finally stepped close enough to lay a gloved hand on Volya's armored hide. Another reached for her wing, caressing the ashy feathers of her thick, muscular wings.

A thought had struck her.

"Would you like to ride her?" Aisling asked, trying to contain the thunderous pounding of her heart.

Yasmin's hand stilled. "You would allow that?"

"I'm curious how you find her."

It melted Aisling's heart a little when Yasmin leaned in close and asked Volya's permission. The winged horse was an incredibly intelligent beast, so much so that Aisling often considered the mare one of her closest friends. She huffed, digging her hoof into the ground twice before lowering her head. An invitation.

By the time Yasmin had taken Volya on an easy ride around valley, Aisling knew the answer to her private question. Fire burned in the Celestian's eyes in a meeting of elemental forces that promised unfettered destruction. Aisling let the others take a ride as well, watching each of them return with the same burning desire.

"She is incredible."

"The *strength*!"

"It's as if the updrafts mean nothing to her. Could you imagine having a mount like that during one of Celeste's rages?"

Aisling's face hurt from grinning, their excitement whipping her own heart into a wicked frenzy. "How difficult would it be to adjust your maneuvers to compensate for a different mount?"

"You'd spend less time calculating and adjusting for changes in the wind. You'd spend less time accounting for the delicacy of their wings."

"Flitting wouldn't work, though," another said. "Too much bulk, and can't turn in a pinch."

"Flitting?" Aisling asked.

"It's a technique we use when subduing larger beasts, like gryphin. Give it too many fast-moving targets that it can't focus on any single one, flitting in and out of its face to obscure its vision while Yasmin goes in for the kill."

"It would still work even if just one of us had a winged horse. Yasmin wouldn't have to watch her mount's wings so carefully if they were stronger like Volya's."

"We could teach you," Yasmin said, looking Aisling over. "We could teach you the patterns, how to measure your striking time. How to get in and out to take the kill without injuring one of us."

If only there was time.

"I would love to learn," Aisling said, "but I think our time would be better spent having at least one of you practice with a winged horse."

Every single one of them stared at her for so long Aisling wasn't sure she'd said what she meant to say.

"You would let one of us ride Volya?" a round-faced witch asked.

"We couldn't. You might not be able to manage on a cunae."

"Wait, she said *at least* one of us. Do you have more of them?"

A collective, hopeful breath. Aisling was shaking with anticipation.

"No. At least not here. There's a small—very small, considering what happened there—but there's a chance my father's herd is still in Dusarn. If I portal, it wouldn't take long to find out. It would be safer, too. I have more armor for them."

And, if she happened to take a few minutes to search for Kaelean while she was there, Eavha would probably appreciate it.

The grin Yasmin adorned was a wild thing, born of the true spirit of a sky witch.

"Then let's go to Dusarn."

CHAPTER FORTY-NINE

AISLING

IN THE CLEAR SKIES OF KERVEDA, THE WORLD AND ITS PROBLEMS SEEMED very, very small. Aisling took a deep breath of clean air and threw her head back, letting go of the reins and throwing her arms wide. Just for a minute, she wanted to pretend there was nothing else but the endless sky and all the freedom it promised.

Yasmin's coven crowed with untamed jubilation, and when Aisling turned to look, all eyes were on her. They recognized one of their own kind, at home in the clouds. They welcomed her.

Standing in the saddle, the whip of wind was softened by the air shield over her face as it pulled her hair into a stream behind her. Aisling grinned. There was no need to keep herself in line up here. There was no need to hold herself perfectly straight, to keep her voice perfectly level, to keep her face in perfect emptiness. Nothing up here could hurt her. Nothing up here could conspire against her.

The princess, the queen, the warrior and the torturer; Aisling shed her roles like snakeskin until there was nothing but her basest self. Until she was nothing but skin and lungs and pounding blood, magic coursing through her veins in a rush like nothing else. Holding her arms out as if they were her own set of wings, she screamed in pure animalistic exultation into the wind and let it swallow the sound whole.

And then Dusarn came into view.

It was her hope that the lengths her father had taken to keep his breeding station secret had saved the mares from the destruction that had ruined the city. Winged horses had been an endangered species for as long as history had books, but Aisling wondered if that was only true inside the wards surrounding Nir. Somewhere beyond the invisible boundary of the faerie ring, maybe herds roamed plentiful and free.

Dropping low on Volya's back, Aisling tucked her moment of joy away to relive later and guided the sky coven over what remained of Dusarn. The Boab's burning had left Eavha distraught, but as Aisling took in the sight of the castle—her childhood home—reduced to rubble . . . She felt nothing. There was no loss to grieve.

The same could not be said for what led up to it.

Scores of black tore through the streets, and on either side, the ashy husks of burned-out buildings. There was no sign of the city's civilians. No sign that there was anything living left at all. Instinctively, Aisling looked toward the inn she used to sneak in and out of the city in her youth, then more recently with Eavha. Most of the building still stood, but the footpath outside was stained red.

"There are no remains," Yasmin noted, voice carrying in the still summer air. "No meat, no bones."

"There!" another of the coven called, pointing to a limb in the middle of an abandoned road.

A leg, Aisling thought as they slowed over it. It too was stained bloody, but as they passed over it, she saw it was not flesh at all. A prosthetic.

"Do you think anybody got out?" one of the younger females asked from toward the back of the formation.

"No," Yasmin answered. "No, I do not."

Aisling thought of the guard in the palace, Foley, who had come to her and offered support. She had told him to leave immediately. Perhaps he and whoever he took with him had made it, but Yasmin was right. Just like at the pass, there would be no survivors; not if Queen Tallula had orchestrated the invasion before succumbing to labor.

Had there been signs? Had Aisling missed a clue to what her mother was doing? How had her father missed it for so long? When had her mother turned? Had there been time or opportunity to stop this if Aisling had simply looked? Why hadn't Davina seen this?

The endless questions forced her attention away from the small wooden leg on the road as they flew past it. She couldn't understand how this had been allowed to happen.

But it had. Right now, that's what she needed to focus on. It had happened, and now she had to make sure it didn't happen again in Hyrsch.

"Come on," Aisling called. "Let's pass over the castle before heading for the stables. I'm wary of traps but we should at least look at see if Wyldeden's high priestess is here."

Nodding, pulling free the bow from her back in anticipation, Yasmin called instructions to her coven in a Celestian language Aisling had never learned.

Even though her parents' castle was half-collapsed piles of rubble, the anxiety that rode her as they approached the center of the city still churned her stomach. The tower holding the throne room where she had seen Chaos born was one of the only things still standing, leaning precariously over the mosaiced courtyard where she had first met Davina.

A lifetime ago. She could not afford to think of it right now.

"Holy Mother." Yasmin's awe was barely audible as they picked up speed, but the sentiment was appropriate.

In the courtyard lay the dead body of a dragon, crushed beneath the remains of the northern tower. Not *a* dragon, but *the* dragon. The one that Byron had arrived on. The one that Kaelean had attacked.

Attacked and defeated.

One hand pulling Volya's reins, the other reaching over her shoulder to grip the handle of her battle-axe, she began a careful descent. One of the spellmarks on Aisling's throat warmed as she focused her magic there, using the air to project her voice.

"Kaelean!"

The sound echoed emptily.

The dragon's wing twitched.

"Not dead." Aisling yanked on Volya's reins, panic echoed in her mount's whinny as the frills around the dragon's neck flared. "Very not dead."

If the dragon woke, if it had the strength to lift its head, it may still be able to reach them. Certainly, its plume of fire could, considering it had managed to burn down Anfar from beyond the wards.

Above, Yasmin had readied an arrow, the head glistening silver in the sun. Such a tiny splinter wasn't going to do anything but annoy the stirring beast, and Aisling's stomach—her heart and lungs and every muscle in her body, too—clenched tight at the reminder that the coven was not prepared for what was to come. They would be dead in seconds if Aisling didn't get them armored.

"Leave it," Aisling called, projecting her voice over the flap of Volya's heavy wings as they rose skyward again. "It's dying anyway."

Yasmin remained focused like a hawk, aim true. "They're bigger than I thought."

"I know," Aisling assured, gliding by. "I have documents at the palace detailing what little was ever recorded about dragon anatomy. We can study where best to aim and how to fight them when we get back. For now, let's get you and your coven mounts that can withstand the downdrafts wings like that are going to cause."

Yasmin nodded. Relaxed her arms.

Aisling took one last look around the courtyard, desperately searching for a glimpse of brownish-red hair or lupanis scales, but she couldn't risk herself or the sky coven if all she was going to find was a body, especially if it was buried beneath the rubble somewhere.

"I'll send someone to find you as soon as we can," she promised, then pulled away to lead Yasmin to her father's secret stables.

Between the easternmost boundary of the city and the river that ran from Kerveda's coast to the northern spine lay farmland protected by the same Sparrow wards that prevented direct portaling into the city. The arid desert to the south and west didn't need protection, but here was where the Terranian witches who chose the Sparrow Coven worked, tending the earth to provide the city with fresh produce. It was among these farms that King Phineas had a loyal acolyte purchase land on his behalf, kept out of the royal name. The men and women who lived there, tending to the cattle, were paid handsomely to keep their mouths shut about the cloaked visitors that sometimes arrived in the middle of the night, stealing into an off-limits barn. They'd been made into some of the wealthiest people in all Kerveda to turn a blind eye to the things that emerged from the stables within.

Even from the sky, Aisling could tell the farms were abandoned. Not destroyed, like the city was; there was less bloodshed soaking the ground and she could see a lone chicken pecking at the ground. Still, there was no sign of people, and *something* had come through. Windows were smashed, doors kicked in.

It wasn't a promising sign that the herd would still be around. Or, worse, if they were, that there was anybody remaining to care for them in the weeks since Dusarn's collapse.

The barn Aisling led them to was just like any other barn, though anyone who knew where to look would see the warding on it. Woven charms with animal bones dangling like windchimes hung over every doorway. The ground had been salted to deter the fae, the hinges and handles forged from silver. Beneath the flaking paint of the walls, spellmarks had been burned into the wood.

The cunae wavered. Sharing a look, Aisling nodded and Yasmin called for the coven to land prematurely. Aisling brought Volya to a stop beside them, stroking her warm hide as she dismounted and drew her weapon.

The sun was growing low. They didn't have much time. Cicadas started their deafening song as the nine witches approached the barn, unaffected by wards not intended against them.

Pushing open the door, Aisling breathed in hay and muck. Snuffling had her heart racing before her eyes even finished adjusting to the low light in the barn, because she knew the sound intimately.

"A miracle," she whispered, stepping aside to let Yasmin in.

The tall, beautiful alpha of the sky coven stood speechless at the sight of exactly eight winged horses waiting patiently in their stables, unperturbed by the invasion, as if they already knew who had come for them.

"I don't care what anybody says," Yasmin managed through her awe, waving the rest of her coven inside. "Morvia is not indifferent. She has a hand in this."

Almost trancelike, the youngest witch stepped forward, hand outstretched to a large dapple-gray mare with wings that darkened to black tips. The horse ruffled her wings and flicked her tail, ear twitching as she watched the approach, but stood utterly calm as the witch placed a palm against her nose.

Aisling tilted her head. The speckled pattern on the horse's face mirrored the spattering of freckles on the witch's. Made for each other. As was the largest witch aside from Yasmin herself, golden hair blending almost too perfectly against the coat of the palomino who welcomed her.

If Davina were here, she would call this a sign. She would call it proof that this was the way forward, that she had done the right thing by coming here. The sky coven were meant to find these mares, were meant to join Aisling in the sky. Maybe, just maybe, there was a way that Aisling survived this. Maybe, when the war was done and she had given away all the land the Sparrows had claimed, she could learn what it truly meant to be Celestian.

A breeze tickled the back of her neck, a whisper on the wind. Closing her eyes for a moment, Aisling uttered a silent prayer for clarity until Celeste's secrets grew louder. Whipping her head around, Aisling locked eyes with the small child peeking out from under a pile of dirty horse rugs in the corner.

A small squeak, and the child disappeared.

Aisling nodded for Yasmin to continue familiarizing her coven with the mares while she took a careful step toward the rugs. She was not good with children. She was not good with comfort.

"You can come out," she said, trying for soft. It still sounded like a demand.

It took a minute. Patience was a virtue as Aisling watched the rugs begin to shuffle, a small body disentangling itself until a young girl no older than eleven stood before her, head down, knees shaking.

"You're the acolyte's daughter." The people who worked the land the barn was hidden on were not permitted inside the barn, but the acolyte who'd bought the plot had left his family behind to tend to the mares. Someone had to feed and brush them, had to muck out their stalls between the king's sporadic visits. Aisling had never seen the family, who were smart enough to keep well out of sight during royal visits, but Celeste knew who cared for her favorite beasts.

The child nodded, finally losing her battle with her knees. "Yes, Your Highness."

So she knew who Aisling was, then.

"Where are your parents?" Again, she tried for gentle, trying to imagine herself talking to Eavha instead, but there was something about having her feet in this barren territory that had her walls raising.

"Everyone ran when we saw . . ." Her eyes widened, her breath hitching as she remembered whatever she'd been able to see of Dusarn's fall from this northern town. "Dragons. Mama said to leave the horses, but . . . But I love them. And I knew Astrid would protect me." Astrid was the largest mare, black as night. The one currently nuzzling Yasmin's outstretched hand. "I'm sorry for intruding, Your Highness."

"She left you?" Aisling asked.

The girl nodded.

"You've been here alone. For weeks."

"Yes, Your Highness."

"You've been taking care of the horses." Their troughs were full, their stalls clean. The girl herself was filthy and reeked of manure, but the horses were all in excellent condition. One small girl for eight horses. "You must be very tired."

"No, Your Highness. I can keep looking after them if you need me to."

Slowly crouching down, Aisling reached out and tilted the girl's chin until her watery gaze was no longer fixed on the ground.

"I would award you a medal of bravery, if I had one. Stand up. If you have anything you wish to keep, collect it now."

She would take the acolyte's daughter back to Hyrsch, then have someone take her out of harm's way, to one of the villages. As soon as she could spare the soldiers, she would send some to find her parents, wherever they fled to.

The young girl looked at Aisling in shock, as if she couldn't believe she wasn't being punished. It wasn't until Aisling practically pulled her to her feet that she nodded, running for the stable doors.

"Have you ever flown with a witchling?" Yasmin asked, a small smile on her lips as Aisling returned, collecting saddles and gear from the walls. The girl was human, through and through, but Aisling knew what Yasmin meant. Riding with Eavha was one thing, even as afraid as she'd been—Eavha had muscle enough to hang on to the saddle, sense enough to shield her face. A child did not.

"No."

"I will take her with me, then."

"That would be best."

Once everybody was saddled and the acolyte's daughter returned with a small rucksack, Aisling and Yasmin led the way out of the stables. The dry air and trot of hooves on the hard earth quickened Aisling's heart. If they had time, she would have loved to fly all the way back to Hyrsch with Yasmin and Ines and the rest. She would have loved to learn the coven's names, their stories, their relationship with Celeste. She'd have loved to learn about the veils they wore and what it was like to live a nomadic life.

But time was not a luxury any of them had.

Outside, the sky was darkening. Cloudless, as was standard during Kerveda's summer. Yet there were no stars. There was no moon.

"We should get back," Yasmin said, staring with the same trepidation that had the hair on the back of Aisling's neck standing on end.

Tonight, they would stay on the parapet. Just in case.

CHAPTER FIFTY

KAELEAN

From the alcove, Kaelean watched Aisling and the coven fly away. It had been difficult not to reveal herself, but she had put too much time into the dragon. She wanted it, and she didn't trust that the princess wouldn't convince her to abandon her plan. She had to see it through now, especially as afternoon gave way to evening.

The new moon had arrived.

Still mostly buried under a mountain of rock, Kari huffed warmly as Kaelean approached, smoothing a hand over the beast's scaled neck.

"You did good," she told her, drawing Cinn's silver blade. "I'll make this quick."

The first cut severed the tendons beneath the dragon's free arm, keeping her from writhing dangerously. It had been an educated guess that Kari's anatomy would have enough similarities with Kaelean's lupanis, but there was no thrill in watching the limb hang limply. Kari roared with naked pain and betrayal, swiveling her head, heat building.

Expecting it, Kaelean leaped onto the dragon's hide and clambering high onto its back. From there, Kari couldn't reach to snap her between those ravaging teeth, nor could she aim her wrathful fire in Kaelean's direction. It didn't stop the dragon from trying. Fire scorched the rubble into ash, the plume of it spearing so far that it blasted apart the last remaining support for the wobbling tower.

It was a stroke of luck that it crumbled away from the two of them, falling into the remnants of the castle's lower levels. The crash of it raked her ears as clouds of dust filled the air.

Maybe, if this hadn't been the dragon to burn her boab to the ground, she might have made a different choice. She had, after all, sworn to never repeat this particular spell again. But every bone in her body was a vindictive one, and so she plunged the silver blade deep between the scales along its back. Making a mental note of where she'd left it, she quickly shifted into her lupanis form and ripped her way down to the dragon's spine. With a single slash, she severed the nerves.

The dragon fire died, Kari's head flopping to the ground with a sickening crunch.

Changing back, Kaelean retrieved Cinn's knife and slid down Kari's heaving side. She crawled under the wing she had freed, listening with her keen ears for where the dragon's heart beat loudest. Again, she shifted, clawing her way through muscle and rib until the panicked heart of the beast was exposed.

This part had to be done more carefully. Returning again to her witch form, Kaelean made sure to leave the arteries and veins intact. To keep the muscle beating. It was all she had been trying to do for weeks.

"May your blood be my blood. May your bones be my bones," Kaelean recited, cutting her palm and smearing the weeping mulberry wound against the boar-sized meal before her. "I give a part of myself to you, and take a part of you for me. May Mother see that we are one and the same."

From the jar of herbs she'd found in the kitchen, she plucked free a handful of ground oregano, stuffing them into the muscle's crevices. It wasn't her favorite mint, but it was better than the taste of raw, still-beating hearts.

CHAPTER FIFTY-ONE

CINN

THE CITY WAS OFFICIALLY EMPTY. EVERY SOUL LEFT IN HYRSCH HAD found either a tent or a dry patch of ground in the encampment outside the city walls, waiting out the new moon's threat. Cinn didn't mind. Trying and failing to sleep in his apartment had only reminded him that Edwina wasn't there. That William wasn't there. At least among the troops there was so much anxiety that his own could get lost in it.

A wasted effort, yet nobody minded. Better to have spent the night waiting for word from the witches that their traps had been sprung, or from the fae that their wards had been breached, than to have succumbed to exhaustion and missed the cue. Daytime was safer for resting. Cinn and Radley stalked through the tents as quietly as they could, letting those who could sleep do so. Neither of them were capable of it, and they were used to long hours of wakefulness anyway.

Eaon had been bullied into the med tent with the phouka and Eavha, and though Cinn missed him dearly, he wasn't ready to face Eavha again yet, nor was he in the mood to be around Aisling. He also didn't want to train with the veteran soldiers today out on the flat. It was pointless. Nothing he'd learned from them had mattered when William had needed it, when Eaon had his throat ripped out. If he couldn't save anyone, then he didn't see the need to dredge up all his harbored hatred, especially if all Cinn had to offer in return was a rage he was too tired to muster. So he went up to the parapet with Radley, carting the barrels of salamander milk that had arrived with the Northern Mountain Clan up the stairwells.

The morning dripped by slowly. Legs trembling from his dozenth trip up and down the stairs, Cinn stopped at the top to rest, fiddling with the charm on his bracelet while Radley fetched them some water. Eyes stinging with the sweat sliding down his brow, he felt more than saw the shadow that flitted over the merciless sun. There and gone in the blink of an eye, it moved too fast to be a cloud. Wiping his face with his sleeve, Cinn frowned up at the sky.

Dark yellow wings spread wide, there soared what was undoubtedly a dragon.

Some dropped the weapons in their hands and ran. Others screamed a warning so loud the troops on the ground could hear it. It was too early. A daytime approach went against everything they understood about beasts. Scanning the horizon, there was no sign of any army, and there was only one dragon in the sky. A scout, perhaps, flying ahead to assess what they were walking into.

A scout that couldn't be allowed to live.

Orders were shouted from one end of the wall to the next as harpoons and crossbows were loaded with silver-tipped bolts. Cinn was barely trained in swordsmanship; had never held a crossbow in his life. But half the archers were still on the ground and the dragon was growing closer, so he shouldered one of the cumbersome weapons and managed to get it loaded.

As if it knew it had been spotted, the dragon began to descend. Arms shaking, sweat sliding down his neck, Cinn took a knee and peered through the eyesight.

Leisurely, the dragon flapped, drawing closer with every beat of its wings. If it was afraid of the scrambling ants below, it didn't show it.

"All aim!" the call came.

It was just the way Eaon had described it. Knowing the beasts were large and being faced with its mass were two different things; three men could easily be crushed beneath one of its feet, claws and teeth shiny black and thick enough to chew through stone. The tiny bolt in Cinn's crossbow would barely scratch its scaled armor, glinting under the midday sun. Only the silver tip steadied his nerves. It might only scratch, but it would fucking hurt.

Eaon had described its stream of fire having enough reach to burn the trees from atop the towers on either side of the Womb. The beast was getting close enough to unleash that destruction on the wall itself, and though Cinn knew he would survive such a thing, he also knew the men and women around him would not be so lucky.

He had to aim true. If, for some reason, his bolt was the only one that hit, it had to be a good shot.

He aimed for the eyes.

Cinn frowned. It was the same dragon Eaon had described, except instead of red eyes, or empty sockets where the phouka had clawed them out, the dragon sported beady black. Utterly unimportant, except they were the same eyes Cinn had seen gleaming behind the grin of a lupanis. Of a fox, and a mouse, and a brownish-red-haired witch he despised with every fiber of his being.

"Steady!" the commander called. "And—"

"Hold!" Cinn screamed, dropping his crossbow.

The nearest soldiers startled, staring at Cinn like he'd lost his gods-damned mind.

"Hold! Hold!" he repeated, running for the stairwell and throwing himself down.

He didn't know if the commanders would listen. Any moment, he expected to hear the call, the twang of unleashed bolts. What was that stupid witch thinking, approaching the city like that?!

By the time he reached the fields again, the dragon was lowering its enormous body to the ground. Cinn ran for her, any doubt that he was wrong eradicated from his mind as the ugly lizard beast grinned at his approach.

Picking up a fist-sized rock, Cinn threw it at Kaelean's scaly face. It fell far short, but the effect was the same. Kaelean snorted, smoke curling around her face.

"They almost shot you out of the sky!" he screamed at her, picking up an abandoned wooden sword and thwacking her enormous foot.

The next huff was startled, heat blistering the air as fire swelled inside her throat. But then the beast's body began to change, scales turning muddy, muscle into clay, and then she was shrinking, shrinking, shrinking, until Kaelean once more stood before him. Naked and clutching a bundle of bloodied cloth, her black eyes were wide as she stared as if she had no idea who he was.

"Did you just yell at me?"

Rather than answer, he resisted the urge to punch her in the face, throwing his arms around her instead. Relief was ice cold in his veins and he hated it.

For a long moment, Kaelean was too stunned to move. Only the slight buckling of her injured leg made her grab hold of him back. Slinging her arm over his shoulders, he kept her steady as she wrapped herself in the bloodied cloth, a macabre makeshift dress. From within its folds, she produced a small parcel of rags.

"Found your voice but lost your toys? Hope there isn't a connection."

The weight was familiar as she placed it in his hands, long and thin and oddly heavy. Pulling it free of the rag, Cinn held his misshapen silver dagger, the handle molded to the fit of his fist. It was the knife he had left in Dusarn. The one he had stabbed Aisling with. The one William had given him—the first bit of safety he'd known in years.

Kaelean may as well have stuck the knife right in his throat for all he could breathe.

Reeking of filth and rotting meat, she stepped closer, voice soft. "What's happened?"

The fragile wall of glass he'd built between him and his grief was shattering again. Clutching the knife to his chest was all he could do to keep it together. He wished he'd never found that farm on the outskirts of Belden. Maybe William would have lived, or if his heart attack was inevitable, at least Cinn wouldn't have to feel like this.

"Oh." It was Kaelean's turn to put an arm around him, half in comfort and half as a crutch as they began their return to the staring army, navigating trenches and spellmarks carved into the ground. "I'm sorry."

A part of him wanted to throw the blade into the Dividing River and forget about the Copelands entirely. It was a small part, though. Mostly, he wished he could absorb the silver into his body so he could keep it safer than he ever could have kept the man himself.

CHAPTER FIFTY-TWO

KAELEAN

Eavha flung herself at Kaelean, whose instincts were only just quick enough to dump her stash and catch her. Grinning into Eavha's hair, she reveled in the fact that while she had claimed all of them some time ago, it now seemed they were claiming her too. First Cinn, now Eavha . . . She had never been so welcomed.

"I knew you'd come back," Eavha said softly.

"Never doubt it."

Letting go, Eavha took a step back. Gasped. "What happened to your hands?"

It was the first Kaelean had seen them too, though she was not surprised. Eavha inspected them as if considering how she could heal the scales embedded in her knuckles, the fingernails that were now black claws.

Taking them back, Kaelean placed two fingers on either side of her black, beady eyes. "Mouse."

She moved her fingers to either side of her nose. "Lupanis."

Dragging her nails through her tangle of brownish-red hair, she said, "Fox."

Then she wriggled her new nails in front of her face. "Dragon."

Eavha swallowed. Paled. "Dragon?"

Kaelean's grin was wicked.

"Did you actually miss the whole fiasco that was her arrival?" Aisling asked, grinning fiercely at Kaelean as she offered her hand. "Volya and I were just making it over the wall when I saw you shift."

"Glad to see you in one piece, Princess," Kaelean said.

"You as well. Where—"

"I was *busy*," Eavha interrupted, cheeks heating. "I was getting ready for *invasion*, not *looking* at it. And can you two catch up later? I need a moment with Kaelean."

Aisling acquiesced gracefully, and only then did it occur to Kaelean that the princess and Cinn were in the same tent. She couldn't imagine a world where the two of them could be in the same place and not try to maim each other, and yet, here she stood.

At some point between their arrival and Aisling's approach, he must have become aware of the predicament and left her side.

Searching the busy med tent for him was an exercise only her eyes needed to perform; as far away as possible, he sat on a cot with Eaon, his back to the reunion he wanted no further part in.

Kaelean lifted a hand. Eaon nodded at her. He looked like a steaming pile of horse shit rolled twice over. Curiosity and guilt warred briefly before her attention was forced back to Eavha.

"Sit down. Eat. Are you hurt?"

Kaelean let herself be led to the nearest cot, a cup of water pushed into her hands while a human ran to fetch something for her to eat.

"I'm alright," she assured Eavha. "Are you?"

"We managed to delay Chaos at least a day, maybe two if the state of the pass is anything to go by. Everyone who went . . . Yvette, Herbe . . . There's been no word, and the fae who went to investigate apparently reported no activity besides the beasts making their way through the rubble. We haven't done anything for them yet, but we should. We had a funeral for everyone who died in the forest. It was beautiful, Kaelean, and I think it helped a lot of people come to terms with this new reality they're in. All the low-blessed and witchlings have gone to Pirevia with Edwina—it's safe, we took it over recently—but even the gardeners wanted to stay behind. They're doing their best to learn with the guardians, but they will be more use bringing soldiers back here for triage and growing herbs for us to use.

"Oh, and here." Eavha took a breath as she lifted the flower crown from her head. "This is for you. I did the best I could."

Before she could do more than lift the wreath of peonies and baby's breath a few inches, Kaelean stilled her hands, returning the crown to its place.

"I'm sure you have done and will continue to do wonderfully."

"I . . . What?"

Tilting her head, Kaelean lifted an eyebrow. Eavha wasn't stupid. She knew what she meant.

"This was just temporary." Eavha's eyes widened. "I couldn't let Lorelei be in charge, but I knew you were coming back—"

"Shh, little one." Kaelean's smile, for once, was warm as she held onto Eavha's hands, clasping them in front of her chest. "It suits you."

"It's yours."

"I am relinquishing it to you."

Eavha clasped Kaelean's fingers in terror. "No."

"Yes."

"But you're our high priestess. You . . . You're Kaelean. You came back to Wyldeden for us after seven hundred years; this is *yours*."

"I came back because Lorelei had no place ruling Wyldeden. And you needed someone to teach you."

Speaking of Lorelei, where was that horrid hag? A matter for later. Right now, Eavha was devolving into utter panic, as if Kaelean didn't know exactly what she was doing. As if she hadn't been planning this moment since the day she asked her to become heir. It was sooner than expected, but on her impossibly fast and thrilling flight across Nir, Kaelean had come to the conclusion that priesthood was no longer her calling. Her rogue years had been painful, but they had also allowed her to find her own truth. To learn a self that had never been given the chance to grow, crowned too young in the midst of war.

"I still need you to teach me," Eavha insisted. "I have no idea what I am doing. We are at war, and you have experience with that. You're what they need. I'm . . . I'm too young."

"I was thirteen; you will do fine. Besides, I'm not going anywhere. I will be with you, to advise, and I will be with them, to fight, but I haven't been one of them for a very long time. I am a witch, but I am also two parts beast and two parts animal. I made Wyldeden, but Wyldeden is gone. I am the past, and that is not what they need anymore. They need the future. They need hope. And you stepped up. You are ready."

"Wyldeden is not gone." With those words, the fear drained from her. Her shoulders straightened, a firmness to her features that demanded Kaelean listen. "It's in all of us."

Smiling so wide she almost couldn't see, Kaelean dropped Eavha's hands to cup her face.

"You're right. Wyldeden was never just a place. You *are* Wyldeden, Eavha, and Wyldeden is you."

Closing her eyes, Eavha rested her forehead against Kaelean's. Every breath was slower and deeper than the last as she came to terms with what Kaelean was doing.

She didn't refute her again.

CHAPTER FIFTY-THREE

EAON

BETWEEN THE PHOUKA'S NAGGING AND EAVHA'S HYSTERICS, TAKING UP space in the med tent set up at the city's perimeter was a compromise Eaon begrudgingly made. It kept Eavha happy, as she could help organize the human physicians and witches volunteering as healers while also keeping an eye on Eaon, waiting for an opportunity to discuss the state of his leg again. It also meant the phouka could hound him while simultaneously bullying promises with Gatty out of the gathering fae nearby, as per Aisling's request—all without forcing another command on him.

Little did the phouka know that his commands couldn't hold Eaon anymore. He didn't want to think about why. He didn't care. Nor did he particularly care what Kaelean and Eavha were talking about in their private corner of the tent. He'd said his hellos, grateful that one of the splinters in his brain could be removed, but otherwise they had nothing to say to each other.

Sitting cross-legged on the makeshift cot, Eaon picked at his food. The day was humid in the aftermath of the summer storm that had blown through and a few degrees too warm to be comfortable. It was the kind of non-perfection that usually put Eaon in a good mood. Today, he could barely feel it. Sure, his shirt had dark patches where sweat made it cling to his body, his mousy curls slicked to the back of his neck, but inside he was cold. Not even the heat from where Killian sat with Tomaii, Reigan and the other Igni-blessed just outside the med tent, working on everlight amulets, could warm him.

He'd brought Dearmead's journal, fingering pages he'd already memorized. Alive. West. It was nothing, and yet it was a balm.

A half-chewed crust hit him in the head.

Pulling his gaze from the leather-bound book, Eaon leveled a glare at Cinn. The heat was taking its toll on him, too. The months of traveling they'd done together since meeting last spring might have brought a tan to Cinn's pale skin, but it didn't shield the bridge of his freckling nose from the sun's harsh kiss. The arches of his ears were also brushed with the soft pink of an early burn—in an attempt to distract him from the grief he wore on his sleeve, Tomaii had spent the early morning trimming Cinn's hair to expose his small ears while telling endless embarrassing stories about Eaon's visits to the Northern Mountain. Only because he was desperate to see Cinn smile again did Eaon suffer through translating Tomaii's broken Nirnish.

It had been worth it.

Meeting Eaon's glare and ripping free another piece of his sandwich's crust, Cinn didn't even try to feign innocence.

{Stop blaming yourself.}

That he managed to sign in a manner that Eaon could interpret with a crust in one hand and his silver dagger clutched tight in the other was testament to Cinn's determination.

Eaon lifted a single brow. "The *audacity*."

Scowling, Cinn threw the second crust at him. A justified attack. Eaon let it hit.

{If I have to hear it, so do you. Stop. Blaming. Yourself.}

"Stop pretending you know what I was thinking about."

{You had your Dearmead face on.}

Eaon stilled. "My what?"

{Your Dearmead face,} Cinn repeated before forcing his own features into some strange combination of a scowl and a pout.

"I do not pull that face."

{It's your Dearmead face. You also have an Eavha face.} Cinn wrinkled his nose and rolled his eyes in an exaggerated gesture that, in all honesty, looked exactly like how Eaon felt most of the time his sister was around.

It took an exorbitant amount of self-control not to laugh, but Eaon managed it. Cinn saw it regardless; he barely contained his own retaliatory smirk. As small and brief as it was, Eaon was glad to see it.

The smile disappeared when Eaon said, "I just feel like I should be doing more to find him. I'm just *sitting* here. It's my fault—"

{No.} Cinn cut him off with a fierce gesture.

"You weren't there. I was *useless*—"

{No,} Cinn repeated before leaning over and flicking Eaon between the eyes.

Eaon blinked at him. "Um, ow."

{Dearmead would not blame you for what happened.}

The sharp pain that had been lodged in Eaon's chest ever since realizing Dearmead was in trouble *twisted*, and he swallowed back bitter words that weren't fair to say: *"Makes no difference what Dearmead would say, since he's not here to say it."*

Cinn was just repeating what Eaon and Sarah, what Siobhan and Edwina and everybody else had been saying to him for days. William would not blame Cinn for what happened that night. For Eaon to insist upon it but reject the notion for himself was a hypocrisy that would only hurt Cinn.

Yet.

"You barely know Dearmead. Have you even exchanged two words with him? Ones that either of you understood?"

{Don't need to.}

Eaon was about to argue again, but the phouka stalked past with a twig-sprite in his fist and gave Eaon a pointed look.

"Eat," he hissed on his way by, putting a little power behind the word. Eaon's hand was moving toward his food before he even finished scowling. A scathing "bite me" sat on the tip of his tongue, but Eaon swallowed it in case the faerie took it as invitation.

By the time Eaon returned his attention to Cinn, the kinner was shaking with repressed laughter. {Now *that* is a face.}

"Fuck you." Then, with his hands, so the male in question couldn't hear, Eaon added, {Don't forget, you've got your own nagging bodyguard watching your every move.}

Two rows of beds over, Radley Lightman had wandered into the med tent, settling down beside a scrawny demi-kin tending to old wounds, only breaking conversation with her to glance at Cinn every thirty seconds. When he caught him at it again, Cinn's eyes softened.

It hurt to look at.

Instead, Eaon returned to Dearmead's journal.

In the end, I stay.

He shut his eyes against the echo of Dearmead's words.

A hand wrapped around his wrist.

Sure enough, a moment later, Eaon felt the sentient magic that the Lover had left inside him stirring, feeding off the dark emotions that always seemed to herald a surge.

"Sorry," Eaon muttered, swallowing the pain down as he shoved the magic back into the depths of his soul. "I've got it."

By the time Eaon opened his eyes again, any hint of happiness was gone from Cinn's face.

"Sorry," he repeated.

Cinn let go of his wrist to flick him between the eyes again.

Two rows over, Radley had gotten to his feet. Humans, demi-kin and kinner couldn't sense magic the way witches could, but Cinn knew Eaon well enough to know when he was losing hold of himself, and Radley clearly knew his brother well enough to know when something was wrong. The phouka, too, had stilled on the other side of the tent, yellow eyes narrowed to slits.

Shame curled Eaon's shoulders as he turned away from all of them.

He was a disaster waiting to happen. Everyone was being so impossibly stupid by refusing to acknowledge it. For not taking advantage, pointing him in the enemy's direction. All these people were preparing for war, for injuries that would undoubtedly come. War and injuries that could be avoided if certain idiots would stop being so sentimental.

He was one person. One measly, wasted life.

Both of Cinn's hands encircled Eaon's wrists, tight enough to pull him out of his spiraling thoughts. All the bright, soft parts of Cinn were gone. This was not the boy who had become so important to Eaon these past six months. No, this was the rabid thing Aisling had made in her dungeon.

"Stop it," Cinn hissed.

Eaon flinched, the cold that had wrapped around his bones melting away. Slowly, Cinn let go of one of his wrists and reached for the button threaded around Eaon's neck. With one finger, he pressed the small metal thing hard into Eaon's chest.

No more words came, but Cinn didn't move his finger.

Slowly, Eaon looked down to the strange gift Cinn had given him so long ago. He still didn't understand what it meant, but he knew how important Cinn's trinkets were to him. With the rest lost to the Womb, he briefly worried Cinn wanted his button back, but that didn't make sense either; Eaon might not understand the message but knew what the act of giving it to him meant. Or at least he thought he did. Maybe it meant something different to Cinn than Eaon had hoped, but when it came to Cinn, Eaon would take what he could get, and it would be enough.

"I thought I imagined it. In the Womb. But you really spoke."

Mentioning it had been a mistake. Cinn seemed to shrink in on himself, glancing around the tent as if afraid someone else had heard him. Eaon swallowed the sick feeling in his stomach. These words Cinn gave him . . . they were not safe. He risked too much by giving them.

"Sorry," Eaon said, quietly, placing a hand over the one Cinn still kept on his chest.

They sat like that a moment as Cinn blinked through wherever he went in his head. It was a relief that he did not get lost there the way he used to, even if the tiny smile he managed was fragile. His lips parted as if to say something else, but it was too much.

Eaon let go of his hand, but what Cinn signed didn't make any sense.

{He is different to you.}

Eaon frowned. "What do you mean?"

{I don't know the word or the sign. But you love Dearmead different.}

It was a sudden shift. A deflection. Curiously, Eaon studied Cinn's face. Did he really not understand, the way he didn't understand attraction, or was he asking for a different reason?

Eaon chose his words very carefully.

"It is rare to find someone you can be . . . true with. Someone who sees you. Who can know you. Dearmead was that person for me for a very long time, so, yes, he is special to me."

Slowly, Cinn nodded, a tiny furrow between his brows. When he met Eaon's gaze again, he knew Cinn had heard what Eaon had not said.

{Am I special too?}

Eaon swallowed, but the words would not come out. He nodded instead.

There was no surprise on Cinn's face, just a deep sadness.

{Then you know why I can't let you do it.}

"Cinn."

Every gesture of his hands was sure and firm and demanded attention. {You are angry like I am angry. You are sad like I am sad. You are a second heart.}

A second heart. Of course Cinn, the boy without words, would find a way to say it.

Closing his eyes, Eaon gave himself a moment to imagine what it would be like. To have everything. To be free to explore the world with Dearmead and with Cinn. To have them both. To be so surrounded by their very different kinds of love that he could forget he'd ever spent a day starving for it.

"If you were me," Eaon started, but stopped when Radley stepped up to the side of the cot.

Facing Cinn but glancing side-long at Eaon, Radley grumbled, "Everything okay?"

For a long minute, Cinn refused to acknowledge his brother. He kept staring at Eaon, once more pressing that button against the hollow of Eaon's throat, *willing* him to understand. But Eaon couldn't, and eventually Cinn dropped his hand and turned his gaze upward.

{I don't want to sit at around feeling sorry for myself anymore.}

Eaon translated without being prompted, though he suspected the sudden request was as much for his sake as Cinn's.

A small smile pulled at Radley's mouth. "Well then. How about we go forget about our problems for a few hours instead."

CHAPTER FIFTY-FOUR

CINN

THEY DIDN'T GO FAR. ONE BLOCK IN FROM THE WESTERN GATE WAS A closed-down tavern that, judging by its ostentatious signage and fancy list of patron requirements scribbled on a chalkboard outside, under normal circumstances, Radley would be forbidden to step foot in. In fact, as they approached, Cinn's brother regaled their small party with a story of how he'd been literally thrown to the curb for daring to stand in line at such a "fine establishment." Cinn had heard it before, and he doubted the dramatized retelling was for Eaon's benefit since his brother still seemed reluctant to acknowledge his existence; no, the show was for the demi-kin who'd tagged along. Cecelia was swimming in borrowed clothes too large, hair a frayed and ratty tail between her shoulder blades. It was painful to look at her; so similar to the way Cinn had been when he'd first emerged from Aisling's dungeon, though he had never worn bruises as long as she did.

The door to the tavern was locked tight, and Radley wrestled with it for a few minutes, trying to show off his non-existent prowess before Eaon cleared his throat.

"May I?"

Lockpicking was not a skill Cinn knew Eaon had. Curiosity peeked through the beaten thing that was his heart as Radley stepped aside with a mocking flourish and Eaon stepped up close to the brass handle.

Hovering over Cinn's shoulder, the phouka was primed to react as Eaon took a shaky breath, fingers trembling slightly as he grabbed hold of the metal. The midday air chilled a few degrees and both the phouka and Cinn took an instinctive step forward. Unnecessary. Eaon had it under control. The handle and its lock rusted against his skin until it crumbled entirely, leaving the heavy door free to swing inward.

The difference between smugness and pride was a difficult distinction on Eaon's face, but Cinn knew. The smirk on the phouka's face suggested he knew too; it was nice to see the curse Eaon had been burdened used for fun instead of horror.

Returning Radley's mocking bow, Eaon herded them all inside.

Deep purple walls, a gilded ceiling, and black leather upholstery spoke to the caliber of patronage the tavern aimed for, but the parquetry floor was just as sticky as any other. Even Eaon's bare feet made a sound as they crossed the empty square toward the bar.

Helping himself, Radley leaped over the counter and began pulling bottles and crystal glasses off shelves.

"Let's see, what have we got. Locked most of it away before they left, cheap bastards. But we've got something brown, something red, something clear, and maybe half a barrel of piss. Not actual piss," Radley assured Cecelia, who wrinkled her nose as she settled on a bar stool. "It's ale. And for you, we have a shot of each. See what you like."

Eaon and Cinn also took seats at the bar while the phouka *popped* into his smaller goblin form and perched instead on the counter itself.

"Have you never had alcohol before?" Eaon asked her, inquisitive and conversational in a way Cinn could never be.

A spurt of hoarse laughter was his answer. "Two weeks ago I ain't barely spent a minute above ground. Then I spent all this new freedom on a ship puking up me guts. I don't even know what alcohol *is*."

Oh. This was more Cinn's speed. Putting his dagger on the counter, he signed a question for Eaon to interpret.

"What are you doing here, then?" Eaon asked for him. "You should run. Find somewhere safe to live your life."

Cecelia laughed so hard she nearly fell off her stool. "Safe? Who are you tryin' to kid? I wouldn't know what to do with meself. Killin' shit's all I know how to do, and if this is where the killin' is happening, then this is where I should be. Owen knew that. That's why he brought me."

With that, she slammed down the shot of whiskey Radley had poured for her. No tentative sips to see what it was like first, just downed it all at once, half throwing the glass across the counter as she spluttered.

"Fuck, alright, that's what alcohol is."

Radley grinned, catching the shot glass before it could roll off the edge. He brought the bottles around to Cinn next.

"Finally time to settle this. Do kinner get drunk?"

"Yes," Eaon answered immediately, smirking at the heat crawling up Cinn's neck.

{I was not half as drunk as you were, and I sobered up very quickly.}

"And yet, you were drunk."

Radley was shaking with glee as he poured out a series of shots for Cinn too. "I need to see it. I need this. It's all I have ever wanted in life."

Rolling his eyes was instinctual, but in all honesty, it was all Cinn had wanted for a long time too. It was no secret that Radley's drinking had spiraled into something worrying after Master Ackford's daughter had tossed him aside the moment he'd been freed, and that it had spiraled further into something ugly since Cinn had been gone, but he couldn't help it—Cinn had grown up wanting to go with Radley on his wild adventures. He wanted to be there when his brother laughed so hard he fell off his seat and couldn't get up again without two people to help. He wanted to see his brother happy. And maybe one day they could do that without the alcohol, but today, for now, he was content to simply be together.

The alcohol burned on the way down and he didn't know whether or not he liked the way it immediately began to loosen the battered thing in his chest. Did he want to shake off the heaviness that had been crushing him slowly since William died? What was beneath it? More worthless tears? A more acute pain? Would it be worse if he found his ability to laugh still intact? He didn't want to be happy, but he didn't want to waste the gift that was this day with Eaon and Radley, either. Not when his brother could meet the Lover any minute—a heart attack, a stray bolt, a lightning strike. Not when Eaon seemed intent on sacrificing himself.

Whatever alcohol the clear one was burned worse than the whiskey, but he drank it down to the sound of Radley's genuine and Eaon's forced cheers.

"How about you, witch boy? You look like a wine drinker."

"Oh?"

"Yeah. Wine is *enjoyable*. Nobody drinks wine to get blindly intoxicated, you drink it for the *experience*. For the snootiness of it."

Cecelia snorted, sniffing at the shot glass of red liquid. "Smells better than the other ones at least."

Betrayed, Radley gaped at her. "Blasphemy."

"Well, speaking from experience," Eaon said, smirking as he turned up his nose, "human wine is vastly less enjoyable than witch wine, and outright paltry compared to faerie wine, so I think I'll decline altogether."

Cinn snorted, putting his forehead down to hide his amusement. Grinning, the phouka leaped off the counter behind the bar to root through the shelves.

"Mother above, I hate having fae in this city," Radley grumbled, watching the goblin run amuck for a moment before rolling his eyes at Eaon. "Suit yourself then. More for Cecelia."

He passed the entire wine bottle to her when she reached for it, then for Cinn, he pulled out a larger glass to fill with—"It's called gin." Once everyone else was sated, Cinn could only stare in wonder and horror as Radley took the whiskey for himself, taking a long drink straight from the bottle.

Cinn took a much smaller sip. His face was growing warm, but rather than forgetting his problems like Radley had promised, every time he glanced across at Eaon, a pang of grief hit him.

Something soft brushed against his ankle. Kicking out, Cinn spat his mouthful everywhere as he slipped off his seat, only keeping off the ground because Eaon grabbed hold of him.

Under the barstool, Gatty grinned.

"Having fun, are we?"

The door opened and Moyra stuck her head in, tucking frizzy curls behind her ears. "Oh, there you all are."

"Has something happened?" the phouka asked, returning to the countertop with a dusty bottle, sliding it closer to Eaon.

Wiping her mouth on the back of her hand, Cecelia stood, ready.

"No, not at all. Your disappearance was noticed, is all, and Eavha sent people out to find you." That was directed at Eaon, specifically. He rolled his eyes and took the phouka's offering, pulling the cork to sniff at the contents.

"Why? So she can try and fail to heal my leg again?" he snapped. "Surely the heir of Wyldeden has better things to do."

"I know why it's not working. If you would just talk to me about—" Moyra started.

"No." The room dropped in temperature. "My leg is fucked, and I don't care. End of conversation. Now if you don't mind, if I'm going to be useless, I can at least be drunk while doing so."

The phouka snatched the bottle back and poured two glasses, keeping one for himself. Cackling, Cecelia sat back down and raised her own glass.

In all his life, Cinn had never seen a demi-kin laugh so much in such a short period of time. Pirevia had broken her.

Reaching over, he took Eaon's hand, squeezing tight. He'd forgotten for a moment that half the reason they'd come here was to distract Eaon, too. Even if Cinn couldn't banish his own misery, he could try to help Eaon with his.

"Fine," Moyra said, losing a little of the patience she'd only pulled out for Eaon's sake to begin with. From the satchel at her hip, she pulled out a deck of cards. "I'm not going to be the one to drag you back, but if you need a distraction, perhaps we could play a game."

"Poker?" Radley asked, perking up.

"Actually, it's called Sol. I can teach you."

Eaon went rigid in his seat, grip tightening painfully in Cinn's hand. The phouka, Gatty and Moyra all noticed.

"Full of surprises, aren't you, witchling?" the phouka asked. "You've heard of it."

"My da taught me. He painted his own deck and we used to play while traveling," Eaon explained. "Said it was something he picked up, up north."

"It is a Morvish game. The emissaries sent to the Sparrow Coven likely brought it with them," Moyra explained, joining Radley behind the bar so the six of them made an elongated circle. "I found this deck in the palace—"

"I found it," Gatty corrected.

Shooting the cat sith a withering glare, Moyra began dealing out cards. "It's a fairly simple game."

"Alright then," Radley said, ignorant to how tense Eaon had grown. "What's your poison?"

~

Cinn did not understand Sol. Possibly because he had never studied the constellations a day in his life and so much of the game required knowing what they were on sight. Eaon, however, was sweeping the floor with them all, phouka included.

"You're cheating," the phouka accused as he picked up another card.

Eaon smirked. "Whatever eases your ego."

Moyra had folded last round, leaning her elbows against the bar, chin in her hands as she watched her nephew with a sad sort of wonder instead. Cecelia and Radley had teamed up, the latter with enough knowledge of the stars to scrape by while the former took great glee in throwing cards on the pile whenever they had a move to make. Twice, Cinn caught Radley's eye across the bar and lifted a brow, looking between the two of them curiously. Radley ignored him the first time. Shrugged the second.

Cinn shook his head and drained the dregs of his glass.

The door creaked open. Cinn watched over his shoulder as Eavha stepped inside. Even unable to understand a word she said, he knew a reaming out when he heard one.

"I know," Gatty drawled, interrupting her mid-rant, "that you speak decent Nirnish. Since three-quarters of the room to which you are cursing don't speak Terranian, you may want to consider including them in the conversation."

Nostrils flaring, Eavha opened her mouth to begin again, but halted when a hand landed on her shoulders. Fingertips blackened with sharp claws, Kaelean stepped into view with a single eyebrow raised.

"To be succinct, we were both wondering what the fuck you all think you're doing?"

"You were just hanging out back there, letting her get it out of her system, huh?" The single glass of wine Eaon had been sipping wasn't enough to do any harm, but it had certainly relaxed his shoulders.

"Both of you can stop talking about me like I'm not standing right here," Eavha snapped, stomping her foot. "Every single one of you have better things to be doing than sitting here *drinking—*"

"Do we, though?" Radley countered.

"It's the middle of the day," Cecelia joined in. "Didn't ya'll fancy people say any attack would come at night?"

"So? You could be training or running drills like Aisling is. You could be practicing with the fae. You could be—"

"Could be winding ourselves up into little anxious balls of stress so that, when it comes time to actually do something, we're completely exhausted," Moyra interrupted Eavha, albeit more gently than the others. "A little like you're doing."

"I am not *stressed.*"

The entire room fell into bouts of laughter, and even Cinn couldn't help a chuckle.

Kaelean shook her head, but she too was smiling.

"They have a point. If you won't get some sleep, the least you could do is relax a little."

"Getting drunk is not relaxing," Eavha argued.

"It is when it's human brewed," the phouka said. "It's not as if any of this is strong. You'll sober up quickly enough that it won't matter."

"Come on." Eaon waved her over. "We're playing a game."

Like watching a house of cards collapse, Cinn watched Eavha give in. She looked to him first, though. Beseeching. Cinn turned back to his cup and refilled it.

"Thatta boy." Radley slapped him on the back.

Kaelean reached the bar first, climbing up to sit on the end of it. "Ah, yes. I'm familiar with this one."

Tentatively, Eavha perched beside Eaon, took one look at the cards in his hand and scowled. "Ugh. Sol."

Eaon choked on air. "You know how to play?"

"No," Eavha spat. "I don't."

Both Gatty and the phouka howled. Moyra covered her mouth, eyes crinkling with quiet laughter.

"I'll teach you," Eaon offered, dumping his cards and collecting the deck to reshuffle.

While he did, Moyra and Kaelean introduced themselves to each other, falling into hushed conversation. Radley and Cecelia did much the same, leaving Cinn to sip at his gin. Was it going straight to his head? Yes. Was he going to be sober again in twenty minutes? Also yes.

By the time Eaon had dealt the cards and explained the rules to Eavha, as well as an in-depth explanation of each of the constellation cards and what they meant—which Cinn would never admit to finding both helpful and fascinating—the door opened again. With fistfuls of everlight amulets to hand out, Killian, Tomaii and Reigan joined them.

Cinn didn't understand a word they said either, but as the noise in the room increased tenfold and more bottles of liquor found their way onto the bar, he smiled anyway. Eaon's friends were a good distraction. Predictable, he knew exactly how the rest of the afternoon was going to go.

The Sol cards scattered on the floor as Tomaii climbed on top of the bar, stomping his feet and vocalizing in a raw, rhythmic beat. Overwhelmed by the frivolity of the Northern Mountain Clan, Cinn had retreated to a booth some time ago, leaving his half-full glass behind. The everlight glowing at his throat and the identical one Eaon wore in the seat beside him brightened the shadowy corner, both content to watch their friends enjoy the afternoon.

On the parquetry floor, Radley coaxed Cecelia into a dance, her movements awkward but honest. Moyra had Kaelean and Eavha with her, hands joined, spinning each other in a complicated knot. Their laughter and Tomaii's improvised music had drawn in half a dozen others who'd come looking for their high priestess, some of them finding drinks while others joined in the revelry. It was a desperate attempt at distraction, a final grab for something pleasant—a reminder of what they were fighting for.

The spinning knot of witches became too tangled. Moyra tripped over her own foot and would have dragged the others down too if Kaelean hadn't planted her feet, holding onto Eavha, whose flower crown flew off her head. Hysterical, Moyra crawled across the floor to collect it for her, ignoring Gatty's revolted expression from where he hid under a barstool.

After helping her aunt back to her feet, Eavha plopped her crown back on, lopsided and a little crumpled. As she looked across the tavern for her brother, taking wobbling steps toward their quiet corner, Cinn watched the blooms plump back into shape.

"How *dare* you sit over here after convincing me to relax a little. It's *rude*," she shouted at them, half collapsing into the opposite booth.

Cinn forced his fingers to play with the bracelet around his wrist instead of the dagger at his hip. Despite her inebriation, she chose to speak to them in Nirnish, including him, and smiled with enough caution to know their unspoken feud had not been forgotten.

"How did you get drunk on human wine?" Eaon mocked.

"I'm not!"

"You are. And I am not carrying you to bed this time," Eaon warned her.

Scoffing, Eavha rolled her eyes. "When have you ever done that?"

"Literally every time you drink."

"That is not true!"

"It absolutely is!" Eaon's almost-smile was the most genuine Cinn had seen on his face in a very long time.

"Well, whatever." Eavha flipped the mess of curls that had spilled from the knot atop her head over her shoulder, shaking her shoulders and sitting up straighter. "I still demand an explanation for why you have abandoned your drinks and why you are both sitting over here like lepers when you should be dancing."

In the booth over, the phouka watched. The moment Eaon had pushed his glass away, the phouka had refused to let Radley rile him about it, snapping threats that had Cinn increasingly on edge. How much of Eaon's decision to join Cinn in isolation had to do with his own desire to step away and how much had to do with separating Radley and the phouka, Cinn could only guess.

"I wouldn't want to ruin the good mood by losing control of myself," Eaon said gently, hands tucked carefully under the table. "But it's good to see you unwind a bit."

Eavha glanced to Cinn, who simply stared until she looked away again.

"I should probably sober up," she said, running her hands down her face.

"Won't take long," Eaon promised.

"Are you hungry? I'm hungry. Are there snacks here?" Eavha made to get up, presumably to find snacks, but froze halfway.

Every muscle in Cinn's body went taut as he scanned the tavern. As far as he could see, the only threat was to anyone who tried to go to the bathroom—Killian and Reigan were leaning against the door, hands in very inappropriate places, tongues twisted in ways Cinn didn't need to see.

"Hey, you!" Eavha spat as she finally got to her feet. Without looking back, she clenched her fists and stormed across the parquetry floor to an older witch with a shaved head. "It's Cleo, right?"

"Oh, shit," Eaon muttered, but didn't make a move to follow her.

The witch in question raised her head at the sound of her name, eyes widening at Eavha's approach. "Oh, shit."

{Who is Cleo?} Cinn asked.

"The brewer who made my tonics when Eavha first came to Hyrsch."

That was all the explanation required. Cinn remembered. The tonics hadn't been made right, the ingredients unblessed. Knowing how seriously Eavha took her work, it was fair to assume that she had shown Cleo how to do it properly—had been very clear, very precise. And Cleo had chosen to be petty instead. Eaon had suffered agonizing migraines. Withdrawals. He had gone into a frenzy. He had endangered the Northern Mountain Clan and almost been burned at the stake for choices he may not have made if he had been properly medicated.

{Oh. Shit.}

Cinn sat back in his seat, crossed his arms and watched Eavha get in Cleo's face.

"You think you're funny, brewing dud tonics for my brother? You think you're better than him? You think you can do whatever you want because he was a laborer?"

Eavha swung. And then she wailed, shaking her hand as Cleo stumbled back, the crack of her nose audible even over Tomaii's theatrics.

"Shit," Eaon hissed, making to get to his feet, but the phouka leaned over the seat separating them and pointed one clawed finger at him.

"No. You sit down."

"I can't let her—"

"It's under control."

"Enough!" Kaelean snapped as the room slowed to silence, everybody staring at where Eavha made to strike at Cleo again, open palm this time. Kaelean caught her wrist in time to stop her, putting herself between the two witches. "It's not Cleo's fault."

"It is *unlawful* to treat laborers like that anymore," Eavha spat. "She needs to be punished."

"Calm down, right now," Kaelean ordered. "Let's talk outside."

"No," she hissed, squirming in Kaelean's grip. "Get off me."

Sighing, Kaelean looked over her shoulder and said, "Go, Cleo."

Dropping her hands, blood ran rivers down her chin, fury blazing. "I won't be punished for doing what I was told."

"Nobody told you to brew intentionally ineffective tonics, you rogue!" Eavha spat.

"We need to talk," Kaelean said, trying to be quiet, but they had the entire room's attention. Privacy was a thing of five minutes ago. Still, she made to drag Eavha toward the booths, allowing Cleo to make a hasty escape through the door.

"Let go!"

"Enough."

"I want her exiled. Immediately!"

"It's not going to happen."

"Why the fuck not?!"

"I literally just made you permanently in charge of our people, and this is how you choose to behave? Do not make a fool of me, Eavha. I will not explain anything to you until you stop behaving like a brat."

"I will not stop until Cleo is excommunicated!"

Pushing Eavha into the booth with the phouka, Kaelean blocked her in, glaring over her shoulder until Tomaii awkwardly began to take up his tune again. It didn't take long for the small crowd to get back to drinking and gossiping, though Cinn didn't doubt all ears were pointed their way.

"Check her hand," Eaon said to the phouka, anxiously leaning over the table.

Between Kaelean refusing to let Eavha out of the booth and the phouka wrestling her into stillness so he could check her swelling knuckles, Eavha settled enough to stop drawing attention. Her face was red, glare filled with unparalleled wrath. Waiting.

Kaelean lifted her chin. "I told her to leave Eaon's tonics unblessed."

Cinn blinked. Blood pounded in his ears.

"What did you say." Eavha's heat banked into a cold that rivaled her brother's. A cold that, surprisingly, wasn't making an appearance as Eaon sat back in his seat.

"I needed him to detox to prove a theory," Kaelean said, shoulders set. There was no shame in those depthless black eyes. "I have suspected for a long time now that your brother may be Morvish, and after speaking with Moyra—"

Eavha lunged, quicker than a whip, her slap heavy across Kaelean's face.

What did it say about him that Cinn's only reaction was to blink?

Beside him, Eaon flinched. The temperature dropped. Cinn took his hand in both of his. The phouka was right there; Eaon didn't need to get involved. Didn't need to risk hurting either of them.

Stepping back, slow and controlled, smoke curled from Kaelean's nose. "How dare you."

"How dare *you*," Eavha retorted. "My brother is not a plaything for you to experiment with."

Forcing herself to look away, Kaelean sought out Eaon. Tried to soften her rage as she took in Eaon's petrified form.

"I knew it from the moment you figured out Aadya was behind your family's curse. I didn't want to say anything until I was sure. I figured you or Cinn would reach out to me if things were too bad during the withdrawal."

Eaon was stone. And then he was bored. The cold retreated and Cinn's hands stopped tingling.

"Sure. Thanks, I guess."

The phouka seemed to grow six inches, letting go of Eavha's hand as she whimpered. Cinn let go of Eaon's hands before this could get worse. Kaelean understood enough sign language for him to get his point across.

{I am very glad you're back, but you need go away for a little while.}

Raising her hands, black tipped fingers spread wide, Kaelean stepped back farther. To Eavha she said, "Send for me when you're in a better mood."

They watched her leave.

Eavha heaved out a breath and wiped her cheeks on the backs of her hands. "I can't believe she did that."

"I can," Eaon said. Empty. "Are you alright?"

"I'm fine. Are you?"

"Sure."

"Come, little one," the phouka said, gently pushing Eavha out of the booth. "Let us fetch us all something to take the edge off. You two will be fine for five minutes, won't you."

Not a question. A demand.

Cinn nodded, taking Eaon's hand again. Lacing their fingers.

The phouka and Eavha made their way back across the room, ignoring the stares that followed them. Still, the party went on. Tomaii's singing was reaching a new fever while Killian and Reigan had disappeared into the bathroom entirely. Moyra sat at the bar, speaking with Gatty while Radley and Cecelia were back mixing liquors and handing them out to whoever asked.

Inch by inch, tension eased from Eaon's body. The emptiness filled with a morose nostalgia that Cinn recognized in his own heart as they watched the crowd. But while Cinn saw people who didn't have to see William gasping down his dying breaths every time they closed their eyes, Eaon looked more like he was trying to absorb as much happiness and joy as he could. As if trying to commit this day to memory, to remind himself of why he thought he had to put himself in so much danger.

{Don't do it.}

Eaon didn't even have to ask what Cinn was talking about.

"You can't tell me you wouldn't do the same thing in my position. That you wouldn't do whatever you had to. For them. To keep them as safe as we can."

Cinn didn't know what he would do. Eaon's position wasn't one Cinn would ever be in. Those moments when he'd bled in Qiri had made him afraid of death in a way he hadn't ever been, and though he'd still prefer it to going back into a cage . . . Not until he made things right for his family. What was left of it anyway.

So maybe he could understand Eaon's choice. Except . . .

Cinn cleared his throat, leaning as close to Eaon as possible. "I want to keep you safe too."

Closing his eyes, Eaon lowered his head until their foreheads pressed together. "I love you for that."

It wouldn't stop him. Nothing would.

Cinn was going to lose Eaon, too.

As if seeing the realization on his face, the pain it caused, Eaon placed his hand against Cinn's cheek. "Knowing you has made this last year—"

Choking, Cinn shook his head. {No goodbyes.}

Eaon nodded. "Can you do something for me?"

{Anything.}

Eaon's eyes grew glassy. He backed away an inch, turning his gaze upward.

"Dearmead. He's out there somewhere. I can't even imagine what he's going through." Eaon's silent words might as well have been screams as he met Cinn's gaze. *But you do.* "Take care of him for me."

Cinn nodded.

"I wrote letters. For him and for Eavha. There's one for Kaelean and Moyra, too. They're in a bag I hid in that other tavern I met you in the other night."

Cinn nodded again. Every part of him wanted to fight Eaon on this. Wanted to scream and scratch and bite until he promised to stay. But he couldn't stop him, and with his track record, he wouldn't be any use trying to save him, either.

"You said . . ." Cinn started, but his voice cracked, and he didn't trust himself to say anymore. {You said in the mountains that if I ever wanted to try kissing someone, I should do it with someone I trust.}

Eaon closed his eyes again, shoulders dropping, chest caving. He nodded. "I did."

With his eyes closed, Eaon couldn't see him sign, so Cinn braced himself and formed words once more.

"I trust you."

Goosebumps shivered down the back of his neck as Eaon rubbed his thumb across Cinn's cheekbone. "Thank you."

His experience with conversations like this was limited, but he thought that maybe Eaon would kiss him now. But he didn't. He sat there for a moment, breathing, before opening his eyes again. Caution ran rampant.

Cinn swallowed. {Is it Dearmead?}

"That's complicated. This is complicated. Is it alright with you if I love you both?"

If anything, Cinn found it endearing. Eaon's heart was so big. {I think it's wonderful. Do you need to ask Dearmead first?}

Eaon shook his head. "He knows. It's just that, I don't want you to do something you don't want to. You said you don't feel that way."

He still wasn't sure that he did. Whatever it was that drove Killian and Reigan into the bathroom, that drove Eavha to Aisling, he didn't understand it.

But he loved Eaon. He loved him and he was going to lose him.

{I don't want to never know what it's like.} He leaned closer. {But if you don't want to—}

"I want to."

Cinn smiled.

Placing both hands on Cinn's face, Eaon watched him for a moment. Excitement was so much like fear—his heart beat so fast he felt it in his fingers, the air on his skin was so warm—the world had shrunk to the two inches of space between them where everything that had ever mattered existed.

It was too much. It was so much, Cinn closed his eyes.

Eaon's lips were warmer than his hands, a gentle press. It was strange but pleasant, and Cinn found he didn't mind it in the slightest. Didn't mind that such a small gesture shut off every other thought in his brain, and for a moment, there was just this. Just him and Eaon.

And then it was over. Cinn opened his eyes as Eaon leaned back. Lowered his hands from Cinn's face to lace their fingers together again.

"You alright?"

Smiling softly, Cinn nodded.

"Thank you. For trusting me."

Raising their hands, Cinn kissed Eaon's knuckles and melted against his side. He needed a moment to switch his brain back on.

From across the room, Eavha stared, crestfallen. Maybe Cinn had said no goodbyes, but anyone watching knew what this was.

CHAPTER FIFTY-FIVE

AISLING

OVER AND OVER, AISLING PUT YASMIN AND HER COVEN THROUGH THEIR paces, making them turn their new, heavier mounts in tighter, tighter circles, making them drop on a whim, teaching them how to roll. The mechanics were the same as what they'd perfected on their cunaes, but response times were slower; they needed to command their mares a full second before they needed the movement. The coven were quick learners, though, and before long they were keeping up just fine, racing each other across the valleys.

They used the opportunity to check the traps the Mare-blessed had left, keeping clear of the mushroom ring marking where the fae had formed their circle. The power radiating off the ground, vibrating in the air, was disorienting. It was good practice though, experimenting with how far they could travel from the wall before they met interference. Where their weak spots would be when the army came up from the horizon, jagged with the spine's mountains.

It was up in the clouds that a spinning leaf found her, whispering incomprehensibly, desperate to reach her.

Catching it, Aisling brought it to her ear. Eavha's soft but panicked voice stopped her heart.

"Meet me at Neve's Inn as soon as you can. Please."

Stuffing the leaf into the neck of her armor, Aisling pushed Volya to catch up to Yasmin, shouting over the wind, "You'll have to excuse me! There's a situation I need to attend to!"

"Need help?" she called back.

"No, thank you."

With a nod, Aisling left the coven to practice their own maneuvers with the new size and muscle of their mounts and speared directly for the city.

~

Eavha sat on a wrought-iron bench outside Neve's Inn, her crown removed and resting beside her. She was chewing her fingernails, eyes rimmed in red and face stained with tears, and when she saw Aisling approaching, still dressed in full silver armor, she jumped to her feet.

"What happened?" she demanded, tying Volya's reins to a nearby lamppost. "Who upset you?"

"No." Eavha shook her head, causing the last of her curls to fall free. "No, nothing like that."

There was a drawl to her words that was too familiar. "Are you *drunk*?"

"No." Sulky. Defensive.

"You are. It's the middle of the afternoon and we are about to go to war, literally any minute. And you're—"

It was at that point that the rowdy laughter coming from inside the tavern made its way outside and Aisling realized it wasn't just Eavha, but a solid dozen or so people.

"That's what I said!" Eavha threw up her hands before dragging them down her cheeks. "But then everyone bullied me . . . It doesn't matter. Listen."

She looked around over her shoulder to the door left ajar, not as if she were making sure nobody could eavesdrop, but as if she were looking for someone.

Sure enough, the phouka came stalking out, yellow eyes narrowed into slits.

"What's going on?" he asked.

"I need to speak with both of you," Eavha explained, falling back into the seat and burying her face in her hands.

Aisling frowned, unsure what she had in common with the phouka that would require the both of them.

"I need your help," Eavha muttered. "With Eaon."

The phouka stilled. Aisling sat beside her and took one of her hands away from her face. "What's wrong?"

"He's still intending to unleash his blessing."

426

Feigning surprise with the lift of her brow, Aisling detested the taste of her silent lie. In one hand she balanced the divine move that was Eaon's unleashing, and in the other she held the bruised remains of her cold heart, begging her to take care of it just this once.

The phouka cursed.

"That's what I said!" A fresh swell of tears streamed down Eavha's face. Turning to Aisling, her big honey eyes pleading, she said, "You know the Lover better than anyone else here. Do you really think, even if Eaon did somehow outsmart the curse, that Death would just let him go? With everything at stake?"

She could offer nothing but the truth. "No."

"No," Eavha agreed. "And Moyra only said it *might* work. And she's so busy sucking up to him, trying to get him to like her, that she would say anything. She hasn't seen what letting in that power does to him. She doesn't understand the toll that taking almost eight-hundred souls and letting them pass through his body is taking. I know we have to win this battle, but using Eaon—"

"Eavha."

Aisling had to stop her. If she was going to conspire with Eaon to get him alone time on the battlefield, the least she could do was save Eavha the humiliation of begging for help.

It would be over. The moment Aisling confessed, she and Eavha would be over. This was a line that, no matter how kind a soul Eavha had, once crossed, could not be forgiven.

"I agree with you," Aisling said. "Using Eaon is not the way to win this."

Shuddering with relief, Eavha looked up to the phouka.

"He thinks he is smarter than everyone else and is such a self-sacrificing idiot . . . He's going to do this. Despite my screaming at him, he's going to do it. So . . . I need your help. Both of your help. I don't trust anyone else to do this; not even me."

"What do you need, little one?" the phouka asked.

"I need you to help me save him from himself."

CHAPTER FIFTY-SIX

EAON

A‌LL GOOD THINGS COME TO AN END.

Someone must have snitched on them because Miika came around, dragging Killian, Reigan and Tomaii back out to the fields. After that, one by one, people went hunting for food. To sober up, to fuel up, to enjoy what may be their last meal together.

Eaon wasn't hungry. He didn't remember the last time he was.

"You should eat," the phouka said, looking directly at Cinn. "I believe your brother and the demi-kin woman he's befriended are about to leave. You should join them."

If Cinn picked up on the severe undertones of impatience, he didn't show it, leaning out of the booth to locate Radley. Eaon heard it though.

{They are, too. You coming?} Cinn asked him.

"I don't know. Am I?" Eaon met the phouka's furious stare and quirked a brow.

"Your expertise is required in the palace."

The trick with fae was learning what a lie sounded like when it wasn't a lie.

Nodding, Eaon kissed Cinn's forehead. Chaste and soft, just like the one they'd shared earlier. He had felt the trembling in Cinn's body as their lips had touched and known he was overwhelmed. That was fine by Eaon. Anything more and he may have changed his mind.

"I'll find you later," Eaon promised, giving Cinn a little push out of the booth.

Familiar with the phouka's antics by now, Cinn rolled his eyes, squeezed Eaon's hand once more, and then let go.

Watching him go was Eaon's own version of a last meal.

"So, where are we really going?" he asked once he was sure they were alone.

"The palace," the phouka insisted. "Aisling has requested your opinion on a matter regarding the harbinger in her dungeon."

That . . . was not what he expected. Then again, Aisling knew full well what the phouka was capable of; this was likely an excuse so they could discuss the details of their plan. Frowning, playing his part, Eaon got to his feet and collected his crutch. Even if the phouka morphed into his horse form, it would take them a solid twenty minutes to reach the palace. Long enough, hopefully, for Eaon to come up with a way to get the phouka out of the room for a little while.

~

Armor set aside, dressed in a tight leather bodysuit, Aisling waited for them at the top of the stairwell that led to the underground dungeon. It was the place she was keeping Aadya, but it was also the place she had kept Cinn.

Eaon didn't want to see it.

In any other life, he would drag Aisling down there by her sweaty braid and put her in that tiny, cramped hole in the ground and let her die there.

"Trust me, I want to be in close quarters even less than you do," Aisling said, reading the murder on his face. "But the sun will be down in an hour or so, and this is urgent."

"What?"

"Aadya."

"What about her?"

Aisling closed her eyes. Took a breath. Opened them again. "It's easier if I show you."

Tilting his head, Eaon shifted his eyed quickly to the phouka and back. Aisling's only response was to dip her chin, turn her back, and begin the descent.

Taking the crutch, the phouka placed it aside and grabbed hold of Eaon's bicep, supporting his weight as they tackled the first step. "Let's get this done."

Down and down and down. Summer couldn't touch the stone walls, and even Eaon felt the cold seeping into his bones. This was a place of rot. Of misery and death. It coated the back of his throat like a sour medicine.

At the bottom, a faint light flickered, casting the rows of empty cells in a warm yellow glow.

"This way," Aisling said, standing in front of the open door of a cell.

This wasn't the place Cinn had described to him, but it would be close. Vivid images built from nightmares induced by Cinn's stories flashed by; a boy so skinny he shouldn't have the strength to stand let alone run, missing parts of his body and growing them back, over and over.

Guiding him forward, the phouka took him to the cell. Tall candles burned in the corner, a traveler's pack leaning against the wall, stuffed full. Eaon noted them without looking, because all he could see was the gibbet bolted to the floor. Door gaping wide, the cage was the size of a man, bars hatched with barely an inch between them. And on each bar, familiar spellmarks.

"What the fuck is this."

Aisling lifted her chin. "It's for your own good."

Before she finished speaking, a lash of power whipped from him, hungry for a kill. He hadn't meant to, but he didn't try to stop it. It didn't matter. The clawed hand clamped around his bicep tightened, twisted, pulling his arm behind his back. Eaon spun to face the phouka and was met with his other hand wrapping around Eaon's throat.

In the same beat, Eaon's back hit the iron bars, the door to the gibbet slammed closed, and his entire body went cold. His stuttering heartbeat was swallowed whole by the foreign rage that swelled beneath his skin—a beast in its own right. Sheer force of will was the only thing that kept the seed's claws retracted; Eaon knew from experience that the spellmarks carved along every bar would send any attack back into himself.

Aisling—the traitorous, two-faced, lying hag—turned and left without a word, but the phouka lingered. Eaon didn't shy away from his slitted eyes.

"I freed you, and this is how you repay me?" The words shook as fiercely as his body. Carefully, Eaon laced his fingers through the small holes between bars, pushing his weight against it. There was no give. There was no space. There was no air.

"You saved my life," the phouka acknowledged. "This is me saving yours."

Something feral pulled his upper lip into a snarl. Inch by inch, he felt himself sinking beneath his skin. This sentient force that dwelled within had grown stronger, sidling up beside him.

Remembering that cell at the bottom of the Northern Mountains, remembering the way the metal had rusted beneath his fingers, no more immune to Death's power than foliage, the magic reached out.

The snap of it back into Eaon's own soul was as painful as he expected it to be. Flinching back, physically, mentally, spiritually, the snarl that ripped from his throat was not his own.

The phouka stepped closer to the bars, looming. "Leave him."

Fight, something else whispered. Something that came from everywhere and nowhere.

Reason evaporated before he could question it. Like a candle blown out, there was only the inner darkness, and from within it, an undeniable rage.

There was no room to move, but that did not stop Eaon from throwing his head against the bars as hard as he could. Again and again and again. His brow split, vision beginning to spot.

"You will stop!" the phouka commanded, his own midnight fingers grasping the bars.

The magic inside Eaon shuddered at the force of the faerie command, but it only gave him pause for a second. Death did not bow. Not even to the Old Ones. And neither did Eaon.

"You are not strong enough to break this cage," the phouka said when he realized his commands held no power right now. "And you will take no lives from within. So if you can hear me, little witch, I give you this promise."

Leaving him for a moment, the phouka picked up the traveler's pack. The clack of bones from within was irrelevant; from the front pocket, he produced a glowing moonstone.

"I will be back. Should the worst happen, I will come back for you, and we will go somewhere no harm can find you. You are mine."

The magic shuddered again, making space for Eaon to find some self-control. Blinking dark, sticky blood from his eyes, he held the phouka's gaze. A weight settled, somewhere deep, somewhere intrinsic. These were not just words the phouka gave him. This was not just a promise. This was something cosmic. Something inevitable. The universe itself was shifting.

"Mine," the phouka repeated, the word barely more than an animalistic growl.

Eaon's lips were so cold they were numb, but he still managed to form a single word. "Mine."

The stars sung.

And the next words that appeared directly inside his head did not

431

come from that voice that was not a voice, from everywhere and nowhere. It was the phouka's voice.

You may call me Dhal.

Eaon was sensible enough to feel the weight of that name. A faerie's name. A true name. He was sensible enough to know the power a name could have.

"You are safe here," the phouka promised. "I will make sure your friends stay that way, too, out on the battlefield. But should you find yourself in danger, you need only call my name. Distance is not a barrier; I will hear you."

Eaon could only stare, not entirely sure he hadn't given himself a concussion. Not entirely sure why he had hurt himself to begin with. The phouka tightened his grip on the bars for a moment, then let go.

CHAPTER FIFTY-SEVEN

AISLING

Mother knew she hated herself.

The worst part was that she couldn't even be sure it was justified. The empty place in her mind reserved for Davina begged her to forgive herself, was proud that she had made a choice out of love, for once, instead of strategy. She'd have been proud of Aisling for putting their biggest weapon in a cage.

It didn't matter what Davina would have thought, though, because Davina was dead. Sacrificed to the moon, willingly, because for her, love and strategy were synonymous. And Aisling might have just wasted it.

Eavha was in the med tent again, waiting for an update on what the phouka and Aisling planned to do about her brother. Oblivious, and to remain so. Eavha said she didn't trust herself to do what had to be done; permission to keep her in the dark about it if Aisling had ever heard it. Still, she couldn't bear to look at her. Guilt and resentment were equal forces revolting in her belly.

How dare Eavha come floating into her life, into her war, offering things like love and peace, letting her taste nirvana when such things were not meant for her. How dare she make Aisling soft.

It couldn't continue.

Especially not as the phouka flapped his enormous wings to land on the parapet. "The first wards have been breached."

Aisling filled her lungs, deep and grounding. The sun had kissed the distant mountain peaks, night not far away.

The night.

Chaos was here.

"We'd best sound the horn, then."

There may have been two armies and half a mile of empty space between them, but Aisling was certain that somewhere on the other side of the valley, Byron was there, looking right back at her.

Equally as certain was the fact that Chaos was among them.

Her skin prickled with the enormity of his presence, her stomach aching at the magnitude of magic being used tonight. There was a balance between using enough magic to be adequately protected and too much that the witches would be incapacitated by it, and Aisling was riding that razor edge so close she wasn't sure if they hadn't in fact fallen to one side.

She had studied war for years, but there were no manuscripts that could truly prepare for the dread settling in her bones. She was afraid, but she was no more afraid of the violence than she was of death—both were staples of her diet. A princess of the Sparrow Coven was raised for bloodshed and cruelty in the name of righteousness. As queen, she was where she had always been going.

This was not the organized armies her grandparents had faced when fighting the Kinner, nor was it the guerrilla warfare her father had waged against the Anfar Forest Clan. It mattered not that she had never fought a real war before. It mattered not that her belly quivered, her knees weak. She had hardened against physical symptoms of fear a long time ago.

The beast army was intelligent enough to band together, but not enough to do so with any sense. The masses writhed, their seething snarls a dull echo from this distance. Scanning the skies, there was no hint of their aerial force, dragons or otherwise, but something would come. Yasmin and the others waited on their winged horses below; Aisling would join them soon. She could not both command and fight, and she knew which she needed to do. The commanders she had chosen to lead the ranks would keep things moving the way they had planned. She trusted them with that.

The cunae, as Yasmin expected, had returned, perched and quivering in the towers, their presence reminiscent of bats in a cave. If things went poorly, they would make for back up, though Aisling had no faith in their ability to withstand the incoming beasts.

The clear skies and countless stars, the tiny sliver of waxing moonlight, was a blessing paid for in blood, and Aisling sent a quiet prayer into the void for those generous souls' safe arrival in the after-realm. It was because of them that the Hyrschan forces had an advantage this night. It was because of them that the numbers were more evenly matched. Because of their sacrifice that, should the worst happen tonight, those who survived had an escape route.

Moyra's last working moonstone was tucked safely in the northern fountain—a rendezvous, and a last resort. Word spread quickly of the meeting place, but only a select few were trusted with the location of the stone; only those who Aisling thought had the wherewithal to wait rather than take it and run. Aisling herself could simply portal, assuming she wasn't too close to a burnout. Portal straight to the moonstone and wait for as many as she could.

A last resort she didn't want to need.

"What do you think?" Aisling asked, passing the spy glass to the witch beside her.

Kaelean Caesarea stood tall and unafraid, draped in a thin robe, the spellmarks drawn with soil on her face her only armor. The glistening of her beady black eyes and the wild anticipation curling her lip had Aisling questioning—not for the first time—how sane a witch could really be after a thousand years.

Taking the spyglass, Kaelean looked to where Chaos's army pushed and writhed within the confines of the faerie ring. Unlike the standard kind, where those who stepped across the threshold were hidden from view, this one was blinding from the inside, allowing Aisling a perfect view of the pain the smallest of fae were unleashing within. Sprites with twigs jumped out of the grass to stab them deep into lupanis eyes, while the traps the river clan had laid turned the ground to mud, sucking in the feet of cawkers, trapping them in place to be trampled.

"I have never seen beasts in such numbers." Kaelean's declaration should have been solemn, but instead, it was thick with smugness. "The more blood that spills, the more likely they are to turn on each other. The harbingers are fools to think they can control so many."

Aisling wasn't convinced. She had seen lupanis and shtryg, usually each other's nemeses, work in tandem back in Dusarn. Perhaps Chaos's presence, the will of their master, held some influence.

"Some may say the same about us," Aisling said. "Sparrows and Anfar and Kinner on the same side? Unfathomable."

The two females, both monarchs in their own right, stood in silence for a moment, watching the seething mass of beasts grow closer. Below, their own armies were assembling.

"Mother is close." Kaelean finally broke the silence. "She watches."

"The Lover, too," Aisling agreed, then prayed, "May they forgive us for the upheaval of their Balance this night."

Kaelean snorted as she shed her robe. "May *we* forgive having to fight this battle on their behalf."

Aisling stared, wide-eyed at such blasphemy, as Kaelean's body turned to clay. Backing away, she watched with fascinated awe as Kaelean grew and grew, the stone of the parapet creaking under her weight.

With a final nod, she left Kaelean and started for the stairwell downward. Volya waited, prancing with barely contained energy. Aisling stroked the mare's neck before climbing into the saddle.

Her next prayer was muttered inside her silver helmet.

"Lover, have mercy on us all."

CHAPTER FIFTY-EIGHT

OWEN

OWEN KNEW THE SILVER CHEST PLATE, THE GAUNTLETS, THE HELMET HE dressed in would be his burial shroud. The soft metal laced his shield and sword as well, but he had no intention of truly wielding them. No intention of stepping off the battlefield. Aisling thought she could bully him into doing whatever she wanted, but unbeknownst to her, this was what Owen wanted too.

To his left, the rebels were decorating their helmets with seven-pointed stars. Among them stood the kinner boy. Briefly, Owen entertained the fantasy that if, all those months ago, he had dragged that feral child out of the Copelands' house and back to the city like he was supposed to, that Nora would have lived. But it made no difference. He hadn't, and she didn't. Instead, the pale, freckled boy twirled a twine bracelet around and around and around, watching Radley Lightman show Cecelia how to paint a star.

"Hey," Radley said once Cecelia was ready, turning back to stop his brother's nervous fidgeting. "We're going to be fine. I'll know if you're in trouble, and you'll know it if I need help, too. We stick together. And if things go wrong, if we get separated, I'll meet you at the northern fountain."

Owen watched, so thoroughly empty, as Radley gripped his brother's hand, the charms on their matching bracelets clinking together. Watched Radley paint a star on Cinn's chest, too.

Once, Owen had been bewitched by the promise of that star. The promise that by endorsing it he could be absolved of his lifetime of sins. Its righteousness had tempted him into a world of rebellion against a ruler who had done no harm to him. Not yet.

Siobhan had taught him how to draw septagrams.

Deep down, he knew the surrogate and their baby should be reason enough to want to come back. He should want to find them. Yet, imagining the taut fabric of her dress against her swollen belly couldn't elicit a single beat in his dead heart.

A horn blew. One long sound that stilled the entire tent.

The beasts were on the horizon.

On Owen's right, the men and women he had trained with, both human and demi-kin alike, rose to their feet and slung their sparrow-adorned shields onto their shoulders. The rebels followed suit.

Owen couldn't feel his feet.

Commander Porter stepped forward, helmet tucked under his arm. The lines around his mouth deepened as he recognized Radley in the crowd, and when he spoke, the words seemed almost directed at him.

"In the name of the Mother, her Lover, and their Balance, may we stand united. By the end of this night, may we be so covered in beast blood that stars and sparrows become meaningless."

A few cheers went up, but Owen remained silent. So did Radley.

As they all began marching out to fill the front lines, Owen overheard Radley's muttering at Porter's side.

"Your sparrow was always meaningless. My star means you'd better watch your back out there, Commander Liar."

Cecelia smirked as she followed him the rest of the way outside.

Somewhere, in the same place he knew he should want to see his child born, he knew he should be pleased that Cecelia had found someone to match her energy. Had found a purpose outside Pirevia's arena.

Still unable to feel his feet, Owen stood. He was the last one out the tent, but he didn't make it very far. *Purpose*—the concept seemed foreign and nauseating, and Owen had to close his eyes against his stomach's revolt.

"Excuse me?"

The words were soft, even if the voice was far from. Owen opened his eyes to find a woman standing in the shadow of the tent, a small everlight glowing at her throat. The witch was unfamiliar to him—tall and lean, with dark skin and full curls, she wore robes of velvet green and bore no weapons beside the hard glint in her unusual eyes. They glowed from within, the colors turning slowly in a hypnotizing display of blue and brown.

"The medics tent is that way," Owen said offhandedly. It was clear she had no intention of facing the beasts.

"I know." Almost mocking, her lips pulled in a tight smile as she stepped closer. "I'm looking for someone, and I believe you may be the man to help me."

He doubted it. He was no help to anyone.

"So sad," she cooed, feet soft and silent on the ground, leaving no footprints in the earth behind her. "So lost. You mourn. I can tell."

"Who are you looking for?" Owen ground out.

Her smile turned knowing, sultry, as she stepped closer still. Closer, until her whisper couldn't possibly be heard by anyone other than him.

"Death not need be forever. It is only so because of Balance. Should that be broken, there would be no need to mourn."

Frowning, Owen leaned away. "What?"

"Help me tip the scales, Owen Turlough, and in return, I can help you. There is a way to bring back the dead. I know someone who can make the impossible happen. Who can turn order into chaos. Who can do whatever he pleases."

Blinking, Owen forgot how to breathe. Was she saying what he thought she was saying?

"Aren't you a Wyldeden witch?" he asked. "Shouldn't you be—"

"I am the rightful high priestess of Wyldeden, despite what some sneaky little foxes may think, and I will bring my people into a greater power. Aadya was very kind to take the fall for the both of us when we were discovered by those troublesome Nemuse brats, and the time has come to repay her that debt. You know where Aisling's secret dungeon is. Help me, and I will give you back Nora."

It wasn't that Owen couldn't breathe, there was just no air left in all of Nir.

Hope was a cruel thing.

"You're lying," he said. "It's impossible."

The witch only grinned. "In this world of Balance, maybe. In a world of Chaos, nothing is impossible. Isn't the possibility worth exploring? Isn't even a small chance of being reunited with your true love better than walking onto a battlefield to die? Maybe you'll find her in the after-realm, or maybe, once Chaos has his throne, I will resurrect Nora and leave you in eternity alone, out of spite."

It wasn't a choice. Not for Owen.

He didn't know much about witches or gods, but she had a point. What difference did it make to him if he died on the battlefield tonight or if he died chasing the lie that Chaos could give him back Nora? At least he would have tried.

"Alright. But . . ." He wavered, his chest aching as his heart tried desperately to beat. Maybe it was madness, but if there was even a possibility that Nora could come back, he couldn't wash their future down the drain. "There's a woman—Siobhan LaTour. I'll help you, but I want your oath that she will be protected."

From within her robes, the witch pulled out a small knife. In one quick motion, she sliced open her palm.

"A blood oath. I, Lorelei Messasure, swear on my life that Siobhan will remain protected until you are reunited with your true love."

No world was worth saving if he couldn't have Nora, and any world with her in it would be alright with him. Cutting open his own palm, he clasped Lorelei's hand.

~

Ever since the rebels had staged the rescue of the kinner boy, Aisling's dungeon within her dungeon was an open secret among those who wore the seven-pointed star. Only a handful of people had been involved in the actual, physical escape, but those who had survived it had been sure to tell whoever they could trust, lest someone end up there again.

So Owen knew where it was. He'd been so angry at the time because it was Siobhan who told him. His wife, second-in-command and loyal to the marrow, had not. There were days she had come home a little more haunted than others, but she had never told him why. It was how he gaged whether or not he could start prodding her to turn.

Now, as he led Lorelei down the dark stairwell, the idea of being angry with Nora for even a second seemed like such a waste.

The night outside was dark, but the dungeon was darker as they finally stepped onto the cold stone floor, and for a moment, Owen's brain was split in half. Leaving him to stew in the festering pit of his mind, Lorelei walked ahead, inspecting the barren cells. All the filthy hay strewn on the floors had been cleaned out, and in the moments Owen was present, he thought he saw candles burning. Scented, if the waft of lemon and honey could be trusted.

It was that—a smell that had no reason to exist in a place like this—

that anchored him. He was fairly sure aromatherapy wasn't standard in Sparrow prisons, especially empty ones.

Almost empty ones.

Lorelei passed the unlocked cell and smirked, moving on toward the end of the row, but Owen took pause. Would he have, if the fog of his own emptiness hadn't been fed a single seed of hope? Would he have noticed or cared that, alone in a cell was a spellmarked gibbet, imprisoning a tall but gangly boy? Barefoot, clothes dark with sweat, his face was hollow and gaunt, spotted with blood as he stared through the small holes in the bars.

"Come on," Lorelei hissed. "We don't have much time."

Dragging himself away stirred the ghost of Owen's morality, but he did it, taking the lead to the cell with the broken door.

"You need magic to open it," Owen told her.

"Not a problem." Lorelei smiled.

Dipping her fingers into her pockets, they came out stained in dirt. He didn't bother watching her unlock the hidden entryway, and opted to stay above ground rather than follow her farther. The smell down there was better suited to a sewer, like the one he'd been born in.

Stepping back out of the cell, he covered his mouth and nose with the hem of his shirt and stumbled closer to one of the burning candles.

A soft cough drew his gaze back toward the gibbet.

Owen was moving before he could think about it. He told himself it was because anything Aisling wanted locked away at a time like this would be a boon for the other side—the side Owen was apparently now on. It had nothing to do with hating cages. Absolutely nothing to do with the darkness twisting present and past. Nothing at all to do with a smuggler named Damien Turlough stopping outside his mother's cage, amid all the screams for help.

"Can you keep quiet?" Owen asked the boy.

Recognition flitted through his eyes, but he didn't speak. Only nodded.

A key dangled from a hook on the wall. Owen kicked the large backpack out of the way and took it. The boy recognized him, but Owen couldn't seem to remember anything that didn't revolve around Nora. It didn't matter. He unlocked the gibbet and threw the padlock aside.

The boy didn't come out immediately. Eyes darkening, skin turning ashen, he simply mouthed the word "go."

A small nod, and Owen left the boy to wreak his havoc.

CHAPTER FIFTY-NINE

EAON

FOR ONCE, THE LOVER'S BLESSING WAITED. AS IF IT KNEW. AS IF IT were privy to Eaon's decision, his promise that the seed could feed to its heart's content very soon.

Everything happened for a reason. He was born Morvish in a place where such magic could not be trained, and in binding it, his da ensured he was the perfect candidate for possession. His family died, he died, so Eavha could bring him back. So the Lover could see him, choose him, and plant their seed in his soul. All of it, so that when this day came, Eaon could stand between the people he loved and their enemy. So that Death could take his body and defend the one they loved too.

And wasn't that just perfect? Wasn't that exactly who he was, who he needed to be—the one to do the undesirable work for the sake of the people. It was what he had been trained to do since the day he came home with a slip of parchment, the word "laborer" scrawled neatly across it.

Stepping out of the cage, his skin tingled. His lips were numb as he glanced to the door where Owen and Lorelei had disappeared. Something about their being down here didn't sit right, but with Eaon's tonics suppressing his Morvish intuitions, he couldn't see any fate lines. And he didn't have time to care.

Every step he took toward the phouka's escape stash sent a pang of pain through his thigh. He couldn't crouch, so he leaned awkwardly against the wall, rifling through the pack until he found the moonstone hidden within; the phouka's escape plan for if everything went to shit.

It wouldn't. Eaon would make sure of that.

Leaving the rest of the supplies, one painful step at a time, Eaon dragged himself to the stairwell and climbed his way to the small room attached to the throne room where prisoners were kept waiting. Even from here, he could feel how empty the palace was. Not a soul lingered on the grounds, or anywhere in the city beyond. Everyone in Hyrsch had either evacuated or gathered at the western boundary.

Through the tiny, barred window, the smallest sliver of waxing moon was visible. The stone in his palm glowed from within.

Just tell it where you want to go.

There were so many places he wanted to go.

But only one where he was needed.

The moonlight spat him out onto muddy grass, the warm night air thick and tingling with magic and humidity. The sheer force of the spellmarks behind him left him weak-kneed and nauseous, but the faerie ring that lay before him was a tantalizing promise of oblivion. Of darkness and warmth where he could wander forever and never be found.

Within the ring, writhing beasts were crushed by their own masses as they scrambled for a way out, clawing and biting at each other for an inch of space. There was no intelligence, no order, just utter rage and hunger that promised to devour everything in its path.

Except one.

Eaon had read about the beasts native to Bernt during his travels—the polpags had exoskeletons reminiscent of a beetles, if beetles were seven feet tall with pincered limbs proportional like spiders legs. A polpag had pushed its way through the chaos and stood at the ward line nearest Eaon, inspecting it. Any moment it would realize what was happening and break its way out, and then all that rage, all that hunger, would swarm toward where his friends, his family, waited to fight.

There was no sign of the harbingers. No sign of dragons, yet, or of Chaos himself. They had sent their rabid animals ahead to set off any traps, likely watching from higher ground to see what they were up against.

That was who Eaon wanted. Those were the souls he wished to take. He had asked the moonstone to take him directly there, but perhaps the moonlight couldn't reach them where they hid. Perhaps this was as close as he could get.

It would have to be close enough.

The blessing inside him stirred, and Eaon didn't bat it down. He could feel its ravaging hunger searching, counting, deep into the masses. He wanted the harbingers. He wanted the rogue who had taken Dearmead. He wanted to taste that filthy soul down his gullet, absorbed into his own, changing him. Preparing him.

Pure death swelled, a hurricane confined in the jar of his flesh, its *need* turning his skin ashen, eyes pits of black as the void shone through. The Lover was close, their warmth only a breath away.

Take him, Eaon begged, picturing the particular harbinger he hated most. It was all he asked in exchange for his body. *Take them all.*

With permission granted, Death blew out of him in an arc that left nothing but brittle dust in its wake. It punched through the faerie wards like they were made of cobwebs and devoured the beasts trapped inside with lethal efficiency.

The first soul to hit Eaon was that of the polpag. It tasted like acid, yet filled him with a euphoria unmatched by any substance he'd ever sampled. Pleasure and pain ripped him apart as another soul hit, and another— dozens in seconds, so fierce and foul and lovely that Eaon lost the strength to stand.

He didn't feel the ache of his poorly healed bones as his knees hit the ground, eyes fluttering against the onslaught of power and weakness, of bliss and agony, of ecstasy and dread.

He didn't see the army falling, but he felt it. Felt every fiber of his being, his essence, his soul, melting away like ice under fire.

All the pain he usually turned in on himself was unleashed, and where it used to claw and shred at him, there was only comfort. A warmth that was not fire, but a soft hand against his cheek. The promise of rest.

You do not need to be afraid, the Lover whispered inside him. *Let me embrace you. Let me embrace the world, so you can rest.*

There was no deceit in the words. The Lover would give them all a peaceful eternity of slumber; all Death needed was to meet Chaos on a level playing field, in a realm they could exist in together, and all they needed in order to do that was Eaon.

The Lover would trap Chaos in his mortal form, the way the kinner were trapped in theirs, and then Death would lay waste to the world. Cleanse it. Take away everything that Chaos wanted so badly; his planet, his toys. Confined in his mortal flesh and deprived of any means to wreak his mayhem, he would not be able to follow Mother and Death to the new world they would build. One where her creatures would not suffer pointless cruelty.

One Eaon would never see.

He would never see what lay beyond Nir's border. None of them would. Cinn, who had only just found his family, would never have the chance to *live*. His sister would never see her quarter-century. And Dearmead . . .

The souls passing through him were endless. He didn't know how many he had taken. Forcing his eyes open, the ring of remains around him stretched so deep he could not see movement.

That was all that would be left.

The glowing flowers that only grew in the deep pit of the Northern Mountains gorge would be gone. The glistening crystal caves beneath Bernt. The towering, sentient trees of the forest, the sharp black desert shrubs of Dusarn, the sapphire waters of the Heart Lake. There would be no more dancing around the bonfire. There would be no more secret kisses behind waterfalls. There would be no more cinnamon biscuits.

Eaon pulled his face away from the Lover's gentle hand and grit his teeth.

Pulling all this power back in was going to hurt.

You cannot deny me. Our union is inevitable.

"Go rogue," he spat, tasting blood on his tongue.

Magic spilled in a violent torrent, its tendrils reaching all the way to the other side of the faerie ring. There were still so many beasts. Polpags. Harpies. Shtryg. Dragons.

Harbingers.

Chaos himself.

Just a few more, Eaon compromised, shuddering against the chill in his bones. It was easy to want more. His power may come from the Lover, but it was a beast in its own right. Ravenous. Insatiable. It would take and take and take—

Then it stopped. Like a rabid dog hitting the end of its leash, his power came to an abrupt halt, turned, and retreated. Spooling back in on itself, tunneling back through his skin, it returned to the void gaping inside him.

The need for more fell away.

Finally, it was satisfied.

Seven hundred and seventy-seven.

It would not take another.

There was no pain.

There was no cold.

Eaon's panting breaths were the only sound for one whole minute before the world began to rumble with the stampede coming his way. Squinting into the dark, Eaon could see a swarm of shadow swallowing up the ashes, the wards of the faerie ring utterly destroyed.

Eaon's legs shook as he climbed to his feet. He had not brought a weapon. Wasn't even wearing any armor. Barefoot and swaying, he would never make it back to the front lines.

Seven hundred and seventy-seven souls. If he died right now, it was over.

This had been a mistake.

Behind him, a piercing shriek. Eaon turned to look. The phouka had taken to his bird form, plummeting toward him, but he wasn't going to make it. Not even the dragon taking wing from behind the city wall—too soon, she was showing their hand too soon—had any hope of reaching him before the swarm of shtryg did.

Along the parapet of Hyrsch's last line of defense, everlight began burning. Their numbers before had been alarming, but now . . . maybe they stood a chance.

If only it mattered.

Eaon heard panting breaths behind him.

The first of the beasts had arrived.

Eaon closed his eyes.

CHAPTER SIXTY

DEARMEAD

His lead on the swarm was only by seconds. Be it panic or rage, elation or disbelief, every hint of exhaustion evaporated as Dearmead burst from the tree line, his bare feet kicking up chilled dust in his wake. To the right, shtryg blew across the empty battlefield toward the lone figure climbing to his feet. To the left, Hyrsch's walls were lit up with thousands of tiny, twinkling lights. They reflected off the feathery spear of pure black racing across the sky, followed by the booming flaps of a dragon.

His friends had a dragon.

There wasn't enough air in his lungs to loose the crow of manic joy bubbling inside him. There wasn't even enough to pant Eaon's name. He could feel the vacuum of the shtryg descending as Dearmead turned his last few steps into a leap.

They hit the ground hard. Dearmead heard the breath rush out of Eaon, crushed beneath him, but the jeering cries of the shtryg soon drowned out everything else. Laying his body over Eaon's, Dearmead endured the raking claws down his back. He could not move under the weight of their presence, but he did not panic; Vy's feral battle cry sounded just as light pushed through the masses. Shtryg shrieked as Vy skidded on her knees to Dearmead's side, slamming the butt of her torch into the earth. It wasn't much protection, but it was enough to give them space to move.

Dearmead pushed against the lingering weight of the shtrygs' vacuum, lifting himself off Eaon to check he was still alive.

Amber eyes, wide with shock, stared up at him.

On his cheek, just below his eye, blistered a mark Dearmead had never seen before, dark as the void.

"Hey," Dearmead managed.

"Hi."

A new sound shook the ground; one Dearmead was too familiar with. A tremendous roar that rattled his bones was their only warning, and then the light of their torch became pitiful as dragon fire scarred the ground. Shtryg became fleeing pillars of flame as the swarm parted.

Their shadows had been hiding what ran beneath.

Lupani were only feet away.

Dearmead met the crazed, hungry eyes of the nearest and braced himself. Vy screamed her millennia of rage at the beasts and hoisted Mustavrick's scythe over her head. Behind her, the phouka collided into the ground and a silver-clad soldier dismounted with a roll, nimbly springing up to swing his sword at the lupanis leaping for Dearmead. With unnatural ease, the silver blade carved through the beast's neck like soft butter.

Poignantly aware that the spear strapped to his back had lost its silver tip, Dearmead lowered himself back down and tucked Eaon's head into his chest. It was all he could do.

A beetle-beast was next to step out of the swirling storm of shtryg shadow surrounding them, one long pincered limb spearing for the phouka. With a *pop*, the giant black raven was replaced by the goat-headed man, who bellowed fiercely, catching the beast's pincer in his hands and tearing it right off its body.

Something bit down on Dearmead's foot. His scream was more of rage than pain as he looked back and kicked at the cawker. Another was trying to peck Eaon's bare feet, chasing them as Eaon flinched away.

Dearmead couldn't stay down. Being a meat blanket wasn't going to be enough to protect Eaon. Keeping low, he raised himself into a crouch and pulled the staff from his back, smacking the cawker latched on his foot with enough force to snap its neck. He batted at the other one but it lacked the same strength, and without silver, without it being *his* spear, the weapon was little more than a glorified stick.

And then a lupanis's head bowled over the carnivorous turkey and the silver-clad soldier swung his sword to finish it off. There wasn't time to thank him; another lupanis loped their way.

The silver-clad soldier dropped his sword in front of Dearmead and snatched his staff out of his hand. Swiping low in a very Wyldeden maneuver, he knocked the approaching lupanis off its feet, punched it in the face, ripped off his helmet, and used it to bash in the beast's skull.

Cinn.

Dearmead blinked once before picking up the sword. It was still an uncomfortable weight in his hands, but with Eaon curled up on the ground at his feet, he needed the silver.

A salamander slithered into their circle of light—not one of the overgrown ones, but it was still half as high as Dearmead. One scratch, and the venom would eat through Eaon quickly.

Dearmead swung in a fierce upward stroke. Too early. His overcompensation for the blade's weight meant it cut the beast's face off instead of slicing through its neck. Still lethal.

Cinn let a lupanis leap at him, dropping below it and using the beast's momentum to send it rolling. A boot to its throat was more brutal than it should have been, all the silver armor making every punch, every kick, so much harder. A shtryg caught hold of Vy's wrist, its shadows pushed back by the torchlight to reveal gray skin blistering from exposure. Still, it held on. Dearmead couldn't leave Eaon, but Cinn whistled sharply and threw his helmet to Vy, who caught it in her free hand and bludgeoned the shtryg into letting go.

Another all-consuming roar of dragon fire lanced the earth. Cinn, Vy and the phouka closed ranks with Dearmead, forming an unkillable ring.

"Get him out of here!" Dearmead shouted to the phouka over the deafening screams of beasts, swinging his sword at a burning beetle-beast stumbling out of the shadows.

He cut one pincer clean off but was too slow to stop the second from piercing through his leg. Breathless and crumpling, he dropped the blade onto the offending limb. Cinn took the sword and left him with a small silver dagger instead, keeping another lupanis back while Dearmead wrenched the pincer out of his body.

"There's no clear path!" the phouka called back, catching a leaping cawker midair and snapping its neck.

They were surrounded on all sides by the black vacuum of shtryg, a writhing mass of beasts beneath. Dragon fire burned in patches, but it was as if the beast knew one of them wouldn't survive a stray blast. If only they could get a clear shot at the sky, the phouka could take Eaon straight up and out, but there just wasn't room.

Vy bludgeoned the skull of a salamander, hissing at the wound closing slowly across her abdomen. It didn't stop her from spinning at the sound of Cinn's pained cry as a lupanis got a claw in the gap of his chest plate. Dearmead spun to take her spot in the defensive circle as she lunged, slamming the helmet down on the lupanis's leg, then up under its canine chin, snapping its head back with so much force the beast fell paralyzed.

Without a second to pause, Cinn turned to smack a ratki with the flat of his sword, stumbling from his own wound. Dearmead stuck the dagger into the creature's jugular, swiped up his abandoned spear and skewered another one trying to sneak up. Doing so left his back exposed, and fresh claws sunk in. The phouka dug his own into the new lupanis and ripped it off, throwing the beast back into the shadows.

Dearmead had never fought like this. He had trained as part of a unit, but this . . . the four of them watching each other's backs as they shredded and cut and ripped . . .

This was what Aisling had wanted a kinner army for.

The four of them were holding their own in the midst of a swarm of beasts, keeping the one mortal being among them safe. Imagine what a hundred could have done.

"Cover me!" Cinn called.

Without waiting, he dropped to his knees and crawled to Eaon.

Dearmead was too busy to see what Cinn was doing, but when Cinn used the phouka as a launch pad to throw himself on the back of a beetle, he was missing a large chunk of his armor.

"Go!" he called out as he drove silver-tipped gauntlets into the beetle's eyes.

Dearmead swung his weapon to clear space as the fae returned to his bird form, grabbed a silver-clad Eaon in his talons, and took wing. Cinn dropped back to the ground and held his sweaty undershirt sleeve against the small fire still burning on their planted torch, eyes hard with a mottled blue-green rage that Dearmead had seen time and again the last few weeks. Gritting his teeth, Cinn let his shirt catch alight, then ran with his fists flying toward the beasts getting too close to the phouka and Eaon.

Dearmead turned off his brain.

He let his training take over. Puss-white blood soaked him, the smell of burning flesh filled his nose, black feathers fell as a claw caught the phouka's wing, but Vy tackled the beast to the ground, holding the helmet with two hands and bringing it down on its head, over and over and over.

There was no room to worry about being overwhelmed. There was no time to think about pain. There was only the next cut. The next kick. The next swing. There was only Cinn, his shirt burned away, pinned to the ground under a lupanis, and Dearmead's sword opening up the beast's belly before it could get its claws into Cinn's abdomen. There was only the beetle knocking the sword away, and Vy throwing him her helmet instead. There were only the cawkers finally knocking down their torch, plunging them into near darkness. Only the shtryg swarming, and Vy disappearing into them, and Cinn's feral screaming as he grabbed a dismembered pincer from the ground and beat the beasts off her.

And then there was the deep rattle of a dragon's breath, leathery wings blocking out what little of the sky they could see.

CHAPTER SIXTY-ONE

KAELEAN

As soon as the phouka had Eaon out of the melee, Kaelean turned back in their direction, sucking down enough air to fuel the fire burning in her throat.

Oh, how she loved this form. It was as if Mother had made dragons just so Kaelean could become something that truly felt like *her*.

She'd meant to keep this new form of hers a secret until the harbingers showed themselves, hoping the shock of being faced with one of their own beasts would give them an advantage. Instead, she'd spent the past fifteen minutes carving arcs of fire in strategic patterns to hold back the stream of escaped beasts, giving the kinners time to get Eaon out.

Stupid boy.

As soon as that tiny flash of moonlight had appeared on the battlefield, she knew who it was. Cinn had known who it was. The phouka had sworn in his old fae language, and she didn't need to understand to know his vocabulary cowed her own.

She couldn't go to Eaon while he was bleeding death all over the place. The phouka could. Cinn could. Perhaps it was shock that kept them standing there while Eaon detonated.

If they survived this, Kaelean was going to throttle him.

But for now, she rallied the wildfire that made up the very essence of this beast she'd consumed and unleashed it without restraint. A satisfying scream of rage that scorched the valley, gouging down to the bedrock where it turned stone molten. The ash of those caught in her fiery release would salt the earth; a wound she would break her bones to rectify later, though she liked to think Terra would forgive her this once.

Burning a path from where she'd last seen the kinners all the way to the wall—or at least as close as she dared let the fire get to the soldiers waiting—Kaelean banked hard so she could watch the three of them, wounded and burning, limping and healing, fight their way out of the throng of beasts scattering under the heat and light of her wrath. Though the smoldering earth scalded their feet and blistered their skin, they ran along the demarcated line to relative safety. Somewhere they could replenish their armor and catch their breath.

It hadn't been exaggeration when she said she'd never seen so many beasts gathered in one place before. Never seen them so focused, so uncaring of the harm that came to them as they crushed themselves against the impromptu wards her fae allies were trying to throw up in the wake of the ring's destruction. A swarm not unlike a bee colony, a million mindless bodies in sync under the whim of their queen. Or in this case, a brutish king.

The kinners' return to the war tents signaled the return to plan; a hundred tiny flames appeared along the parapet, casting a faint glow over the faces of the Igni-blessed. As one, they released their burning arrows. Arcs of fire rose and fell, descending into the mass of scales and teeth; lupani, frothing at the mouth, and behind them, hordes of salamanders the size of horses, their weight crushing the bones of their fallen brethren. Shiny, beetle-shelled polpags stalked cautiously behind the feral front lines, and among them all, a cloud of writhing shadow—shtryg.

The archers aim was precise, their arrows' silver tips slicing through cawkers like butter. One good shot speared straight through a salamander's eye, lodging in the back of its skull. Its collapsed form was nothing but another hurdle to jump to the lupanis scrambling behind it.

As the fire from the first volley petered out, a second rained down.

Soaring above it all, Kaelean felt the first signs of fatigue setting in. It was a lesson learned as she'd flown down the length of the spine; the problem with being so big was that she tired quickly. Then, it hadn't mattered. She knew she could rest once she reached Hyrsch, but here and now, she had to pace herself.

The archers could hold the line. Kaelean waited for the gap between rounds of arrows before folding in her wings and diving for the ground. Body turning to clay, she was herself again within seconds of her feet touching grass.

While her dragon rested, she would fight the way she'd won her wars before. Terra was, after all, a fiercer spirit than Mother could ever hope to be.

Crouching low, burying her hands in the earth, Kaelean took in the spill of beasts breaking through the fae's desperate wards, disintegrating beneath the shtryg pouring in a sea of shadow.

She had a second. Observing her allies sprinkled all down the hill—nymphs with grassy hair and stockpiles of rocks; tiny sprites tiptoeing around the near invisible spellmarks carved into the ground—her attention caught on one in particular. Hunched among them all, swamp-reed hair hanging down to her waist and a cape of hawthorn flowers spread behind her, Kaelean recognized the swamp hag from Vertlyn. Judging by the black-toothed grin the hag gave her, the Old One recognized her too.

Lowering her lips to the soil, Kaelean whispered her prayer.

"Spirit of the earth, from thee I am descendent and to thee I give my all. Terra, keeper of our foundation, bless me once more. Take my enemies."

Beneath her hands, the earth roiled like a tempestuous sea. The shtryg were unaffected, but the lupanis and salamanders slinking in their shadows relied on the ground; it clung to them, dragging them beneath the surface inch by inch until it swallowed them whole. Their panicked clawing only forced them down faster, but Kaelean dug her hands deeper into the soil, muttering her prayer over and over, just to be thorough.

Hissing in her own fae language, the hag buried her hands in the soil too, and from the quicksand Kaelean had made, roots speared into the air, wrapping around the shtryg to slam them into the hungry earth.

The ash of their bones may be poison, but it was balanced by the fresh flesh delivered for Terra to fertilize herself with.

Learning quickly, a cawker flapped its wings, unable to attain flight but able to hop across the liquid ground with relative ease. Finding solid earth gave it no respite though; the nymphs and sprites attacked with all the fury of the scorched forest, stabbing twigs into its eyes and bullying it onto a spellmark. Kaelean watched as the cawker fell into one of the river-clan's traps, its squawking silenced as water gurgled up its throat to spill from its beak, its eyes and ears. For a second, it convulsed where it fell. Then it was still.

Life may be Mother's most sacred gift, but Kaelean would not mourn the beasts. Kari, she would atone for, but not the cawker. Not the ratki that hopped across the drowning salamanders' backs. Not the shtryg, tangled in the hag's vines, wrinkled gray flesh consumed into the ground even as its shadow cloak dissipated. They chose their fate when they sided with the harbinger who burned her forest.

As much as Kaelean would have loved to drag the entire army underground, her reach only went so far. And there was only one hag. Shtryg were slipping past, lupani and polpags sneaking around the patches of earth devouring their comrades. The nymphs had no fear, smashing skulls with rocks, encasing any injured beast in a net of grass and dragging them back to the quicksand, but they were delicate things. One blow from a lupanis was enough to tear the field nymphs in two, their bodies transforming into boulders upon impact. The number of small branches and random piles of petals suggested sprites had found similar fates.

It didn't stop the rest from pushing forward, and Kaelean swore that if she ever got a chance to rebuild Anfar, to bring Wyldeden back, she would find a safe place for the sprites and nymphs too. She had misjudged them, nine hundred years ago.

Before Kaelean had time to worry about the beasts getting past, the front lines of the Hyrschan army moved forward.

Who knew that Nir's inhabitants could rally like this. For a millennia, Kaelean had warred against other clans, against humans and beasts and fae and rogues. For over a millennia before her birth, there had been no peace. Kinner and demi-kin and Fair Folk had fought, beside each other and against each other, over territory, over philosophy and theology. And yet, on this night, none of it mattered.

On the same field where Aisling waited with the sky coven, Cinn had found new armor, rejoining Dearmead and the strange kinner woman once more at the front line. Following him, two demi-kin—Radley, from the south, and Cecelia, from the north—joined other Hyrschan rebels bearing shields for Sparrow soldiers, pressing back against an enormous salamander. At their side, Wyldeden guardians threw their spears with alarming precision as the shtryg closed in, downing the vile beasts before their vacuum could take effect.

Was this what Yomra saw, when she asked Kaelean to let her die? This unity? Was this what her sacrifice had been for?

From the city wall, a horn blared, alerting the sky coven that their moment had come. Kaelean turned her head to watch as the remaining members of Yasmin's sky coven sent their new mounts galloping. Soaring. And among them, Aisling flew.

Between the fae and the army, there were thousands on the ground.

Only nine took to the sky.

Refreshing her spellmarks, the change only took a moment. Kaelean shook her large head and stretched her wings, taking to the stars once more.

CHAPTER SIXTY-TWO

AISLING

THERE WERE A DOZEN HARPIES ALREADY IN THE SKY BY THE TIME Aisling got Volya airborne. In the minutes it took to pass the masses of her army, hundreds of winged beasts had joined them. The faerie ring had broken apart, but it had done its job; the beasts hadn't seen what Aisling had prepared until it was too late, and as the first harpies saw the fae and the front lines cutting down their ground-bound brethren, they hesitated.

Axe drawn, Aisling didn't.

With the sky coven in formation around her, the nine of them plowed into the enemy's midst, the silver of their armor better than a battering ram. Trusting Aisling to protect her wings, Volya brought her right into striking range, the twirl of her blade the first of many.

Keep swinging, keep moving. Calculated blasts of air kept the harpies back as they began to orient themselves, to swarm, swallowing the coven whole. The beat of wings and shrieking cries drowned out the sky coven, but they didn't need to communicate to know what to do. Yasmin flew point, and the rest followed with unwavering faith, blasting their way out of the cocoon of feathers and claws over and over.

There were just so many, though. As many in the skies as they had on the ground. Too many for the nine of them to fight individually.

A streak of fire, and the next group of harpies descending on the coven became ash. Banking sharply, Yasmin led them away from the worst of the heat, but Aisling still scowled across at where Kaelean flew behind them.

Not a single beast bothered her; in fact, as the harpies realized the dragon was not one of theirs, they scattered.

"We're never going to get anywhere like this!" Yasmin shouted, using the reprieve to drop back to Aisling's side. "We can keep going, but we're going to run out of steam before they run out of bodies to throw at us."

Kaelean spewed another plume of fire, but the harpies were giving her a wide berth, darting out of danger's way.

Aisling knew what had to be done.

"I'm going to do it now," she warned Yasmin.

Wild eyed, the alpha nodded, falling back. No question. No doubt. They had discussed waiting until the harbingers revealed themselves, but Aisling had a feeling that so long as their front lines were pushing ahead, the hybrid traitors would wait.

Squeezing Volya with her thighs, Aisling put some distance between herself and the coven. Arrows flew past her, skewering anything that got too close as Aisling put her axe away and rallied her reserves.

Even covered in leather and silver, she knew the exact shape of every tattoo on her body. Felt them prickling as she turned her attention inward.

She had not trained enough. She knew she hadn't. The small, secret moments she had stolen to experiment had left her afraid of what would happen if she lost control. Fear had made an idiot of her, wasting the time she'd been given worrying about doing it wrong, of burning herself out before time. Having Davina's ghost watching over her had been the only thing keeping her sane over the past six years, but it had also been a pressure to not squander her sacrifice. But, if there was one thing Aisling had learned from the incorrigible healer she never meant to fall in love with, it was that, while training and practice were worthwhile endeavors, sometimes a witch had to take a risk. Had to embrace the caged thing that beat in her chest. Had to set it wild and trust it knew what to do.

It was time to see exactly what the gifts Davina had given her were capable of.

Her spine tingled as the line of spellmarks down it sunk deeper into her skin, the weight of them across her shoulders curling her over. Her bones trembled and creaked under the force brewing, the armor on her back restrictive but necessary.

Around her, the air came to a complete still—paused to consider what Aisling was asking of it.

The flapping that filled the night sky became deafening as winged beasts and horses struggled with the sudden lack of current. Maybe grounding the harpies and gryphin would be enough. Maybe she didn't have to risk this thing Davina had marked her body to do.

"There!"

The call wasn't meant for her, yet Aisling looked to where one of Yasmin's coven pointed.

In the far distance, the last lines of Chaos's army shadowed the crest of a hill. Three large shapes, larger than anything else on the battlefield below, pushed up into the sky.

Three dragons. Three harbingers.

With the hundreds of harpies and gryphin crowding in, more and more taking wing every second, Aisling would never be able to focus long enough to deal with the biggest threat beside Chaos himself.

She had to clear the skies.

"Get back to the wall!" Aisling called out.

Yasmin whistled, sharp and clear into the night, and the coven fell back.

Stroking the strip of unarmored shoulder where Volya's wing began, Aisling whispered, "Just like we practiced, girl."

Finally, making its decision, the still air stirred. Celeste kissed her cheek before whipping by, drawing the summer humidity upward. The stars that had shone so brightly in the clear sky winked out, disappearing behind thick cloud blooming like an ink spill. Aisling's abdomen tightened as the spellmarks there darkened and burned, cramping so fiercely her hips came up off Volya's back. Pressure curled her into a ball as she prayed again, closing her eyes, trusting Volya as they swooped away from panicking harpies making desperate grabs for her, the rest chasing after the sky coven—directly into the archers' range.

Only Kaelean followed Aisling into enemy airspace, and in their wake, the storm cloud thickened. Thundered. The updraft tugged at the wagons forced to halt, beasts hunkering against the punishing wind that spun faster and faster until the black cloud came down to meet it. As the two forces kissed, Aisling released a cry of relief. The weight on her shoulders lifted, the cramp in her belly dropped; her body whole body arched as the up and downdrafts of the storm she'd made chased each other into a tight funnel.

Whinnying, Volya fought against the pull of the wind. Aisling grit her teeth and *pushed*, forcing an unnatural current to help. But where they flew, the small tornado followed.

Alright. She could play that game, too.

Kaelean bellowed for attention before climbing her way higher into the sky, disappearing into cloud cover. Good. Aisling had never done this before and she had no idea what kind of control she had over this force of nature; by its size, she didn't think the tornado could do too much damage to a dragon of Kaelean's stature, but it was still safer for her allies to distance themselves.

Sweating, Aisling urged Volya onward, leading her storm on a path of destruction through the mass of beasts below. Narrow but powerful, it sucked harpies and gryphin alike into its vortex, spitting them out mangled and broken. Watching over her shoulder, Aisling shook her head.

She did that.

She really did that.

Light-headed, she lay down over Volya's back and gasped down a breath. She felt fragile and insubstantial, like a wispy cloud. The gush of magic slowed to a trickle; forcing it any further was going to kill her. The spellmarks on her skin stopped burning as Aisling called them to stop, shouting over the wind for Volya to take her back to their side of the valley.

She needed a moment. Needed to rally. She needed Eavha to lay hands on her.

CHAPTER SIXTY-THREE

KILLIAN

RELEASE, REACH BACK, NOCK, DRAW, AIM, RELEASE.

He had been practicing this single, fluid movement his whole life. To his left, Miika was a mirror. Behind them, Tomaii and Reigan swallowed mouthfuls of liquor before banging on their chests, spewing fire onto the arrow heads, passing them forward at exactly the right moment, without fail, every time.

Silver was not naturally flammable. It didn't matter. Ignatius burned in his friends' blood, and his fire was irrefutable.

Reach back, nock, draw, aim, release.

Fire rained down on the cloud of shadow, scale, and claw. Even from the top of the parapet he could hear the beasts' vicious screeching, hungry for the fae turning the land into a weapon, and hungry for the army behind them. He could hear the bellowing of the witches, demi-kin and humans alike who stayed to protect their home, and he heard the terror of those who dropped their shields and ran. There were too many of the latter. If Aisling's commanders were calling them back, their voices were drowned out under the sea of violent sound.

Reach back, nock, draw, aim, release.

Killian's aim was true, but it didn't have to be exact, even with Yasmin and the coven in the skies. The shields Celeste provided would redirect any stray arrows.

It only helped him breathe a little easier as Aisling loosed a tornado behind enemy lines.

Killian had never seen anything like it.

Beasts chased the sky coven back toward the city, but as burning arrows found homes in the gryphins' chests, they changed direction again. Fleeing to the north and south wasn't an option; the first few harpies to fly into the wards that had funneled the army to the western side shattered and fell to the ground like a sack of boneless meat. Others tried flying straight upward, but they'd never find the top of the wards before the archers caught them.

Draw, aim, release, reach back . . .

An arrow didn't immediately fall into his hand.

Killian looked back. Tomaii held a batch of arrows, face sweaty, smoke curling from his nose as he swayed.

"You good?" Killian asked.

Tomaii grinned, more smoke billowing between his teeth.

"Take a milk break," Killian snapped. Salamander milk waited nearby for when the Igni-blessed reached their boiling point.

Snatching an arrow directly from the barrel, he finished the movement. Nock, draw, aim, release. Reaching for another, a flaming arrow slapped his knuckles. Killian scowled over his shoulder at Tomaii, who had not done what he was told. Of course he hadn't.

Killian took the offering but warned, "Don't be stupid."

In the valley, Aisling's storm was petering out. The tornado chased her for a few minutes, but she had clearly used up whatever power she had; the mare was flying her back in their direction, and without Aisling, the storm couldn't sustain itself.

Reach back, nock, draw, aim, release.

Glancing back to check on Tomaii, his friend was distracted, fierce gaze raking the skies. Killian followed his line of sight, high up into the clouds.

"Miika," Killian warned. "Twenty-eight clicks out, thirty skyward."

His oldest brother looked. Swore.

"Ready the crossbows!" he shouted down the line.

Somewhere, a horn blew.

Draw, aim, release, reach back, nock, draw, aim, release.

Five tons of muscle and scales fell through the dissipating storm clouds.

Nothing that big, nothing that *heavy* should be able to fly, and yet, two dragons were tangled together, clawing at bellies and biting at throats, trying to stop each other from gathering their breath. Wings flapped awkwardly as they tried to stay airborne, but they plummeted toward the ground at a velocity that would likely crack it open like an egg.

At the last minute, one of them pulled free, gliding so close to the ground that their clawed feet dragged trenches through the earth. The other managed to slow down but crashed into the ground, rolling once before springing to its feet and chasing after the first dragon, uncaring that it had just crushed at least a hundred beasts beneath its thick hide.

"Burn and fucking stake me," Reigan breathed.

Killian forgot to reach back again as the clouds finally cleared and two more dragons descended.

"Oh, *shit*," Tomaii wheezed behind him.

Killian looked back to find Tomaii turning an unnatural shade of gray. Beside him, Reigan met his panicked stare. A plead sat on the tip of his tongue—*Run to the fountain, now*—but his mouth stayed firmly shut. Neither of his friends knew when to back down. They weren't made for it. In fact, Reigan turned her glare from Killian to the sky as if her wrath alone could ground the threats.

Tomaii broke into the most feral grin Killian had ever seen.

"I want one," he said, voice crackling with strain.

"Milk. Now." Killian gave his friend a shove toward the barrel nearby and reached for another arrow.

It was only then that he saw Miika staring at him. He said nothing, but Killian saw the same plead burning behind his brother's clenched jaw. Killian shook his head and nocked his arrow.

Miika mirrored him.

On the ground, the arrival of the dragons hadn't gone unnoticed. The beasts were invigorated, throwing themselves against Hyrsch's army. Rallying into a single cloud, the shtrygs speared through, their shadows swallowing the soldiers whole. Only the tiny pinpricks of everlight burning at their throats proved their numbers weren't immediately decimated.

Killian steadied his eye. He took an extra second to choose his target. Looking through the shadows, he found a soldier crumpling under the gravity of a shtryg and loosed his arrow right into the beast's face.

Reach back, nock, draw, aim, release.

A rogue witch tackled a lupanis off one of the Terranian guardians and landed beneath the beast's claws. Killian loosed his next arrow into the lupanis's mouth and saw the Terranian guardian pull the rogue to her feet before smacking a leaping cawker down with his staff.

Reach back, nock, draw, aim, release.

The arrows were coming too slowly.

Killian looked back again.

Tomaii's lips were blistering.

He opened his mouth to shout at his friend again, but his brother's scream drowned out whatever he was going to say. Killian whipped his head around, first to check that Miika was okay, then to follow his gaze to the sky.

One of the enemy's dragons—he could tell now that they were closer, the small riders on their backs visible—had targeted Kaelean, loosing a stream of fire that she banked hard to miss. Twisting back, they met in the sky again with a meaty crash, both flapping madly to keep aloft as they clawed and bit at each other.

The other two dragons glided directly for the city, and one member of the sky coven broke formation to give chase. The tiny everlight amulet was not enough, the rider too far away to identify, but Miika knew it was Yasmin regardless.

Aisling had been aiming for the ground, for the med tent, but one look at what was coming their way had her pulling back on Volya's reins. She met Yasmin in the sky and the two winged horses flew fearlessly to meet the harbingers.

Nock. Draw. Aim. Release.

Along the wall, the crossbows fired. Spears of silver tore through the sky, farther than any of their arrows could hope to reach. The two dragons heading their way swerved to avoid them, and their turn exposed the small figures on the dragon's backs—a rider, also wielding a bow.

Killian reached back. Nocked. Took aim.

They were too far.

"Come on," Killian hissed against the bowstring, fingers trembling.

"Miika, where are you going?!"

Reigan's shout was only a brief distraction. Killian loosed his arrow, not waiting to see if it landed before looking to where his brother was running for a cunae. A *cunae*.

"What the fuck are you doing?!" Killian screamed after his brother, already reaching for another arrow. "That thing will be shredded in seconds!"

His brother spared him a look as he leaped onto the cunae's back, the giant moth's antennae quivering. "Cover me."

Taking off into the sky, Miika flew for Yasmin.

"*Fuck!*" Killian screamed after him, nocking another arrow.

Any harpy within ten meters of Miika's mad dash across the battle's airspace met a fiery arrow. Another round of crossbow bolts loosed into the sky. One struck home.

The screech of pain from the nearest dragon shook the wall beneath their feet, but the beast didn't go down. Its raging maw opened wide, fire building in its throat as it finally noticed them.

Killian took another arrow and aimed for the rider he had missed before. Closer now, the rider had twisted around, back to the wall, aiming at Yasmin instead.

Miika's arrow found home first.

Twitching to the left, Killian didn't waste his shot, burying it in another harpy instead.

Nock, draw, aim, release.

Reach back.

No arrow.

Killian turned to find Tomaii on his knees, skin cracking over the glowing embers beneath. Tossing his bow aside, Killian ran for the barrel of salamander milk. Reigan dropped to her cousin's side, placing one palm against his burning forehead and screaming obscenities in his face.

Returning, Killian skidded to his knees and poured the milk down Tomaii's throat, ignoring the scalding heat of his skin. But Tomaii wasn't looking at either of them. His dark eyes widened as he looked beyond.

Killian turned, scrambling for his bow.

The two dragons had come into range. They were close enough for Killian to watch Aisling standing in her saddle as she flew along a dragon's underside, dragging her axe along its belly. Close enough that the beast's agonized roar shook the nearest tower loose, parts of it crumbling into the parapet. Something burst in Killian's ear, but he didn't care. Yasmin was firing arrows into the riderless dragon's face, but they weren't going deep enough. Miika was screaming at her to move, his cunae close enough for him to leap across, tackling her out of the way.

It didn't matter.

Annoyed, the dragon opened its maw, the fire within turning his brother into a silhouette.

And then Miika and Yasmin were gone, and the fire that consumed them lanced right for the wall.

Killian's legs wouldn't work.

Tomaii shoved him down. Shoved Reigan down. Then he stood, arms stretched wider than the grin on his face, smoke curling off his flaking skin.

All around them, the wall blew apart. Stone burned.

But not where Killian and Reigan lay. A hundred meter chunk of the wall was gone, except the narrow pillar where the three of them had been stationed.

And when the stream ended and the dust settled, ash was all that was left of Tomaii.

Reigan slowly, achingly, got to her hands and knees. Trembling, she leaned over the edge of the pillar and puked.

Killian couldn't feel yet. Couldn't, until they got down.

But there was no way down. The stairwells were gone and the sections of wall still standing were too far. They needed help.

Carefully, he stood. One of the dragons was flailing over the city, raining blood from its torn belly. Its rider was abandoning it, getting ready to leap from their dying mount to the one mourning its harbinger. The one who had consumed Miika and Yasmin, destroyed the wall and taken Tomaii with it. Aisling was still there, blood soaked and banking hard to come back for another attack.

Over the battlefield, the sky coven had disappeared.

"I don't—"

Something hit him. He stumbled, but the ground was gone. Shock and pain ripped a scream from his lungs, terror pulling one from Reigan as Killian rose into the sky and she was left alone on the pillar.

Up and up and up.

Claws hooked deep into Killian's shoulder, the wind battering his bleeding ears, he struggled against the harpy dragging him over Hyrsch. The roof of Neve's Inn was the size of a thumbnail, the road thin as a snail's trail.

He didn't have time to grab his dagger before it let him go.

CHAPTER SIXTY-FOUR

EAVHA

"You're going to be fine," Eavha promised, even as the ground rocked so terribly that every jar of salve rattled off the workbench, shattering at her feet.

Fior stared up at her, bleeding out on the cot, too deep in shock to speak. The wound opening the river witch's belly had cut all the way through her spine, and though Eavha knew she could heal it with her hands pressed against the torn flesh, it was taking too long. There were a hundred people being triaged inside the tent, more doing their best to keep themselves in one piece outside, and every minute the battle wore on saw even more soldiers dragged her way.

She didn't have time to be gentle, so she reached inside the gaping wound of Fior's belly and grabbed hold of either side of her broken spine.

"The wall's been breached!" someone screamed.

Inside, Eavha shuddered against Sanni's whisper.

Run.

She needed a minute.

Focused, trying to remember everything she knew about spinal nerves and synapses, Eavha pictured what she wanted Fior's spine to look like, keeping half an eye on the river witch's pulse.

The rest of the med tent was pandemonium.

"Eavha! Did you hear?" Moyra ran to her side, covered in blood and other bodily fluids, blanching when she realized Eavha was elbow deep in someone's gut.

"I heard," Eavha ground out. "Whoever can move, move. Start getting people to the fountain."

If Moyra hesitated, she didn't notice. If people were leaving the tents, she didn't see. The spine was whole and working, but Fior had passed out from the pain. Piece by piece, Eavha pulled her innards back into place.

Run, now, Sanni told her.

"Just let me finish."

Fior's intestines were leaking bile into the abdominal cavity. Cursing, Eavha wrapped one hand around the perforation while scooping what she could out with the other.

But nothing happened. The undercurrent of healing magic that had been coursing through her veins since the first horn blew now lay dormant.

"Sanni!" Eavha snapped.

Run.

"I'm nearly done!"

But the spirit didn't care. And without her help, without her permission, Eavha didn't have the strength to do much at all.

The insults that flew from her lips could sour milk as she looked around for a needle and thread. She would heal the old-fashioned way if she had to.

"Eavha." Moyra again.

"Pass me that," she snapped, nodding to a wad of bandages.

"*Eavha.*"

Outside, the groans of the injured and the battle cries of the soldiers had given way to only screaming terror and snarling beasts. Most of the tent had been abandoned, but those who lingered were frozen as dark shadows crept across the west-side threshold.

"We need to get to the moonstone," Moyra said, voice shaking.

Everlight hung in woven cradles, keeping the shadows back. Buying them time.

Removing her hands from Fior's belly, Eavha wiped her hands on her shirt and reached for the small dagger at her hip. She could not remember a single thing Aisling had ever tried to teach her about fighting. Could not think of a single thing Eaon might have ever told her about shtryg.

From within the impossible darkness filling the doorway, tendrils of it creeping over the outside of the tent, the canvas buckling under an enormous weight, long, sharp pincered limbs reached inside. Puss oozed from its joints, weeping from the plates of elytra coating its body, and as the beast pushed inside, rearing to its full height, it knocked the everlight lanterns from the ceiling. Watching the ball of glass roll across the ground, the beast lunged, shattering it with its pincer.

The light went out.

The shadows seeped in.

In the front half of the tent, the lingering healers abandoned their patients and ran. The panicked cries of the injured became shrieks of agony as the shadows consumed them, only one able to climb off their cot and hobble after the fleeing healers.

Dominic, from the sea-shore clan.

Pushing past Moyra, shrugging off her desperate fingers, Eavha got to him before his bandaged knee gave out and pulled his arm over her shoulders.

"Let's go."

"Run. Leave."

Behind her, the monstrous beetle-shelled beast was breaking more everlight cradles, letting the shtryg deeper into the med tent.

Not all shadows bore enemies, though.

From under Fior's bed, Gatty solidified. His soft black fur was matted with curdled white blood, claws chipped, scales stuck between his toes. He didn't seem to care as he rubbed himself against Moyra's shin.

"Go to the fountain, my pet. I will find you when this is done."

"Are . . . Are you sure?" The Morvish witch looked to the invading beasts behind Eavha, then back at the cat sith, doubt finding room in her otherwise petrified face.

Gatty scoffed and flicked his tail. As darkness enveloped the tent, he seemed to grow larger, his grin widening until it split his face in half. His fangs lengthened with every step he took toward the seething shadows.

"Go, Moyra," Eavha snapped, chasing the last of the everlight. "I'm right behind you."

Stumbling, Moyra turned her back and ran. The east-side entrance to the tent let out to the city's gate, half closed and half ruined by whoever was desperate enough to break it down—beast or deserter. The Morvish witch disappeared into the throng of people fleeing the battle.

The cat sith turned his buttercup eyes to Eavha as she hurried past. Winked.

"See you soon, witchling."

Huffing, Eavha bulled past, half dragging Dominic who grew heavier by the second. As did the air, thick and suffocating, worse with every light crushed. The hair at the back of her neck stood up, her skin gooseflesh. She couldn't stop. She could feel the vacuum of an impossible gravity drawing her back, bending her knees, and if she stopped, they were done.

Something laughed, and she swore it was right in her ear. Dominic took her little knife from her free hand and swatted lamely at something behind them, but the laughter was drowned out by a low, feline hiss.

Dominic stumbled. "Holy Mother of all."

Eavha couldn't look. Couldn't stop.

Couldn't breathe until they fell out of the tent, scrambling desperately. Fresh air brought with it freedom from whatever horror had been breathing down her neck, but inside the med tent was pitch black. Pure midnight seethed within.

A mighty roar shook the cobblestone beneath her feet.

And then the tent was burning.

Stumbling back, shielding her face, heat blistered the air.

Dominic tugged her arm, and Eavha forced her feet to move.

She looked back only once.

The shadows were gone. The tent was gone.

Gatty was gone. Where he had last stood, a rough chunk of obsidian glass remained, cracking under the heat. There was nothing else left to show he had ever been there.

CHAPTER SIXTY-FIVE

AISLING

GUTTING BYRON'S DRAGON HAD BEEN A VICTORY, BUT HE KNEW HER tricks now, smirking as he refused to let her get beneath him again. Smug. He was *smug*, even as the dragon she'd killed collided into the western quarter, mewling weakly as its blood soaked the main road. If Byron cared how much of Chaos's forces were being wasted on this detour, he didn't show it. Wasn't impressed with the force Aisling had rallied and wasn't interested in dealing with her, making an obvious beeline for the palace.

For Aadya.

Aisling couldn't afford to chase him deeper into the city. Not with her army flagging, the rest of the sky coven dead or missing. More and more beasts were breaching the crumbling wall, and as she looked across the killing field, she saw no end.

This night was always going to be costly. It didn't stop the fact of it grating against her resolve.

Kaelean may have come out of her fight alive, but not well. Her large dragon body wept from deep gouges in her side, one wing snapped in half, yet she clawed her way up the still-standing portion of the city wall, perched above the masses, and breathed a scorching demarcation line between theirs and the enemy. It bought the soldiers some time to push back the beasts already in their midst, but it wasn't going to be enough. Nine smaller dragons weaved their way westward, but they were no less dangerous than their parents; when they reached the city, they would burn it to the ground, along with everyone inside.

The deserters, hiding. The healers, working.

Eavha.

The sky coven was gone, and Aisling couldn't fight *nine* dragons on her own.

And then the world rippled.

Aisling buried her face against her mare, who whinnied and flared her wings as, from far below, a shifting mass of claws and shadow rose. Twisted, rippling arms of exposed vein and muscle formed, reaching out from within.

Chaos was here. Chaos was joining the fight.

Even if Aisling could figure out how to lure him away, she would be abandoning what remained of her people to a losing battle. The beasts would not stop just because their king was not there to watch.

Davina had seen her standing on the bridge between towers over the Womb, facing Chaos. Whether or not it ever came to pass, it was not to be this night.

"We have to retreat," she said the words softly, grimacing at the taste of them, preparing herself for how they'd feel when she sent the call down. A mere flurry was all that was left of her Celeste-blessing, her voice carrying to every pair of ears who needed to hear her. "Retreat! Now! Get to the moongate Everybody, now!"

Kaelean roared, agreement and command, and immediately began to shrink.

Magic fizzled in Aisling's veins, her edges fraying, and if she forced it any further, she'd risk dissipating entirely. She didn't have enough left to portal, so she flew Volya down, timing it right so that she flew past the wall just as Kaelean grew small enough to latch on. She carried Wyldeden's founder over the shadows spilling through the city streets, unable to help the soldiers caught beneath their vacuum. Beasts of every kind thundered in their wake, devouring the few soldiers trying to escape inside buildings. One man was still bleeding out from the wound a shtryg had left in his throat when a pack of cawkers found him, tearing chunks of flesh from beneath his armor.

She couldn't help them all. She couldn't do anything but swing her axe at a harpy who dared fly too close. Couldn't do anything but pray for the witch who plummeted from the sky, splattering against the cobblestones ten feet in front of her. She couldn't make Volya fly any faster, and she didn't question when Kaelean leaped from the saddle down onto a nearby rooftop. It was a waste of energy to doubt her, and a waste of time looking back to see what caught her attention.

As Volya barreled through the western quarter, Aisling kept her eyes peeled for a curly-haired healer who would no doubt be exactly where she shouldn't be.

There.

Barefoot and covered in blood, Eavha dragged Dominic inch by inch toward an abandoned apartment building. Singularly focused on her task, she didn't notice the people streaming past her, nor did she notice the heavy gallop of Aisling's mare as she touched down on the cobblestones. Shucking her axe into its holster, Aisling leaned to the side, one arm out, and braced herself.

Her shoulder screamed, threatening to snap as Aisling scooped Eavha around the chest and hauled her onto the horse's back. The scream Eavha loosed was only half terror, half rage as she swung clenched fists at whatever part of Aisling she could reach. At least until she realized it wasn't a beast. Her wide honey eyes finally locked on Aisling, but there was only panic and fear to be found there.

"We have to go back!" she screamed. "Aisling! Go back!"

Aisling ignored her.

"Up!" she commanded, pulling the reins tight and digging her heels into Volya's side. Her mare spread her filthy wings, tucking her hooves as she leaped skyward.

A whisper brushed her spine a second before impact.

It was enough warning for Aisling to lean sideways, pinning Eavha as hard as she could as Volya squealed. On her left wing, right by the joint connecting it to the thick muscle of her shoulder, a lupanis dangled, claws ripping through flesh and feather. A few inches farther and those claws would have torn through Aisling's thigh.

Letting loose her own cry of frustration and panic, Aisling leaned the other way, pulling Volya to the right before they could collide into the side of a building. The mare was falling, unbalanced and bleeding, and at the same time Aisling risked releasing the reins, reaching back for her axe, Eavha squirmed farther over Volya's back and slapped a hand onto the ruined wing.

Two inches from the lupanis's claws.

Lurching up, the beast released Volya's wing to swipe for Eavha.

She didn't think. Standing in the saddle, Aisling swung.

The jolt of their landing on the cobblestone road was ill timed—the axe took off the lupanis's front leg before those lethal claws could touch her, but it followed through, cutting through Volya's wing, too.

The horse buckled, careening to her side. The snap of bone as she landed awkwardly on her other wing was audible even through the growing chorus of screams throughout the city streets. Volya's high shrieking rattled Aisling's skull worse than the impact her elbows and knees made on the road, Eavha rolling to a stop bedside her.

"Get up!" Aisling screamed, clambering to her feet. "Now! Get up!"

Hauling Eavha to her feet, Aisling dragged her to Volya. Even disoriented, Eavha fell to the mare's side, hands closing over the shoulder wound spurting blood.

"Please," she begged in her native tongue. "Please."

Aisling ran to Volya's other side, stroking her mare's snout. "I'm sorry, girl. Come on. I need you."

At the end of the street, the night grew darker, shadows flitting along alcoves, avoiding the little light emitted from the everlight amulets still hanging from bodies scattered on the road. Among them lurked a beetle-beast, scraping gore off the length of its pincer before twisting its hideous face in their direction.

"Come on," Aisling pleaded, tugging the reins. "Come on."

"Please," Eavha begged louder. "I'm sorry. Please."

They could run, but they'd be dead before they reached the next block. Aisling dug deep for a scrap of power, just enough to portal once, just to the northern quarter. The marks on her skin blistered with cold and her skull creaked with the agony of it, her edges fraying. She couldn't do it.

Clicking and groaning, the beetle-beast hunkered down, loping toward them.

"Please," Eavha sobbed, burying her face in Volya's side. "Sanni, please."

Rising to her feet, Aisling fisted the everlight at her throat and collected her axe from where it had skidded into the middle of the road.

"Eavha, darling. Now would be a really good time for one of your miracles."

CHAPTER SIXTY-SIX

EAON

THERE WAS A WHOLE FUCKING WAR GOING ON, AND THE ONLY THING the phouka cared about was dragging Eaon back down to the palace's dungeons. When he realized where he was being taken, Eaon threatened to bring his seventh death upon himself if the phouka didn't put him down immediately and go back for the others.

Fury was caustic in the Old One's voice as he informed Eaon that he wasn't taking him back to the cage, but was going back for the pack, and then getting Eaon the fuck out of this city.

The pack. The traveler's pack full of bones that he'd left in the dungeon.

"Are you *fucking* with me?" Eaon screamed at him. "Go back! Dhal! Right now!"

The phouka shuddered at the sound of his name, but blatantly ignored Eaon's request. Apparently it didn't hold the same power as when the fae used *his* name. Unfair.

Folding his wings and tucking his talons as tight as he could while still holding onto Eaon, the phouka nosedived straight through the stained-glass window of Aisling's throne room, *popped* into his goat form, threw Eaon over his shoulder, loose bits of armor and all, and bolted down the stairwell.

"I should have chained you to a fucking tree in the northern mountains!" The phouka cursed as he ran, claws digging into Eaon's thighs.

"I should have wrapped your fucking head in chloroform, put you in a silver chest, and nailed it to the bottom of the womb!"

"My sister is back there!" Eaon shouted back. His Dearmead. His Cinn.

Reaching the bottom of the stairwell, they stormed to the cell Eaon had been confined to. Dhal finally put him down, inspecting the key still sitting in the lock.

"Who let you out."

"Just get your stupid bones so we can go," Eaon spat.

He didn't really remember being let out of the gibbet. Everything up to the point where his magic had stopped working felt hazy, like a very long dream he'd just woken up from. He was *awake*. He was *clear*. There was no cold blistering in his veins, no ravenous beast clawing at his lungs. He could *breathe*.

Shoving the pack into Eaon's chest, the phouka paused. Grabbed his chin and glared down with such undiluted hatred it should have wilted Eaon on the spot. One clawed thumb rubbed his cheek, weirdly gentle.

"I've seen this somewhere before."

"What?" Eaon asked.

The phouka only scowled, pushing his face away.

A sound like a mountain breaking in two rumbled through the dungeon, shaking the ceiling and walls. Instinctively, Eaon ducked. His leg barked, giving way, and Eaon dropped the pack to catch himself as he fell.

"We need to go," the phouka growled, hovering over him as a layer of dust floated down.

Biting his tongue, Eaon didn't argue. He let the phouka haul him onto his back and tried not to think about how silly it felt. How childish. Tried not to think of his da, carrying a seven-year-old Eaon through Wyldeden's forests on his shoulders.

Tried and failed.

"What's that?" he'd asked, pointing into the canopy, giggling as Kailevi skipped over a fallen branch, jostling him on purpose.

"What's what?"

"That purple thing?"

His da had looked up and frowned. *"There's nothing there, Eaon."*

"Da!" Eaon had laughed. *"That purple thing! The purple rainbow. It's pretty."*

Kailevi had looked at the canopy for a long time. *"You're right, buddy. It is pretty. Should we follow it? See where it leads us?"*

In the dungeon, Eaon's head throbbed, vision spotting.

"Wait," he croaked.

Halfway crouched for the pack, the phouka paused.

He could see it.

The phouka picked up the pack, took him to the stairwell, and halfway up there would be a man. A male with dark hair and dark eyes, small dragon wings dragging behind him where a scaled tail swept the steps.

There would be a fight. The phouka would win. Eaon would die again.

He couldn't die again.

"Dhal, wait," Eaon said again. "Just wait. Blow out the candles."

Maybe it was the certainty, the calm in Eaon's voice, but this time, the phouka did what he was told. Carefully, he put Eaon back down. Put the pack down and blew out the candles. Unable to hold his own weight, Eaon leaned against the wall and dragged his leg, putting himself in the farthest corner and hunkering down. Relying on the shadow.

The phouka loomed, crouching low, arms spread wide, shielding Eaon. With his toe, he drew a line in the dust. Part of a circle, arching around the two of them.

A minute passed, two, and hurried footsteps echoed from the stairwell.

"Aadya!" the call came. "Aadya, are you down here?"

Sucking in a breath, Eaon held it. Silent. He had to be silent.

The scrape of claws on stone, the brush of scales on the floor, and the call again, louder, then quieter as he passed by. The phouka moved, but Eaon grabbed hold of his wrist.

Not yet.

The pain in his head was so sharp he wanted to vomit, but he refused to open his mouth. Refused to shift his weight an inch.

A scream of rage rattled the unstable foundation.

"Fucking *bitch*! I'm going to burn this whole city! She's not even here! Burn this whole place to nothing!"

Footsteps again, closer, then farther.

Gone.

The phouka looked over his shoulder, eyes narrowed.

"*Now* you have self-preservation instincts."

Eaon let out his breath.

CHAPTER SIXTY-SEVEN

CINN

CINN HAD SPENT MUCH OF HIS LIFE RUNNING, BUT NEVER THIS FAST. Oxygen was irrelevant; he could run forever and never take a breath. His limbs knew nothing of exhaustion. He barely felt his body at all as Hyrsch blurred by.

Shedding armor had slowed them down momentarily, but it was a risk worth taking. The restriction, the weight, could mean the difference between life and death—for Radley and Cecelia, anyway. For Cinn, escape was freedom. Being caught held a fate worse than death, or at the very least, put his brother at risk when he inevitably came to rescue him. The noise the clunky armor made also drew too much attention, and unlike the everlight at their throats, it wasn't an attention balanced with cost.

Radley and Cecelia kept pace like they'd been born running, and the seconds they lost dumping their outer layers were made up swiftly. The sword in Cinn's hand was cumbersome, but he had given his dagger to Dearmead. They'd been separated in the melee, and though Cinn had never been a big fan of the Wyldeden guardian, he was special to Eaon. William's knife would keep him safe.

Him, and the woman with him.

The woman with mottled blue-green eyes and a silver mark on the back of her neck.

He couldn't think about it. Not now. Couldn't think the word *mother* and keep from tripping over his own feet.

All their years running the streets as children finally came to good use as Cinn spotted the narrow gap between stores that didn't truly qualify as an alley. Radley remembered, too, cursing as he dragged Cecelia behind him. Remembered the shortcut through the old breeders complex and the garden outside that shaved two minutes off the run, the clock counting down to when Master Ackford would come to the servants' room to unchain them. They were bigger now than they'd been back then, but Cinn pushed into the space anyway, scraping himself raw on the brick.

Falling out the other side, Cinn skidded to a halt, shoving his brother back in the gap before twirling around to cut the first of three ratki in half. Oversized rats that they were, all they saw was flesh to eat; the moment the ratki's innards hit the ground, they were on their brethren like hounds on a rabbit.

Cinn took no risks, killing the other two while they were distracted.

Of all the beasts he'd seen this night, all the claws and teeth he'd had in him, the ratki were nothing. There to clean up the mess, to be distractions while the larger beasts crippled Hyrsch's army.

Anyone else would be dead a thousand times over, yet Cinn blew through Hyrsch's northern quarter without a scratch to show for the blood he'd shed on the battlefield.

"There!" Radley called as they reached the breeder's gardens, across which waited the northern courtyard. The fountain where Moyra and Aisling had opened their moongate. Where they had hidden the last moonstone in case they had to make another one.

From what Cinn could see, nobody else had made it to the rendezvous yet.

The growls and shrieks that had chased them through the city ebbed and grew as the beasts hunted; they couldn't be allowed to occupy the courtyard.

Leaping over the rusty iron gate of the complex, Cinn trampled shrubs and flowers as he ran. The light at his throat made him a beacon to anything nearby, but it was also all he had to see by and would give any shtryg pause. As dark as it was, they still had the stars. Still had a scrap of moonlight.

A shadow blocked it out.

Looking up, Cinn shuddered at the silhouette of a dragon gliding overhead.

"Fuck. Fuck, fuck, fuck," Radley spat.

How long he swore for, Cinn didn't know. Light came first, casting the northern quarter in a red haze; then the sound of flame roaring through the night drowned out everything else.

The stream hit the breeder's complex like a star falling to earth. One second the building stood large and ominous, and the next Cinn was on the ground, blinking red spots out of his vision. Panic pulled a rasping scream from his throat, vaguely reminiscent of Radley's name as he searched for his brother.

He was there, on his hands and knees, shaking his head. Cecelia was rolling on the lawn, trying to orient herself.

Good. That was okay.

Climbing to his feet, Cinn looked to the courtyard. Chunks of brick and stone scattered across the garden, spilling into the courtyard, but the fountain stood intact.

The leathery flap of wings warned that they were not alone. Searching the sky for silhouettes, Cinn spotted one turning back for another run. Did it know what this place was, somehow? Or was it chasing them? Him, specifically? Did it have a rider? It looked like one of the smaller ones, but he couldn't be sure.

Didn't matter.

Sprinting across the garden, leaping over debris, Cinn raced the dragon's shadow.

He was fast, but he was not faster than fire.

The dragon let loose another devastating stream into the nearest storefront. Cinn found himself on his hands and knees again, but this time the destruction sent rubble careening deeper into the courtyard. The top half of the marble centerpiece featuring in the fountain was knocked clean off, the rest crumbling.

He didn't remember finding his feet again. Didn't remember running the final meters to the fountain. Somewhere, Radley was screaming his name, but Cinn was flying, falling, submerged under water as he scrambled for the velvet sack hidden within.

The world fell on top of him. Every bone in his back cracked under the weight of a thousand pounds of marble and stone, his lungs unable to expand, unable to find air. But he had it. He had the moonstone.

The bubbling water burned brightly, heating his skin. The fountain trembled and cracked, the groan of it collapsing around him loud enough to split his head open. But as it eased, the water drained, and Cinn wheezed down a thin breath. Another, too quick, because there was no room in his chest for it.

The courtyard was nothing but rubble. Cobblestone charred to dust, brick smoldering.

The weight pinning him meant he could barely turn his head at the call of his name. Radley. Radley was alright. Arms outstretched in front of him, Cinn could only lay there in the damp remains of the fountain's base, fist clenched around the velvet sack. With trembling fingers, he pulled out the stone, hiding its luminescent winking in the palm of his sweaty hand.

"Ry? Cinn? Fuck, please?" Radley begged, closer.

Cinn wheezed as loud as he could, sucking in a series of short, hungry breaths as his vision darkened.

"There you are." Hysterical. Cinn had never heard his brothers voice pitched quite so high. "There you are. It's alright. Breathe. Fuck. Cecelia! Help me with this!"

Radley's boots were in front of his face, then his knees. His calloused fingers pushed Cinn's damp hair away from his face, crouching down to meet his eye.

"You're alright."

Cinn managed a nod. Took Radley's hand in his free one and squeezed tight.

One handed, Radley shoved at chunks of marble. Cecelia shoved her entire weight against it, moving it a bare inch at a time. Then she paused.

"There's someone! Over here! We're over—"

Her call was cut short by a gurgling scream. Shadow—a different kind, the heavy kind, so much heavier than the marble even—fell over them.

A voice like silk over gravel chuckled. "There you are."

Cinn's grip on Radley's hand tightened as he squirmed uselessly, unable to feel his legs at all. Pupils blown wide, Radley couldn't move beneath the crushing weight of the shtryg's vacuum.

Wrinkled gray skin loomed over them, and then Radley was screaming. Bloody spittle splattered over Cinn's face, but he held on, *held on*, as the shtryg tried to drag his brother away. A tug of war Cinn could not lose, not even as his shoulder burned, the joint popping out of its socket. Not even as his vision went completely dark, his ears ringing.

And then it stopped. The pull dropped, the vacuum ebbed. Radley's hand was still warm in Cinn's. Every thready breath he sucked down cleared his vision until he could see the little charm dangling from his brother's wrist. Blinking a few times, he waited for the rest of him to reappear. But he didn't.

Beyond the elbow, Radley was gone.

Not gone.

A dozen feet away, bloody pulp dressed in Radley's clothes lay beneath the corpse of a dried up shtryg, a silver dagger sticking out of its skull.

Drenched in the same combination of putrid white beast blood and the darker red of his own that stained Cinn's clothes, Dearmead perched on a boulder of nearby rubble, hand still outstretched from when he'd flung William's knife.

Cinn stared at him. Because looking at anything else was going to break him in a way that wouldn't heal.

Somewhere, a lupanis howled.

The sound spurred Dearmead back into motion, jumping down and running for the shtryg, yanking the dagger free. Behind him, the other kinner woman came running, a stolen silver sword slung across her shoulders.

"We're going to have unfriendly company in less than two minutes," she snapped. "Where are these powerful witches you spoke of?"

"They'll be here," Dearmead barked back, crouching at Cinn's side. The ground shifted beneath his feet as he braced himself against the crushing stone and shoved.

If it moved, Cinn didn't feel it.

Distantly, he was aware of others beginning to bleed into the courtyard. Aware of them fighting an increasing number of beasts that had followed their blood trail. Aware of them dying.

Cinn watched the muscles in Dearmead's calves as he moved the pieces of broken fountain off Cinn's numb body.

Nothing else existed, until another shadow fell over him.

He must have made a sound, because Dearmead's voice was a gentle assurance. "It's just the phouka with Eaon."

A panicked cry. "Cinn!"

Pain flooded into Cinn's chest. He couldn't breathe.

"Dea?"

"I'm working on it."

The way Eaon fell to the ground suggested he was dumped, rather carelessly, but it put him at eye level with Cinn. Shucking off the traveler's pack on his back, Eaon's eyes fell on the limp hand Cinn still clutched tightly. His face paled under the little black spellmark on his cheek.

"Is that . . ." Eaon stopped. Placing a hand over Cinn's other clenched fist—the one housing the moonstone—he wrestled for words. As the phouka bellowed a war cry, he looked away. "We have to get out of here."

"I'm trying," Dearmead huffed. Something shifted, and this time Cinn felt it. A broken cry cracked from his wasted lungs as whatever Dearmead had moved dug deeper into his spine.

"Stop, stop, stop," Eaon begged, needlessly. Dearmead had stilled so completely he could have been a statue himself.

Then the guardian swore, pulling the dagger free again and disappearing from Cinn's view. All he could see was Eaon's face, eyes darting everywhere as he followed whatever horror was happening now.

Finally, he looked down at Cinn again. "Do you have the stone?"

Cinn nodded.

"I don't know that we can get you out. There's too many . . . And I can't . . . But you've got the stone. We'll hang onto you, and you can get us out. Right?"

Again, Cinn nodded. He could do that.

Eaon's breath hitched. Guilt carved a line between his brows.

"Promise me we won't leave without Eavha."

Cinn closed his eyes. It was easier to pretend the limp hand in his wasn't growing clammy that way.

"I'm sorry," Eaon breathed. "I'm so sorry. Fuck, Cinn, I'm so sorry."

He had only enough breath for one word, and he gave it to Eaon.

"Promise."

There was nothing either of them could do but wait. Time was measured in the number of times Dearmead returned to try and get Cinn free, but the time between visits was longer and longer as more and more people flooded into the courtyard. They were fodder for the beasts tracking them.

The only thing Cinn opened his eyes for was the sudden loss of Eaon's hand on his. A cawker had reached them and Eaon had let go to wrap his hands around its throat. Contact didn't mean instant death anymore, though feather and flesh still rotted slowly beneath his hands. Half the size of Eaon and frenzied from killing, the cawker scratched and snapped wildly; Eaon's magic was taking too long, so he resorted to grabbing a jagged chunk of stone and bludgeoning the beast to death instead.

Then his shaking hand was on Cinn's again, the phouka looming furiously over them, matted with gore.

"We have to go. Now."

He grabbed hold of Eaon's shoulder, other hand extended to Dearmead, who held onto the kinner woman. Nobody else was nearby. Not a single soldier or healer. Every second they waited was one he spent risking everybody's lives, but if they left without Eavha, Eaon would not forgive him.

"Wait," Eaon croaked.

"We can't," the phouka insisted. "We can't hold them back forever!"

"Eavha's coming," Eaon pleaded. "She's coming. She's . . . She's there! She's there!"

The phouka looked. Scowled. "Across the garden still! They'll never get here!"

"She's nearly here," Eaon begged. "And . . . and there's Kaelean! She's got Moyra. They're right behind them. They're coming. We have to wait. There's no other way out of here."

"Kaelean can shift and fly them out, and Aisling can portal," the phouka argued.

"Then why isn't she?!" Eaon screamed back. "They're running here for a reason, and I'm not leaving without my sister!"

Their bickering meant nothing. Cinn was the one holding the moonstone, and the phouka could pry it out of his cold, dead hand. Unable to draw breath, unable to sign, all he could do was twist his neck to glare up at them and hope they got the point.

"Look, Aisling's mare is hurt," Dearmead added.

Cinn's teeth snapped so hard he thought he chipped them.

If anyone deserved to die here, in this city she had sentenced to death, it was Aisling.

Gods, he wanted to leave her.

Eaon had known. Had conveniently not mentioned Aisling's presence. He knew that if he told Cinn who was approaching, he would not wait. Clenching his eyes tighter than his shaking fists, he knew if he caught sight of her, it was over. He wouldn't care who he left behind, he would go.

And then Eaon was screaming in his ear.

"Go! Cinn, go!"

He sucked down another breath, but a word wouldn't form in his mind. His tongue wouldn't move. All he knew was that he wanted to be safe.

The world went white.

CHAPTER SIXTY-EIGHT

KAELEAN

Kaelean's ears popped. Moonlight spat them out into the silent dawn—or near silent. Neither she nor Aisling's mare had stopped running as they approached the fountain, and their momentum sent them sprawling into the grass. Kaelean released Moyra's hand, released her grip on Volya's tail, rolling into the fall and springing up into a crouch, prepared to shift.

A burbling stream was nearby, and the startled cry of birds taking to wing set her racing heart into palpitations, but then they were gone.

It was too dark to see where Cinn had taken them, but she didn't need to. She knew the smell of the pines and firs, the feel of the earth beneath her feet. She had spent more time roaming these forests than she'd ever spent in Wyldeden. And if all that wasn't enough, the crawl of Sparrow-magic on her skin, of a far-too-pungent ward, gave it away.

After all this time, The Mark of Things Unwanted still protected the Copeland farm.

Wheezing, Moyra pushed herself to her hands and knees. Behind her, Aisling's battered mare collapsed, sending its two blood-soaked riders tumbling off. The creature gave a pained whinny, red staining its coat from the scabbed-over wound of its missing wing.

"That's it?" the strange kinner woman asked, looking around at the panting mess of them expectantly.

Dearmead lowered himself to the grass and closed his eyes, unable to do more than simply breathe. Eaon swayed where he sat; only the phouka's

485

grip on the back of his neck keeping him upright. Face-down on the ground, Cinn heaved, clutching the now-bland moonstone in one hand and a severed arm in the other.

The kinner woman stared at him for a moment, then shook her head in disappointment. "What now?"

Hoping the Morvish witch among them had some insight, Kaelean met Moyra's wide-eyed gaze. The tiny shake of her head sent straw-colored curls falling out from behind her ears.

"What now?" the woman repeated a little louder, perhaps doubting anybody had heard.

Kaelean looked to Aisling next. This grand stand had been her idea. She'd had plans upon plans, but looking at her now, staring at her injured mount, Kaelean saw only a ghost. The fight had left her.

At the Sparrow queen's side, Eavha trembled, staring at her bloody hands.

Kaelean shook her head. "That's a very good question."

ACKNOWLEDGMENTS

From the very beginning I wanted to write a story about climbing back up after hitting rock bottom, about what happens when you're supposed to get your "happily ever after" and instead lose everything, because when it happened to me, I needed to know that the story went on.

My story, like this one, is not done yet.

I owe a world of thanks to the people who stood by me during my darkest days, who supported me, because without you I never would have had the chance to do this thing I love doing. It isn't easy to love someone through all of grief's ugliness; to all my family, both blood and not, I know I don't tell you often enough but I love and appreciate you endlessly.

To the friends who were patient when I didn't have space for them, who continued to invite me to things they knew I wouldn't come to, who'd already forgiven me by the time I found my feet again, thank you. And to my son, who I live and breathe for, thank you for being so unapologetically you.

A huge thank you also goes to my amazing editor, Kat from Element Editing Services. I've said it before and I'll say it again, your work is incredible and greatly appreciated. Without you, this book never would have come together and I can't wait to work on the next instalment with you.

Last but not least, a great thanks is also owed to my readers—knowing how much you love this series and these characters is all the reward any author needs. They're my heart, and it's my honour to lay it bare for you.

Until next time,

Alex.

ABOUT THE AUTHOR

Alex Clifford has spent the past decade studying creative writing, interior design, sociology, psychology and secondary education, bringing it all together to do what they have always loved to do best—tell stories. As a neurodiverse, queer, widowed, single parent, Alex is excited to bring their perspective and experience to the fantasy genre for many years to come.

For more on Alex Clifford's upcoming work, visit: www.alexclifford.com.au

You can find them on social media at:
  Facebook: facebook.com/AfsCliffordBooks
  Twitter (X): @AfsClifford
  Instagram: @almost_alex
  TikTok: @alexcliffordwrites

THEY WERE NOT
ENOUGH

TIME TO FIGHT FIRE WITH FIRE

THE
MARK OF
SOULS
UNDEPARTED

ARRIVING

2024

9 780645 020199